THE READER'S DIGEST ASSOCIATION LIMITED
Berkeley Square House, London W1X 6AB

THE READER'S DIGEST ASSOCIATION
SOUTH AFRICA (PTY) LTD
Reader's Digest House, 130 Strand Street, Cape Town

Printed by BPCC Petty Ltd, Leeds
Bound by BPCC Hazell Books Ltd, Aylesbury

Original cover design by Jeffrey Matthews FSIAD

For information as to ownership
of copyright in the material of this book see last page

CONDENSED BOOKS

LONGSHOT

Dick Francis

PUBLISHED BY MICHAEL JOSEPH

NO HARP LIKE MY OWN

Marjorie Quarton

PUBLISHED BY COLLINS

TRIAL

Clifford Irving

PUBLISHED BY HAMISH HAMILTON

THE FLIGHT OF FLAMINGO

Elizabeth Darrell

PUBLISHED BY CENTURY

CONTENTS

LONGSHOT

Dick Francis

A girl has been strangled at a party; a second victim, a stablegirl, goes missing and is later found dead . . . Racehorse trainer Tremayne Vickers is thankful for the help of his young biographer, John Kendall, when several of his family and close associates fall under suspicion. Every male amongst them could, it seems, have had a motive. So which one is capable of murder? John discovers the surprising truth only when he himself has become the killer's final target.

Dick Francis is at the height of his form with a gripping new mystery which will delight his many fans.

page 9

NO HARP LIKE MY OWN

Marjorie Quarton

The offer of a job on a sheep farm in Yorkshire is a welcome prospect for Benedict Glyn. Above all, it's a chance to escape from Cloninch, the farm in Ireland where his stubborn grandmother, Agatha, rules with a will of iron. But Ben's new life is quickly shattered by a tragic accident. Facing dark depths of despair, he must learn to depend upon the devotion of a very special girl—and the exceptional courage and loyalty of a Border collie named Meg.

A memorable and moving novel that celebrates the conquering power of hope and love.

page 123

TRIAL

Clifford Irving

Defence lawyer Warren Blackburn badly needs a legal case that will put him back on his feet. Being assigned to the low-key trial of Hector Quintana, a homeless immigrant, is a start. But the next case to come his way is Houston's big murder trial. Warren can't believe his luck. Until suddenly, while he is preparing his defence, he has the sickening feeling that his two cases are linked . . . When the guilty start to appear innocent, and the innocent guilty, it puts a conscientious lawyer like Warren in an impossible position.

Scintillating courtroom drama packed with suspense.

page 227

THE FLIGHT OF FLAMINGO

Elizabeth Darrell

In the 1930s the world of aviation is full of promise—especially for Kit Anson, young test pilot for Kirkland Marine Aviation. Handsome and daring, Kit wins many a heart, including that of Sir Hector Kirkland's daughter, Leone. But when he threatens to reveal a secret that will shake the foundations of the Kirkland empire, he is publicly disgraced.

This enthralling novel tells how Kit regains his honour, by flying once again, in tests of courage that take him from the jungles of Africa to the icy fiords of Norway during World War II.

page 355

LONGSHOT

by Dick Francis

ILLUSTRATED BY JACK McCARTHY

At the time, it seemed to John Kendall, an amateur survival expert, a good idea to throw in his well-paid job in order to become a novelist. Many hungry months later, it seemed an even better idea to accept a commission to write a biography of racehorse trainer Tremayne Vickers.

But when John moves into Tremayne's Berkshire mansion, he finds himself plunged into the middle of a murder inquiry, with suspicion focused chillingly close to home . . .

The killer will, it seems, stop at nothing to cover his tracks. And when John starts to get tantalisingly close to the truth, it is his survival skills, rather than his writing talents, which are put to the ultimate test.

Chapter 1

I accepted a commission that had been turned down by four other writers, but I was hungry at the time.

Although starving in a garret had seemed a feasible enough plan a year earlier, the present realities of existence under the frozen eaves of a friend's aunt's house in a snowy January were such that without enough income to keep well fed and warm I was a knockover for a risky decision.

My state, of course, was my own fault. I could easily have gone out looking for paid employment. I didn't have to sit shivering in a ski suit, biting the end of a pencil, hunched over a notebook, unsure of myself, of my ability and of the illuminations crashing about in my head.

The spartan discomfort was not, either, a self-pitying morass of abject failure, but more the arctic doldrums between the high elation of the recent acceptance of my first novel for publication, and the distant date of its launch into literary orbit. This was the downside after the heady receipt of the first advance payment and its division into past debts, present expenses and six months' future rent.

Give it two years, I'd thought, kissing farewell to the security of a salary: if I can't get published in two years I'll admit that the compulsion to write fiction is fool's gold and settle for common sense. Tossing away the pay-cheque had been a desperate step, but I'd tried writing before and after work, and at weekends, and had produced only dust. A stretch of no-excuse solitude would settle things one way or another. Incipient hypothermia wasn't in any way diminishing the intense happiness of having put my toe into the first crack of the rockface.

I did, as it happened, know quite a lot about survival in adverse circumstances, and the prospect of lean times hadn't worried me. I just hadn't realised that sitting and thinking made one cold. I hadn't known that a busy brain sneakily stole warmth from inactive hands and feet. In every freezing configuration I'd lived through before, I'd been moving.

The letter from Ronnie Curzon came on a particularly cold morning when there was ice like a half-descended curtain over the inside of my friend's aunt's attic window, with its high view over the Thames at Chiswick. 'Dear John,' the letter said. 'Care to drop into the office? There's been a suggestion about American rights in your book. You might be interested. I think we might discuss it, anyway. Yours ever, Ronnie . . . Why can't you have a telephone like everyone else?'

American rights! Incredible words.

The day warmed up miraculously. American rights happened to successful authors, not to people afflicted by self-doubts, with a need to be told over and over that the book is OK, it's OK, don't worry so much.

'Don't worry,' Ronnie had said heartily, summoning me to his presence after reading the manuscript I'd dumped unheralded on his desk a couple of weeks earlier. 'Don't worry, I'm sure we can find you a publisher. Leave it to me. Let me see what I can do.'

Ronnie Curzon, authors' agent, with his salesman's subtle tongue, had indeed found me a publisher, a house more prestigious than I would have aimed for.

'They have a large list,' Ronnie explained kindly. 'They can afford to take a risk on a few first-timers.'

On the day of the American-rights letter I walked as usual from the friend's aunt's house to Ronnie's office four miles away in Kensington High Street and, as I'd learned a thing or two by that time, I went late in the morning, so as to arrive at noon. Shortly after that hour, I'd discovered, Ronnie tended to offer wine to his visitors and to send out for sandwiches.

I misjudged things to the extent that the door of his office was firmly shut, where normally it stood open.

'He's with another client,' Daisy said.

Daisy smiled easily, an unusual virtue in a receptionist. Big white teeth in a black face. Wild hair. 'I'll let him know you're here,' she said, lifting her telephone, pressing a button and consulting with her boss.

'He wants you to wait,' she reported, and I nodded and passed some time on one of the two chairs arranged for the purpose.

Ronnie's suite of private offices was approached through a large outer room, partly furnished with Daisy's desk, box-files on shelves and a large central table scattered with published books.

Eventually one of the doors opened and out came Ronnie's head, his neck and a section of shoulder. 'John? Come along in.'

I went down a passage to his office which contained his desk, swivelling armchair, two guest chairs, a cupboard and roughly a thousand books.

'Sorry to keep you,' he said. He was as expansively apologetic as if I'd had a definite appointment.

Ronnie was rounded and enthusiastic. Cuddly was almost the word. Short, with smooth dark hair and soft dry hands, wearing always a business suit over a white shirt and a striped tie. Authors, his presentation seemed to say, could turn up if they pleased in ski suits and snow-defeating moon boots, but serious business took place in sober worsted.

His other client remained settled in his chair. It seemed to me that Ronnie was stifling exasperation under a façade of aplomb.

'Tremayne,' he was saying jovially to his guest, 'this is John Kendall, a brilliant young author.'

As Ronnie described all his authors as brilliant, even with plentiful evidence to the contrary, I remained unembarrassed.

Tremayne was equally unimpressed. Tremayne, sixtyish, grey-haired, big and self-assured, was clearly not pleased at the interruption. 'We haven't finished our business,' he said ungraciously.

'Time for a glass of wine,' Ronnie suggested, ignoring the complaint. 'For you, Tremayne?'

'Gin and tonic.'

'Ah . . . I meant, white wine or red?'

With annoyed resignation Tremayne said, 'Red, then.'

'Tremayne Vickers,' Ronnie said to me noncommittally, completing the introduction. 'Red do you, John?'

'Great.'

Ronnie bustled about, moving books and papers, clearing spaces, producing glasses, bottle and corkscrew and presently pouring with concentration.

'To trade,' he said with a smile, handing me a glass. 'To success,' he said to Vickers.

'Success! What success? All these writers are too big for their boots.'

Ronnie glanced involuntarily at my own boots, which were big enough for anyone.

'It's no use you telling me I'm not offering a decent fee,' Tremayne told him. 'They ought to be glad of the work.' He eyed me briefly. 'How much do you know about horse racing?' he demanded.

'Well,' I said. 'Not a lot.'

'Tremayne,' Ronnie protested, 'John isn't your sort of writer.'

'A writer's a writer. Anyone can do it. You tell me I've been wrong looking for a big name. Very well then, find me a smaller name. You said your friend here is brilliant. So how about *him*?'

'Ah,' Ronnie said cautiously. 'Brilliant is just . . . ah . . . a figure of speech. He's inquisitive, capable and impulsive.'

I smiled at my agent with amusement.

'So he's *not* brilliant?' Tremayne asked ironically, and to me he said, 'What have you written, then?'

I answered obligingly, 'Six travel guides and a novel.'

'Travel guides? What sort of travel guides?'

'How to live in the jungle. Or in deserts. That sort of thing.'

'For people who like difficult holidays,' Ronnie said. 'John used to work for a travel agency which specialises in sending the intrepid out to be stretched.'

'Oh.' Tremayne looked at his wine without enthusiasm and after a while said testily, 'There must be someone who'd leap at the job.'

I said, more to make conversation than out of urgent curiosity, 'What is it that you want written?'

Ronnie made a gesture that seemed to say 'Don't ask,' but Tremayne answered straightforwardly. 'An account of my life. You'd think those racing writers would be falling over themselves for the honour, but they've all turned me down.' He sounded aggrieved. 'Four of them.'

The truculence in Tremayne's voice was one of the reasons, I reflected, why he was having trouble. I lost interest in him, and Ronnie, seeing it, suggested sandwiches for lunch.

'I hoped you'd be lunching me at your club,' Tremayne said grouchily, and Ronnie said vaguely 'Work,' with a flap of the hand to indicate the papers on his desk. He went over to the door and put the same section of himself through it as before.

'Daisy?' He called to her along the passage. 'Phone down for sandwiches, would you? Usual selection. Everyone welcome.'

He brought himself in again. Tremayne went on looking disgruntled and I drank my wine with gratitude.

It was warm in Ronnie's office. That, too, was a bonus. I took off the jacket of the ski suit, hung it over a chair back and sat down contentedly in the scarlet sweater I wore underneath. Tremayne went on niggling away at his frustration.

'I offered to have them to stay,' he complained. 'They all said the sales wouldn't be worth the work, not at the rate I was offering. Arrogant lot.' He gloomily drank and made a face over the taste. 'My name alone would sell the book, I told them, and they had the gall to disagree.'

He seemed to think I should know who he was, that everyone should. I hardly liked to say I'd never heard of him.

He partially enlightened me. 'After all,' he said, 'I've trained getting on for a thousand winners. The Grand National, two Champion Hurdles, a Gold Cup, the Whitbread, you name it. I've seen half a century of racing. There's stories in all of it. Childhood . . . growing up . . . success . . . My life has been *interesting*.'

Words temporarily failed him, and I thought that everyone's life was interesting to themselves, tragedies and all. Everyone had a story to tell: the trouble lay in the few who wanted to read it.

Ronnie soothingly refilled the glasses and gave us a regretful summary of the book trade, which was in one of its periodical downswings on account of current high interest rates.

Daisy at length appeared in the doorway to say the food had arrived, and we all went along to the big room where the central table had been cleared of books and relaid with plates, knives, napkins and two large platters of healthy-looking sandwiches.

Ronnie's associates emerged from their offices to join us, which made seven altogether, including Daisy, and I managed to eat a lot without, I hoped, it being noticeable. Fillings of beef, ham, cheese, bacon: once-ordinary things that had become luxuries lately. I wished Ronnie would write summoning notes more often.

Tremayne harangued me again over the generic shortcomings of racing writers, while I nodded in sympathetic silence and munched away as if listening carefully. He made a great outward show of forceful self-confidence, but there was something in his insistence which curiously belied it. It was almost as if he needed the book to be written to prove he had lived.

'How old are you?' he said abruptly, breaking off in mid-flow.

I said with my mouth full, 'Thirty-two.'

'You look younger. Could you write a biography?'

'I don't know. Never tried.' If there was one biography I didn't want to cut my teeth on, I thought, it was his.

Ronnie fetched up beside him and wheeled him away, and in between finishing the beef-and-chutney I watched Ronnie across the room nodding his head placatingly under Tremayne's barrage of complaints. Eventually, when nothing was left on the plates, Ronnie said a firm farewell to Tremayne, who, with ill grace, finally left. Without any hint of relief Ronnie said to me, 'Come along then, John. Sorry to have kept you all this time,' and led the way back to his room.

'Tremayne asked if I'd ever written a biography,' I said, taking my former place on the visitors' side of his desk.

Ronnie gave me a swift glance, settling himself into his own padded dark green leather chair. 'Did he offer you the job?'

'Not exactly.'

'My advice to you would be not to think of it.' He gave me no time to assure him that I wouldn't, and went straight on. 'It's fair to say he's a good racehorse trainer, well known in his own field. It's fair to say he's a better man than you would have guessed today. It's even fair to agree he's had an interesting life. But that isn't enough. It all depends on the writing.'

'Will you find him someone?' I asked.

'Not on the terms he's looking for. He's asking for a writer to stay in his house for at least a month, to go through all his cuttings and records and interview him in depth. None of the top names will do that, they've all got other lives to lead. Then he wants seventy per cent of royalty income. No top writer is going to work for thirty per cent.'

'Thirty per cent . . . including the advance?'

'An advance no bigger than yours, if I could get one at all.'

'That's starvation.'

Ronnie smiled. 'Comparatively few people live by writing alone. I thought you knew that. Anyway'—he leaned forward, dismissing Tremayne and saying more briskly—'about these American rights . . .'

It seemed that a New York literary agent, an occasional associate of Ronnie's, had asked my publishers whether they had anything of interest in the pipeline. They had steered him to Ronnie. Would I, Ronnie asked, care to have him send a copy of my manuscript to the American agent, who would then, if he thought the book saleable in America, try to find it an American publisher.

'I . . . er . . . I'd be delighted,' I said.

'Thought you would. Not promising anything, you realise. He's just taking a look.'

'Yes.'

He went on for a while discussing technicalities and possibilities that I only half understood. He would let me know, he said, as soon as he got an opinion back from the New York agent.

'How's the new book coming along?' he asked.

'Slowly.'

He nodded. 'The second one's always difficult. But keep going.'

He rose to his feet, looking apologetically at his waiting paperwork, shaking my hand warmly in farewell. I thanked him for the lunch and walked along the passage to the lift, saying goodbye to Daisy on the way. I went down two floors and out into the bitter afternoon air, thinking of the steps that had led to Ronnie's door.

The six small books I'd previously written, though published and on sale to the public, had all been part of my work for the travel firm, who had paid me pretty well for writing them besides sending me to far-flung places to gather the knowledge. The travel firm wasn't in the market for novels.

I'd taken my precious typescript personally to a small but well-known publisher (looking up the address in the phone book) and had handed it to a pretty girl there who, having read it, suggested I should take it to an agent. She gave me a list of names and addresses.

'Try one of those,' she said. 'Good luck with it.'

I tried Ronnie Curzon for no better reason than his office lay on my direct walk home. Impulse had led to good and bad all my life, but when I felt it strongly, I usually followed it. Ronnie had been good. Opting for poverty had been so-so. Accepting Tremayne's offer was the pits.

Chapter 2

As I walked back to the friend's aunt's house in Chiswick, I hadn't the slightest intention of ever meeting Tremayne Vickers again. I thought of the present book I was writing: especially of how to get one character down from a runaway helium-filled balloon. The book that had been accepted,

Long Way Home, was about survival in general and in particular about the survival, physical and mental, of a bunch of people isolated by a disaster. Hardly an original theme, but I'd followed the basic advice to write about something I knew, and survival was what I knew best.

I opened the front door with my key and met the friend's aunt in the hall.

'Hello, dear,' she said. 'Everything all right?'

I told her about Ronnie sending my book to America, and her thin face filled with genuine pleasure. She was roughly fifty, divorced, a grandmother, sweet, fair-haired and undemanding. She'd been introduced to me as 'Aunty' and that's what I called her, and she seemed to regard me as a sort of extension nephew. We had lived in harmony for ten months.

'It's very cold . . . are you warm enough up there?' she asked kindly.

'Yes, thank you,' I said. The coin-in-the-slot electric heater she had installed for me ate money. I almost never switched it on.

She said, 'Good, dear,' amiably, and we nodded to each other, and I went upstairs thinking that I'd lived in the Arctic Circle and if I hadn't been able to deal with a cold London attic I would have been ashamed of myself. It was writing that made me cold.

Up in my eyrie I struggled for a couple of hours to resolve the plight of my man in the helium balloon. I thought I'd have to invent a range of mountains dead ahead for him to come to grief on. Then he would merely have the problem of descending from an Everest-approximation with only fingers, toes and resolution. Much easier. I knew a tip or two about that.

My attic had a worn pink carpet and cream wallpaper sprigged with pink roses. The resident furniture of bed, chest of drawers, wardrobe, two chairs and a table was overwhelmed by a veritable army of crates, boxes and suitcases containing my collected worldly possessions: clothes, books, household goods and sports equipment, all top quality and in good shape, acquired in carefree, bygone affluence. Two pairs of expensive skis stood in their covers in a corner. Wildly extravagant cameras and lenses rested in dark foam beds. My helicopter pilot's licence lay in a drawer, automatically expired now since I hadn't flown for a year. A life on hold, I thought. A life suspended.

I thought occasionally that I could eat better if I sold something, but it seemed stupid to cannibalise things that had given me pleasure. They were mostly tools of my past trade, and I might need them again.

Helium balloon . . .

The second half of the advance on *Long Way Home* wasn't due until publication day, a whole long year ahead. My small weekly allotted parcels of money wouldn't last that long, and I didn't see how I could live on much less. My rent-in-advance would run out at the end of June. If, I thought, if I could finish this balloon lark by then and if it were accepted and if they paid the same advance as before, then maybe I'd just manage the full two years. Then if the books fell with a dull thud, I'd give up and go back to the easier rigours of the wild.

THAT NIGHT THE AIR temperature over London plummeted still further, and in the morning Aunty's house was frozen solid.

'There's no water,' she said in distress when I went downstairs. 'The central heating stopped and all the pipes have frozen. I've called the plumber. He says he can't do anything until it thaws.' She looked at me helplessly. 'I'm very sorry, dear, but I'm going to close the house. I'm going to stay in a hotel until this is over. Can you find somewhere else for a week or two?'

Dismay was a small word for what I felt. She let me use her telephone to look for another roof. I got through to her nephew, who still worked for the travel firm. 'Do you have any more aunts?' I enquired.

'Good Lord, what have you done with that one?'

I explained. 'Could you lend me six feet of floor to unroll my bedding on?'

'Why don't you gladden the life of your parents on that Caribbean island?'

'Small matter of the fare.'

'You can come for a night or two,' he said. 'But Wanda's moved in with me, and you know how tiny the flat is.'

I also didn't much like Wanda. I thanked him and said I would let him know, and racked my brains for somewhere else.

It was inevitable I should think of Tremayne Vickers.

I phoned Ronnie Curzon and put it to him straight. 'Can you sell me to that racehorse trainer?'

'What?'

'He was offering free board and lodging.'

'Take me through it one step at a time.'

I took him through it and he was all against it.

'Much better to get on with your new book.'

'It's too cold to invent stories.'

'Don't do it,' he said.

'I might as well learn about racing. Why not? I might use it in a book. And I can ride. Tell him that.'

'Impulse will kill you one of these days.'

I should have listened to him, but I didn't.

WHEN I PHONED AGAIN at noon, Ronnie was mournfully triumphant. 'Tremayne agreed you can write his book. He quite took to you yesterday, it seems.' Pessimism vibrated down the wire. 'He's agreed to guarantee you a writing fee.' Ronnie mentioned a sum which would keep me eating through the summer. 'It's payable in three instalments—a quarter after a month's work, a quarter when he approves the full manuscript, and half on publication. He's agreed you should have forty per cent of any royalties after that, not thirty. He's agreed to pay your expenses. You can drive one of his cars. He was pleased you can ride. He says you should take riding clothes with you and also a dinner jacket, as he's to be guest of honour at some dinner or other and he wants you to witness it.'

'When does Tremayne expect me?' I asked.

'He says he'd be happy for you to go as soon as you can. Today, even, he said. He lives in a village called Shellerton, in Berkshire. He says if you can phone to say what train you're catching, someone will meet you at Reading station. Here's the number.' He read it out to me.

'Fine,' I said. 'And Ronnie, thanks very much.'

'Don't thank me. Just . . . well, just go on writing fiction. That's where your future is.'

'Do you mean it?'

'Of course I mean it.' He sounded surprised I should ask. 'For someone who's not afraid of jungles you exhibit the strangest self-confidence deficiency.'

'I know where I am in jungles.'

'Go and catch your train,' he said, and wished me luck.

I caught, instead, a bus, as it was much cheaper, and was met outside Reading bus station by a young woman in a padded coat and woollen hat who visually checked me over from boots via ski suit to dark hair and said, 'You're the writer?' She was used to authority, not unfriendly.

'John Kendall,' I said, nodding.

'I'm Mackie Vickers. Your bus is late.'

'The roads are bad,' I said apologetically.

'They're worse in the country.' It was dark and extremely cold. She led the way to a chunky Jeep parked not far away and opened the rear door. 'Put your bags in here. You can meet everyone as we go.'

There were already four people in the vehicle, all cold and relieved I had finally turned up. I stowed my belongings and climbed in, sharing the back seat with two dimly seen figures who moved up to give me room. Mackie Vickers positioned herself behind the wheel, started the engine, released the brake and drove out into a stream of cars. A welcome trickle of hot air came out of the heater.

'The writer says his name is John Kendall,' Mackie said.

There wasn't much reaction to the introduction.

'You're sitting next to Tremayne's head lad,' she went on, 'and his wife is beside him.'

The shadowy man next to me said, 'Bob Watson.' His wife said nothing.

'Next to me,' Mackie said, 'are Fiona and Harry Goodhaven.'

Neither Fiona nor Harry said anything. There was an intense quality in the collective atmosphere, as if the very air were scowling.

Mackie drove for several minutes in continuing silence. Eventually she said to me, 'We're not good company. We've spent all day in court. Tempers are frayed. You'll just have to put up with it.'

'No trouble,' I said. Trouble was the wrong word to use, it seemed.

As if releasing tension Fiona said, 'I can't *believe* you were so stupid.'

'Give it a rest,' Harry said. He'd already heard it before.

'But you know damned well that Lewis was drunk.'

'Everyone says he was drunk,' Harry said, 'but I don't *know* it, do I? I didn't *see* him drinking too much.'

Bob Watson beside me said 'Liar' on a whispered breath, and Harry didn't hear.

'Nolan is going to prison,' Fiona said. 'All because of you.'

'The jury haven't found him guilty yet,' Harry complained.

'But they *will,* won't they? And it will be *your fault*. All you had to do was say Lewis was drunk. Now the jury thinks he wasn't drunk, so he must be able to remember everything. Nolan's whole *defence* was that Lewis can't remember. How could you be so *stupid*?'

Harry didn't answer. The atmosphere worsened and I felt as if I'd gone into a movie halfway through and couldn't grasp the plot.

Mackie, without contributing any opinions, turned from the Great West Road onto the M4 motorway and made better time westwards along an unlit stretch between snow-covered wooded hills.

'*Bob* says Lewis was drunk,' Fiona persisted, 'and he should know, he was serving the drinks.'

'They should have had you in the witness box,' Harry said defensively. 'Then you could have sworn he was paralytic and had to be scraped off the carpet, even if you weren't there.'

Bob Watson said, 'He wasn't paralytic.'

'You keep out of it, Bob,' Harry snapped.

'Sorr-ee,' Bob Watson said, again under his breath.

'You let that prosecutor tie you in *knots* . . .' Fiona ran on and on, the rage in her mind unabating.

I began to feel mildly sorry for Harry.

We reached the Chieveley interchange and left the motorway to turn north on the A34 to Oxford.

Silence had mercifully struck Fiona's tongue by the time Shellerton showed up on a signpost. Mackie cautiously turned off the main road into a very narrow secondary road where snow had been roughly pushed to the sides but still lay in shallow frozen brown ruts over much of the surface. The tyres scrunched on them, cracking the ice. Mist formed quickly on the inside of the windscreen and Mackie rubbed it away impatiently with her glove.

There were no houses beside the lane. There were also no cars: no one was out driving if they could help it. For all Mackie's care, one could sometimes feel the wheels sliding, losing traction for perilous seconds.

'It's worse than this morning,' Mackie said, sounding worried. 'This road's a skating rink.'

No one answered her. With extra care she took a curve to the right.

Caught by the headlights, stock-still in the middle of the road, stood a horse. A dark horse buckled into a dark rug, its head raised in alarm. The moment froze like the landscape.

'Hell!' Mackie exclaimed, and slammed her foot on the brake.

The vehicle slid inexorably on the ice. The horse, terrified, tried to plunge off the road into the field alongside. Intent on missing him, and at the same time fighting the skid, Mackie miscalculated the curve. The Jeep slid to the side of the road, spun its wheels on the snow-covered grass shoulder, mounted it, tipped over sideways into an unseen drainage ditch, cracking with noises like pistol shots through a covering sheet of ice.

We'd been going slowly enough for it not to be an instantly lethal crunch, though it was a bang hard enough to rattle one's teeth. The nearside wheels, both front and back, finished four foot lower than road level, the far side of the ditch supporting the length of the roof of the vehicle so that it lay not absolutely flat on its side. I was opening my door, which was half sloping skyward, and hauling myself out before the engine had had time to stall.

The wind stung my face sharply with a freezing warning. Wind-chill was an unforgiving enemy, deadly to the unwary.

Bob Watson had fallen on top of his wife. I reached down into the Jeep and grasped him, and began to pull him out.

He tried to free himself from my hands, crying 'Ingrid' urgently, and then in horror, 'It's wet . . . she's in water.'

'Come out,' I said peremptorily. 'Then we can both pull her. You'll never get her out like that.'

He let me yank him out far enough so that he could stretch back in for his wife. Between the two of us we brought her out onto the roadway.

The ditch was almost full of muddy freezing water under its coating of ice. Even as we lifted Ingrid out, the water deepened fast in the vehicle, and in the front seat Fiona was yelling to Harry to get her out. Harry, I saw in horror, was underneath her and in danger of drowning.

The one headlight still shining suddenly went out.

Mackie hadn't moved. I pulled open her door and found her dazed and semiconscious, held in her place by her seat belt.

'Get us out!' Fiona yelled.

Harry, below her, was struggling in water and heaving. I felt around Mackie until I found the seat-belt clasp, released it, hauled her out bodily and shoved her into Bob Watson's arms.

'Sit her on the verge,' I said. 'Shield her from the wind.'

Bob took Mackie's weight and helped her to sit down. She began moving and moaning, showing welcome signs of life.

Fiona, halfway panic-stricken, put her arms up to mine and came out easily into the air, lithe and athletic. I leaned in for Harry, who now had his seat belt unfastened and his head above water and had got past the stage of abject fright. He climbed out and went dripping over to Mackie.

Ingrid stood in the road, soaked, thin, frightened, helpless and crying. The wind was piercing, relentless . . . infinitely dangerous. It was easy to underestimate how fast cold could kill.

I said to Bob Watson, 'Take all your wife's clothes off.'

'What?'

'Take her wet clothes off or she'll freeze into a block of ice. Start at the top. Take everything off and put my jacket on her, quickly. It's warm.' I unzipped it and took it off. The cold bit through my sweater and undershirt as if they were invisible. I was infinitely grateful to be dry.

'I'll help Ingrid,' Fiona said, as Bob still hesitated. While the two women unbuttoned and tugged I went to the rear of the overturned vehicle and found to my relief that the luggage door would still open. I pushed up my sleeves and literally fished out my two bags.

'Everything will be wet,' Harry said close beside me.

'No.' Waterproof, sandproof, bugproof were the rules I travelled by, even in rural England. I asked Harry, 'Would you prefer bathrobe or dinner jacket?'

He actually laughed.

'Strip off,' I said, 'in case the iceman cometh. Top half first.'

Harry began to struggle out of his sodden clothes wincing with pain as the cold hit his wet flesh. I handed him a navy blue silk undershirt and long johns, two sweaters, grey trousers and the bathrobe. No one ever dived into clothes faster.

Fiona had changed Ingrid to the waist and was waiting to do the second half. I took off my boots and then my ski pants, which Fiona put on Ingrid after trying to shield her brief lower nakedness from my eyes, which amazed me. It was hardly the time for fussing. The boots looked enormous, once they were on, and Ingrid was nine inches shorter than my ski suit.

I dug into the bag again for a navy blazer, jodhpur boots and jodhpurs, black socks and a sweatshirt. 'These any good to you?' I asked Fiona.

She took all the clothes gratefully and hid behind Ingrid to change. I put on my black evening shoes, which were all that remained in the way of footwear, and the dinner jacket: a lot better than nothing.

When Fiona reappeared she still had too few layers, even if now dry. The only useful thing still unused in my belongings was the plastic bag which had contained my dinner jacket. I pulled it over Fiona's head, widening the hole where the hanger usually went. At least it stopped the wind a bit and kept some body heat in.

'Well,' Harry said with remarkable cheerfulness, 'thanks to John we should live to see Shellerton. All you lot had better start walking. I'll stay with Mackie and we'll follow when we can.'

'No,' I said. 'How far is it to the village?'

'A mile or so.'

'Then we all start now. We'll carry Mackie. It's too cold, believe me, for hanging about. How about a chair lift?'

So Harry and I sat the semiconscious Mackie on our linked wrists and draped her arms round our necks, and we set off with Bob Watson carrying all the wet clothes in one of my bags, Fiona carrying dry things in the other and Ingrid shuffling along in front in the moon boots, lighting the way with the dynamo torch from my basic travel kit.

'Thank God it isn't snowing,' Harry said, but there were ominous clouds hiding the stars. I was glad it wasn't too far to the village. Mackie wasn't heavy, but we were walking on ice.

'Doesn't any traffic ever come along this road?' I asked in frustration when we'd gone half a mile and still seen no one.

'There are two other ways into Shellerton,' Harry said.

Harry's hands and mine were going numb carrying Mackie. If I'd brought any more socks we could have used them as mitts.

'It's not far now,' Bob said after a while. 'Once we're round the bend you'll see the village.'

He was right. Electricity twinkled not far below us, offering shelter and warmth. Mackie suddenly awoke to full consciousness on the last stretch and began demanding to know what was happening.

'We skidded into a ditch,' Harry said succinctly.

'The horse! Is the horse all right? Put me down.'

We stopped and set her on her feet, where she swayed and put a hand to the side of her head. 'Did we hit the horse?'

'No,' Harry answered. 'It ran off across the Downs. Come on, Mackie, we're literally freezing to death here.' He hugged his body and tried to warm his hands in his armpits. 'Let's get on.'

Mackie refused to let us lift her up again, so we began to struggle on towards the village, a shadowy band slipping and sliding, holding on to each other and trying not to fall, cold to the bone.

'You'd better all come to our house,' Fiona said in a shaking voice. 'It's nearest.'

No one argued.

Presently we turned into a driveway which wound round behind some cottages and opened into a snowy expanse in front of a big Georgian-looking house.

Fiona said, 'This way,' and led a still-silent procession round to a side door, which she unlocked with a key retrieved from under a stone.

The relief of being out of the wind was like a rebirth. The warmth of the extensive kitchen we filed into was a positive life-giving luxury, and there in the lights I saw my companions clearly for the first time.

Chapter 3

Everyone except Ingrid was visibly trembling, myself included. All the faces were bluish-white, suffering.

'That was hell,' Fiona said.

Fiona was older than I'd thought. Forties, not thirties. The plastic bag reached nearly to her knees, bordering on farcical.

'Take this thing off me,' she said. 'And don't bloody laugh.'

Harry obligingly pulled the cleaner's plastic bag up and over her head, taking her knitted hat with it, freeing heavy silver-blonde hair and transforming her from a refugee into an assured, charismatic woman in jodhpurs and blue blazer.

She stared at me across her kitchen, looking with curiosity at the man whose clothes she wore, seeing, I supposed, a tallish, thinnish, youngish brown-eyed person in scarlet sweater and incongruous dinner suit.

I smiled at her and she, aware of the admiration in my expression, swept a reviving glance round her other unexpected guests. The bad temper of the journey had disappeared.

'Hot drinks,' she said decisively. 'Harry, fill the kettle.'

Harry, my height but fair and blue-eyed, complied with the instructions as though thoroughly accustomed to being bidden, and began rooting round for mugs, spoons, instant coffee and sugar. Swaddled in my blue bathrobe, he looked ready for bed; and he too was older than I'd thought.

Mackie sat down uncertainly at the big central table, her fingers gingerly feeling her temple. 'Is the Jeep all right?'

'Shouldn't think so,' Harry said without emotion. 'The door on my side buckled when we hit. Filthy ditchwater just rushed in.'

'Damn,' Mackie said. 'That on top of everything else.'

She huddled into her padded coat, still shivering, and it was hard to tell what she would look like warm and laughing. All I could see were reddish curls over her forehead, closed eyes, pale lips and rigid muscles.

'Is Perkin home?' Fiona asked her.

'He should be. God, I hope so.'

Fiona went across to a wall telephone and pressed buttons. Perkin, whoever he was, apparently answered and was given a variety of bad news.

'Yes,' Fiona said, repeating things, 'I did say the Jeep's in a ditch . . . I don't know whose horse, damn it . . . No, we had an *abysmal* day in court. Look, just come down here and collect everyone. Mackie's all right but she hit her head. Just *come*, Perkin.' She hung up the receiver with a crash.

Harry poured steaming water onto instant coffee in a row of mugs and then picked up a milk carton in one hand and a bottle of brandy in the other, offering a choice of additives. Everyone except Ingrid chose brandy.

The deep trembles in all our bodies abated. Bob Watson took off his cap and looked suddenly younger, a short, stocky man with wiry brown hair and rounded cheeks, and a natural insolence not far from the surface but controlled enough to keep him out of trouble. He had called Harry a liar, but too quietly for him to hear. That rather summed up Bob Watson, I thought.

Ingrid, swamped in the ski suit, looked out at the world from a thinly pretty face and sniffed at regular intervals. She sat beside her husband at the table, unspeaking and forever in his shadow.

Standing with his backside propped against the warm Aga, Harry looked at me with the glimmering amusement that, when not under stress from giving evidence, seemed to be his habitual cast of mind.

'Welcome to Berkshire,' he said.

'Thanks a lot.'

No one had a great wish to talk, and there was a return to the pre-crash gloom, so it was a relief when slammed doors and approaching footsteps announced the arrival of Perkin.

He hadn't come alone. It was Tremayne Vickers who advanced first into the kitchen, his loud voice and large personality galvanising the subdued group drinking coffee.

'Roads too much for you, eh?' he boomed with a touch of not wholly unfriendly scorn.

The man who followed Tremayne through the door looked like a smudged carbon copy: same height, same build, same basic features, but none of Tremayne's bullishness. If that was Perkin, I thought, he must be Tremayne's son.

The carbon copy said to Mackie crossly, 'You ought to have more sense than to take that short cut.'

'It was all right this morning,' Mackie said. 'It was the horse . . .'

Tremayne's gaze fastened on me. 'So you got here. Good. You've met everyone? My son, Perkin. His wife, Mackie . . . Why on earth are you wearing a dinner jacket?'

'We got wet in the ditch,' Harry said briefly. 'Your friend the writer lent us dry clothes.'

Tremayne looked briefly bewildered. He asked Fiona if she'd been hurt in the crash. 'Fiona, my dear . . .'

Fiona, his dear, assured him otherwise. He behaved to her with a hint of roguishness, she to him with easy response. She aroused in all men, I supposed, the desire to flirt.

Perkin belatedly asked Mackie about her head. She gave him a tired understanding smile, and I had a swift impression that she was the one in that marriage who did the looking after, who was the adult to her good-looking husband-child.

'But,' he said, 'I do think you were silly to go down that road.' His reaction to her injury was still to blame her for it, but I wondered if it wasn't really a reaction to fright, like a parent clouting a much-loved, lost-but-found infant.

Tremayne said, 'What's done's done,' as if announcing his life's philosophy, and added that he would 'give the police a ring' when he got home.

'About your clothes,' Fiona said to me, 'shall I send them to the cleaners with all our wet things?'

'Don't bother,' I said. 'I'll come and collect them tomorrow.'

'All right.' She smiled slightly. 'I do realise we have to thank you. Don't think we don't know.'

Mackie stood up, clearly much better for the warmth and the stiffly laced coffee. 'Tomorrow,' she said slowly, 'which of us is going back to Reading?'

'Oh,' Fiona said. 'For a minute I'd forgotten.'

'Some of us will have to go,' Mackie said. It was clear no one wanted to.

Harry stirred. 'I'll go. I'll take Bob. Mackie . . .' He stopped.

'I'll come with you,' she said. 'I owe him that.'

Fiona said, 'So will I. He's my cousin, after all. Though after what Harry did today I don't know if I can look him in the face.'

'What did Harry do?' Perkin asked.

Fiona shrugged and retreated. 'Mackie can tell you.'

'Let's be off,' Tremayne said. 'Come along, Bob.'

'Yes, sir.'

Bob Watson, I remembered, was Tremayne's head lad. He and his Ingrid went over to the door, followed by Mackie and Perkin. I put down my mug, thanking Harry for the reviver.

'Come this time tomorrow and fetch your clothes,' he said. 'Come for an ordinary drink, not an emergency.'

'Thank you. I'd like that.'

He nodded amiably, and Fiona also, and I picked up my dry-clothes bag and followed Tremayne and the others out again into the snow. The six of us squeezed into a large Volvo.

At the end of the village Tremayne, who was driving, stopped to let Bob and Ingrid get out, Ingrid giving me a sketchy smile and saying Bob would bring my suit and boots along in the morning.

Tremayne started off again. 'Not much of a welcome for you, John, eh?' he said over his shoulder. 'Did you bring a typewriter?'

'No. A pencil, actually. And a tape recorder.'

'I expect you know what you're doing.' He sounded more sure of that than I was. 'We can start in the morning.'

After another mile of cautious crawling, he turned in through a pair of imposing gateposts and stopped outside a very large house where many lights showed dimly through curtains. We went in at the side, into a warm carpeted hall leading to doorways in all directions.

Tremayne walked through a doorway to the left, looking back for me to follow. 'Come on in. Make yourself at home. This is the family room, where you'll find newspapers, telephone, drinks, things like that. Help yourself to whatever you want while you're here.'

The big room looked comfortable in a sprawling way. There was a mixture of patterns and colours, a great many photographs, and a glowing log fire in a wide stone fireplace. Tremayne picked up a telephone and briefly told the police that his Jeep was in the ditch in the lane and he would get it picked up in the morning. Duty done, he went across to the fire and held out his hands to warm them.

'Perkin and Mackie have their own part of the house, but this room is where we all meet,' he said. 'If you want to leave a message for anybody, pin it to that board over there.' He pointed to a chair on which was propped a cork board. Red drawing pins were stuck into it at random, one of them anchoring a note which announced in large letters BACK FOR GRUB.

'That's my other son,' Tremayne said, reading the message from a distance. 'He's fifteen. Unmanageable.' He spoke however with indulgence. 'I expect you'll soon get the hang of the household.'

'Er . . . *Mrs* Vickers?' I said tentatively. 'Your wife?'

'My wife took a hike. Can't say I minded. I've a daughter, married a frog, lives outside Paris. She's the eldest, then Perkin. Gareth came later.'

He was feeding me facts without feelings, I thought. He was glad I was there, but jerky, almost nervous. Almost—now we were alone—shy.

Mackie, coming into the room, restored him to his confident self. Carrying an ice bucket, she went over to a table bearing a tray of bottles and glasses and began mixing a drink.

She was wearing a blue jersey dress over knee-high black boots. Her red-brown hair, cut short, curled neatly on a well-shaped head and she was still pale, without lipstick or vivacity.

The drink she mixed was gin and tonic, which she gave to Tremayne. 'For you?' Mackie said to me.

'The coffee was fine,' I said.

Truth to tell I was hungry, not thirsty. I began to hope that Gareth's return, 'BACK FOR GRUB', was imminent.

Perkin appeared carrying a full glass of brown liquid that looked like Coca-Cola. He sank into an armchair and began complaining again about the loss of the Jeep, not seeing that he was lucky not to have lost his wife.

'The damned thing's insured,' Tremayne said robustly. 'The garage can tow it out of the ditch in the morning and tell us if it can be salvaged.'

'How will we manage without it?' Perkin grumbled.

'Buy another,' Tremayne said.

This simple solution silenced Perkin, and Mackie looked grateful. She sat on a sofa and took her boots off. She massaged her toes and looked across at my black shoes.

'Those shoes of yours are meant for dancing,' she said, 'and not for carrying females across ice. I'm sorry, I really am.'

'Carrying?' Tremayne said, eyebrows rising.

'Yes, didn't I tell you? John and Harry carried me for about a mile, I think. It's a bit of a blur . . . it was like dreaming.'

Perkin stared, first at her, then at me. Not pleased, I thought.

'I'll be damned,' Tremayne said.

I smiled at Mackie and she smiled back, and Perkin very obviously didn't like that. I'd have to be careful, I thought. I was not there to stir family waters but simply to do a job.

Thankful for the heat of the fire, I shed the dinner jacket, laying it on a chair and feeling less like the decadent remains of an orgy.

'Sit down, John,' Tremayne said, waving to an armchair. I sat as instructed. 'What happened in court?' he asked Mackie.

'It was awful.' She shuddered. 'Nolan looked so . . . so *vulnerable*. The jury think he's guilty, I'm sure they do. And Harry wouldn't swear after all that Lewis was drunk . . .' She sighed deeply. 'I wish to God we'd never had that damned party.'

'What's done is done,' Tremayne said heavily. He glanced at me and asked Mackie, 'Have you told John what's going on?'

She shook her head and enlightened me a little. 'We gave a party here last year in April to celebrate winning the Grand National with Top Spin Lob. Celebrate! There were a lot of people here, well over a hundred, including of course Fiona and Harry, who you met. I train horses for them. And Fiona's cousins were here, Nolan and Lewis. They're brothers. No one knows for sure what happened, but at the end of the party a girl died. Nolan swears it was an accident. Lewis was there . . . he should have been able to settle it one way or the other, but he says he was drunk and can't remember.'

'Is Nolan being tried for murder?' I asked.

'For assault resulting in death,' Tremayne said. 'The prosecution are trying to prove intent, which would make it murder. Nolan's lawyers are pressing for involuntary manslaughter, which could be called negligence or plain accident. The case has been dragging on for months. At least tomorrow it should end.'

Tremayne told me, 'Mackie and Harry walked together into Mackie and Perkin's sitting room and found Nolan standing over the girl, who was lying on the floor. Lewis was sitting in an armchair. Nolan said he'd put his hands round the girl's neck to give her a shaking, and she just went limp and fell down.'

'The pathologist said in court today that she died from strangulation,' Mackie said, 'but that sometimes it takes very little pressure to kill someone. He said it's always dangerous to clasp people suddenly round the neck, even in fun. But there's no doubt Nolan was furious with Olympia—that's the girl—and the prosecution produced someone who'd heard him say, "I'll strangle her" . . .' She broke off and sighed again. 'The pathologist's original report said it could so easily have been an accident that there wasn't going to be a prosecution, but Olympia's father insisted on bringing a private case against Nolan.'

'If he'd had his way,' Tremayne confirmed, 'Nolan would have been behind bars all this time, not out on bail.'

Mackie nodded. 'It's Olympia's father who deserves to be strangled for all the trouble he's caused.'

It seemed to me that on the whole it was Nolan who had caused the trouble, but I didn't say so.

'You won't put all this Nolan business in my book, will you?' Tremayne asked.

'I shouldn't think so,' I said, 'not if you don't want me to.'

Tremayne just nodded. Seen in his own home, standing by his own fire, he was a big-bodied man of substantial presence, accustomed to taking charge and ruling his kingdom. This was the persona, no doubt, that the book was to be about: the face of control, of worldly wisdom and success. So be it, I thought. If I were to sing for my supper I'd sing the songs he chose. But meanwhile, where was the supper?

'In the morning,' Tremayne said to me, 'I thought you might come out with me to see my string at morning exercise.'

'I'd like to,' I said.

'Good. I'll wake you at seven. The first lot pulls out at seven thirty. At present, with this freeze, we can't do any schooling but we've got an all-weather gallop. If it should be snowing hard, we won't go.' He turned to Mackie. 'I suppose you won't be out for first lot?'

'No, sorry. We'll have to leave early again to get to Reading.'

He nodded, and to me he said, 'Mackie's my assistant.'

I glanced at Mackie and then at Perkin.

'That's right,' Tremayne said, reading my thought. 'Perkin doesn't work for me. Mackie does. Perkin never wanted to be a trainer and he has his own life. Gareth . . . well . . . he's too young to know what he'll want. But when Perkin married Mackie he brought me a damned smart assistant.'

Mackie looked pleased at his audible sincerity and it seemed the arrangement was to Perkin's liking also.

'This house is huge,' Tremayne said, 'and as Perkin and Mackie couldn't afford much of a place of their own yet, we divided it, and they have their private half. You can have the dining room to work in. Tomorrow I'll show you where to find the cuttings, videotapes and form books.'

'Fine,' I said. Food in the dining room would be better, I thought.

Gareth at long last blew in with a gust of cold air and, stripping off a dazzling psychedelic padded jacket, asked his father, 'What's for supper?'

'Anything you like,' Tremayne said, not minding.

'Pizza, then.' His gaze stopped on me. 'Hello, I'm Gareth.'

Tremayne told him my name and that I would be writing the biography and staying in the house.

'Straight up?' the boy said, eyes widening. 'Do you want some pizza?'

'Yes, please.'

Gareth was perhaps five foot six with a strong echo of his father's self-confidence and a voice still half broken, coming out hoarse and uneven. He gave me an all-over glance as if assessing what he'd got to put up with for the length of my visit and seemed neither depressed nor elated.

'Right.' Gareth took his Joseph's coat with him out of the door and almost immediately returned. 'I suppose there isn't the faintest chance,' he said to me, 'that you can cook?'

Chapter 4

In the morning I went downstairs to the kitchen.

It wasn't palatial like Fiona's but did contain a big table with chairs all round it as well as an Aga solid-fuel cooker whose warmth easily defeated the pre-dawn refrigeration. On a chair I found my boots, gloves and ski suit with a note attached by a safety pin, 'Thanks ever so much'.

Smiling, I unpinned the note and put on the suit and boots, and Tremayne, in a padded jacket, cloth cap and yellow scarf came in, generally bringing the arctic indoors.

'Ah, there you are,' he said, puffing. 'Good. Bob Watson brought up your clothes when he came to feed. Ready?'

I nodded.

'It's as cold as I've ever known it. We won't stay out long.'

As we went through the hall I asked him about the feeding.

'Bob Watson comes at six,' he said briefly. 'All horses in training get an early-morning feed. High protein. Keeps them warm. Gives them energy. A thoroughbred on a high-protein diet generates a lot of heat. You rarely find a bucket of water frozen over in a horse's box, however cold it is outside.'

As we stepped out into the open, the wind pulled his last words away and sucked the breath out of our lungs. A short walk took us straight into the stable yard, dark the night before and dimly seen, now lit comprehensively and bustling with activity.

'Bob Watson,' Tremayne said, 'is no ordinary head lad. He has all sorts of skills. Any odd job, carpentering, plumbing, laying concrete, anything to improve the yard—he suggests and mostly does it himself.'

The object of this eulogy came to meet us. 'All ready, guvnor,' he said to Tremayne.

'Good. Bring them out, Bob. Then you'd better be off to Reading.'

Bob nodded and gave some sort of signal, and from many open doors came figures leading horses, riders in hard helmets, horses in rugs. In the lights and the dark, with plumes of steam swirling as they breathed, with the circling movements and the scrunching of icy gravel underfoot, the great elemental creatures raised in me such a sense of enjoyment and excitement that I felt for the first time truly enthusiastic about what I'd set my hand to.

Bob moved through the scene giving a leg-up to each lad and they resolved themselves into a line.

'Splendid,' I said to Tremayne, almost sighing.

He glanced at me. 'Horses get to you, don't they?'

'To you too? Still?'

He nodded and said, 'I love them,' as if such a statement were no more than normal, and in the same tone of voice went on, 'As the Jeep's in the ditch we'll have to go up to the gallops in the tractor. All right with you?'

'Sure,' I said and got my introduction to the training of steeplechasers perched high in a tractor over chain-wrapped wheels. Tremayne drove with the facility of long custom. His house and stables, I discovered, were right on the edge of the grassy uplands, so that the twenty or so horses had merely to cross one public road to be already on a downland track. We lumbered onwards and upwards over frozen rutted mud as the day broke clear and high over the rolling, snow-dusted hills.

Tremayne stopped the tractor and told me that today they would be doing only half-speed gallops on the all-weather track, and he led the way on foot across a stretch of powdery snow to a low mound from where we could see a long dark ribbon of ground winding away down the hill.

'They'll come up here towards us,' he said. 'The all-weather surface is wood chips. Am I telling you what you already know?'

'No,' I said. 'Tell me everything.'

He grunted noncommittally and raised a pair of binoculars powerful enough to see into the riders' minds. I looked where he was looking, to spot three dark shapes moving over the dark track. They seemed to be taking a long time to come up head-on towards us but the slowness was an illusion. Once they drew near and passed us their speed was vivid, stirring, a matter of muscles stretching and hoofs thudding urgently on the quiet surface.

Two or three at a time they all came up in their turn. 'The one on the left of this next three is my Grand National winner, Top Spin Lob,' Tremayne said from behind the binoculars.

With interest I watched the pride of the stable go past us.

Tremayne began to walk up beside the gallop in the direction of the horses, and I followed, and we soon came over the brow to where his whole string was circling on snowy grass, silhouetted against the eastern sun, steam swirling in clouds from their breath after their exertions.

Tremayne reached his horses and spoke to his lads. 'Walk on back to the yard. Take care crossing the road.'

They nodded and began to walk off in self-generated mist.

We went down to the tractor and in due course drove it back and parked it where it had been before we started out.

In the now sunlit kitchen Tremayne took off his coat, scarf and cap, revealing a big diamond-patterned golfing sweater over a boldly checked open-necked shirt.

'Coffee?' he said, going towards the Aga. He slid the heavy kettle onto the hot plate and went along to a refrigerator which disgorged sliced bread, a tub of yellowish spread and a pot of marmalade. 'Toast?' he said, putting two slices in a wire-mesh holder which he slid under the second hot plate lid of the cooker. 'There's cornflakes, if you'd rather. Or cook an egg.'

Toast would be fine, I said.

'Hang your jacket in the cloakroom, next door.' He went out into the hall. 'Dee-Dee,' he shouted. 'Coffee.'

He came back, finished making the toast and sat down to eat, waving to me to join him, and presently in the doorway appeared a slight, brown-haired woman who wore jeans and a huge grey sweater reaching to her knees.

'Dee-Dee,' Tremayne said, 'this is John Kendall, my writer.' To me he added, 'Dee-Dee's my secretary.'

I stood up politely and she told me unsmilingly to sit down. My first impression of her as she went across to the Aga to make her own coffee was that she was like a cat, soft-footed, fluid in movement and self-contained.

Tremayne watched me watching her and smiled. 'You'll get used to Dee-Dee,' he said. 'I couldn't manage without her.'

She sat half on a chair as if about to retreat.

'The Jeep's in a ditch on the south road to the A34. Skidded last evening with Mackie. No one hurt. Get the garage to fish it out.'

Dee-Dee nodded.

'John, here, will be working in the dining room. Anything he wants, give it to him. Anything he wants to know, tell him.'

Dee-Dee nodded.

'Check that the haulage people will be on time delivering the hay. We're running low. Don't take snow for an answer.'

Dee-Dee smiled, which looked feline also, although far from kittenish. I wondered fleetingly about claws.

Tremayne went on giving sporadic instructions which Dee-Dee seemed to have no trouble remembering. When the spate slowed she stood and said she would finish her coffee in the office while she got on with things.

'Utterly reliable,' Tremayne remarked to her departing back. He lowered his voice. 'An amateur jockey treated her like muck. She's not over it yet. I make allowances. If you find her crying, that's why.'

I was amazed by his compassion and felt I should have recognised earlier how many unexpected layers there were to Tremayne below the loud executive exterior: secret, unrevealed privacies which maybe I would come to in time, and maybe not.

He spent the next half-hour on the telephone. It was the time of day, I later discovered, when trainers could most reliably be found at home. Toast eaten, coffee drunk, he told me that I could set things up in the dining room, arrange things however I liked. As all racing was off, he could, if I agreed, spend the afternoon telling me about his childhood.

'Good idea,' I said.

'Come along, then, and I'll show you where things are.'

We went out into the carpeted hall and he opened a door. 'This is my dining room. We don't use it much. You'll have to turn the heating up.'

I looked into the room I was to get to know well; a spacious room with mahogany furniture, swagged crimson curtains, formal cream and gold striped walls and a plain dark green carpet.

He closed the door again. 'This passage leads to Perkin and Mackie's half of the house. Come along, I'll show you.' He walked along a wide, pale-green-carpeted corridor with pictures of horses on both walls and opened double white-painted doors at the end.

'Through here,' he said, 'is the oldest part of the house.'

We passed onto a big wood-blocked expanse of polished floor from which two graceful wings of staircase rose to an upper gallery. Under the gallery, between the staircases, was another pair of doors, which Tremayne opened, revealing a vista of formal gold and pale blue furnishings.

'This is the main drawing room,' he said. 'We share it. We hardly use it.

We used it last for that damned party . . .' He closed the drawing-room doors and pointed straight across the hall.

'That's the front entrance, and those double doors on the right open into Perkin and Mackie's half. We planned it as two separate houses, you see, with this big common section between us.'

'It's great,' I said to please him, but also meaning it.

He nodded. 'It divided quite well. No one needs houses this size these days. Most of this was built about nineteen six. My father bought the place for peanuts during the Depression. I've lived here all my life.'

'Was your father a trainer also?' I asked.

Tremayne laughed. 'God, no. He inherited a fortune. Never did a day's work. He liked going racing, so he bought a few jumpers and engaged a trainer for them. When I grew up, I just took over the horses. Built another yard, eventually. I've fifty boxes at present, all full.'

He led the way back to his own domain.

'That's more or less all,' he said, 'except for the office.'

Once back in his own hall I followed him into yet another big room in which Dee-Dee looked lost behind a vast desk.

'This used to be the billiards room,' Tremayne said, looking at his watch. 'I'll leave you to Dee-Dee. See you later.'

He went away purposefully, and Dee-Dee said, 'How can I help you?' without any great enthusiasm.

'Don't you approve of the biography project?' I asked.

She blinked. 'I didn't say that.'

'You looked it.'

She fiddled lengthily with some papers, eyes down.

'It's important to him,' she said finally. 'I think . . . if you must know . . . that he should have held out for someone better . . .' She hesitated. 'Better *known,* anyway.' She looked up, suddenly fierce. 'He deserves the best.'

I looked round the jumbo office, seeing the remains of the classical decorative style overlaid by a host of modern bookshelves, filing cabinets, computer, telephones, television, tapes by the dozen, cardboard boxes, and another corkboard with red drawing-pinned memos. Pictures of horses passing winning posts inhabited the walls alongside a bright row of racing silks hanging on pegs. I ended the visual tour where I'd begun, on Dee-Dee's face. 'The more you help,' I said, 'the more chance he has.'

She stared at me, her antagonism still clear. She was about forty, I supposed. Thin but not emaciated, from what one could see via the sweater. Good skin, bobbed straight hair, unremarkable features, pink lipstick, no jewellery, small, strong-looking hands. General air of reserve, of holding back. Perhaps that was habitual; perhaps the work of that amateur jockey.

'What I chiefly need,' I said, 'are cuttings books.'

'The cuttings are not in books, they're in boxes.' She turned her head, nodding directions. 'In that cupboard over there. Help yourself.'

I went across and opened a white-painted door and inside found stacked on shelves from floor to head height a whole array of uniform white cardboard boxes about eight inches deep, all with dates written on their ends in black marker ink. 'Can I take them all into the dining room?'

'Be my guest.'

I ferried the boxes to the dining room until the whole lot was transferred. Dee-Dee meanwhile went back to her work, which largely consisted of the telephone. I arranged the boxes of cuttings chronologically and took the lid off the first. Tattered, yellow pieces of newsprint informed me that Mr Loxley Vickers, of Shellerton House, Berkshire, had bought Triple Subject, a six-year-old gelding, for the record sum for a steeplechaser of 1,200 guineas. A house, an astonished reporter wrote, could be bought for less.

I looked up, and found Dee-Dee standing in the doorway.

'I've been talking to Fiona Goodhaven,' she said abruptly.

'How is she?'

'All right. Thanks to you, it seems. Why didn't you tell me about your rescue job?'

'It didn't seem important.'

'If you turn that thermostat,' she said, pointing, 'it will get warmer in here.'

She whisked away before I could thank her, but I understood that peace had been declared, or, at the very least, hostilities temporarily suspended.

Tremayne returned in time. He strode into the dining room. 'How are you doing?' he asked.

'Reading about your father.'

'A lunatic. Had an obsession about how things would look in his stomach after he'd eaten them. He used to make his butler put an extra serving of everything he was going to eat in a bucket and stir it round. If my father didn't like the look of it, he wouldn't eat his dinner. Drove the cook mad.'

I laughed. 'What about your mother?'

'She'd fallen off the perch by then. He wasn't so bad when she was alive. He went screwy after.'

'How old were you when she . . . er . . . fell off the perch?'

'Ten. Same age as Gareth when *his* mother finally hopped it. Except *his* mother's still alive and he sees her sometimes.'

'You said your father inherited a fortune. Did he leave it to you?'

Tremayne laughed in his throat. 'A fortune seventy or eighty years ago is not a fortune now. But yes, in a way he did. Left me this house. Taught me the principles of landowning which he'd learned from *his* father but hardly practised. My father spent, my grandfather accumulated. I'm more like my grandfather, though I never knew him. I tell Gareth sometimes that we can't afford things even if we can. I don't want him to turn out a spender.'

'What about Perkin?'

'Perkin?' For a second Tremayne looked blank. 'Perkin has no money sense at all. Lives in a world of his own.'

'What does he do,' I asked, 'in his world?'

'He makes furniture,' he said. 'Designs it. Makes it himself, piece by piece. Chests, tables, screens, anything. Two hundred years from now they will be valuable antiques.' He sighed. 'Best thing he ever did was marry Mackie. She sells his pieces, makes sure he makes a profit. He used to sell things sometimes for less than they cost to make. Absolutely hopeless.'

'As long as he's happy.'

Tremayne made no comment on his son's state of happiness but asked about my tape recorder. 'Didn't it get wet last night? Won't it be ruined?'

'No. I keep everything in waterproof bags. Sort of habit.'

'Jungles and deserts?' he asked, remembering.

'Mm.'

'Then you go and fetch it, and we'll start. And if you want any lunch,' he added, 'I nearly always have beef sandwiches; I buy them by the fifty, ready made, and put them in the freezer.'

We both ate mostly thawed, uninteresting beef sandwiches in due course and I thought that even if Tremayne's housekeeping were slightly eccentric, at least he hadn't stirred his food up first in a bucket.

Chapter 5

At about six thirty that day I walked down to Shellerton to collect my clothes from the Goodhavens, Fiona and Harry. Darkness had fallen but the air temperature hadn't, and there was less wind than in the morning.

I had by that time taped three hours' worth of Tremayne's extraordinary childhood. When I reminded him that I was going down to Fiona and Harry's he offered me his car.

'I quite like walking,' I said. 'I'll cook when I get back.'

'You don't have to,' he protested. 'Don't let Gareth talk you into it.'

'I said I would though.'

'I don't care much what I eat.'

I grinned. 'Maybe that will be just as well. I'll be back soon after Gareth, I expect.'

I'd discovered that the younger son rode his bicycle each morning to his friend Coconut's house, from where both of them were driven to and from a town ten miles away, as day boys in a mainly boarding school. The hours were long and Gareth was never home much before seven, often later. His notice BACK FOR GRUB' seemed to be a fixture. He removed it, Tremayne said, only when he knew in the morning that he would be out until bedtime.

I reached the main street of Shellerton and tramped along to the Goodhavens' house, passing three or four cars in their driveway and walking round to the kitchen door to ring the bell.

After an interval the door was opened by Harry, whose expression changed from inhospitable to welcoming by visible degrees.

'Oh, hello. Forgot about you. Fact is, we've had another lousy day in

Reading. But home without crashing, best you can say.'

I stepped into the house and he closed the door behind us.

'Nolan and Lewis are both here,' he said. 'Nolan got convicted of manslaughter. Six months' jail suspended for two years. He won't go behind bars but no one's happy.'

'I don't need to stay,' I said. 'Don't want to intrude.'

'Do me a favour, dilute the atmosphere.'

'If it's like that . . .'

He nodded, and walked me through the kitchen to a pink and green chintzy sitting room beyond.

Fiona, turning her silver-blonde head, said, 'Oh, good heavens, I'd forgotten.' She came over, holding out a hand, which I shook.

'These are my cousins,' she said. 'Nolan and Lewis Everard. A friend of Tremayne's,' she said to them briefly. 'John Kendall.'

Mackie, sitting in an armchair, waggled acknowledging fingers. Everyone else was standing and holding a glass. Harry pressed a pale gold drink into my hand. Whisky, I found, tasting it.

Nolan and Lewis were both short, Nolan handsome and hard, Lewis swollen and soft. Late thirties, both of them. Dark hair, dark eyes, dark jaws. Nolan's aristocratic-sounding speech was essentially violent and consisted of fifty per cent obscenity. The gist of his first sentence was that he wasn't in the mood for guests. If Nolan had spoken like that in court, I thought, it was no wonder he'd been found guilty. One could quite easily imagine him throttling a nymph.

Harry said calmly, 'John is writing Tremayne's biography. He knows about the trial. He's a friend of ours, and he stays.'

'Anyone can know about the trial,' Mackie said. 'It was in all the papers this morning, after all.'

Harry nodded. 'To be continued in reel two.'

'It's not a joke,' Lewis said. His peevish voice was like his brother's though a shade higher in pitch.

'The public won't remember by next week,' Harry told him.

Nolan said between four-letter words that everyone who mattered would remember, including the Jockey Club.

'I doubt if they'll actually warn you off,' Harry said. 'It wasn't as if you hadn't paid your bookmaker.'

'Harry!' Fiona said sharply.

'Sorry, m'dear,' murmured her husband.

I had read two accounts of the previous day's proceedings, one in a racing paper, another in a tabloid, and I had learned a few facts left out by the Vickers family the evening before.

Fiona's cousin Nolan, for starters, was an amateur jockey ('well-known', in both papers) who often raced on Fiona's horses, trained by Tremayne Vickers. Nolan Everard had once briefly been engaged to Magdalene Mackenzie (Mackie). 'Sources' had insisted that the three families, Vickers,

Goodhavens and Everards, were on friendly terms. The prosecution, not disputing this, had suggested that indeed they had all closed ranks to shield Nolan from his just deserts. A demure photograph of Olympia (provided by her father) showed a fair-haired girl, immature, an innocent victim.

'I still think you ought to appeal,' Lewis said.

Nolan's pornographic reply was to the effect that his lawyer had advised him not to push his luck, as Lewis very well knew.

I looked speculatively at Mackie, wondering about her sometime engagement to Nolan. She showed nothing for him now but concerned friendship: no lingering love and no hard feelings.

Fiona said to me, 'Stay to dinner?' but I shook my head.

'I promised to cook for Gareth and Tremayne.'

Mackie put down her glass and stood up tiredly. 'I think I'll go too. Perkin will be waiting to hear the news.' To me she said, 'Did you come in Tremayne's car?'

'No, walked.'

'Oh! Then . . . do you want a lift home?'

I thanked her and accepted. Harry came with us to see us off.

'Here are your clothes in your bag,' he said, handing it to me. 'Can't thank you enough, you know.'

'Any time.'

Harry and I looked at each other briefly with the sort of appreciation that's the beginning of friendship.

'He's not always like that,' Mackie said shortly, as she steered out of the drive. 'Nolan, I mean. He can be enormously good fun.'

'I read in today's paper that you were once engaged to him.'

She half laughed. 'Yes, I was. For about three months, five years ago. We met at a hunt ball. I knew who he was. Fiona's cousin, the amateur jockey. I'd been brought up in eventing. Had ponies before I could walk. We spent the whole evening together and . . . well . . . the whole night. It was sudden, like lightning. Don't tell Perkin. Why does one tell total strangers things one never tells anyone else? Sorry, forget it.'

'Mm,' I said. 'What happened when you woke up?'

'It was like a roller coaster. We spent all our time together. After two weeks he asked me to marry him and I said yes. Blissful. My feet never touched the ground.'

'Then what?'

'I don't know. Maybe we just got to know each other. I just said one day, "It won't work, will it?" and he said, "No" so we had a few tears and I gave him his ring back.' She turned into Tremayne's drive and came to a halt. 'We've been friends ever since, but Perkin has always been uncomfortable with him. He does tend to be jealous.'

She sighed and got out of the car. 'I'm going in through our own entrance. Perkin and I will probably be along for a drink. We often do, at this time of day.' She nodded and walked off, and I went round and into Tremayne's side of the house as if I'd lived there for ever. Tremayne, standing by the log fire in the family room with his gin and tonic, listened with disillusion to the outcome of Nolan's trial.

'Guilty but unpunished,' he observed. 'Newfangled escape clause. Help yourself to a drink.'

'Thanks.'

Mackie and Perkin came through from the central hall while I was dithering between the available choices of whisky or gin, neither of which I much liked. Perkin solved the liquid question for himself by detouring into the kitchen and reappearing with a glass of Coke.

'What do you *like*?' Mackie asked, seeing my hesitation.

'Wine, I suppose. Red for preference.'

'There will be some in the office. Tremayne keeps it for owners when they come to see their horses. I'll get it.'

She went without haste and returned with a Bordeaux-shaped bottle and a sensible corkscrew, both of which she handed over.

Tremayne said, 'If you like the stuff, put it on the shopping list.'

'The shopping list,' Mackie explained, 'is a running affair pinned to the kitchen corkboard. Whoever does the shopping takes the list with them.'

Perkin, slouching in an armchair, said I'd better get used to the idea of doing the shopping myself, particularly if I liked eating.

'Tremayne takes Gareth to the supermarket sometimes,' he said. 'Or Dee-Dee goes, if there's no milk for the coffee three days running.' He looked from me to Mackie. 'I used to think it quite normal until I married a sensible housekeeper.'

Perkin, I thought, as he reaped a smile from his wife, was a great deal more relaxed than on the evening before, though the faint hostility he'd shown towards me was still there. Looking at him and Tremayne, the differences were as powerful as the likenesses. Physically they were of one cloth; but where Tremayne radiated strength, Perkin was soggy; where Tremayne was a leader, Perkin retreated. Tremayne's love was for living horses, Perkin's was for passive wood.

Gareth came home with his usual air of a life lived on the run and eyed me with disapproval as I sat in an armchair drinking wine.

'I thought you said—' he began, and stopped, shrugging his shoulders with disappointment.

'Let him alone,' Mackie said mildly. 'Let him finish his drink.'

Perkin reacted to this harmless remark with irritation. 'As he said he'd cook, let him do it.'

'Of course,' I said cheerfully, getting up. I glanced at Tremayne. 'All right with you?'

'You're all right with me until further notice,' he said. Perkin didn't like that testimony of approval either, but Gareth did.

'You're home and dry with Dad,' he told me happily, steering me through the kitchen. 'What did you do to him?'

'Nothing.'

'What did you do to me?' he asked himself comically, and answered himself. 'Nothing. I guess that's it. You don't have to do anything, it's just the way you are. The freezers are through here, in the utility room.'

There were two freezers, both upright, both with incredible contents. The first was stacked with pizzas and nothing else, though only half full.

'We eat our way down to the bottom,' Gareth said reasonably, 'then fill up again every two or three months.'

He shut that freezer and opened the other, which proved to contain four packs of beef sandwiches, fifty to a pack. There were also about ten sliced loaves (for toast, Gareth explained), pints galore of chocolate ripple ice cream (Gareth liked it) and bags of ice cubes for gin and tonics.

'Well,' I said in amusement, 'what do we have in the larder?'

'You'd better look,' Gareth said, closing the second freezer's door. 'What are you going to make?'

I hadn't the faintest idea, but what Tremayne, Gareth and I ate not very much later was a hot pie made of beef extracted from twenty defrosted sandwiches, chopped small, then mixed with undiluted condensed mushroom soup (a find) and topped with an inch-thick layer of sandwich breadcrumbs fried crisp.

Gareth watched the simple cooking with fascination, and I found myself telling him about the techniques I'd been taught of how to live off the countryside without benefit of shops.

'Fried worms aren't bad,' I said.

'You're kidding me.'

'They're packed with protein. Birds thrive on them.'

'Could you really live off the land? You yourself?'

'Yes, sure. But you can die of malnutrition eating just rabbits.'

'How do you *know* these things?'

'It's my business, really. My trade.' I told him about the six travel guides. 'The company used to send me to all those places to set up holiday expeditions for real rugged types. I had to learn how to get them out of all sorts of disasters.'

'How did you ever start on something like that?'

'My father was a camping nut. A naturalist. He worked in a bank, and still does, but every spare second he would head for the wilds, dragging me and my mother along. Actually I took it for granted, as just a fact of life.'

'You are *lucky*,' Gareth said.

I paused from cutting up the beef. 'Yes.' I agreed, thinking about it. 'And grateful. And you've got a good father, too.'

He seemed extraordinarily pleased that I should say so, but it seemed to me, unconventional housekeeping or not, that Tremayne was making a good job of his younger son.

Notwithstanding Tremayne's professed lack of interest in food, he clearly enjoyed the pie, which three healthy appetites polished off to the last fried crumb. I got promoted instantly to resident chef, which suited me fine. Tomorrow I could do the shopping, Tremayne said, and without ado pulled out his wallet and gave me enough to feed the three of us for a month. I stowed the money away and Gareth told his father about fried worms and asked me if I had any of the travel guides with me.

'No, sorry, didn't think of bringing them.'

'Couldn't we possibly get some? I mean, I'd buy them with my pocket money. I'd like to keep them. Are they in the shops?'

'Sometimes, but I could ask the travel company to send a set.'

'Yes, do that,' Tremayne said, 'and I'll pay for them. We'd all like to look at them, I expect.'

'But Dad . . .' Gareth protested.

'All right,' Tremayne said, 'get two sets.'

I began to appreciate Tremayne's simple way of solving problems and in the morning, after I'd driven him on the tractor up to the Downs to see the horses exercise, I phoned my friend in the travel agency.

'Today?' he said, and I said, 'Yes, please,' and he said he would Red-Star-parcel them by train. Tremayne told me to get them sent to Didcot station where I could pick them up when I went to do the shopping.

'Fair enough,' the friend said. 'You'll get them this afternoon.'

'My love to your aunt,' I said, 'and thanks.'

The day slowly drifted into a repetition of the one before. Dee-Dee came into the kitchen for coffee and instructions and I returned to the boxes of clippings in the dining room.

I decided to reverse yesterday's order and start at the most recent clippings. I worked through the previous year, which had been a good one for Tremayne, embracing his Grand National win with Top Spin Lob. Tremayne's face smiled steadily from clipping after clipping including, inappropriately, those dealing with the death of the girl, Olympia.

Drawn irresistibly, I read a whole batch of accounts of that death from a good many different papers. In total, they told me not much more than I already knew. Olympia had been twenty-three, had come from a 'secure suburban background' and had worked as an instructor in a riding school in Surrey. Her parents, not surprisingly, were said to be 'distraught'.

Dee-Dee came into the dining room and saw what I was reading. 'That Olympia was a sexpot bimbo,' she remarked flatly. 'I was there at the party and you could practically smell it.'

'Really?'

'Her father made her out to be a sweet innocent little saint. Perhaps he even believes it. Nolan never said any different because it wouldn't have helped him, so no one told the truth.'

'What was the truth?'

'She had no underclothes on,' Dee-Dee said calmly. 'She wore only a long scarlet strapless dress slit halfway up her thigh. Do you want any coffee?'

'Yes, please.'

She went out to the kitchen and I continued reading clippings: 'Olympia's father brings private prosecution' and 'Magistrates refer Nolan Everard case to Crown Court'.

It was after a bunch of end-of-jumping-season statistics that I came across an oddity from a Reading paper published in June.

'Girl groom missing' read the headline, and there was an accompanying photo of Tremayne, still looking cheerful.

Angela Brickell, 17, employed as a 'lad' by prominent racehorse trainer Tremayne Vickers, failed to turn up for work on Tuesday afternoon and hasn't been seen in the stables since. Vickers says lads often leave without notice, but he is puzzled that she didn't ask for pay due to her. Anyone knowing Angela Brickell's whereabouts is asked to get in contact with the police.

Angela Brickell's parents, like Olympia's, were reported to be 'distraught'.

Chapter 6

By the following week Angela Brickell's disappearance had been taken up by the national dailies, who all mentioned the death of Olympia at Shellerton two months earlier but drew no significant conclusions.

Angela, I learned, lived in a stable hostel with five other girls, who described her as 'moody'. An indistinct photograph of her showed the face of a child, not a young woman. There was no account of her having been found, and after a week or so the clippings about her stopped.

In August Nolan, 'the well-known amateur now out on bail . . .', had ridden a winner on one of Fiona's horses.

In early September Nolan had hit the news again, this time in giving evidence at a Jockey Club enquiry in defence of Tremayne, who stood accused of doping one of his horses. It had tested positive to traces of the stimulants theobromine and caffeine, prohibited substances.

The horse in question had won an amateurs' race back in May. Belonging to Fiona, it had been ridden by Nolan, who had himself been in charge of the horse that day, since Tremayne hadn't attended the meeting. The Jockey Club's verdict had been that there was no way of determining who had given the drugs or how, since the groom in charge of the horse, Angela Brickell, could not be found.

Angela Brickell. Good grief, I thought.

Tremayne had nevertheless been adjudged guilty as charged and had been fined £1,500. A slapped wrist, it seemed. The drug theobromine, along with caffeine, commented the reporter, could commonly be found in chocolate. Well, well, I thought. Never a dull moment in the racing industry.

The rest of the year seemed an anticlimax after that. I was sitting and thinking when Tremayne breezed in.

'How are you doing?' he said.

I pointed to the pile of clippings out of their box. 'I was reading about last year. All those winners.'

He beamed. 'Couldn't put a foot wrong. Amazing.'

'Did Angela Brickell ever turn up?' I asked.

'Who? Oh, her. No, silly little creature, God knows where she made off to. Every last person in the racing world knows you mustn't give chocolate to horses in training. Pity really, most of them love it. A Mars bar here or there isn't going to make a horse win a race, but there you are, by the rules chocolate's a stimulant, so bad luck.'

'Would the girl have got into trouble if she'd stayed?'

He laughed. 'From me, yes. I'd have sacked her, but she'd gone before I heard the horse had tested positive. It was a routine test; they test all winners.' He paused thoughtfully. 'It could have been anyone, you know. Anyone here in the yard. Or Nolan himself, though God knows why he should. It's a risk every trainer runs. Risk of crooks. Risk of plain malice. You take what precautions you can and pray.'

'I'll put that in the book, if you like.'

He looked at me assessingly. 'I got me a good writer after all, didn't I?'

I shook my head. 'You got one who'll do his best.'

He smiled with satisfaction and we got down to work again on taping his early life with his eccentric father.

About midafternoon, when we stopped taping, he lent me his Volvo to go to Didcot. I shopped with luxurious abandon for food and picked up the parcel of books from the station, getting back to Shellerton while Tremayne was still out in his yard at evening stables.

He came into the house with Mackie, both of them blowing onto their fingers as they discussed the state of the horses. He asked me if the books had arrived. They had, I said.

'Great. Bring them into the family room. Come on, Mackie, gin and tonic.'

The big logs in the family-room fireplace never entirely went cold: Tremayne added a few small sticks and a fresh chunk of beech to renew the blaze. Perkin arrived as if on cue and collected his Coke.

With flattering eagerness Tremayne opened the package of books. Slightly larger than paperbacks, they had white shiny hard covers with the title in various bright black-edged colours: *Return Safe from the Jungle* in green, *Return Safe from the Desert* in orange, *Return Safe from the Sea* in blue, *Return Safe from the Ice* in purple, *Return Safe from Safari* in red, *Return Safe from the Wilderness* in a hot rusty brown.

'They must have taken a lot of work,' Mackie observed.

'There's a good deal of repetition in them,' I said. 'A lot of survival techniques are the same wherever you find yourself.'

'Such as what?' Perkin asked, faintly belligerent as usual.

'Lighting fires, finding water, making a shelter. Things like that.'

‘ “Survival begins before you set out,” ’ Tremayne said, reading the first page of *Jungle*. He looked up, amused, quoting, ‘ “Survival is a frame of mind.” ’

‘Yes.’

All three of them went on reading with obvious interest. Gareth erupted into the peaceful scene like a poltergeist. ‘Boy, oh *boy*. They’ve come!’

He grabbed *Return Safe from the Wilderness* and I sat drinking wine and wondering if I would ever see four people reading *Long Way Home*.

‘This is pretty earthy stuff,’ Mackie said after a while, laying her book down. ‘Skinning and degutting animals . . . ugh.’

‘You’d do it if you were starving,’ Tremayne told her.

‘There’s an awful lot about first aid,’ Gareth said, turning pages. ‘How to stop wounds bleeding . . . pressure points. A whole map of arteries. How to deal with poisons . . . swallow *charcoal*!’ He looked up. ‘Do you mean it?’

‘Sure,’ I said. ‘Scrape it into water and drink it. The carbon helps take some sorts of poison harmlessly through the gut.’

‘Did you ever rely on all this stuff to save your life?’ Tremayne asked.

‘Not entirely,’ I said. ‘I lived by these techniques for weeks at a time, but someone always knew roughly where I was. I had escape routes. I was basically testing what was possible in each area where the agency wanted to set up adventure holidays.’

‘But,’ Mackie said, ‘did things ever go wrong?’

‘Sometimes. A bear smashed up my camp in Canada once and hung around it for days. I couldn’t reach anything I needed. It was a shade fraught there for a bit.’

‘Do you mean it?’ Gareth was open-mouthed.

‘Nothing happened,’ I said. ‘The bear went away.’

‘Wow,’ Gareth said.

‘Bears eat people,’ his brother told him repressively. ‘Don’t get any ideas about copying John.’

‘Let Gareth dream,’ Tremayne said. ‘It’s natural. I don’t suppose for one moment he’ll go chasing bears.’

‘Boys do stupid things, Gareth included.’

‘Hey,’ his brother protested. ‘Who’s talking? Who climbed onto the roof and couldn’t get down?’

‘Do give it a rest, you two,’ Mackie said wearily. ‘You always quarrel.’

‘We’re nothing compared with Lewis and Nolan,’ Perkin said. ‘They can get really vicious.’

Diffidently, because it wasn’t really my business, I asked, ‘Why do they quarrel?’

‘Why does anyone?’ Tremayne said. ‘But those two envy each other. You met them last night, didn’t you? Nolan has the looks and the dash, Lewis is a drunk but when he’s sober he’s a whiz at making money. Lewis would like to be the glamorous amateur jockey and Nolan would like to be disgustingly rich. Neither will ever manage it, but that doesn’t stop the envy.’

'You're too hard on them,' Mackie murmured.

'But you know I'm right.' He turned to me and with a swift change of subject said, 'How well do you ride?'

'Er . . .' I said. 'I haven't ridden a racehorse.'

'What then?'

'Hacks, dude-ranch horses, Arab horses in the desert.'

'Hm.' He pondered. 'Care to ride my hack with the string in the morning? Let's see what you can do.'

'OK.'

He nodded. 'Mackie, tell Bob to have Touchy saddled up for John, if you're out in the yard before me.'

'Right.'

'Touchy won the Cheltenham Gold Cup,' Gareth told me.

'Oh, did he?' Some hack.

'Don't worry,' Mackie said, smiling, 'he's fifteen now and almost a gentleman.'

'Dumps people regularly on Fridays,' Gareth said.

WITH APPREHENSION I went out into the yard on the following morning, Friday, in jodhpurs, boots, ski jacket and gloves. I hadn't sat on a horse for almost two years, and my idea of a nice quiet return to the saddle wasn't a star steeplechaser.

Touchy was big, with bulging muscles. Bob Watson gave me a helmet and a leg-up, and it seemed a fair way down to the ground.

Oh, well, I thought. Enjoy it. I'd said I could ride: time to try to prove it. Tremayne, watching me appraisingly, told me to take my place behind Mackie, who would be leading the string. He himself would be driving the tractor. I could take Touchy up the all-weather gallop at a fast canter when everyone else had worked.

'All right,' I said. I collected the reins and a few thoughts and tried not to make a fool of myself.

'All out,' Bob Watson said, and out they all came from the boxes, circling in the lights, breathing plumes, all as before, only now I was part of it.

I followed Mackie out of the yard and across the road and onto the downland track, and found that Touchy responded better to pressure with the calf than to strong pulls on his tough old mouth. I circled with the others as it grew light and we waited for Tremayne to reach the top of the hill.

Snow still lay thinly over everything and it was another clear morning, stingingly, beautifully cold. January dawn on the Downs; once felt, never forgotten.

Section by section the string set off in twos or threes up the wood-chippings track until only Mackie and I were left.

'I'll ride on the right of you,' she said, coming up behind me. 'Then Tremayne can see how you ride.'

'Thanks very much,' I said ironically.

She swayed suddenly in the saddle and I put out a hand to steady her. 'Are you OK?' I asked anxiously. 'You should have rested more after that bang on the head.' She was pale. Huge-eyed.

'No . . . I . . .' She took an unsteady breath. 'I just felt . . . oh . . .'

She swayed again and looked near to fainting. I leaned across and put my right arm round her waist, holding her tight to prevent her falling. I took hold of her reins in my left hand, and her horse moved his rump sideways away from me until she slid off out of her saddle altogether and finished half lying across my knee and Touchy's withers.

With both hands I pulled and heaved her up onto Touchy until she was half sitting and half lying across the front of my saddle, held in my arms. Mackie's horse had backed away sharply to the length of his reins and was on the edge of bolting. Touchy got an unmistakable signal from my leg and obediently turned towards home. As if by magic Mackie's horse got the going-home message and decided not to object any further.

We had gone perhaps three paces when Mackie came to full consciousness as if a light had been switched on. 'What happened . . . ?'

'You fainted. Fell this way.'

'Let me down,' she said. 'I feel awfully sick.'

She rolled against me onto her stomach and slid down slowly until her feet were on the ground. She turned away from me suddenly and vomited convulsively onto the snow.

I hopped down off Touchy with the reins of both horses held fast and tried to help her.

'I haven't felt well for days,' she said weakly, searching for a tissue.

'Concussion,' I said.

'No, even before that. Tension over the trial, I suppose. I feel perfectly all right now. I don't understand it.'

She was looking at me in puzzlement, and I quite clearly saw the thought float into her head and transfigure her face into wonderment and hope . . .

'Oh!' she said ecstatically. 'Do you think . . . I mean, I've been feeling sick every morning this week . . . and after two years of trying I'd stopped expecting anything to happen . . . I mean, I didn't even *suspect*. . . I'm always wildly irregular.' She stopped and laughed. 'Don't tell Tremayne. Don't tell Perkin. I need to make sure. I can't believe it. I think I'll burst.'

I thought that I had never before seen such pure uncomplicated happiness in anyone, and was tremendously glad for her.

She seemed to wake suddenly to our whereabouts. 'Tremayne will be going mad because we haven't appeared.'

'I'll ride up and tell him you're not well and have gone home.'

'No, definitely not. I *am* well. Gloriously well. Give me a leg-up.'

I lifted her lightly into the saddle, scrambling up myself onto Touchy's broad back. She shook up her reins as if nothing had happened and set off up the wood chippings at a medium canter. I joined her, expecting to go the whole way at that conservative pace, but she quickened immediately I reached her. I could hardly hang back and say hold on a minute, I hadn't done this in a while and could easily fall off. Instead, I tucked in my elbows and relied on luck.

Towards the end Mackie kicked her horse into a frank gallop and it was at that speed that we both passed Tremayne. I was peripherally aware of him, though all my direct attention was acutely focused on balance, grip and what lay ahead between Touchy's ears.

Touchy, I thanked heaven, slowed when Mackie slowed and brought himself to a good-natured halt without dumping his rider, Friday or not. I was breathless and also exhilarated.

'Where did you get to?' Tremayne enquired of me, joining us and the rest of the string. 'I thought you'd chickened out.'

'We were just talking,' Mackie said.

Tremayne looked at her now glowing face as she took her place at the head of the string. 'What were you and Mackie talking about?' he demanded.

'She'll tell you,' I said, smiling.

He said belligerently, 'Mackie's off limits.'

'We were not flirting, or whatever else you care to call it.'

After a grudging minute he said, 'All right then,' and I thought that in his way he was as possessive of Mackie as Perkin was.

A short while later, back in the kitchen, munching the toast I'd made for him, he seemed to have forgotten it.

'You can ride out every morning,' he said, 'if you'd like.'

He could see I was pleased. I said, 'I'd like it very much.'

The day passed in the way that had become routine: clippings, beef sandwiches, taping, evening drinks, Gareth home, cook the dinner.

On Saturday morning I rode Touchy again but Mackie didn't materialise, having phoned Tremayne to say she wasn't well. But she and Perkin appeared in the kitchen during breakfast, he with an arm round her shoulders in a surprisingly proprietorial way.

'We've something to tell you,' Perkin said to Tremayne.

'Oh, yes?' Tremayne was busy with some papers.

'Yes. Do pay attention. We're having a baby.'

Tremayne paid attention abruptly and was clearly delighted. Not an overdemonstrative man, he didn't leap up to embrace them but purred in his throat like a cat and beat the table with his fist. Son and daughter-in-law had no difficulty in reading the signals and looked pleased with themselves. They looked more in love with each other, more relaxed, as if the earlier failure to conceive had caused tension between them, now relieved.

On Sunday morning Fiona and Harry came to the stables to see her horses and drink with Tremayne afterwards in the family room. Nolan came with them, but not Lewis. An aunt of Harry's, another Mrs Goodhaven, tagged quietly along. Mackie couldn't keep her good news to herself, and Fiona and Harry hugged her while Perkin looked important and Nolan gave halfhearted congratulations. Tremayne opened champagne.

At about that time, ten miles away in lonely woodland, a gamekeeper came across what was left of Angela Brickell.

Chapter 7

The discovery made no impact on Shellerton on that Sunday because at first no one knew whose bones lay among the dead brambles.

In Tremayne's house, when the toasts to the future Vickers had been drunk, Gareth showed Fiona and Harry a couple of the travel guides. Nolan picked up *Safari* absent-mindedly and said that no one but a bloody fool would go hunting tigers in Africa.

'There aren't any tigers in Africa,' Gareth said.

'That's right. He'd be a bloody fool.'

'Oh . . . it's a joke,' Gareth said. 'Very funny.'

Nolan, though the shortest man there, physically dominated the room. His strong animal vigour and powerful saturnine features seemed to charge the very air with static. One could see how Mackie had been struck by lightning. One could see how Olympia might have died by violent accident. One's reactions to Nolan had little to do with reason, all with instinct.

Harry's aunt was looking into *Ice* in a faintly superior way as if confronted with a manifestation of the lower orders.

'How frightfully *rugged*,' she said languidly.

'Er,' Harry said to me. 'I didn't introduce you properly. I must present you to my aunt, Erica Goodhaven. She's a writer.'

There was a subterranean flood of mischief in his eyes, as though I were about to be thrown to the lions.

'Erica,' Harry said, 'John wrote these books.'

'And a novel,' Tremayne said defensively, coming to an aid I didn't realise I needed. 'It's going to be published. And he's writing my biography.'

'A *novel*,' Harry's aunt said. 'How *interesting*. I, also, write novels. Under my unmarried name, Erica Upton.'

Thrown to a literary lion, I perceived. A lioness. Erica Upton had a five-star, prize-winning reputation. She was a slender, intense-looking grey-haired woman in a wool dress with flat shoes and no jewellery. A quintessential aunt, I thought; except that most people's aunts weren't Erica Upton.

'What is your novel *about*?' she enquired of me. Her voice was patronising but I didn't mind that: she was entitled to it.

The others all waited with her to hear my answer.

'It's about survival,' I said politely. 'It's about some travellers cut off by an earthquake. It's called *Long Way Home*.'

'How *quaint*,' she said dismissively.

I felt again the same mild recklessness that I had had riding Touchy:

even if I lacked confidence, I should relax and have a go.

'My agent says,' I said neutrally, 'that *Long Way Home* is really about the spiritual consequences of deprivation and fear.'

She knew a gauntlet when she heard one. I saw the stiffening in her body and suspected it in her mind.

She said, 'You are too young to write with authority of spiritual consequences. Too young to have learned the intensity of understanding that comes only through deep adversity.'

I said, 'Shouldn't contentment be allowed its insights?'

'It has none. Unless you have suffered or are poor or can tap into melancholy, you have defective perception. You are not a serious writer.' A dire accusation; her worst.

'I write to entertain,' I said.

'I,' she said simply, 'write to enlighten.'

I could find no answer. I said wryly, with a bow, 'I am defeated.'

She laughed with pleasure, her muscles loosening. The lion had devoured the sacrifice and all was well. She turned away to begin talking to Fiona, and Harry made his way to my side.

'You didn't do too badly,' he said. 'Nice brisk duel.'

'She ran me through.'

'Seriously,' he said, as if he thought my ego needed patching, 'these survival guides are good. Do you mind if we take a few of them home?'

'They're Tremayne's and Gareth's, really.'

'I'll ask them, then.' He went off to talk to Tremayne.

ANGELA BRICKELL'S REMAINS lay on the Quillersedge Estate at the western edge of the Chilterns. The Quillersedge gamekeeper arranged on the telephone for the local police to collect him from his cottage on the estate and drive as near to the bones as possible on the estate's private roads. From there, everyone would have to go through the woods on foot.

IN TREMAYNE'S HOUSE, Fiona began to say goodbyes, chiefly with kisses. She stopped beside me and put her cheek on mine.

'How long are you staying?' she asked.

Tremayne answered for me. 'Three more weeks. Then we'll see.'

'We'll fix a dinner,' Fiona said. 'Come along, Nolan. Ready, Erica? Love you, Mackie, take care of yourself.'

When they'd gone, Mackie and Perkin floated off home on cloud nine.

Gareth said, 'I'll make beef-sandwich pie for lunch.'

AT ABOUT THE TIME we ate lunch, two policemen and the gamekeeper reached the pathetic collection of bones and set nemesis in motion. They radioed for more instructions. Detective Chief Inspector Doone, Thames Valley Police, decided that first thing in the morning he would take a pathologist for an on-site examination and a photographer for the record.

IN TREMAYNE'S HOUSE Gareth and I went up to my bedroom because he wanted to see the survival kit I'd brought with me.

'Is it just like the ones in the books?' he asked as I brought out a black waterproof pouch that one could wear round one's waist.

'No, not entirely.' I paused. 'I have three survival kits at present. One small one for taking with me all the time. This one here for longer walks and difficult areas. And one that I didn't bring, which is full camping survival gear for going out into the wilds. I'll show you the smallest kit first, but you'll have to get it. It's in my ski-suit jacket pocket in the cloakroom.'

He went willingly but presently returned doubtfully with a flat tin, smaller than a paperback book, held shut with insulating tape. 'Is this it?' he said.

I nodded. 'Open it carefully.'

He did as I said, laying out the contents on the white counterpane on the bed and reciting them aloud.

'Two matchbooks, a bit of candle, a little coil of thin wire, a piece of jagged wire, some fish-hooks, a small pencil and piece of paper, needles and thread, two bandages and a plastic bag folded up small and held by a paperclip.' He looked disappointed. 'You couldn't do much with those.'

'Just light a fire, cut wood, catch food, collect water, make a map and sew up wounds. That jagged wire is a flexible saw.'

His mouth opened.

'Then I always carry two things on my belt.' I unstrapped it. 'One is a knife, one is a multipurpose survival tool.'

'Can I look?'

'Yes, sure.'

The knife, in a black canvas sheath with a flap fastened by Velcro, was a strong folding knife with a cunningly serrated blade, very sharp indeed, nine inches overall when open, only five when closed. The other object was a flat metal rectangular object about three inches by two and a half.

'What's this?' he asked, taking it out onto his hand.

'I carry that instead of an ordinary penknife. It has a blade slotted in one side and scissors in the other. That little round thing is a magnifying glass for starting fires if there's any sun. With those other odd-shaped edges you can make holes in a tin of food, open bottles, screw in screws, file your nails and sharpen knives. The back is polished like a mirror for signalling.'

'Wow.' He turned it over and looked at his own face. 'It's really cool.' He began to pack all the small things back into the flat tin and remarked that fish-hooks wouldn't be much good away from rivers.

'You can catch birds on fish-hooks. They take bait like fish.'

He stared at me. 'Have you eaten birds?'

'Chickens are birds.'

'Well . . . ordinary birds?'

'You eat anything if you're hungry enough.'

Gareth had no idea what it was like to be primevally alone with nature, and it was unlikely he would ever find out. I'd spent a month once on an island without any kit or anything modern at all. It was then that I'd discovered for myself that survival was a matter of mind rather than body.

Gareth replaced the coil of fine wire in the tin and said, 'I suppose this wire is for all the traps in the books?'

'Only the simplest ones.'

'Some of those traps are really sneaky. There you are, a harmless rabbit hopping along about your business, and you don't see the wire hidden in dead leaves and you trip over it and suddenly, pow! You're all tied up in a net or squashed under logs. Have you done all that?'

'Yes, lots of times.'

'I like the idea of the bow and arrows better,' he said.

'Yes, well, I put in the instructions of how to make them effectively, but it's not easy to hit anything if it's moving. I've always preferred traps.'

I handed kit number two to him, the black pouch, and let him open its three zipped and Velcroed pockets, to lay the contents on the bed. Although the pouch itself was waterproof, almost every item inside it was further wrapped separately in a small plastic bag, fastened with a twist tie; safe from sand and insects. Gareth undid and emptied some of the bags.

'Explain what they are,' he said. 'I mean, twenty matchbooks are for lighting fires, right, so what are the cotton-wool balls doing with them?'

'They burn well. They set fire to dry leaves.'

'Oh. The candle is for light, right?'

'And to help light fires. And wax is useful for a lot of things.'

'And this? This little jar of whitish liquid packed with the sawn-off paintbrush.'

I smiled. 'That's in the *Wilderness* book. It's luminous paint. If you have a camp and you want to leave it to go and look for food or firewood, you want to be able to find your way back again, don't you? Essential. So as you go, you paint a slash of this on a tree trunk or a rock, and then you can find your way back even in the dark.'

'Cool,' he said.

'That little oblong metal thing with the handle,' I said, 'that's a powerful magnet. Useful but not essential. Good for retrieving fish-hooks if you lose them in the water. You tie the magnet on a string and dangle it.'

What really fascinated him was a tiny blowtorch which shot out a fierce blue flame hot enough to melt solder.

'Cool,' he said again. 'That's really *ace*.'

'Infallible for lighting fires,' I said, 'as long as the butane lasts.'

Gareth had come to the last thing, a pair of leather gloves, which he thought were sissy.

'They give your hands almost double grip,' I said. 'They save you from cuts and scratches. And they're invaluable for collecting stinging nettles.'

'I'd hate to collect stinging nettles.'

'No, you wouldn't. If you boil the leaves they're not bad to eat, but the best things are the stalks. Incredibly stringy. You can thrash them until they're supple enough for lashing branches together, for making shelters and also racks to keep things off the ground away from damp and animals.'

'You know so much,' he said.

'I went camping in my cradle. Literally.'

He methodically packed everything back as he'd found it. A thought struck him. 'You haven't got a compass!'

'It's not in there,' I agreed. I opened a drawer in the chest of drawers and found it for him: a slim, liquid-filled compass set in a clear oblong of plastic which had inch and centimetre measures along the sides. I showed him how it aligned with maps and made setting a course relatively easy, and told him I always carried it in my shirt pocket to have it handy.

'But it was in the drawer,' he objected.

'I'm not likely to get lost in Shellerton.'

'You could up on the Downs,' he said seriously.

I doubted it, but said I would carry it to please him.

We returned to the family room, where Tremayne was getting ready to walk round his yard at evening stables. He invited me to go with him.

'It's thawing,' he said. 'Everything's dripping. Thank God.'

The world did indeed turn from white to green during the night, bringing renewed life to Shellerton and racing.

Out in the melting woodlands, Angela Brickell spent her last night in the quiet undergrowth.

Chapter 8

That Monday morning, Tremayne promoted me from Touchy to a still actively racing steeplechaser, a nine-year-old gelding called Drifter. I was also permitted to do a regular working gallop and by great good fortune didn't fall off.

When we returned from the newly greenish-brownish Downs there was a strange car in the yard and a strange man drinking coffee in the kitchen. He was young, short, thin, angular and bold, wearing self-assurance as an outer garment. He was also, I soon found, almost as foul-mouthed as Nolan but, unlike him, funny.

Tremayne said to me, 'This is Sam Yaeger, our jockey.' To Sam Yaeger he explained my presence and said I'd been riding out.

Sam Yaeger wore jodhpurs, along with a brilliant yellow sweatshirt. A multicoloured anorak, twin of Gareth's, hung over the back of his chair. Nothing shy or retiring about Sam.

Dee-Dee, appearing for her coffee, brightened by fifty watts at the sight of him. 'Morning, lover-boy,' she said.

Lover-boy made a stab at pinching her bottom as she passed behind him, which she seemed not to mind. Well, well, well, I thought. She made her coffee and sat at the table beside the jockey, very aware of him. I made the toast, which had become my accepted job, and Sam Yaeger watched with comically raised eyebrows.

'Didn't Tremayne say you were a writer?' he asked. 'You don't look like a bloody writer.'

'So many people aren't what they look like,' I said. 'Bloody or not.'

'What do I look like?' he demanded.

'Like someone who won the Grand National among eighty-nine other races last year and finished third on the jockeys' list.'

'You've been peeking,' he said, surprised.

'I'll be interviewing you soon for your views of your boss.'

Tremayne said with mock severity, 'And they'd better be respectful.'

'They bloody well would be, wouldn't they?'

'If you have any sense,' Tremayne agreed, nodding.

Sam's extremely physical presence dominated breakfast and I wondered briefly how he got on with Nolan. I asked Dee-Dee that question after Sam and Tremayne had gone out with the second lot.

'Get on?' she repeated ironically. 'No, they do not.' She paused, considered whether to tell me more, shrugged and continued. 'Sam doesn't like Nolan riding so many of the stable's horses. Whatever else you can say about Nolan, no one denies he's a brilliant jockey. He's been top of the amateurs' list for years.'

'Why doesn't he turn professional?' I asked.

'The very idea of that scares Sam rigid, but I don't think it will happen. Nolan prefers his amateur status. He thinks of Sam as blue collar to his white. It isn't just riding,' she said calmly. 'It's women.'

'Women?'

'They're rivals there, too. The night Nolan—I mean, the night Olympia died . . .'

They all said, 'when Olympia died', and never 'when Nolan killed Olympia', though Dee-Dee had just come close.

'Sam set out to seduce Olympia,' Dee-Dee said. 'Nolan brought her to the party and of course Sam made a beeline for her.'

'Did he . . . er . . . know Olympia?'

'Never set eyes on her before. She took one look at Sam and *giggled.* Sam has that effect on females.' She raised her eyebrows. 'Don't say it. I respond to him too. Can't help it. He's fun.'

'I can see that,' I said.

'Can you? Olympia did. Putty in his hands, which of course were all over her the minute Nolan went to fetch her a drink. When he came back, she'd gone off with Sam. Nolan went looking for them, but without results. He came back cursing and swearing and telling me he would strangle her because, you see, I think he blamed *her*, not Sam, for making him feel a fool. So, anyway, there you are, that's really what happened.'

'Which no one,' I said slowly, 'brought up at the trial.'

'Of course not. Not many people knew, and it gave Nolan a *motive*.'

'Yes, it did.'

'But he didn't mean to kill her. Everyone knows that. If he'd attacked and killed *Sam*, it would have been a different matter. It wasn't the first time he and Nolan had bedded the same girl, and sometimes Nolan had pinched one of his, and it was a bit of a lark on the whole, not a killing matter.'

'More of a lark to Sam than to Nolan,' I suggested.

'Probably.' She shook herself. 'I'm getting no work done.'

'You've done some of mine.'

'Don't put it in the book,' she insisted, alarmed.

'I promise I won't,' I said.

I retired to the dining room and began to map out the book into sections, giving each a tentative title with subheadings. I still hadn't, as yet, put an actual sentence on paper.

OUT IN THE WOODLAND Detective Chief Inspector Doone looked morosely at Angela Brickell's jumbled bones while the pathologist told him they were those of a young female, dead probably less than a year.

Under a blanket of dead leaves two constables came across some wet filthy jeans, a small-sized bra, a pair of panties and a T-shirt with the remains of a pattern on the front. The girl, Detective Chief Inspector Doone reckoned, had been naked when she died.

He sighed deeply. He didn't like these sorts of cases. He had daughters of his own.

TREMAYNE CAME BACK from second lot in a good mood, whistling between his teeth. He came into the dining room to let me know the state of play and to ask a favour or two, taking it (correctly) for granted that I would oblige.

The ditched Jeep had gone to the big scrapheap in the sky: a replacement had been found in Newbury, a not new but serviceable Land-Rover. If I would go to Newbury in the Volvo with Tremayne, I could drive the substitute home to Shellerton.

'Of course,' I said.

The racing industry was scrambling back into action, with Windsor racecourse promising to be operational on Wednesday. Tremayne had four horses entered. He would like me to come with him, he said, to see what his job entailed.

'Love to,' I said.

He wished to go out for the evening to play poker with friends, and he'd be back late: would I stay in for Gareth?

'Sure,' I said.

'He's old enough to be safe on his own, but . . . well . . .'

'Company,' I said. 'Someone around.'

He nodded. 'Dee-Dee thinks we take advantage of you,' he said bluntly.

I was surprised. 'I like what I'm doing. I'd rather be a part of things, and useful. OK?'

He nodded.

'And,' I said, 'this way I get to know you better for the book.'

For the first time he looked faintly apprehensive, as if perhaps he didn't want his whole self publicly laid bare; but I would respect any secrets I learned, if he didn't want them told.

The day went ahead as planned, and in the evening, after Tremayne had departed to his card game, Gareth asked me to teach him to cook.

'It's easy,' I said. 'What do you want to eat?'

We went into the kitchen where Gareth tentatively asked for 'real' shepherd's pie, 'not that stuff in supermarket boxes that tastes of cardboard and wouldn't feed a pygmy.'

'Real easy shepherd's pie,' I assented. 'First of all, catch your shepherd.'

He grinned and watched me assemble some minced beef, an onion, gravy powder and a jar of dried herbs.

'The gravy powder's sort of cheating,' I said. 'But it thickens the meat and tastes good.'

I dissolved some powder into a little water, added it to the beef, chopped the onion finely, added that, sprinkled some herbs, stirred it all round in a saucepan, put the lid on and set it to cook on a low heat.

'Next thing to decide,' I said, 'is real potatoes or dried granules. How are you with peeling potatoes? No? Granules, then. Follow the directions,' I added, giving him the packet.

'Will you write down all you bought last week, so I can get them again and cook when you're gone?'

'Sure thing.'

'I wouldn't mind if you stayed.'

Loneliness was an ache in his voice. I said, 'I'll be here another three weeks.' I paused. 'Would you like, say perhaps next Sunday if it's a decent day, to come out with me into some fields and woods? I could show you a few of the things in the books . . . how to do them in real life.'

His face shone: my own reward. 'Could I bring Coconut?'

'Absolutely.'

'Mega cool.'

He whipped the potato granules happily into the hot water and we piled the fluffy result onto the cooked meat mixture in a round pie dish. Put it under the grill to brown the top. Ate the result with mutual fulfilment.

'Can we take the survival kit?'

'Of course.'

'And light a fire?'

'Perhaps on your own land, if your father will let us.'

'I really can't wait,' he said.

ON TUESDAY MORNING the pathologist made his report to Detective Chief Inspector Doone.

'The bones are those of a young adult female, probably five foot four or five; possible age, twenty. Could be a year or two younger or older.'

'How long since she died?' Doone asked.

'I'd say last summer.'

'And cause of death? Drugs? Exposure?'

'Her hyoid bone is fractured.'

Depression settled on Doone. 'You're sure?'

'Positive. She was strangled.'

ON TUESDAY AFTERNOON Doone sent his men to search the whole area where the bones had been discovered. He told them to look for shoes, also for anything else man-made. They were to mark on the map where each artefact was found, and also tag the artefact, being careful not to destroy evidence. This was now a murder investigation, he reminded them.

ON WEDNESDAY MORNING when we came in from first lot, Sam Yaeger was again in the kitchen. He had come with a borrowed pick-up truck in which he proposed to collect some Burma teak that Perkin had acquired for him at trade discount.

'Sam has a boat,' Tremayne told me drily. 'An old wreck that he's slowly turning into a palace fit for a harem.'

Sam Yaeger grinned cheerfully and made no denials. 'Every jockey's got to have an eye to the bloody future. I buy clapped-out antique boats and make them better than new.'

Life was full of surprises, I thought.

'Where do you keep the boat?' I asked, making toast.

'Maidenhead. On the Thames. I bought a bankrupt boatyard there a while back. It looks a right shambles but a bit of dilapidation's a good thing. Thieves think there's nothing worth stealing.'

'So I suppose,' Tremayne said, 'that you're taking the wood to the boatyard on your way to the races.'

Sam looked at me in mock amazement. 'Don't know how he works these things out, do you?'

'That'll do, Sam,' Tremayne said, and one could see just where he drew the line between what he would and would not take from Sam Yaeger. He began to discuss the horses he would be running at Windsor races that afternoon, telling Sam that 'Bluecheesecake is better, not worse, for the layoff,' and 'Give Just the Thing an easy if you feel her wavering. I don't want her ruined while she's still green.'

'Right,' Sam said. 'What about Cashless? Do I ride him in front again?'

'What do you think?'

'He likes it better. He just got beat by faster horses, last time.'

'Go off in front, then. Nolan rides Telebiddy in the amateur race,' Tremayne added. 'Unless the Jockey Club puts a stop to it.'

Sam scowled but spoke no evil. Tremayne turned to me. 'We'll leave for Windsor at twelve thirty.'

At about that time, Detective Chief Inspector Doone went into the formerly unused office that had been dubbed 'Incident Room' for the bones investigation and laid out on a trestle table the bits and pieces that his men had gleaned from the woodland.

There were the clothes found originally, now drying out in the centrally heated air. There was also a pair of well-worn trainers, still sodden, which might once have been white. There were four old empty and dirty soft-drink cans, a pair of broken sunglasses, a puckered leather belt with split stitches, a gin bottle, a blue plastic comb uncorrupted by time, a well-chewed rubber ball, a gold-plated ball-point pen, a pink lipstick, chocolate-bar wrappers, and a broken dog collar.

Detective Chief Inspector Doone walked broodingly round the table, staring at the haul from all angles.

'Speak to me, girl,' he said. 'Tell me who you are.'

The clothes and the shoes made no answer.

He called in his men and told them to go back to the woods and widen the search, and he himself went through his lists of local missing persons.

He had a list of twelve persistent adolescent runaways: all possibles. A list of four defaulters from youth custody. A list of six missing for 'various reasons'. One of those was Angela Brickell. The reason given was: 'Probably doped a racehorse in her charge. Skipped out.'

Chapter 9

Tremayne told me that the only place he couldn't take me on Windsor racecourse was into the weighing room. Everywhere else, he said, I should stay by his side.

Accordingly I followed him doggedly, at times at a run. Where he paused briefly to talk to other people he introduced me as a friend, John Kendall.

His four runners, as it happened, were in four consecutive races. He began a darting progress: into the weighing room to fetch his jockey's saddle, off at a trot to the saddling boxes to do up the girths himself, into the parade ring to join the owners and give last-minute orders to the jockey, off up to the stands to watch the horse run, down again to the unsaddling areas, hoping to greet a winner, and then off to the weighing room to start all over again.

Nolan was there, anxiously asking if Tremayne had received any thumbs-down from the Jockey Club.

'No,' Tremayne said. 'And don't ask questions. Don't invite a no. They'll tell you quick enough if they want you off. Apply your mind to winning, eh?'

Tremayne dived into the weighing room, leaving me outside with Nolan, who had come dressed to stifle criticism. Sam Yaeger slouched up beside us and annoyed Nolan by patting him on the back. Sam, too, was transformed by tidiness and I gradually observed that most of the jockeys arrived and departed from the racecourse dressed for the boardroom. Their working

clothes might be pink, purple and the stuff of fantasy but they were saying they were businessmen first.

The physical impact of Nolan and Sam was diluted by the open air that was still as cold as their relationship.

'Go easy on Bluecheesecake,' Nolan said. 'I don't want him loused up before the Kim Muir at Cheltenham.'

Sam answered, 'I'm not nannying any bloody amateur.'

He made no concessions on Bluecheesecake, progressing smoothly,

staying in third or fourth place. The steeplechase course at Windsor proved to be a winding figure of eight, which meant that tactics were important. Coming round the last of several bends, Bluecheesecake made a mess of one fence, his nose going down to the ground, but both horse and jockey righted themselves miraculously without falling. Sam rode over the last two fences with what even I could see was total disregard for his own safety and pressed Bluecheesecake unceremoniously for every ounce of effort. In the last few strides Bluecheesecake's nose showed decisively in front.

After Tremayne had received his due congratulations in the winners' enclosure, he followed Sam into the weighing room to fetch the saddle again for Just the Thing.

When he came out he was escorted by Nolan, who fell into step beside him complaining ferociously that Sam had spoiled his, Nolan's, chances with Bluecheesecake at Cheltenham.

'Cheltenham is six weeks off,' Tremayne said calmly. 'Sam did exactly right. Go and do the same on Telebiddy.'

Nolan stalked away, still looking more furious than was sensible in his position, and Tremayne allowed himself a sigh but no comment.

Sam rode Just the Thing in the next event, providing the green mare with a clear view of the jumps and urging her on at the end to give her a good idea of what was expected. She finished a respectable third.

Telebiddy was running in the next race. In jockey's clothes Nolan still looked chunky, strong and powerfully arrogant, but the swagger seemed to stop the moment he sat on the horse. Then professionalism took over and he was concentrated, quiet and neat in the saddle.

Nolan gave a display of razor-sharp competence that made most of the other riders look like Sunday drivers. He saved countable seconds over the fences, his mount gaining lengths by always seeming to take off at the right spot. Judgment, not luck. As if determined to outride Sam Yaeger, he hurled himself over the last three fences and won by ten lengths.

In the next race Cashless set off in front as expected, a position he held until right where it mattered, the last fifty yards. Then three jockeys who had been waiting behind him stepped on the accelerator and passed him.

Tremayne shrugged. 'Too bad.'

We reached the parade ring, where the unsuccessful runners were being unsaddled. Sam, looping girths over his arm, gave Tremayne a rueful smile and said Cashless had done his best.

'I saw,' Tremayne agreed. 'Can't be helped.' We watched Sam walk off towards the weighing room, and Tremayne remarked thoughtfully that he might try Cashless in an amateur race, and see what Nolan could do.

'Do you play them off against each other on purpose?' I asked.

'I do the best for my owners,' Tremayne said. 'Let's go home.'

AT ABOUT THE TIME we were driving home, Detective Chief Inspector Doone was poring over the increased pickings from the woodland.

Among some insignificant, long-rusted detritus lay the star of the whole collection, a woman's handbag. Total satisfaction had been denied him, as the prize had been torn open on one side, probably by a dog, so that most of the contents had been lost. All the same, he was left with a shoulder strap, a corroded buckle and at least half of a brown plastic school-style bag which still held a small mirror and a folded photograph frame.

With careful movements Doone opened the frame and found inside, water-stained along one edge but otherwise sharply clear, a coloured snapshot of a man standing beside a horse. Doone reviewed his lists again, and provisionally paused on Angela Brickell, stablelad . . .

THE BOMBSHELL BURST on Shellerton on Thursday.

Tremayne was upstairs dressing before going to Towcester races when the doorbell rang. Dee-Dee went to answer it and presently came into the dining room looking mystified.

'It's two policemen,' she said. 'They won't say what they want. I've put them in the family room until Tremayne comes down. Go and keep an eye on them, would you?'

'Sure,' I said, already on the move.

The two men might have invented the word grey, so characterless did they appear. Ultimate plain clothes, I thought. 'Can I help you?' I said.

'Are you Tremayne Vickers?' one of them asked.

'No. He'll be down soon. Can I help?'

'I am Detective Chief Inspector Doone, Thames Valley Police,' he said. 'This is Detective Constable Rich.'

'How do you do,' I said. 'I'm John Kendall. Would you care to sit down?'

They perched gingerly on chairs and said no to an offer of coffee. Doone appeared to be about fifty, with grey-dusted, light brown hair and a heavy medium-brown moustache. He had light brown eyes, big bony hands and, as we all slowly discovered, a habit of talking a lot.

Tremayne came downstairs buttoning the blue and white striped cuffs of his shirt and carrying his jacket between forearm and chest.

'Hello,' he said, 'who's this?'

Doone introduced himself before I could do so. 'We'd like to speak to you alone, sir.'

Tremayne asked me with his eyes to leave, shutting the door behind me. I returned to the dining room but presently heard the family-room door open and Tremayne's voice calling, 'John, come back here, would you?'

I went back. Tremayne said to Doone, 'I want him to hear it. Will you repeat what you said?'

Doone shrugged. 'I came to inform Mr Vickers that some remains have been found which may prove to be those of a young woman who was once employed here.'

'Angela Brickell,' Tremayne said resignedly. 'They have a photograph. They're trying to identify the man.' He turned to Doone. 'Show it to him.' He nodded in my direction. 'Don't take my word for it.'

Unwillingly, Doone handed me a photograph in a plastic holder.

'Harry Goodhaven?' I said.

Tremayne, looking unconcerned, nodded. 'That's Fiona's horse, Chickweed, the one they said was doped.'

'How can you recognise a horse?' Doone asked.

Tremayne stared at him. 'Horses have faces, like people.'

'Who is this man, this Harry Goodhaven?' Doone demanded.

'The husband of the owner of the horse.'

'Why would Angela Brickell be carrying his photograph?'

'She wasn't,' Tremayne said. 'It was the *horse*'s photograph she was carrying. She looked after it.' Doone looked completely unconvinced.

'To a lad,' I said, 'the horses they look after are like children. They love them. It makes sense that she carried Chickweed's picture.'

Tremayne glanced at me in surprise. I'd been listening to the lads for a week.

The attendant policeman, Constable Rich, was all the time taking notes, though not at high speed, not shorthand.

'I'm already running late,' Tremayne said, making moves to leave. 'Stay as long as you like, talk to whoever you want.'

'I don't think you understand, sir,' Doone said with a touch of desperation. 'Angela Brickell was *strangled*.'

'What?' Tremayne stopped dead, stunned. 'I thought you said . . .'

'I said we'd found some remains. And, sir'—he hesitated briefly as if to summon courage—'only last week, sir, we had a Crown Court case about another young woman who was strangled . . . strangled here in this house.'

There was silence.

Tremayne said finally, 'There can't be any connection.'

Doone said doggedly, 'Did Mr Nolan Everard have any connections with Angela Brickell?'

'Yes, of course he did. He rides Chickweed, the horse in that photograph. He saw Angela Brickell quite often in the course of her work. Where did you say her . . . remains . . . were found?'

'I don't think I said, sir.'

It occurred to me that Doone was hoping someone would *know*, and anyone who knew would very likely have strangled her.

'Poor girl,' Tremayne said. 'But all the same, Chief Inspector, I do now have to go. John, tell Mackie and Bob what's happened, will you? Right, I'm off.'

He continued purposefully on his way, and in some bemusement Doone watched him go: his first taste of the difficulty of deflecting Tremayne from a chosen course.

'Well, Chief Inspector,' I said neutrally, 'where do you want to begin?'

'Your name, sir?' I gave it again.

'And your . . . er . . . position here?'

'I'm writing a history of the stables.'

He seemed vaguely surprised. 'Very interesting, I'm sure. And . . . er . . . did you know the deceased?'

'Angela Brickell? No, I didn't. She vanished last summer, I believe, and I've been here only just over a week.'

'But you knew about her, sir,' he said shrewdly.

'Let me show you how I knew,' I said. 'Come and look.'

I led him into the dining room and showed him the clippings.

'This is my workroom,' I said. 'Somewhere in *that* pile of cuttings,' I pointed, 'is an account of her disappearance.'

He seemed reassured about me personally, and I got the first hint of the garrulity to come.

'Well, sir,' he said, relaxing, 'you can start introducing me to all the people here and explain why I'm asking questions and, since I've found on other cases when only remains are found that people tend to think the worst and imagine all sorts of horrors so that it makes them feel sick and wastes a good deal of time altogether, I'll tell you, sir, and you can pass it on, that what was found was *bones*, sir, quite clean and no smell, nothing horrible, you can assure people of that. Animals and insects had cleaned her, you see.'

'Thank you,' I said, a shade numbly.

'And, if you don't mind, sir, will you please just tell everyone she's been found, not that she was strangled.'

'All right. We'd better start with Mr Vickers's secretary, Dee-Dee.'

I steered him into the office. Detective Constable Rich followed everywhere like a shadow, taking notes. I explained to Dee-Dee that Angela Brickell had probably been found.

'Oh, good,' she said spontaneously, and then, 'Oh, dear.'

'The poor lass has been dead six months or more,' Doone said to Dee-Dee. He asked if Dee-Dee knew of any reason for Angela Brickell's disappearance. Had the girl been unhappy? Having rows with a boyfriend?

'I've no idea. We didn't find out until after she'd gone that she must have given chocolate to Chickweed. Stupid thing to do.'

Doone looked lost. I explained about the theobromine.

'Is that what was meant in our notes by "possibly doped a horse in her charge"?' Doone asked.

'Spot on,' I said.

'Chocolate!' he said disgustedly. 'Not worth dying for.'

Doone said he'd like to talk to the rest of the stable staff, asking Dee-Dee meanwhile not to break the news to anyone else.

'I like to get people's first thoughts, first impressions, not hear what they think after they've spent hours discussing something with all their friends. First thoughts are clearer and more valuable, I've found.'

Doone asked to be taken out to the stables.

Bob Watson was outside the tack-room door, beavering away with saw, hammer and nails, making a new saddle-horse. I introduced Bob to Doone, Doone to Bob. Doone told him of Angela Brickell's remains.

'No!' Bob said. 'I always thought she'd just scarpered. Who found her?'

'She was found by chance,' Doone said. 'Was she unhappy over a boyfriend?'

'Not that I know of. But truth to tell, I can't remember much about her, except she was sexy. Ask the other girls here, some of them lived in a hostel with her. Why do you want to know about a boyfriend? She didn't take a high jump, did she?'

Doone didn't say yes or no, and I understood what he'd meant by preferring to listen to unadulterated first thoughts, to the first pictures and conclusions that minds leaped to when questioned.

He talked to Bob for a while longer but as far as I could see learned nothing much. 'You want to see Mackie,' Bob said in the end. 'That's young Mrs Vickers. The girls tell her things they'd never tell me.'

Doone nodded and I led him and the ubiquitous Rich round the house to Mackie and Perkin's entrance, ringing the bell. It was Perkin who came to the door, appearing in overalls, and smelling of wood and linseed oil.

'Hello,' he said, surprised. 'Mackie's in the shower.'

Doone introduced himself formally. 'I came to let Mrs Vickers know that Angela Brickell's been found,' he said.

'Who?' Perkin said blankly. 'I didn't know anyone was lost. I don't know any Angela . . . Angela who did you say?'

Doone patiently explained.

'Good Lord. Really?' A thought struck him. 'I say, is she the stablegirl who ran off some time last year?'

'That's the one.'

'My wife will be glad she's found. I'll give her the message.'

Doone said he would like to see Mrs Vickers himself.

'Oh? All right. You'd better come in and wait.'

He led the way into a kitchen-dining room, and offered us rattan armchairs round a table made of a circular slab of glass resting on three gothic plaster pillars. The curtains and chair covers were bright turquoise overprinted with blowsy grey, black and white flowers, and all the kitchen fitments were faced with grey-white streaked Formica; thoroughly modern.

Mackie arrived with damp hair at that point, looking refreshed and pleased with life. Her reaction to Doone's first cautious words was, 'Great. Where is she?'

The gradual realisation of the true facts drained the contentment and the colour from her face. 'You're telling us, aren't you,' she said flatly, 'that either she killed herself . . . or somebody killed her?'

'I didn't say that, madam.'

'As good as.' She sighed desolately. 'We've just had months and months of trouble and anxiety over Olympia and Nolan, we're only just beginning to feel free of it all . . . I can't bear it . . . it's *starting all over again*.'

Chapter 10

I borrowed the Land-Rover and, at Doone's request, led him down to Harry and Fiona's. He explained a little solemnly that he found people felt less *threatened* by a police officer if he turned up with someone they knew.

'Don't you want them to feel threatened?' I asked. 'Many policemen seem to like it that way.'

'I'm not many policemen.' He seemed uninsulted. 'I work in my own way, sir, but I do tend to solve things, I assure you.'

'I don't doubt it, Chief Inspector,' I said.

'Never make assumptions,' he said absent-mindedly, as if giving me advice. 'You know the two most pathetic words a policemen can utter when his case falls apart around him?'

I shook my head.

' "I assumed",' he said.

As it happened, only Fiona was home, coming to the kitchen door in a dark blue tailored suit and an air of rush.

'John,' she said. 'What can I do for you? I'm going out to lunch. Can you make it quick?' She smiled apologetically.

'Er . . .' I said, 'this is Detective Chief Inspector Doone, Thames Valley Police. And Constable Rich.'

'Policemen?' she asked anxiously. 'Nothing's happened to Harry?'

'No. No. Nothing. It's not about Harry. Well, not exactly. It's about Angela Brickell. They've found her.'

'*Angela . . . ?* Oh, yes. Well, I'm glad. Where did she go?'

Doone was very adroit at letting silence break the bad news.

'Oh, my dear,' Fiona said after a few seconds, 'is she dead?'

Doone nodded. 'I need to ask you a few questions, madam.'

'Oh, but . . .' She looked at her watch. 'Can't it wait? It's not just a lunch, I'm the guest of honour.'

We were still standing on the doorstep. Doone produced the photograph and asked Fiona to identify the man if she could.

'Of course. It's Harry, my husband. And that's my horse, Chickweed. Where did you get this?'

'From the young woman's handbag.'

Fiona's face was full of regret. 'She loved Chickweed,' she said.

'Perhaps I could come back when your husband's at home?' Doone suggested.

Fiona was relieved. 'Oh, yes, do that. After five tonight or tomorrow morning. He'll be here. Bye, John.'

She hurried back into the house, leaving the door open, and presently, from beside our own cars, we saw her come out, lock the back door and drive away in a neat BMW.

'If you had to describe her in a word,' Doone said to me, 'what would it be?'

'Staunch,' I said. 'Steadfast.'

'Mm.' He pondered. 'I read the transcript of part of that trial before I came here. Loyalty is strong here, wouldn't you agree? Staunch, steadfast loyalty, wouldn't you say?'

Doone might look grey, I thought, but there was a cunningly intelligent observer behind his disarming chattiness.

He said he would like to speak to all the other stablegirls before they heard the news from anyone else, and also the men.

I took Doone and Rich to the small, modern house in the village which I knew the girls called their hostel. He sat paternally on a flower-patterned sofa in the sitting room, at home among the clutter of pot plants, satin cushions, fashion magazines and endless photographs of horses, and told them without drama about Angela Brickell.

Only four of the six girls had been employed at the yard in Angela's time, they said. She hadn't been their close friend. She was moody and secretive, they all agreed. They didn't know of a steady boyfriend. They thought Sam Yaeger had probably had her, but no one should read much in that.

'Did Angela and Sam Yaeger quarrel?'

'You don't quarrel with Sam Yaeger,' the brightest of them said boldly. 'You go to bed with him. Or in the hay.'

They were all in their teens. Light-framed, hopeful, knowing.

The bold girl said, 'But no one takes Sam seriously. It's just a bit of fun. He'd never try to force anyone. It's casual with him, like.'

I wondered if Doone was thinking that maybe with Angela it hadn't been casual after all. We travelled back through the village to a bungalow where the unmarried lads lived.

The living room in the lads' hostel, in contrast to the girls', was plantless, without cushions and grubbily scattered with newspapers, empty beer cans, dirty plates and muddy boots.

The lads all knew that Angela Brickell had been found dead, as one of them had learned it from Bob Watson. None of them seemed to care about her personally (exactly like the girls) and they had no information and few opinions about her.

'She rode all right,' one of them said, shrugging.

'She was a bit of a hot pants,' said another.

After we'd left, Doone demanded of me, 'Well, what do you think?'

'It's *your* job to think,' I protested.

He half smiled. 'I'll listen to everything anyone wants to say. I'm not proud. I don't mind the public telling me the answers.'

I DIDN'T SEE DOONE ON FRIDAY, but on Saturday I learned that he had spent the day before scattering fear and consternation.

Tremayne had asked if I would like to go to Sandown with Fiona, Harry and Mackie. He himself would be saddling five runners at Chepstow. 'To be frank, you'd be under my feet. Go and carry things for Mackie.'

With old-fashioned views he persisted in thinking pregnant women fragile. I wondered if Tremayne understood how little Perkin would like my carrying things for Mackie.

'Fiona and Harry are taking Mackie,' Tremayne said, almost as if the same thought had occurred to him. 'I'll check that they'll take you too.'

They had room. They collected Mackie and me at the appointed time and they were very disturbed indeed.

Harry was driving. Fiona twisted round in the front seat to speak to

Mackie and me directly and with deep lines of worry in her face told us that Doone had paid a menacing visit to them the day before and more or less accused Harry of strangling Angela Brickell.

'What?' Mackie said. 'That's ridiculous.'

'Doone doesn't think so,' Harry said gloomily. 'Did he show you that photo of me with Chickweed?'

Mackie and I both said yes.

'Well, it seems he got it enlarged. I mean, blown up really big, just of me, not the horse. He asked me to confirm that I was wearing my own sunglasses in the photo. I said of course I was. Then he asked me if I was wearing my own belt, and I said of course. Then he asked me if the pen clipped onto the racecard I was holding in the photo was mine also . . .' He stopped for a moment. 'You won't believe it . . . but they found my sunglasses and my belt and my gold pen lying with that girl. I don't know how the hell those things got there.'

Fiona said, 'Doone demanded to know precisely where Harry had been on the day that girl went missing.'

'He thinks I killed her,' Harry said. 'It's obvious he does. I don't know where I was that day.'

'We keep a big appointments diary,' Fiona said fiercely. 'I dug up last year's. There's nothing listed at all on that day.'

'No work?' I suggested. 'No meetings?'

Harry and Fiona simultaneously said no. Harry, whose personal fortune seemed to equal Fiona's in robust good health, passed his time lucratively as occasional consultant to private firms. He couldn't remember any consultations for most of June.

'We went to see Nolan ride Chickweed at Uttoxeter near the end of May,' Fiona said worriedly. 'Angela was there looking after the horse. That was the day someone fed him theobromine and caffeine, and if she didn't give Chickweed chocolate herself then she must have let someone else do it. Sheer negligence, probably. Anyway, Chickweed won and Angela went back to Shellerton with him. And I can't remember seeing her again after that.'

'Nor can I,' Harry said.

'Someone must have put those things there to incriminate Harry,' Mackie said unhappily.

'Doone believes it was an unpremeditated murder,' Harry said. 'I asked him why and he just said that people who commit unpremeditated murder often drop things from extreme agitation and don't know they've dropped them.' Harry, trying to sound balanced, was clearly horribly disconcerted.

AT SANDOWN IT WAS a subdued little group that stood in the parade ring watching Fiona's tough hunter, the famous Chickweed, walk round before the Wilfred Johnstone Hunter Chase.

No one, one hoped, had given him chocolate.

Fiona had told Nolan about Doone's accusations. Nolan told Harry that now that he, Harry, knew what it was like to have a charge of murder hanging over him he would have more sympathy for him, Nolan. Harry protested that he, Harry, had not been found with a dead girl at his feet.

'As good as, by the sound of things,' Nolan said, rattled.

'Nolan!' Fiona wasn't amused. 'Put your mind on the race. Harry, not another word about that *bloody* girl. Everything will be sorted out. We'll just have to be patient.'

Harry gave her a fond but rueful glance and over her shoulder caught my eye. There was something more in his expression, I thought, and after a moment identified it as fear.

Mackie, *in loco* Tremayne, saw Nolan into the saddle and the four of us walked towards the stands to see the race. With Mackie and Fiona in front, Harry fell into step beside me.

'I want to tell you something,' he said, 'but not Fiona.'

'Fire away.'

'Doone said . . . he said the girl had no clothes on when she died. He asked what I was doing with my belt off.' The shock still trembled in his voice.

We reached the stands, Harry falling silent in his torturing troubles amid the enfolding hubbub of the gathering crowd. The runners cantered past on their way to the starting gate, Nolan looking professional as usual on the muscly chestnut. Chickweed, now running in the first hunter chase of the spring season, was going to win three or four times before June, Tremayne hoped.

We were joined at that point by pudgy, unfit Lewis, who asked if the Jockey Club had said anything about Nolan going on riding.

'Not a word,' Fiona said. 'Fingers crossed.'

'If they were going to stop him,' Lewis opined judiciously, 'they'd surely have let him know by today, so perhaps he's got away with it.'

'Brotherly love,' Fiona remarked ironically.

'He owes me,' Lewis said darkly and with such intensity that all of us, I thought, recognised the nature of the debt. 'I am the best bleep bleep actor of you all.'

Fiona starkly faced the certainty that Lewis had not after all been too drunk to see straight when Olympia died. Mackie's clear face was pinched with dismay. Harry had known all along.

'What would you have had me do?' Lewis demanded, seeing the general disapproval. 'Say he called her every filthy name in the book and shook her by the neck until her eyes popped out?'

No one answered him, me included.

Fiona said, 'They're off,' a split second before the official announcement, and concentrated through her raceglasses.

Chickweed was easy to spot, I discovered, with the white blaze down his chestnut face that so clearly distinguished him in the photograph, nodding away on the rails at every galloping step. He flew the first fence and all the next six down the far side. A length in front of his nearest pursuer, he swept round the long bend at the bottom end of the course and straightened himself for the third fence from home.

'Oh, come on,' Fiona said explosively, the tension too much. 'Chicky Chickweed . . . jump it.'

Chicky Chickweed rose to it as if he'd heard her, his white blaze showing straight on to us before he veered right towards the second-last fence and the uphill pull to home. Chickweed made short work of the second-last fence but didn't shake off his pursuer, who closed the gap coming to the last fence.

'Oh, no,' Fiona groaned. 'Oh, Nolan, come on.'

Chickweed made a spectacular leap, leaving unnecessary space between himself and the birch, wasting precious time in the air. His pursuer, jumping lower in a flatter trajectory, landed first and was fastest away.

Fiona was silent, beginning to accept defeat.

Nolan had no such thoughts. Nolan was crouching like a demon over Chickweed's withers delivering the message that losing was unacceptable. Nolan's whip rose and fell twice, his arm swinging hard. Chickweed took up the struggle again. The jockey and horse in front, judging the battle won, eased up fractionally too soon. Chickweed caught them napping a stride from the winning post and put his head in front.

It was Nolan, I saw, who had won that race. Nolan himself, not the horse. Through Nolan I began to understand how much more there was to riding races than fearlessness and being able to stay in the saddle. Winning races, like survival, began in the mind.

WE ARRIVED BACK at Shellerton before Tremayne returned from Chepstow. Fiona dropped Mackie off at her side of the house and I walked round to Tremayne's, unlocking the door with the key he'd given me and switching on lights. In the family room I poured some wine and felt at home.

A knock on the back door drew me from comfort to see who it was. A young woman with a shy enquiring smile, pretty in a small way, brown-haired, self-effacing . . . Bob Watson's wife, Ingrid.

'Come in,' I said warmly. 'But I'm the only one home.'

She came over the threshold tentatively and I encouraged her into the family room, where she stood nervously and wouldn't sit down.

'Bob doesn't know I'm here,' she said anxiously.

She seemed to be screwing herself up to something.

'You were ever so kind to me that night. Bob reckons you saved me from frostbite at the least . . . and pneumonia, he said. Giving me your own clothes. I'll never forget it. Never.'

'You looked so cold,' I said.

'I knew you'd come back just now . . . I saw Mrs Goodhaven's car come up the road . . . I came to talk to you. I've got to tell someone . . . '

'Go on then. Talk. I'm listening.'

She said in a small burst, unexpectedly, 'Angela Brickell was a Roman Catholic, like I am.'

'Was she?' The news meant very little.

Ingrid nodded. 'After she'd vanished last year Mrs Vickers asked me to clear all her things out of the hostel and send them to her parents, and I did.' She stopped, staring searchingly at my face for understanding.

'What,' I asked, feeling the way, 'did you find in her belongings? Something that worries you . . . because she's dead?'

'I threw it away,' she said. 'It was a do-it-yourself kit for a pregnancy test. She'd used it. All I found was the empty box!'

Chapter 11

Tremayne came home and frightened Ingrid away like Miss Muffet and the spider. 'What did she want?' he asked, watching her scuttling exit. 'She always seems scared of me. She's a real mouse.'

'She came to tell me something she thinks should be known,' I said reflectively. 'Angela Brickell was perhaps pregnant.'

'What?' He stared at me blankly. *'Pregnant?'*

I explained about the used test. 'She was a Roman Catholic, Ingrid says. They're against abortion.'

He stared into space.

I said, 'Harry's in trouble. Have you heard?'

'No, what trouble?'

I told him about Doone's accusations, and also about Chickweed's way of winning and about Lewis's more or less explicit admission of perjury. Tremayne told me in his turn that he'd had a rotten day at Chepstow. 'One of the runners went crashing down at the last fence. Sam said he was absolutely OK from the fall but the damned doctor thought he looked concussed and he's stood him down until Tuesday.'

He flopped into an armchair and stretched out his legs, thinking things over. Mackie and Perkin came through for their usual drink and news exchange and even Chickweed's win couldn't disperse the general gloom.

'Angela pregnant?' Mackie shook her head, bewildered.

'Damned careless of her,' Perkin said. 'That bloody girl's nothing but trouble. It's all upsetting Mackie just when she should be feeling relaxed and happy, and I don't like it.'

Mackie stretched out a hand and squeezed her husband's in gratitude, the underlying joy resurfacing, as persistent as pregnancy itself.

Gareth gusted in full of plans for an expedition I'd forgotten about, a fact he unerringly read on my face. 'But you said we could light a fire.'

'Um,' I said. 'Ask your father.'

Tremayne listened to Gareth's request for a patch of land for a campfire and raised his eyebrows my way.

'I suggested it, in a rash moment,' I said.

Gareth nodded vigorously. 'Coconut's coming at ten.'

SUNDAY MORNING crept in greyly on a near-freezing drizzle, enough to test the spirits of all would-be survivors, and Tremayne elicited a promise from me to bring everyone home at the first sneeze.

Coconut arrived in brilliant yellow oilskins with a grin to match. It was easy to see how he'd got his name. He stood in the kitchen, dripping, and pulled off a sou'wester to reveal a wiry tuft of light-brown hair sticking straight up from the top of his head. Nearly fifteen, he had bright intelligent eyes, a big nose and a sloppy, loose-lipped mouth, as if his face hadn't yet synthesised with his emerging character.

'There's a bit of wasteland at the top of the apple orchard,' Tremayne said. 'You can have a campfire there.'

'But, Dad . . .' Gareth began, raising objections.

'It sounds fine,' I said firmly. 'Survivors can't choose. But February's a bad month for food, so we'll cheat a bit and take some bacon with us. Bring gloves and a penknife each. We'll go in ten minutes.'

Tremayne came to the door to see off the intrepid expedition, all of us unequipped except for my survival kit (with added bacon) and the penknives in their pockets.

The cold drizzle fell relentlessly. Gareth led us through a gate in a wall, through a patch of long-deserted garden, and up a slow gradient through about fifty bare-branched apple trees, fetching up on a small bedraggled plateau with ruined dry-stone walling on one side and the remains of a hawthorn hedge round the rest. I thought Tremayne had chosen pretty well. Whatever we did, we couldn't make things much worse.

'First of all,' I said, 'we build a shelter for the fire.' I brought the basic survival tin out of my pocket and gave Gareth the coil of flexible saw. 'We passed at least four dead apple trees on the way up here. Slide a couple of sticks through the loops at the ends of this saw, and you and Coconut go and cut one down and bring it up here. Cut it near the ground.'

They bounced off, and I wandered round, seeing everywhere possibilities of a satisfactory camp. By the time the boys returned, puffing, red-faced and dragging the result of their exertions, I'd wrenched out a few rusty old metal fence posts, cut a lot of living hawthorn switches from the hedge and harvested a pile of dead grass stalks. We made a short trip down to the deserted garden to reap a patch of old stinging nettles for bindings, and, about an hour after setting off, were admiring a freestanding four-foot-square shelter made of a metal frame with a slightly sloping roof of closely latticed hawthorn switches, thatched on top with bundles of dried grass. The drizzle dripped off to one side, leaving a small rain-free area underneath.

'OK,' I said. 'Next, we find some flat dry stones from that broken-down wall to make a floor for the fire. Then we go round looking for anything very small and dry that will burn. Dead leaves. Bits of fluff caught on fences. When we've got enough tinder, we'll feather some kindling sticks. We also need dry wood, if you can find any. And bring any old cow pats you come across: they burn like peat.'

After another hour's labour with a match, a piece of candle, the tinder of dead leaves and flower heads, the feathered kindling sticks and a good deal of luck (but no cow pats), a bright little fire burned healthily against the drizzly odds and Gareth and Coconut looked as if the sun had risen where they didn't expect it. The smoke curled up and out over the edges of the thatched roofing. I remarked that if we'd had to live there for months we could hang spare meat and fish under the roof to smoke it.

'We couldn't live out here for months,' Coconut said.

'It wasn't always sunny in Sherwood Forest,' I said.

Lunch, after a long forage, consisted mainly of finds from the old garden: some tubers of wild parsley, comfrey and Jerusalem artichoke, a handful of very small Brussels sprouts (ugh, Gareth said) and a rather bitter green-leaf salad of plantain, dock and dandelion (double ugh). Both boys fell on the bacon, threaded and grilled on sharpened peeled sticks, and such was their hunger that they afterwards chewed for ages on strips of the inner sweet bark of a young birch tree. Birch bark was good nourishing food, I said. Gareth said they would take my word for it.

We were sitting in the shelter, the fire burning, the drizzle almost a permanence, the end of the experiment not far ahead.

'Survival isn't really much fun, is it?' Gareth said.

'Often not,' I agreed. 'Just a matter of life or death.'

'If we were outlaws in Sherwood Forest,' he said, 'the Sheriff's men would be hunting us.'

Coconut involuntarily looked around for enemies, shivering at the thought. I thought that perhaps for a second or two they'd had a vision of a much older, more brutal world where every tomorrow was a struggle, where hunger and cold were normal and danger ever present and cruel. A primitive world, where the strong ate and the weak died; the bedrock and everlasting design of nature.

When a dark shade of iron seeped into the slate-grey light we pulled the fire to pieces and doused the hot ends in wet grass. It was with leaps and whoops that Gareth and Coconut ran down from the shelter to re-embrace the familiar constraints of civilisation.

'Lead me to a pizza,' Gareth said, barging in through the back door. 'To two pizzas, maybe three.'

Laughing, I peeled off my ski suit and left them to it in the kitchen, heading myself for warmth in the family room; and there I found a bunch of depressed souls contemplating a different sort of disastrous tomorrow.

Harry, Fiona, Nolan, Lewis, Perkin, Mackie and Tremayne. Tight-knit, they looked at me vaguely, at the stranger within their gates.

'Ah . . . John,' Tremayne said, 'are both boys still living?'

'More or less.'

I poured myself some wine and sat on an unoccupied footstool, feeling the oppression of their collective thoughts.

'If Harry didn't do it, who did?' It was Lewis's question, which got no specific reply, as if it had been asked over and over before.

'Doone will find out,' I murmured.

Fiona said indignantly, 'He's not trying. He's not looking beyond Harry. It's disgraceful.'

Proof that Doone was still casting about, however, arrived noisily at that point in the shape of Sam Yaeger, who swept into the house in a high state of indignation.

'Tremayne!' He stopped in the doorway. 'Oh. You're all here.'

'You're supposed to be resting,' Tremayne said repressively.

'To hell with bloody resting. There I was, quietly resting my bruises according to orders, when this Policeman Plod turns up on my doorstep. And d'you know what little gem he tossed at me? Your bloody stablegirls told him I'd had a bit of how's-your-father with Angela Brickell.'

The brief silence which greeted this announcement wasn't exactly packed with disbelief.

'Well, did you?' Tremayne asked.

'That's not the point. The point is that it wasn't any Tuesday last June. So this Doone fellow asks me what I was doing that day, as if I could remember. Is this man for real? He said he had to check every possibility, so I told him he'd have a long job considering old Angie's opportunities, not to mention willingness.' He paused. 'She was even making goo-goo eyes at Bob Watson at one time.'

'She wouldn't have got past Ingrid,' Mackie said. 'Ingrid looks meek and mild but you should see her angry. She doesn't trust any girl in the yard. I doubt if Angela got anywhere with Bob.'

Gareth and Coconut came in, busily stoking their furnaces with pizza wedges. Tremayne raised his eyebrows at the food.

'We're starving,' explained his younger son. 'We ate *roots* and birch bark, and no one in their right mind would live in Sherwood Forest, being chased by the Sheriff.'

Sam looked bewildered. 'What *are* you on about?'

'Survival,' Gareth said. He marched over to a table, picked up *Return Safe from the Wilderness* and thrust it into Sam's hands. 'John wrote it,' he said, 'and five other books like it. So we built a shelter and made a fire.'

'What about Sherwood Forest?' Harry drawled.

Coconut explained, 'We might be cold and hungry but there weren't any enemies lurking behind the apple trees.'

'It makes you realise how lucky you are to have a bed and a pizza to come home to,' Gareth said thoughtfully.

'Next time,' Coconut enquired, 'why don't we make some bows and arrows?'

'What for?' asked Perkin.

'To shoot the Sheriff's men, of course.'

'You'd wind up hanged in Nottingham,' Tremayne said. He looked at me. 'Is there going to be a next time?'

Before I could answer, Gareth said, 'Yes.' He paused. 'Well, it wasn't all a laugh a minute, but we did *do* something. I could do it again.'

'Next Sunday,' I said, 'we could go out, do something else.'

The vague promise seemed enough for both boys, who drifted back to the kitchen for further supplies, and Sam, leafing through the book, remarked that some of my more ingenious traps looked as if they would kill actual people, not only big animals like deer.

I agreed. 'Some traps aren't safe to set unless you know you're alone.'

MONDAY FOUND DOONE on our doorstep, wanting to check up on the dates when Chickweed had won and Harry had been there.

Tremayne sorted the way through the form book and his memory, saying finally that there had been no occasion that he could think of when Harry had been at the races without Fiona.

'How about the fourth Saturday in April?' Doone asked slyly.

'The what?' Tremayne looked it up again. 'What about it?'

'Your travelling head lad thinks Mrs Goodhaven had flu that day, when the horse won at Uttoxeter but failed the dope test later. If Mr Goodhaven went alone to Uttoxeter, and Mrs Goodhaven was at home feeling ill . . .'

'You don't know what you're talking about,' Tremayne interrupted. 'Angela Brickell was in charge of a *horse*. She couldn't just leave it.'

'But I understood from your head lad, sir,' Doone said with deadliness, 'that they had to wait for Angela Brickell that day because when they were all ready to go home she couldn't be found. She *did* leave her horse unattended, sir. She turned up just in time, and wouldn't say where she'd been.'

Tremayne said blankly, 'I don't remember any of this. There's no privacy for anything odd on racecourses. I don't believe a word of what you're hinting.'

'Angela Brickell died about six weeks after that,' Doone said, 'by which time she'd used a pregnancy test.'

'Stop it,' Tremayne said. 'This is supposition of the vilest kind, aimed at a good intelligent man who loves his wife.'

'Good intelligent men who love their wives, sir, aren't immune to sudden passions,' Doone said.

'I don't want to hear any more of this,' Tremayne announced. 'You're inventing a load of rubbish.'

'Mr Goodhaven's belongings were found with the lassie, and she carried his photograph, and that's not rubbish,' Doone sombrely replied.

BY TUESDAY THE PRESS had been drenched with leaks from all quarters. Trial by public opinion was in full swing: Harry Goodhaven had 'allegedly' bedded a stablegirl, got her pregnant and throttled her to save his marriage to a 'wealthy heiress'.

Wednesday's papers were even worse. Harry phoned me soon after lunch. 'If I come and pick you up, will you come out driving with me?'

'Sure,' I said.

'Fine. Ten minutes.'

Harry came in his BMW, twin of Fiona's, and I climbed in beside him, seeing new lines of strain in his face and also rigidity in his neck muscles.

'John, good of you,' he said. 'Life's bloody.'

I tried a shot at comfort. 'Doone knows there's something wrong with his case, otherwise he would have arrested you already.'

He glanced my way as he put the car into gear and started forward. 'Do you think so? He's on our doorstep every day, building a cage round me.'

'He's trying to break your nerve,' I said, guessing.

Harry turned the car towards Reading to travel by the hilly route that would take us through the Quillersedge Estate.

'Fiona says not to let him rattle me, she's being splendid, absolutely marvellous, but he *does* rattle me, I can't help it. He tosses out lethal questions as if they were harmless afterthoughts . . . "Did she undress willingly?" How can I answer? I wasn't there.'

'That's the answer.'

'He doesn't believe me.'

'He isn't sure,' I said. 'Something's bothering him.' I paused. 'Why are we going this way?'

The question surprised him. 'To get to where we're going, of course.'

'So we're not just out for a drive?'

'Well, no.'

A long stretch of the road was bordered on each side by mixed woodland, looking bare-branched and bedraggled in the scrag end of winter, wild and open to anyone caring to push through the tangle of trees, saplings and their assorted undergrowth. Five yards into that, I thought, and one would be invisible from the road.

We drove a fair way through villages unknown to me. From a mostly uninhabited lane we turned through some broken gateposts into a rutted drive leading to a large sagging barn, an extensive dump of tangled metal and wood, and a smaller barn to one side. Beyond this unprepossessing mess lay a wide expanse of muddy water.

'Where are we?' I asked, as the car rolled to a stop.

'That's the Thames,' Harry said. 'Almost breaking its banks after all that rain and melted snow. This is Sam's boatyard.'

'This?' I remembered what Sam had said about useful squalor: it had been an understatement.

'He keeps it this way on purpose,' Harry confirmed. 'We all came here for a huge barbecue party he gave to celebrate being champion jockey . . . eighteen months ago, I suppose. It looked different that night. One of the best parties we've been to . . .' There was sweat on his forehead.

'What's making you nervous?' I asked.

'Come with me,' he said jerkily. 'I want someone with me.'

He pointed to the smaller of the barns. 'That big place on the left is Sam's

workshop and dock. The boathouse isn't used much, though Sam made it into a grotto the night of the party. I'm going to meet someone there. I'm a bit early.'

'Who are you going to meet?'

'Someone,' he said, and got out of the car. 'I don't know who. Look,' he went on, as I followed him, 'someone's going to tell me something which may clear me with Doone. I just wanted *support* . . . a witness, even. I suppose you think that's stupid.'

'No. How was the meeting arranged?'

'On the telephone,' he said. 'This morning. I didn't know the voice. Don't even know if it was a man or a woman.'

'Why here,' I asked, 'of all places?'

He frowned. 'I've no idea. That's why I wanted company.'

'All right.' I shrugged. 'Let's wait and see.'

With relief he smiled wanly and led the way across some rough ground of stones and gnarled old weeds. Close to, the boathouse was, if anything, less attractive than from a distance. The construction was mostly of weathered old brick, the long sidewalls going down to the water's edge, the whole built on and into the river's sloping bank.

True to Sam's philosophy, the ramshackle wooden door had no latch, let alone a padlock, and pushed inwards, opening at a touch.

Windows in the walls gave plenty of light, but inside all one could see was a bare wooden floor stretching to double glass doors leading to a railed balcony overhanging the swollen river.

'Don't boathouses have water in them?' I enquired mildly.

'The water's underneath,' Harry said. 'This room was for entertaining. There's another door down by the edge of the river for going into the boat dock. That's where the grotto was. Sam had put coloured lights all round and some actually in the water . . . it looked terrific.'

'Did Sam invite Nolan to his party?'

'He asked everyone. Even Angela . . .' He stopped and looked at his watch. 'It's just about time.'

He turned and took a step towards the far-end balcony, the ancient floorboards creaking underfoot.

There was a white envelope lying on the floor about halfway to the balcony and, saying perhaps it was a message, he went towards it and bent to pick it up. With a fearsome crack, a whole section of the floor gave way under his weight and shot him into the dock beneath.

Chapter 12

It happened so fast that I nearly slid after him, managing only instinctively to pivot on one foot and throw myself headlong back onto the boards still remaining solid behind the hole.

Peeling off my jacket, I wriggled until I could peer over the edge into the wet depths below and I couldn't see Harry at all. I yelled to him. No reply.

I kicked off my boots and swung down below, holding on to a bared crossbeam that creaked with threat. All that was visible was brownish opaque muddy water. I dropped with bent legs so as to splash down softly and felt the breath rush out of my lungs from the iciness of the river. I stretched my feet down to touch bottom and found the water came up to my ears; took a deep breath, put the rest of my head under and reached round for Harry, unable to see anything at all.

He had to be there. Time was short. I stood up for a gasp of air, ducked down again, searching with fingers, with feet. I could feel things, pieces of metal, sharp, spiky things, nothing living.

Another gasp of air. I looked for bubbles rising, hoping to find him that way, and saw a red stain in the water a short way off.

I dived towards the scarlet streaks and touched him at once, but there was no movement in him. I slid my arms under Harry's and yanked him upwards as fiercely as I could until whatever had been holding him released its grasp and he came shooting to the surface.

He still wasn't breathing. I laced my arms round his back, under his own arms, letting his face fall on mine, and in that awkward position I blew my own breath into him, into his open nostrils, into his flaccid mouth, into either or both at once, as fast as I could, trying to pump his chest in unison.

They tell you to go on with artificial respiration for ever, for long after you've given up hope. Don't give up. Don't ever give up.

He was heavy in spite of the buoyancy from the water. I blew my breath into him rhythmically, squeezing him, telling him, ordering him, come back, come back . . . Harry, come back . . .

I felt the jolt in his chest and for a long second couldn't believe it, but then he heaved again in my arms and coughed in my face and a mouthful of dirty water shot out in a spout and he began coughing in earnest and choking and gasping for air . . . He opened his eyes and began groaning, and I started looking about to see how we were going to get out of what appeared to be uncomfortably like a prison.

Another door, Harry had said, down by the river's edge. I could see it, its bottom edge barely six inches above the water.

Across the whole end of the building, stretching from the ceiling down into the river, was a curtain of linked metal like thick, oversized chicken wire. Beyond it flowed the heavy main stream.

The dock itself was deeper than usual because of the height of the river. The door was still six inches above it, though . . . it didn't make sense to build a door high if the water was usually lower . . . not unless there was a step somewhere . . .

Taking Harry gingerly with me, I moved towards the wall, and with relief found that there was a shelf there about waist high. I lifted Harry until he was sitting on the walkway and then, gripping him tightly, wriggled up beside him so that we were both sitting with our heads wholly above water.

Harry was semiconscious, confused and bleeding. The hole through which he had fallen was in the centre of the ceiling. Even if I stood up on the walkway, I wouldn't be able to reach it. There seemed to be part of a beam missing in the area. Rotted through, no doubt.

Harry had stopped coughing, but still looked dazed. The blood was from one of his legs. I was debating whether to try to stop the bleeding first or to leave him while I found a way out, when I heard the main door creak open directly above our heads; the way Harry and I had come in.

My first natural impulse was to shout, to get help from whoever had come, but a stream of thoughts suddenly left me silent.

Thoughts. Harry had come to this place to meet someone. He didn't know who. He'd walked into the boathouse and tried to pick up an envelope and the floor had given way beneath him and a piece of beam was missing, and if I hadn't been there with him he would certainly have drowned in the dock, impaled on something beneath the surface. I guessed at an enemy above our heads, not a saviour.

There was silence. Then the creak of a step or two, then the sound of the door being quietly closed. Eerie.

In a short while I heard a car door slamming and after that an engine starting up and being driven away.

Harry suddenly said, 'I'm f-freezing.'

'Are you awake enough to sit here on your own for a bit?'

'John, for God's sake . . .'

'Not long,' I said hastily. 'I'll not leave you long.'

I waded along the walkway in the direction of the lower door and the river. There were indeed steps by the door. I went up and tried the doorlatch.

No easy exit. The door was solid as rock.

On the wall beside the door there was a row of three electric switches. I pressed them all without any results. There was also a central box with cables leading to the top of the metal curtain. I opened the box and pressed the button; again nothing happened.

'Harry?' I called.

'John . . .' His voice sounded weak and strained.

'Sit there and don't worry. I'll come back.'

'Well . . . hurry.' There was fear in his voice but also control.

I slipped back into the water and swam to the curtain. Tried standing up, but the water was much deeper there. Hung on to the wire, feeling the tug of the eddies from the river.

With luck, with extreme luck, the curtain wouldn't go all the way down to the riverbed. I took a breath and pulled myself hand over hand down the curtain, seeking to find the bottom of it with my feet: and there was indeed a gap between the bottom edge of the curtain and the mud, but only a matter of inches, and there was clutter down there, unidentifiable, pressing against the barrier, trying to get past it. I came up for air.

'Harry? There's a space under the metal curtain. I'm going out into the river and I'll be back for you very soon.'

'All right.' More control this time; less fear.

Deep breath. Dived, pulling myself down the wire. Came to the end of it, felt the mud below.

Go under it, I told myself. The temptation to return safely back up where I'd come from was enormous. Go *under* . . .

I decided to go headfirst, face-up, curling my back down into the soft riverbed, *praying* that the links wouldn't catch on my clothes . . . Head under, metal lying on my face, take care, don't rush, don't snag clothes, hold on to the wire outside, don't let go. The current in the river was appreciable, tugging. Keep straight, *hang on*, shoulders through, back through, legs . . . short of breath . . . lungs hurting . . . feet catching . . . *through*.

I came up into the air, gasping deeply, panting, aching lungs swelling, clinging on to the curtain in a shaky state.

'Harry?' I called.

'Oh, John . . .' His relief was beyond measure. 'Thank God.'

'Not long now,' I said, and heard the strain in my voice.

I edged along the curtain and by hauling my way up the links at the side managed to scramble up out of the water to roll at last onto the grassy bank. I stood up with knees that felt like buckling and tried to open the door into the dock. It was as immovable from outside as from in. The best thing to do was to find a telephone and get help. If I couldn't find a telephone in Sam's big workshop I could drive Harry's car to the nearest house . . .

Big snag. Harry's car had gone.

Before I did anything, I thought, I needed to put on my boots. Went into the boathouse through the top door.

Another big snag. No boots. No ski-suit jacket either.

There was now no doubt about murderous intention on someone's part and the certainty stimulated renewed strength. I ran along the stony path to Sam's large shed, and found to my relief that I could get inside easily enough—no lock on the door.

The space inside looked as much like a junkyard as the space outside. The centre was occupied by a large boat on blocks covered with plastic sheeting. I searched for a telephone, but couldn't find one. All around lay old and rusting tools and equipment, but among the junk I found, almost at once, two perfect aids: a tyre lever and a heavy mallet.

With those I returned at speed to the boathouse and attacked the lower door, hammering the toe of the tyre lever between the wooden doorframe and the surrounding brickwork just below the keyhole. The old wood of the doorframe splintered, freeing the tongue of the lock, and I pulled the door open towards me, swinging it wide. I stepped down into the boathouse, the shocking chill of the water again a teeth-gritter.

Harry's head was lolling only just above the surface.

'Come on,' I said urgently. 'Harry, wake up.'

He looked at me apathetically through a mist of weakness and pain. I floated him along in the water to the steps and there strained to pull him up them and out onto the grass.

'God, Harry, what do you weigh?' I asked, lugging.

'None of your bloody business,' he mumbled.

I laughed, relieved. If he could say that, he wasn't in a dying frame of mind. His leg seemed to have stopped bleeding, but all the same the faster I could get him to a doctor the better.

As far as I remembered, the boatyard lay down a lane with no houses nearby. On the other hand, only a few feet off I could see the upturned keel of an old clinker-built rowing boat. Small. Maybe six foot overall. A one-man job, big enough for two. If it weren't full of holes . . .

I heaved the dinghy over right side up. It looked seaworthy, but naturally there were no rowlocks and no oars. Never mind. Any piece of pole would do. Plenty lying about. I picked up a likely length and laid it in the boat.

'Come on, Harry. Let's get you in the boat.'

'In the *boat*?'

'Yes. Someone's taken your car.'

He looked bewildered, but he made feeble efforts to help me get him to his left foot, and with my almost total support he made the few hops to reach the boat. I helped him sit down on the one centre thwart.

'Hang on tight to the sides,' I said. 'Tight.'

'Yes.' His voice was vague, but his hands tightened.

I tugged and lugged the dinghy until it was sliding backwards down the bank. When the stern hit the water, I jumped in myself and simply hoped against all reasonable hope that we wouldn't sink at once.

We didn't. The current took the dinghy immediately and started it on its way downstream, and I edged past Harry into the stern space and retrieved my piece of pole, trailing it behind in the water like a rudder. The steering was rudimentary, but enough to keep us travelling bow-first downstream.

Downstream was always the way to people . . . Bits of the guidebooks floated familiarly to the surface. *Some traps are horrific*. Some of the traps described how to arrange for the prey to fall through seemingly firm ground into a pitful of spikes beneath.

Everyone had read the guides.

There was some water in the boat now, sloshing about under our feet. The wide river narrowed abruptly with a notice on our left saying DANGER in huge letters, and a smaller notice saying LOCK with an arrow to the right.

I steered the dinghy powerfully to the right. DANGER led to a weir. A lock would do just fine. Locks had keepers.

We floated on as if in a timeless limbo. The water in the bottom of the boat grew deeper. Finally, blessedly, on the right, there were moorings for boats wanting passage through the lock.

I took the dinghy as far as we could go, right up near to the lock gates. Tied it to a mooring post and stepped up out of the boat.

'Won't be long,' I told Harry. He merely nodded. It was all too much.

I climbed the steps up onto the lock and knocked on the door of the lock-keeper's house, and through great good fortune found him at home.

'Fell in the river, did you?' he asked cheerfully, observing my soaked state. 'Want to use the phone?'

Chapter 13

I went with Harry in the ambulance to Maidenhead hospital, both of us swathed in blankets, Harry also in a foil-lined padded wrap used for hypothermia cases, and from then on it was a matter of phoning and reassuring Fiona and waiting to see the extent of Harry's injuries, which proved to be a pierced calf, entry and exit wounds both clean and clotted, with no dreadful damage in between. The doctors stuffed him full of antibiotics and put stitches where they were needed, and he was warm and responding nicely in a recovery room somewhere by the time Fiona arrived and wept briefly in my arms.

'You're damp!' She disengaged herself and held me at arm's length. 'Did you fall through the floor too?'

'Sort of.' The hospital's central heating had been doing a fine job of drying everything on me and I felt like one of those old-fashioned clothes horses, steaming slightly in warm air. Still no shoes or boots; couldn't be helped.

A nurse came to fetch Fiona to see Harry, and she went anxiously, calling over her shoulder for me to wait for her. When she returned half an hour later she looked dazed.

'Harry's sleepy,' she said. 'He kept telling me silly things . . . How could you possibly get to this hospital in a *boat*?'

'I'll tell you on the way home. Would you like me to drive?'

'But . . .' She looked at my feet dubiously.

'It's quite easy with bare feet. I'll take off my socks.'

'Go straight to Shellerton House,' she said. 'I'll drive home from there.' She handed me the keys. As we headed for Shellerton in the early dark I told her calmly the gist of what had befallen us in Sam's boatyard.

She listened with a frown. I pulled up outside Tremayne's house and, while I put on my socks again, she said she would come in for a while for company, 'to cure the trembles.'

Tremayne, Mackie and Perkin were all in the family room for the usual evening drinks.

'I think someone tried to kill Harry,' Fiona said starkly.

'What?' There was general shock on all the faces.

'He went to Sam's boatyard and was nearly drowned . . .' She told it to them much as I'd told her myself.

Tremayne said robustly, 'My dearest girl, it must have been the most dreadful accident. Whoever would want to kill Harry?'

'No one,' Perkin said, his voice an echo of Tremayne's. 'I mean, did Harry say someone tried to kill him?'

Fiona shook her head. 'Harry was too dopey.'

'Does John think so?' Perkin asked.

Fiona glanced at me. 'John didn't actually say so. It's what I think myself. What I'm afraid of. It scares me to think of it.'

'Then don't, darling.' Mackie put an arm round her and kissed her cheek. 'It's frightening, but Harry *is* all right.'

They all spent time reassuring Fiona until the worst of the worry unwound from her body, and I made no attempt to throw in doubts because it would have achieved nothing good.

WITH DOONE, EARLY the next afternoon, it was a different matter. He came into the dining room where I was working and sat down opposite me at the table. 'I hear from Mr Goodhaven that you're a hero,' he said.

I stared back blandly.

'Accident or attempted murder?' Doone asked, apparently seeking a considered answer.

I gave him one. 'The latter, I'd say. Have you found his car?'

'Not yet.' He frowned at me with a long look in which I read nothing. 'Where would you search for it?' he asked.

After a pause I said, 'At the top of a cliff.'

He blinked.

'Maybe a metaphorical cliff,' I said. 'What would you have thought if Harry Goodhaven had disappeared for ever yesterday afternoon and you'd found his car later by a cliff, real or metaphorical?'

'Suicide,' he said promptly. 'An admission of guilt.'

'End of investigation? Books closed?'

He stared at me sombrely. 'Perhaps. But there would also be the possibility of simple flight. We would alert Australia . . . look for him round the world. The books would remain open.'

'But you wouldn't investigate anyone else, because you would definitely consider him guilty.'

'The evidence points to it. Flight or suicide would confirm it.'

'But something about that evidence bothers you, because you've made no arrest. I can only guess, but I'd say perhaps Harry's sunglasses and pen and belt were with Angela Brickell because she took them there herself.'

'Go on,' he said neutrally. It wasn't, I saw, a new idea to him.

'Suppose,' I said, 'that she did have a thing about Harry. Suppose she did carry his photo. Suppose she'd managed to acquire personal things of Harry's, and wore them or carried them with her. They'd only be evidence of her crush on Harry, not of his presence at her death.'

'I considered all that, yes.'

'Suppose someone couldn't understand why you didn't arrest Harry, and decided to remove any doubts you might be showing?'

He sat for a while without speaking.

'Whoever took Harry's car,' I said, 'removed my jacket and boots as well. I took them off before I went through the floor into the dock. I would think that whoever took those things is very worried indeed now to find that Harry and I are alive. I'd say it was an attempt to confirm Harry's guilt that went disastrously wrong, leaving you with bristling new doubts and a whole lot more to investigate.'

He said formally, 'I would like you to be present at the boatyard tomorrow morning. Mr Yaeger is meeting me there at nine o'clock.'

I nodded.

'You know,' Doone said slowly, 'I had indeed started to question others besides Mr Goodhaven.'

'Sam Yaeger told us. Everyone knew you'd begun casting wider.'

TREMAYNE LENT ME HIS VOLVO to go to the boatyard in the morning, reminding me before I set off that it was the day of the awards dinner at which he was to be honoured. Most of the racing world, it seemed, would be there to applaud.

Sam and Doone were already in the boatyard by the time I'd found my way there, radiating a mutual absence of civility.

'Right, sir,' Doone said, as I got out of the car. 'Please take us through your actions of Wednesday afternoon.'

'Harry said he was due to meet someone in the boathouse, so we went over there.' I walked where we'd gone, the others following. 'We opened this main door. It wasn't locked.'

'Never is,' Sam said.

I pushed open the door and we looked at the hole in the floor.

'We walked in,' I said. 'Just talking about a great party Sam gave here once. Harry began to walk down to the windows and saw an envelope on the floor and when he bent to pick it up the floor creaked and gave way.'

Sam looked blank.

'Is that likely?' Doone asked him. 'How long ago was the floor solid enough to hold a party on it?'

'A year last July,' Sam said flatly.

'Quick bit of rot,' Doone commented.

'Anyway,' I said, 'I took off my boots and jacket and left them up here and I dropped into the water. You can see better from the lower door,' I remarked, turning to go down the path. 'This door leads into the dock.'

Sam disgustedly fingered the splintered doorframe. 'Did you do this?' he demanded. 'It wasn't locked. The key was in the keyhole on the inside.'

'Absolutely not,' I said.

Sam pulled the door open and we looked into the scene that was all too familiar to my eyes: an expanse of muddy water, the hole in the ceiling overhead and the curtain of iron mesh across the exit to the river.

'There's a sort of walkway along this right-hand wall,' I told Doone. 'If you care to walk along there,' I suggested, deadpan, 'I'll show you an interesting fact about that hole.'

They both stared at the water with reluctance stamped all over their faces, then Sam thought of a more palatable solution. 'We'll go and look in a boat.'

'How about the curtain?' I said. 'What happens to the rubbish lying in the dock when you roll it up?'

'What are you talking about?' Doone asked.

'The bed of this dock is mud, and it slopes downwards towards the river,' I said. 'When the curtain's rolled up, there's nothing to stop things drifting out by gravity into the river and being moved downstream by the current. You of all people must know that those who drown in the Thames are probably taken by undercurrents down through London and out to sea.'

Doone nodded. 'We lose a few holidaymakers every year.'

'Harry's leg was impaled on something,' I said mildly. 'He was stuck underwater. He'd have been dead in a very few minutes. Next time Sam rolled the curtain up, Harry would have drifted quietly out of here, I should think, and no one would ever have known he'd been here.' I paused, and asked Sam directly, 'How soon would you have rolled up the curtain?'

He answered at once. 'Whenever I'd found the hole in the floor. I'd have gone to take a look from beneath. Like we're going to now. But I hardly ever come over here. Only in summer.' He gave Doone a sly look. 'In the summer I bring a mattress.'

'And Angela Brickell?' Doone asked.

Sam, silenced, stood with his mouth open.

I asked him, 'What's under the water in the dock?'

He said vaguely, 'Haven't a clue.'

'If you raise the curtain we may never know what Harry got stuck on.'

'Ah,' Doone said. 'It's a matter for grappling irons, then.'

Sam said, 'There's nothing in the dock except maybe beer cans . . .'

'Harry wasn't impaled on a beer can,' I said.

Doone said uneasily, 'This could have been an accident.'

I nodded. 'A good trap never looks like one.'

'Are you quoting someone?'

'Yes. Me. I've written a good deal about traps. How to set them. How to catch game. The books are all over Shellerton. Everyone's dipped into them. Follow the instructions and kill your man.'

'I'll have to see those books.'

Above us the weathered old grey beams crossed from side to side, holding up the planks of the floor above, except where the hole was.

'There's a bit of beam missing,' I said, 'isn't there?'

Sam nodded. 'Looks like it. But I didn't know about it. How could I?'

Doone said meaningfully, 'You yourself, sir, have all the knowledge and the tools for tampering with your boathouse.'

'I didn't.' Sam's response was belligerence, not fear. 'Everyone knows this place. Everyone's been here. Everyone could cut out a beam that small, it's child's play.'

'Who, precisely?' Doone asked. 'Besides you?'

'Well . . . anybody. Perkin! He could. Nolan . . . I mean, most people can use a saw, can't they? Can't you?'

Doone said merely, 'I'll take another look upstairs now, if you please.'

We went in gingerly, but as far as one could tell the floor was solid except for the one strip over the missing bit of beam. The floorboards themselves were grey with age, but not rotten.

Sam said, 'The floorboards aren't nailed down much. Just here and there. They fit tightly most of the time because of the damp, but when we have a hot dry summer they shrink and you can lift them up easily. The last time I took the floorboards up was for the party, installing coloured lights in the ceiling underneath.'

I went down on my knees and edged towards the hole. The way the floorboards had been laid, I saw, had meant that the doctored beam had been a main load-bearer. Several of the planks, including those that had given way under Harry's weight, had, without that beam's support, simply been hanging out in space, resting like a seesaw over the previous beam but otherwise supported only by the tight fit of each plank against the next. The floorboards hadn't snapped, as I'd originally thought: they'd gone down into the dock with Harry. I tested a few planks carefully with the weight of my hand, then retreated and stood up on safer ground.

'Well?' Doone said.

'It's still lethal just each side of the hole.'

'Right.' He turned to Sam. 'I'll have to know, sir, when this tampering could have been carried out.'

Sam gave it some thought. 'A week last Wednesday I dropped off a load of wood here on my way to Windsor races. Friday I spent some time here, half a day. Saturday I raced at Chepstow and had a fall and the doctor stood me down until Tuesday. Monday I spent here, pottering about. Tuesday I was back racing at Warwick. Wednesday I went to Ascot, yesterday Wincanton . . .' He paused. 'I've never been here at nights.'

'What races did you ride in on Wednesday?' Doone asked.

'The two-mile hurdle, novice hurdle, novice chase.'

Doone pulled out a notebook and wrote down the reply as given.

Sam, upon whom understanding had dawned, said, 'I wasn't here driving Harry's car away, if that's what you're thinking.'

'I'll need to ascertain a good many people's whereabouts on Wednesday afternoon,' Doone said placidly. 'But as for now, sir, we can proceed with our investigations.'

'Class dismissed?' Sam said with irony.

Doone, unruffled, said we would be hearing from him later.

Sam came with me to where I'd parked Tremayne's car on stone-strewn grass. The natural jauntiness remained in his step but there was less confidence in his thoughts, it seemed. 'Do you think I set that trap?' he said.

'You certainly could have.'

'Sure,' he said. 'Dead easy. But I didn't.' He looked up into my face, partly anxious, partly still full of his usual machismo.

'Unless you killed Angela Brickell,' I said, 'you wouldn't have tried to kill Harry. Wouldn't make sense.'

'I didn't do the silly little bimbo any harm.' He shook his head as if to free her from his memory. 'She was too intense for me, if you want to know. Old Angie took everything seriously, always going on about mortal sin, and I got bloody tired of it, and of her, tell the truth. She wanted me to marry her!' His voice was full of the enormity of such a thought. 'A bit of a hellcat, she could be, old Angie.'

I listened with fascination. The moody Miss Brickell suddenly became a real person, a mixed-up young woman full of strong urges and stronger guilts who'd piled on too much pressure, loaded her need of penitence and her heavy desires and perhaps finally her pregnancy onto someone who couldn't bear it, and who'd seen a violent way to escape her.

Someone, I thought, who knew how easily Olympia had died from hands round the neck.

Sam said cheerfully, as if shaking off murder as a passing inconvenience, 'Are you going to this do of Tremayne's tonight?'

'Yes. Are you?'

He grinned. 'Are you kidding? I'd be shot if I wasn't there to cheer. And anyway'—he shrugged as if to disclaim sentiment—'Tremayne deserves it. He's not all bad, you know.'

'I'll see you there, then,' I said, agreeing with him.

'If I don't break my neck.' It was flippantly said, but an insurance against fate, like crossed fingers. 'I'd better tell this bloody policeman where the main electric switch is.' He bounced off towards Doone, who was writing in his notebook, and I drove away.

Back at Shellerton House I returned to my slowly growing first chapter. But I couldn't concentrate. The trap in Sam's boathouse kept intruding, and so did Angela Brickell. Under the day-to-day surface of ordinary life in Shellerton the fish of murder swam like a shark, silent, unknown, growing new teeth. I hoped Doone would net him soon, but I hadn't much faith.

Fiona telephoned during the afternoon to say that she'd brought Harry home and he wanted to see me, so with a sigh, but little reluctance, I abandoned the empty page and walked down to the village.

Fiona hugged me like a long-lost brother and led me into the pink and green chintzy sitting room where Harry, pale with blue shadows below the eyes, sat in an armchair with his bandaged leg elevated on a large upholstered footstool. 'Hello,' he said, raising a phantom smile.

'How's the leg?' I asked, sitting down.

'Lousy. Weighs a couple of tons. Still, no gangrene as yet.'

He meant it as a joke but Fiona looked alarmed.

'Darling,' he said placatingly, 'I'm bloated with antibiotics, punctured with tetanus jabs and immunised against cholera, yellow spotted mountain fever and athlete's foot. I have it on good authority that I'm likely to live. How about a stiff whisky?'

'No. It'll curdle the drugs.'

'For John, then.'

I shook my head.

'Take Cinderella to the ball,' he said.

'What?'

'Fiona to Tremayne's party. You're going, aren't you?'

I nodded.

'I'm not leaving you,' Fiona protested.

'It wouldn't be the same for Tremayne if you weren't there. He dotes on you. John can take you. And'—his eyes brightened mischievously—'I know who'd love to use my ticket.'

'Who?' his wife demanded.

'Erica. My sainted aunt.'

Chapter 14

The Lifetime Award to Tremayne was the work of a hotel chain aiming to crash the racing scene with sponsorship in a big way. They, Castle Houses, had arranged the award dinner at Newbury racecourse, in the grandstand with its almost limitless capacity; and the whole affair, Mackie had told me, was frankly only a giant advertisement, but everyone might as well enjoy it.

Before we went, we met in the family room, Tremayne pretending nonchalance and looking unexpectedly sophisticated in his dinner jacket, his grey hair smooth, strong features composed, bulky body slimmed by expert tailoring. Perkin's jacket, by contrast, looked a shade too small for him and, in hugging his incipient curves, diminished the difference between the sizes of father and son.

Gareth's appearance in a dinner jacket no one knew he had, surprised everyone, and he looked neat, personable and much older than fifteen.

'Where did you get that?' his father asked, marvelling

'Sam said I was the same height as him now and he happened to have two. So he lent me one, OK?'

'It's great,' Mackie said warmly, herself shapely in a shimmering black dress edged with velvet. 'And John's jacket, I see, survived the ditch.'

The ditch seemed a long time ago: two weeks and three days back to the lonely, silent, abandoned struggle in the attic.

Tremayne, happy with life, said to me, 'You feel confident riding Drifter now, don't you?'

'More or less,' I agreed.

'Tomorrow you can ride Fringe. I own a half-share in him. He's that five-year-old in the corner box. You can school him over hurdles.'

'If you think so,' I said, astonished. Mackie was smiling, and I knew she and Tremayne must have discussed it.

'If you stay here a bit longer,' Tremayne said, 'and if you ride schooling satisfactorily, I don't see why you shouldn't eventually have a mount in an amateur race, if you put your mind to it.'

'Cool,' Gareth said fervently. 'Say you will.'

'I shouldn't think he wants to,' Perkin remarked. 'You can't make him.'

Here goes impulse again, I thought, a headlong plunge into a new dimension of existence.

'I will.' I looked at Tremayne. 'Thank you.'

We all loaded into the Volvo and went down to Shellerton Manor to see Harry. Tired but cheerful, he held court from his chair.

'I'm so glad you're alive,' Mackie said, with a suspicion of tears, and he stroked her arm and said lightly that he was too.

'What did it feel like?' Perkin said curiously, glancing at the bandaged leg.

'It happened too fast to feel much,' Harry said. 'If John hadn't been there I'd have died without knowing it, I dare say.'

'Don't!' Fiona exclaimed. 'I can't bear even to think of it. Tremayne, off you go or you'll be late. John and I will pick up Erica and see you soon.' She swept them out, following them, and Harry and I looked at each other across the suddenly empty room in a shared fundamental awareness.

'Do you know who did it?' he asked, stress visible.

I shook my head.

'Couldn't be someone I know.' He meant that he didn't want it to be. 'They meant to *kill* me, damn it. It's pretty awful to know someone hates me enough . . . That hurts more than my leg.'

'Yes.' I hesitated. 'It was maybe not hate. More like a move in a chess game. And it went wrong, don't forget. The strong presumption of guilt has changed to a stronger presumption of innocence. Entirely the wrong result. That can't be bad.'

Fiona returned, pulling on a fluffy white wrap over her red silk dress, saying she really didn't want to go to the dinner and being persuaded again by her husband. He would be fine, he said, goodbye, have a good time, give Tremayne the evening of his life.

Fiona drove her own car, the twin of Harry's (still lost), and settled Erica Upton in the front beside her when we collected her on a westerly detour.

'Harry told me to lay off you, as you'd saved his life,' the five-star novelist announced baldly. 'A proper spoilsport.'

I said in amusement, 'I don't suppose you'll obey him.'

I heard a chuckle from the front seat, quickly stifled. The battle lines, it seemed, had already been drawn. Hostilities however were in abeyance during arrival at the racecourse, disrobing, hair tidying and first drinks.

Half the racing world seemed to have embraced the occasion. Glittering black and silver ceiling-to-floor curtaining transformed the workaday interior of the grandstand into something ephemerally magnificent.

Background music made a change from bookies' cries. I drifted around, seeing a few people I knew by sight and hundreds I didn't. Bob Watson was there, dapper in a dark grey suit, with Ingrid shyly pretty in pale blue.

'Couldn't let down the guvnor,' Bob said cheerfully. 'You're riding Fringe tomorrow. Schooling. The guvnor just told me.'

'Yes.'

'Fringe will look after you,' he said inscrutably.

I noticed all evening that Ingrid stuck very closely to his side, and I remembered Mackie saying that meek little Ingrid never gave Bob much chance to stray with the likes of Angela Brickell and God help him if he did.

Sam Yaeger, ever an exhibitionist, had come in a white dinner jacket, having lent Gareth his black. He also had a frilled white shirt, a black shoestring tie and a definite air of strain. Doone, it appeared, had more or less accused him straight out of sabotaging his own boathouse.

'He says I had the tools, the knowledge, the opportunity and the location, and he looked up those races I rode at Ascot and worked out that I could have had time between the first two and the last to drive to Maidenhead and remove Harry's car.'

'He's persistent.'

'He whistled up his cohorts after you'd gone,' Sam complained, 'and they dredged up a lot of muck from the dock. An old broken bicycle frame, some rusted railings, an old disintegrating metal gate. He thinks I put it all in the water hoping Harry would get tangled in it.'

'Which he did.'

'How come *you* didn't get spiked when you went down there?'

'I learned how to jump into shallow water very young. I didn't go down far. Put my feet down cautiously after I was floating.'

He stared. 'How do you do that?'

'Jump shallow? The second your feet touch the water you raise your knees and crumple into a ball. The water acts as a brake.'

'Doone asked me if I'd left your jacket and boots in Harry's car. Tricky bastard. He got me so riled I lost a race this afternoon I should have won.'

He seemed to have let out sufficient resentment and turned to flirt obligingly with a middle-aged woman who touched his arm in pleased anticipation. Nolan, glowering routinely at Sam from a few feet away, switched his ill humour to me.

'Why don't you clear out of Shellerton?' he said forcefully.

'I will in a while.'

'I told Tremayne there'll be trouble if he gives you any of my rides.' He glared at me. 'I don't understand what Fiona sees in you. You keep away from her horses, understand?'

He stomped away, his place almost immediately taken by his brother, who gave me a malicious imitation of a smile and said, 'Nolan doesn't like you.'

'You don't say.'

'Nolan likes to be the centre of attention and you've usurped his pinnacle,' Lewis said. He gave me a sly leer. 'Don't put your neck within my brother's reach.'

'You stuck *your* neck out for him, anyway.'

'Sometimes I hate him,' he said with undoubted truth, and wheeled away as if he had said enough.

Glasses in hand, the chattering groups mixed and mingled, broke and re-formed, greeted each other with glad cries. Tremayne, large smile a permanence, received genuinely warm congratulations with modesty.

The throng began moving towards dinner. At table number six I found myself placed between Mackie and Erica Upton, who were already seated.

'I asked to sit next to you,' Erica remarked as I sat down.

'Er . . . why?'

'Do you have so little self-confidence?'

'In a desert, plenty. With pencil and paper, little. And you?'

'I don't answer that sort of question.'

I listened to the starch in her voice, recognised the ramrod will. 'I could take you across a desert,' I said. She gave me a long piercing inspection. 'You've found your courage since I met you last.'

She turned away, satisfied, to talk to Nolan on her other side, and I, abandoned, found Mackie smiling on my right.

'She's met her match,' she said.

I shook my head. 'If I could write like her . . . or ride like Sam or Nolan. . . if I could do *anything* that well, I'd be happy.'

Her smile sweetened. 'Try cooking. I hear the power of your *flambéed* bananas made Gareth oversleep.'

Perkin, on her other side, murmured something to get her attention and for a while I watched Tremayne make the best of our table having been graced by the sponsor's wife, a gushing froth of a lady in unbecoming lemon. Lewis on the lady's other side put away a tumblerful of vodka poured from a half-bottle in his pocket. Fiona watched him with a frown.

Fidgeting between Lewis and Perkin, Gareth ate everything fast and looked bored. Perkin with brotherly bossiness told him to stop kicking the table leg and Gareth uncharacteristically sulked. Mackie made a placatory remark and Perkin snapped at her too.

She turned her head my way. 'What's wrong with everyone?'

'Tension.'

'Because of Harry?' She nodded. 'We all pretend, but no one can help *wondering* . . . Nothing feels safe any more.'

'You're safe,' I said. 'You and Perkin. Think about the baby.'

Her face cleared automatically; the thought of the baby could diminish to trivia the grimmest forebodings.

Dinner wound to a close, speeches began. Cultured gents from the Jockey Club paid compliments to Tremayne and bowed low to the sponsor. He, the lemon lady's husband, eulogised Tremayne, who winced only slightly over

Top Spin Lob being slurred to Topsy Blob, and a minion in the livery of Castle Houses brought forth a tray bearing the award itself, a silver bowl rimmed by a circle of small galloping horses.

Tremayne was pink with gratification. He made a brief speech of all-round thanks, and everyone cheered and clapped loudly.

The background music became dance music. People moved about, flocking round Tremayne. Perkin took Mackie to shuffle on the square of dance floor adjoining the table. Nolan took Fiona, Lewis got drunker, Gareth vanished, the sponsor retrieved his lady. Erica and I sat alone.

She looked out at the still-alive party. 'Someone tried to kill Harry. That's extremely disturbing.'

'It was premeditated. Angela Brickell's death may or may not have been, but the attack on Harry was vastly thought out.'

She seemed to relax.

'My God!' I said, stunned.

'What? What have you thought of?' She was alert again.

'I'll have to talk to Doone.'

'What? Do explain.'

'Wood floats.'

She looked bemused. 'Well, of course it does.'

'The floorboards that went down to the water with Harry, they stayed under. They didn't float.'

'Why not?'

'Have to find out,' I said. 'Doone can find out.'

'What does it matter?'

'Well,' I said, 'no one could be certain that Harry would be spiked and drown immediately. So suppose he's alive and swimming about. He's been in that place before. He knows there's a door and he has daylight. So how does he get out?'

She shook her head. 'Tell me.'

'The door opens outwards. If you've got three or four floorboards floating about, you use one of them as a battering ram. When the enemy came to the boathouse,' I said, 'there wasn't any sound of Harry battering his way out.'

She began to say something but never completed it. Instead our heads turned in unison towards the dancers, among whom there was a crash and a scream. Bizarrely against the unrelentingly cheerful music two figures could be seen fighting. Sam . . . and Nolan.

Sam had blood on his white jacket and down the white ruffles. Nolan's shirt was ripped open, showing a lot of hairy chest. They were exchanging swinging blows not ten feet from table six and I stood up automatically.

Perkin tried to pull them apart and got knocked down by Nolan, quick and tough with his fists as with his riding. I stepped in and tried words instead. 'You stupid fools,' I said: not the most inventive sentence ever.

Nolan took his attention off Sam for a split second, lashed out expertly at my face and whirled back to his prime target. With instinct more than thought I barged into Nolan bodily, pushing him off line. He turned a face of mean-eyed fury in my direction and easily transferred his hatred.

I was acutely conscious that Nolan knew volumes more about bare-knuckle fisticuffs than I did. As the band came to a straggling sharp-flat unscheduled halt, Lewis's drunken voice could be heard drawling, 'Five to four the field.'

Everyone laughed. Everyone except Nolan. He was high on the flooding wave from the bursting dam of his dark nature, all the anxiety, guilt, hate and repressions sweeping out in a torrent. I was a punchbag for his escaping fury, the interloper, usurper, target.

I turned my back on him and took a step or two away. All I knew about fighting was ruse and trickery. I could see from the onlooking faces that he was coming for me, and I went down fast on one knee and whirled and punched upwards hard into the bottom of his advancing rib cage and then shifted my weight into his body and upwards so as to lift him wholesale off the floor. I had one of his wrists in my hand and he ended up on his feet with me behind him, his arm in a nice painful lock and my mouth by his ear.

'You stupid idiot,' I said intensely. 'The Jockey Club are here. Don't you care about your permit?'

For answer he kicked back and caught me on a shin.

'Then I'll ride all your horses,' I said unwisely.

I gave him a hard releasing shove in the general direction of Sam, Perkin and an open-mouthed Gareth, and at last watched a dozen restraining hands clutch and keep him from destroying himself entirely. But he turned his vindictive face my way and shouted in still-exploding rage, *'I'll kill you.'*

I stood unmoving, and thought of Harry.

Chapter 15

I apologised to Tremayne.

'Nolan started it,' Mackie said, peering anxiously at the reddening bruise on Perkin's cheek, a twin to one on mine.

Perkin sat in angry confusion at table six while the racing crowd drifted away and got the band restarted. Nolan was nowhere in sight. Sam took off his stained jacket, wiped his bloody nose and began making jokes.

'I bumped into him, that's all I did,' he proclaimed with tragicomic gestures. 'Well, say I then took Fiona off him and maybe I told him to go find himself another filly; next thing was he was bopping me on the nose.'

'Nolan's a violent man,' Tremayne stated, the shambles of his splendid evening aggravating him. 'You don't go poking a stick at a rattlesnake if you don't want to get bitten.' He looked at me. 'Are you all right?'

'Yes.'

'John was splendid!' Mackie exclaimed, and Perkin scowled.

'Let's go home,' Tremayne said abruptly. He stood, picked up the box containing his silver bowl and waited for obedience from his sons, his daughter-in-law and his prospective biographer. We stood. We followed him meekly. He made a stately exit, his displeasure plainly visible to all around, yet he, in many respects, was the stoker of the ill feeling between his warring jockeys, and putting me among them wasn't a recipe for a cease-fire.

'Perhaps I'd better not ride schooling in the morning,' I suggested, as we reached the gate to the car park. 'Nolan and Sam don't like it.'

He stared at me. 'Do you want to ride in a race or two, or don't you?'

'I do.'

'School Fringe tomorrow, then. And as for now, you'd better go back with Fiona. Make sure she gets home safe.'

'Right.'

I RODE DRIFTER with the first lot in the morning and crashed off onto the wood chippings halfway up the gallop. Tremayne showed a modicum of anxiety but no sympathy, and the anxiety was for the horse.

'Concentrate,' he said. 'You weren't keeping him straight. Get up.'

I wriggled back into the saddle. I supposed he was right about not concentrating: sleep had come slowly with anxiety dreams. I felt unsettled.

I rode Drifter back with the rest of the string and went in to breakfast. Tremayne's mood appeared to be a deepening depression over the evening's finale, and I was sorry because he deserved to look back with enjoyment.

As I made the toast, he said, 'Are you fit enough to ride Fringe?'

'If you'll let me.'

He studied me. 'Look,' he said, a touch awkwardly, 'I don't mean to take my bad temper out on you. If you hadn't been here we'd all be in a far worse pickle. Best thing I ever did, getting you to come.'

In surprise I searched for words to thank him but was forestalled by the telephone ringing. Tremayne picked up the receiver and grunted 'Hello?'

His face changed miraculously to a smile. 'Hello, Ronnie. Calling to find out how the book's going? What? Yes, he's here. Hold on.' He passed me the receiver, saying unnecessarily, 'It's Ronnie Curzon.'

'Hello, Ronnie,' I said.

'How's it going?'

'I'm riding a good deal.'

'Keep your mind on the pages. I've got news for you. My colleague in America phoned. He says he likes *Long Way Home* very much indeed. He will gladly take it on, and is certain he can place it with a good publisher.'

'Ronnie!' I swallowed. 'Are you sure?'

'Of course I'm sure. I always told you it was all right. It's all beginning.'

He disconnected and, ridiculously, I felt like crying.

'What happened?' Tremayne asked. 'What did he tell you?'

'I'm going to be published in America. Well . . . probably.'

'Congratulations.' He beamed, pleased for me, his gloom lifting. 'But you will still write my book, won't you?'

I saw his anxiety begin to surface and promptly allayed it. 'I'll write it. I'll do the very best I can and hope it does you justice. And will you excuse me if I run, jump and do handsprings? I'm bursting . . . Ronnie said it's all beginning!' I looked at him. 'Did you feel like this when Top Spin Lob won the National?'

'I was high for days. Kept smiling. Topsy Blob, I ask you!' He stood up. 'Back to business. You'll come up with me in the Land-Rover, Fringe's lad can ride him up, then change with you.'

Ronnie's news, I found, had given me a good deal more confidence in Fringe than I had had on Drifter, illogical though it might be.

It's all beginning . . .

Fringe was younger, whippier and less predictable than Drifter. I gathered the reins and lengthened the stirrup leathers a couple of holes while Fringe made prancing movements, getting used to his new and heavier rider.

'Take him down below the three flights of hurdles,' Tremayne said, 'then bring him up over them at a useful pace. You're not actually racing. Just a good half-speed gallop. Bob Watson will be with you for company. Fringe jumps well enough but he likes guidance. Don't forget, it's you that's schooling the horse, not the other way round. All ready?'

I nodded.

'Off you go, then.'

I tried telling myself that ahead lay merely a quick pop over three undemanding obstacles, not the first searching test of my chances of racing. I'd ridden over many jumps before, but never on a racehorse, never fast, never caring so much about the outcome.

Bob was circling on his own horse, waiting for me. Both his horse and Fringe, aware they would be jumping, were stimulated and keen.

'Guvnor says you're to set off on the side nearest him,' Bob said briefly. 'He wants to see what you're doing.'

I nodded, slightly dry-mouthed. Bob expertly trotted his mount into position, gave me a raised-eye query about readiness and kicked forward into an accelerating gallop. Fringe took up his position alongside with familiarity and eagerness.

First hurdle ahead. Judge the distance . . . give Fringe the message to shorten his stride . . . I gave it to him too successfully, he put in a quick one, got too near to the hurdle, hopped over it nearly at a standstill, lost lengths on Bob. Damn, I thought. *Damn.*

Second hurdle, managed it a bit better, gave him the signal three strides from the jump, felt him lift off at the right time.

Third hurdle, the distance was awkward. I couldn't make up my mind whether to get him to lengthen or shorten and in consequence we floundered over it untidily, his hoofs rapping the wooden frames, my weight too far forward . . . a mess.

We pulled up at the end of the schooling stretch and trotted back to where Tremayne stood with his binoculars. He offered no direct opinion. Instead he said, 'Second pop, Bob. Off you go,' and I gathered we were to go back to the beginning and start again.

I seemed to have more time to get things together the second time and Fringe stayed beside Bob fairly smoothly to the end. I felt exalted.

Tremayne said nothing until we were driving back to the stable and then he asked me if I was happy with what I'd done.

'I'll learn,' I said grimly, and he didn't answer.

When we reached the house, however, he brought a paper into the dining room, plonked it on the table and instructed me to sign. It was, I saw, an application for a permit to race as an amateur jockey. I signed it without speaking, incredibly delighted, grinning like a maniac.

Tremayne grunted and bore the document away, coming back presently to say I should go with him to Newbury races. Also Mackie would be coming with us and we'd be picking up Fiona.

'All right,' I said.

He departed again and, after a moment's thought, I went into the office to put through a call to Doone's police station. He was off duty, I was told. I could leave a message.

'Ask him,' I said, 'why the floorboards didn't float.'

We went to the races and watched Nolan ride Fiona's horse, Groundsel, and get beaten by a length into second place, and we watched Sam ride two of Tremayne's runners unprofitably.

'There's always another day,' Tremayne said philosophically.

Fiona told us that the police had phoned Harry to say they'd found his car in the station car park at Reading. 'They said it looks OK but they've towed it off to search for clues.'

From Reading station one could set off round the world. Metaphorical cliff, I thought. A guilty disappearance had been the intended scenario, not a presumption of suicide.

By osmosis of information, both Sam and Nolan knew details of Fringe's schooling. Sam said, 'You'll be taking my bloody job next,' without meaning it, and Nolan, bitter-eyed and cursing, saw Tremayne's warning glare and subsided with festering rancour. I was truly disconcerted to have acquired so violent an enemy without meaning to and could see no resolution short of full retreat; and the trouble was that since that morning's schooling, any inclination to retreat had totally vanished.

I looked back constantly to the morning with huge inward joy; to Ronnie's phone call, to the revelation over hurdles. Doors opening all over the place. All beginning.

THE NEXT DAY, SUNDAY, Gareth held me to my promise to take him and Coconut out on another survival trip.

The weather was much better; sunny but cold still, with a trace of a breeze, a good day for walking. I suggested seven miles out, seven miles back; Gareth with horror suggested two. We compromised by borrowing the

Land-Rover followed by walking as far as their enthusiasm took them.

'Where are you going?' Tremayne asked.

'Over the hills towards Reading,' I said. 'There's some great woodland there, unfenced, no signs saying keep out.'

Tremayne nodded. 'It's all part of the Quillersedge Estate.'

'We'd better not light a fire there,' I said, 'so we'll take our food and water with us. But it will be survival food. Things you could pick or catch.'

'OK,' Gareth said. 'How about chocolate instead of dandelion leaves?'

I agreed to the chocolate. The day had to be bearable. We set off at ten, collected Coconut and bowled along to the woods.

There were parking places all along the road, small inlets of beaten earth formed by the waiting cars of many walkers. I pulled into one of them, put on the handbrake and, when the boys were out, locked the doors.

Gareth wore his psychedelic jacket. Coconut's yellow oilskins had been superseded by an equally blinding anorak and I looked camouflaged against the trees in stone-washed jeans and a roomy olive-drab Barbour.

They slid the straps of bright blue nylon knapsacks over their shoulders, and we stepped straight into the tangled maze of alder, hazel, birch, oak, pine, fir and laurel. It was scrub woodland as nature had made it, the real thing as far as the boys were concerned.

We went about a mile before they tired of the effort involved, and according to the map I had in my pocket, we were by then in about the centre of the western spur of the Quillersedge woods. Gareth stopped in a small clearing and mentioned food hopefully.

'Sure,' I said. 'We can make some seats with dead twigs to keep our bottoms off the damp ground, if you like. No need today for a shelter.'

They made flat piles of twigs, finished them off with evergreen, then emptied their rucksacks and spread the blue nylon on top. We sat comfortably and ate the things I'd bought for the occasion.

'Smoked trout!' Gareth exclaimed. 'That's an advance on roots.'

'You could catch trout and smoke them if you had to,' I said.

'How do you smoke them?'

'Make a fire with lots of hot embers. Cover the embers thickly with green fresh leaves: they'll burn slowly with billows of smoke. Make a latticed frame to go over the fire and put the trout on it or hang them over the smoke.'

Gareth had brought a camera and he took photos of everything possible: the seats, the food, ourselves. We ate the trout with unleavened bread and healthy appetites, and afterwards filled up with pre-roasted chestnuts and almonds. The boys declared it a feast compared with the week before and polished off their chocolate as a bonus.

Gareth said casually, 'Was it in a place like this that someone killed Angela Brickell?'

'Well . . . I should think so. But five miles or so from here.'

'She wanted to kiss me,' he said with a squirm.

Both Coconut and I looked at him in astonishment.

'I'm not as ugly as all that,' he said, offended.

'You're not ugly,' I assured him, 'but you're young.'

'She said I was growing up.' He looked embarrassed, as did Coconut. 'She was always out there in the yard. Always looking at me. I told Dad about it, but he didn't listen. It was Grand National time and he couldn't think of anything but Top Spin Lob.' He looked at me anxiously. 'I suppose it's wrong to be relieved someone's dead.'

'Is relieved what you feel?'

'I was afraid of her,' he said finally. He looked ashamed.

'It won't be the last time someone makes a pass at you,' I said prosaically. 'Next time, don't feel guilty.'

Easier said than done, I supposed. Shame and guilt tormented the innocent more than the wicked.

As I packed away our food wrappings I asked, 'Which way to the Land-Rover?'

'That way,' said Gareth immediately, pointing east.

'That way,' Coconut said, pointing west.

'Which way is north?' I asked.

They both got it instinctively wrong, but then worked it out roughly by the sun, and I showed them how to use a watch as a compass. 'Point the hour hand at the sun, then halfway between the hand and twelve o'clock is the north–south line.'

Coconut looked at his watch and around him. 'That way is north,' he said, pointing. 'But which way is the Land-Rover?'

'If you go north you'll come to the road,' I said.

'What do you mean "you"?' Gareth demanded.

'I thought that it would be more fun for you to find your own way back. And,' I went on as he tried to interrupt, 'so as you don't get lost if the sun goes in, you can paint the trees as you go with luminous paint. Then you can always come back to me.'

'Cool,' he said, entranced. He told Coconut about finding one's way back to places by blazing the trail.

'I'll follow you,' I said, 'but you won't see me. If you go really badly wrong, I'll tell you. Otherwise, survival's up to you.'

I unzipped the pouch round my waist and gave Gareth the small jar of paint and the sawn-off paintbrush.

'Paint so you can see the splash from both directions, coming and going, and don't get out of sight of your last splash.'

'OK.'

'Let's go back the way we came,' Coconut said to Gareth.

'Easy!' Gareth agreed.

I watched them decide on the wrong place and paint the first mark carefully round a sapling's trunk. Tracking backwards was incredibly difficult. All the identifiable marks of our passage, like broken twigs and flattened grass, pointed forward into the wood, not out of it.

They consulted their watches and moved north through the trees, looking back and painting as they went. They waved once and I waved back, and for some time I could see their bright jackets in the afternoon sun. Then, when they had gone, I began slowly to follow their splashes.

I could go much faster than they could. When I saw them again I dropped down on one knee, knowing that they wouldn't see me at that low level, in my nature-coloured clothes.

Besides the map, I'd brought along my faithful compass, and by its reckoning checked the boys' direction all the time. They wandered off to the northeast a bit but not badly enough to get really lost, and after a while made a correction to drift back to north. The pale cream splashes were easy to spot, never far apart. I kept the boys in sight intermittently all the way.

As I slowly followed the trail, I felt at home and at peace. There were birds singing, and the quiet was as old and deep as the land.

It was a slow-going mile, but towards the end one could hear cars along the road ahead and Gareth and Coconut, with whoops, crashed through the last few yards, as the week before, relieved to be back in the space age. I speeded up and stepped out behind them, much to Gareth's surprise.

'We thought you were miles back,' he exclaimed.

'You laid an excellent trail.'

'The paint's nearly finished.' He held it up to show me and the jar slipped out of his hand, rolling the remains of its contents onto the earth. 'Hey, sorry,' he said. 'But there wasn't much left.'

'Doesn't matter.' I picked up the jar, and, screwing its lid on, dropped it with the brush into a plastic bag before stowing it again in my pouch.

We found the Land-Rover round the next bend, and rode back in euphoric good spirits.

'Terrific,' Gareth told Tremayne, bursting into the family room after we'd dropped Coconut off and returned to Shellerton.

Tremayne, Mackie and Perkin received a minute-by-minute account of the whole day. Tremayne listened with veiled approval, Mackie with active interest, Perkin with boredom.

'It's real wilderness,' Gareth said. 'You can't hear *anything*. And I took lashings of photos—' He stopped, suddenly frowning. 'Hold on a minute.'

He sped out of the room and came back with his blue knapsack, searching the contents worriedly. 'My camera's not here!'

'Perhaps Coconut's got it,' Perkin suggested languidly.

'Thanks.' Gareth leaped to the telephone in hopes that were all too soon dashed. 'He says he didn't see it after lunchtime.' He looked horrified. 'We'll have to go back at once. I must have left it where we had lunch. I hung it on a branch to keep it from getting damp. I just forgot it.'

'No,' Tremayne said positively. 'It'll be getting dark soon.'

'But it's *luminous* paint,' Gareth begged. 'That's the whole point, you can see it in the dark.' He turned to me. 'Can't we go back?'

I shook my head. 'Your father's right. We could get lost in those woods at night, paint or no paint.'

'*You* wouldn't get lost.'

'I might,' I said. 'I'll get it tomorrow afternoon.'

'Will you? Oh, *great*.' He thought of something. 'Isn't it lucky I dropped all the paint, because now you can see where the trail starts.'

'All right then,' Tremayne said. 'Let's talk about something else.'

'Grub?' Gareth asked hopefully. 'Pizza?'

Chapter 16

On Monday morning, first lot, I was back on Drifter.

'He's entered in a race at Worcester the day after tomorrow,' Tremayne said as we walked out to the yard in the half-dawn. 'Today's his last training gallop before that, so don't fall off again. The vet's been here already this morning to test his blood.'

Tremayne's vet took small blood samples of all the stable's runners prior to their last training gallop before they raced, the resulting detailed analysis being able to reveal a whole host of things from a raised lymphocyte count to excreted enzymes due to muscle damage.

'You can gallop Fringe this morning, second lot.'

'Thanks.'

'And thanks to you for giving Gareth such a good day yesterday.'

We reached the yard and stood watching the last preparations.

'That's a good camera,' Tremayne said regretfully.

'I'll get it back.'

He smiled, shaking his head. 'You're the most competent person . . . Fiona says you put calamities right. Give Drifter a good gallop.'

We went up to the Downs and at least I stayed in the saddle, and felt indeed a new sense of being at home there, of being at ease. Drifter flowed up the gallop in a smooth, fast rhythm.

When I'd left the horse in the yard and gone in for breakfast I found both Mackie and Sam Yaeger sitting at the table with Tremayne, all of them discussing that day's racing at Nottingham. The horse that Tremayne had been going to run had gone lame; Sam's other ride had been withdrawn.

'I hear you played cowboys and Indians all over Berkshire with Gareth and Coconut yesterday.' Sam grinned at me.

'News travels,' I said resignedly.

'I told him,' Mackie said, smiling. 'Any objections?'

I shook my head and asked her how she was feeling. She'd stopped riding out with the first lot because of nausea on waking.

'I feel sick,' she said to my enquiry. 'Thank goodness.'

Sam said to me, 'Doone spent all Saturday afternoon at the boatyard. He got a message from you, it seems.'

'What message?' Tremayne asked.

'I asked him why the floorboards didn't float.' I told them what I'd told Erica at Tremayne's dinner, and said it might not lead to anything helpful.

'But it certainly might,' Mackie said.

Sam said to me thoughtfully, 'If you hadn't stopped me, I'd have rolled up the curtain so as to go into the dock in a boat, and all that stuff under the water would have slithered away.'

'Fiona's sure John will find out, before Doone does, who set that trap for Harry,' Mackie said.

I shook my head. 'I don't know who it was. Wish I did.'

'Matter of time,' Tremayne said confidently. 'Talking of time: second lot.' He stood up. 'Sam, I want a trial of that new horse Roydale against Fringe. You ride Roydale, John's on Fringe.'

'OK,' Sam said easily.

'John.' Tremayne turned to me. 'Don't try to beat Sam as if it were a race. This is a fact-finder. Go as fast as you can but if you feel Fringe falter, don't press him, just ease back.'

'Right.'

'Mackie, talk to Dee-Dee or something. I'm not taking you up there to vomit in the Land-Rover.'

'Oh, Tremayne, as if I would,' she protested, but she might as well have argued with a rock. He determinedly left her behind and drove Sam and me up to the gallops.

On the way, Sam said to me drily, 'Nolan usually rides any trials. He'll be furious.'

Tremayne said repressively, 'I've told Nolan he won't be riding work here again until he cools off.'

Sam raised his eyebrows comically. 'Do you want John shot? Nolan's a whiz with a gun.'

'Don't talk nonsense,' Tremayne said, a shade uneasily. He drew the Land-Rover to a halt on the smooth upland grass. 'Keep your mind on Roydale. He belongs to a new owner. I want your best judgment.'

Sam nodded. We took Roydale and Fringe from the lads and when Tremayne had driven off and positioned himself on his hillock we started together up the all-weather gallop, going the fastest I'd ever been. Fringe, flat out at racing pace, had a wildness about him I couldn't really control and I guessed it was that quality which won him races. Whenever Roydale put his nose in front, Fringe found a bit extra. It seemed there wasn't much between them, and with the end of the wood chippings in sight the contest was still undecided. I finished literally breathless but Sam pulled up nonchalantly and trotted back to Tremayne for a report in full voice.

'He's green,' he announced. 'He has a mouth like elephant skin. He shies at his own shadow and he's stubborn. Apart from that, he's fast.'

Tremayne listened impassively. 'Courage?'

'Can't tell till he's on a racecourse.'

'I'll enter him for Saturday. We may as well find out.'

We handed the horses back to their lads, went down the hill again with Tremayne and found Doone waiting for us.

'Which of us do you want?' Tremayne enquired bullishly.

'Well, sir. All of you, if you don't mind.'

'You'd better come in, then,' Tremayne offered, shrugging.

Doone followed us into the kitchen, removed a grey tweed overcoat and sat by the table in his much-lived-in grey suit. Tremayne suggested coffee, and I made a mug of instant for each of us.

Mackie came through saying she wanted to know how the trial had gone. She wasn't surprised to see Doone. I made her coffee and she sat while Doone picked a piece of paper out of his pocket and handed it to Sam.

'A receipt, sir,' he said, 'for three lengths of floorboard retrieved from the dock in your boathouse.'

'Why didn't they float?' Tremayne asked bluntly.

'They didn't float, sir, because they were weighted with pieces of paving stone. There are similar pieces of paving stone scattered on a portion of your boatyard property.'

'*Paving* stone?' Sam sounded bemused, then said doubtfully, 'Do you mean broken slabs of pink and grey marble?'

'Is that what it is, sir, marble?'

'It might be.'

Doone pondered, made up his mind, went out to his car and returned carrying a five-foot plank which he laid across the kitchen table. The old grey wood was still dampish. Towards one end, on the surface that was now uppermost on the table, rested a long, unevenly shaped, darkish slab.

'Yes,' Sam said, glancing at it. 'That's marble.'

'It's stuck on,' Doone said. 'Superglue, we think.' He asked Sam conversationally, 'Did you stick the marble onto the floorboards, sir?'

'No, I bloody well did *not*,' Sam said explosively.

The plank on the table was about eight inches across. Harry had taken three of them down with him; according to Doone, five had been doctored.

'Have you finished snooping around my place now?' Sam demanded. 'I want to work on my boat.'

'Go ahead, sir. Never mind my men, if they're there.'

'Right.' Sam stood up with bouncing energy. 'Bye, Tremayne. Bye, Mackie. See you, John.'

He went out to his car, carrying his jazzy jacket, and tooted as he drove away. The kitchen seemed a lot less alive without him.

'I'd like to talk to Mr Kendall alone,' Doone said placidly.

Tremayne made no objection. He suggested I take Doone into the dining room while he told Mackie about Roydale's gallop, and Doone followed me docilely, bringing the plank.

It appeared to me that Doone was troubled rather by indecision as to which side I was now on, them or us. He seemed to settle finally for us, us being the police, or at least the fact-seekers, and, clearing his throat, he asked forthrightly, 'Do you know who did it?'

'No,' I said truthfully.

'You must have opinions. I'd like to hear them.'

'I'd assume the trap-setter had been a guest at Sam Yaeger's boatyard party,' I said, 'only you warned me never to assume.'

'Assume it,' he said, almost smiling.

'And,' I went on, 'I'd assume it was the person who killed Angela Brickell, who wanted to fix the blame on Harry, only . . .'

'Assume it,' he said.

'Anyone could have killed Angela Brickell, but only a hundred and fifty or so people went to Sam's party, and half of those were women. What woman could have lured Angela Brickell and persuaded her to take all her clothes off in the middle of a wood?'

He sucked his teeth. 'All right,' he said, 'I agree, a man killed her.' He paused. 'Motive?'

'I'd guess . . . to keep a secret. I mean, suppose she went out into the woods with . . . *him*, and they were going to make love, and she said, "I'm pregnant, you're the father, what are you going to do about it?" She was full of jumbled religious guilts, but it was she who was the seducer . . .' I paused. 'I'd think perhaps she was killed because she wanted too much, and because she wouldn't have an abortion.'

'All right,' he said again. 'Method: strangulation. Guaranteed to work, as everyone around here knew, after the death of that other girl, Olympia. Opportunity?'

'No one can remember what they were doing the day Angela Brickell disappeared.'

'Except the murderer,' he observed. 'What about opportunity on the day Mr Goodhaven fell through the floor?'

'Someone was there to drive his car away . . . no fingerprints, I suppose?'

'Gloves,' he said succinctly.

Perkin in his overalls appeared in the open doorway, hovering.

'Is Mackie over here?' he said. 'I can't find her.'

'In the kitchen with Tremayne,' I said.

'Thanks.' He swept a gaze over Doone and the plank and said with irony, 'Sorting it out, then?'

Doone said, a shade heavily, 'Mr Kendall's always helpful,' and Perkin made a face and went off to join Mackie.

'About Harry's car,' I said to Doone. 'There must have been just a small problem of logistics. I mean, perhaps our man parked his own car in Reading station car park, getting from there to the boatyard . . .'

'We don't know when the car arrived at Reading. It could have been parked somewhere else on Wednesday and repositioned when our man discovered Mr Goodhaven was still alive.'

'That means our man had a lot of time available for manoeuvring.'

'Racing people do have flexible hours,' he observed.

'I don't suppose my jacket and boots were still in the car?'

'No sign of them. Sorry.' He was looking round the room again. 'About those guidebooks of yours. I'd like to see them.'

I went to fetch them from the family room and returned with only three I'd found, *Jungle, Safari* and *Ice*. He opened *Jungle* and quickly flipped through the opening chapters, which had straightforward advice for well-equipped jungle holidays: 'Never put a bare foot on the earth. Shower in slippers. Sleep with your shoes inside your mosquito netting.'

' "Never get exhausted"!' Doone read aloud. 'What sort of advice is that?'

'Exhausted people can't be bothered to stick to lifesaving routines. If you don't drive yourself too hard you're more likely to survive.'

' "Food," ' Doone read out. ' "Fishing, hunting, trapping." ' He flicked the pages. ' "Don't forget bait. You always need bait." ' He looked up. 'That envelope was bait, wasn't it?'

I nodded. 'Good bait.'

'We haven't found it. That water's like liquid mud.'

He went back to the book. ' "It's possible to bring down game with a spear or a bow and arrow, but these take considerable practice and involve hours spent lying in wait. Let a trap do the waiting . . ." ' He read on. ' "The classic trap for large animals is a pit with sharpened staves pointing upwards. Cover the pit with vegetation and earth, and suspend the bait over the top." ' He looked up. 'Very graphic illustrations.'

'Afraid so.'

He silently read several pages, occasionally shaking his head, not, I gathered, in disagreement with the text, but in sorrow at its availability. He put down *Jungle* and flipped through *Safari* and *Ice*. Many of the same suggestions for traps appeared in all the books, modified only by terrain.

'Well, sir,' he said, laying the books aside, 'we can trace the path of ideas about the trap, but who do you think put them into practice?'

I shook my head.

'If I throw names at you, give your reasons for or against.'

'All right,' I said cautiously.

'Mr Vickers.'

'Tremayne?' I must have sounded astonished. 'All against.'

'Why, exactly?'

'Well, he's not like that.'

'As I told you before, I don't know these people the way you do. So give me reasons.'

I said, thinking, 'Tremayne Vickers is forceful, a bit old-fashioned, straightforward, often kind. Angela Brickell would not have been to his taste. If, and to my mind it's a colossal if, *if* she managed to seduce him and then told him he was the father-to-be, it would have been more his style to pack her off home to her parents and provide for her. As for trying to kill Harry . . .' Words failed me.

'All right,' Doone said. He brought out a notebook and methodically wrote *Kendall's Assessments* at the top of the page. Underneath he wrote *Tremayne Vickers*, followed by a cross.

'Nolan Everard,' he said.

Not so easy. 'Nolan is dynamic, determined . . . and violent.'

'And he threatened to kill you,' Doone said flatly.

'Who told you that?'

'Half the racing world heard him. And when he attacked you, you picked him up like a baby in front of all those people. A man might not forgive that.'

'We're talking about Angela Brickell and Harry,' I pointed out.

'Talk about Nolan Everard then. *For*, first.'

'*For* . . . Well, he killed Olympia, not really meaning to, but definitely by putting her life at risk. He couldn't afford another scandal while waiting for trial. If Angela Brickell had threatened a messy paternity suit . . . Nolan and Sam Yaeger often bed the same girl, more or less to spite each other, it seems. Nolan regularly rides the horse Chickweed, that Angela Brickell had care of, and there would have been opportunities. As for the trap for Harry, Nolan would be mentally and physically capable. *Against*. He's Fiona's cousin, and they're close. He depends on Fiona's horses to clinch his amateur-champion status. He couldn't be sure she would have the heart to go on running racehorses if she were forced to believe Harry a murderer . . . and if she was also haunted by the thought of Harry with Angela Brickell.'

'Would Everard have stopped to consider all that?'

'The trap was well thought out.'

Doone wrote Nolan's name and a question mark. He wrote *Bob Watson* under Nolan.

'*For* him being our man,' I said dubiously, 'is, I suppose, his wife Ingrid. She wouldn't put up with shenanigans with Angela Brickell. Also he's an extremely competent carpenter, as you saw yourself. He was serving drinks at the party when Olympia died and went to the boatyard party as a guest.'

'Against?'

I hesitated. 'Killing Angela Brickell might have been a moment's panic. Setting the trap for Harry took cunning and nerve. I don't know Bob Watson well enough for a real opinion.'

Doone nodded and put a question mark after his name also.

Gareth Vickers, he wrote.

I smiled. 'It can't be him. Angela Brickell's sexuality frightened him. He would never have gone into the woods with her. Apart from that, he hasn't a driving licence, and he was at school on Wednesday afternoon.'

'Actually,' Doone said calmly, 'he is known to be able to drive his father's Jeep on the Downs expertly, and he was out of school last Wednesday afternoon on a field trip to Windsor Safari Park. That's not miles from the boatyard. The teacher in charge is flustered over the number of boys who sneaked off to buy food.'

I considered Gareth as a murderer. 'You asked me for my knowledge of these people. Gareth couldn't possibly be our man.'

He wrote a cross against Gareth's name, and then, as an afterthought, a question mark also. Under Gareth's name he wrote *Perkin Vickers*.

'Perkin . . .' I sighed. 'He lives in another world, half the time. He works hard. *For*, I suppose, is that he makes furniture, he's good with wood. I don't know that it's *for* or *against* that he dotes on his wife. He's very possessive of her. He's a bit childlike in some ways. She loves him and looks after him. *Against* . . . he doesn't have much to do with the horses. He didn't remember who Angela Brickell was, the first morning you were here.'

Doone pursed his lips judiciously, then nodded and wrote a cross against Perkin, and then, again, a question mark.

'It might be reasonable to assume that Mr Goodhaven didn't set the trap himself, to persuade me of his innocence,' he said, writing *Harry Goodhaven* on the list.

'A hundred per cent,' I agreed.

'However, he took you along as a witness.' He paused. 'Suppose he planned it and it all went wrong?'

'Who drove his car away?' I said, a shade aggressively.

'A casual thief.'

'I don't believe it.'

'You like him,' Doone said. 'You're unreliable.'

He put a question mark against Harry.

I said reflectively, 'Have you worked out when the trap was set? Raising the floorboards, finding the marble and sticking it on, cutting out the bit of beam . . . It would all have taken a fair time.'

'When would *you* say it was done, then?' he asked.

'Any time Tuesday, or Wednesday morning, I suppose. You'd begun to spread your investigation outwards . . . which must have horribly alarmed our man. Sam Yaeger spent Monday at the boatyard because of a fall, but by Tuesday he was racing again, so the boathouse was vulnerable all day Tuesday and again Wednesday morning.'

Doone looked at me from under his eyelids. 'You're forgetting something,' he said, and added *Sam Yaeger* to his list.

Chapter 17

'Put a cross,' I said.

Doone shook his head. 'You admire him. You could be blinded.'

I thought it over. 'I do in many ways admire him, I admit. I admire his riding, his professionalism. He's courageous. He's a realist.' I paused. 'I'll agree that on the *For* side he has all the skills to set the trap and the perfect place to do it. And you'd begun actively investigating him.'

Doone nodded. 'Yes, I had.'

'He'd rolled around a bit with Angela Brickell,' I said, 'and that's where we come to the biggest *against*. He wouldn't have taken her out into the woods. He told you himself he moves a mattress into the boathouse on such occasions. And I wouldn't think he'd need to cover his sins with strangulation. Everyone knows he seduces anything that moves. He would pass off an Angela Brickell sort of scandal with a laugh.'

At the bottom of his list Doone wrote *Lewis Everard.*

'That's a long shot,' I said.

'Give me some *fors* and *againsts.'*

I pondered. *'Against* first. I don't think he's bold enough to have set that trap, but then'—I hesitated—'there's no doubt he's both clever and cunning. I wouldn't have thought he would have gone into the woods with Angela Brickell. I'd think he'd be too fastidious, especially when he's sober.'

'For?' Doone prompted, when I stopped.

'He gets drunk . . . I don't know if he'd tumble Angela Brickell in that state or not. He would have seen her at the races. And he is a good liar. According to him, he's the best actor of the lot.'

'A question mark, then?' Doone's pen hovered.

I slowly shook my head. 'A cross.'

'The trouble with you,' Doone said with disillusion, looking at the column of negatives, 'is that you haven't met enough murderers.' He put away the notebook and stood up. 'Well, Mr Kendall, thank you for your time. I don't discount your impressions. You've helped clarify my thoughts.'

He shook my hand and let himself out, a grey man in grey clothes following his own idiosyncratic path towards the truth.

I worked on and off on Tremayne's book for the rest of the morning but found it hard to concentrate. Tremayne put his head in to say he was going to Oxford to see his tailor. Mackie came through saying Perkin had gone to Newbury to collect some supplies, and presently she and Dee-Dee went off to lunch together, leaving me alone in the great sprawling house.

I felt restless and uneasy. I went upstairs, showered and changed out of riding clothes into the more comfortable jeans and shirt I'd worn the day before, then pulled on trainers and my red sweater for warmth. After that I wandered in a desultory fashion into the family room. Gareth's BACK FOR GRUB message was still pinned to the corkboard, and it was with a sense of release that I remembered I'd said that I would go back for his camera.

The unease vanished. I left my own message: I'VE BORROWED THE LAND ROVER TO FETCH GARETH'S CAMERA. BACK FOR COOKING THE GRUB! With a light heart I went upstairs again to change back into jodhpur boots to deal with the terrain and to pick up the map and the compass in case I couldn't find the trail. Then I skipped downstairs and went out to the wheels, locking the back door behind me.

It was sunny like the day before but with more wind. I drove over the hills on the road to Reading and coasted along the Quillersedge Estate until I thought I'd come more or less to where Gareth had dropped the paint.

The splash was dusty but still visible. Without much trouble, I found the beginning of the trail about twenty feet straight ahead in the wood and followed it easily through the tangled trees and undergrowth.

Gareth a murderer . . . I smiled to myself at the absurdity of it.

Wind rattled and swayed the trees and filled my ears with the old songs of the land. I wound my slow way through the maze of unpruned growth. The trail eventually reached the small clearing. Almost at once I spotted Gareth's camera, hanging, as he'd said, from a branch. I walked across to collect it and something hit me very hard indeed in the back.

Moments of disaster are disorientating. I didn't know what had happened. The world had changed. I was falling. I was lying face down on the ground. There was something wrong with my breathing. I had heard nothing, but I thought incredulously, *someone had shot me*.

From total instinct as much as from injury I lay as dead. There was a zipping noise beside my ear as something sped past it. I shut my eyes. There was another jolting thud in my back.

So this was death, I thought numbly; and I didn't know who was killing me, and I didn't know why.

Breathing was terrible. My chest was on fire. A wave of clammy perspiration broke out on my skin. My face was on dead leaves and I could smell the musty earth. Someone, I thought dimly, was waiting to see if I moved, and if I moved there would be a third thud and my heart would stop. If I didn't move someone would come and feel for a pulse and, finding one, finish me off. Either way, everything that had been beginning was now ending, ebbing away without hope.

I lay still. Not a twitch.

I couldn't hear anything but the wind in the trees. Could hear no one moving. Breathing was a shaft of pain. In a while I would go to sleep.

A long time seemed to pass, and I was still alive. I felt cold.

Nothing happened in the clearing. After countless ages I came to a real realisation that I was continuing to breathe, even if with difficulty, and didn't seem in immediate danger of stopping.

My certainty of the waiting gun began to fade. He wouldn't be there after all this time. He believed I was dead.

He had gone. I was alone. If I didn't move I would die where I lay.

With dread I moved my left arm. It *hurt*. I moved my right arm. Even worse. No more thuds in the back, though. No final curtain.

I put both palms flat on the decaying undergrowth and tried to heave myself up onto my knees.

Practically fainted. The effort was too excruciating. My weight settled back on the earth and I felt nothing but staggering agony. Something was odd, I thought finally. It wasn't only that I couldn't lift myself off the ground but that I was stuck to it in some way. Cautiously, sweating, with fiery stabs in every inch, I wormed my right hand between my body and the earth, and came to what seemed like a rod between the two.

I must have fallen onto a sharp stick, I thought. Slowly I slid my hand out again, and then after a while, hardly believing it, I bent my arm and felt round my back and came to the rod there also, and faced the grim certainty that someone had shot me not with a bullet but an *arrow*.

I LAY FOR A WHILE simply wrestling with the enormity of it.

I had an arrow right through my body, somewhere in the region of my lower ribs. Through my right lung, which was why I was breathing oddly. Not, miraculously, through any major blood vessels or I would by now have bled to death internally. About level with my heart, but to one side.

Bad enough. Awful. But I was still alive.

Survival begins in the mind.

I'd written that, and knew it to be true. But to survive an arrow a mile from a road with a killer around to make sure I didn't make it . . . where in one's mind did one search for the will to survive that?

I thought about rescue. No one would start looking for me for hours; not until after dark. Theoretically the luminous trail should lead rescuers to the clearing even at night . . . but any sensible murderer would have obliterated the road end of it after he'd found his own way out.

I couldn't realistically be rescued before tomorrow. I thought I might die while I waited: might die in the night.

Better die trying.

All right. Next decision. Which way to go.

The trail seemed obvious enough, but my intended killer had come and gone that way—must have done—and if he should return for any reason I wouldn't want to meet him.

I had a compass in my pocket. The distant road lay almost due north and the straightest line to the road lay to the left of the paint trail.

Next decision: get up.

The tip of the arrow couldn't be far into the earth, I thought. I'd fallen with it already through me. I shut my mind to the consequences, positioned my hands, and pushed.

The arrow tip came free and I lay on my side in frightful suffering weakness, looking down at a sharp black point sticking out from scarlet wool. The length of a finger. Hard and sharp.

Only one arrow. Only one all the way through, at least.

A mile to the road seemed an impossible distance. Moving an inch was taxing. Still, inches added up. I retrieved the compass carefully from my pocket and took a bearing on north.

I rolled with effort to my knees and felt desperately, appallingly, overwhelmingly ill. I stayed on my knees, sitting back on my heels, head bowed, breathing as little as possible, staring at the protruding arrow.

There was a pale slim rod sticking into the ground beside me. I remembered the thing that had sung past my ear.

An arrow that had missed me.

It was about as long as an arm. A peeled fine-grained stick, dead straight. A notch in its visible end, for slotting onto a bowstring. No feather to make a flight. Even without flights, the aim had been deadly enough.

The guidebooks all gave instructions for making arrows. 'Char the tips in hot embers to shrink and toughen the fibre for better penetration . . .' Illustrations thoughtfully provided.

Gingerly, sweating, I curled my left hand behind my back and felt for the third arrow, and found it sticking out of my sweater though fairly loose in my hand. With trepidation I took a stronger hold of it and it came away altogether but with a sharp dagger of soreness, like digging out a splinter. I reckoned it hadn't gone in further than a rib or my spine. I only had the first one to worry about.

Only the one. Quite enough.

It would have been madness to pull it out, even if I could have faced doing it. A puncture let air rush in and out, spoiling nature's enclosed vacuum system. With holes to the outer air, the lungs collapsed and couldn't breathe. With the arrow still in place, the holes were virtually blocked, and bleeding was held at bay. I might die with it in. I'd die quicker with it out.

The first rule of surviving a disaster, I had written, was to accept that it had happened and make the best of what was left. All right, I told myself, accept that it hurts, that every movement will hurt for the foreseeable future. Take that for granted. Go on from there.

Still on my knees, I edged round to face north. The clearing was all mine: no man with a gun. No archer with a bow. I slowly shifted on my knees across the clearing, aiming to the left of the painted trail.

It wasn't so bad . . . It was awful.

Ignore it. Get used to it. Think about north.

Hauling on branches, I stood up. I clung hard to a sapling with my eyes closed, waiting for things to get better.

North.

I took the compass out of my jeans pocket, where I'd stowed it to have hands free for standing up. I took a visual line ahead from the north needle to mark into memory the furthest small tree I could see, then put the compass away again and with infinite slowness clawed a way forward by inches and after a while reached the target and held on to it for dear life.

I had travelled perhaps ten yards. I felt exhausted.

'Never get exhausted,' I had written. Dear God.

In a while I consulted the compass, memorised another young tree and made my way there. I wiped sweat off my forehead with my fingers and stood quietly, holding on, trying to let the oxygen level in my blood climb back to a functioning state.

A functioning mode, Gareth might have said. Gareth . . .

Sherwood Forest, I thought, eight hundred years ago. Whose face should I pin on the Sheriff of Nottingham . . . ?

I went another ten yards, and another, careful always not to trip, holding on to branches as if on to railings. My breath began wheezing from the exertion. Pain had finally become a constant.

Stopping again for things to calm down, I began to do a few unwelcome sums. I had travelled perhaps fifty yards. It had taken me fifteen minutes. At a speed of fifty yards in fifteen minutes it would take me another eight hours to reach the road. It would then be half past midnight, and that didn't take into account long rests or crawling.

Despair was easy. Survival wasn't.

To hell with despair, I thought. Get on and walk.

North. Ten yards visible at a time. Go ten yards. Five times ten yards. Short rest. The sun sank lower and the blue shadows of dusk began creeping in among the sapling branches and the alders. In the wind the shadows threw barred stripes and moved like prowling tigers.

Fifty yards, rest. Fifty yards, rest. Fifty yards, rest.

Dusk deepened until I could no longer see ten yards ahead, and I stopped and sank slowly to my knees, resting my forehead against a young birch trunk, drained as I'd never been before.

Perhaps I would write a book about this one day, I thought.

Perhaps I would call it . . . *Longshot*.

A long shot with an arrow.

Perhaps not so long, though. No doubt from only a few yards out of the clearing, to get a straight view. A short shot, perhaps.

He'd been waiting there for me, I concluded. I'd walked up to the carefully prominent bait and presented him with a perfect target, a broad back in a scarlet sweater, an absolute cinch.

Traps. I'd walked into one, as Harry had.

Who was the Sheriff of Nottingham? . . .

I tried to find a more comfortable position but there wasn't one, really. To save my knees a bit I slid down onto my left hip, leaning my head and my left side against the tree. It was better than walking.

The darkness intensified down in the wood, though I could see stars between the boughs. I listened to the wind. Grew cold. Felt extremely alone.

I hovered on the edge of consciousness, semi-asleep. I sat for what seemed a long time in the cold darkness. Eventually there was a lightening of the shadows and a luminosity in the wood, and the moon rose clear and bright in the east. To eyes long in the dark, it was like daylight.

Time to go. I pulled out the compass. Everything was sore, every muscle seemed wired directly to the arrow.

Ignore what it feels like, concentrate on the Sheriff . . .

I pulled myself to my feet again, rocked a bit, sweated, clung on to things. Put one foot in front of the other, the only way home.

I couldn't always see so far ahead by moonlight and needed to consult the compass more often. I plodded on methodically, breathing carefully, aiming performance just below capability so as to last out to the end.

Slowly, slowly, I went north. Then one time when I put my hand in my pocket to bring out the compass, it wasn't there. I'd dropped it.

I couldn't go on without it. Had to go back. Doubted if I could find it in the undergrowth. I felt swamped with despair.

Get a bloody grip on things, I told myself. Work it out.

I was facing north. If I turned precisely 180 degrees I would be facing where I'd come from. Elementary. *Think*.

I stood and thought and made the panic recede until I could work out what to do, then I took my knife out of its sheath on my belt and carved an arrow in the bark of the tree I was facing. An arrow pointing skywards. I had arrows on the brain as well as through the lungs, I thought. The tree arrow pointed north. The compass had to be somewhere in sight of that arrow. I would have to crawl to have any hope of finding it.

I went down on my knees and carefully turned to face the other way, south. I crawled a foot or two, casting about, trying to part the undergrowth, hoping desperate hopes. I looked back to the arrow on the tree, then crawled another foot. Nothing. The compass had to be *somewhere*.

The cold of the night was deepening and I was weaker than I'd been when I set out. When I turned to check on the arrow on the tree, I couldn't see it. I no longer knew which was north.

I stopped and slumped dazedly back on my heels, facing utter defeat. I was wounded to death and dying on my knees, scrabbling in dead grass, my time running out with the moonlight, the shadows closing in. I had no will left. One couldn't survive unless one believed one could, and belief had leaked out of me.

Chapter 18

Time . . . unmeasured time . . . slid away.

I moved in the end from discomfort, from stiffness, made a couple of circling shuffles on my knees. I looked up and saw again the arrow cut into the tree. It wasn't far away, almost out of sight behind a group of saplings.

Apathetically, I thought it of little use. The arrow pointed in the right direction, but ten feet past it, which way was north?

The arrow on the tree pointed upwards.

I looked slowly in that direction, as if instructed. Looked upwards to the sky, and there was the constellation of the Great Bear . . . and the Pole Star.

No doubt from then on my route wasn't as straight or as accurate as earlier, but at least I was moving, inching a slow way forwards. I didn't know at what rate I was now travelling and no longer bothered to work it out. All that I was really clear about was that this time I would go on as long as my lungs and muscles would function. Survival or nothing.

The archer had to have a face . . .

In splinters of thought, unconnectedly, I began to look back over the past three weeks. I thought of Angela Brickell's death and of the attacks on

Harry and me, and it seemed that all three had had one purpose, which was to keep things as they were.

One foot in front of the other . . .

Angela Brickell had probably been killed to close her mouth. Harry was to have died to cement his guilt. I wasn't to be allowed to do what Fiona and Tremayne had both foretold, that I would find the truth for Doone.

They all expected too much of me.

The archer had to be someone who knew I was going to go back for Gareth's camera. It had to be someone who knew how to find the trail, who could follow instructions to make an effective bow and sharp arrows, who wanted me gone. Who had a universe to lose.

One step, and another. There was fluid in my lungs, rattling and wheezing at every breath. Hold on to branches. Breathe by fractions. Midnight.

Grapevine around Shellerton. A mass of common knowledge. Yet this time . . . this time . . .

I stopped. Doone would have to juggle with alibis and charts, proving opportunity, searching for footprints. Doone would have to deal with a cunning mind in the best actor of them all.

I tortoised onwards. No one but a bloody fool would try to walk a mile with an arrow through his chest. Meet J. Kendall, bloody fool.

Light-headed. The moon, I thought briefly, had come down from the sky and was dancing about in the wood not far ahead. I could see it.

Lights. Travelling along the road. I had actually got there.

I reached the last tree and leaned feebly against it, wondering what to do next. Crawl out onto the road and risk getting run over? Hitchhike? Give some poor passing motorist a nightmare?

I slid down to kneeling, leaning head and left shoulder against the tree. By my reckoning, the Land-Rover was way along the road to the right, but it was pointless and impossible to reach it.

Car lights came round a bend from that direction. I tried waving an arm to attract attention but only a weak flap of a hand was achieved.

The car braked suddenly with screeching wheels, then backed rapidly until it was level with me. It was the Land-Rover itself.

Doors opened. People spilled out. People I knew.

Mackie running, calling, 'John, John,' and reaching me and saying, 'Oh, my *God*.'

Perkin behind her, looking down, his mouth open in shocked speechlessness. Gareth saying, 'What's the matter?' urgently, and coming down scared and wide-eyed on his knees beside me.

'Run and fetch Tremayne,' Mackie told him, and he sprang instantly to his feet and sprinted away along the road to the right.

'Surely we must take that arrow out,' Perkin said, and put his hand on the shaft and gave it a tug. He hardly moved it in my chest but it felt like fire.

I yelled . . . it came out as a croak only . . . 'Don't.'

I tried to move away from him but that made it worse. I shot out a hand

and gripped Mackie's trouser leg and pulled with strength I didn't know I still had left. Strength of desperation.

Mackie's face came down to mine, frightened and caring.

'Don't let him move . . . the arrow.'

'Oh, God.' She stood up. 'Don't touch it, Perkin. It's hurting him.'

'It would hurt less out,' he said obstinately. The vibrations from his hand travelled through me, inducing terror as well.

'No. No.' Mackie pulled at his arm in a panic. 'You must leave it. You'll kill him. Darling, you *must* leave it alone.'

Without her Perkin would have had his way, but he finally took his dangerous hand off the shaft.

A car pulled up behind the Land-Rover and disgorged Gareth and then Tremayne, who moved like a tank across the earthy verge. He took charge of things. 'Right, I'll call an ambulance on the car phone. Keep still,' he said to me unnecessarily. 'We'll soon have you out of here.'

I didn't answer him. He sped away back to the car and we could hear his urgent voice, though not the words. He returned shortly, telling me to hang on, it wouldn't be for long.

'We've looked for you for hours,' he said. 'We telephoned the police and the hospitals and then we came out here . . .'

'Because of your message,' Mackie said, 'on the corkboard.'

Gareth's camera was swinging from Perkin's hand. Mackie saw me watching it and said, 'We found the trail, you know.'

Gareth chimed in, 'The paint by the road had gone but I remembered pretty well where it started. And Perkin found it.'

'He went all the way with a torch,' Mackie said, stroking her husband's arm, 'clever thing—and he came back after absolutely ages with Gareth's camera and said you weren't there.'

'I wouldn't let them go home,' Gareth said, with a mixture of stubbornness and pride in his voice. Thank God for him, I thought.

'What happened exactly?' Tremayne asked me bluntly.

'Tell you . . . later.' It came out not much above a whisper.

They waited beside me making worried encouragements until the ambulance arrived from the direction of Reading. Tremayne and Mackie went to meet the men in uniform. Gareth took a step or two after them and I called to him in an explosive croak, 'Gareth. Stay with me.'

It surprised him but he said, 'Oh, OK,' and stayed a pace away.

Perkin said irritably, 'Oh, go on, Gareth.'

I said, 'No,' hoarsely. 'Stay.'

After a pause Perkin put his back towards Gareth and his face down near mine and asked with perfect calmness, 'Do you know who shot you?'

I didn't reply. I looked straight into his moonlit eyes, and I saw Perkin the son, the husband, the one who worked with wood. Saw the man who thought he'd killed me . . . saw the archer.

'Do you really know?' he asked again.

He showed no feeling, yet my knowledge held the difference between his safety and destruction. After a long moment, in which he read the answer for himself, I said, 'Yes.'

Something within him seemed to collapse, but he didn't outwardly fall to pieces or rant or rave. He straightened and said, 'I love Mackie very much.'

He'd said everything, really.

I SPENT THE NIGHT thankfully unaware of the marathon needlework going on in my chest and drifted back late in the morning to a mass of tubes and machines. It seemed I was going to live: the doctors were cheerful, not cautious. A nurse told me visitors had been barred until tomorrow.

By tomorrow, I was breathing without mechanical help, sitting propped up sideways, attached to drainage tubes and, they said, doing just fine.

The first person who came to see me was Tremayne. He looked white, fatigued and many years older.

He said, 'Something awful happened yesterday.' He was trembling.

'What?' I asked apprehensively.

'Perkin . . .' His throat closed. His distress was overwhelming.

He fumbled his way into the visitors' chair and put a hand over his lips so that I shouldn't see how close he was to tears.

'Perkin,' he said. 'He was carving part of a cabinet by hand, and he cut his leg open with the knife. He bled . . . he tried to reach the door. There was blood all over the floor . . . an artery. Mackie found him.'

'Oh, no,' I said in protest.

'She's in a terrible state.' Tears filled his eyes. 'Fiona's with her,' he said. 'She's been marvellous.' He swallowed. 'I have to go back now, but I wanted to tell you myself.'

'Yes. Thank you.'

'There's so much to see to.' His voice wavered again. 'I wish you were there. The horses need to go out. I need your help.'

'In a few days,' I said, and he nodded.

'There has to be an inquest,' he said wretchedly. He sighed deeply, pushed himself to his feet and, with a wan smile, departed.

Doone arrived very soon after Tremayne had gone and came straight to the point. 'Who shot you?'

'Some kid playing Robin Hood,' I said.

'Be serious.'

'Seriously, I didn't see.'

He sat in the visitors' chair and looked at me broodingly. 'I saw Mr Vickers in the car park,' he said. 'I suppose he told you their bad news?'

'Yes. Dreadful for them.'

'You wouldn't think that this could be another murder?'

He saw my surprise. 'I hadn't thought of it,' I said.

'It looks like an accident,' he said, 'but he was experienced with that knife, was young Mr Vickers, and after Angela Brickell, after Mr Goodhaven, after your little bit of trouble . . .' He left the thought hanging and I did nothing to bring it to earth. He sighed after a while and asked how I was.

'Fine.'

'Hm.' He bent down and picked up a paper bag that he'd laid on the floor. 'Thought you might like to see this.' He drew out a sturdy transparent plastic inner bag and held it up to the light to show me the contents. An arrow, cut into two pieces. One half was clean and pale, and the other stained and dark, with a long black section sharpened at the tip.

'Our lab says there are no distinctive tool marks. It could have been sharpened by any straight blade in the kingdom. But charring the point, now, that's in your books, isn't it?'

'Yes. And in other books besides mine.'

Doone nodded. 'Yesterday morning, at Shellerton House, I told Mr Tremayne Vickers and young Mr and Mrs Perkin Vickers not to worry, I would go on working with you as soon as you were conscious and we would see our way together to a solution of the whole case.'

I made no comment and he looked disappointed. You don't seem to care.'

'I'm tired,' I said.

'You wouldn't be interested then in the glue.'

'What glue?' I asked. 'Oh, yes, glue.'

'For sticking marble to floorboards,' he said. 'We had it analysed. Regular impact adhesive. On sale everywhere. We're working on the alibis, but everyone moved about so much except poor young Mr Vickers, who was in his workroom all the time.'

He seemed to be waiting for me to react, rather as if he'd floated a fly in front of a fish.

I smiled and displayed no interest. His moustache seemed to droop further from the lack of good results. He rose to go and told me to take care. He would proceed, he said, with his enquiries.

I wished him luck.

When he'd gone I lay and thought about poor young Mr Vickers, and of what I should have told Doone, and hadn't. Perkin, I thought, was one of the very few people who'd known about the camera and the trail. I'd listened to Gareth tell him in detail on Sunday evening.

On Monday morning Doone had turned up at Shellerton House with the plank. Perkin knew it was I who had remembered that the floorboards should have floated, and on Monday he'd seen the plank on the dining-room table and heard Doone and me talking. Everything Fiona and Tremayne believed of me must have looked inevitable at that moment: John Kendall would lead Doone to the quarry. Any quarry was entitled to take evasive action: to pre-empt discovery by striking first.

By lunchtime Perkin had driven off, going to Newbury for supplies, he'd said. Going to the Quillersedge woods, more like. I'd abandoned the empty house and walked joyfully into the woods.

I imagined Perkin threading along that trail at night, being secretly pleased with himself because if he had inadvertently left any traces of his passage the first time, they could be explained away naturally by the second. That satisfaction would smartly have evaporated when he reached the clearing and found me gone. A nasty shock, one might say. He might have been intending to go back to his family and appear utterly horrified while breaking the news of my death. Instead, he'd looked shocked and utterly horrified at seeing me still alive.

If I'd tried to walk out along the trail, I would have met Perkin face to face. I shivered. Some things were better unimagined.

For Perkin, making arrows would have been as simple as filing his nails. He must have constructed a pretty good strongbow too (according to my detailed instructions), which would by now, no doubt, be broken in unidentifiable pieces in distant undergrowth.

Random thoughts edged slowly into my mind for the rest of the day. For instance, Perkin thought in wood, like a language. Any trap he made would be wooden. Perkin had had to get over the shock of finding my familiar ski jacket and boots in the boathouse and then the far worse shock of the cataclysmic reversal of his scheme when Harry and I both lived. The best actor of them all, he had contained those shocks within himself.

Never assume . . .

Perkin had always been presumed to be busy in his workshop, and yet there were hours and days when he might not have been, when Mackie was out of the house seeing to the horses. On the Wednesday of Harry's trap, Mackie had been at Ascot.

I thought of Angela Brickell and of all the afternoons Perkin had spent alone in the house. Intelligent men in love with their wives weren't immune to blatantly offered temptations. Sudden arousal. Quick, casual gratification. End of episode.

Except not the end of the episode if the result was conception. Not the end if the woman could and would destroy the man's marriage. Say she enticed him into the woods and became demanding in every way and heavily emotional, piling on pressure. Perkin had not long before seen Olympia lying dead at Nolan's feet. He'd heard over and over again how fast she'd died. Say that picture had flashed into his mind. The quick way out of all his troubles lay in his own two strong hands.

I imagined what Perkin might have been feeling, might have been facing. Mackie at that time had been unable to conceive and was troubled and unhappy because of it. Angela Brickell, however, was carrying Perkin's child. Perkin loved Mackie and couldn't bear to hurt her so abominably.

Irresistible solution: a fast death for Angela too. Easy.

Long before Doone came knocking on the door, Perkin could have decided, in case the girl's body were ever found, to say he didn't remember her. No one had thought it odd: he was seldom seen with the horses.

His one catastrophic mistake had been to try to settle the mystery for ever by making Harry disappear.

By his actions shall you know him . . . By his arrows.

I thought that Doone might not think of looking in Perkin's workroom for a match to the arrow's wood. Perkin would have used a common wood, not exotic, but all the same, there would be more of it to be found.

Perkin would know that a wood match could be made. Doone, with his promise of instant detection once I woke up, must have been the end of hope. He did love Mackie. His universe was lost. One way out remained.

I thought of Tremayne and his pride in Perkin's work. Thought of Gareth's vulnerable age. Thought of Mackie, her face alive with the wondrous of joy of discovering she was pregnant. Thought of that child growing up, loved and safe.

Nothing could be gained by trying to prove what Perkin had done. Much would be smashed. They all would suffer. The families always suffered most. All of them would live more happily if they and the world remained in ignorance, and to try to achieve that, I would give them the one gift I could.

Silence.

AT THE SHORT, uncomplicated inquest on Perkin a week later the coroner found unhesitatingly for 'Accident' and expressed sympathy with the family. Tremayne came to collect me from the hospital afterwards and told me on the way to Shellerton that Mackie had got through the court ordeal bravely.

'The baby?' I asked.

'The baby's fine. It's what's giving Mackie strength. She says Perkin is with her, will always be with her that way.'

'Mm.'

Tremayne glanced briefly across at me and back to the road.

'Has Doone found out yet who put that arrow through you?'

'I don't think so,' I said.

'You don't know, yourself?'

'No. Doone came to see me twice. I told him I didn't know who shot me. I told him I had no ideas of any sort any more.'

'You don't think,' Tremayne said painfully. 'I mean, it had to be someone who knew you would fetch Gareth's camera.'

'I told Doone it was a kid playing Robin Hood.'

'I'm . . . afraid . . .'

'Block it out,' I said. 'Some kid did it.'

He knew, I thought. He was no fool. He could have worked things out the way I had, and he'd have had a hellish time believing it all of his own son.

'About my book,' he said. 'I don't know that I want to go on with it.'

'I'm going to write it,' I said positively. 'It's going to be an affirmation of your life and your worth, just as intended. It's all the more important now, but for Gareth, for Mackie and your new grandchild.'

'You do know,' he said.

'It was a kid.'

He drove without speaking the rest of the way.

FIONA AND HARRY were with Mackie and Gareth in the family room. Mackie looked pale but in charge of things, greeting me with a sisterly kiss.

'Hi,' Gareth said, very cool.

Harry said, 'How are you feeling?' and Fiona put her arms carefully round me. Mackie brought cups of tea for everyone; a very English balm in troubles.

It was a month yesterday, I thought, that I came here.

A month in the country . . .

Harry said, 'Has anyone found out who shot at you?'

I gave him the simple answer that eventually became official. 'Doone is considering it was a child playing out a fantasy,' I said. 'Robin Hood, cowboys and Indians. That sort of thing. No hope of ever really knowing.'

'Awful,' Mackie said, remembering.

I looked at her with affection and Tremayne patted my shoulder and told them I would be staying on to write his book.

They all seemed pleased, as if I belonged; but I knew I would leave them again before summer, would walk out of the brightly lit play, and go back to the solitude of fiction. It was a compulsion I'd starved for, and I would feel for ever.

After a while I left the family room and wandered through the great central hall and on into the far side of the house. The door to what had been Perkin's workroom was open and I entered.

It smelled aromatically of wood. Tools lay neatly. A glue pot was cold on a gas cooker against one wall. Everything was tidy and there were no stains on the polished wood-block floor to show where his life had pumped out.

I felt no hatred for him. I thought instead of his talent. Thought of consequences and seduction. I couldn't wipe out an enveloping feeling of pathetic waste. A copy of *Return Safe from the Wilderness* lay on a workbench, and I picked it up idly and looked through it.

Traps. Bows and arrows. All the familiar ideas.

I flipped the pages resignedly and they fell open, as if from use, at the diagram in the first-aid section showing the pressure points for stopping arterial bleeding. I stared blankly at the carefully drawn illustration of exactly where the main arteries could be found nearest the surface in the arms and wrists . . . and in the legs.

Dear God, I thought numbly. I taught him that too.

DICK FRANCIS

During the past year, the subject of survival—especially under extreme conditions—has occupied much of Dick Francis's attention. He was inspired to write *Longshot*, his twenty-ninth novel, when his son, Felix, a schoolteacher, was planning a trip to the jungles of Borneo. 'Felix took about fourteen pupils, boys and girls, on an expedition. They had to slog through the jungle for a month with heavy kit on their backs, but they loved it. There were two schoolmasters with them, and a Ghurka and another soldier who acted as escorts. So there was no chance of them getting lost.' Fortunately, there were no serious mishaps either, thanks in part, to the many survival books which Felix read before the trip—and then passed on to his father. They included the *SAS Survival Handbook*, a manual compiled by an ex-member of the highly trained Special Air Services. The handbook explains, amongst other things, how to make a raft or set a trap.

Like John Kendall, hero of *Longshot*, ex-jockey Dick Francis has had experience of writing a racing biography. In 1986, *Lester*, his official account of the life of Lester Piggott, was published. 'Of course, John Kendall knows less about the racing world than I did when my book was published!' he adds quickly. He then explains, 'Writing a biography is very different from writing a novel: you have to check so many facts. In Lester's case, it was complicated because of the hundreds of horses he rode during his career.'

Dick and Mary Francis have been living on the coast of Florida for four years now. 'We like the weather,' Dick says. 'We also like the way of life, and the Americans. We've made a lot of friends out here.' But the couple still visit the UK regularly to see their two sons and five grandchildren, and Dick takes great pleasure in keeping up-to-date with his first love: the English racing scene. Will it provide the setting for his next novel too? Dick Francis won't say, but he already has an idea for the plot . . .

No Harp Like My Own

by Marjorie Quarton

ILLUSTRATED BY PETER JONES

When 27-year-old Benedict Glyn finds employment on Charlie Thorpe's sheep farm at Middlegarth in Yorkshire, he's over the moon. At last, he can make his own life, free from the oppressive rule of his 82-year-old grandmother back home in County Kildare.

But three encounters lie ahead which alter Ben's life in totally unexpected ways. There's Lesley, a local girl with a heart of gold; Meg, an unforgettable collie; and Anagram, a horse with a terrifying will of its own . . .

Irish-born Marjorie Quarton has captured the spirit and determination of country folk, in this moving tale of a young man's triumph over personal tragedy.

No harp like my own could so cheerily play,
And wherever I went was my poor dog Tray.

Thomas Campbell—*The Harper*

Prologue

I was late for dinner today, or lunch, as Grandmother calls it. Eighty-two she is, and still boss. She's the one with the money, and she keeps us all at home, getting under each other's feet, trying to make some kind of living out of the farm. I wish to God I could get full-time work with Terry.

I rode out two of Terry's horses today, so I should have hurried. But I stopped, as I always do, to look back, before turning Dancing Lady's head down Tinker's Lane for the last mile home.

The farm stands in the dead centre of a hundred acres of fertile land. From the T-junction where you turn off, you can see the whole place—Cloninch. You can see the grey, two-storeyed house, with the copper beeches in front of it, the new silage yard and milking parlours, the fields with cows and sheep. You can see the river flowing right round the boundary like a great horseshoe. The water is deep brown bogwater, and sallee trees hang out over it. The undrained bog beyond the river has more colours than a rainbow. When the light catches the dry sedges and the birch trees, it's just as beautiful as the lakes and mountains the travel agencies go on about.

I turned the mare's head for home, and she trotted away down the lane to her stable and her bit of hay like a two-year-old. I was so happy I felt like singing, in spite of the old lady waiting to tell me off like a child when I showed up late.

It was a great day for me when Terry gave me Dancing Lady. Her tendon isn't too bad—no good for racing, or Terry'd have kept her—but it doesn't bother her at exercise. If it wasn't for her and for Terry I'd be gone long ago. The sun was shining, and little sparks of green and red seemed to dance on her black mane. Her ears twitched all the time; forward as if she could see with them, then back to hear what I was saying to her. It went through my mind that Dancing Lady means more to me than my own family. I don't want it that way, but they make it hard for me.

I put the mare in her stable, pulled off her saddle and threw a rug over her as quick as I could. The happiness had left me. I'd never once raised my voice to my grandmother, but the temper's there. It's piling up inside me like steam in a boiler. I'm afraid of my temper, and Grandmother knows it, just as she knows everything about everybody. Grandfather never stirs out now, and Mother and Father are afraid to open their mouths. Mike and Brian keep out of her way, and Denis is careful not to vex her, even when she grumbles about Sheila.

I could hear them all at their dinner as I crossed the yard. Old Shep was lying out on the flagstones by the door. He lolled out his tongue, grinning at me. When I opened the door, they all stopped talking, and looked at me, waiting for Grandmother to say something. Mother was setting out pudding plates; the meat was cleared away.

When Grandmother's in a room, you don't notice the other people much. It's not just the funny clothes she wears, there's something about her.

She said, 'Late again, Benedict.'

I'd been going to say, 'Sorry I'm late,' but changed my mind. I went into the scullery and took off my old black sweater and washed in the sink.

'Hurry on, Ben,' my sister-in-law, Sheila, said, with that whiny note in her voice. 'Your dinner's getting cold.'

'Shut the door, Ben, you'll catch your death.' That was Mother.

'Coming.' I left the muddy sweater beside the sink, rolled my shirtsleeves down, and smoothed my wet hair with my hands. They say Grandmother's hair was black like mine once. She didn't have any wedding photos, of course, and it's been white as long as I can remember. The looking-glass was steamed up, but I didn't bother to wipe it. I have to crane my neck to see in it. I'm a head shorter than any other man in the house, and not allowed to forget it.

When I came back into the kitchen, I found a place at the table, and carved two slices of nearly cold mutton for myself. I made a face at the cool, greasy gravy and the cold cabbage and potatoes. Grandmother won't allow Mother to keep dinner hot for anyone who's late.

'What kept you, Ben?' asked Mother. 'You finished the sheep hours ago.'

'I rode out an extra horse at Terry's. A young one—green as a cabbage.' The mutton was leathery and unappetising. Only unsaleable animals found their way into our freezer.

Grandmother, bolt upright at the head of the table, turned her steel-grey eyes on me. I looked straight back at her. Nobody else in our house does that. 'That horse of yours, Benedict,' she said. 'It must cost a great deal to feed. I would have thought that riding was a rich man's occupation.'

I nearly said, We'd all be richer if you weren't boss. If you didn't own the farm and everything on it.

I said, 'She doesn't eat much, Grandmother. Just a bit of hay and a bag or two of nuts. Anyway, I pay for her keep.'

'Hm. You'll break your neck one of these days.'

I paid no heed to the old threat. I reached for the teapot. My gift-horse saves petrol, and Terry pays me. If he didn't, I'd have nothing but pocket money like my brothers. I felt my face turning red with anger.

'Some girl telephoned you this morning, Benedict. She said her name was Maura. Why people will not give their full names, I cannot think. Maura.'

'She should've known I'd be out.'

'That would be the young woman who picked you up at the Spring Show, I dare say. She has the manners I would expect.'

I set down my teacup carefully. Stood up. I heard myself say, 'I don't know why we put up with you.'

I was tied in a knot inside, and had a hard job to keep my voice steady. I knew she was despising the way I talk. Temper brings out the brogue.

I watched her face, with the big nose and the crisscross of wrinkles, turn slowly white. I saw all the other faces, gaping with their mouths open. Sheila was feeding some mashed-up food to little Sarah and didn't raise her head. Sarah pushed away the spoon and began to cry.

Grandmother got up slowly, glaring at me. She didn't say anything at all. I slammed my chair in against the table, and walked out of the house.

I was trembling, sweating; my heart pounded. I jumped into the Renault van that Denis had bought cheap, and stalled it twice before I got it going. Rage made me clumsy.

My grandmother is powerful, very likely immortal. I can't imagine life without Grandmother. She ran off with Grandfather nearly sixty years ago, and made enemies of two sets of parents. Poor old Grandfather lost his old friends and never made any new ones. She tried to teach him bridge! Grandfather! And she seems so clever in some ways.

While I was thinking, I was driving—fast. I didn't have anywhere in mind, so I went into town. There'd be a pub open, and I'd get chips maybe, or a burger and a bottle of ale. If the pubs were shut, I'd go back to Terry's, and give him a hand bringing in the mares. The sheep didn't take up much of my time in January; they were still out, getting a little hay in the racks.

I stopped the van at Browne's Bar. The Odeon is just across the street. I'd taken Maura to the pictures at the weekend, *Out of Africa*. I'd really liked it—all the wild animals and everything, but the woman's clothes had reminded me of what Grandmother wears year in, year out. Long jacket, floppy blouse, long tweed skirt. I suppose they were the latest thing when she eloped, and that was when the clock stopped for her.

Billy Browne was behind the counter, reading *The Irish Stockbreeder*. The iron stools have green plastic tops, and the tables look like pink marble. I asked for something hot, and Billy said, 'The microwave's on the blink. What are you doing out in your shirtsleeves this time of year?'

I'd come out without my jacket, without even noticing. I bought a beer and drank it down in big gulps. I was still boiling with anger.

Billy doesn't talk much, and I was glad of it. I moved to one of the pink marble tables. Billy passed his paper over to me, folded open at an advert.

SEE BRITAIN'S TOP FLOCKS
VISIT FAMOUS SHEEP FARMS
Three days for £129, including ticket for fatstock
show at Middlegarth, Yorkshire. . .

'Like a coach trip, Ben? See some more sheep. The brother was going across, but he has the flu. Paid an' all. I was thinking of ringing you. Liverpool boat tomorrow night.'

I opened my mouth to say that I couldn't afford it; that I was busy; that I'd have no time to make arrangements.

'Thanks, Billy,' I said. 'I'd like to go.'

One

A biting east wind, straight from Siberia by way of Scarborough, had replaced the sleety drizzle of the morning. It swept over the acres of frost-bitten kale, over the bent shoulders of the huddled group of Irish farmers, and scoured Charlie Thorpe's meaty face. Charlie stood four-square to the wind. His fur-lined parka was unzipped, showing his thick neck and open shirt. He was hatless, and strands of his grey hair were tugged this way and that by the gale.

Charlie Thorpe was 'the Guvnor' to everyone within five miles of Middlegarth Farm. He spoke with the authority of a cabinet minister, and could hold an audience, even out of doors in Yorkshire in January. He was talking about sheep.

The journalist from the *Hangleby Tribune* said, 'Bring 'em in now, Guvnor, they're too cold to listen.'

'Let's move on to the pedigree flock, Charlie,' said Ted Wilkes, the Guvnor's partner and son-in-law.

Charlie shrugged his big shoulders angrily. He turned and stumped into the barn, muttering, 'No colder for them than for me.'

The barn was large and chilly, but coming into it from outside was like stepping into a warm bath. Charlie marched over to the pens, and began to talk again. The party from County Kildare split up into smaller groups as they moved from pen to pen. Their green anoraks and Hunter boots might almost have been a uniform; only in the matter of headgear was there much variety. Tweeds hats were favoured.

There were a few cloth caps, a knitted Aran hat with a pompom, and one or two trendy denim affairs.

Charlie looked them over with a hard, dispassionate stare. There was only one bare head. It belonged to a broad-shouldered young man he'd noticed right at the start. Only a little fella, thought the Guvnor, but there's ways about him.

Ben was enjoying himself. He looked down at the pen beside him, where a ewe stood within reach. He scratched her hard black skull, and pulled her ear. 'Well, old girl,' he said, 'that's a fine pair of lambs you have.'

The Guvnor stopped talking. His watery blue eyes focused on Ben. There was a moment's silence. 'Have you anything more to say to that sheep?' he asked. 'If not, we'll get on.'

Ben straightened up, and returned glare for glare. He edged out of the group and walked out of the barn.

He had noticed a dog kennel close to the entrance. It appeared to be empty—but Ben had seen some movement on the way in. Standing well back, he looked into the kennel. Hostile eyes stared back. A tooth gleamed in the shadow.

'Hello boy. Come on, Shep. Come here then.'

As a schoolboy, Ben had made bets with other boys who staked their pocket money that their dogs wouldn't leave them when Ben called. They'd always lost.

The dog—whose real name was Roy—felt the pull of Ben's will, as tangibly as the pull of his chain. He stood up, and slowly came to the door of the kennel.

Ben had seen dogs like Roy on television and at the local sheepdog trials. Nobody near Cloninch kept a border collie. Old Shep at home was a heavy, lazy dog. Fat and idle.

AFTERWARDS, THEY ALL WALKED back to the farmhouse, where the minibus was waiting.

There were two stables in the courtyard, with horses' heads looking over half doors. The light outside the back door shone on the white-blazed face of the nearest. Ben went at once to the horse, and rubbed its face. The horse bent its head in recognition of something it couldn't define. Ben looked over the door, and saw that the horse stood with its weight on its right foreleg, the left fetlock was puffy.

He was alone. Everyone else had gone into the house. The Guvnor turned back, and came with purposeful strides. He was about to give the young man what he called a bit of straight Yorkshire, but Ben spoke first.

'Has he something in his foot? Is he gravelled?'

'God knows, lad. Vet says it's ligaments.'

'I thought it was hurting him even when he had no weight on it, like an abscess.'

'If I want another opinion, I'll ask for it.' Charlie turned away. He was tired. He made up his mind to put a stop to these capers. He was sick of lecturing busloads of strangers.

He left the group to their tea in the kitchen, went into the front room and dropped into his armchair.

'WAKE UP, FATHER!' Charlie felt his daughter Mandy shaking his shoulder. 'They're going. Aren't you coming to see them off?'

'Suppose I better had.' Grumbling, he went out to the yard.

The wind had dropped, and it was snowing. The fourteen members of the group piled into the minibus. They were going down to the Turpin Arms in Middlegarth for drinks, then back to their hotel. Charlie Thorpe watched them stonily. Last to board the bus was the little fella; the one who had been talking to a sheep. The first person who'd had anything sensible to suggest about the lame horse.

'You, lad! You there behind!'

The young man looked round. 'Talking to me?'

'What do they call you, lad?'

'Ben. Benedict Glyn.'

'Ben. Sensible name. Had a goodish dog called Ben. Know a bit about horses, do you?'

'A bit.'

'You drive?'

'I do.'

'Not looking for a job, are you?'

Ben stopped, holding the door of the minibus. Huge flakes of snow drifted down, settling on his hair. He didn't seem to mind. 'I might be,' he said.

'See you in the pub,' said Charlie. He turned on his heel, and disappeared into the house.

HIS SON-IN-LAW WAS AGHAST. 'What do we know about him?'

'Nowt. But there's ways about him.' Charlie and Ted Wilkes faced each other across the kitchen table.

'But Guvnor,' said Ted, 'he can't do Peter's work. I mean, Peter was a good lambing shepherd and did the horses as well. How do we know that he's any use with sheep?'

'He'll do. Doesn't chatter. Doesn't mind a bit of snow. See him as we came through back barn second time? Old Roy came out of kennel to him. There's ways about the lad.'

'For God's sake make sure he realises it's only temporary,' pleaded Ted. 'Peter might come back in a month.'

'Might he hell. What good'll he be just out of plaster?'

Ted tried again. 'That's another thing. How do you expect this Irish chap to ride Anagram? Nobody's even tried since he put Peter in hospital. If he was my horse, I'd beef him.'

'He's not your horse,' said Charlie. He shrugged on a heavy overcoat, took his cloth cap from its peg, and marched out.

IN THE CROWDED BAR at the Turpin Arms, Charlie saw Ben at once, although he was in the furthest corner of the smoky room. He was finishing a pint of ale.

Charlie pushed his way across the room to the bar. He ordered another pint for Ben and a grapefruit juice for himself, and took it over.

Charlie prided himself on his snap decisions and judgment of character. He sipped his soft drink, and watched Ben closely as they talked. He was pleased, but not surprised, to see that the young man was not disconcerted by his scrutiny. His vitality was extraordinary. He seemed to displace more than his share of the air around him.

Anagram wouldn't have broken this chap's legs, thought Charlie. The horse was wick as an eel, and Peter must have been dreaming. Serve him right. Good riddance.

Two

Back in the soullessly new hotel in Leeds where the group was staying, Ben changed his black jumper for an olive one, and put on his drab cords. He didn't own a suit. Grandmother had once offered to have one made for him, as mass producers don't cater for five-foot-five men with forty-two-inch chests. Ben had refused, and asked if he might have the cash instead. He'd finished up with neither.

Ben was taking his time. He wanted to think about the offered job. It was tempting, more than tempting. The Guvnor hadn't mentioned wages, but any wage was better than none. At home, he got what Grandmother called 'cigarette money'—although he didn't smoke—his keep, and a bonus when the lambs were sold. Last year, he'd earned £250. Why, Terry had paid Ben almost double for riding work in his spare time. And riding work was Ben's favourite occupation.

Ben sat down in front of the white-painted vanity unit. He brushed his hair, looking in the mirror. The eyes that looked back at him were as grey as his grandmother's, but warmer. The brows were straight and heavy, the lashes long, thick and black. Both of his parents had indeterminate sandy colouring. I must be a throwback, thought Ben.

Eight o'clock. Grandmother would be in her bedroom now. She never sat downstairs after tea. She and Grandfather shared the best bedroom, and that was where the old lady kept the few possessions she had brought with her as a bride. After tea, Grandfather would go to bed and doze.

Grandmother would sit erect in her basket chair by the window, reading. She read six books a week. She bicycled to Kilmoon on Tuesday, Thursday and Saturday, to change two books at the library. Shortsighted now, she wore a pince-nez for reading and for fine needlework.

When Ben was a little boy, he used to go into her room and look at the picture, *Young Girl in a Garden*. There were pictures everywhere at Cloninch, the horse pulling a haycart in the hall, the holy pictures in the kitchen, a big framed photo of Arkle and another of Red Rum. But *Young Girl in a Garden* was in another league altogether. She sat on the grass with her skirts spread round her and her lap full of yellow flowers. Her back was as straight as Grandmother's. Her dress was greener than the grass, and the flowers were just dabs of colour, but you could almost smell them. The girl's face was pale as ivory on a long neck. There were pearls in her red hair. The sun streamed into the picture, but you felt that it had been raining and that the grass was damp. Grandmother was as nearly pleased as she ever was when Ben told her that the picture was his favourite thing in the whole world. He'd been six years old then.

As Ben grew older, he gave up going into the room. When he'd decorated it just lately, and seen the picture once more, it was like meeting a dear friend again . . . Ben jumped up. He'd forgotten all about supper and he was hungry.

AGATHA LOGAN SAT PERFECTLY still in her basket chair. Every five minutes, she turned a page. She was reading a life of Marcel Proust. Agatha sighed. She had read three lives of Proust. The library had a limited selection of books and she had read them all, with the indiscriminate appetite of a vacuum cleaner. She thirsted for information as some thirst for drink or drugs. But at eighty-two, she could only assimilate three serious books a week if she alternated them with cheap thrillers.

Agatha laid down her book, took off her pince-nez, and rose stiffly. Michael was sound asleep, had been for hours. He slept more as he grew older, she slept less. Agatha crossed to the big brass bed, tall and severe in her long tweed skirt and pink crepe de Chine blouse. She looked down at Michael with a curious expression compounded of pity, impatience and affection.

Fascinating, Michael had been. His dark good looks and compelling personality had more than made up for his deficiencies. Agatha jerked her shoulders, shrugging off uncomfortable memories, and returned to her chair. She stared at the picture on the wall, as if she was seeing it for the first time. The girl's fiery hair, loosely twisted into a coil, spilled onto her bare shoulder in a thick, shining ringlet. Almost three-dimensional, she turned, or seemed to turn, her long, greenish eyes on Agatha. She smiled, not coyly nor mockingly, but with pure happiness. She was probably about seventeen years old.

'If that picture's so valuable, I wonder you don't sell it.' The voice, coming from the apparently sleeping Michael, would have made most people jump.

'I trust,' said Agatha, 'that my circumstances are not so reduced that I must sell my grandmother. As I am obliged by the terms of my father's will to leave the farm to Denis, I have nothing but this picture within my power to bestow as I like. I do not regret my decision to bequeath it to Benedict.'

'He won't thank you for it,' muttered Michael on a yawn. He spoke indistinctly without his false teeth. 'Poor old Ben. Needs a farm and gets a picture. Shame—he's a good lad.'

Agatha, whose teeth were her own and excellent, snapped back, 'Even in a recession it must be worth considerably more than Cloninch.'

But Michael had gone to sleep again.

Michael blamed her, she knew, because Benedict had gone to England, and had telephoned earlier that evening to say that he would not return. He had dared to suggest that she was unfair to Benedict and singled him out for criticism. Perhaps she did, but who else was worth her criticism? She had no son of her own; Muriel was her downtrodden daughter. Muriel had married Myles, who hovered between the pub and the greyhound track. Agatha seldom troubled to speak to him.

The four grandchildren were of the same pattern as their parents, except for Benedict . . . A seven-months' child, despaired of by all the doctors, he had insisted on continuing to live, against all odds. Dark, while they were fair, short while they were tall, alert while they were sluggish; he was the only one that Agatha cared about. She hoped and dreamed for him, but could not help him.

Agatha slowly began to prepare for bed. Her clothes, made to last, were folded away in tissue paper, her T-bar shoes placed side by side. She put on an ancient handmade silk nightdress. Even in January, nothing would have induced her to sleep in Viyella or interlock.

Quietly, she slid into bed beside Michael.

EVEN IN HIS WILDEST DREAMS, Ben had never imagined having a house to go with his job.

He had spent the first few days at the farm, under Charlie's cold eye. Today, he'd been instructed to ride Anagram in the straw yard. Ben knew that this was the horse which had thrown the absent Peter, but he was surprised when the entire staff turned out to watch. Ben had disappointed his audience—or rather Anagram had. After an experimental plunge and a buck which was no more than light-hearted, he had settled down, and trotted around as quietly as a riding-school hack.

And now Eric, the head shepherd, had driven Ben up to Peter's cottage with his luggage.

The cottage had many defects, but Ben didn't care. He could do what he liked within its four thick walls. He could do handstands on the stone floor, dance, sing—he wished he'd brought his guitar with him.

The cottage was icy. It was heated by a solid-fuel cooker, which had been out since Peter's departure twelve freezing January days earlier. There wasn't much room to manoeuvre in the cramped kitchen, but he soon had the fire roaring cheerfully, with a tin of stew warming in a saucepan on the hotplate.

Ben drew the curtains, and went to the bedroom. He glanced around. There were hooks on the wall, and a pull-out drawer under the feather bed. The window was set so deeply that the sill provided as much space as the small table. These two rooms were the original cottage. A built-on room with a tin roof was divided into scullery and lavatory. There was a tin bath under the draining board, and a hose to fill it.

Ben ate the stew and a tin of mushy peas. This was all the edible food that Peter had left. Mandy Wilkes had given him some eggs which he was saving for breakfast. He hadn't got any bread.

Ben rinsed his plate. He said aloud, 'I've never been so happy in my life; never.'

There was no television or radio in the cottage, and Ben had nothing to read. So he put on his gumboots and jacket and went out. There was a little frozen snow on the ground, and it was a beautiful starry night. From the cottage door, he could see the lights of Middlegarth, half a mile away, down the steep lane. He checked his money—£4.

In Kilmoon, it would have been perfectly possible to buy supplies at 9pm. Not in Middlegarth. Disappointed in his search for bread, milk and tea, he went into the Turpin Arms. The dozen or so occupants of the bar turned and studied him. He asked for a shandy. Two girls and a man were sitting in the corner, and there was a crowd of men gathered round the darts board.

One of the girls jumped to her feet, and came across to the bar. 'No, it's my turn,' she was saying. As she reached the counter, she looked at Ben, and he looked back. She said, 'Hi,' and turned away as he replied. He noticed her hair was pale gold and very smooth. She had a long nose and a short chin, and you couldn't call her pretty.

Ben said, 'Cold night,' to make her turn her head. She did, and he saw her broad forehead, and that she had intelligent eyes and a gentle mouth. She wore long flashing earrings, a big red sweater and black ski pants. He thought he had glimpsed her up at the farm, but it was hard to be sure.

'You got Peter's job, eh?' she said.

'I have,' he said. 'For a while anyway.'

'I was up at the Guvnor's,' she said, 'seeing about a puppy. They told me you'd been riding Anagram. You want to mind that brute; he'll kill you.'

The other girl at the corner table called out, 'What about those drinks, Dogsbody?'

The girl said, 'Hang on,' counting her change.

'Who's Dogsbody?' enquired Ben.

'Oh, that's me. Silly nickname.' She grinned.

'They can't call you Dogsbody,' said Ben angrily. 'I never heard such a thing.'

'A nice girl like me?' She mocked him. 'It's just a joke—I help with dogs part time. Guide dogs for the blind.' She picked up the glasses. 'Join us?' she suggested.

Ben shook his head. How could you join anybody with four quid in your pocket? He sipped his drink, his mild interest in the girl evaporating, although he knew she was still watching him. He hated thinking about blind people. A world without light seemed to him like a living death. To Ben, a blind man with a dog was a lost soul, wandering through limbo; haunted by the bogies of poverty, dependence and humiliation.

Ben remembered being terrified as a child by an old blind tramp whose daughter had led him about, begging for him. Ben had never forgotten those milky eyes with their sightless gaze. Even now, the horror he had felt hadn't quite left him. He finished his drink, and left.

AGATHA ATTENDED THE PROTESTANT church every Sunday. The unusual feature about this dedication was that Agatha was a Roman Catholic. True, her grandfather had been a Protestant archdeacon, but she had been obliged to change her religion when she eloped with Michael.

The service would be taken by young Tony Robinson, recently ordained. He tried to scuttle into the vestry, unobserved by Agatha who was parking her bicycle by the side door. He was unsuccessful. Callow fool, thought Agatha, as the young man took her proffered hand rather as he might have accepted a loaded gun.

She went inside and knelt, painfully, in the family pew. She stood, and sat, and endured the cold and the choir. She didn't hear the words being said and sung. She was thinking about Ben.

Agatha came back to the present when Major Arnold quavered out a reading from the Apocrypha. Like her, he was over eighty. Unlike her, he was fragile and wheezy.

'The wisdom of the scribe depends on the opportunity of leisure; And he who has little business may become wise. . .'

Agatha thought of Ben working eighteen hours a day in lambing time. He'll never become wise, she thought.

'How can he become wise who handles the plough. . . And whose talk is about bulls?'

Or horses. Or ewes.

Poor Benedict. What had she done to him? And the farm would never be his. Entirely preoccupied, Agatha knelt through the Creed, a hymn, some prayers, another hymn . . .

During the sermon she shut her eyes, as it was her habit to sleep openly when the young vicar was preaching. At once, she saw her picture in her mind's eye. Beautiful thing—she loved it more than any living thing except Benedict. She opened her eyes. 'I shall sell it,' she said aloud, and marched out of the church.

She collected her bicycle and rode home.

Three

Lesley Peabody woke with a headache; her alarm clock was bleeping insistently. She stretched out a sleepy arm and stopped it, thinking about the day ahead. Today, she would visit Henrietta, George Bull, and hopeless, weepy Mrs Betts; then lunch, then the children's Day Centre. A typical day.

She'd slept badly. The evening at the Turpin Arms had gone sour on her. Her friends Bob and Tina liked to go out for a drink after working all day at the Training Centre. Often, they asked Lesley to join them.

Lesley went on thinking about the evening as she dressed. Normally a serene person, she felt edgy and ruffled. She felt she'd made a fool of herself as she remembered the dark young man and Bob's teasing and her own sharp retorts. She had snapped at Tina, 'Don't call me Dogsbody—I don't like it.' And Tina had laughed and said, 'Your young man didn't like it either, did he?' Lesley had flushed with annoyance.

She couldn't get the man out of her mind; his springy, compact build, his vitality, his unreasonable anger.

She brushed her hair and walked into the kitchen, bracing herself for Hazel's morning face.

Lesley shared her flat in Leeds with Hazel, a moody, swarthy girl who came and went at odd hours. Lesley disliked her quite a lot, but Hazel paid her share, and there seemed to be no valid reason for asking her to go. She ate muesli with her mouth open, but you didn't have to watch.

When Mark had walked out, Lesley had needed a tenant to help pay the rent, and Hazel had taken Mark's place in the flat. His place in Lesley's life was still vacant. Now, as she walked into the kitchen, it occurred to her that she might resume her maiden name. Why should she be lumbered with Mark's name? And if she stopped being Peabody, perhaps she'd stop being Dogsbody as well.

Hazel, for once, was up first. She was gloomily stirring a mug of coffee. Thank God, she'd finished her muesli. She annoyed Lesley, who was twenty-six, by persisting in calling her Mrs Peabody. She did it now. 'Morning, Mrs Peabody; I laid breakfast.'

'Thanks. And Hazel, look, if you can't get round to Lesley, would you mind calling me by my old name? It's Grant.'

'Right.'

Hazel stirred and stirred, peering into her mug as if she were telling fortunes. She didn't so much sit at the table, as collapse beside it and spread herself over it.

Lesley drank her coffee, ate a piece of toast, and made notes. Restlessly, she moved about tidying things up (Hazel was untidy) and switching things off. 'I might go away for a few days,' she said. 'I'm due a long weekend . . .'

'Right, Mrs Grant,' Hazel said. 'Have fun.'

Lesley grabbed her diary and rushed out of the room. Her thoughts skidded about uncharacteristically. Whenever she let herself relax, her mind went back to the same thing—'What about those drinks, Dogsbody?' and the young man's sudden anger.

SHE WALKED THE TWO BLOCKS to Henrietta's flat. Since Mark's humiliatingly public affair and departure, Lesley had filled her waking hours with work. All her social work was in Leeds. Her work with The Guide Dogs for the Blind Association was voluntary. She was highly thought of as a social worker with the blind. Her cool, unsentimental approach was ideal for the exacting tasks involved, and it was a measure of her skill that she had been allocated to look after Henrietta.

Poor Henrietta, people said. But that was patronising, even insulting. She'd had more to lose than most; not only her looks but her high-powered job as foreign correspondent for a national weekly. She was the youngest and most reckless, and she'd got too close to the scene of action. Lesley had never heard exactly how she got the burns.

Lesley rang the bell. From upstairs, the voice came through the intercom. 'Lesley? Come on up.'

Lesley spent twenty minutes every day making up Henrietta's face. Trying to make the undamaged lower half of it blend into the upper; masking the scars with heavy make-up. 'You could do this yourself, except perhaps the lipstick,' she said. 'When are you going out?'

'Never. Perhaps after dark, wearing a fencing mask.'

'No, listen. You're getting better every day. All you really need now is cleanser, foundation and make-up. The cleanser's liquid, in a bottle; the cream foundation's in a jar; the make-up's a stick. They're in that order, left to right on the dressing table. Try it tomorrow, and I'll tell you how it looks.' Lesley arranged the jars and bottles, tissues and cotton wool. 'If you could do your own face, you could fix your hair without waiting for me.'

'Put on my wig, you mean.'

'Your own hair's growing like mad. I'll give you a home perm as soon as there's enough of it if you like.' Lesley was creaming Henrietta's throat. 'I don't want to nag, but you could go out in this cold weather easily, wearing a woolly hat well pulled down. Lots of people wear dark glasses in the snow.'

'You *have* to nag, I suppose.'

'Any washing?'

'On the bed. Oh, Lesley, you know that stuff you put on tape for me to learn, so that I could recognise my groceries? I think I've sent it to the *Illustrated Manchester News,* right in the middle of a piece about race riots.' She laughed, a clear happy sound. 'I'm a clot, aren't I?'

'I hope you learned it first.' Lesley laughed too as she stuffed clothes into a laundry bag. 'I'm going to the laundrette now. I'll bring this lot back tomorrow. See you then.'

'Yes, Nanny.'

Lesley ran downstairs. She left the flat feeling encouraged. It was only a matter of time until the other girl would overcome her fear of going out. Lesley was pretty sure that the day would soon arrive when she would no longer be needed.

GEOFF MERCHANT LUNCHED at his usual place, in Leeds, the Kosy Kitchen. He was pleased with the dog, Pepper. She led him confidently to an empty table. Geoff told her to lie down, dropped the harness, and went to collect his meal from the self-service counter. He was too good a trainer to glance back and make sure that Pepper was staying where he'd left her. He helped himself to liver and bacon and a cup of tea, and sat down, facing the street.

Geoff, a heavily built man with bristly grey hair and enormous bushy eyebrows, enjoyed his reputation as a brilliant dog trainer. As a younger man, training dogs for police work, he had felt obscurely dissatisfied. He disliked teaching dogs to attack. After having taken early retirement from the police, he had turned to guide-dog training. Geoff had a wife and two daughters. They all knew their place in his scheme of things—next after the dogs and those that used them.

Geoff raised his hand as Lesley came through the door. They often lunched together. To Geoff, she was not an attractive woman, he didn't think in those terms. She was simply a good social worker who never wasted his time and didn't chatter. When her husband had left her, she had grown quieter, smiled less and become even more efficient. She collected a salad at the counter, and came over to his table.

As Lesley spoke, Geoff looked at her sharply. She was more animated than usual. 'How's it going?' he asked.

'Fine. I believe Henrietta Lake will venture out soon. She's simply rushing about with her cane. Must be practising.'

'D'you reckon she'll be wanting a dog?'

'No, I don't. You don't know her, Geoff; she's the last person. George Bull, now, he could do with one any time.'

'He's down for the next training course,' said Geoff. 'Did you see him today?'

'Yes. I put his dinner in the oven and set it for him. When he gets the hang of the Braille temperature setting, I won't even have to do that. He's quick.'

'Well, he's a policeman,' said ex-policeman Geoff.

Lesley laughed at him. 'Don't tell me there aren't any slow policemen,' she said, sparkling at him.

Something up, thought Geoff. A man—sure to be. 'What about Mrs Betts?' he asked.

'Hopeless. She can see more than most of my lot, but she does nothing but cry.'

They pushed away their plates, sitting at the iron-legged table with its mottled Formica top.

'Where are you off to this afternoon?' Geoff asked.

'To the Day Centre until four o'clock. Then I thought I'd go to Middlegarth and see how the puppies are getting on.'

'Again? Thought you went Tuesday?'

'I did as it happens,' said Lesley, 'but Bob hasn't seen them yet.'

'Tell you what,' said Geoff. 'I'll come with you.'

They agreed to meet at the Training Centre, collect Bob and drive out together. Geoff picked up Pepper's harness, and immediately began to imitate the actions of a blind man. Walking slightly ahead and to the left of him, the big dog led the way out of the café.

IT WAS QUIET AT THE Training Centre when Lesley drove into the yard behind the square Georgian house which formed the main building. The dogs were mostly out in the runs at the back of their sleeping quarters. Geoff had taken another dog out, and hadn't yet returned.

Bob, the senior puppy-walking supervisor, was a placid, smiling man in his late thirties. His loud, jolly laugh, which went 'ho ho!' like Santa Claus, was well known and widely imitated. Tina, his wife, was in charge of the catering.

'I don't see much point in looking at those puppies yet,' grumbled Bob.

'Come on,' said Tina, 'it's a drive out.' She dragged him out of his chair. 'Why don't we take Meg with us? Mandy Wilkes would love to see her again.' So Bob fetched Meg from her kennel.

The only purebred Border collie at the Centre, Meg was a big dog for her breed. One ear was pricked, the other bent over at the tip. She had a white-blazed face, with a bright tan spot over each eye. Her coat was fine and silky, shining with health. 'She needs another month to six weeks,' said Bob. 'Geoff thinks she may be overpossessive. She's still a bit funny if anyone goes near him.'

Geoff arrived, and an hour later the four of them pulled up at the back door of Middlegarth Farm. The house, built of weathered yellow stone, was as old-fashioned as the farm buildings were modern. The kitchen floor was of worn brick, and hams hung from hooks in the smoke-blackened ceiling. Mandy offered sandwiches, apple pie and Christmas cake. Lesley had been at school with Mandy Wilkes and the friendship had survived. Privately, Lesley thought that Mandy's much older husband, Ted, was a bore, but then Mandy hadn't liked Mark either.

Lesley sat on the window seat drinking tea, looking across the brightly lit courtyard towards the double Dutch barn, while Mandy took Bob to see the puppies. 'One at a time,' she said, 'Old Nell isn't so keen on strangers.'

Lesley was aware of someone walking towards the house, whistling a tune she didn't know. Then the door opened, and a familiar stocky figure came into the kitchen. 'Did you get that pen-strep?' he asked Mandy, who had reappeared, cuddling a puppy.

All day, while Lesley got on with her work, stray thoughts had intruded. Did Ben ever smile? How would he look if he did? Now, seeing her unexpectedly, Ben gave her a wide grin which lit up his whole face.

Mandy went to the cupboard and fetched a bottle and a hypodermic. Lesley swallowed the rest of her tea. Her insides had given a violent lurch when she encountered Ben's smile. She hoped she hadn't turned red. Ben went out taking a basin of warm water, a towel, soap, the hypodermic and the bottle of penicillin. Lesley watched him go. In another week, she thought, it would be two years since Mark had left. Far too long to be alone.

MEG SLUMBERED FITFULLY under the table where Geoff, her person, had told her to lie. Meg was happy with her person. She was learning new words every day, and dimly understood that there was some purpose in what she was doing. She didn't care at all for seeing other dogs taking her person for walks; sometimes running him into trees and that. She meant to take such care of Geoff that he'd stop taking other dogs. That would be champion. She dozed off.

Meg woke as the back door opened and the man came in. The man who had gone out with a basin half an hour since. The man you might like to take for walks if you had no person of your own. Meg noticed that all three of the females in the room reacted to him in their different ways. Missus told him to come and warm himself by the fire. Tina pricked her ears, insomuch as a person can, and the lass at the window watched him like a good dog with a bunch of sheep that might be fettling for breaking away. The man, Ben, noticed Meg and snapped his fingers. She got up, remembered, and lay down again.

Old Nell had been given to Mandy by the Guvnor because, he said, she wasn't worth a cartridge. Her first litter of puppies by old Roy had been unplanned. Meg was the only one of them to take after her mother. The other three, inheriting Roy's genes, were so good that Charlie had allowed Mandy to breed a second litter from Nell. In Meg's make-up, the herding instinct was missing.

Meg felt, however, that had she been the sort of dog that works sheep, she would have enjoyed helping the short, stocky man who was washing his hands at the sink.

THE GUVNOR, DEVELOPING his usual winter bout of bronchitis, had heard Ben from the front room where he'd been sitting over the fire. Coughing, he entered the kitchen. 'Finished up outside, have you?' Charlie asked Ben.

'I have at last. I'll be off home now.'

'Stay and have supper with us,' suggested Mandy.

'Thanks, but I'd rather get back to the cottage. I left a stew on the range.' Ben went over to Lesley. 'I was rude to you the other night,' he said. 'I'm sorry. It's none of my business what your friends call you.'

Lesley said, 'You weren't rude; my friends call me Lesley. I hope you approve.'

'I do,' said Ben. He did. He approved of what he saw, and wanted badly to know her better. But this one has money, he thought. She was wearing an ink-blue wool dress this time, and she had a gold necklace and earrings which came from a jewellers, not a chain store. Out of my league, thought Ben, sadly.

'Do you ever come to Leeds?' asked Lesley. 'There's lots of buses.'

Small talk or invitation? He couldn't be sure. 'I might go Saturday week,' he said. 'Do some shopping.'

'Why don't we all meet up?' asked Tina brightly. 'We could go to that new place, the Hart Royal.'

Ben felt Lesley's tension as she waited for his reply. She wore rings on almost every finger; thin ones, thick ones, twisted ones. There was a plain one on the fourth finger of her left hand. He counted; she was wearing six rings altogether. So perhaps it wasn't a wedding ring. Her hand was trembling slightly.

'Thanks,' he said. 'I'll come unless something crops up.' He took his anorak off the hook and put it on. There was a rent in the back of it, mended with insulating tape. 'I'll catch an early bus and get myself something decent to wear, or I'll be thrown out of the Hart Royal.'

AS HE RODE TO LEEDS on the bus over a week later, Ben's mind was taken up with Lesley. She'd been to the farm twice more; she seemed to be visiting Mandy a lot. Both times, they'd exchanged a few commonplaces, both knowing that there would be more than this. Mandy was matchmaking, Ben thought.

Ben was no fool, but he was puzzled. On what terms did Lesley want him? He knew little of women. True, he was pursued by girls at home, but he didn't believe in letting them catch him. Love and marriage, in Ben's limited experience, did not go together like a horse and carriage. He thought of love as a sort of bonus in marriage; the exception, not the rule.

He was going to have to ask her if she was married, and soon. Unless he was greatly mistaken, Lesley was not a girl for casual affairs.

Suddenly, he thought of Agatha, always icily remote, except when moved by anger. He wondered what she had been like as a girl, when love for Michael had made her throw family, position and fortune to the winds. He thought he might be like her some day—he knew there was much of her passion in his own make-up.

IN LEEDS BEN BOUGHT a blue sweater, black cords and a sleeveless jacket. They cost less than he expected, so he bought a pair of shoes as well. He put on the new clothes, had the old ones wrapped, and went to the Hart Royal.

It was large, low and lavishly decorated; self-consciously new. The bar was in the shape of a horseshoe; black, with a laminated top. Some of the chairs in the centre of the lounge were suspended from the ceiling, but along the walls were oak settles bolted to the floor, slightly too far away from the heavy oak tables.

Lesley was there already, standing at the far end of the bar. She hadn't seen him. She was wearing a white dress, a gold belt, and earrings, Ben thought, as big as horse-brasses. She was talking to the landlady, an overripe blonde whose low-cut dress appeared to be fashioned out of kitchen foil. A tall man was leaning on the counter beside Lesley and, as far as Ben could tell, was trying to chat her up.

Ben saw the man place a large white hand on Lesley's arm. She moved her arm away sharply. The stranger was youngish, fattish, and his clothes suggested a race meeting. Ben felt uncertain of himself. What, after all, did he know about Lesley's circle of friends? Too shy to approach them, he ordered a drink and looked hard at Lesley. She turned round at once, and their eyes met and held. She spoke to the landlady, ignored the man and walked over to Ben. The dim lights glimmered on her smooth pale hair; she looked expensive and assured. Out of my league, he thought again.

Lesley glanced round to see if the other man had followed her. It was a devil, she thought, when you couldn't wait five minutes for a friend without being pestered.

Ben was watching her, his face illuminated by one of his rare smiles. 'I thought I was going to have to fight for you.'

What was it about Ben, she asked herself. There was a crackling vitality about him which made the other drinkers at the bar look lifeless and cold.

'That man's a right pain,' she said. 'He embarrasses the staff, annoys the customers and never goes far enough to be thrown out—unfortunately.'

'I'll throw him out if you like,' said Ben. She saw by his face and his bunched muscles that he wasn't joking.

'Oh, Ben, forget him. He isn't worth bothering about.'

'I'm glad Bob and Tina aren't here yet,' said Ben. 'I've never seen you without a lot of people round. Could we go out on our own another time? I've no car, but I can bus into Leeds.'

She guessed that he didn't want to be collected in her car, so she didn't offer. 'I'd like that,' she said.

While they waited for Bob and Tina, Ben asked questions, and Lesley answered. 'You're inquisitive, aren't you?' she said at last.

'I'm not inquisitive, I'm curious. There's a big difference. I'm taking a short cut to knowing you better.'

Any minute now, he'd ask if she was married, Lesley thought. She didn't want to talk about Mark, and Ben was sure to disapprove of divorce. She'd heard they didn't have it in Ireland.

'Are you a Catholic?' she asked. 'Not inquisitive—just curious.'

'A bad one. Protestants don't get called Benedict.'

'Benedict? I imagined you were Benjamin. Benedict's much nicer.'

'Don't call me by it,' he begged. 'Only my grandmother does that—the old devil.'

'Why do you call her an old devil?'

'It's nothing to what my brothers call her; she runs all our lives.' There was a note of reluctant admiration in his voice. He laughed, and said, 'I left home because I had a row with her. She kicked up over what my horse cost to keep.'

'Ben, that reminds me, are you still riding that wretched horse, Anagram?'

'When I get time. Don't worry, he's harmless. If I could cure him of shaking his head, he'd be a decent horse.'

'Listen, Ben, Anagram went over backwards with Peter. They said he screamed out and reared up for no reason—he must have a tile loose. Please don't ride him.' She pictured Ben spread-eagled under the crashing horse so vividly that she caught her breath.

'I'll watch every move,' said Ben. 'Why does the Guvnor keep the horses anyway? Nobody else rides them, and Flycatcher isn't much good. He's hardly ever sound.'

'They belong to Stephen, Mandy's brother. He and the Guvnor had a flaming row, so he cleared off to New Zealand last year. Charlie keeps the horses on because he's sure he'll be back; the only son, you see. Ted's a poor substitute but he does as he's told. Steve was too like his dad.'

Ben said, 'It's me and my grandmother over again, only she's not keeping Dancing Lady and hoping I'll go home.'

Lesley had her back turned to the man who'd annoyed her earlier. As she wondered aloud what was keeping Bob and Tina, Ben's face told her that he was coming towards them. A meaty hand dropped on her shoulder. 'Do you mind?' she said coldly, moving away.

The stranger shouldered in between her and Ben. 'What's it to be, my lovely?' he asked. 'Vodka?'

'Get lost,' said Lesley angrily. 'I'm not drinking with you.'

'That's what you think.' His face was flushed.

Ben intervened, making an effort to be polite. As always when he was fighting his temper, his accent was more noticeable than usual. 'Please go away,' he said. 'This lady is with me.'

The newcomer looked him up and down offensively. 'Sorry, Paddy,' he said. 'You could have fooled me.'

Ben knocked him down.

The man levered himself up slowly onto his hands and knees. Ben picked him up by his collar and the seat of his trousers, carried him to the door and tossed him outside. He landed at the feet of Bob and Tina, arriving late.

Proud and delighted, Lesley went to meet him as he walked back, wiping his hands down the sides of his cords. 'Thank you, Ben, I didn't know there were any knights in shining armour left.' A group of men raised a cheer, and there were shouts of 'Well done, lad!' and 'About time he was thrown out!' Bob and Tina were both talking to Ben at once.

Gloria, the landlady, leaned across the counter. 'You can have whatever you like on the house for that,' she said. 'He's been in every night since we opened and we're all dead sick of him.'

Ben favoured her with one of his devastating smiles. 'Anything?' he said.

Lesley watched her with a twinge of jealousy. 'Shall we order our meal then?' she said. 'It's getting late.'

At the mention of food, Ben lost interest in Gloria and turned his attention to the menu. When they'd finished eating, a singsong started round the piano and they joined the group.

When the pianist played 'Loch Lomond', Ben joined in. His voice was strong, unexpectedly deep. He broke off when he saw Lesley looking at him.

BOB AND TINA made excuses and left early.

'I mustn't miss the last bus,' said Ben regretfully.

'It's only half past ten,' Lesley said. 'My car's outside—don't worry about the bus. Can't I give you a lift?'

Ben glanced at her doubtfully. She could tell he was sizing up the position. He lived twenty-five miles in the opposite direction. 'Thanks,' he said.

Half an hour later, they went out together. Lesley unlocked the car, Ben beside her was silent. But as always, his stillness was that of a coiled spring. Suddenly he said, 'Haven't you a fellow somewhere? You must have.'

'No,' said Lesley carefully. 'No boyfriend.' They got into the car, and she slowly put the key in the ignition. 'I've got a husband somewhere. He went off with another woman two years ago.' Silence, almost visible, stretched between them.

Ben said at last, 'Do you still mind?' She knew he meant, 'Do you still love him?'

'No, I don't now. I did mind—it was hurtful and humiliating.'

She pulled out of the car park and into the traffic.

Ben said angrily, 'The bastard. You were well rid of him.'

'I know. I'm glad now that he's gone.' Lesley was surprised by the anger in Ben's voice. He constantly surprised her.

When she pulled up at the cottage, Ben took her hand in his, and she thought wildly, What am I getting myself into? This isn't a bit of fun—it's serious. I could love him. Her heart thumped violently—when had it last done that?

Ben said, 'Are you coming in?'

She answered, in a voice that sounded like someone else's, 'Do you want me to stay?' She looked down at his hand holding hers. It was hard to meet his eyes.

'I hope you will,' he said gently.

She got out of the car without a word.

In the cottage it was cold, and Ben made up the fire. It was easier to talk to him when his back was turned. Lesley wondered where her self-confidence had gone. 'Does Mark—my husband—make a difference to you?' she asked.

'He makes a difference—he might come back.' Ben slammed the door of the cooker.

'We weren't married in church, if that's any help.'

'Where I come from, plenty of people would say you hadn't been married at all.' Ben straightened up and turned to take her in his arms, and she knew a moment of joy unlike anything she'd ever experienced. She wanted desperately to say, 'I love you,' but Mark had cheapened the words for her. Believing that a girl who valued her independence should never commit herself verbally, she said, 'If you think I'm going to sleep with you, Ben, you can think again.'

'I know you are,' said Ben, 'and so do you.' He picked her up and carried her into the bedroom, and she was reminded of him carrying the drunk out of the Hart Royal.

'Why are you laughing?' he asked suspiciously.

'No reason. Just happiness.' You couldn't be coy with a man like Ben, she realised. It had to be yes or no.

'I love you, Ben,' she said. 'I'm yours.'

Four

Ben woke with a start. Then he thought he was still dreaming. He had never shared his bed with anyone. Lesley was cuddled against him, breathing quietly. He held her gently—you wake up from dreams.

It was still dark, but with the shimmering darkness that comes with snow. Ben felt stupefied with happiness. If only she would stay, he thought. But her work was miles away, and she was used to comforts that the cottage couldn't provide. Perhaps the occasional Saturday. . . She was waking up, turning to him, murmuring the loving things again. He couldn't take in all she was saying—surely she didn't mean it, it was too good to be true.

'I love you too,' he said, unhappily aware that he couldn't express himself in words as easily as she could. He felt he'd been given a dazzling gift and that words were inadequate. He hoped with all his heart that she wouldn't be disappointed in him, get sick of him. He shut his eyes, holding her close.

The alarm clock, a dreadful thing on legs with bells on top of it, jangled violently. Lesley shot upright.

'What on earth. . . It's Sunday—what's the time?'

'Six. I'd forgotten. I'm doing an early stint.'

As Lesley retreated under the faded quilt, Ben slid down beside her, saying, 'You meant all that, didn't you? Things you said to me?'

'Of course I did.' She looked up at him in surprise. 'The first time I saw you, I was sunk. Remember at the Turpin Arms? I didn't know anything about you, not even your name, but I felt we were lovers already.'

'I did too,' said Ben.

'I know. I thought it was just that you're wildly attractive and I was lonely, but I found out different.'

Ben grinned at her and then he sat up and reached for his shirt. 'I'm hungry, aren't you? There's rashers and eggs in the kitchen.'

He switched on the light, pulled on trousers and jersey and padded barefoot into the other room where he started to cook breakfast. He sang softly as he worked.

What luck, what amazing luck! A job, a house, and now a girl who behaved as if she loved him. He had never imagined such a thing.

Then he remembered the absent husband. What kind of man could have left Lesley for another woman? He must be stark staring mad. Ben filled the teapot, and scooped rashers, eggs, fried bread and tomatoes onto two plates. These he carried into the bedroom.

Lesley ate a piece of fried bread with her fingers. Ben ate all the rest. 'You'd get on well with the Guvnor,' she said. 'He eats cold beef and apple pie for breakfast. Sometimes, he eats leftover cold cabbage and chips.' She yawned.

'I have to go now,' Ben said when both plates were clean.

Lesley was falling asleep. He kissed her, tucked in the quilt round a bare shoulder, switched off the light and went out into the chilly morning.

Funny, he thought, as he trudged along the snowy path towards the lighted sheds, how his own home had dwindled in his mind. He got on well enough with all his family except his grandmother, but she was the only one he ever spared a thought for. He wondered how she and Lesley would get on.

EDWARD RYDER SAT, chain-smoking, in the dark old office where generations of Ryders before him had dealt with the legal problems of Kilmoon. Edward's father had retired after coping with the legal procedures that cut off Agatha Logan from her family. The disinheritance, the entail, the wills and codicils, the plots and counterplots had left John Ryder mentally exhausted.

At last, all was in order. Agatha Vere-Lanigan and the workman, Michael Logan, were married and settled at Cloninch Farm, while Agatha's father, Sir Arthur Vere-Lanigan, paid his lawyer's bill remarking, 'Well, Ryder, that's the end of the business. I shall not trouble you again.'

Ever since, the Vere-Lanigan file had lain unopened, gathering dust.

Agatha's father had been dead for forty years. His son had sold Castle Lanigan to pay death duties, and gone with one of his sisters to live in England. He had died almost penniless, his title dying with him. Edward didn't know if the sisters were alive or not.

There was a tap on the door, and Agatha Logan swept into the room wearing an almost ankle-length Burberry and a brown leather cloche hat which hid all of her white shingled hair.

'I cannot imagine how you work in all this dust and smoke,' she said. 'It's extremely bad for you. You do still work?'

Edward stood up. Talk of the devil! 'Good morning, Mrs Logan,' he said stiffly. 'Sit down. What can I do for you?'

Agatha's derisive glance took in the cobwebs, the papers impaled on spikes, the curling calendar for the previous year.

'I have a painting by Tissot. You go to Dublin, don't you?'

'Ah, Tissot,' said Edward, who knew nothing about him. 'What have you in mind?'

'I wish to sell the painting. When next you go to Dublin, you shall take it with you and have it valued for me. I may accompany you,' she added.

'Impossible,' said Edward hastily. 'That is, I couldn't accept the responsibility. You should write, inviting a valuer to your house. You could ask Barney Mangan's advice. He would know about specialists in art valuation. The picture is insured, I take it?' He was trying to see what it was that Mrs Logan had brought into the office with her. Something large in a case.

Agatha stood up. The grey eyes shrivelled Edward as he too rose to his feet. 'If I wished to ask Mangan to my house, I should have done so,' she said. 'And yes, the painting is insured, but inadequately. The premiums required are ridiculous. You have been most unhelpful. Good day.'

Giving Edward no chance to reply, she marched out of the office, closing the door with an angry snap. Edward saw that she was carrying a guitar.

AGATHA HAD NO FAITH in Barney Mangan, a cheerful villain with a fondness for greyhounds. It was he who encouraged her son-in-law Myles in his gambling.

Agatha had bought the guitar at one of Barney's auctions some years earlier. It was the only present she had ever given Benedict.

When he was a little boy, she used to allow him to play his favourite, 'Ol' Man River', on an old HMV gramophone. As he grew older and his voice broke, he began to sing at his work in a deep baritone, velvety soft. Michael had had the temerity to suggest that the boy might turn his singing to good account, but no grandson of hers would be a mountebank, singing for his supper. The operatic stage, possibly, nothing less. Michael said no more, and Ben, sensing friction, had kept quiet. Only the sheep and Dancing Lady heard him sing.

The shop at the corner of Kilmoon Square was called Sound and Fury. It pulsated with sound, and Agatha supplied the fury as she stormed in. 'Turn that thing off,' she commanded.

The teenage girl in charge obeyed, looking terrified. 'I want this instrument restrung immediately,' said Agatha, shouting in the sudden hush, and took the guitar out of its case. It was old and scratched. She would have it repaired, and write and tell Benedict. He might be persuaded to return.

Driving home in the van beside Myles, Agatha brooded silently. It would require more than a restrung guitar to induce Benedict to come home. If she could not turn the painting into money, Benedict would be lost. A temporary undershepherd, he had told Denis on the telephone, living in what sounded like the most primitive cabin, and riding two horses, one unsound and the other thought to be dangerous.

Even as Agatha reviewed these things in her mind, she knew that she was not facing up to her biggest worry. Benedict was possessed of the same sort of magnetism that had made her leave everything for Michael. And there was something less superficial than mere charm in his rare smile. Some scheming hussy would snare him and he would be lost for ever.

Back at Cloninch, Agatha climbed the stairs to her room, sat down at the little rosewood writing table and began to write.

BEN ARRIVED AT THE LIGHTED sheds where two yawning students, who'd been taken on to help with the lambing, were bedding up the lambing pens before going off duty. More than twenty ewes had chosen the small hours to produce.

Ben would be working on his own until late afternoon, but Eric, the head shepherd, was in the far yard if extra help was needed. Ted never came down to the sheds. He supervised the field work and attended four markets a week.

Ben moved quickly and quietly among the sheep. They barely roused as he passed, not bothering to get up, accepting him. A sharp bleat behind him made him return to the shed. Another ewe was starting to lamb. Ben walked quietly up to her. She got up, rolling her eyes at him, but made no attempt to run away. Quickly, he caught the heavy animal and flipped her down on her side.

Ben knelt by the sheep, gently examining her. As he did so, he softly sang an old spiritual—*'Oh, by and by . . . by and by . . . I'm gonna lay down this heavy load . . .'* He delivered the lamb as he did everything, tidily and without fuss. It raised its head almost at once, sneezing and flapping its ears. Ben tipped the ewe back onto her feet and hefted her belly gently with his hands. Another lamb there—maybe two. Number one was a little one. He decided to put her in a big pen, or she might lie on one lamb while she was having another. He worked happily, humming to himself. He wished he owned just a few sheep of his own.

A sudden shuffling and tension among the sheep made him turn round. The Guvnor was standing there. 'You should be farming,' he said abruptly.

'Thought I was,' said Ben, shaking out straw.

'I'm farming, you're earning wages,' said Charlie. 'You should be giving somebody else orders. Students do just what you say. So does the flaming dog. You should rent a bit o' land in Ireland.'

'Tired of me?'

'Nay, I don't want rid of you. Trying to advise you.'

'Where I come from,' said Ben, 'landlord's a dirty word. Anyway, I couldn't pay the rent.'

'Stay on then. But stop bloody well humming. Drive anybody mad. Now where are you off?'

'Going to get Roy and go round the big lambs in the back field,' said Ben.

He let Roy off his chain, and the two men walked together. Ben sent the dog round the sheep, brought them into the open and began to count them. The Guvnor suddenly called Roy to him. Roy glanced enquiringly at Ben. Ben, who had lost count and was annoyed, made no sign. Roy ignored Charlie, and continued to work.

Charlie grudgingly liked Ben, but this was more than he could stand. 'Keep the bloody useless dog then!' he roared. 'Rotten devil wants shooting.' He turned on his heel, and Ben could hear him coughing all the way back to the house.

As Ben continued his rounds, Roy at his heels, he wondered how long it would be before he fell out with his employer. A few days earlier, Charlie had told him off in front of the students. Ben had been eating his 'lowance, as the midmorning sandwiches and tea were called, and Charlie had been hunched, wheezing over the fire. Not a good time to tell him that Anagram's head-shaking was getting worse. Charlie told him he was mutton-fisted, and advised a rubber snaffle, adding, 'Our Stephen never had any bother.' Ben had shut up, but his anger had reduced everyone except Charlie to embarrassed silence.

It wouldn't do to get the sack, thought Ben. He might lose Lesley as well as his job. He must try to control his temper.

Ben called Roy to his side, and headed back towards the buildings. He began to hum again and then, softly, to sing.

LESLEY'S CAR WAS GONE. Ben found his cottage warm and tidy, with snowdrops in a mug on the windowsill. There was no note. Agatha's letter lay on the table where he had left it yesterday. Some sort of superstitious misgivings had prevented him from reading it before he set off for Leeds. Ben picked it up and opened it.

Dear Benedict,

I have come to a decision. Since you choose to live elsewhere, I will sell the painting which I had intended should be yours when I die. I must ask you to open a bank account and inform me when you have done so. A sum of money will be paid in shortly. This money is to ensure that you do not live in squalor. I shall be displeased if you squander it on unessentials.

Your loving Grandmother

Ben's first thought was: loving? That's a good one. Then it was borne in on him that she proposed to part with her most cherished possession on his account. He hadn't told Denis what a generous wage he was getting, it would have looked like boasting. But Agatha must be told, and quickly. Ben was a poor writer. He dialled, and spoke to Agatha herself.

'Where are you telephoning from, Benedict?'

'My own house,' replied Ben. He didn't add that the telephone had been installed so that the shepherd could be summoned at night. 'Don't sell the painting, Grandmother.'

But Agatha replied, 'My mind is made up.'

Ben knew that Agatha's mind, once made up, stayed made up, so he wasted no more words, merely asking her to bank the money in Ireland for her own use. Agatha snorted and hung up.

Ben set about preparing a meal for himself. The rest of the day was his own. He ate his meal without tasting it, sat by the fire and waited for Lesley.

After a while, he began to have doubts. This husband, he thought, I wonder if he's really gone for good. Ben no longer had a conscience about him, because of the way he had walked out. But would he walk back? And would Lesley decide to return to him? She had said he was a sales rep—how could he compete? When he reached this point in his thoughts, Lesley arrived.

'I've brought a suitcase,' she said. 'I want to stay with you, Ben.'

He held her gently. 'I didn't dare hope you would,' he said.

LESLEY SET ABOUT TURNING the bleak little house into a welcoming home. Every day, she brought things back from her flat—a lamp, cushions, a duvet, pots and pans. She was light-hearted, finding everything easy.

February came and went, it seemed to her, in a flash. Ben came home with a big bunch of primroses for her. The snow had gone, and she'd seen him from the window, picking the flowers. Mark had sometimes bought her flowers in the early days, but she couldn't imagine him picking them. She buried her face in their damp coolness. 'My favourite scent—they're beautiful.' She put them in a milk mug. 'I'll get us some more mugs—we've only got two.'

'I like it like that,' said Ben. He looked round the room fondly. 'This place is just grand.'

GEOFF NEEDN'T HAVE FEARED that Lesley's work would suffer. Her happiness infected almost all the people she visited. She met him at the Kosy Kitchen less often, but when she did she always had progress to report. One day as they sat at one of the pink-mottled tables, she told him she had seen a lawyer about a divorce. 'He didn't think there'd be any problem,' she said.

Geoff studied her. A great lass, Lesley, and wonderful at her job. She managed to achieve a relationship of mutual confidence and trust with almost all her charges, without allowing herself to be worn out by their emotional difficulties.

'I think your young man would make a good dog trainer,' he said. 'You can often tell. He's a silent bloke though, isn't he? Nothing to say for himself.'

Lesley said, 'I thought he was rather dour and touchy at first, always on his guard. But that's not the real Ben. He's had a hell of a life in Ireland under his grandmother's thumb, no freedom and expected to do all the work. Of course he was on the defensive. He's quite different now he's happy.'

Meg was lying under the table, wearing her harness. She was aware that the lass feeding with her person was now the property of the youth she'd seen in the kitchen at Middlegarth. The one who, with a snap of his fingers, had almost, but not quite, made her disobey Geoff. Her gaze travelled from Geoff's well-polished shoes to the pair of long nylon-covered legs at her other side. What had this woman done to deserve a person of her own? Nothing as like as not. And she, Meg, had to share Geoff with a kennel full of other dogs.

When Lesley left the café, Geoff watched her retreating back, hoping fervently that the new boyfriend wouldn't carry her off to Ireland. She had told Geoff that Ben liked everything about her except her job. She'd have to be pretty far gone to give it up to please him, thought Geoff.

AT NIGHT LESLEY ALLOWED herself to think ahead. Ben was content to live each day as it came. She had to face the fact that, after two months, she was

still more committed than he was. Plainly, he loved her, but not helplessly and totally as she loved him.

Obviously, Ben had hang-ups concerning her. She had thought they were religious, but apparently not. Her marriage didn't count, he had said. There was the thing about money. She had discovered that Ben thought she was loaded. She'd explained that she had some good clothes which didn't date, but that she made her own dresses. Still there was something bothering him. She felt dimly that it was to do with his grandmother, and dismissed the ridiculous thought. She fell asleep.

Lesley woke at first light with the feeling, now familiar, of floating calm. I never knew, she thought. I might have spent my whole life not knowing, but for Ben.

Ben had got up quietly and was dressing. She watched him pull his jersey over his head, taking pleasure in everything he did, however trivial.

When he left the cottage, she knelt up in bed and watched him going up the path. It was blowing hard—a blustery March morning, a Saturday. Ben never bowed his head against the wind, he walked straight into it.

Lesley planned to go to her flat for her sewing machine and some material. She meant to surprise Ben with new curtains. The existing ones were rubbed almost through at the edges, as rotten as cobwebs. She got up, contentedly planning ahead—but only a few days ahead. She hoped as usual that Ben wasn't going to ride Anagram.

As Ben walked up the lane to the farm, he could hardly contain his happiness. He hummed to himself as he walked, but when he saw that the Guvnor was there, he stopped.

Charlie had been looking over Anagram, but couldn't see anything wrong with the horse. How could there be anything wrong with a horse he and Stephen had bought?

'Nowt wrong with him that regular work won't cure.' Charlie's aggressive greeting didn't disturb Ben. The Guvnor didn't believe in wasting breath on 'good mornings'.

Ben studied the horse, standing, rugs off, in the yard. Anagram was dark brown, with the bumpy forehead which sometimes goes with a sulky temperament.

'You may be right,' he said, 'but he's changed since I first rode him. He'd have a go then if you didn't watch him. Now, he rides like an old pensioner up off the grass. And the rubber snaffle hasn't stopped him shaking his head.'

'Don't know what I pay a vet for,' said Charlie nastily. 'Take him out when you've finished in buildings.' He tramped off.

'Bloody old fool,' murmured Ben. 'He should try riding him himself.'

Ben saw Lesley's car go out shortly after he started work. He didn't expect her home to lunch, so he made do with a pile of beef sandwiches, half an apple pie and several mugs of tea in the farmhouse kitchen.

After his meal, Ben saddled Anagram, noting that the brown hadn't eaten his feed. This was a new development. Oh well, thought Ben, a quiet hack down by the Ings won't hurt him.

Riding on Middlegarth Farm was boring, because there were sheep everywhere, and miles of electric fencing. Ben preferred to ride down the back lane, past his cottage, to the Leeds road. On the other side of the road was a broad strip of rough grazing, known as Killington Ings. It was a good place for a canter.

He swung himself onto the horse's back. The brown gelding sidled uneasily. Ben shortened the reins, and kicked him forward. The response was lethargic. Anagram switched his tail and plodded off. He shook his head up, down and sideways. Ben thought, This is the last time I ride the devil. Blast the Guvnor.

He noticed Lesley's dark blue Fiat turning in off the Leeds road. He rode past the cottage onto the lane. It was wide enough for a horse to pass a car, with a shallow ditch on either side. As the car came towards him, Ben raised his hand to Lesley in greeting.

Then it happened. Anagram stopped dead and backed. He flung his head from side to side. He slid onto his hocks and, with a shrill scream, reared up until he was almost vertical. Ben's reactions were quick. He dropped the reins and threw his weight forward, wrapping both arms round Anagram's neck. For a long second it seemed as if the horse must topple over backwards, then he righted himself. As his forefeet touched the ground, he stretched out his neck, laid his ears flat back and bolted.

Lesley's car was only yards away; the brute was tearing straight at it. Ben saw Lesley dragging the wheel over, the car on the edge of the ditch. Anagram slammed against the side of it, banging Ben's leg painfully. The car crashed into the ditch.

The main road was scarcely a hundred yards away and on it heavy traffic roared to and fro. There was a gate onto the road with a cattle grid. It always stood open. Beside it was a narrower gateway without a grid. Between them was a three-foot-square pillar of yellow stone. As Anagram raced along the edge of the ditch, out of control, Ben knew he would be wise to throw himself off into the ditch. He dismissed the idea. He must keep trying to turn the horse until the last possible second. There would be an appalling pile-up if he galloped onto the road.

There wasn't time for weighing alternatives. Ben turned the bolting horse fractionally. Now he was heading for the stone pillar. He galloped straight into it. Ben had learned how to fall off a runaway horse. He knew how to tuck his head in to avoid a broken neck, how to roll up like a hedgehog to lessen the danger of internal injuries. But there was no time. Automatically, he kept his head down, shielding his face. The bang on the back of his skull knocked him out.

Five

Lesley's head ached vilely, and the plaster on her forehead was pulling the stitches underneath. She made a move to touch it, and saw that her right forearm was encased in an elastic bandage. Memory came back unevenly with consciousness. A charging horse, the car heeling over, Ben's face, mouth open, as his leg struck the car. The car had rocked perilously, and she had unfastened her seat belt with some idea of jumping clear, just as it nose-dived into the ditch. She had been thrown violently forward—she recalled the pain as her head had struck the windscreen. Semiconscious, she had heard a dreadful thudding crash, then there had been silence. She had tried to shout Ben's name, but no sound came. Then a man's voice had said clearly, 'He's broken his neck.'

Her right knee was bandaged too, it was hurting like hell. Fuzzy-brained, she attempted to focus on her surroundings. She was in a large light ward, full of people. The light hurt her eyes and she shut them again. There was a movement beside her, someone was sitting there, reading a book. 'Ben?' She rolled her head sideways.

'No, sorry, it's Mandy. Thank heaven you've come round. I'll call a nurse.' Mandy laid aside the book she was reading. 'Ben's OK,' she added.

Lesley's head swam as she struggled to sit up. 'What do you mean, Ben's OK?' Her voice rose. 'He's broken his neck—I heard someone say so. Is he dead? He is, isn't he?'

'Take it easy.' Mandy put her arm round Lesley's shoulders. 'Ben's all right. He's been sitting with you for ages. I took over while he went to get something to eat; he'll soon be back. Do lie down and let me get a nurse.'

Lesley dropped back wearily against the pillows. 'I don't need a nurse. Thank God he's all right. Oh Mandy, I was certain he'd broken his neck.'

'The horse broke its neck. By, you should have heard Father! Poor brute, it had a brain tumour. Father knows he made a mistake, so he's cursing everybody into heaps.'

Lesley felt her forehead cautiously. 'I seem to be in a mess,' she said. 'Have I got a broken leg?'

'Your kneecap was out of place,' said Mandy. 'It's been put back. You've ever so many stitches in your head—eighteen I think—and a sprained wrist.' She spoke with involuntary relish; Mandy thrived on disaster. 'Thank goodness it wasn't any worse,' she said. 'Ben prevented the horse from galloping onto the main road. It ran slap into the gatepost, and Ben clonked his head. He must have a skull like iron.' She went on to describe the damage to Lesley's car and to speculate about insurance.

Lesley had stopped listening. Ben was coming.

BEN HAD BEEN KNOCKED out for only a minute or two. He had picked himself up, alarmed by the blood on his clothes and hands, but it came from the horse. There was nothing to be done for Anagram. Ben had run back to the car to get Lesley out. The back of his head throbbed. His jeans were torn at the knee. He had driven to Leeds with Charlie, following the ambulance with Lesley inside. Ben had gone reluctantly for an X-ray; there was no fracture. Then he had been taken to the ward where Lesley lay, paper-white and with a dressing covering her forehead. He had stayed with her until his rumbling stomach had reminded him that he was hungry. Chased away by Mandy, he had gone to find a canteen.

When he came back, Mandy withdrew with exaggerated tact. Lesley's shaky smile somehow touched Ben's heart more than anything she could have said or done. He felt he'd been taking her for granted—he never would again. He bent to kiss her, and saw that there were tears in her eyes. She asked Ben faintly if he was sure he was all right.

'I'm fine—but you . . . I couldn't do a thing; the horse went crazy.'

She clutched his hand. 'Never mind, love, you're all in one piece, that's all that matters,' she said.

The doctor arrived to examine Lesley. Ben would have to wait until the following afternoon to see her again, he was told.

Ben missed Lesley more than he would have imagined possible that night.

He slept badly, worrying about the cut on her head. Supposing it were to affect her sight? It didn't bear thinking about. He got up early, and reported for work, insisting that he didn't need a holiday. But the Guvnor's orders were clear. Ben hung about, his head aching mildly, waiting for the afternoon.

He packed Lesley's suitcase, thinking how pretty, how delightfully silky and scented her clothes were. He took his time, enjoying the task. As he shut the case, he allowed himself for the first time to think seriously about marriage.

When he arrived at the hospital, carrying the suitcase, a box of chocolates and a white azalea in a pot, Lesley had been moved to a private room. The Guvnor had been giving orders concerning her as well.

Ben hugged her cautiously; even so she cried out, 'Mind my knee! I'll have to go to the flat when I get out of here, I'm afraid.'

Ben's face darkened. 'Ah no, I'll mind you at the cottage,' he said. 'The Guvnor wants me to take time off.'

'It isn't easy. I'm to be discharged tomorrow, but I'll have to come back for physiotherapy for my knee. I won't be able to drive for a bit—anyway, the car's out of action. Move over, Ben, I'm getting up.'

Lesley got out of bed and tested her knee. 'Goodness, I'm shaky. I'm supposed to walk about, but I can't seem to manage the crutch.' She draped her arm round his neck.

After two turns round the ward, she was glad to climb back into bed.

WHEN HE REACHED HOME that night, Ben remembered his telephone call to Agatha, and how she had hung up on him. The accident had driven it out of his mind.

Ben found a Biro in a jar on the living-room windowsill, and a small notebook of Lesley's. He filled seven of the small pages with his painstaking handwriting.

> *Denis got the wrong idea about my job. I have good pay and a nice house. Please don't sell the* Young Girl, *I don't need the money.*
>
> *I wasn't going to say anything yet, but I might get married. It wouldn't be for a long time yet. I like the picture so much, and I think my girlfriend would like it too. So I would sooner have the picture than the cash when it comes to me which I hope won't be for a long time. . .*

Ben read over what he had written. He could imagine Agatha snorting, and hurling the letter into the fire. Let her snort. He had done his best. He finished, 'hoping this finds you in the best of health,' and signed it 'Benedict'.

He posted it first thing in the morning.

ON BANK HOLIDAYS when the library was closed, Agatha usually had her hair cut. This was done by Miss Bond who lived with her sister in the little house by the Protestant church. They were both over seventy and Miss

Miriam made all her clothes, copying the styles out of *Weldon's Home Journal* dated 1933. Miss Clare could cut and wave hair in the styles of her youth—the Eton crop, the marcel wave.

On Easter Monday, Agatha seated herself in her accustomed place where she could see out onto the street. Miss Clare combed and snipped and clipped. Then she offered Agatha a mirror. Agatha favoured her reflection with the same arctic glare which so unnerved the Misses Bond. Without comment, she returned the mirror and sat tight-lipped while the sisters encased her hair in a net, and removed the towel from her shoulders.

Two men had appeared in Agatha's line of vision, her son-in-law Myles, and the auctioneer Barney Mangan. They stopped in a doorway and conferred together. Myles glanced furtively this way and that. Then he took out his wallet and counted money into Barney's palm. In all probability, it was to be expended at the dog track.

Agatha rose slowly to her feet. Still in silence, she handed £1 to Miss Clare. In the same instant, Myles noticed the familiar bicycle outside, and both he and Barney looked at it in horror. Agatha hurried to the door and threw it open. 'Myles,' she said, not loudly, but with withering scorn. 'A word with you, if your business will allow it.'

Myles crossed the road, his expression a mixture of defiance, sulkiness and fear. Barney hurried away, tucking the money into his pocket. She watched Myles coming towards her, and noticed that his jacket was frayed at the cuffs. Her perception seemed heightened, as if she had just had a glass of champagne. She stared at Myles, taking in his round shoulders, greying hair and shambling gait. She wondered what to say to him. Perhaps nothing—what was there to say?

A long shudder ran through Agatha. She felt suddenly piercingly cold, with the chill of the grave. For a moment she tottered, almost falling, trying in vain to speak. Myles reached her in two strides and put an arm round her.

Agatha thought, I am dying, and I have not yet sold the picture. Benedict. She fainted.

DR BLAKE HAD ATTENDED Agatha's daughter for years, and Muriel's four children at one time or another. He would never forget the time when he had been called out to attend Ben's premature birth. He hadn't believed that such a small baby could live without benefit of hospital equipment, but Agatha had refused to allow the child to be moved. Dr Blake had come back the next day, expecting to find a dead or dying infant, and had heard Ben's angry yells before he was out of his car. Never had he heard a child bawl quite as loudly as Ben when he was hungry.

He had not had occasion to attend the old lady. She was never ill, so he was surprised when old Miss Bond burst into his surgery.

'Come quickly, Doctor; Mrs Logan's had a stroke.'

Dr Blake found Agatha lying on Miss Miriam's bed, with the son-in-law sitting beside her.

Agatha was lying perfectly flat and straight like a crusader's effigy on a tomb. She was quivering with rage. 'There is nothing whatever the matter with me,' she said, speaking clearly but with evident difficulty. 'Go home, Myles,' she added, as if speaking to a dog.

Dr Blake sat down beside her. Myles obeyed his mother-in-law with alacrity, making for the door with obvious relief.

'Wait,' said the doctor. 'You'll have to drive Mrs Logan home.'

'Won't she be going to hospital?'

'I doubt it.' Dr Blake knew his Agatha.

'I refuse to go to hospital. I prefer to die a natural death.'

Agatha suffered examination without protest, but her bleak hostility was worse than the outburst Dr Blake had expected.

'A mild attack,' he said at last. 'You've been fortunate. But you must have a thorough checkup, and you'll have to take it easy.'

'No.'

'Be reasonable, Mrs Logan. I know you must be over eighty, and you must be prepared for your own good to slow up a little. For a start, you'll have to give up cycling.'

'Am I dying, or am I not?'

'No, you—'

Agatha sat up. 'In that case,' she said, 'I will dispense with your no doubt well-intentioned advice.'

Dr Blake stood up. 'If you don't take my advice,' he said, 'you must be prepared to take the consequences.'

'I always expect to take the consequences of my actions,' said Agatha, her voice vibrant with loathing. 'Kindly leave.'

Dr Blake found Myles outside, loading Agatha's bicycle into the van. 'Can you stop her cycling?' he asked. 'A very mild stroke, but a second would probably be much more serious, perhaps even fatal.'

'I'll try,' said Myles doubtfully, and on the way home, he mentioned it.

Agatha didn't bother to reply. Her mind was with Benedict. If she were to die, Myles and Barney might well dispose of the painting unwisely. She determined to write to Sotheby's, and ask them to send a valuer to Cloninch immediately.

THE NEXT TIME Ben visited Lesley, she had been sent home. He hadn't been to the flat before, and was impressed by its size and comfort. Lesley looked thin and tired, and it was the first time Ben had seen the scar on her forehead. She put up her hand to it. 'I'm going to change my hairstyle,' she said. 'Hide it with a fringe.'

'Don't,' said Ben. 'I like your hair the way you wear it, and the mark will soon fade.'

Ben found she was disinclined to talk. She curled up on the sofa, resting her head against his chest. 'Tell me about yourself, Ben love.'

'I've told you all about me. There isn't much to tell.'

'There must be. I want to know all the little things—it's amazing how little I know. I want to know about when you were a little boy, everything that's ever happened to you.'

'I'm not a great one for talking about myself,' said Ben. 'Why don't we wait until we're back at home for my life story—we have all our lives before us, haven't we?'

There was a pause. Lesley turned her head sharply to look at him. 'What?' she said. 'All our lives? We've got until you finish your job here, isn't that more like it?'

She had turned even paler than before. Ben wondered if she was going to faint. He said comfortingly, 'Don't look so tragic, I'll stay as long as you want me. And you say you can get a divorce, no problem; I thought we might get married. I haven't much money, but I can work, and there's nothing for me at home. You do want to marry me, don't you?'

'Yes,' said Lesley, 'I do.'

THE FORTNIGHT THAT LESLEY spent in her flat, attending a clinic three days a week, was a busy one for Ben. The Guvnor had changed his mind about a holiday. Ben had found himself back at work two days after his fall. He went to see Lesley every evening by bus, but he had to catch the last bus home. They didn't have many hours together. Sometimes they stayed in the flat. Sometimes they went to a small park, sat on a bench and talked.

Lesley gradually found out a lot about Ben's life. He had left Kilmoon Primary School at thirteen years old. He was needed to help with the harvest in the summer holidays, and somehow he had never gone back to school. It had never bothered him until he grew up and realised that it was idle for him to dream of being a vet, even if his grandmother could have been induced to pay for his training. He had resigned himself to unpaid labour at home, and helping Terry school his horses.

Lesley too had a farming background. Her father, a crop farmer from the other side of Middlegarth, was killed by an overturning tractor, only months after her mother's death from leukaemia. By then, Lesley was already earning, and living in lodgings in Leeds. Shortly afterwards, while the shock of her parents' death was still fresh, she had married Mark.

A FEW DAYS AFTER BEN went back to work, the Guvnor went out to the fields with him. As they were leaving the yard, Roy came out of his kennel. He greeted Ben with guarded enthusiasm and the Guvnor with civil indifference. Charlie ignored the dog. 'Lambs look well,' he said. 'Contented. They do you credit, lad. Still have a chat with them, do you?'

'I do,' said Ben, glancing up for signs of mockery, but there were none. He walked ahead, humming a tune, but checked himself.

Charlie said, 'Hum away lad, aye, sing if you want.'

Ben knew that this was as close as Charlie was likely to come to an apology, so he said, 'Thanks, Guvnor.' He thought there was something else on Charlie's mind, so he waited in silence. He hadn't long to wait.

'I've nowt against that lass of yours,' said Charlie. 'I meant telling you she'd have to go, but I've had another think. You can stay in cottage as long as you're working here, and she can stay and look after you.'

'That's good of you,' Ben said, 'but I have to look after her. I'm not hurt, she is.'

'Nursemaid each other then,' said Charlie. 'It's matterless to me, so long as sheep don't suffer. Sheep come first—never forget that.' He turned on his heel and went away.

Ben watched him go. He rubbed his right eye with the back of his hand. Black dots danced in front of him, and a little shower of blue sparks. I must have looked straight at the sun, thought Ben.

LESLEY DIDN'T EXPECT to go back to work for at least a week, so they decided it would be a good opportunity for Ben to see more of Yorkshire. They borrowed Tina's car and went out into the countryside, seeing as many places as possible on the long spring evenings, and returning in time for Ben's bus home.

Sometimes they drove between enormous unfenced fields, where rippling green barley stretched unbroken for miles; sometimes they went up to the moors. They went to places with quaint names—Agglethorpe, Kettlewell. They went to Scarborough and watched the giant waves thundering against the sea wall, then along the coast to Robin Hood's Bay, where pieces of the town occasionally slid into the sea.

Ben's eye still wasn't right, but he could almost forget the annoyance of the mysterious spots as he took in everything he saw.

The last place they went to was Aysgarth Falls. Ben felt a surge of excitement when he heard the roar of the rapids. Lesley had brought her camera, and they took pictures of each other against the background of wild water. They were immensely contented and at ease.

Friday that week Ben had his day off. Lesley would be at the hospital, having her last session with the physiotherapist. So he caught a bus and went to York. He walked along the city walls, gazing curiously down on the back gardens below, then he found his way to The Shambles, and joined the throng of tourists. He stopped outside a small dark shop with antique jewellery in the window. An aquamarine ring had caught his eye. Ben thought of Lesley. The colour was exactly right, cool and clear in an uncluttered setting. He went in and bought it. The price startled him, but fortunately he had enough money with him. The jeweller put the ring in a blue leather box lined with cream velvet, and Ben put it in the pocket of his anorak. He treated himself to two pork pies and a pint of beer, and returned to Middlegarth with ten pence in his pocket.

ON SATURDAY, BEN COLLECTED Lesley's car from the garage, and drove into Leeds to fetch her home. He wasn't a bad driver, but he found the heavy traffic alarming because he wasn't altogether familiar with the way. Also, his eye was worse. Black spots like smuts drifted diagonally across his field of vision.

Lesley was standing in her doorway. Her face lit up when she saw him. He pulled up and jumped out of the car shouting, 'We're going home!'

Ben fingered the leather box in his pocket. He meant to wait for exactly the right moment to give her the ring. 'Think you can drive?' he asked.

'Probably, but I'd rather you drove me home. I've been looking forward to that.'

'Shall we have something to eat first?' Ben said.

They left the car and walked together to the Kosy Kitchen, where they dawdled over an early lunch.

'Is there something wrong with your eye?' asked Lesley. 'You keep rubbing it.'

'I'm seeing spots. It's no harm, just a nuisance.'

'Shouldn't you see the doctor about it? You got a terrific bang on the head after all. It might be delayed concussion.'

'Ah, it's nothing,' said Ben impatiently. He wasn't best pleased a few minutes later when the dog trainer, Geoff, came in with Meg, the collie bitch he'd brought to Middlegarth. Geoff gave Lesley a run-down on the progress of her cases and Ben took no part in the conversation. Instead, he made friends with the dog, Meg. She was the picture of health, unlike her sire Roy, whose coat never shone.

Geoff sensed Ben's antagonism. Searching for a point of contact, he said, 'I hear the old dog has left the Guvnor for you, Ben!'

Ben looked up, smiling reluctantly. 'I don't think the Guvnor minds, unless maybe the hurt to his vanity. Do Border collies make good guides then? I'd've thought they'd be too independent.'

'They often are, and some of them are too possessive or too nervous. We have plenty of Border crosses though.'

'I don't like to think of training the working instinct out of a dog,' remarked Ben. 'I think it's terrible.'

'Don't you think that taking charge of a disabled person is more important than picking up a pheasant or bringing the cows home?'

'I suppose it is,' said Ben sulkily. He stopped stroking Meg, who thrust her nose under his hand, begging him to continue. 'There's one thing I've wondered,' he said. 'How do you transfer a dog you've trained from yourself to somebody who isn't a trainer?'

Geoff said, 'It can be traumatic for the dog, but it generally works out. I never call myself a trainer—I'm an instructor. We breed a quality into our dogs, we call it generosity. When a dog works through generosity rather than self-preservation, he'll do anything the instructor tells him to, no matter how fond of him he is. You'd make a good instructor yourself. There's something about you that dogs recognise.'

Ben shrugged and returned to stroking Meg's smooth head.

As they walked back to the car, Lesley said, 'I know you've a thing about my work, Ben, but you aren't planning to ask me to give it up, are you?'

'I'm not that narrow-minded,' said Ben, 'nor that selfish. But you mustn't mind if I don't want to talk about it. It gives me the creeps. That's the way I am. I'm sorry.'

At the cottage, Ben insisted on making a fuss of Lesley, making coffee for her, rebandaging her knee. She laughed at him, but it was plain that she enjoyed it. Later on, he asked her why there was never any music at the Turpin Arms. 'I like a bit of music,' he said.

'Sing me an Irish song, then.'

'Ah, no,' said Ben. 'I might if I had a guitar, or if I was half jarred. Some other time.'

IN THE MORNING A LETTER arrived from Ben's father. Agatha had had a slight stroke. Apparently it was nothing serious.

Ben's eye was worse. The sparks and flashes had gone, but the drifting black spots were bigger. It was no longer possible to ignore them. He had managed to forget his fears during the hours of darkness with Lesley in his arms, but when he got up he was afraid.

It was Sunday, Ben's turn for the morning foddering. He loaded meal onto the trailer, and set off to the field with the tractor.

Experimentally, Ben put his hand over his good eye. It was like driving through a slanting rain of black, coin-sized blobs. With his heart beating violently, he pulled up the tractor at the troughs, and jumped down. As his feet touched the ground, a jet-black curtain descended across his field of vision. The spots stopped drifting. Petrified, he stood stock-still. Again, he put his hand over his left eye.

With his right eye he could see nothing at all.

Six

Agatha was feeling unwell. Possibly she would have to give up bicycling after all. She snorted.

Alone in the sitting room, she read Benedict's letter for perhaps the twentieth time. Well, she would respect his wishes. She had written to Sotheby's, saying that she had changed her mind about the valuer. She who never changed her mind!

It was just as she had thought. The woman, whoever she was, had wasted no time. Agatha did not intend to keep the painting for a scheming hussy to enjoy; she intended to make it clear in her will that the picture was for Benedict himself to dispose of as he pleased. Pointless now to request him to return. His guitar was in her bedroom; she had wasted money on having it restrung for him.

The restlessness which had affected her since Benedict left was increasing

daily. She was sure that he was in need of her help. He had written and told her that all was well with him, but she was unable to believe it. Something was wrong; terribly wrong.

Muriel came into the room. Agatha stood up, a head taller than Muriel, her long putty-coloured linen dress making her seem taller still. 'Now that the rest of my family are dead, I see no reason why I should not visit my sister,' she said aggressively.

'Your sister?'

'My sister Flora. I would not have considered it while my sister Constance was alive—she took my father's part against me. I saw her death in the *Irish Times* recently. Flora lives in Yorkshire, I believe. I have not spoken to her since nineteen thirty-three.'

'In Yorkshire?'

'Muriel, must you repeat every word I say? Have you lost your wits?'

'No, Mother, but—' Muriel dared not ask whether her mother intended to travel alone, so she said brightly, 'Yorkshire! Why, you can call on Ben, can't you?'

'I could if I wished to do so,' snapped Agatha.

WHILE BEN WAS DOING his Sunday work among the sheep, Lesley made a stew and put it on the hotplate, then she washed the clothes Ben had been wearing the day before.

She changed into a clean dress which Ben hadn't seen before and was waiting in the kitchen when he came in. He would be free for the rest of the day and she wondered how they would spend it.

Ben charged up the path and into the cottage, barely greeting her. She glimpsed his savage expression and guessed he'd had a row with the Guvnor. She decided to wait and let him tell her about it in his own good time.

Lesley dished up the lunch. Ben seemed to have recovered his temper. In fact he was extra affectionate, extra cheerful, positively chatty.

He gave a sprightly account of the morning, and suggested going to the cinema that evening. Lesley poured tea and pushed the milk jug towards him, but he ignored it. A moment later, he knocked the jug over with the back of his hand. 'Sorry,' he said, getting up to fetch a dishcloth, 'I didn't notice it.'

'Ben,' said Lesley, 'are you still seeing spots?'

'No,' said Ben. 'Devil a spot. Which movie would you like to go to? You choose.' He pushed away his plate.

As Ben stood up and walked about restlessly, Lesley sat looking at the table, her own appetite gone. Ben put his hands on her shoulders, and kissed the top of her head. 'I don't know what I'd do without you,' he said quietly.

She turned in the chair, looking up at his troubled face. 'You won't have to do without me,' she said.

'I wish I could be sure of it,' said Ben. He turned away and sat down by the fire.

Lesley had loved Ben almost at first sight. But since his fall her feelings had deepened and strengthened; she could no more stop loving him than fly. Mark had had the power to make her suffer and he had used it. Ben, she knew, had the power to break her heart.

Lesley wondered whether Ben had heard something more from Ireland and was concealing it from her. He had been visibly upset when he heard of Agatha's illness. Lesley had never quarrelled with him, but their occasional arguments were always, in one way or another, concerned with his grandmother. She told herself she was having ridiculous fancies, but had to admit she was glad that Agatha was old, ill and elsewhere.

Thank goodness, she thought, Ben's eye was better. She'd been really worried about that. She suggested a drive and Ben agreed. He took the wheel and drove carefully, but faster than usual, turning up the radio. Pop music filled the car.

'Do you like that?' shouted Lesley.

'No!' shouted Ben.

She selected a tape. 'What about this?' she said, holding it out.

'Don't show me,' said Ben. 'Put it on. I haven't an eye to spare.' He was laughing as she slotted the tape into place. It was an old Johnny Cash, and for the first time, Lesley heard Ben sing out freely. *'No, no, no, it's not me, Babe,'* sang Ben. *'It's not me you're looking for, Babe.'* He sounded very cheerful about it.

He drove up to the moors above Rosedale, a desolate place. When they got out of the car, the wind almost knocked them over. Ben's strange mood of elation continued. He climbed alone onto a wall made of flat slabs of grey stone, and looked down the green dale to the village below. A single pine tree grew beside the wall. He leaned into the wind, resting one hand on the scaly bark. Lesley wished he'd come back to the car; it was cold up there. But he lingered, silhouetted against the milky sky, his hair whipped about by the wind, a wild look on his face. At last he jumped down and they went back to the car, his arm round her shoulders.

Ben drove all afternoon. Instead of going to a movie, he took her to a big roadhouse on the main road. There was a group, and dancing, so they danced. It was a rock number, and Ben threw himself about, guying the antics of the other dancers. Lesley contented herself with twitching her hips, and occasionally twirling round with her weight on her good leg. She twirled, and there was nobody to catch her hand—she'd lost Ben. He emerged from among the dancers. 'Where did you get to?'

'Nowhere,' said Lesley. 'You lost me.'

'I'll take care not to lose you again,' said Ben. The music changed to a slow number, and she linked her hands behind his neck while he held her closely. 'This is how I like to dance,' said Ben. 'Close as butter on bread.' To the tune of the dance, he sang, '*You are the butter, darling, I am the bread.*'

Lesley chuckled. 'You should be up there with the group,' she said. 'You're good.'

They had supper, but Ben still wasn't hungry. He ate a small piece of pie and drank whisky instead of beer. Lesley was relieved when he allowed her to drive home.

BEN AND LESLEY shared a companionable breakfast as usual. Both were tired.

'I suppose I'd better be going, or the Guvnor will play hell,' Ben said at last.

'He will. I'll be off myself in ten minutes.'

Still Ben hung about. He took Lesley's hand in his, and turned the rings round and round. 'Such a lot of rings—why do you wear so many?'

'I don't know. I seem to collect them.'

Ben thought about the aquamarine in its leather box. He longed to give it to her there and then, but fear held him back. He knew he could get by with one eye, but supposing the trouble, whatever it was, spread to the other?

'Dearest Ben, I *must* go. Oh . . .' She emerged breathlessly from a violent embrace. 'We're not parting for ever, bless you. See you later.' She jumped into the car and drove away.

AS THE DAY WORE ON, Ben's mood had improved. He set off for the north meadow to take up an electric fence and close the field for hay. He took the tractor and trailer, with Roy sitting at his feet in the cab.

As he worked, rolling up the wire and pulling up the stakes, Roy followed. Generally, he stayed in the tractor cab unless he was needed. Today, he was at Ben's heels, always within a yard of him.

'That's that,' said Ben aloud, hoisting the last of the wire onto the trailer. 'Up you go, old dog.' Roy obeyed, jumping into the cab ahead of Ben. But instead of lying down, he put a paw on Ben's knee, looking up searchingly into his face. Ben looked down at the wary light brown eyes, and read concern in them. 'You know, don't you?' he said. 'It's no good trying to hide anything from you.' Roy retreated to the corner of the cab, and Ben drove back to the yard.

He decided that he would tell Lesley about his eye—but not yet.

FOR MORE THAN A FORTNIGHT, Ben got on with his work cheerfully, and Lesley began to wonder whether she'd been stupid to worry about him. He was sweet-tempered and loving, going out of his way to please her.

Lesley wondered why she wasn't happier. She and Ben seemed to have everything going for them, but there was something preventing perfect harmony.

One day, she came home from work and told Ben, 'I met Charlotte in Leeds. You know—the girl who went off with Mark.'

'I hope she doesn't want to give him back.'

Lesley laughed. 'She can't do that; he's ditched her too. He's shacked up with some rich widow now. I can get a divorce any time. Mark's hoping to marry her.'

Ben was down on his knees, fixing a board onto the bottom of the door. He looked up sideways at her. 'That's good,' he said. 'Except for the widow.'

'Ben—we can get married. I—I thought you'd be glad.'

He stood up and put his arms round her, holding her tightly. 'I think of you as my wife already,' he said. 'You *are* my wife. Is there a big rush about making it legal?' He kissed her mouth and the scar on her forehead.

Lesley drew back, looking into his eyes. 'I know, love, I feel I'm your wife too. But don't you want a proper wedding? You suggested it, not me.'

Ben's gaze narrowed suddenly as he looked at her. 'Orange blossom, champagne and six bridesmaids,' he said in a hard voice she'd never heard before.

'Don't be so selfish,' said Lesley, firing up. 'I don't know what's the matter with you.'

'No, you don't, do you,' said Ben slowly. 'I'm going to have to tell you.'

Seven

Sweat stood on Ben's forehead. His heart knocked against his ribs. He stood frozen in horror. Lesley was wearing a light blue cotton dress. He saw the blue dress through drifting black spots, like a snow shower seen on a negative. Emotions crowded in on him.

He wanted to get married as soon as Lesley's divorce came through, but only if his sight was in no danger. He sensed her need for a secure foundation, for a life free of Mark, free of the flat with its memories of Mark, free to have children.

Ben could have pinpointed the exact moment when he began to love Lesley. It was when she had given him a brave, lopsided grin in hospital after the accident. Ben, who thought he was in love already, had experienced the real thing for the first time. And he had been worried in case the blow to her head might affect her sight.

'I'm going blind,' he said.

Lesley's face seemed to shrink behind the rain of black snowflakes.

She took a deep breath and asked, 'Is it those spots again?'

He nodded. 'This is worse than the other. Much quicker. The right one hardly bothered me at first.' His voice was expressionless. He might have been discussing a sick sheep.

'You mean this is your *left* eye? What about the other?'

'The right one's gone,' he said. 'You asked me if I was seeing spots the day we drove all that way and went dancing. I wasn't seeing anything.'

'Darling, don't panic. There's nearly always something that can be done nowadays.' He sensed her own panic and thought dully, This is how she's been trained to talk.

'Your retina must be detaching. Oh God, Ben, why didn't you tell me? Why didn't you see a doctor?' There was anguish in her voice, but she controlled it. 'Listen. You mustn't make any sudden movement. Go slowly to the bed and lie down on your back while I ring the doctor. Don't rub your eye; keep as still as you possibly can. Please, darling.'

Ben obeyed. He sat on the side of the bed and pulled off his shoes. He could hear Lesley speaking urgently on the telephone. As the second shoe came off with a slight jerk, he became aware of a thin sliver of jet black at the topmost edge of his left eye. He lay down on his back and shut his eyes.

Lesley came back and knelt on the floor beside him. He found her hand—it was icy and trembling.

'I phoned the hospital where I used to work,' she said. 'They've got one of the best men in Yorkshire there—Dr Stroud. They're sending an ambulance. They repair retinas all the time; I'm sure they can mend it. Is there any pain?'

'No,' said Ben. 'It doesn't hurt, it never has. But the shutter's coming down. Now, while I'm speaking to you.'

She gripped his hands and went on talking, trying to reassure both of them. The curtain descended, cutting off the last of his perception of light. He struggled to fight off panic, unable to speak. And instead of Lesley's horrified face he saw the blind tramp at Kilmoon fair, the old man's daughter pointing to his eyes with one dusty hand, while the other clutched his ragged sleeve. The girl's practised beggar's whine, 'A copper for the blind man and I'll say a prayer for you,' was clearer in his ears than Lesley's voice.

THE HOURS THAT FOLLOWED were pure nightmare. He had feared to be left in the dark, but the blackness had gone. Instead, he knew the colourless gloom experienced behind closed lids in daylight. Sometimes the no-colour nothingness was prickled with tiny sparks.

Ben wasn't cheered by the reassurances coming from all sides. He couldn't believe that anything so final could be cured. His future stretched ahead, an endless grey vista, perhaps fifty years or more. He'd have to leave the cottage, go home to his family, an object of pity, a financial burden. The idea of continuing to live with Lesley he dismissed out of hand. There was no way he would shackle the woman he loved.

He tried to move his head, but something was holding it, some kind of frame. He had been lifted on and off a stretcher, driven somewhere, wheeled somewhere. He heard Lesley say, 'I have to leave you now, love. You'll be all right, you're in good hands. I'll come back later.'

He was given the first injection in all his twenty-seven years. It hurt less than he expected. He began to feel calm and uncaring. After a time, he slept.

LESLEY WENT BACK to the cottage. She packed Ben's belongings, to take them to her flat. The cottage went with the job; she couldn't see the hardheaded Guvnor allowing her to keep it warm for Ben.

Next day, she talked to Dr Stroud.

'But my dear girl,' said the doctor, 'if you're living with this man, why on earth didn't you persuade him to get help? His right eye is likely to be beyond repair; we've a good chance of saving the other one. But there was no need to lose either. Didn't you realise the danger of delay?'

'I didn't know anything about it,' said Lesley. 'He didn't tell me. Scared, I think.'

Ben was to have an operation in three days' time. Meanwhile, tests were being carried out on him.

She wondered about the family in Ireland. Probably his mother had a right to know, but she didn't mean to summon his relatives over unless Ben wanted them to come. She asked him, and he said, 'I think you should let my grandmother know.'

'But Ben, won't it be a shock, at her age?'

'It'll be a bigger one if this op doesn't work and she finds out when I go home with a white stick. She'd die of shock and come and haunt you.' The words were light, but he gripped Lesley's fingers painfully as he spoke.

She said, 'Oh, all right then. I'll ring her when I go home.'

A flustered female voice answered the telephone. Ben's mother, Lesley supposed. It seemed dreadful not to tell her. She asked for Mrs Logan.

There was a long delay. At last, a chilly voice said, 'Yes?'

'Lesley Grant speaking. Are you Ben's grandmother?'

'Benedict Glyn is my grandson, yes. Who are you?'

'I'm his fiancée,' said Lesley, wondering if she still was. 'I'm afraid Ben's had an accident.'

'I suppose he has fallen off a horse again.' The voice would have cut glass, thought Lesley.

Lesley cautiously tried to explain matters, softening the details in deference to Agatha's age.

'Am I to understand that Benedict has gone blind?' There was no quaver in the uncompromising tones, but there was unmistakable shock.

Lesley said that the operation should restore the sight of one eye, and might be partially successful on the other.

'Balderdash,' said Agatha. 'Either one can see, or one can not.' She hung up.

That night the old woman's razor-edged voice haunted Lesley's dreams.

EVERYTHING AT CLONINCH was in Agatha's name. All cheques were made payable to her and cashed by her. She drew whatever cash she considered necessary for the household, and paid Denis a regular allowance.

Myles and Denis had sold a pen of calves at the market a few days before Benedict's young woman telephoned. The cheque had arrived that morning. Agatha had no trouble in persuading Myles to drive her to Kilmoon—she never did when there was a cheque to pay in.

As usual, he waited for her outside the bank. She carried an old pigskin handbag, cracked and stiff with age, initialled in silver.

It was ten minutes before Agatha reappeared. She looked distracted, unlike her usual self, but once in the van she began to speak with confident authority.

'Myles, I shall be travelling to Yorkshire. Muriel may have told you that I wish to visit my sister.'

'But Mother, the doctor—'

Agatha talked on and over the interruption. 'I have asked Edward Ryder to drive me to the airport. He has agreed. I have decided to sell my picture immediately. You had better take it to Morgan's Sale Rooms in Dame Street. I have made arrangements there for the day after tomorrow. You will be expected.'

'But Mother, the silage—'

Agatha turned her head and looked him up and down. 'The silage,' she said, 'can go to the devil.'

Agatha had no faith at all in Benedict's recovery. The young woman would not have telephoned had she really been confident of a successful outcome. She had sounded tense and strained. Possibly she was fond of

Benedict. Perhaps she imagined herself to be in love with him. She would soon change her mind if the operation did not succeed. Agatha was determined that, if Benedict could not see the *Young Girl in a Garden,* neither should this woman.

AGATHA CLIMBED THE STAIRS SLOWLY, using the banister rail. She was pleased to find that Michael was asleep. The room was frowsty; the red-haired girl more than ever out of place.

She fetched a dusty Gladstone bag from the wardrobe, and placed two changes of underwear in it, night attire, washing things and clean blouses. Michael snored on.

She checked the cash she had drawn from the bank. Seven hundred pounds. She had heard that it was illegal to take any quantity of money out of the country. Agatha smiled grimly. Once the notes were pinned inside her camisole, it would take an intrepid customs man to remove them.

She sat down by the window and picked up her library book: *The Human Eye: an Everyday Miracle.*

EDWARD RYDER HAD BEEN prepared to find the old woman in her Burberry and her cloche hat, and had steeled himself for the journey and for the looks he would get at the airport—please God he wouldn't meet any other clients. He was not prepared for the Gladstone bag or the guitar. He got out of the car and opened the door for Agatha, thinking that she looked ill; pinched about the mouth. He put the bag and the guitar in its case into the boot.

Edward started the car, remarking, 'It's a long time, fifty-four years, but I'm sure your sister is looking forward to your visit.'

'Unlikely,' said Agatha. 'She knows nothing about it.'

'Oh.' Edward gritted his teeth hard, and didn't speak until he had deposited her at the check-in desk. Then he said, 'Have a pleasant journey, Mrs Logan.'

'Journeys are never pleasant,' she said. 'I have successfully avoided them for half a century.' Then she added, 'It was good of you to bring me here. Thank you.'

More astonished than by anything that had gone before, Edward said, 'I'll meet you when you come back if you like.'

Agatha was watching the revolving belt bearing her Gladstone bag and Benedict's guitar out of sight. 'Possibly I shall not return,' she said.

AGATHA WAS TIRED. Early that morning, she had telephoned Benedict's cottage. A Mrs Amanda Wilkes had supplied the name of the Waterloo Street Hospital. Agatha had said that she was flying to Leeds that day, and rung off.

She was not prepared to find Benedict's young woman waiting at the airport. Not a painted Jezebel, but a tall, pale girl who might have been attractive but for an unsightly scar on her forehead.

As they crawled through heavy traffic to the hospital, the girl explained that she had been living with Benedict almost since his arrival. Agatha greeted this admission in stony silence. The girl flushed and said something about a divorce. Agatha said that her grandson had not informed her that he was living in sin with a married woman.

Benedict's mistress made a visible effort to control her temper. Her name, she claimed, was Peabody, although she preferred Grant. She asked Agatha to call her Lesley. Was she deliberately trying to be confusing? She said that Benedict had a great respect and admiration for his grandmother; that she had hoped that Agatha would be broad-minded.

Agatha explained, patiently she thought, that she had been broad-minded as a girl, but had outgrown it.

At the hospital, Agatha was obliged to wait, while Lesley disappeared. She sat down, choosing an upright chair with its back to the wall, and accepted a cup of tea—it would not do to fall asleep.

After a while, she noticed that Lesley had returned. Perhaps she was not a bad lot after all. She thought Agatha was asleep, and the despair on her face was plain to see.

Agatha felt a long icy tremor pass through her. She sat, bolt upright, her eyes closed, her hands tightly clasped in her lap. The tremor passed. Will-power, she thought, conquers most things.

THE GUVNOR WAS OF THE OPINION that a cheque, if it was big enough, was a cure for most human ills. As soon as he heard about Ben's condition he went straight to Leeds, taking his cheque-book.

Ben was already in a private room, so there wasn't much that Charlie could do. Dr Stroud told him patiently that nothing further could be done for Ben for several days. He had been sedated to keep him quiet. Would Mr Thorpe please keep his voice down?

The next day and the next, the story was the same. Charlie found he couldn't bulldoze his way into Ben's room.

At the farm, Ted imported a towheaded student called Gideon. Lesley had packed up and left the cottage, but when Ted suggested that Gideon might move into it, Charlie cursed him for several minutes.

Early the following week, the Guvnor could stand it no longer. He got out the Range Rover and drove to Leeds. His plan was to find the eye doctor and ask him why the flaming hell he didn't operate on Ben and get it over with.

The woman at the desk called out, 'Yes?' as he was about to march straight through the reception area. Charlie stopped unwillingly and told her his business. He was directed to the waiting room.

The room was large, with chairs set round the walls. There was nobody there except an old woman who looked so ill and so odd that Charlie hesitated, taking her to be a mental patient.

'Good evening,' he said politely, wondering if the old boiler was violent.

'And who might you be?' enquired Agatha.

Eight

Lesley knew something about surgery for retinal detachment. She was aware that, once the retina was separated from its blood supply, it would die for lack of oxygen in a short time. She had little hope for Ben's right eye.

Ben had done just about everything he could to endanger his sight. He had caught sheep, jumped off tractors. He had refused to take care because he would not accept what had happened. She knew too that a reattached retina took as long to become secure as a set limb. There was no chance that, after the operation, Ben's sight would be immediately restored. He would be kept immobilised for days, perhaps for weeks.

It was a pretty thought—the sufferer, his eyes unbandaged, looking up ecstatically at his beloved—but it was a fairy tale. First came the waiting.

She wondered how she would endure it.

For hours that Monday he had been out of his ward having tests. Lesley had been hanging about at the hospital waiting for news ever since collecting Ben's awesome grandmother. She wondered what was to be done with her.

Lesley had had a bad day. After a restless night, she'd gone to the hospital, hoping for a glimpse of Ben before she went to work. She was told that he had gone for further tests and that the operation was planned for the following morning. 'Ben's granny is coming to see him, isn't that nice?' said the nurse. 'She's flying over from Ireland today.'

Fortunately, Lesley could take the day off. Ben's granny. How cosy it sounded. She didn't intend to offer Mrs Logan a bed for the night. She was still smarting after their exchange on the way from the airport.

As she went towards the waiting room, she heard the Guvnor's familiar voice. Who on earth could he be talking to? She opened the waiting-room door in time to hear Agatha's reply.

'I am fully in agreement with you, Mr Thorpe. A most refreshing viewpoint in these decadent days.'

Charlie and Agatha were sitting together. Charlie was smiling broadly, and Agatha's austere features had relaxed into a near smile. When she saw Lesley's face, she made a quick movement to rise, asking, 'How is he?' But she swayed as she stood.

Charlie and Lesley caught hold of her arms. 'I'm afraid I haven't any more news,' said Lesley.

'A good night's sleep, Mrs Logan, and you'll be like a new-catched 'un,' said Charlie encouragingly.

'I doubt it,' said Agatha. 'I have not yet engaged any accommodation.'

'Take you back to farm,' said Charlie. 'Less than an hour in Range Rover. Plenty of room.'

'I should prefer to be closer to Benedict,' said Agatha. 'I have travelled a long way at great personal inconvenience to be near him. I have brought his guitar with me.'

Lesley thought, She cares. Almost as much as I do, in her own dried-up way. She said, 'I'll put you up if you like, Mrs Logan. I'm only ten minutes from here. Do come.'

Agatha appeared to consider. 'Very well, I will,' she said.

AT CLONINCH, EVERYBODY was blaming everybody else because Agatha had gone without leaving a forwarding address. The family, knowing nothing about Ben's state, presumed she was with her sister, but nobody knew where she lived except that it was in Yorkshire. They presumed she would come back when it suited her. Probably soon; they were certain to quarrel. In the meantime, there was a shortage of ready cash.

But even in her absence, Agatha's word was law. Myles took the *Young Girl in a Garden* down from the bedroom wall, wrapped it in a piece of sacking and put it in the back of the van. He lived only an hour's drive from Dublin, but his visits there were mostly to the greyhound track. He had never once driven into the city centre. The idea made him nervous.

Myles followed the airport signs, knowing they would lead him to the river where he could get his bearings. He recognised the great grey shape of Houston Station with gratitude, and the one-way signs with alarm. He would have to cross the Liffey here, and he had somehow got himself onto the wrong side of the road. He began to nudge his way to the right.

Safely on the Quays, he drove slowly, hugging the kerb, searching for a handkerchief to mop his forehead. And to reach Dame Street, he would have to cross the river again!

After a while, he noticed the friendly frontage of a pub on his left. The Crock of Gold. He hadn't meant to stop, but he felt that he needed a drink as never before. He drove round the block, and found a vacant site, filled with cars. He slid into a space and got out. He wished the steering would lock. Never mind, it would only take a minute to swallow a brandy. He locked the doors.

The pub was allegedly closed for the afternoon, but Myles knocked and a young woman let him in. The lounge bar was in semidarkness.

'Myles, you old devil! Where were you since? I didn't see you these ages.' The voice came from a corner where a hugely fat man in a pinstriped suit was relaxing in front of an army of empty glasses. 'What'll you have?'

'Dan! Am I glad to see you. This one's on me.'

'No, let me.' Dan heaved himself up and lurched to the counter. 'What's wrong with you, Myles? Run over somebody? You're shaking.'

'I'm all right,' said Myles. 'All I need is a drink. I mustn't stay long. I have a picture to deliver. Belongs to the mother-in-law.'

Dan knew all about mothers-in-law. He knew a number of jokes about them, and he told them all. 'Same again,' he shouted.

'I hope the old van's all right,' said Myles, going to the window. 'I can't see it from here.'

Dan laughed. 'Old van? Safe as houses. Don't you worry, take your time.'

Myles took his time.

When he went to the site, the van had gone.

The Garda was unimpressed. 'Renault 4 van,' he said, writing. 'Year of registration nineteen seventy-six. Colour chocolate. Dented rear. Rear lights broken. What kind of a picture? Oil painting, gilt frame. Woman sitting on the ground holding a bunch of flowers. Right. Leave it with us. No problem.'

Myles badly needed another whisky. He had yet to face Morgan Fine Arts. Two whiskies later, Myles phoned them.

'You left a Tissot in an old van on a derelict site?' cried Pascal Morgan, head of the firm. 'You're a bright one, aren't you? Get the crime squad onto it at once, if you haven't already.'

'The crime squad?' said Myles, astonished. 'Even if the picture was worth a grand, they'd hardly bother.'

Pascal Morgan seemed to be about to have a fit. 'Have you any notion of the value of that picture?' he asked.

'I think my mother-in-law had it insured for eight hundred pounds,' said Myles. 'She'll slaughter me.'

'So she should,' said Pascal Morgan. 'The last Tissot sold at public auction fetched a quarter of a million.'

BEN KNEW THAT HE WAS more or less permanently sedated. Night melted into day, into night. The day after his operation, there was no difference. He was still bandaged, still immobilised.

'Lesley, are you there?'

'Yes, love, I'm here.'

'Have you heard anything about the operation? They haven't told me.'

'No, nothing,' said Lesley. 'I don't suppose they know themselves yet. Ben, your grandmother's here. She stayed at my place last night; she'd like to talk to you.'

He felt the touch of her fingers on his shoulder, heard the tap of her shoes, then nothing. He would never see again, he thought. Never see Lesley again. She wouldn't want him, would she? Oh, she'd pretend she did, perhaps even convince both of them for a time. Then one day he would sense her true feelings, know that he was pitied. He would rather die than accept that.

Slow footsteps: a voice. 'Well, Benedict, this is a sad state of affairs.'

Ben said, 'Lesley told me you were here—I never dreamed you'd come. Is Mother with you?'

'No. I did not inform your mother. If you can be cured, she will be spared needless worry; if not, she will come.'

Ben heard her seat herself, give a small sigh. He heard the rasp of her stockings as she crossed her legs, the sound of her breathing.

'I'm not going home,' he said suddenly.

'I did not suppose you would. I was incensed when I discovered that you had taken a mistress, but she seems to be a capable young woman, and is obviously besotted. You would be well advised to remain with her.'

'I couldn't do that. I want a wife, not a nurse.'

Agatha ignored this. 'I have always disliked horses,' she said, 'and have warned you repeatedly that you would injure yourself.'

Ben felt the quiver of a smile. If he had expected any softening in Agatha, he would be disappointed. 'How long do you mean to stay?' he asked her.

'I shall remain here until you recover your sight,' said Agatha.

A flip-flop of soft-soled shoes and a woman's voice saying, 'You must go now, Mrs Logan. Time for Ben's injection.' There was a brief, bitter argument. Ben heard Agatha's feet as she left the room, protesting all the way.

He was used to injections now. He said, 'You'll make an addict of me.' Then came the sleep.

DR STROUD WAS A SLIGHT, olive-skinned man with clever brown eyes. He was sitting beside Ben's bed. Ben's bandages were off, his head no longer immobilised. The doctor shone a bright light into Ben's right eye. Ben gave no response. Dr Stroud directed the light at the other eye.

'There's a light somewhere,' said Ben.

'A bright one?'

'No. A kind of paleness—hardly anything.'

'Any difference now?'

'It's gone . . . it's back again.'

'Can you see anything else? Anything at all?'

'No.'

Dr Stroud sat back and considered Ben. A fine chap, he thought. He knew Ben was a farm labourer, but would have guessed it anyway from his short, square hands and calloused palms. Ben seemed an unlikely mate for Lesley, whom Dr Stroud remembered as a bright, rather sensitive girl. It was to be hoped that Ben would understand that he was not the only one needing help.

He said, 'The news isn't too good, Ben. There's nothing to be done about your right eye, and the left—well, we reattached the retina, but it detached again almost at once. There's only a slight chance that further surgery will help—do you understand?'

'I don't understand anything,' said Ben flatly. 'I don't even know exactly what a retina is.'

Dr Stroud sat back, putting the ends of his fingers together. 'The seat of vision is at the back of your brain,' he said. 'Think of your brain as a computer which won't work unless it's fed with information. The retina gathers information in the form of a picture. It photographs the information through the lens in your eye, and the optic nerve passes it back to the brain. An eye without a retina is like a camera in which the film has slipped. But don't forget that's only a fraction of what your brain does. You taste, feel, smell, hear—all your senses pass messages back to your brain in their various ways.'

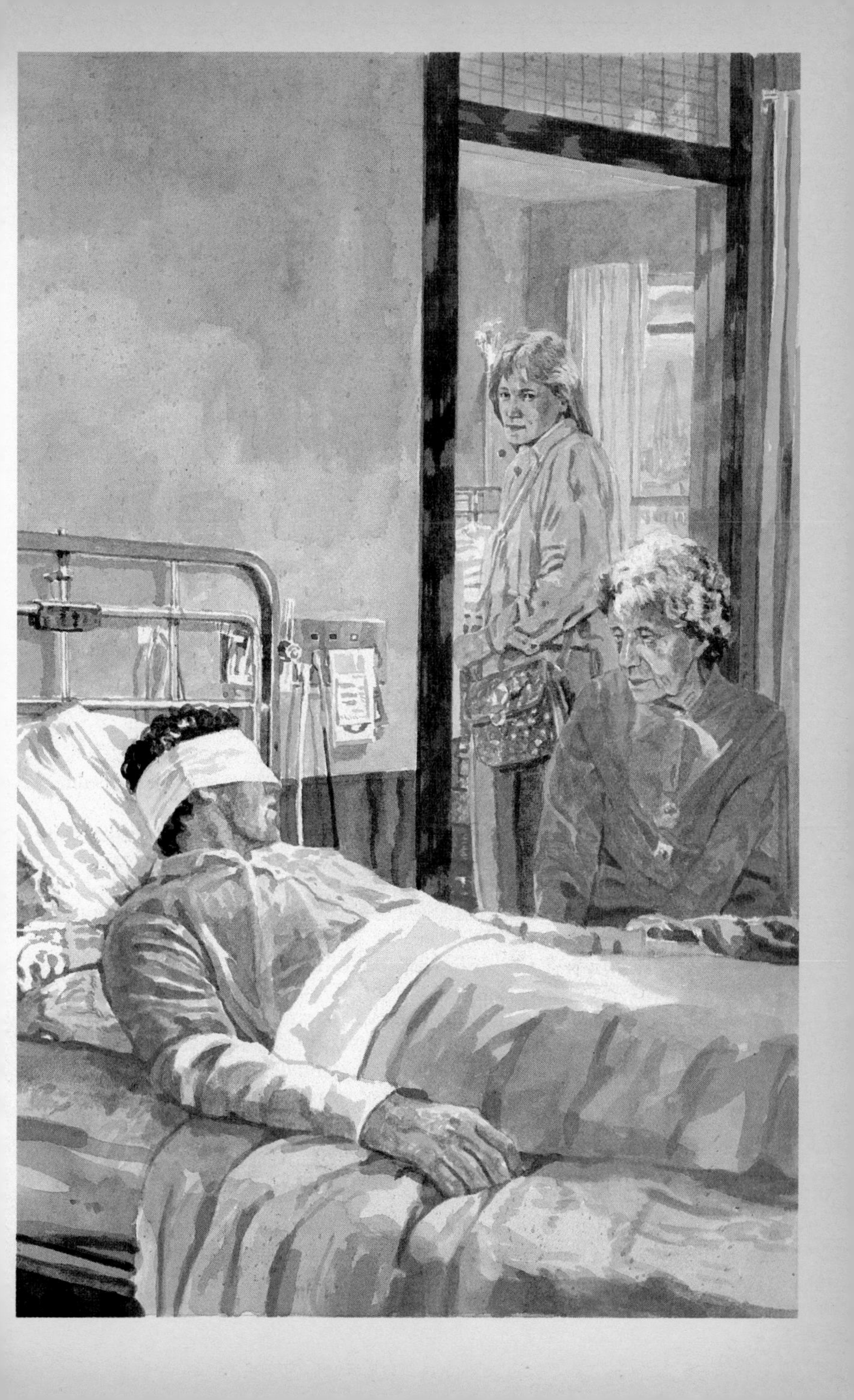

'Aren't you going to have another crack at loading the camera? Lesley said you reattached retinas all the time.'

Dr Stroud wished he knew Ben better. The true verdict might turn natural incredulity to depression and withdrawal—perhaps even suicide. The doctor knew that there was virtually no hope for Ben's sight, but he softened the verdict.

'We may be able to do something further,' he said. 'It depends. As you are, there's no disfigurement. If we persist in trying to patch you up, there may be.'

Ben's hands clenched. 'No disfigurement? You're sure of that?'

'Certain. Let's hope that in the future some means will be devised for grafting a new retina. Medicine advances all the time, and there is almost always some hope, however slight, for the unsighted.' Dr Stroud felt that he had done his best to let Ben down lightly. He got up and left, saying 'Goodbye' from the door.

Ben sat up in bed, staring in the direction the voice had come from. 'You liar!' he yelled. 'I'm blind! I'm blind, man. Blind!'

TO THE SURPRISE OF BOTH, Lesley and Agatha had formed a sort of alliance. Friendship was definitely not the word for it. Agatha had settled herself in, had unpacked, and the next day had summoned a taxi to take her to the hospital. There she had been allowed only a few minutes with Ben, after which she had returned to the flat.

On the second day, she went through the same routine. When Lesley got back from work, she found Agatha reading a paper by the window. They exchanged looks which told that there was no further news of Ben.

Lesley prepared a meal, and they ate sparingly. After a while she said, 'I wonder where Hazel's got to.'

'I was obliged to complain about her table manners,' said Agatha. 'She was extremely uncivil to me, and has gone to seek accommodation elsewhere.'

'She owes me a month's rent,' said Lesley. 'I agree she's a pain, but this flat's expensive and I need the money.'

Agatha stood up. 'I appear to have been thoughtless,' she said, and went into her bedroom.

Lesley sighed, wishing that she and Ben's grandmother could share their grief. She supposed they did in a way, but there wasn't much comfort in it. Ben had told her about Agatha's elopement and disinheritance. He had said that those events had unhinged her. What would the trauma of blindness do to Ben? She shuddered. For in Agatha's bitterness she could see traces of Ben's passion; in her spite, there were echoes of Ben's aggression.

Agatha came out of the bedroom and laid five Irish ten-pound notes on the table.

'You may consider this a month's rent in advance,' she said. 'Take it.'

The last words were an order. Lesley did as she was told.

THAT EVENING, AGATHA watched Lesley leaving the flat with real regret. She no longer considered her as Benedict's concubine . . . a pretty word, she thought, it sounds like a climbing plant. What was the matter with her today? Her thoughts were tangled, and she was not always able to find the word she needed.

She had talked to Lesley today—*really* talked for the first time. Lesley insisted that there was hope for Ben's sight. Agatha knew somehow that there was none.

Lesley had gone to spend the evening with a blind girl named Henrietta. She had left a pie in the oven for Agatha's supper, and an evening paper on the table.

As Agatha picked up the paper, she shivered, although the flat was warm. The cold tremors were getting more frequent. Difficult to ignore. She had put Dr Blake's words out of her mind, but they returned now. 'A mild attack . . . another could be far more serious, even fatal.'

Agatha went to Lesley's desk and found writing paper, envelopes and a pen. She began to write:

> *To whom it may concern: If I should die, I may as well be buried or burned here whichever is the cheaper. I want no religious service.*
>
> *My grandson, Benedict Glyn, who by the terms of my will is to receive my unencumbered property, may also have my wedding ring. He may give it to Mrs Lesley Peabody if they marry. The ring will save him unnecessary expense.*
>
> *My daughter Muriel may have my clothes. To my husband Michael I consider I have already given more than enough.*
>
> *Somebody should inform my sister, Miss Flora Vere-Lanigan, of my death. She lives in Harrogate; I have forgotten the address.*

Agatha read the letter through, wrote *To be opened in the event of my death* on the envelope, and propped it up against an ornament. She opened the paper and sat down at the desk again.

As she sat in the wing chair, Agatha found that her thoughts were straying back to her childhood. She must be getting feeble. Her thoughts were not allowed to stray.

She and her sisters had been virtual prisoners at Castle Lanigan, while their brother had gone to an English public school. Constance had married a master of hounds from Yorkshire; Flora had seemed content to spend all her time in the garden. But Agatha, apart from her music, had no outlet for her stormy personality. Her sisters read and talked about romance. Agatha dreamed of a grand passion—the world well lost for love.

She was twenty-seven when, at harvest time, her eye fell on an amazingly handsome young man pitching sheaves up onto the ricks. As the load grew lower, Michael Logan had to throw the sheaves higher. Agatha watched fascinated.

The cart empty, Michael jumped down and saw Miss Agatha watching him. He smiled at her—a brilliant smile which lit his sunburned face. Poor devil, from that moment his fate was sealed.

Agatha had been thrilled by the runaway match, careless of her father's rage. Michael's main concern had been to run as fast and as far as possible.

Agatha had ignored her pregnancy until it became impossible to ignore any longer. Then she had fixed her hopes on a son—a little boy with Michael's looks and her own iron determination.

She and Michael had moved to Cloninch with its farmhouse and its hundred fertile acres. Her little boy would start his career as a farmer. But he would not be satisfied to plod along. No, he would excel in everything he did, and be all that she had hoped Michael would be. He would fulfil her dreams.

When Muriel had been born, something in Agatha snapped. She would have no more children, she would run the farm (and Michael) herself, she would ignore the passage of time. She would exist independently, and never allow anything or anyone to touch her emotions again.

She had succeeded. A picture of Benedict came to her mind. She amended her thoughts—she had almost succeeded.

She sat back, feeling very tired, and began to glance through the paper.

IT WAS ALMOST MIDNIGHT when Lesley let herself into the flat. An acrid smell met her at the door. She ran to the stove. Black smoke poured out. Agatha had forgotten the pie, and it was burned to a cinder. Then she saw that Agatha was sitting at the writing desk, in the wing chair. Couldn't she smell the smoke?

Lesley thought Agatha must have fallen asleep. She picked up the newspaper from the floor, pausing as a headline caught her eye: ART TREASURE DUMPED IN FIELD. VALUED AT £250,000.

'Wake up, Mrs Logan,' she said, gently shaking her shoulder.

Agatha's head was propped in the angle of the wing back. On her face was an expression of fury. She was dead.

Nine

Lesley had gone to bed when the ambulance had taken Agatha away, but it was as if the old woman was still there in the flat. Even when Agatha had been laid on the bed with her eyes closed, Lesley had been conscious of her cold scrutiny.

When the doctor had examined Agatha's body, he had found nearly £700 fastened to her underwear with safety pins.

Lesley had found and read the letter. The doctor told her to take care of the money for funeral expenses. He eased the wedding ring off the knotted finger. 'You'd better take care of this too,' he said. 'Had she any relations besides Ben?'

Lesley had said she'd notify them, and tell Ben in the morning. She lay with aching throat and dry, burning eyes, wondering how she would break the news to Ben.

IN THE MORNING, Lesley arranged for a week's holiday. She looked up Miss Flora Vere-Lanigan in a Harrogate directory, and left a message.

She put the cash and the wedding ring in the bank for safekeeping, returned to the flat and packed Agatha's clothes in the Gladstone bag. Her feelings of regret surprised her. She sat on the floor on her heels with a cameo brooch in her hands, wondering what to do with it.

You may as well keep it. It is of little value.

Lesley started, and dropped the brooch. She picked it up, pinned it to the neck of a blouse and returned both to the bag. She mustn't start imagining things.

At the hospital, Ben was absent from his room. A house doctor told her that he'd turned violent, put his fist through a pane of glass and was having it stitched. She sat down and put her head in her hands.

Lesley looked up and saw Ben walking towards her, a nurse leading him by the arm. He walked with his head high. His right hand and wrist were bandaged. On his face was an expression of rage.

The nurse guided Ben to a chair.

'Got it into his head there's something wrong with his granny,' the nurse whispered to Lesley.

'What? Who's there? Lesley?'

Lesley pushed past the nurse. 'I'm here, Ben.' She announced herself as she'd been trained to do, staying still so that Ben would be spared talking to the place where he thought she was, and being answered from somewhere else.

'Tell me,' said Ben. 'For God's sake tell me. Is she ill? Is she dead?'

'She's dead, Ben. She had a stroke last night at my place. The doctor thought she must have died at once—she was still sitting in her chair. Oh, I'm sorry, love. I was—not fond of her exactly, but we got on. She loved you, Ben.'

'She didn't love anybody,' said Ben in a low voice, 'but I can't imagine life without her.'

THE WHOLE FAMILY came from Ireland for the funeral. They respected Agatha's wishes in so far as they didn't take her body back to Ireland, but they insisted on a conventional funeral service. Not cremation.

They were waiting for the hearse to arrive, the family all together like a flock of cornered sheep. They'd been waiting for years for Agatha to die. Now that she had, they didn't know where to turn or what to do without her tyrannical rule.

Ben was still not allowed out, to Lesley's relief.

Lesley, neat in a charcoal suit and her most restrained earrings, stood despondently, waiting. She hated to see Agatha's wishes ignored. She had nearly quarrelled with Mandy, whose exclamations, 'Isn't it awful? Oh, the poor thing and all alone too,' had almost driven her to screaming point. As she waited, she thought about Mandy, and how friendship could become a habit. She had turned to the other girl when her father had died, and Mandy's kindness had helped her. But even then, there'd been that vicarious thrill, that feeding on misfortune.

A taxi drew up, and a large, fat old woman scrambled out of it. She shut her coat in the door, freed it and dropped her handbag. Lesley bent to help pick it up.

'Are you Miss Vere-Lanigan?' she asked.

In a welter of half-finished sentences, the old woman said she was. She stood up and smiled. Wildly untidy, she seemed to have thrown on the first garments that came to hand: a flowered cotton skirt, a blue cardigan over a pink jumper over a red blouse. She had covered it all up with a shapeless black coat. A perfect shell-pink rose was pinned to the coat. Her broad face was pink under layers of powder. Lipstick of a cruel shade of cyclamen was slashed across her mouth.

'I'm so sorry about your sister,' said Lesley. 'She was staying with me when she died.'

Flora burst into tears. She flung herself at Lesley, who was obliged to submit to being kissed on both cheeks.

Lesley glanced at Ben's family. But they had shied away from Flora like frightened horses. She was relieved when the hearse arrived.

At the graveside, Lesley had a light-headed feeling of unreality. The funeral seemed too bogus to be sad.

A vulgar charade. Hypocrites.

For a moment, the scornful voice sounded clearer than the priest's.

Then they all went to see Ben. Myles, Muriel, Denis, Brian, Mike and Flora. Sheila had stayed at Cloninch to look after old Michael and little Sarah.

Mandy insisted on going along too, but the Guvnor refused. Instead, he took Lesley to a café and ordered a pot of strong tea and beef sandwiches.

'I been thinking, lass,' he said. 'Ben isn't likely to get his sight back, is he?'

'No,' said Lesley. 'I don't believe he will.' She swallowed a mouthful of tea, and looked at her plate.

'What about cottage then? D'you reckon he could make out living there? He can have it for nowt—aye, and you can stop with him, same as before.'

Lesley looked up. 'It's a wonderful offer,' she said. 'I think it would be perfect for Ben. As for me, we'll have to wait and see what he wants.'

'Oh aye? He wants you, doesn't he? Fair soft about you. You want to get shut of that Peabody, then you can get wed.'

'I wish it was that simple. Thank you anyway. Ben should stay in the place he knows; he's had a shock to recover from, a double shock. His reactions are extreme. He alternates between aggression and dull acceptance.'

'You've had too much schooling,' said Charlie. 'Lad's gone blind; he wants his own home and the woman he's used to. Isn't that what you mean?'

Lesley gave him a shaky grin. 'Something like that,' she said.

CHARLIE WENT TO THE HOSPITAL when he judged that Ben's family would have left it. He was wrong.

Ben was standing with his back to the wall and an expression of bewilderment on his face. His parents, his brothers, Flora and Mandy were all talking at once, suggesting cups of tea, tranquillisers, a drink, a rest. They crowded round him, speaking loudly as if he were deaf.

Charlie heard Muriel say, 'You mustn't worry any more, Ben. We'll look after you properly, won't we, Myles? You mustn't be unhappy any more.'

Charlie stormed into the group. 'What's got into you?' he shouted. 'Why shouldn't he be miserable? Be a pretty rum lad if he weren't, wouldn't he? He's gone blind—of course he's unhappy! Let him get over it his own way. You make him worse.'

There was a stunned silence. Ben looked gratefully in the direction of the shouting.

Mandy nervously put her hand on Charlie's arm. 'Don't worry, Father,' she said. 'We understand Ben, really we do.'

Charlie shook her off. He turned to the others who were standing gaping. 'You don't understand nowt about him. I've had my say; if you've owt to say to me, say it.'

Nobody had anything to say to him. One by one, they sidled past him and out of the room.

'Have they all gone?' asked Ben.

'Aye, they've gone. I scattered 'em,' said Charlie. 'How do you come to have such a set of clodpolls for a family? The old 'un was worth the lot of them, she was that.' He saw that Ben was smiling.

'Mother didn't mean any harm,' said Ben defensively. Then he felt himself grinning. 'Thanks,' he said. 'Why were they bullying me like that, I wonder?'

'Blood's thicker nor water,' pronounced Charlie. 'We'll be glad to see you back in cottage.'

'I'll be glad to get out of here,' said Ben. 'I don't see that I can come back to your cottage, though. It goes with the job.'

'You'll have to if you aren't off back to Ireland. Or would you sooner stop in Leeds at Lesley's place?'

'I can't do that.'

'You aren't going to ditch poor lass, are you?'

'I wouldn't put it like that,' said Ben. 'There's a chance I might get back the sight of one eye. When I do—if I do, we'll get married.'

He sensed Charlie's angry incredulity. 'You're a fool if you wait,' he said. 'Her husband will be here for divorce. Don't wait too long.' He said goodbye, clapping Ben on the shoulder. The door banged.

'Guvnor?' said Ben. There was no answer. Hands extended, he made for the door. The bed was in his path—it skated away. Some piece of furniture grated on the vinyl floor. He grabbed the iron frame of the bed and stood listening. Then he threw himself down on the bed, which suddenly seemed to be the most desirable place in the world. He dragged at the covers, kicking his way between the tidy sheets. He was back in the limbo of the first days.

As sleep evaded him, Ben found that there was nothing he could bear to think about, so he tried to make his mind a blank. He could remember what people looked like, but when he tried to examine them in his mind's eye, their likenesses slid away. Their voices were clear enough.

I trust you will play your guitar, Benedict. I have brought it at considerable inconvenience.

'I SHALL NEVER FORGIVE MYSELF—never,' said Flora.

I shall go mad, thought Lesley. She had heard Charlie routing the Job's comforters from Ben's room. She had seen the family leave. When Flora trotted towards her, she had felt guiltily obliged to help.

They sat in the waiting room where Agatha and Charlie had talked. Flora clutched Lesley's hand like a child and repeated that she wouldn't forgive herself ever.

Lesley patted the fat hand. 'Please don't worry, Miss Vere-Lanigan. I'm sure you've nothing to blame yourself for.'

'I'm eighty years old, alone and bereft,' said Flora with a tragic smile. 'I deserve it, I suppose.'

Hell, thought Lesley, she's enjoying herself. 'Mrs Logan wasn't an easy person,' she said.

Flora stared. 'Agatha?' she said. 'I'm not talking about Agatha. I'm talking about my painting. I know our dear mother would have wished me to have it.'

Lesley said, 'Do you mean the *Young Girl in a Garden*? Mrs Logan left it to Ben in her will.'

For answer, Flora went off into peals of laughter. 'There's poetic justice for you,' she said.

Lesley wondered if she should call a doctor or slap her face. 'Shall I call a taxi to take you to your hotel?' she asked.

Flora stopped laughing as suddenly as she'd begun. 'Oh my goodness,' she cried. She plunged into her oversized handbag, scooping out a mass of papers and crumpled hankies. 'I've left my purse and my cheque-book at home, and I haven't booked in anywhere.'

Lesley took a deep breath and said, as calmly as she could, 'I can put you up for the night, but you'll be on your own. I won't be in until late. You can get some money in the morning when the banks open.' She evaded Flora's grateful embrace, and led the way rapidly to the car park.

In Lesley's flat, Flora asked for a mug of cocoa. She sat down in the wing chair and opened the paper.

'That's Thursday's,' said Lesley. 'I haven't bought a newspaper since

Mrs Logan died. I haven't even read that one.'

Flora was staring at the page. 'I suppose that was what finally killed her,' she said.

Lesley put down the cocoa. 'What did?' she said.

Flora pointed. ART TREASURE DUMPED IN FIELD. Lesley had noticed the headline when she found the paper beside Agatha's body. She bent to look.

Valued at in excess of a quarter million, the painting by fashionable Victorian artist James Tissot was in the back of a van stolen from the

rear of the Crock of Gold premises on Thomond Quay last Monday.

Discovered by schoolchildren, the canvas had been almost destroyed by a herd of cows, the property of Mr Thomas Mullins, 71, who also owns the land.

The van has not been recovered, and it would appear that the painting, which was wrapped in sacking, was thrown over the hedge by the thieves.

'I had no notion it was worth all that,' said Myles Glyn, 56, farmer, of Cloninch in County Kildare. The painting had been insured for a mere £800. Mrs Agatha Logan, 82, owner of the picture, is at present unavailable for comment.

There was a photograph of Myles, looking sheepish; holding in one hand the splintered frame, in the other a tattered object which might have been anything.

'Owner of the picture!' cried Flora. 'The audacity of it.'

'Do you know if Ben was told about this?' Lesley asked.

'I don't know . . . I don't think . . . Does it matter?'

'If the painting was left to Ben, it matters quite a lot.'

'Oh nonsense, dear. It was mine.'

Lesley bit her lip. She showed Flora her bedroom, lent her a nightdress, and went out.

THERE WAS NO LIGHT in the upstairs flat, but Lesley could hear the stereo. Henrietta greeted Lesley affectionately, and turned down the sound. Her movements were totally assured now, and Lesley visited her only twice a week to do her shopping.

'I've come for sympathy and understanding,' said Lesley. 'Role reversal. Are you on?'

'You sound as if you need it. Are you going to tell me you've quarrelled with Ben and beg for advice?'

'No,' said Lesley. 'Much more serious than that. It's the sort of coincidence you read about in trashy books. He's gone blind. You're the only person I know who won't give me a lot of baloney about grit and stamina and courage. Me being so capable and Ben being so brave. You know.'

'Lesley, I'm shattered—what can I say? I've been so happy for you and Ben.'

'I wish I thought he'd make out as well as you do.'

'You're joking. My Owen's stuck by me for two years, he phones me twice a day and he's given me this stereo, but I still can't make my mind up to let him see me like this. If I don't decide soon, he'll stop wanting to see me. Serve me right if he did.'

'He won't,' said Lesley.

'I'm not so sure. I think perhaps we should say goodbye.' Henrietta leaned back in her chair, thinking. 'I'd get by,' she said. 'I'm tough—probably tougher than Ben, and from what you say he hasn't many resources. Thank God he's got you.'

'Yes, well. He has and he hasn't. I'm not sure that I'm the person to help him; I don't feel that I've enough patience. His mad great-aunt is staying in my flat by the way.'

'Oh, *that's* why you're here. Did you say you were short of patience? You don't know what you're talking about.'

They listened to music and talked until late. When Lesley got home, she found a wilting rose on her pillow and a note which read, 'Bless you, dear. Sweet dreams.'

She dreamed about Agatha.

Ten

One evening, a week after Agatha's funeral, Geoff called at Lesley's flat. She opened the door looking haggard in shirt and slacks. He thought there was something missing, and realised he'd never seen her without earrings before.

'Come in, Geoff, I'm delighted to see you,' she said. Geoff followed her into the living room, where an untidily dressed old woman was sorting through a boxful of papers. She looked up, and Geoff was startled by her garish make-up.

Lesley introduced them, saying, 'This is Geoff Merchant, who instructs at the Training Centre, Aunt Flora,' and to Geoff, 'Miss Vere-Lanigan is Ben's great-aunt.'

Lesley offered to make a pot of tea, but Flora asked for, and downed, a large gin and French. While Lesley was making the tea, Flora talked to Geoff, hardly pausing for breath.

'Poor dear Lesley,' she said. 'I felt I had a duty to stay for a while and take care of her. You know all about the tragedy? Two young lives blighted at one stroke ... Never mind, our dear Father knows best.' In response to Geoff's surprised look, she added, 'I refer of course to our heavenly Father.'

Geoff muttered something noncommittal, as Flora launched into the story of the stolen picture and suddenly began to weep. Lesley silently handed her a full box of mansize tissues and Flora dragged out a handful. Lesley's eyes met Geoff's above Flora's bent head.

'What about a walk, Lesley?' said Geoff. 'It's still light.'

Hardly giving Geoff time to say goodbye to Flora, Lesley hurried him out into the street.

They went to a café which was almost deserted, and Geoff ordered more tea. 'Why did you ask the old lady to stay?' he asked.

'I didn't. Well, only overnight. In a way she's company, she takes my mind off Ben. She's a perfect nuisance but very kind, and I feel obliged to do something for her.'

'Where's Ben then? I thought he was going back to Middlegarth last week, then I thought he might be with you.'

'He's still in hospital having treatment. Apparently he's still in shock. He was in bed and hardly speaking when I had to tell him about the picture being stolen. He didn't seem to care.'

'Poor chap, he couldn't see it anyway.'

'No,' said Lesley, 'but it was worth a fortune and the insurance had run out. I wonder what else can go wrong for him.'

'Once he gets discharged from hospital he should manage. He couldn't have anyone better than you to look after him.'

Lesley didn't smile. 'That's what I want to talk to you about,' she said. 'I don't think he wants me.'

'Oh, come now. I can't believe he said that.'

'If I try to carry on where we left off, I'll mess things up worse than they are now. I think he should have a dog.'

'You aren't usually in a hurry for people to get a dog.'

'No. But Ben's so fit, so active and quick. Losing his freedom's going to hit him harder than losing his sight in the long run. My opinion, for what it's worth, is that he should have a guide dog and the sooner the better. He's good with dogs too.'

Geoff nodded. 'You can see to anything he needs before you go to work, and again in the evenings. We can send a Mobility Officer to assess him for a dog in a week or two.'

'But Geoff, you don't understand. I'm sure he doesn't want me to stay with him.'

Geoff stirred his tea. 'Why not stay at the farm for a bit? You could still look after Ben.'

Lesley looked up. 'Listen, Geoff, I'd do anything for Ben, but this isn't on. Not when we've talked about getting married. I love him too much.'

'Well, my dear, you've got a choice. Either ask the boss to allocate him another social worker or bully him into having you back. Surely you can handle it.'

'No,' said Lesley. 'I've never gone overboard for anyone like this before. I can't manage it. I can't cope with my feelings—they're coping with me. Please persuade him to have a dog. A nice undemanding dog that'll settle for a pat on the head and a tin of dogfood.'

'Hey up,' said Geoff. 'Don't you start crying. I'll talk to Ben as soon as I can. Try and talk sense into that thick head of his.'

'Don't talk to him about me, talk to him about a dog. What about Meg?'

'She'd be perfect for him—if he treats her right,' said Geoff. 'But if you're wrong—if he wastes her . . .'

'You'll never forgive me,' finished Lesley. 'I'll risk it.'

GEOFF FOUND BEN ALONE. He was neatly dressed, shaven and had had his hair cut. He had been in the cottage for a week now, and the anger seemed to have gone. He was sitting with his guitar on the table beside him.

'It's Geoff,' he said. 'May I come in?'

'Geoff. Come in; sit down. Thought it was Mandy. She isn't with you, is she?'

'No. What's she been doing?'

Ben's hands clutched the edge of the table. 'Nothing,' he said. 'I shouldn't talk like that. She's Charlie's daughter after all. Very kind, very sympathetic, very understanding.'

'I thought the shepherd was looking after you,' said Geoff.

'Eric? He is. Grand fellow. Funny, isn't it, how much easier it is to tell if a person's genuine if you can't see him.'

Geoff said, 'When I was training, I was blindfolded for three days and nights. It should give one an idea, but it doesn't, because you know you can take the blindfold off. I came to talk to you about a guide dog. Has Lesley talked to you about it?'

'She mentioned it,' said Ben sulkily. 'I don't want one.'

Geoff said, as if he hadn't heard, 'The way you walk is perfect. You hold up your head, and you walk quickly. People who have been blind for some time often start poking their heads forward, shuffling their feet. It wouldn't suit you to be like that, Ben.'

'A dog wouldn't suit me either. It would be like a leper's bell; like a label round my neck. Blind. Be kind to him." '

'I didn't think you'd take that attitude,' said Geoff. 'The dog is a sign that you're independent of human help, not a badge of dependence. What does Lesley think about it?'

Ben stood up. 'Leave Lesley out of it,' he said loudly. 'She's not going to waste any more of her life—not if I can help it.'

'I'd let her be the judge of that if I were you. Lesley knows her job. She wouldn't let you get overdependent; she'd encourage you to help yourself.'

'Help myself?' shouted Ben. 'I can't. I can't read or write or drive a car. I can't even tell if I'm properly dressed. Better if I'd split my skull that time. What's left for me to do? Beg?'

'Calm yourself down, Ben. There are plenty of skills to be learned nowadays, and in the meantime you can look after Meg, feed her and groom her, and get yourself some exercise taking her out.' Geoff stood up. 'She's that collie, you know, bred at Middlegarth. I'll give you until the end of the week—three days—to think about it, then she'll go to somebody else.'

'I don't want a dog,' said Ben sullenly.

Geoff went to the door. 'Think about it.'

Ben listened to Geoff's car going away. He picked up his guitar and began to strum an old pop song, 'Garden of Eden'. As he played, gaining confidence with every note, he began to sing the words.

But then he remembered another garden, and a girl with red hair. He stopped playing, and tried to concentrate on bringing the picture—his picture—into focus in his mind's eye. It was there, yet not there. Tantalisingly, he knew every brushstroke in memory, but it refused to be held still and examined. He played six notes down the scale in a minor key.

'Young girl in a gar-den,' sang Ben.

The familiar sound of Lesley's car made him start guiltily, as if caught out. He laid the guitar aside and waited for her.

LESLEY WAS THE ONLY PERSON whose presence never irked Ben. Her voice betrayed nothing except affection—no irritation, no sorrow, no pity. He wondered if it came naturally or if she had to work at it.

She said, 'I've only come for a few minutes; I brought you some food. Mandy tells me you're getting tired of mince.'

'I am. She thinks I have to be fed like an invalid.' He heard her moving about. 'What are you doing?'

'Picking up your socks. You'll never sort yourself out if you chuck your things down when you undress.' Her voice came from low down; close. He could smell her hair.

Off his guard, he said, 'I'd rather undress you.'

She came to him saying, 'Do. I wish you would.'

For one moment his resolve left him; his arms went round her. Then he forced himself to turn away saying, 'It won't do. You know it won't.'

'Why won't it do, love? I know you want me.'

'Of course I want you. But it's all wrong.'

'Blind people have lovers. They often marry one another.'

'That's different.' Ben deliberately made his voice impatient.

Facing him, she said angrily, 'Am I supposed to stick around while you find a blind woman?'

'Shut up.' Anger helped; he made no effort to check it. 'You know very well what I mean.'

Lesley felt ill. All her training and experience pointed the same way. Never, never allow yourself to become emotionally involved. Be friendly with your cases, care about them, have compassion, even affection for them. But love? Love was out.

She tried again, controlling her voice with a fierce effort. 'My place is with you—we both know that. I—I need you, Ben.' She wondered what had happened to her pride.

Ben laughed loudly, without a trace of mirth.

'Don't laugh like that, Ben. Please don't.'

'Sorry. Thought you were trying to be funny.'

This new mood was much harder to take than anger. She wanted to tell Ben that she had real friends who had once been despairing patients. Friends whose laughter was true and genuine, like Henrietta's.

Ben spoke for her. 'Don't bother to tell me about all the blind people out there, singing and dancing and holding down highly paid jobs,' he said, 'because I don't want to know.'

'You will,' she managed to say, 'one day.'

He didn't answer.

Lesley said, 'You laughed when I said I needed you, but it's true. I can't help it if you don't believe me.'

'I don't believe you,' Ben whispered. 'I wish I was dead.'

Lesley had heard these words so often that they had lost their power. She would like to have told him, Everybody says that—it doesn't last. Life is still sweet. But she didn't trust her voice. This was plain stupid. She must go away, for a time at least.

She pretended she hadn't heard him. With an effort, she said, 'I've left food on the table. There's scones, pork pies, sausage rolls and apples. Eric and Mandy will see to you until I can arrange something else. I'm not the person to do it. I'm going now.'

She went out and sat in her car, where she found that the desperate urge to burst into tears had gone. She drove to the farm, left a message for Mandy who was out, and went home to Leeds.

BEN SAT DOWN, his hands gripping the arms of the chair. The strain of sitting still, of not holding out his arms to Lesley and begging her to stay with him, had left him feeling ill. He had been brutal, he knew, but the slightest weakening would have been fatal. He would have been done for, and so would she. One day, he thought, she would thank him for his ruthlessness. He wished fiercely that Lesley would come back. Not to stay—but to give him a chance to say he was sorry.

He got up, felt his way into the other room and lay down on the bed. He discovered that eyes which could not see could shed tears.

It wasn't in Ben's nature, however, to give himself up to self-pity for long. He soon found that he was thinking of Agatha and how, already ill, she had come to him. Such dedication deserved recognition. He got up and found his guitar.

Ben had never taken music lessons, but he had a good ear and a natural feeling for music. The melody was putting itself together, and words to go with it. In his mind, he was looking into the garden of the picture. And as he looked, the girl jumped to her feet; he caught a glimpse of her smile, then she was gone. As he added line to line, he thought that perhaps the song was about the lost Lesley, or Agatha, or even his lost sight. Maybe it was about all three.

Putting the guitar down, he went outside. It was warm, with a gentle breeze. He felt his way round the cottage until he reached the back wall where he was invisible from farmhouse and road alike. He sat down on the ground with his back against the sun-warmed stone, put his arms round his knees and wondered how to set about returning to Ireland. It was unfair to Lesley and to the Guvnor to stay where he was.

There was a movement close to him. He became aware of the smell of an elderly dog, not overclean. 'Roy?' he said.

He felt a hot dry nose in his hand. Ben rubbed the head, and the base of the scruffy ears with their matted locks of hair. What a mess the dog was in. He might trim him with nail scissors, he thought. Roy whined, and Ben felt a paw placed hesitantly on his instep. It was cold and wet, with overgrown toenails. It smelt of silage.

'Off you go, Roy,' he said. 'Run away home.'

He felt Roy stiffen. The paw and the nose were removed at once, but the smell of dog was still there. Even as he reached out to push the dog away, he sensed Roy's bewilderment. 'Silly old fool,' he said. 'Hurt your feelings, have I? Come here then.'

But Roy had gone. Ben heard the scatter of gravel as he galloped away.

Roy was not the sort of dog to inspire love, but Ben was fond of him. He was angry with himself for driving the animal away. He could have recalled him as easily as he could have recalled Lesley; self-contempt prevented him.

Why should dog or man—or woman—put up with his moods?

Ben's dour reflections were interrupted by a skittering noise, accompanied by bleating, and the sharp reek of sheep.

Ben scrambled to his feet, hands held out. The sheep closed in, all round him, closer and closer. One of them squeezed between him and the wall at his back. Ben toppled forward, saving himself from falling by putting both hands on a woolly back. The back jerked away and his hands met the ground. For a frightening moment, he sprawled there as the startled animals piled round him.

Suddenly, Ben realised what was happening. Roy, driven away for no fault that he could understand, was doing something which he was certain would please Ben. Who could fail to be cheered by a beautiful flock of sheep?

Ben shouted, 'That'll do, Roy, that'll do!'

Answering immediately to the command, the dog came straight round the flock to Ben's side. Ben heard the sheep wheel, and race away into the distance. Roy, uncertain of his welcome, kept out of reach. Ben held out his hand, and received a brief nudge from the hot nose. 'Thanks, Roy,' he said. 'That was just what I needed. I'll get that daughter of yours to keep me out of trouble. No human being would put up with me.'

Eleven

Geoff let Meg out of her run. She was not given to displays of affection. A working dog, like her father Roy, she knew she had a purpose, though she didn't yet know what it could be. She was devoted to Geoff, but would never wriggle or slaver as some of the young dogs did.

Geoff put on Meg's harness, and let her lead him along the obstacle course. A series of planks were leaning against poles of varying heights. Meg, leading Geoff under or round these obstacles, knew his height to a centimetre and never made a mistake. Geoff knew that she would quickly learn Ben's height too.

Geoff had cut a few corners in order to get Ben accepted for the next residential course, but Ben's association with Lesley and his ability with working dogs were both in his favour.

When Geoff had shut Meg up in her sleeping quarters, he went to the office and checked her individual score sheet once more. Each dog was assessed for hearing and body sensitivity, for nervousness and for various forms of aggression, for concentration, willingness and initiative. Meg had top scoring for everything except protective aggression, but for that, Geoff had been obliged to knock off two points. However, the last time he had been to see Ben he had taken Meg with him, and she had been only slightly uneasy when Ben's simmering temper had begun to show.

'It isn't Meg that worries me, it's Ben,' Geoff said to himself.

LESLEY, WHO HAD BECOME short-tempered, impatient and inclined to lapses of memory, was having problems with all her charges except Henrietta. She hadn't been to see Ben again.

After Flora's departure back to Harrogate, Lesley was obliged to meet Mark, in order to discuss the lease of the flat. The encounter was an anticlimax. There was no emotion, no resentment. Mark had put on weight, and had bags under his eyes. He obviously expected recriminations; when they didn't come, he was affable and impersonal.

Lesley had taken trouble with her appearance, fearing that Mark might blame his desertion for her loss of weight and her pallor. She had had her hair permed for the first time in years, and set in a tumble of curls and waves, hiding the scar and most of her forehead. She wore a gaily patterned dress and sealing-wax-red lipstick. She could see that Mark hardly recognised her.

The lease of the flat was sold. Mark told Lesley she could keep any furniture she liked, and she replied that she wouldn't need much. She had enough of her own to furnish a smaller flat.

'I'd like the wing chair, though,' said Lesley. 'That's where Ben's grandmother was sitting when she died.'

'Ben?'

'Ben and I hope to get married eventually,' she said.

'You seem to have fallen on your feet,' said Mark. 'What does this Ben do for a living?'

'He's a farmer,' said Lesley recklessly.

When Mark left, she realised that she'd probably thrown away financial support, but rather than tell him that Ben was blind, she would have lived on bread and water.

The next day, Lesley took a two-roomed flat in the street where Henrietta lived, and started to move her belongings there.

BEN'S RESIDENTIAL COURSE was to start in late July. He had learned to manage very well for himself in the cottage. Mandy did his shopping and washed his clothes, and he needed no other help. On the narrow path at the back of the cottage, he sometimes jogged to and fro, fifteen paces each way.

Various well-wishers had assured Ben that he would develop a sixth sense. As he had suspected, this was nonsense, but the four senses left to him had sharpened immeasurably. He found he could orientate himself easily now. He knew where the barbed wire was, and had a fresh crop of scars to prove it. The traffic on the Leeds road behind his home and the farmyard noises in front of it were about half a mile apart. The smells of sheep, silage, diesel oil, grain and chemicals were enough to guide him around the buildings. His nose had learned to separate the smells in an almost uncanny way.

Although Charlie had rushed to Ben's defence after Agatha's funeral, he had found the young man's blindness so upsetting that for a time he had hardly visited him. Then he had taken to calling every evening for a short visit. He talked with a sort of false jollity, but before he left, he usually said in his normal voice, 'By, it's a bad job, is this,' and departed muttering to himself.

Charlie came down to the cottage the night before the course. 'By, it's a bad job, is this,' he said, for perhaps the twentieth time. 'Don't you move, lad, I'll mash tea.'

Ben said, 'I've been blind for three months now. Can't you give it a rest?'

'What are you on about?' demanded Charlie.

'You told my family I wanted time to be sorry for myself. You were right and I'm grateful. But now I've had enough sympathy. It slows me up; stops me trying to get around and make the best of it.'

There was silence as the Guvnor digested this. Ben wondered if he'd said too much. At last Charlie said slowly, 'Aye, you're in the right of it. If you don't find your feet soon, you'll be like a dog tied up all the time. Let him off chain and he'll stop in kennel as like as not. Well, get on then, mash tea. I'm dry if you're not.'

Ben mashed it.

AT THE CENTRE IN LEEDS, Ben's first impressions were so confused that afterwards he could remember only the barking of dogs, and Geoff's familiar voice among a babble of unfamiliar ones.

Geoff took Ben along a corridor, showing him the lounge on the right (first door), the dining room second on the left, the two telephones near the door; the lavatories at the end of the passage. They went upstairs—thirteen steps—and turned left. Three doors and eight paces from the landing, Geoff stopped. 'This is your room,' he said.

'Where's my dog?' Ben asked.

'You don't get your dog until you've been here for a day or two,' said Geoff. 'We have to be sure that you suit one another. Wait in here until you hear a bell, then come down for lunch.'

This was Ben's first time in a strange room since he had left hospital. He found that he had made more progress than he would have thought possible. He knew where the window was by the current of air from its open top. He could tell which surfaces were hard and which were soft by the way that sounds bounced back or were absorbed. He made a thorough investigation, then sat down on the bed. He tried to remember what Geoff had told him. 'Walk on the right—your dog will be on the left. Stop at the top and bottom of the stairs, as your dog will have been trained to do. Knock before you open a door, and never leave it half open for someone else to run into.' There was a lot more he'd forgotten.

When they were summoned to lunch Ben made unerringly for the door, shut it behind him and paced eight strides along the passage, keeping to the right. Thirteen steps—he rattled down them, wondering if he needed a dog after all.

A woman's voice said, 'Look out!' as he walked into a group of three or four, stepping heavily on somebody's foot. A hand grasped his arm, and the same harsh voice said angrily, 'Here, look where you're going!'

'Can't,' said Ben. 'That's why I'm here.'

'Sophy Fryton. Instructor. Not yours, I'm glad to say.' The woman led him along with a hard grip on his arm. 'Here's the dining room. Here's your chair. Sit down and stay sitting down. The students have quite enough to cope with on their first day without someone charging about like a bull in a china shop.' She was gone.

This was back to school but worse. He'd meant to learn faster than anyone else, to be the star pupil. Now he was deflated; ticked off by a prefect, and a girl at that.

It was a good lunch. He ate it all.

Afterwards, Geoff lectured the whole group in the lounge. Ben was sitting next to somebody large who was eating peppermints. There were two women behind him who whispered together and were shushed, somebody in front of him whose eagerness was as obvious as the women's lack of interest. He didn't know if it was a man or a woman.

Ben felt lost—he didn't belong, he wanted to go home to the cottage.

After the talk, Geoff took the students, ten in number, to the dogs' quarters. They were shown the way to the room where the dogs were groomed, and told something about their care and feeding.

'Have you any questions?' asked Geoff.

'When do I get this damned dog?' said Ben.

'I've told you: when you're ready to work with her. Anything else?'

'No,' said Ben.

BRIAN AND MIKE between them filled a tape with news from Cloninch for Ben. They felt guilty about the meeting in the Leeds hospital, each wishing he could have talked to Ben alone. So they took turns with the tape, talking to Ben as if he'd been there. They told him that Grandfather was up, sitting in Agatha's chair and bossing Dad about, that he had taken all Grandmother's funny old dresses and burned them, that Sheila was pregnant and in a shocking temper, that Denis had been robbed all ends up when he sold all the sheep.

They asked Muriel to contribute, but she shook her head, so they said that Mam was in great form and asking after Ben, and sent the tape with a blank one for a reply to Middlegarth Farm.

'They haven't any labels—I wonder what's on them,' said Mandy.

The Guvnor put them in his pocket. 'Go on wondering,' he said.

MEG WATCHED FROM HER RUN AS the class came out on their second day. Each student had the construction of the harness explained to him and was told how to hold the handle in his left hand, along with the dog's lead.

Then Geoff did his dog imitation. The exercise, called a 'handle walk', taught the students, without the risk of bewildering and upsetting the dogs.

The instructor was the 'dog'. As Geoff put the harness in the hands of the broad-shouldered man with the dark curly hair, Meg suddenly knew who he was.

Here was the man that Meg had thought would be good to work for. The man, Ben, took hold of the handle and charged straight at Geoff's broad back. Meg felt the fine hairs on her shoulders prickle as Geoff staggered, but he merely laughed and said, 'Try again. You're getting a collie, not a greyhound.'

Meg would have torn out the throat of anyone who tried to hurt Geoff. The difficulty was to learn the difference between hurting and helping. She had learned, slowly and painfully, that she must not be possessive, or try to prevent people from touching her person. Her wish to please him by her obedience was now stronger than her instinct to defend him.

ON THE SECOND EVENING, after tea, Geoff took most of the students to a local hotel, where the management was used to people from the Centre.

Ben, drinking a shandy, amused himself by isolating the different voices, trying to visualise their owners. He listened for Geoff, and heard him greeting somebody who had just come in. He said, 'You'll see a big difference in him already.'

'It's a bad job,' was the reply. 'Poor lad. A bad job.'

'Guvnor!' Ben got up, carefully setting down his drink. He knew better now than to charge towards the voice.

'Eh, Ben lad, I'm pleased to see you.' Ben's hand was crushed, his shoulder thumped. 'Where's dog, then?'

'It's great to see you,' said Ben. 'No dog yet. They say we're not ready for them.'

'If you ask me, they think more to dogs than folks.' The jolly note was back in Charlie's voice. 'Brought something for you; from Ireland.'

A small flat object was pressed into his hand.

'A tape?' he hazarded.

'Aye. Summat o' that. There's nowt on label; just your name.'

They sat down, and Charlie's voice gradually lost its heartiness.

'Seen Lesley lately?' Ben asked.

'Nay, more's the pity. I hear she's moved house.'

'Still in Leeds?'

'Reckon so. She's shut of that Peabody now—divorced.'

'Remember me to her if you see her,' said Ben, choosing the formal words with care.

Charlie didn't stay long. He'd been at a wool-growers' meeting and had to go home, he said, but Ben knew he was bothered and embarrassed by the other students. Ben stood up as Charlie did, half sorry, half relieved that he was going so soon.

'It'll be grand to have you back at Middlegarth,' said Charlie.

'Thanks. When I get there, I'll find out what kind of work I can do,' said

Ben. 'Geoff says I'll be able to go by bus once I've got a dog, and there are jobs going in the factories. I won't live on your charity.'

'Aye, that you won't,' agreed Charlie. 'Ask anyone round Middlegarth if Charlie Thorpe's a charitable man. They'll tell you he'd skin a louse for its pelt.' He laughed heartily. 'Soon as you can earn any brass, I'll be after you for rent.'

A wink went with this promise. Through the closing doors, Ben heard faintly, 'A bad job . . .'

Somebody started haltingly to play the piano, and Geoff said, 'Sing us a song, Ben.'

'No. I'm no good.'

'Come on, Ben, what used you to sing to the Guvnor's old ewes?'

Ben laughed. '*O by and by, by and by—I'm gonna lay down this heavy load* . . . Might have been written for them.'

There was laughter followed by calls for a song. Ben was shy of singing in public—Agatha had seen to that. But an audience he couldn't see wasn't nearly so alarming.

A woman's voice said, 'I love the old spirituals—do you know any more?' Almost before he knew it, he was playing and singing, 'Michael row the boat ashore', while the room resounded with Hallelujahs.

He began to enjoy himself, to be warmed by the enthusiasm of his companions and he was sorry when it was time to go home.

When he was alone he played his tape. His brothers' familiar tones gave him a shock. They might have been trying to amuse a backward child. It wasn't what they said, it was their bright, encouraging voices.

He put on the blank, hummed the melody he'd been working on, recited the lyric and finally sang a verse. Then he recorded a 'letter' home.

ALL THE STUDENTS got their dogs on the same day. Almost a week had passed and the occasion was looked forward to by the instructors nearly as much as the students. Geoff assembled the ten, and told each the name, breed and description of his or her dog. As his eyes travelled from one eager face to another, he thought of the first lecture of the course, only six days earlier. Then, those faces had shown anxiety, puzzlement, even fear.

Geoff never tired of seeing worried faces break into smiles when their owners first had their dogs described to them. It was one of the compensations which made the punishing hours, hard slog and responsibility worthwhile. And Ben's smile was worth waiting for.

'Ben, your dog Meg is a Border collie bitch. She's medium-coated, with one ear pricked and the other bent over at the tip. She's a tricolour—black, white and tan, with a white collar, legs and tail tip. Oh, and she has a white stripe down her face. She's almost two years old.'

The smile came. 'Is she like Roy?' asked Ben.

'Very like him to look at—you saw her once—but she's more generous and outgoing by far.'

'I wish I could have had Roy,' said Ben. 'His daughter's the next best thing.'

'You're joking. He'd have guided you round flocks of sheep, and bitten anyone who tried to help you.'

The instructors issued the chattering students with slip chains, leads and grooming equipment. Then Geoff told them to go to their rooms where their dogs would be brought to them.

Ben's room was the third on the corridor, so Geoff had handed over two dogs to their new owners when he reached it. As he passed the first two doors with Meg at his side, he could hear a variety of sounds from the rooms. Dogs were whining and panting, while the students' voices were raised in excitement as they exclaimed to the dogs. He could hear sobbing, but he was used to tears from students of both sexes. Tears of happiness and relief.

Geoff wondered how he would get out of Ben's room without Meg. He would order her to stay, of course, but Meg was *his*. She had been his throughout her training; she was special.

He knocked, and opened the door. 'Here's Meg, at last,' he said. 'Call her by name.'

'Meg?' Ben spoke quietly, seeking her by the sound of her paws. Meg left Geoff's side and went to Ben. There was no need to say 'stay'. As Ben stretched out his hand, Meg lowered her head, pressing it against his palm. She sat down with her back to Geoff. She half turned her head, rolled an eye in his direction. She rested her chin on Ben's knee.

With a pang remarkably like jealousy, Geoff closed the door.

Twelve

Lesley had been allocated a fresh case to look after: Ron Watson, a teenage boy who had been blinded in a street fight. He lived on a new housing estate in the suburbs—so new that the houses were still going up, and the gardens were littered with broken bricks and rubble.

His mother kept up a furious tirade against the gang who had blinded her son, never pausing for breath or to listen to Lesley. Ron was bitter and silent. Lesley hated the job.

As she drove away from the brightly painted little house with Mrs Watson's outraged cries ringing in her ears, Lesley saw the familiar minibus from the Training Centre turning into the estate, with Geoff driving it. Bob was following, driving a small pick-up van with two bicycles in the back.

Lesley stopped her car. Her heart thumped, her hands sweated on the wheel. She knew to the day how far the course had progressed. This was the third week; the students would soon be going home. The minibus, bicycles and pick-up were to be used as traffic hazards, bricks and uncovered drains as natural hazards.

Meg was first off the bus, followed by Ben. Both exuded confidence. Ben hadn't changed in appearance. He looked, not happy, but determined.

Meg led Ben within ten yards of Lesley's car, waited as Bob cycled out of a side alley and swerved across her path, walked on. She and Ben walked quickly. Ben's head was held high, his hand on the harness sensitive but firm.

Unreasoning rage filled Lesley. He's mine—mine. How dare he take that dog home and leave me out . . . throw me out? Blast him, with his self-confidence and his clever dog. Who but a besotted fool would hanker for a blind man who didn't want her when there were plenty who both saw and wanted . . . If only she could go on being angry with him, the rest would be easy. She would be free of him for ever. Free to—well, free, anyway.

Lesley wrenched the steering wheel of her car round and drove home. It was lunchtime but she didn't feel like eating, so she walked down to Henrietta's place. When she rang, Henrietta's voice came joyfully, 'Come on up; surprise.'

Lesley wasn't surprised, she'd seen it coming for weeks. Owen was there.

'I've been such a fool, Lesley,' said Henrietta. 'Such a fool. Ring up your Ben and tell him what a fool he is.' She stretched out a hand, and Owen held it tightly.

'Do stay,' they both said, while plainly longing for her to go away.

'I can't,' said Lesley. 'Another time. I can't tell you how happy I am for you.' She kissed them both and left.

IT WAS SATURDAY EVENING. The next week would be Ben's last at the Centre. Lesley pushed him firmly to the back of her mind, and opened a tin of spaghetti. She had grown careless of what she ate, or when. As she turned off the gas, the bell rang. Lesley started, splashed the sauce, burned her fingers and swore. If I get any jumpier, I'll have to resign, she thought, opening the door. Henrietta and Owen were there.

'Come in,' said Lesley, with forced enthusiasm. 'Lovely to see you.'

'Spaghetti,' said Henrietta, sniffing. 'Is there any left?'

'I haven't started. I can open another tin or make something else. What would you like?'

Owen, tall, stooping, with dark hair and thick glasses, led Henrietta to the sofa. 'Don't bother about food,' he said. 'We don't want to put you out.'

'Do her good,' said Henrietta. 'She deserted a poor blind girl who needed her gentle pity and understanding.'

'Oh, do shut up,' said Lesley, not quite joking. 'I've never seen anyone less in need of pity. I've got some cold chicken—we'll have that. If Owen sees his poor blind girl winding spaghetti round her neck, he might change his mind.'

They ate chicken and cheese. Owen had brought a bottle of wine. 'We mean to get married as soon as I can get it organised,' he said. 'You'll come, won't you? We're not asking anyone else except parents.'

'I warn you, our mothers will weep like fountains. Bring plenty of tissues,' said Henrietta.

'How did you talk Henrietta into this, Owen?' said Lesley. 'I could do with a few hints.'

'She was using her disability as an excuse to refuse to make an honest man of me. When cajolery failed, I tried threats. Caveman stuff. You will come to our wedding, Lesley, won't you?'

'Yes, of course. I wouldn't miss it for anything.'

As the evening passed, Lesley felt that some of their happiness was rubbing off on her. Although she could hardly bear to look at them, she was sorry when they went, and that night she cried herself to sleep. For weeks, she had choked back tears whenever they threatened to spill over. Though red-eyed and headachy in the morning, she felt a great release of tension. She washed her face in cold water and remembered gratefully that it was Sunday.

When Lesley had drunk three cups of coffee, she came to a decision. She drove to Middlegarth at illegal speed.

CHARLIE SAW LESLEY'S CAR outside Ben's cottage. He went in and discovered her cleaning the cooker.

'Now then, Lesley, what's to do? Ben seen sense yet?'

'No, Guvnor, I don't think so. I'm just cleaning up the place for him, then I'll go away.'

Charlie looked at her critically. 'Why did you get your hair frizzled up?' he said. 'You look like a stranger.'

Lesley smiled faintly. 'I thought a change would cheer me up,' she said.

'It's good to tell it hasn't. Face as long as a wet fortnight.'

Lesley returned to the cooker. 'I'll finish this job, if you'll excuse me,' she said politely.

Charlie watched her, his thick red hands resting on the table. 'Tell you what,' he said, 'I'll fetch Ben home myself, and you can come along o' me. Break the ice like, me being there. Talk about dog. Talk about weather if you must. Then I'll leave you both here, and you can get him his tea. If you can't carry on from there, he isn't worth bothering with.'

He saw the colour rise into Lesley's face, and recede, leaving it whiter than before. He knew he was witnessing suffering which was beyond his understanding.

'May I think about it?' Lesley said.

'Aye, but think sense if you can. This last month'll have changed lad. Maybe he'll have seen sense hisself. Went down to see him early on; he was asking about you.'

'What did he say?'

'Nowt much. He's same as you. You two want your heads jowling together. Knock some sense into you.'

AS BEN'S COURSE neared its end, he thought more and more about his homecoming. He and Meg were perfect partners. Meg had treated Ben with patience, had looked after herself as well as him, had ignored his commands when they were obviously wrong. Ben had learned quickly, and formed a strong bond with her.

Ben was the only one of the ten who was unsure what he was going home to. The cottage, yes, but beyond that he knew nothing. He felt energy build up in him as they waited to be collected and taken home; the bottled-up energy which had so often led to fits of temper. He couldn't keep still, so he went right round the outside of the building with Meg, dodging obstacles with ease. It came so easily now that his mind was left free for thoughts which he would have preferred not to think. He had thrown away his chance of living with Lesley, and he was beginning to realise he had made a mistake.

Ben decided that he would achieve something remarkable—he didn't yet know what—and when Lesley congratulated him . . . provided she hadn't found somebody else . . .

'Ben.' It was Geoff's voice. 'The Guvnor's come for you.'

Ben, saying goodbyes all round, kept an ear cocked for Charlie's voice saying that it was a bad job. But what he heard was the Guvnor saying that he never would've believed it and that you could have knocked him down with a feather.

'By, lad, Ben, it's good to see you.' The thump on the shoulder made Meg move closer to Ben. 'Come on then.'

'Leave him to the dog, Mr Thorpe,' said Geoff. 'Don't ever take hold of Ben's left arm when he's with Meg, and if you want to thump his shoulder, thump the right one.' To Ben he said, 'I'll be round to see you soon.'

Ben sat beside the Guvnor in the Range Rover with Meg at his feet. Charlie said that he wouldn't have believed it, that the farm hadn't been same without Ben.

'You haven't seen Lesley about, have you?' asked Ben.

'I have that. I thowt she were coming along to bring you home, but she couldn't make it. Phoned Mandy at last moment. Happen she'll be coming round to see you.'

'Happen she won't,' said Ben glumly.

Ben listened to the traffic as they drove. His ears had learned to pinpoint different sounds. His nose registered diesel oil, plastic, tweed, tobacco, his own smell and Meg's. There were dozens of fainter scents from outside. Straw, tar, grass. It occurred to Ben that half the things he could hear or smell were invisible anyway.

AT THE FARM, Eric greeted him as if he'd been on holiday. Mandy exclaimed over Meg, going down on her knees to pat and cuddle. Meg endured politely. Ben could sense her boredom.

'How's old Roy?' asked Ben.

'Dead,' said Charlie. 'Poor old dog missed you, I reckon. He used to hang about cottage, then he wandered out on road. Never knew him to do it before. Eric found him, dead as a nit.'

Ben said nothing. Meg moved closer; automatically, he caressed her.

'He was getting on,' said Charlie. 'Ten, maybe twelve. Decent dog—always was. Don't take on, lad; it's only a dog.'

'I'd like to go home now,' said Ben.

'I'll take you,' cried Mandy.

'Meg will take me,' said Ben firmly, 'thanks all the same.' He shook Mandy's eager hand off his left arm fairly gently, and left the house. He found his way home easily enough. He put the key in the lock without fumbling, went in, sat down and took off Meg's harness.

It was ridiculous to be so affected by the death of an old, not very likable dog. He slumped in his chair, remembering how Roy had sensed his misery and brought him a flock of sheep. He buried his fingers in Meg's ruff, twisting a lock of hair until she whined.

He unpacked, fed Meg, let her out, and spent ten minutes grooming her. He considered ringing up Lesley—hers was the only phone number he could remember. What business was so urgent that it had kept her from coming to meet him at the last moment, he wondered. In this mood, he didn't feel like risking a rebuff. He went to bed early.

LENA DANBY, TECHNICAL OFFICER, called on Ben next day. She asked him a great many questions.

'Is there anything useful I can do?' asked Ben. 'I haven't had much education.'

'It depends on you. If you want an interesting job with a decent wage though, you'll have to learn Braille. Then you could use computers, typewriters—all sorts of things.'

'I'd better learn to weave baskets,' said Ben.

'What about music? Somebody said you played the guitar.'

'I don't play well. It's there somewhere—can you see it?'

'No. I'm blind.'

'*You're* blind?' Ben was staggered.

'It's a help in assessing people. I can't see you, but I may know more about you than if I could. Let's find that guitar.'

Ben found it. 'I sing better than I play,' he said.

'Sing then.'

After a weak protest, he began to sing with confidence, because nobody was watching or sympathising.

'Why is she waiting alone out there
In the empty garden?
The sun's rays spark on her shining hair,
The grass is wet but she doesn't care.
She is waiting for somebody—not for me.
Whose is the face her green eyes see
In the sunny garden?'

'Sorry. I'm not much good.'

'Yes you are. Love the song—what is it? I've never heard it before. Go on.'

But Ben wouldn't. When she'd gone, he tried another verse.

'Where have you gone to, girl of mine,
Gone from the garden?
I was only away for a minute or less
And I caught just a glimpse of your long green dress
And the edge of a smile like sun in the rain,
And now I'm alone, alone again
In the shadowy garden.'

Ben again tried to recall the garden in Agatha's picture, but it was all muddled. Lesley was sitting on the grass in an ink-blue dress and the earrings like little silver fans, with the sun on her fair head. But he'd sent Lesley away.

'When I slept I dreamed you were in my arms—
Spring in the garden.
I held your body close to my own—
Don't vanish, my love, and leave me alone.
But you slide away like a falling tear,
The rain pours down and my arms hold air.
Night in the garden.'

The song was coming into shape. He had never tried to compose a tune before, and now, already, another was forming in his mind; a cheerful thing with a good beat to it. He began to improvise, sitting on the corner of the table, his back to the door.

MEG WISHED THAT BEN would stop singing and playing. She could put up with it but she didn't like it. She wished he'd let her go outside, where there were interesting smells, including that of another dog. Although trained to disregard other dogs and smells of all kinds when at work, when her harness was removed she was off duty.

Ben didn't hear the car pull up. He was making so much noise that he didn't hear the tap on the door. Meg swallowed the growl which rose to her throat. The woman Lesley had no business to be there. She had given Ben away to Geoff who had passed him on to Meg. He was Meg's person now, and she had no intention of giving him back.

The door opened. The woman was happy, laughing. She spoke to Ben in a warm, loving voice. Ben jumped off the table, spun round.

Meg tucked in her tail, and with her ears flattened to her head, pushed open the bedroom door with her nose and crawled under the bed. She could hear their voices rising and falling, two people who wanted to be together. Ben had forgotten about Meg. He would remember her when the woman had gone away.

AFTERWARDS, BEN COULDN'T be sure how the quarrel started. He loathed being watched, and hadn't wanted Lesley to hear the song until it was finished. But she'd only just arrived, he should have known she wouldn't spy on him. Then he forgot everything but the joy of her presence, her voice, her scent. When she spoke he could see her in memory. He had always loved to smooth the hair back from her forehead as he kissed her—its silkiness gave him special pleasure. His hand touched her face . . . then his fingers tangled in a mass of curls, right down to her eyebrows.

'What have you done to your hair?'

'Had it permed. It hides that scar and I felt like a change. A new hairstyle's a cure for depression.'

Ben felt shocked out of all proportion. He held the bunch of curls in his hand, not silky but springy. 'It isn't a cure for mine,' he snapped. 'How could you? I don't know what you look like now. Why did you have to change?'

'I haven't changed.' Lesley's voice rose. 'You've changed—I never have. You're being childish, I wish I'd stayed away.'

And that was only the beginning. Like any quarrel between people in love, it was bitterer and nastier than if either of them had cared less. Meg padded out of the bedroom and stood in front of Ben.

Lesley realised that she might be throwing away her last chance of staying with Ben. She said, 'I'm sorry, darling, I didn't mean it, forgive me,' but it was too late.

Ben said, 'I'm sorry too, but what chance have we got? Half an hour together and we're fighting.' He stepped back, caught his foot in the chair leg and nearly fell. Lesley grabbed his arm. Meg, goaded beyond endurance, growled.

'That dog should know better than to growl,' said Lesley. 'Over-protective and jealous.'

'How dare you find fault with Meg!'

'Oh, she's perfect, is she? Give her a kick in the ribs and she'll come crawling back and lick your feet. OK, if that's what you want—'

'Lesley, wait—'

'Here, I brought you a pocket recorder.' A hard object was banged down on the table. 'You have my phone number and Geoff's. I'll be there if you learn to control your foul temper, but I won't play second fiddle to your wretched dog.'

The door slammed.

BEN DROPPED INTO THE LARGER of the two chairs, shaking violently. He had been selfish, cruel, childish—everything Lesley had said was true. He didn't blame her—he had started the row.

A cold nose was pressed into his trembling hand. He thought of Roy. In that black moment, he felt responsible for everything that had happened since he left Ireland. If he hadn't quarrelled with Agatha, he wouldn't be blind. Agatha herself would probably still be alive, the picture hanging in her bedroom. Lesley would be happy with somebody else, Roy would never have wandered onto the main road.

'I think we'll go for a walk, Meg,' he said.

Ben's fingers shook so that he was clumsy adjusting the harness, but he managed at last. Meg waited while he fumbled with the key and locked the door. He lifted the handle of the harness from Meg's back and told her to turn left. She led him down the farm lane towards the traffic noises, through the gate beside the cattle grid, and stopped at the edge of the road.

Ben considered. He didn't want to go to the village where he would meet people he knew. 'Turn left, Meg.'

They walked along the road for about half a mile, then Ben heard the screech of brakes as a bus overtook them and drew up. He raised his arm, saying to Meg, 'Onto the bus, girl.'

'Hup-up . . .' Three steps. He took a seat, felt in his pocket, held out a dozen coins. A hand selected some of them as a voice asked, 'All the way?'

'All the way,' said Ben.

Thirteen

'I've had a row with Ben,' said Lesley.

'You what?' Charlie looked up from the *Yorkshire Post*. 'You two were in that house quarter of an hour at most and you fell out. What about?'

'Nothing much. It was a straightforward slanging match. And now he's disappeared.'

Lesley walked about the kitchen restlessly. 'I wanted to say I was sorry,' she said. 'So I went down to the Turpin Arms and rang him up. There was no answer. I went back to the cottage and he'd gone out. You haven't seen him, have you?'

'Nay. He'll have taken dog out.'

'But where? If he'd been on the road, I'd have seen him.'

'Gone down to Ings and drowned hisself, like as not,' Charlie said impatiently. 'Daft enough for owt.' He turned to the factory report.

Lesley went back to her car. Ben wasn't the type to kill himself, but he was in a temper and might easily have gone to the Ings. The beck was deep, with treacherous banks—no place to go walking.

She crossed the road and hurried down to the beck. A pair of mallard flying up almost under her feet made her jump, she laddered her tights and got burrs in her skirt.

There was no sign of Ben or Meg.

Lesley drove home slowly. It was stupid to be so worried. Even at the height of their quarrel, common sense had told her, This isn't the end, we can sort this one out; it might even clear the air. She was bitterly ashamed of herself, and badly wanted to tell him so.

When she got home, she washed her hair, dragging out the curls, combed it back and plaited it in two pigtails. She rang the Centre, but Geoff wasn't there. He wasn't at home either. She determined to find him.

It was late afternoon. Ben will come back home when he gets hungry, thought Lesley.

BEN FOUND THE SWAYING of the bus soothing. His unreasoning guilt had gone, and his anger was now all directed against himself. Why, why quarrel with Lesley? He loved her, he wanted her, he had shouted at her and kept a row going when he could have stopped it.

Ben knew she would come back. He had a curious feeling of triumph. There had been no pity in her today. You don't yell at someone you pity. But he simply wasn't ready to share his life with Lesley—not yet. He still felt a compulsion to prove himself in some way.

'Give you a hand, lad?' The bus was emptying. Lost in his thoughts, Ben had sat on.

'I'm OK,' he said, jumping up. 'Out, Meg.' A hand clutched his elbow as Meg led him down the steps.

'Where are we?' Ben asked the owner of the hand.

'Runcie Sands. The seaside. Didn't you know? Come on then, I'll take you down to beach.' It was a man, elderly, with ill-fitting dentures.

'That's all right. My dog'll find it.'

'No trouble,' said the man, taking a firm grip on Ben's arm.

Ben heard the sea, hissing on the sand about fifty yards away. 'Please let go of my arm,' he said, his voice tight with controlled annoyance.

'It isn't a bit o' trouble to walk you down. Never know when you might fall over this or that; dog can't do it all, can it? Now, you wait here, lad, don't move. I'll get you a deck chair. Don't want to go nearer when tide's on turn.'

The man's feet receded, crunching pebbles. Ben listened like a hunted animal. 'Turn left, Meg. Walk on, quick.'

Meg turned left, guessed the meaning of the rest, hurried. Almost running, Ben followed. The sea was on the right now, voices of children playing.

'Straight on, Meg.' Ben walked on ribbed sand. This sand would be submerged at high tide. He wondered if it was coming in or going out.

The voices dropped behind. Meg stopped. 'Straight on, Meg.' Meg led him onto loose stones, he slipped and tripped. She bore left again, and there was a path underfoot. It felt like asphalt.

He was hungry. He had smelt chips down there, but the deck-chair man had driven him away. The path climbed and twisted. After a while, it became a dirt track; long grass brushed Ben's legs.

'Straight on, Meg.' They reached high ground—a strong wind struck them suddenly. Meg stopped.

They must have come the best part of a mile. Ben sat down, and Meg leaned against his knees. The crash of waves was very close. Ben thought he heard a distant hail. He jumped to his feet. Why couldn't he be left in peace for five minutes?

'Straight on, Meg.' Meg stood her ground, firmly ignoring the wrong command as she had been trained to do. Ben had been trained too. In a case like this, trust the dog. Check carefully before attempting to go any further. 'Shift, can't you?' Meg sat down. Ben stepped forward, trod on her tail, withdrew his foot and took a long step forward.

It was a sheer drop. As he fell, Ben let go of Meg's harness. He landed flat on his stomach on the water, winding himself. A mouthful of salt water roused his survival instincts and he began to swim, probably in a circle, he thought.

Ben could swim moderately well and he supposed he could keep afloat for some time. But he couldn't protect himself from bangs on rocks he couldn't see. He wondered how long it took to drown.

The sea wasn't rough; probably this was a small cove where the waves were forced in through a bottleneck of rocks. Ben felt the nearness of a cold, dank wall of rock before he reached it. Then his face and hands scrubbed against the stone. This must be the cliff he'd fallen from. He could hear Meg barking, not so very far above him—six feet? Ten? Too far, anyway. The sea picked Ben up and threw him carelessly against the high, wet wall of rock. Then it dragged him back and ducked him. Automatically, he began to swim again.

Self-pity began to return, bringing with it a kind of warped comfort. Why bother to swim? Agatha gone, Lesley driven away. Blind. Helpless.

A small wave ducked him like a cold hand on the back of his neck playfully pushing him under. It receded, taking him out into the open with it, and banged him agonisingly against something sharp and large. He reached out, and hooked his right arm round a slimy, limpet-encrusted lump of rock. He spat out water and shook his head.

Self-pity evaporated. Pain turned it to anger. And a picture came to his memory with sudden vividness. Agatha at the head of the table. For a moment, he thought he heard her voice.

Weakling.

MEG STOPPED BARKING. She was standing on the cliff edge, overlooking a small bay with a rock in the middle of it. Ben was clinging to the rock. Beyond the headland, on the right, lay sand and safety.

Meg had to make a conscious decision between training and instinct. On one hand, Ben, for whom she was responsible, had fallen into the sea and, if no help came, he would drown. Instinct told her to go to him. Whether or not she drowned was beside the point.

On the other hand, Meg was on duty and in harness. She should remain at the spot where her last command had been given, right or wrong. She could bark to attract attention; she had barked herself hoarse. The sea drowned her voice, the wind carried it away.

It was a fair drop—about twice Ben's height. Nothing, if she hadn't been in harness. There was no way of bringing Ben up to where she stood, but if she tried to swim towards that headland, she might be able to tow him within sight of the cheerful seaside crowd around the point.

She hesitated, her paws at the very edge. The wiry, silvery grass was smooth as glass, the cliff eroded by centuries of salt, wind and water.

Meg jumped.

BEN DIDN'T HEAR the splash. He was concentrating on his piece of rock. He clung to it like a barnacle. If the tide was coming in, he would soon know, and he would have to let himself be carried out into the open sea and hope to be seen—some hope!

He'd noticed that Meg had stopped barking. Thank God he hadn't pulled her in with him. The thought of Meg drowning as a result of his own carelessness was unbearable. Then, suddenly, she was there beside him, panting and paddling. His hand closed on the handle of her harness. 'Oh, Meg, Meg, you bloody fool!'

She was trying to drag him away from the rock; trying to swim out to sea with him. Ben pulled her back, got his left arm round her. He hoisted her up as high as he could, until her front paws were hooked over his left shoulder, her head level with his own.

Every few seconds, a wave washed right over both of them. In one of the intervals, Ben said to Meg, 'I think the tide's going out,' and in the next, 'I hope I'm right.'

Ben felt stinging pain all over him as the salt found a dozen cuts. His right elbow and knee were numb with bruises, his fingernails broken. Yes, the tide was going out all right—only about one wave in seven was breaking over their heads.

After a long fifteen minutes, the waves hit him chest-high. Meg anxiously licked his ear.

'We've got a chance, Meg. Don't worry, I won't let you drown—nobody's going to drown today.'

Down, down. There was ground under Ben's feet at last. Carrying Meg, Ben waded painfully to the cliff, guided by the sound of the waves receding on the shingle. The water was just above his knees when he reached the cliff, turned left and began to work his way along it.

Meg struggled to be put down, the water was only just above Ben's ankles. He fell into a small rocky pool and she fell underneath him.

They scrambled out, and Ben wondered how much he had hurt her. He sorted out harness and lead. 'Carry on, Meg. Back to the bus. Clever girl.'

It took them half an hour to round the point. Again and again, Ben fell, as the smooth wet stones slid about. One of his shoes was gone, the sole torn from the other. In places, he was shuffling through piles of loose pebbles, then there would be a patch of smooth wet sand, then they were paddling through tepid shallow water.

Now that he was out of danger, Ben's thoughts were all of Lesley. He might have drowned—almost had—leaving her nothing but rejection and hard words to remember.

'Lesley,' he said aloud. Meg walked faster.

As they rounded the point, the bathers had gone. It must be evening. The smell of frying chips was still there. Ben headed for it.

'It's been a long time since breakfast, Meg,' he said.

PHIL MONK HAD GONE to Bridlington that day to watch the Duchess of York bestow her name and her blessing on the new Maritime Museum. He had searched in vain for anything to say about the event that every other reporter there wouldn't have said too, got bored, phoned the evening paper, and had finally driven up the coast to kill some time. He had a dinner to cover in Leeds, but that wasn't for hours yet.

At Runcie Sands, Phil met a talkative elderly man who seemed the type to know everything interesting—if there *was* anything interesting—about the place. The man accepted a beer at the Three Jolly Tars, and Phil began to wish he'd gone straight to Leeds. The old devil's teeth clacked like castanets.

'One of those guide dogs he had. I told him wait, because it stood to reason dog couldn't fetch him chair, could it? Got chair—he'd gone, just like that. Well, for all you and me know, poor fellow's gone and drowned. This beach is dangerous, you know. It's not fair on folks, blind men running about losing themselves.'

'When was this? Where did you see him last?'

'Two hours since, maybe more. I'm from Bridlington, me, come to see my sister. That's my bus out there, it's the last 'un.'

'Well, Mr Green, it's been nice meeting you, but you don't want to miss that bus, do you?' He firmly led Mr Green to the bus, then looked idly across towards a group by the chip van. He took a number of pictures with a telephoto lens. Intrigued by one man's appearance, he went nearer. Good-looking chap—or would be when he was cleaned up—and packed with personality. His jeans and shirt were in ribbons. His face and chest were streaked with blood, dirt and weed. The dog was lying down, licking its paws.

Phil had been a journalist for thirty years. He didn't put on a special voice for anybody. 'You look as if you could do with a lift home,' he said.

The young man gave him a smile which illuminated his stern features. There'll be a girl somewhere, thought Phil.

'I'm catching a bus.'

'You're out of luck. The last one's just gone. Where are you going?'

'A village called Middlegarth.'

'That's a bit of luck. I'm going to Leeds, and it's on my road. Good pub there, isn't there? The Turpin Arms.' Phil noticed that the guide dog was hurt. It got up stiffly and stood on three legs; it had a cut over one eye. 'Lovely dog that—mind if I take a photo?'

'I don't, but she must be all to hell; we've been half drowned. She's called Meg. I'm called Ben.'

Phil drove slowly and, without ever seeming to pry, learned a great deal about Ben.

'Put me down at the bus shelter, please,' said Ben. 'It's this side of a notice saying "Middlegarth Farm".'

'Can't I drive you to your door?'

'No thanks. I'd sooner walk up.'

Five minutes later, Phil was at the telephone in the Turpin Arms. 'Lorraine? Phil. Get me the news desk—quick.'

BEN FOLLOWED MEG at her slow pace up the path to the cottage. He put his hand under the tub of hydrangeas Lesley had bought, feeling for the key. It wasn't there. She'd come back! He charged through the door.

'What the hell have you been doing to that dog?' demanded Geoff.

Fourteen

Ben had been seen boarding the bus for the coast at noon. Lesley, who had tracked Geoff down in the Kosy Kitchen, had persuaded him to meet the last bus when it reached the stop outside Middlegarth. When it arrived without Ben, he began to be really worried and questioned the conductor.

The conductor remembered Ben well, and said he'd got off at Runcie Sands. 'That's as far as we go,' he had said. 'Godforsaken spot. Some families go there to picnic, but the rip tide and the quicksands keep the swimmers away.'

'Is there a pub there, or a guesthouse?'

'Just the pub where we stop. The Three Jolly Tars.'

By this time, Geoff was almost as frightened as Lesley. He drove to the cottage, found the key and went in. Meg's belongings were unpacked and tidily laid out, there was a mug with some tea in it on the table. Geoff picked up the telephone and asked Enquiries for the number of the Three Jolly Tars. He was dialling when he heard Ben looking for the key under the tub of hydrangeas.

Geoff's temper never got the better of him, he was too good a dog trainer for that. But when he saw Meg, her fur clotted with dry blood, limping into the kitchen, he told Ben exactly what he thought of him.

'You frightened Lesley out of her wits, and let down your friends who got you the best dog I've ever worked with. Have you ever given a thought to what our dogs cost to rear and train? Don't you know how many people there are waiting for a dog, who would look after one properly?'

Geoff filled a basin with water and gently bathed Meg's cuts and sores. 'I don't think she's broken anything,' he said, 'but she'll have to go to the vet. She can stay at my place tonight.'

He looked up from inspecting Meg's swollen paw, and for the first time saw the extent of Ben's injuries. 'What about you? Shall I clean up those cuts for you?'

'Thanks. And Geoff, I'm as sorry about Meg as you are.'

As Geoff washed and refilled the basin, he said, 'I should have seen to you first, Ben. Sorry about that.' He began to bathe Ben's cuts, but when he'd washed away the blood and saw the deep dirty grazes, he stopped and said, 'I'll get you to bed, Ben. It's the doctor for you.'

'I'm all right. I'll be fine.' Reluctantly, Ben allowed Geoff to help him. Suddenly he said, 'Do you really think I tried to drown both of us on purpose? Does Lesley think I did?'

'We didn't know what to think. And you aren't helping much.'

'I fell into the sea. Meg jumped in after me off a cliff. She tried to rescue me, but in the end, I suppose, I rescued her. We saved each other.'

'She jumped off a cliff? With her harness on? I don't believe it.'

'That's what happened.' Ben got into bed.

'I'm going for a doctor, Ben. Dr Richards from Hangleby.'

'I don't need a doctor.'

'Do you want tetanus and pneumonia and Mandy to nurse you?'

Ben smiled reluctantly. 'You win. But get me the one who came when the Guvnor had pleurisy. Boozy old lad, but I liked him.'

'Dr Strang? I don't think he has any patients left besides the Guvnor. He lives in the Turpin Arms. I'll get down there while he can still stand.'

DR STRANG HAD MET Geoff Merchant before and liked him, and he liked Charlie Thorpe. The list of people he liked was short. He had met Ben once, had heard a fair amount about him from Charlie, and was secretly pleased to be sought out. He was usually sent for only when nobody else was available.

Dr Strang was about seventy, short, red-faced and fat, with thin little legs. He was completely bald, and his mouth was set in a downward turn of surliness. He was a steady drinker whose temper was vile.

Geoff drove him to the cottage. He shook his head testily at the multicoloured bruises appearing all over Ben, then he examined him thoroughly, taking no particular pains not to hurt him. He gave Ben an anti-tet, a shot of penicillin and a prescription.

'Why did you do it?' he asked abruptly.

'If Geoff told you I tried to drown myself, I didn't.'

Dr Strang sat down on the bed. 'You deserved to drown—chasing about on the top of a cliff like a lunatic. What's driving you, I wonder? Charlie told me a bit about you.'

'I need to do *something*,' said Ben, 'and I don't know what. It's sending me mad. If only I knew if I was going to be able to see again one day.'

'What, with totally detached retinas six months back? No chance, lad.'

'But the eye doctor said—'

'Medical science is wonderful? New cures every year? That's called letting you down lightly. By the time you've found out it's all moonshine, you're supposed to have found something or somebody worth living for.' He laughed shortly. 'Doesn't work of course.'

'It'd be rough having to give up hope,' said Ben. 'That's what's kept me going.'

Dr Strang looked down at the man in the bed, wondering whether he would bother to try to help him. It was a long time since he'd bothered much about anybody. But there was a brilliance and forcefulness in the young man that touched some chord in the grumpy old doctor. He thought of his own youth; wasted chances, lost opportunities. He made up his mind.

'Ben,' he said. 'I'll tell you something that may help you.'

'You've just told me I haven't any hope.'

'I did no such thing. I told you there was no hope for your sight. That's not the same at all. Until you accept that, there's no hope for you as a man.'

'What were you going to tell me?' Ben's voice was friendlier.

The old man seemed to be searching for words. At last he spoke in a low voice. 'My wife left me and the boy years back. We didn't hit it off—my fault I dare say. Our son Keith—Keith was sixteen when it happened. Some virus—they can cure these things now, but that was thirty years back. He was ill, paralysed, for six months. When he died, I felt like any father losing his only son . . .'

'I didn't know; I'm sorry,' said Ben.

Dr Strang sat up straight. 'Listen. As long as Keith was alive, there was hope. I lived on it, same as you're doing. When he died, and this is the point, hoping for a miracle was over. I had to start living again. I'd been no good to anyone, couldn't practise—couldn't keep off the bottle. But when Keith was dead and buried, I got back on the tracks again.

'Oh, I was younger then, had some strength of purpose left, some zest for life. Couldn't face it now . . .' His voice trailed off. 'Think about it, lad,' he said, almost kindly. 'You've a girl fair silly about you, so I've heard, and if you don't feel the same about her, make no mistake, there'll be others.' Dr Strang's grim chuckle was seldom heard. 'Give it time. Don't rush yourself—look after your dog instead.' He stood up. 'Can't stay all night. Remember the saying about one door closing and another opening.'

'What if it doesn't?' asked Ben.

Dr Strang turned as he went out. 'Kick it down,' he said. 'Start living.'

Fifteen

Lesley looked at her watch. Geoff had promised to let her know if Ben was found. What could have happened? She watched the local news, and sighed with relief when there was no account of bodies washed up. She switched the set off. Why hadn't Geoff telephoned?

'Too worried about that stupid dog, I suppose,' she said aloud.

She was standing by the telephone, wondering whether to try Geoff's number, when it rang.

Startled, Lesley snatched the receiver, clumsy in her haste. 'Geoff?' But it was Ben himself.

Relief seemed to cloud her brain. She wiped her eyes with the back of her hand. 'Oh, Ben love, I've been so scared, I thought you were dead.'

Ben said he hadn't meant to frighten her.

'Tell me what happened,' she said.

Ben told his story quickly, as if he wanted to get on to something more important. She exclaimed in astonishment when he told her that Dr Strang had attended him.

'That old soak? You should have had a proper doctor.'

Ben said, 'Thank God I didn't. Now listen; this is what he told me.'

Lesley listened obediently. When Ben had finished, she said, 'I thought the surgeon was wrong about you. He was sure you were too shocked to stand the truth.'

'You mean you knew all the time? Why didn't you say anything?'

'I was like you. Hoping for the impossible. I'm sorry, Ben.'

She waited anxiously for an outburst, but he said, 'We spend our time apologising when we aren't fighting. It's not going to be like that any more. When I get a real life worked out you'll be in it—if you still want to be.'

'You know I do.'

'Will you wait a bit longer then?'

'I'll be here,' said Lesley.

'I've treated you rotten, but I couldn't help it. The old doctor knew. He said I was afraid of being poor and idle.'

'I've never known you to be afraid of anything,' said Lesley.

'He was half right,' said Ben. 'I'm used to being poor, but without any work I wouldn't be fit to live with. I can't adapt or adjust—whatever it is they tell me to do. But with Meg's help, I have to fight this thing . . . When I ask you to come back, you're going to be proud of me, I promise you that.'

There was more, but she couldn't take it all in. She'd imagined him dead, and he was alive, excited, exalted.

SHE OVERSLEPT AFTER A WAKEFUL night, skipped breakfast and went down to the corner to do some shopping. She glanced absently at the *Leeds Morning Echo* on the counter.

BLIND SHEPHERD BENEDICT GLYN IN CLIFF FALL RESCUE
'I couldn't let Meg drown,' says Ben.

The picture showed Ben's bare torso, romantically battered, his expression remote but pleased. Inset was a picture of Meg, one eye half closed, one swollen paw raised, her fur spikily on end.

Lesley bought the paper and read it in the shop. The article was factual—obviously the reporter had talked to Ben himself. The Guvnor and Geoff were mentioned by name; there was no reference to her.

She got through the day's work automatically and, on her way home, saw the headlines in the evening papers. They were divided in opinion.

GUIDE DOG PLUNGES TO RESCUE OF BLIND MASTER
BLIND MAN'S LEAP FROM CLIFF TO RESCUE DOG FROM SEA

She bought both versions, and walked down to Henrietta. They would laugh together over them.

Something of Dr Strang's philosophy struck her. Henrietta had never had any hope of restored sight, but she and Owen were to be married the following week. Perhaps the cranky old devil had known what he was talking about after all.

Owen let Lesley in. He was all welcoming smiles and so was Henrietta, but they both had a slightly shamefaced air. A tall grey-haired man was standing by the window drinking whisky.

Owen introduced Phil Monk.

It was impossible to hide from him who she was—he guessed at once. Fearing she might feature in a sequel—I STILL LOVE HIM, SAYS SOCIAL WORKER GIRLFRIEND—Lesley kept quiet.

Phil exerted his considerable charm to win her over. By degrees she relaxed, glad of an opportunity to talk about Ben to somebody who had obviously been impressed by him.

'Pity he's such an outdoor type,' said Phil. 'The best jobs for blind people are in offices. Has he any other skills that he might turn to account?'

'He can sing,' said Lesley. 'I mean, *really* sing. Well enough to earn a living by it.'

Phil smiled pityingly. 'My dear girl, have you any idea what that entails? He'd have to be good—exceptionally good—and he'd need capital behind him.'

'He *is* good.' Lesley was getting angry. 'And he plays well enough to get by, too.'

'Well enough isn't good enough,' said Phil. 'He might be able to earn a few pounds playing in the pub, but it's a hard nut to crack, that world. Even if you can see.'

'Blind harpists, singers and fiddlers. The old stories are full of them. I thought that was one thing blind people did long ago,' said Henrietta.

'Audiences weren't so selective before radio and television,' said Phil. 'They were thrilled when the blind harper arrived with his faithful dog Tray, even if he did sing flat. But people know better now. No matter how beautifully Ben sings, you can't expect him to make it big. It's a hard cruel world, you know.'

PHIL HAD BEEN MEANING to visit Ben ever since meeting Lesley. He'd been intrigued by him at the time of his accident, and now he was wondering if there was another story in Ben, about his future. He left his car on the road and walked up to the cottage.

Ben wasn't a pretty sight. His bruises had turned green and yellow, his lip was cracked. He was walking about outside his door, giving quiet instructions to Meg, who appeared to have recovered.

Ben heard him, his face lighting up with that extraordinary smile. When Phil spoke, the smile faded. Ben had been expecting somebody else—Lesley, perhaps. But he accepted Phil's sympathetic enquiries.

Ben invited him in. They sat down, and Phil's eye fell on the guitar. 'Do you play that guitar?' he asked.

'A little. I wish I'd learned it properly. It's good to sing to.'

'You can get computerised sheet music in Braille.'

'I never learned to read music at all,' said Ben. 'I can play for a singsong and that's about it.'

'Why don't you ask Sid Walker at the Turpin Arms to take you on—lunchtime, say? If you're good enough, that is. He can but say no.' Phil was already writing in his mind the heart-warming piece which would help to launch Ben.

'Too near home,' Ben said. 'I'm living in Mr Thorpe's cottage, on his charity. He'd hit the roof if I did that—and offer me money instead, which would be worse.'

'Get on a bus and go to Leeds then. Try the Hart Royal. If they like you, there might be a modest living in it. If you're shy, get a song down on tape.'

'I've recorded a song already,' said Ben, 'but the quality isn't good. Listen to it and tell me if you think it's worth offering.' He handed a pocket recorder to Phil.

Phil hoped Ben could sing in tune. He switched on the tape.

What is she doing alone out there . . .

'You're right about the quality,' said Phil when it was over, 'but any fool could tell you've got a good voice—more than good. Not my kind of song, but it's something. Have you a copy I could look at?'

'No. I made it up lately.'

'You what? The lyric or the tune?'

'Both. Is it any good? I know loads of old favourites I could sing instead.'

'It's good. Just the right amount of pathos, but not sugary. Ben,' Phil said, 'the pub's OK for starters, but I'd like to see you on a stage—I might be able to help.'

It occurred to Phil that he no longer saw Ben as just a possible story. He had a blazing talent which must not be wasted, but he was also a man in need of help. Getting altruistic in my old age, he thought.

'Would you like to come out for a drink, Ben?'

'Thanks, Phil,' said Ben. 'I could do with one.'

IN THE HART ROYAL, Ben renewed acquaintance with Gloria, the gaudy blonde lady behind the horseshoe bar. Phil watched him curiously. He noticed that some of the drinkers were over-friendly, causing Meg to sit up straight with her ears laid back. Others slid away.

Meg was feeling miserable. Noise and smoke filled the room. She hated the brightly lit place they had come to. She would have liked Ben to have stayed at home where she could have him to herself.

Ben was drinking beer and laughing with a fat golden-haired woman. Fortunately the bar was between them: Lesley was bad, thought Meg, but this one wouldn't do at all.

The place got fuller and noisier every instant. Ben made jokes, and some people laughed. Meg sensed that there were others who felt uncomfortably that he shouldn't joke.

Phil led Ben towards the piano—Meg could have done it if asked. She was deeply unhappy, sensing his uncertainty. He didn't want to sing, but he was going to. Meg didn't want anyone to sing. Her ears were highly sensitive and she had no way of keeping the noise out. She flattened one of them against Ben's leg, and felt that he was trembling.

Phil wanted Ben to sing the song he often sang at home, but he wouldn't. He sang a song that everybody seemed to know. More songs were called for. People crowded round and there were glasses all over the piano. As Meg endured, she felt Ben relax and start to enjoy himself.

The applause was going to Ben's head. He sang out, and forgot all the worries and fears that Meg had tried in vain to share with him. For the moment he was happy. Meg tried to be happy with him, but instinct told her that nothing would ever be quite the same again.

BEN KNEW THAT HE couldn't have sung as well if he had been able to see his audience. Their invisibility made them into an anonymous mass. He couldn't be upset by the faces of those who were tone-deaf, anti-Irish or plain bored. The warmth and positive reaction of the others worked on him like strong drink—without the disadvantages.

Once he asked where Phil was, and was told he'd been buying up the phone for the last half-hour. He had come back; Ben heard him ask if he might take some photos. Whatever for?

Shortly afterwards, they left. People made way for Meg to lead him out.

Back in Phil's car, Ben could hardly speak because of jawbreaking yawns.

'The landlord talked of giving you a trial run, two evenings a week for four weeks,' said Phil.

'Will he pay?' Ben struggled with another yawn.

'Of course. Probably not very much, but it'll be cash and you'll get a free meal and drinks.'

Ben tried to find words to thank Phil. 'You've started me off,' he said. 'It's up to me to keep going . . .' He yawned hugely, and fell asleep.

When he woke they were at Middlegarth. Some sort of commotion was going on, and Meg was sitting on his lap.

'What's up?' he said.

‘We’re home,’ said Phil. ‘I tried to shake you awake, and the dog thought I was attacking you. Too well trained to bite—she just showed her teeth. I’d rather argue with a shark.’

Sixteen

Practice was improving Ben’s playing and he sang from the heart, buoyed up by the response he received. He’d recently been asked to sing at the Cock and Lion at Hangleby three times a week. Even Meg, surly to start with, was now part of the act. Ben sensed that she was proud of him, eager to show him off, like a mother with a precocious tot.

He was busy tinkering with his song, which he hadn’t yet sung in public, and was completing another.

The coffee tin on the shelf, where Ben kept his money, was almost full. Lesley was constantly in his thoughts, but he couldn’t and wouldn’t approach her until he was making enough to support both of them. In the meantime, he feared he might lose her to someone else. If only she would wait . . .

Ben was asked to sing at the Hangleby Christmas concert. The Boy Scouts’ Hall in Hangleby, about halfway between Middlegarth and Leeds, was a dingy spot. There was olive-green high-gloss paint on the walls, a good many faded flags drooping in corners, and a small stage at the end. A concert was held there every Christmas, consisting of a popular group eked out with local talent.

Mandy was a nuisance. He had to be civil to her because she kept the cottage clean and did his laundry, but she constantly hung about chattering, especially when he had a half-formed idea taking shape in his head.

The day of the concert, Charlie banged on Ben’s door.

Charlie sat down. ‘I’ve never been to hear you sing in pub, lad, so I thowt as how I might go to concert and take you along o’ me. T’other lot can come by bus. And I think—don’t fly out at me now—you could do with a new outfit.’

Ben burst out laughing. ‘No, Guvnor, this’ll have to do for the concert. I’ll spend my fee on clothes if I’m that shabby.’

Charlie went away shortly afterwards, and returned at about six o’clock with the Range Rover. They drove to Hangleby in companionable silence, each thinking his own thoughts.

‘Penny for ’em,’ said Charlie.

‘I was thinking I might sing my own song tonight,’ said Ben.

LESLEY WAS GROWING used to living in a sort of limbo. She had gone to hear Ben sing more than once, but had not made herself known. Seeing Ben hit her hard. She didn’t know which was worse, going or staying away.

Lesley sat with Owen and Henrietta. Along with Phil Monk who was there too, they had done their best to promote the concert in the press and on local radio. The hall was cold and musty and they were the first arrivals. The stage was screened by limp curtains.

Phil said, 'I almost hope Ronnie Hyde doesn't come.'

Ronnie was agent for many internationally famous pop groups. Now he was turning his attention to Country and Western. Phil had interviewed some of his discoveries, and it was to please him that Ronnie had come, on a cold December night, to Hangleby Boy Scouts' Hall.

The hall filled up fast. The rector made a speech. Then the curtains, jerkily drawn, revealed Big Harry and the Dalesmen, standing in a semicircle. They were greeted with applause by the mainly local audience.

At the back of the hall, a latecomer was looking for a seat. 'Up here,' mouthed Phil. He'd been keeping the place between him and Henrietta for Ronnie Hyde. Ronnie, a loose-limbed character, wrapped in a variety of scarves and cardigans, topped with a cape, sat down.

'God, what a circus,' he muttered.

The Dalesmen offered a selection guaranteed to offend nobody and please most people over fifty years old. When it was over, there was a fair amount of shouting and stamping, and then Big Harry introduced Ben.

The curtains were tweaked shut by more or less invisible Boy Scouts, and Meg appeared in the gap in the curtains. She walked through, followed by Ben with his guitar. He looked preoccupied because he was counting his steps towards the central spotlight.

Meg turned her head and thumped her tail.

Ben took three even steps, bent, and just touched her head. Then he started his opening song.

When it was over, there was fairly enthusiastic clapping. Nothing like as much as the Dalesmen's.

Ben turned his head this way and that, assessing the reaction, then he said, 'I hope you all have handkerchiefs with you. If not, they have them on sale at the door.'

One or two halfhearted titters greeted this.

He's nervous, thought Lesley.

'This song is called "Girl in a Garden",' said Ben briefly, and he began to sing. There was total silence in the hall.

'You slide away like a falling tear,
The rain pours down and my arms hold air—
Night in the garden.'

Ben sang the words softly, sadly. He felt the reaction from the hall.

At the end, the audience were hesitant. Was there another verse? Then the applause started and swelled.

There was shouting and stamping and whistling. Under cover of the applause, Ronnie Hyde said to Phil, 'You were right, he's a winner—where's he been hiding?'

Lesley turned to Henrietta. 'I don't know how much more of this I can stand.'

Henrietta whispered, 'He's singing for *you*. Can't you tell?'

'I wonder if he is.'

'Who else? Meg?'

'Perhaps.'

The clapping died away and Ben said, 'I'll sing you a song about friends. My best friend is my dog Meg here. This is her song, and I call it "The Best Friend Game".'

He pulled the stool he'd sat on earlier towards him and Meg jumped onto it. Her expression was one of suffering bravely borne. The song had a swing and a beat and a neat punchy lyric. When it was over, Meg jumped down, Ben waved his hand and followed her through the curtains to the accompaniment of clapping, shouting and cheers.

Lesley stood up with a muttered apology and went out.

IT WAS DARK OUTSIDE, and a thin sleet was falling. She backed into a doorway. Steps behind her. She stood still, searching in her bag for a hanky; she didn't want to talk to Owen or Henrietta.

It was Geoff. He put a clumsy arm round her shoulders and she turned and pressed her face against his jacket.

In the hall, a spatter of clapping greeted the announcement of the Nativity Play by the schoolchildren.

'Let me take you home,' said Geoff. He added gruffly, 'Ben doesn't deserve such devotion.'

Lesley said bitterly, 'Doglike devotion. It's not enough.'

For a minute, he held her without speaking, feeling her wretchedness as if it had been his own.

Finally he said, 'I don't blame you for a minute for resenting her. Ben looks to be starting out on a career which includes Meg, but not you—of course you're upset.'

Lesley blew her nose. She disengaged herself. 'With any luck I'll outlive my rival,' she said flippantly.

Geoff was shocked. 'I should hope so,' he said seriously. 'No, Lesley, you must try to think of Meg as a specially trained nurse-companion, tiding Ben over the rough patches. He doesn't want you on the same terms as before. Give him six months and he'll be making as much money as you are—maybe more. I was sitting behind Ronnie Hyde. He wants to buy the performing rights of the song. I'm not musical, but I do know something about blind people. I tell you, it'll be the saving of Ben. Come back into the hall.'

They returned quietly to their seats in time to hear an aggressively Yorkshire angel telling the Christmas story to a class of infant shepherds.

Ronnie was missing from his seat. He had gone backstage for a word with Ben. After the play he came back and asked Phil if a woman called Lesley Grant was in the audience.

'Here,' said Lesley.

'I can't get any sense out of Ben. He won't discuss his songs and says if there's anything to be signed he wants you to do it for him.'

AFTER THE SHOW, Ben went with Phil's party and Ronnie to the Cock and Lion, where they all assembled in a private room. Lesley kept behind the others, but when Ronnie produced a document for signing they made way for her and she and Ben stood side by side.

Ben was still high on applause, but when he heard Lesley's voice, he knew that success was hollow without her. 'Lesley,' he said, 'will you do whatever you think best about the songs? I can probably do my own negotiating, but I need somebody to sign things. Will you?'

'What does that make us, business partners?' asked Lesley.

'In a way. This may be a flash in the pan; don't do it if you'd rather not. Ask Phil.' Ben knew his words were brisk and dismissive, but wondered if she sensed the depth of feeling behind them. 'Please, Lesley,' he said.

'I'll see to it,' she said. She talked to Ronnie, who wanted to act as Ben's agent, and it was decided that all three of them should visit a lawyer the next day.

They'd forgotten Charlie until they heard him out in the street, bellowing

Ben's name. Lesley ran out to fetch him in, and he thumped Ben's shoulder violently. 'Good lad, good lad,' he kept repeating.

Congratulations came from all sides. Ben felt bewildered and overwhelmingly sleepy. He sat on a settee with Meg lying at his feet, her chin on his instep. He listened to fragments of conversation, and sipped his beer, sleepily enjoying it.

Charlie said loudly, 'Time we went home, I reckon. Drink up, Ben.'

Ben emptied his glass obediently.

'Good night, Lesley,' he said.

As they went out through the saloon bar, somebody accosted Ben, standing in his path. Meg stopped.

'Kicked the door down, I see,' said Dr Strang.

'I suppose I did,' said Ben.

Charlie said, 'What brings you to Hangleby, Albert?'

'I came to hear Ben sing. Well done, lad. I enjoyed it.'

'God helps them that helps theirselves,' said Charlie, with the air of one who has just coined a telling phrase. 'Come to farm. Plenty of whisky there.'

Dr Strang struggled into his overcoat with a grunt of thanks. The three of them climbed into the Range Rover.

'What's the date?' Ben asked suddenly.

'Seventeenth,' said Charlie. 'Christmas tomorrow week, and eleven months to the day since you came to Yorkshire.'

Ben said, 'St Patrick's Day's three months off. I'll know by then if I'm going to be any good.'

'You *are* good!' Charlie shouted.

'He wants recognition in Ireland, I should think,' remarked the doctor. 'That's it, isn't it, Ben?'

'You read my mind once before,' said Ben.

Ben, sitting in the back seat, spoke to Meg, and she leaned her head against his leg. His hand smoothed her head, rubbed the backs of her ears. 'Meg,' he said, too softly for the others to overhear, 'you're a comfort to me.' He had thought that a dog would be a tedious responsibility; he couldn't imagine how he had been so mistaken.

She was a support, a companion, filling much of his time. But Ben wished, with painful intensity, that Lesley was beside him, driving back home with him. Meg whined, nosing his hand, trying with every nerve to communicate with him. Almost, he thought, as though she knew what he was thinking.

'WHAT ABOUT A NIGHTCAP?' asked Charlie, whisky bottle poised.

'As long as you drive me home.'

Charlie poured a generous dollop of whisky for Dr Strang, and levered the top off a bottle of grapefruit juice for himself. Ben had been invited in but had refused. He'd been half asleep anyway.

Dr Strang studied the grapefruit bottle with concentrated loathing. 'You'll poison yourself with that rubbish, Charlie. Acid muck.' He tipped water into his whisky and drank it off like medicine.

'He'll go far, Ben,' he said suddenly.

'Don't see how he can, the way he is. Oh, he'll try,' said Charlie. 'Stubborn youth—always was. Got a temper too.'

Dr Strang's harsh chuckle surprised him. 'You'd be angry yourself if you lost your sight, Charlie Thorpe,' he said.

'I would that. But what real future is there for him, blind?' Charlie filled the doctor's glass. 'Too late for poor lad now,' he said.

Dr Strang gulped, and set down the empty glass. 'Poor lad, nothing,' he said. 'Ben's not a poor lad—never could be. He's too much character.'

'He treated that girl of his shameful,' said Charlie. 'Must make allowances, I suppose.'

'H'm. Probably knows what he's doing. Chances are he'll outgrow her and leave her behind. If fame's what he's after.' He thoughtfully rubbed his stomach. 'She'd best try to forget him if he makes the grade with this singing lark.'

'Forget him? You might as well tell sun to forget to rise,' Charlie muttered as he stood up, steadying the doctor's elbow.

Seventeen

As filming of the *Late Late Show* began, the studio audience knew what to expect. The St Patrick's Day concert at the Gaiety Theatre in Dublin had been televised, and indeed some of them had been there. The name was being talked about all over Ireland; a new name and one with a lilt to it. Benedict Glyn.

'The Best Friend Game' had been an overnight success early in the new year. With its bouncy rhythm and singable tune, it was played at every party and in every pub. 'Girl in a Garden' also caught on, and sales were soaring.

Ben's parents had been invited to appear on the *Late Late Show* too. Both were overcome with stage fright and were tongue-tied. Gay Byrne, the presenter, did his professional best with Myles and Muriel, putting Muriel at her ease, and playing Myles along with questions about greyhound racing. On the subject of Ben, neither seemed to have much to say.

'Yes, he used to play the guitar sometimes.'

'He wanted to be a jockey but he was too heavy.'

'He was good with sheep.'

When it was Ben's turn, he played and sang 'The Best Friend Game'. Meg sat beside him, looking self-conscious.

When the applause had died away, Gay Byrne, smiling and gently clapping his hands, said, 'Wasn't that beautiful? Wasn't it? Thank you, Benedict.'

'I'm always called Ben.'

'Oh? But you like to be billed as Benedict. Why?'

'It's my name,' said Ben. If he'd said it was because his grandmother, now dead, would have wanted him to, they'd have thought he was crazy.

When Ben stood up to sing 'Girl in a Garden', he felt supremely confident. Not happy exactly; happiness would have to wait.

He felt he must continually drive himself to achieve more. He was learning Braille and how to use a home computer. He listened to talking books half the night and he was educating himself. He had tried to fight his blindness and he knew he had won.

MEG LED BEN off the plane with great care. Ben's right hand was in his pocket. Meg knew that he carried a small cube-shaped box in it. Sometimes, when they were alone, he would open it and take out the ring inside, turning it round, almost as if he could see the pale blue stone in it. The corners of the box were scuffed from handling.

The reporters were taking photographs. Meg posed looking up, ears pricked, at Ben. She had learned to enjoy posing for the cameras.

One of them held out a microphone and said, 'Haven't you brought back an Irish colleen with you? I hear they mobbed you at your last concert.'

Ben said, 'No. I prefer Yorkshire lasses now.'

The reporter said, 'Oh, I see; lasses in the plural—not just one then?'

'No, two,' said Ben. 'The other one is my dog, Meg.' He added, 'Walk on, Meg,' and she steered him round and through the eager strangers.

As Ben spoke, Meg had seen the woman, Lesley, quite close. She was pushing her way through the crowd towards Ben.

Meg gave one of her wide, yawning sighs. She had always known that one day she would have to share Ben with a human female. But sharing love with a human is the lot of most men's dogs. Meg had hoped, by making herself indispensable, to postpone the woman's return. She knew, as she heard their voices and saw Ben's face light up, that she had failed.

Doglike devotion had not been enough.

MARJORIE QUARTON

'The way some people are with antique shops, I was with horse fairs. I couldn't go to one without wanting to buy, and I cannot remember a time when I imagined I would be anything but a horse dealer.' Horse dealing, a very tough profession for a woman, is just one of Marjorie Quarton's talents, acquired through hard work and determination.

She was brought up near Nenagh in County Tipperary where, sixty years later, she still lives and farms. An only child, she was educated at home until she was eight by a succession of governesses, though her father, she says, taught her 'some Latin and useful things like how to navigate by the stars'. At fifteen, she was sent to boarding school to prepare for entrance to Trinity College Dublin, but after two 'quite wretched' years, returned home to take over the running of the farm from her father who had fallen ill. Before long, in order to supplement a very meagre income, she began horse dealing. Her memories of the colourful world of the Irish horse fairs are recorded in her recently published autobiographical book, *Breakfast the Night Before*. Among her customers were the Household Cavalry, several of Britain's police forces, and the Swiss Cavalry—until they changed their steeds for motorbikes.

In 1965, a Yorkshire horse dealer visited Marjorie in Ireland, bringing with him a farmer named John Quarton. Two years later, John, a widower with seven children, and Marjorie were married. Their very happy union lasted until John's death in 1985, and they had one daughter of their own, Diana, now twenty-one.

It was John Quarton's Yorkshire background that provided the setting for *No Harp Like My Own*, and it was he who introduced Marjorie to Border collies. 'I was fascinated by their herding ability: I'd been used to running or riding after my sheep!' she remembers. Both Roy and Meg in the novel are based on the first two dogs that John gave her, and which formed the basis for her current dog-breeding business. Today she keeps eleven collies, plus several pups. With the cattle and 300 breeding ewes in her care, it's quite a handful. But then Marjorie Quarton, who is also a journalist in her spare time, is not easily daunted!

TRIAL

by Clifford Irving

ILLUSTRATED BY DON DAILY

Warren Blackburn was once an up-and-coming attorney but now, with his career in ruins, he is grateful for any legal cases that come his way. Imagine his surprise when, suddenly, he is assigned to represent the defendants in two separate murder trials. One, a shrewd former beauty queen, can probably win an acquittal. But is she really innocent? The other, a homeless Mexican immigrant, will probably be convicted. But is he truly guilty? During one sizzling Texan summer, Warren finds his whole world on the line: his career, his marriage, even his trust in the law . . .

1

In Houston, Texas, in the early winter of 1985, a petty thief named Virgil Freer devised a scheme to swindle the chain of K-Mart stores. Using a bootleg electronic-pricing gun, he drastically lowered the bar codes on such items as expensive fishing equipment and lawn mowers, bought the goods in one branch of K-Mart and then returned them in other branches for a full refund. Like most crooks with a workable scam, Virgil Freer did it once too often. He was arrested, and jailed.

Virgil was a small, wiry man with pale eyes and yellowed teeth. He seemed beaten down by life, humbled, pitiable. He made enquiries around the Harris County Jail from the knowledgeable inmates.

'I need a real smart lawyer. But I ain't got much money, so he'd better be on the young side.'

He hired Warren Blackburn, twenty-nine, a criminal defence attorney toiling his way towards the top of his profession. Virgil had heard that Warren Blackburn was a friend to the friendless, that he was stubborn and he got things done.

On a cool January morning the young, dark-haired lawyer, wearing a leather windbreaker and corduroys, sat opposite Virgil in one of the visiting cubicles of the Harris County Jail. There was a persistent smell of meat loaf and disinfectant in the air.

Warren Blackburn said to Virgil, 'If you're straight with me, Mr Freer, I can help you. If you lie to me—well, I've known liars so that one more won't crater me. It'll be your butt on the line, not mine.'

Virgil liked this lawyer immediately. Confident, calm, wry in speech and keen of eye, he was not one of those fast-talking counsellors who kept saying 'Don't worry' and never quite bothered to explain the snares that lay ahead in the legal undergrowth. An honest man, Virgil decided, with a college education. The man I need.

'I swear I'll tell you God's truth,' Virgil said. 'But please, you got to spring me outa here right away. My wife's in the hospital with cancer. If I don't git back home, my kids'll starve.'

Warren commiserated, probed, asked basic questions. 'Virgil, do you have any prior convictions?'

Shamefacedly, Virgil admitted that some years ago up in Oklahoma he had been convicted of drunk driving, and then later copped a plea for passing a few bad cheques.

'That's just a little misdemeanour trash,' Warren said, 'so let's see what I can do.' They arranged a small fee.

Warren checked with Ben Taub Hospital and discovered that Freer had told the truth: his wife was about to be operated on for bone cancer. That saddened the young lawyer but it also made him feel he could trust his client's word. He put on a dark suit and went to the assistant district attorney who was prosecuting the case. The prosecutor slapped down a computer print-out that listed the two prior convictions. He demanded $20,000 bail.

Warren shook his head mournfully. 'Don't you want to be able to sleep nights? This is the man's first felony. His wife's in the hospital, he's got kids to support. Give the guy a break.'

The prosecutor agreed to $5,000 bail. Using a bondsman who owed him a favour, Warren got Virgil Freer out of jail.

The case had fallen into Judge Louise Parker's 299th District Court. Lou Parker, as the judge called herself, was probably the most harsh and obdurate magistrate in the Harris County Courthouse. Warren kept plea-bargaining, delaying, hoping for a break. And he got one—Judge Parker's number-two prosecutor, a young black woman named Nancy Goodpaster. She was sincere and ambitious but overwhelmed by the crowded court agenda.

In her small office piled high with papers, Nancy Goodpaster and Warren began plea-bargaining. 'Freer's a first offender, isn't he?' the prosecutor enquired. She answered her own question. 'I'm sure he is—I can't find any priors in his file.'

The computer print-out citing Freer's Oklahoma misdemeanour convictions evidently was buried deep, perhaps even lost. A little startled, Warren changed the subject.

'If we could come out of this with probation and a fine,' he said, 'we could live with it. The man's wife may die of cancer. He's got four little children to support.'

Nancy Goodpaster had heard around the courthouse that Warren was a scrupulous, trustworthy lawyer. She wilted, offering thirty days probated for a year, plus a $500 fine. A good deal.

Warren worried it over in his mind a while and then returned to Freer, who was biting his chipped fingernails on a back bench in the 299th.

Warren's eyes were hard and stern. 'Virgil, are you going to keep that job you've got?'

'Yes, sir.'

'You swear on the Bible and all that's holy that you're going to stay out of trouble?'

'Yes, sir! I swear it!'

'Well, you better, because I'm putting a lot on the line for you.' Warren explained the state's offer and said, 'My advice is take it. Look after your kids and pray for your wife. Sign fast, Virgil, before I change my mind.'

The paper to be signed was an affidavit that stated Freer had no prior convictions. Warren signed it too.

Warren's career proceeded along its steady upward track. He forgot about Virgil Freer until one night nine months later, when Freer was caught attempting to hijack a truckful of television sets. He was carrying a .38-calibre pistol. He exchanged six frenzied shots with the arresting officers before he was wounded in the leg and begged to surrender.

A zealous young Harris County assistant district attorney studied the full file and noticed something peculiar about Freer's last probation. He said to Virgil, 'Look here, in this affidavit in the K-Mart case last year, you swore you didn't have any priors. You lied.'

'Yeah, but my lawyer told me to.'

Warren, when he heard the charge, sank his head into the darkness of his cupped hands. He could say that Freer had never told him. But one more lie would be more than he could stomach.

That evening, at home, he told the tale to his wife, Charm, a young woman of slender grace and strong opinions. Under her maiden name, Charmian Kimball, she was a reporter for the local independent TV station. The Blackburn house on Braes Bayou was red brick with a small back-yard pool surrounded by banana trees. In the shadows, standing by the pool, Warren stared up at the silent and indifferent universe.

'I feel such a fool,' he said. 'I put my whole career in jeopardy for a man I knew I'd never see again.'

'You thought he owed you something,' his wife said quietly, with some reproach. 'You forgot about human nature.'

My God, Warren thought. How could I have been so wrong?

He was technically guilty of aggravated perjury, a felony. If convicted, Warren would be disbarred. Humiliated, disgusted with himself to a degree that no one at the courthouse fully realised, he cut a deal: aggravated perjury reduced to a Class A misdemeanour, party to false swearing. The agreement was for one year's suspended sentence.

Wearing his most conservative grey suit, he pleaded before Judge Lou

Parker, since hers was the court where the offence had taken place. In her black robes of authority, Judge Parker sat upright in her big leather chair behind the judicial bench, glasses dangling from a gold chain that she fondled with stubby fingers. She had a mannish voice, a deep South Texas accent. She called Warren 'a disgrace to the legal profession'.

'Mr Blackburn,' Judge Parker intoned, 'before I'll consider the state's recommendation, I want to hear just why you think I shouldn't drop three years in the penitentiary on your bowed head. And I don't want any namby-pamby standard baloney like y'all always throw up at me when you're pleading for some low-life dog who sold cocaine to children. Make an effort, counsellor.'

Warren squared his shoulders and said, 'I relaxed my ethical standards, your honour. And I bought a sob story. I'm ashamed not only because I perjured myself as an officer of the court but because it was an extreme error of personal judgment.'

'You finished, counsellor? That's it?'

'Yes, your honour. And it's a lot.'

Scowling, Judge Parker honoured the deal that Warren had made with the Office of the District Attorney. But she added on her own that he be suspended for one year from practising law.

Despite his dark mutterings of protest, Warren's wife had been in the courtroom when Lou Parker sentenced him to the year's exile. At home later, in their bedroom, Charm kicked off her shoes and said heatedly, 'From what I hear, if every lawyer who signed a false affidavit got suspended for a year, they could turn the Harris County Courthouse into a parking lot!'

Warren said, 'Honey, I knew what I was doing. I paid the price.'

'Too facile. I think maybe the reason you helped Freer was a little deeper than you realise.'

Deeper? He had wanted to save a handful of human lives. He asked what she meant.

She said, 'What I'm trying to say is, Warren, you were weak. You find it painful that people go to prison.'

'Not all of them,' he grumbled. He realised that he was evading her point.

So did Charm. 'I'm not talking about the evil ones,' she said. 'Most of your clients are just common sleazeballs. Nine times out of ten they did something either horribly wrong or unforgivably stupid. The law says if they're guilty they have to go to jail. If you feel too sorry for them, maybe you weren't cut out to be a criminal lawyer.'

'Lay off,' he muttered to his wife. 'I feel like hell already. I don't need to be told I should quit practising my profession.'

During the twelve months of official disgrace he reported once a month to his probation officer. He worked as an occasional part-time investigator for another lawyer, an old friend named Rick Levine. He joined a gym and pumped iron. He took a cordon bleu cooking class. In the summer he drove down to Mexico for a month and took a course in intensive Spanish.

Charm stole a week's vacation from reporting and flew down to join him in the mountain town of San Miguel de Allende. They stayed in a little inn on a narrow cobbled street where purple bougainvillea climbed over the balcony, with a view of the cathedral. Warren remembered it as the best week of his marriage, even better than their honeymoon on Maui. Charm said, 'You're a good man. When this is all over, you'll be fine.'

At last, banishment ended. Warren appeared at the courthouse to inform the world that he was again ready to practise law. Except for the judges and prosecutors, everyone was friendly, backslapping. But it was referrals he needed: clients, not lunch companions. An occasional misdemeanour came his way, but most of the time he sat in his office, a converted residential cottage on Montrose, annotating his cookbooks and reading current volumes of the *American Criminal Law Review*.

Charm organised dinner parties for lawyers and their wives and husbands. Warren prepared escargots and coq au vin. The dinners were lively. Rick Levine—short, black-haired, with a flaring moustache and the beginnings of a paunch—gravely said, 'Maybe you should open a restaurant.'

Warren and Rick had been schoolmates together, then at South Texas College of Law in Houston. One night after dinner Warren drew Rick outside to the terrace. 'So I made a mistake once, but I'm still a damned good lawyer. Don't people remember that?'

'I imagine,' Rick said, 'that prospective clients may think that some judges are a little prejudiced against you. And that might be true. Everyone wants an edge, not a liability.'

Warren realised that Rick had heard something. Maybe he *would* be a liability to a client. Maybe I'm not tough enough: that, he realised, was what Charm had been trying to say. It could be that in this business you needed skin of leather and no heart.

Warren began to doubt whether he had it, whatever it was. But to prove to his peers and his betters that one lapse in judgment had diminished neither his skills nor his respect for the law, he began hustling court appointments.

The Houston courts employed no public defender's office. If an accused claimed he was too poor to hire counsel, the judge would appoint a lawyer and order a legal fee paid out of public funds. Each morning at eight o'clock, hungry defence attorneys left their business cards on the bench at the judge's elbow, then crowded round the desks of the court coordinators who helped to dispense the cases. Some lawyers, fresh out of law school, sought court-appointed work in order to gain experience. Older lawyers hustled for it when their collars were frayed.

When he was younger, more brash, Warren had likened the older lawyers to vultures waiting for dead meat. Now he was more forgiving. He was one of them.

Warren did court-appointed work for two years. It was survival. He never went to trial: all the cases were plea-bargained. He dealt with drunken drivers, vagrants, addicts, and small-time crack dealers, the trash of the streets and ghettos.

Some days Warren wanted to smash his fists against the courtroom walls in frustration. I'm a trial lawyer, he thought bitterly, that's where I shine, that's what I love! And I gave all that up for the sake of a son of a bitch like Virgil Freer who was now doing thirty years at Huntsville Prison for armed robbery and attempted murder of a police officer.

RAIN BEAT ON THE ROOF, lightning and thunder crackled across the horizon. Charm Blackburn cried out softly and it woke Warren, who calmed her with whispers and touches until she subsided into uneasy sleep. The digital bedside clock showed 3.30am.

Shortly after six o'clock, Warren woke again. Usually Charm kept far to her own side of the bed. But this morning she was pressed against his shoulder blades. He took that closeness to be a hangover from the storm and the unnamed fears it had aroused in her.

'What time is it?' she murmured.

'Six fifteen.'

She turned away from him and pulled the duvet over her head. Sliding out of bed, Warren embraced Oobie, his arthritic old golden retriever, and then slipped into his grey track suit. With Oobie joyfully limping and panting at his side he jogged for twenty minutes along Braes Bayou. At home again he showered, brewed coffee, and with it ate a bowl of cereal and a banana from the tree by the pool.

He dressed quietly, careful not to wake Charm. Looking down at what he could see of his wife—some strands of dark blonde hair, a curve of ivory cheek, he whispered, 'I love you.'

A few minutes after seven he was driving down the Southwest Freeway under a blue sky scrubbed by the night's rain. As he drove, Warren dreamed that he was married to a woman who still adored him, that his office telephone never stopped ringing, that he was in control of his life. He knew that his life had lately unravelled out of control and that he had to make a move or the centre would fall apart.

From a telephone in the courthouse, he retrieved messages from his office answering machine. The only message of consequence was a request to call Scoot Shepard's office. Dropping another quarter into the slot, Warren returned the call. A secretary informed him that Mr Shepard was in a pre-trial hearing in the 342nd District Court.

'And what's happening in the 342nd?' Warren asked.

'A setting for bail in the Ott case,' the secretary said.

Scoot Shepard was the dean of Houston criminal defence attorneys. He'd defended major drug dealers and Mafia *capos* and got them off when there was little more than a hazy hope or a muttered Sicilian prayer. He'd been profiled in *Time* and been asked by a dozen New York publishers to write a book about his cases.

Warren took the elevator up to the fifth floor and the 342nd District Court. The current presiding resident of that court, Judge Dwight Bingham, was one of Harris County's four black judges. His courtroom was the most spacious and dignified in the courthouse; he had earned it by seniority. Warren liked and admired Judge Bingham. He had compassion.

Ten days ago, Judge Bingham had drawn the plum of the current season, the Ott murder case. The accused, the owner of a topless nightclub, had killed her lover, Dr Clyde Ott, a multi-millionaire gynaecologist. The State of Texas was charging wilful murder; Scoot Shepard, on behalf of the defendant, had pleaded self-defence. For weeks the murder had been a lead story on the evening news. The trial was on the agenda for late July—guaranteed to make headlines every day, the kind of trial a lawyer loved.

Nearing seventy years of age and ready to retire, Judge Bingham sat on the high walnut bench. Warren squeezed into one of the spectators' pews, noting that more than a few attorneys had come to hear Scoot Shepard, the maestro.

Chunky, about five foot ten, Scoot had a pale, domelike forehead and slightly bloodshot eyes. His nose was large and fleshy. Today he wore a wrinkled suit. Warren had always thought he could pass for an oil-rig operator on holiday in Vegas.

Dim yellow lights from the high panelled ceiling gleamed onto Judge Bingham's bald brown head. He looked up from some papers and said gently, 'All right now, Mr Shepard. You want me to reduce your client Ms Johnnie Faye Boudreau's bail from three hundred thousand dollars to fifty thousand. I'm not sure I can do that.'

Scoot Shepard scrambled to his feet. 'Your honour, my client's got the best reason a defendant can have. She's broke.'

Judge Bingham looked across the courtroom at the assistant district attorney, Bob Altschuler, chief prosecutor in the 342nd. 'I take it,' the judge said, 'that the State of Texas disagrees.'

'Yes, your honour, and for the best reasons the state could have.' Altschuler was already standing, feet planted wide apart like a wrestler. A bulky, handsome man of forty-five, with snapping brown eyes and a full head of pepper-and-salt hair, he folded his arms in a truculent posture. 'This is a murder charge. No question that the defendant, Ms Boudreau, shot the victim, Dr Ott, who wasn't armed. She's admitted it.'

'Well,' Judge Bingham said to the prosecutor, 'these papers claim that Ms Boudreau lives in town, is gainfully employed, and isn't going anywhere. She's showed up today. What's your contention, Mr Prosecutor? Here today, gone tomorrow?'

'The state's contention,' Bob Altschuler said, 'is that the defendant can afford the three-thousand-dollar bail set by this court. Especially if the defendant can afford to hire Mr Shepard.'

The judge peered down at the defendant, Johnnie Faye Boudreau, sitting alone at the defence table. 'Ma'am, you claim you don't own that topless nightclub out on Richmond that everybody says you own. What's it called?' Adjusting his horn-rimmed bifocals, he rustled the papers set before him. ' "Ecstasy"! What a provocative name. Is that your contention?'

Scoot walked back and bent to whisper to his client. Then he said to the court, 'Your honour, Ms Boudreau has a slight sore throat, and this is a mighty cavernous courtroom. I don't want her to have to shout and aggravate her condition. May we and Mr Altschuler approach the bench for this discussion?'

'Of course you may, Mr Shepard,' the judge said.

Johnnie Faye Boudreau rose slowly from her chair. This May morning in the air-conditioned courtroom she wore a white linen suit with high heels to match, one strand of cultured pearls and an emerald ring. She had admitted she was forty years old but could have passed for thirty. She had high breasts, flaring hips and a remarkably narrow waist. Her most remarkable feature, however, was the colour of her eyes. The left one was hazel, the right one a cool grey-blue.

As she approached the judge the courtroom grew still. Everyone strained to hear.

'That's right, your honour,' Johnnie Faye Boudreau said in a husky, relaxed voice. 'I don't own Ecstasy. I just work there.'

Scoot took over. 'She's on a salary, your honour—forty thousand dollars a year, paid monthly. Her only current assets are a bank account with under two thousand dollars, some jewellery and a car.'

'Her car is a Mercedes four-fifty SL,' the judge pointed out.

'She's got good taste,' Scoot said.

Bob Altschuler, scowling, leaned towards the defendant. 'Ms Boudreau, are you telling this court that you have no stocks, bonds, savings accounts, or any other negotiable assets?'

Johnnie Faye Boudreau's wide mouth curved into a smile. 'No, sir. Nothing except my account at Bank of America and the clothes on my back.'

'And a few clothes in your closets at home, I'm sure.'

'A few,' Johnnie Faye said. 'Do y'all want me to sell some?'

The reporters from the *Post* and the *Chronicle* heard this and scribbled in their notebooks. That was quotable.

Judge Bingham said, 'Mr Altschuler, these papers tell me that if the bail is reduced, Ms Boudreau's employer—this corporation owned by some oil people over in Louisiana—is ready to lend the money to Ms Boudreau. Then she can pay Mr Shepard and we can get on with this case. What do you say to that?'

Altschuler wheeled smartly on the defendant. 'Ms Boudreau, do you swear that you have no controlling interest in the corporation that owns Ecstasy? No shares at all?'

'No, sir. Neither. Just like the papers say.'

Judge Bingham gently responded, 'And you're not going to run away before or during the trial, are you, Ms Boudreau?'

'No, sir,' Johnnie Faye said firmly.

'Well, then, I believe the request has merit. I'm going to reduce bail to a hundred thousand dollars.' Judge Bingham tapped his mahogany gavel.

Warren Blackburn managed to intercept Scoot just outside the broad swinging doors of the courtroom. 'Can't talk now,' Scoot explained, dramatically placing a finger on his lips and gesturing at the reporters about to corral him. 'You available for lunch next week, young fellow?'

'Any day,' he said.

'I'll call you after the weekend,' Scoot said regally, 'and tell you where.'

LATE THAT SAME FRIDAY AFTERNOON Johnnie Faye Boudreau dug under the mattress in her guest room, stuffed $50,000 in hundred-dollar notes in her big ostrich-leather handbag, and went out on a spending spree.

In Sakowitz, opposite the Galeria shopping mall, she bought a ruby brooch. In the cool of Lord & Taylor, she bought a Russian sable jacket and a T-shirt with a leopard motif. And then, in Neiman-Marcus, she bought a grey shantung suit and a blue silk dress that she thought would be appropriate to wear in court for the Ott murder trial. She paid cash.

AT ABOUT THE SAME HOUR a man named Dan Ho Trunh was installing a pool timer in the back garden of a house off Memorial Parkway. A twenty-seven-year-old Vietnamese, Dan Ho had been in Houston for five years and would be eligible for citizenship in August. He was an electrician who worked cheap and liked to be paid in cash. With the job finished and an extra three twenty-dollar notes in his wallet, he edged his old Ford Fairlane station wagon onto the Southwest Freeway going eastwards.

Close to the Wesleyan exit, Dan Ho remembered that he had to pick up laundry and dry-cleaning. With a quick glance into the rearview mirror, he flicked his indicator, stepped on the gas and veered from the middle lane towards the exit ramp. This should not have been difficult. In his experience, Texans were courteous and forgiving drivers.

But the car to the right of him seemed to accelerate rather than slow to give him room. He felt a mild jolt, as if his rear bumper had grazed another driver's front bumper.

It was not possible to stop. Cars were surging right and left. Dan Ho powered down the exit ramp and swung the station wagon into the parking lot of a mini-shopping-mall, pulling up in front of the Wesleyan Terrace Laundry & Dry-Cleaners. It was after eight o'clock and except for a wino propped in a loose sitting position against an optician's façade, the parking lot was empty of people.

Through the plate-glass window of the dry-cleaners Dan Ho Trunh saw the half-turned back of an Indian woman in a green and gold sari. She was stacking cardboard boxes.

Then he became aware that another car had pulled up alongside in the parking lot, and a woman in the car was shouting and cursing at him. He rolled down his window. 'What's the problem?' Dan Ho said quietly.

The woman snarled, 'Don't get smartass with me, you yellow slant-eyed sleazeball!'

He shook his head and said quietly, 'Lady, you're crazy.'

'Who the hell do you think you're talking to?'

Sighing, Dan Ho Trunh turned away, reaching into his back pocket for his wallet which contained his laundry ticket. From the car parked a few feet to his left, he heard a shriek. He looked up and beheld a small black circle, the barrel of a pistol. He felt a terrible pain. He went down backwards on the seat, spurting bright blood on the dashboard.

THE NAME OF THE SMILING WINO propped against the optician's shop in the mini-mall was James Thurgood Dandy—known back in his native Beeville, Texas, of course, as Jim Dandy. As the station wagon and then the second car pulled into the parking lot, Jim Dandy had clambered to his feet and yawned a couple of times. Then he heard a woman's scream followed by a sharp crack that could only be a gunshot.

Instinctively he ducked, turning his head towards the street, then, after a moment, he walked slowly over to the station wagon. The front window was wide open. He peered inside. Someone in that car looked awfully dead.

On the seat, the man's outstretched right hand clutched an open leather wallet. A laundry ticket protruded from it and a fat sheaf of wrinkled green was exposed in the billfold part. Jim Dandy took the wallet. 'Hot damn,' he whispered. Clutching it, he turned and ran.

AN HOUR LATER, Hector Quintana, a homeless man, rolled his Safeway shopping cart between Buildings C and D of the Ravendale Apartments in the Braeswood district.

Ravendale rented out furnished apartments on a month-to-month basis to visiting yuppies and divorcées. The residents drank wine and played volleyball in the pool on hot summer evenings. No one paid attention to strangers.

Good trash cans here, Hector Quintana had learned. Gringos threw things out which back in El Palmito his people would battle to own. Once he found a toaster; another time, running shoes with a hole in the toe. Tonight he had even better luck. Rummaging in the trash can, he dug out a pair of dirty white tennis socks, a half-finished jar of Planters salted peanuts, and then a bottle of Old Crow about four inches full. He opened it. The aroma of bourbon whisky filled his nostrils.

Hector dug further. Amid lemon peel and coffee grounds, his brown hand closed on something cool and metallic: a pistol.

He looked at it and knew he had a prized possession, something which could change his life—if he could find the courage to use it correctly. Hector sat down on the fresh-mown grass next to the parking lot and ate the jar of peanuts, which he washed down with big swallows of Old Crow until the bottle was empty. Then abandoning the shopping cart, he stuffed the little pistol into his back pocket and set out on foot for the Circle K convenience store just up the block on Bissonet.

ON THE HUMID MAY TUESDAY morning following the reduction of bail for Johnnie Faye Boudreau, Warren Blackburn returned for the first time in two years to the 299th District Court, the scene of his crime. He stood for ten minutes in the anteroom of Judge Lou Parker's chambers. He had avoided her court assiduously until now, but now it was time. Can't duck her for ever, he decided, and I've paid my dues. Warren wore his best dark-blue suit and his shoes had been shined by the bootblack in the courthouse basement.

Finally the court coordinator, Melissa Bourne-Smith, shot him a radiantly false smile.

'Might have something good for you. The judge said she wants a young lawyer on this one.' She glanced down at the agenda sheet. 'Defendant's name is Hector Quintana. Capital murder, case number 388-6344. Can you come back at noon?'

Surprised, not quite believing what he had heard, Warren wrote quickly on his yellow legal pad. Capital murder was top of the line, differing from ordinary murder in that there were aggravating circumstances: murder during the commission of another felony, murder of a police officer. The fees averaged a decent $750 for every day's appearance in court. 'Who's the victim?' he asked Bourne-Smith.

'Some Vietnamese. Shot in the parking lot. It's a nothing case, it'll go real fast. Just let me get the judge's OK.'

'I'll be here at noon,' Warren said. 'Thank you.'

2

Warren had first met Charmian Ellen Kimball by the side of the Shamrock Hilton pool one September Sunday afternoon in his twenty-sixth year. Charm had just graduated from the University of Pennsylvania as a journalism major—a willowy, blonde young woman with serious blue eyes and a strong, clear voice. Her stepfather, a Boston stockbroker, had brought the family to Houston when a branch of his firm opened in the Galeria mall. Charm had fought for the right to go back East to college; no idea was more foreign to her than that of marrying a Texan. But Warren touched a yearning spot deep inside her.

He lived in a bachelor studio apartment on the edge of Hermann Park. She was in her first season as a television reporter. Throughout the summer before their wedding they debated about where to live. 'I miss the East,' Charm said wistfully, but they agreed to stay in Houston, where Warren was making a name for himself as a young criminal defence attorney, and they pooled their money for the house on Braes Bayou.

Charm progressed to co-anchor on the evening news. Warren chose their few investments and took care of the mortgage from a joint account. But after the year of suspension handed to him by Lou Parker, he had to ask his wife for money. After his suspension was lifted he was going over the credit-card statements one month when he saw $1,200 for Marshall Field and $1,600 for Lord & Taylor. He asked her what they were for.

'I bought two new suits,' Charm said.

'That's a lot for just a couple of suits. I haven't bought a suit in two years.'

Charm's eyes grew hooded. 'You can't afford a suit,' she said, 'and I can. I need good clothes for my job, which is what's supporting us these days.' She paused. 'You know, you really irritate me, Warren. You've given up on your life. And I don't think you even realise what's happening to you.'

They were in the den. Oobie lay on her mat, watching them carefully with wet eyes. Warren stood framed in the arched doorway, his hands stuffed in the pockets of his jeans.

'You're doing that court-appointed stuff all the time,' Charm said. 'You think it's demeaning but you still do it. You're bright. You've got a mind that cuts right to the heart of a problem. But you've let that drift away from you. You're only thirty-three, but you've lost your zest.'

He tried to keep his fury in check. 'Zest for what?'

'For *everything* . . . including me. We used to talk about having children.'

'Are you saying you're ready to have a baby?'

'Actually, I'm saying the opposite, Warren, I don't want children if our marriage is going down the drain. I love you, but your life's so screwed up you can't find the energy to love me back. I don't know if I want your kids. You're depressed, you're irritable, you snap at people. What kind of a father would you be? Get your act together.'

No one had ever hurt him more deeply. He hadn't been able to reply. He walked out of the room into the kitchen and poured a glassful of whisky, which he drank in five minutes. And then another.

There is a winding-down in an unhappy marriage, a struggle to define what's wrong, a reluctance to relinquish what's right. Another year passed. His marriage, Warren realised, seemed to have gone from elegance and passionate gaiety to the drab business of getting on with things. A faded glory, he thought, like his love affair with the law.

But then, one Friday in May, he listened to Scoot Shepard plead for reduction of bail for Johnnie Faye Boudreau, and the following Tuesday a court coordinator he hardly knew asked him to defend a homeless man named Hector Quintana against a charge of capital murder.

That same Tuesday, Warren called Scoot Shepard's secretary, who told him that the lunch date was set for the next day. 'If you could pick him up in the 181st around twelve thirty, he'd appreciate it.'

'I'll be there,' Warren said.

He had time for a cup of coffee before his noon meeting with Judge Lou Parker. He manoeuvred around a pack of waiting jurors into the elevator. When it stopped on the fourth floor, Rick Levine darted inside, his brown eyes shining with good humour.

In the basement cafeteria, they sipped coffee from plastic cups. Warren said: 'Lou Parker's looking for a young lawyer to appoint to a capital—a Mexican shot some Vietnamese. I walked in at the right time. Or maybe the wrong time.'

Rick's olive-coloured face split into a frown. 'You ready to put on the gloves again with the lady hyena?'

'It's not my heart's desire, but I'll handle it.'

A bleak look showed on Rick's face. 'Listen to your old buddy,' he said. 'If you go to trial in the 299th and the jury awards probation, Lou Parker automatically gives your client thirty days in jail as a condition of it. She's telling you, "Dare to waste my time, I'll teach you a lesson." '

Warren checked the time on the wall clock. He drained the last sip of coffee. 'I have to go.'

'Watch yourself,' Rick counselled. 'She's got a long memory. If there's a way she can hurt you, she'll dig a tunnel to find it.'

WARREN KNOCKED ON THE OAK DOOR of Judge Parker's chambers, then twisted the brass knob and walked in. The room was spacious, its windows facing westwards framed the rotunda of the civil courthouse and the gothic rise of the Republic Bank Building. On the wall, flanking her diplomas, Judge Parker displayed oversized framed photographs of George Bush and John Wayne.

Lou Parker sat behind her cluttered desk, square-faced, frowning, and holding a long filter cigarette in one hand. She waved Warren into a leather armchair.

With no preamble, she asked, 'You want this capital?'

Warren stayed silent a moment. Why would he *not* want it? It was a way to crawl back from the basement of criminal law into the high-rent district. He wondered what Parker had in mind. A lawyer who would do what he was told? Someone she could step on? He would have to take that risk.

'I want it,' he replied.

'What do you really know about me?' Judge Parker asked. He knew that she was divorced with grown children, had been one of the first women defence attorneys in the county, ran the 299th like a German railway station. And doesn't like me.

'Twenty years a defence attorney.' Judge Parker stubbed out her cigarette in an ashtray already overflowing. 'Got my court seven years ago. I'm not popular like Dwight Bingham and I don't care. I do as I please, I say what I please. I run a tough courtroom. I get things done and I know what I'm doing.'

There was a certain amount of truth to that, Warren knew.

'This is my courtroom—you better get that straight,' Parker rasped. 'No speeches for the peanut gallery. No tricks. Hint of a stunt like you pulled four years ago, you're out on your butt.'

Parker waited, but this time Warren did not nod his head.

'I'm giving you this capital,' she said, 'because you finally had the guts to walk in and ask for a case, and I suppose every fool on this earth deserves a second chance. It's no great shakes, because it's a whale in a barrel for the state. I'm not saying the defendant's guilty—I'm not allowed to say that. But don't waste my time, you understand? Just move it along. I expect you to plead it out for whatever you can get.'

Lou Parker's dark eyes glinted. She blew cigarette smoke in the general direction of his face. 'Now go see your client.'

IN THE PARK OPPOSITE the ugly granite monolith of the courthouse, Warren bought a hot dog from a vendor and ate it while he studied the Quintana file. Some mustard dripped onto the pages. Warren wiped it off with his handkerchief. An hour later he settled into a steel-backed chair in a Harris County Jail visitors' cubicle as he once had with Virgil Freer. At a shiny bare metal desk under fluorescent lighting so garishly bright that it made his eyes ache, he talked to Hector Quintana through a metal grille.

Quintana had smooth skin, black hair, an uncomplicated face. Warren guessed they were about the same age.

'Mr Quintana, do you understand English?'

Quintana nodded, but Warren saw uncertainty in his eyes.

He kept his speech simple. 'Mr Quintana, my name is Warren Blackburn, and I'm a lawyer appointed by the court to represent your interests. The State of Texas will pay my fee but I don't want you to think for one minute that means I work for them. I work for you, Mr Quintana. There's nothing you tell me about this case that I'll ever repeat to another living soul unless I have your permission. I'm bound by a solemn oath—what we lawyers call confidentiality and lawyer-client privilege. You understand what I'm saying?'

'Sir,' Quintana said, 'I didn't do what they say I did.'

Warren ignored that. He would never ask Quintana if he had done it. That was the first rule of a criminal defence attorney.

'Do you trust me?' Warren said.

'Yes, sir.'

Warren formally told Hector Quintana that he had been accused of murdering a man named Dan Ho Trunh, an electrician, twenty-seven years old, married, the father of two children—

'I doan know this man,' Quintana said.

'Let me finish, please.'

Slowly, now and then using some of the Spanish he had learned in Mexico, Warren explained that the indictment returned by the grand jury was for capital murder, because it was believed that the offence took place during the course of a robbery—Dan Ho Trunh's wallet had not been found on his person or in his car. Texas law mandated that if Hector Quintana stood trial and was found guilty of capital murder, or instead pleaded guilty to the court, there were only two possible penalties: life in prison or death by injection.

Quintana gasped. 'But I doan kill this man. I doan know him. I try to rob a store, *nada más*.'

'Hector, suppose you tell me your version of what happened on the evening of May twenty-six. First, where do you live?'

Quintana lived with friends near the stables in Hermann Park. In the evenings, behind a shed, he told Warren, they fried pork cracklings in a pot of deep fat. He had worked as a handyman in a 7-Eleven store. The 7-Eleven was a good job, but the franchise had been sold to a Vietnamese who paid Hector a week's wages and let him go because a brother-in-law wanted the job.

'Did that upset you?' Warren asked.

'I had no work. It wasn't fair.'

Bad, Warren thought. If the DA's office didn't know it now, they would surely find out.

Since February he had lived by doing odd jobs, but in April he gave up his bed in a rooming house in the Spanish district in order to save the rent and send money back to Francisca, his wife. That was when he began to sleep with his friends Pedro and Armando in the park by the stables. He found a shopping cart one day from the Safeway—

'Found? Where did you find it, Hector?'

'In the street, I doan remember . . .' But Quintana flushed, looked ashamed.

'You stole the shopping cart, isn't that so?'

'I found it. Maybe someone else stole it. *Yo no*—not I.'

A stubborn man. But maybe it was true. You never knew.

Quintana related to Warren the various treasures and staples he had inherited from apartment-house trash cans. He went often to Ravendale and it was there, on that night, that he had found what was left of a bottle of whisky. And *la pistola*.

After finishing the last swallow of Old Crow, Hector Quintana said he decided to rob the Circle K up on Bissonet. He shrugged, as if to say to Warren: these are hard times. A man grows weary and relaxes his principles. The pistol was not loaded, and he was glad of that.

'There is something I wish you to understand,' Quintana said, looking at his lawyer with a clear gaze. 'If I had not been a little drunk, I would not have done this thing.'

The clerk in the Circle K claimed he couldn't open the cash register. It often jammed like this, there was nothing to do but bang away. He said, Hector recalled, 'Please don't shoot me, I'm doing my best.' Finally, the drawer crashed open. He handed Hector a little over $120 in small notes and change.

'I was so happy,' Hector told Warren, 'that I thanked him. I went out into the street. But by then the police were there. They were so quick! I couldn't believe it. . .'

Two Houston Police Department (HPD) cops leaped from a blue and white squad car, revolvers drawn. 'Police! Freeze. Drop the weapon at your feet!'

Without being asked, he turned to lean against a nearby car so that they could frisk him and handcuff him.

'Did they tell you that you had the right to remain silent, the right to a lawyer, and so forth?'

'Yes, it was the same as on TV.'

Only late the next day, here in jail, did the matter of murder arise. He couldn't believe they were serious. He told them they had the wrong man. But it was clear that they didn't believe him.

Warren asked him where he had been earlier on the evening of May 26, before he arrived at Ravendale.

Walking around, just thinking about Francisca and his children. He was from El Palmito, a village in north central Mexico.

'And in those hours before you found the gun in the trash can, did you talk to anyone? Did you meet anyone you knew?'

He had knocked on a few doors, Quintana recalled, to ask if anyone wanted their car washed. No one had wanted.

Warren thought diligently for a minute. 'Let's focus on *la pistola*, Hector. It's the same one that was used to murder a Vietnamese man earlier that evening, and the fact that you had it in your possession is very bad. You understand that, don't you?'

'There were no bullets in it,' Quintana said. 'I tole you.'

'Did you ever show that pistol to anyone? To any of your friends at the stables?'

'How could that be?' Quintana asked, puzzled.

'It would be foolish of you to lie to me about the pistol.'

Quintana looked him in the eye. It was a look he had not shown before: it was slightly menacing. 'If you think,' he said in Spanish, 'that you can make me say I killed a man, or ever fired that pistol, you are betting on a lame cock.'

'Don't get your feathers ruffled,' Warren said sternly, gathering up his papers. 'I'll be back.'

WARREN'S FATHER HAD ONCE TOLD HIM a story of an old mountaineer who said of his pancakes, 'No matter how thin I mix 'em, there's always two sides.' Warren would have to find out the other side of Hector's pancakes. Unfortunately, the best person to ask was the prosecutor, Assistant District Attorney Nancy Goodpaster, to whom he had lied four years ago.

Warren entered the windowless 299th District Court, just as Judge Lou Parker was calling the roll of defendants and attorneys. 'No talking in court,' the judge said in her spikiest tone to some women on the rear bench. He caught Nancy Goodpaster's eye and walked back with her to her cool little office next to Parker's chambers.

'The judge is not in a good mood today,' Warren said.

Settling herself behind the desk in a steel-backed swivel chair, Goodpaster looked at him calmly. 'The judge is in the mood she's always in. We all live with it.'

Her thin hands were steady on the papers in front of her.

'Mr Blackburn,' she said, 'I'm looking to settle the Quintana case. So let's get down to it.'

Five years with Lou Parker and the State of Texas, he thought, and she's a gunfighter.

He nodded at the file on her desk. 'What have you got?'

What she had, she said flatly, was a good case. She had motive, opportunity, and possession of the murder weapon.

The motive for the murder was money. When he left the house that morning, Dan Ho Trunh had more than fifty dollars in his wallet, and it had been established that during the course of that day he had been paid at least ninety dollars in cash for electrical repair work he had done. His wallet had not been found.

As for opportunity, an hour after the murder Hector Quintana had been picked up within a mile from the crime scene. If he had an alibi, it had not yet surfaced.

Warren coughed, said nothing.

Ballistics confirmed that the murder weapon was the same .32-calibre Diamondback Colt clutched in Hector Quintana's hand when he ran out of the Circle K on Bissonet. They had traced the gun and discovered it was purchased five years ago from a pawnshop in Dallas. The buyer had given phoney ID.

'And when Quintana walked into the Circle K the gun was empty, right?'

Goodpaster nodded. 'He was drunk, the police offence report says. Maybe too drunk to think of reloading.' Then Goodpaster said smugly, 'Anyway, Quintana's not under indictment for drunk and disorderly or armed robbery of a store. This is capital murder.'

Warren leaned back in the wooden chair, making a steeple of his hands. 'But you have no witnesses.'

'What makes you think so? We have a witness who saw him at the crime scene, and two days later she picked him out of a line-up. Sorry, Mr Blackburn.'

Goodpaster reached into the file, plucked out a stapled sheaf of papers and tossed them across the desk to the unhappy defence attorney.

The next morning, once again, Hector Quintana glared at Warren through the metal mesh. 'You didn't tell me,' Warren said quietly, 'that you'd been in a line-up.'

'What is a line-up?'

'The police make you stand with a bunch of other guys facing a mirror. Each of you holds up a number.'

'Oh,' Quintana said wearily, unconcerned. 'That happened. I held up Number Five. I didn't know what it meant.'

'What happens in a line-up,' Warren explained, 'is that there are people on the other side of the mirror. They can see you but you can't see them. In this instance, an Indian woman named Singh picked you out. She said, "That's him." '

Him meant the man whom Siva Singh had seen running away from the shopping complex on Wesleyan. Singh had been in the back of the Wesleyan Terrace Laundry & Dry-Cleaners and had heard what she later realised was a gunshot. Coming up to the front of the store a minute later, she had noticed a man standing by a station wagon parked in the lot. And the next minute: 'My goodness, he was running away very fast.'

A few minutes later a customer came in to drop off some dry-cleaning. The police offence report noted the customer's name as Rona Morrison, a clerk at Better Buy Motors on Bissonet. On her way back to her car, Morrison had glanced in the window of the station wagon.

Siva Singh heard a scream. She hurried outside and found Morrison on her knees, gagging. Singh then peered inside the station wagon and saw the dead man. She brought Morrison into the store, settled her on a chair and dialled emergency.

When the HPD squad car arrived, Singh was interviewed by Homicide Sergeants Hollis Thiel and Mitch Douglas. That was when she described the man she had seen running away as 'about five foot ten inches tall, with long black hair, and he wore just a pair of trousers with a shirt. He wore no jacket. He looked, if I may say so, to be poor and homeless. I thought he might have been Hispanic.' She had never seen him before in her life. Downtown at Harris County Jail the next morning she picked Hector Quintana out of a line-up of six men.

Warren related most of this to Quintana, whose hair was black and could be described as long.

'What were you wearing that night, Hector?'

'A shirt and pants.'

'No jacket?'

'Was a hot night. My jacket was in my shopping cart.'

'This is not good.' Warren shook his head gloomily. 'The Indian woman says it was you she saw running away.'

'She saw someone else,' Quintana grumbled. *'Yo no*. If you doan believe me—'

'I know, I know. I'm betting on a lame cock.' Quintana's denial of guilt was beside the point. Men had been known to deny guilt until the very moment they stepped into the courtroom and saw the grim faces of the jury. Texas juries killed. That was part of their heritage.

'Hector, I believe you. But I'm a lawyer, not your mother. I have to look at the evidence. This Indian woman is going to get on the witness stand and point a finger in your face and state that she saw you running away from the scene of the crime. And the HPD Ballistics expert is going to say that the gun you had in your hand an hour after the murder was the gun that killed this Vietnamese man. That's bad, very bad.'

Quintana nodded gravely.

'Now, as your defence lawyer, I can't tell the jury you were somewhere else when the murder was committed, because I can't produce a single live body who can verify it. I can't say you're a peace-loving citizen, because you were caught robbing a store with a gun. You were drunk, but that won't help you.'

This was usually the moment when the defendant lowered his head, because he finally understood the terrifying price he had to pay, then said, 'What can you do for me if I plead guilty?'

That Hector Quintana was guilty of murdering Dan Ho Trunh, Warren had almost no doubt. The qualifier was there only because he liked Quintana, but he was all too wary now of the consequences that might arise from liking a client.

He had one more idea. 'Hector, I know that when men get drunk they get crazy. Maybe you bumped into this Vietnamese guy in that parking lot. Maybe he insulted you—said something nasty to you about your being a Mexican. Is that possible?' Warren felt his cheeks warm up with enthusiasm. 'If it is, and if you're straight with me, and I'm straight with the jury, they'll understand why what happened happened . . .'

Quintana said in his soft voice, 'There will be a trial?'

Warren ground his teeth. This guy was stubborn.

'There can be a trial by jury. Twelve men and women.'

'Can I speak to the jury?'

'You have that right. It will be testimony under oath.'

'Then I will tell the jury that this woman makes a mistake, and that I doan ever know this man and doan kill him.'

Leaning forward to the mesh, Warren cleared his throat to hold back his impatience. 'If there's a trial, and they find you guilty,' he said quietly, 'the jury will sentence you either to death by cyanide injection or to life in the penitentiary. That's the law.'

'But I will tell them, and they will believe me even if you doan. I will tell them,' Quintana repeated desperately.

WARREN WALKED at a slow pace through the twisting underground tunnel that connected the Harris County Jail with the courthouse. Thinking about Hector Quintana, he felt a barbed pain in the upper part of his back. No wonder. It was a hopeless case. The judge had been clear: *'Don't waste my time. I expect you to plead it out for whatever you can get.'*

It occurred to him then that Hector Quintana had never asked what would happen if he were willing to plead guilty.

Warren would have said, 'I can plea-bargain, Hector. I could try to get the prosecutor to reduce the charge to plain murder. I'd try for thirty years. You could be out in fifteen.'

If Quintana agreed, that would be a minor blessing for everybody. Warren would be in Lou Parker's good graces. Word would spread. A small start, but still a start. And Quintana would stay alive and one day see his Francisca again.

But if Warren took the case to a jury and they gave his man death, which seemed an excellent possibility, he would be worse off than when he started. They would say he had thrown away a defendant's life for the chance to play to the crowd. Not easy to live with. A lawyer's responsibility in a capital case was to see that the client came out of it alive. And I can't take it to trial, he thought, reaching the end of the gloomily lit tunnel, pausing at the door to the courthouse. That's the deal with Lou Parker.

3

He took the elevator up to the 181st on the third floor. With Scoot Shepard at work, the courtroom was crowded.

When the judge declared a break for lunch, Scoot immediately came up to Warren, squeezed his hand and said, 'Let's trot over to my office. I'll have Brenda send out for sandwiches.'

In his office Scoot pulled two cans of beer from a diminished six-pack in the little refrigerator behind his desk. Brenda was dispatched into the heat for turkey sandwiches. Scoot lit a cigarette, popped the beer can and dropped with a sigh into his leather armchair. He was probably sixty-five years old, but his hair was still full and black with small silver-grey wings above the ears. 'What do you know about the Dr Ott case? And my client, Johnnie Faye Boudreau?'

'Whatever I read in the *Chronicle*,' Warren said. 'And of course I remember the Underhill murder.'

Between pulls at the can of beer and puffs on his cigarette, Scoot gave him a synopsis. The victim, Clyde Ott, had been a successful Houston gynaecologist. In his early thirties he had married one of his patients, Sharon Underhill, the forty-year-old widow of an oil-and-gas baron and the mother of two teenaged children. With Sharon's money Dr Ott built the Underhill Clinic for drug addicts, and then a series of expensive retirement homes. There was a waiting list to get into all of them.

'I knew Clyde Ott,' Scoot said. 'Before Clyde married Sharon he'd had more women in Harris County than the whole Houston Astro infield put together. Marriage didn't stop him. But his main squeeze in recent years was Johnnie Faye Boudreau. You saw her in the courtroom. She runs a topless bar out on the strip behind the Galeria. Maybe she owns it, maybe she doesn't—who really knows? Won a couple of beauty contests when she was younger, then became a model, then a dancer. Couple of brothers got killed in Vietnam—she talks about them all the time. Married twice, no kids. First husband she divorced on grounds of nonsupport. Second husband was a drug dealer. She divorced him after he got sentenced to a thirty-year rap up in Dallas. Then she took up with Clyde Ott.'

Almost two years ago, on a sunny October morning, Clyde's wife, Sharon Underhill Ott, had been shot down in a parking lot on her way to an aerobics class. A high-powered rifle had done the killing. A man in a black Lincoln saloon was seen speeding away from the scene. Clyde Ott was in San Diego at the time, at a medical convention. Johnnie Faye Boudreau was visiting her mother down in Corpus Christi. Airtight alibis.

'Johnnie Faye had another part-time boyfriend then,' Scoot said, 'David Inkman, called Dink. He was an assistant manager at her club, an ex-Marine. Dink drove a black Lincoln saloon. Naturally, he fell under suspicion. But he had an alibi too. A couple of hookers swore his Lincoln was parked in their garage the night before.'

Scoot popped another can of beer. 'About three months after Sharon Ott was killed, Dink was shotgunned to death in the driveway of his home from a passing pick-up.'

Warren blew out his breath. 'You're saying—'

'Not me. Others did. Said that Johnnie Faye was behind it all, that she wanted to marry Clyde Ott, and the first thing she had to do was get rid of her husband, which was easy—there was a story that she'd told the law where he was picking up dope in Dallas—and then Clyde's wife, which was hard. And then after Dink had done that for her out of the blackness of his loyal heart, she had to get rid of Dink too. Around the time of the Inkman murder there was another guy named Bobbie Ronzini who also worked for her at the club. Ronzini fell under suspicion but the cops couldn't prove anything. Then he vanished. Maybe into a hole in the ground. No one knows.

'So now we come to the Ott case,' Scoot went on. 'But here we know that Johnnie Faye Boudreau pulled the trigger. She admitted it. Called HPD to tell them. Of course, Clyde's stepdaughter was in the house when it happened, so it would have been a tricky business for Johnnie Faye to cut and run.'

She had shot Clyde Ott twice with a .22-calibre pistol, her own gun, which she normally carried in her handbag. She had a permit. At her club, she had to deal with some bad people.

'Now, I can see in your face that you want to know how come I'm talking to you.' Scoot leaned back in his tall leather chair, while cigarette smoke spiralled lazily towards the air-conditioning vents. Bob Altschuler, the prosecutor, was a first-rate trial lawyer, and the DA's office had the full resources of a bureaucracy. Against that, Scoot couldn't handle the case alone. There was law to research, potential witnesses to be hunted down and interviewed. The two younger lawyers in his office who would normally assist him were tied up with major litigation.

'You had a bad break,' Scoot said to Warren. 'But I've been watching you for years and I think you're a fine lawyer. If you're free, I'm asking you to assist me, to sit second chair with me in *Boudreau.* I'll pay you twenty grand up-front against your hourly rate. Trial's set for July twenty-fourth. You might have fun. You might learn something. Is it a deal?'

Warren never hesitated. If Scoot trusted him, others would. It was a real step to a comeback. Significantly better than struggling for a homeless Mexican who refused to see that he was doomed. 'Deal,' he said. 'What's the theory of the defence?'

'The defence,' said Scoot, 'is the oldest in Texas—the son of a bitch needed killing. A little hard to do nowadays, but you can still try it. *I'd* listen.' He handed Warren a copy of the thick file marked *Texas v. Boudreau.* 'Take this home and read it.'

IN HIS OFFICE Warren turned the air conditioning up a notch against the afternoon heat, and began reading the file.

On Sunday evening, May 14, according to the transcript of Johnnie Faye Boudreau's first interviews with Scoot Shepard, the defendant had been invited by Dr Clyde Ott to dinner at the Hacienda, a Tex-Mex restaurant just off the I-10. It was one of Johnnie Faye's favourites, a big place with several dining rooms. Before dinner Clyde had a couple of drinks, and during dinner a few more, and there was no telling what he'd sipped before he got there.

Clyde drank, she said, and he sniffed cocaine. He was the sort of drunk who never fell down or slurred his words; he just got mean. Last Christmas he had hit her with a clenched fist, right across the nose. Before she knew what was happening—Pow! There was blood all over her silk blouse.

Clyde had beat up his wife too, and one of his other girlfriends, a cocktail waitress at the Grand Hotel. Knocked out three of her teeth, had to pay her $25,000 to shut her up. And he'd threatened Johnnie Faye more than once, raised his fist and said, in front of two friends, 'You slut, I could kill you!'

She wanted to marry him, that was a fact. Love is a funny thing—you don't always pick the most upstanding person to lavish it on. His being that rich had nothing to do with it.

If he could get a divorce and not lose his clinics in the process, absolutely, he'd marry Johnnie Faye. He was crazy about her. She was the most exciting woman he had ever known. He said that often, when he was sober.

Then Sharon was shot down outside her aerobics class by some mad killer. Clyde didn't mourn her. He was a louse, but no hypocrite. He stayed out of public places for a month or so, then he stepped out into the world again. Now he could marry Johnnie Faye.

But he didn't.

'It upset me. I can't lie about that.' She put it to him: 'Are we or aren't we going to do it, and when?'

'I need some time.'

'Time to make the decision or time before we get married?'

'Both, I guess, sweetheart.'

That bothered her. She never could get Clyde to tell her what really was the problem.

'Let's have a quiet dinner,' she said. 'And we'll talk about getting married. We'll make a timetable we can live with.'

That was the purpose of their dinner at the Hacienda on the evening of May 14. They arrived about nine o'clock. But Clyde got drunk and nasty. Accusations flew across the table over *fajitas* and sizzling onions. 'Take me home,' she said.

By home she meant her apartment, but Clyde had other ideas. Drunk or stoned or sober, he couldn't get enough of her. She drove and they made it to the house on River Oaks Boulevard without incident and went up to the bedroom. But when he couldn't follow through, he bellowed with frustration and began calling her names again. She climbed out of bed and got dressed. 'I can't take this any more, Clyde. I'm leaving you.'

Usually when she said that he became contrite, begged her to give him yet another chance. But not that night. He yelled, 'I'm sick of your threats!' and slapped her in the face.

In his black silk pyjama bottoms he followed her downstairs to the living room. He was a big man, six foot tall and two hundred and twenty pounds, with thick shoulders and a gut. He waddled when he walked, but he was quick enough. In the living room he got between Johnnie Faye and the front door. His eyes were bloodshot. He was gasping. He raised his fist and she backed across the carpet towards the fireplace.

Resting against one of the andirons was a poker; Johnnie Faye snatched it up to defend herself. Clyde twisted it out of her hand like a twig. Stumbling across the room, screaming, she positioned herself behind a white Italian sofa, with bookcases at her back. She hoped the noise would wake his stepdaughter, Lorna, occupying one of the guest suites. But the house was huge.

In her handbag Johnnie Faye had the .22 compact she always carried. She fumbled among the keys and make-up, then pointed the pistol at him. 'Clyde,' she said, 'if you come near me, I'll shoot.'

His response was to lift the poker like a baseball bat. She yelled, '*Don't!*'—but the drunken fool kept coming. In her panic she pulled the trigger and let loose three shots. The .22, when it was manufactured in 1928, had been a semiautomatic. But long ago some previous owner had filed down the sear—the piece that held the hammer cocked—thus making the pistol fully automatic. She'd forgotten about that, she said. That was the tragic part. She couldn't stop it from firing.

Believe it or not, he still took a swing at her with the poker. When she raised her head she saw him tumbling onto the white sofa. One bullet missed, one had hit him almost between the eyes and the other in the chest.

Scoot asked, What about the safety?

She must have released it without thinking when she grabbed the gun out of her handbag.

And did she know it was illegal to file that sear?

I didn't do it, she explained.

Clyde lay on his knees, head pillowed on the sofa.

From the telephone in the TV room she dialled emergency, gave her name and the address in River Oaks, and said, 'I just killed a man. He was about to assault me, and I shot him.'

She told a briefer version of that tale to the Homicide detectives when they arrived. If there's no one to contradict her, Warren thought, we'll win this case. Can't lose unless Scoot goes to sleep in the courtroom, and that had never happened.

AT HOME THAT EVENING he warmed up last night's chicken stew in the microwave, fed Oobie, then read the file a second time and went to bed. Charm hadn't come home: of late she had her own social life, a gang of friends from the TV station, a separate schedule.

She was there in the morning, asleep beside him, blonde hair tangled on the pillow. He studied her face. He knew it down to the tiny scar where the branch of a blueberry bush had hooked the corner of her mouth when she was thirteen. And he had loved it for eight years. He wanted to talk to her. The oaths of confidentiality, he believed, did not extend to man and wife. And she had always helped him to see more clearly. But she treasured her sleep in the morning, and he didn't wake her.

Running with Oobie along the bayou, heels pounding the concrete, he came to a decision. Working with Scoot on the Ott case was the major leagues, and he had earned the chance without even realising it. He had lost self-esteem, had toiled like a humble peasant in the fields of the law, and finally it had paid off. He was going to do a good job. Going to prevail.

But two murder trials was one too many. Get rid of *Quintana,* he concluded. Stop being sorry for the guy—he's guilty. Plead him out, fast.

The next day in Judge Bingham's court, Warren was registered as co-attorney of record for the defendant in *The State of Texas v. Johnnie Faye Boudreau.* He shook hands with a dark-suited Bob Altschuler, whose grip was like that of a heavyweight wrestler trying for an armlock. 'Congratulations,' the prosecutor rumbled. 'Let's sit down and cut a deal. You know this woman's a killer. She's a cannibal, a homicidal maniac!' He refused to let go of Warren's hand. 'She knocked off Ott's wife and the guy who did it for her and the guy who knocked off *that* guy, and we think that back in eighty-two she offed some Korean kid who worked in her club and gave her some back talk when she wouldn't give him a raise. You want to do a service to society, help me put her away. Tell your partner I'll settle for fifty years.'

Warren sighed. 'Are you finished? Can I go?'

'You don't believe any of it?'

'It's not for me to believe or disbelieve,' Warren said. 'It's for you to prove it.' He shook his hand loose from Altschuler's, and walked briskly up the stairs to Judge Parker's court. He drew Nancy Goodpaster off into a private corner of the hallway. 'Cards on the table, Nancy. What will you give if Hector Quintana pleads out? I need something to offer him.'

'What do *you* want, Warren?'

'Reduce the charge to simple murder. Twenty years. Drop the charges of armed robbery and possession of a weapon.'

'You're wasting my time, counsellor.' Nancy Goodpaster looked at her gold wristwatch.

'The Siva Singh ID won't stand up. It was dark in that parking lot—I checked it out. There are a thousand guys who have black hair and wear shirts and trousers on a summer night. I don't think Singh really saw the man's face.'

'She claims she did.'

'Nancy, what makes it a capital is the assumption of robbery. So tell me this—what did Quintana do with all the money from Trunh's wallet? He didn't have it on him when he robbed the Circle K. You can't make capital murder stick.' He waited for a moment. 'You want to settle this, don't you?'

'Naturally.'

'Then give a little. Give with a good heart.'

'Fifty years.'

'My man will never buy it. He has no record.'

She sighed. 'You feel sorry for him, that's all.'

'And if Quintana gets up there on the witness stand,' Warren said, 'the jury's going to feel sorry for him too. A jury will never go for the capital.'

'Forty years,' Goodpaster said. 'My final offer.'

'You're a hard woman.'

'No, I'm doing my job. Like you're doing yours.'

'You'll drop the charge of armed robbery?'

'I'll think about it, Warren. Now I have to go.'

Warren sighed. He hoped he was masking his feeling of triumph. He was saving a man's life.

IN HIS OFFICE late the following Monday afternoon, Scoot Shepard asked, 'You know the statute on self-defence?' In one hand he held a cigarette, in the other a glass of bourbon.

Warren nodded, frowning. 'And I know there's a provision in the penal code that calls for "the duty to retreat". Seems to me that one question a prosecutor might ask a jury to focus on is this: if Clyde Ott was drunk and abusive that night, why did Johnnie Faye Boudreau ever enter the house with him? Why didn't she just go out the door before he blocked her path? And if her story's true, that he once said in front of two witnesses that he would kill her—that's good for us, but it's got a flip side. The state will say that's why she carried the gun in her handbag on a dinner date. They'll call it premeditation.'

'True, true.' Scoot smiled delicately. 'Of course this is still Texas. People pack guns and everybody thinks he's the second cousin of Wyatt Earp. No Texas man or woman has to back down in the face of a threat, regardless of what the law says.'

Scoot refilled his glass.

'Don't fret too much about "the duty to retreat". You have no duty to retreat. Especially when the son of a bitch needed killing. I want to sell that theory to the jury and walk my client right out of Dwight Bingham's courtroom.'

'You think Johnnie Faye's story is true?'

'Hard to say. So far it's all I've got to work with. I want you to talk to her, then go nosing around and talk to anyone else you have to. Find out where we can be hurt. When I go before that jury, I don't want any unpleasant surprises.'

'When do I meet her?'

Scoot looked at his Rolex watch. 'In about two hours' time we're all going to the Dome for the Astro game—you and me and Johnnie Faye and her new boyfriend. Her idea, her treat. Between innings, you can get to know the lady.'

DRIVING HOME TO CHANGE, Warren avoided the crowded freeway and took a route along Main Street and Holcombe. He would be at Braes Bayou by seven fifteen, at the Astrodome by eight. He had had to break a dinner date with the Levines. When he turned the corner into the cul-de-sac leading to his house, he saw Charm's car in the driveway. It meant she had driven home immediately after work. She was not expecting him; he had told her about meeting the Levines for dinner. Charm was invited too. 'I doubt I can make it,' she had said, 'but if I can, I'll call Shepard's office.'

In the hazy evening heat Warren saw that Charm and a man he didn't know were standing by a car parked further up the street on the same side as the house. Charm's back was to him. The door of the car was open and the man was leaning on it, gesturing emphatically. Warren touched the brakes.

The man put his hand on Charm's shoulder, seemed to squeeze it. Then he placed his palm on her cheek and kept it there a few moments. Charm bowed her head slightly.

The man bent to kiss Charm briefly on the lips, and ducked into his own car. He drove past Warren with not even a glance. Hands tight on the wheel, Warren stared at him as the car moved by. He saw a suntanned man of about forty with a moustache.

Charm turned and walked quickly, heels clicking down the driveway, into the house. Further up the block, children shouted at each other. Roller skates rasped on concrete.

Warren parked, got out of the car, unlocked his front door and stepped into the cool hallway that led to the living room. Oobie stumbled up to him, wagging her tail.

Charm was seated in a rocker at the pine kitchen table, drinking a glass of cold white wine. She looked up with blurred eyes. There was a certain wild look too and an anger equal to his.

'I saw you out there,' he said. 'I was in my car.'

She stared at him in silence.

Warren's heart fluttered but everything else felt numb. 'Can we talk in the bedroom, Charm? I have to change.'

She followed him, carrying her glass of wine. She sat on the edge of the kingsize bed while Warren took off his suit and folded the edges of his trousers violently into the press of the wooden hanger. I don't know what to say or do, he thought.

'He's a man I've been seeing,' she said quietly.

'Seeing?'

'Having an affair with.'

Warren felt the blood hum through his veins.

'What are you going to do?' Charm asked. Her eyes had misted with tears.

'Tell me about it,' he said.

'Just what is it that you want to know?'

He said gently, 'How you feel. What you're going to do now.'

She cried for about five minutes. He was used to that: she was a woman with deep emotions, and sometimes she couldn't stop. The sobs made her throat hoarse. She had summed it up once: 'I'm insecure. It's common among kids from divorced families—my real father jerked us up and down the whole east coast until I was ten years old. I never could keep a friend. And then I got hauled out here. I have no roots.'

'You do,' Warren would reply. 'Here, now, with me.'

But now in the fading light he didn't comfort her with his hands or soothe her with his words. He no longer knew how.

She went to the bathroom to wash her face. During that time Warren put on a pair of jeans, a clean shirt and his cotton windbreaker. He sat on the floor and worked his feet into the old cowhide boots.

When she came out, he repeated, 'Tell me about it.'

'That won't help.'

'Maybe it will help *me,* Charm.'

She was thoughtful for a while. 'All right. Maybe it will.'

He was a lawyer—civil, not criminal. A partner in a big firm. He was from New York. A few months ago he'd begun some business at the station. They had started an affair. He was in love with her, he claimed. She wasn't sure how she felt about him. She might be in love with him too.

Her lover was separated from his wife back in Manhattan, awaiting a final divorce decree. He had three children.

'Three children,' Warren muttered.

'Is that meant to be a snide comment?'

'It just slipped out. How do you feel about all this?'

'Confused.'

'I can imagine. And what about our marriage?'

That was at the root of everything, wasn't it? She had lost faith in Warren—she saw him as a man going nowhere, a man, as she'd said a while ago, with no zest left in him. Their sex life had waned. Outside work, her life was dull. Unfulfilled. He bored her. Probably, doing all this court-appointed stuff, he bored himself. That was the impression he gave. Maybe she wasn't in love with him any more.

'Do you want to leave me and marry this guy?'

'I don't know what I want to do.'

He glanced at his watch. It was ten minutes to eight. 'I'm sorry,' he said. 'I guess I've been letting you down. Maybe you've been letting me down too. I want to talk to you about all that. I have to go now. We'll talk when I get back.'

Charm's blurry eyes took on heat. 'You're going? Now? Where?'

'To the ball game, with Scoot Shepard and a client.'

'To the ball game? When our lives are falling apart?'

'It's business.' He hated the words even as he said them.

She jumped off the bed furiously and hurried after him. When his hand was on the knob of the front door, he turned to touch her shoulder, but she jerked back from him.

He opened the door and stepped outside into the thick evening warmth. It had grown nearly dark. Driving to the Astrodome he felt a fool, a cuckold, a homeless man. As homeless as Hector Quintana. In the car, he cried.

THE ASTROS TOOK AN EARLY lead against the New York Mets, and the crowd in the air-conditioned Dome grew boisterous. From the box seats behind third base, Warren cheered and hooted. He had a particular rooting interest tonight against the Mets.

'Pile it on!' Warren yelled. 'Let's go! No mercy!'

At his side, Johnnie Faye Boudreau gave a snort of laughter. 'You sure are having a good time, Mr Blackburn.'

Scoot drank Wild Turkey from a silver flask. Warren and Johnnie Faye and a man named Frank Sawyer drank beer from plastic cups. Sawyer was clean-shaven, about thirty, with light-blue eyes and close-cropped fair hair. Military, Warren decided. A bouncer at her club, Johnnie Faye said. His black T-shirt revealed a weightlifter's biceps, and he was tattooed on both arms: a blue and red spitting dragon on one, an anchor and the word 'Rosie' on the other.

Warren chatted idly with Johnnie Faye, but images of Charm kept invading his mind like mosquitoes swarming through a torn screen. In the bottom half of the fourth innings, Johnnie Faye asked him if they should be talking about the case.

'This isn't exactly the right time and place,' Warren said, as cordially as he could. 'But why don't you tell me about yourself?' He could see her eyes flicker with appreciation. 'Scoot told me you were a beauty queen,' he prompted.

'One of the high points of my life,' she said.

She had been brought up in Odem, a little town west of Corpus Christi, with her beloved twin brother Garrett and her older brother Clinton. Daddy was a part-time Baptist preacher who ran the filling station there.

When Johnnie Faye got out of high school along came Vietnam. Her brother Clinton had been blown up by a mine at Da Nang, sent home to Texas in a body bag. And now all those gooks were *here,* buying up everything from shrimp boats to convenience stores, and their deadpan kids were nailing down all the scholarships that real American kids couldn't get any more.

She pumped gas until she'd saved enough money to move to Corpus Christi, where she waitressed at an International House of Pancakes. 'I wanted to go to college,' she told Warren, 'but I couldn't afford it. Biggest regret I've got.'

When she was twenty-one, Johnnie Faye won Miss Corpus Christi and qualified for the Miss Texas Pageant, coming up in Austin. There was one problem: in the local gym she had met a curly-haired young fiddler with a country-music band—his name was Bubba Rutherford. Bubba promised her the world, and two weeks later she married him. Her friends warned her to shut up about it. All Miss Texas contestants had to be single.

The pageant officials instructed her to be more dainty, and lose a few pounds. Johnnie Faye made it to the final eight, and in the talent portion, when she sang 'He's Gone, and He Took Everything but the Blame', she won second place. Accepting the prize, Johnnie Faye stood up at the microphone, flashed her white teeth at the TV cameras, and revealed that she was really Mrs Bubba Rutherford, but she'd kept that under her hat.

She was stripped of her runner-up title, which she had expected, and picked up some modelling offers from a Houston advertising agency, which she hadn't expected. Soon she became bored with Bubba. 'So I got a divorce and stayed on here. Meanwhile my brother Garrett showed up and moved in with me. I supported him. He had nightmares and he was a junkie. The war did that to him. He went off one weekend with some of his buddies and OD'd on heroin. I loved that kid, and that was the worst thing ever happened to me. I was dancing by then and I was worn out. Found a backer for Ecstasy a while ago, and the rest is history. I still go down to Odem three times a year to see my mama, and I'm loyal to anyone who's loyal to me. That's my creed,' Johnnie Faye concluded.

When the game was out, they filed up the ramp towards the exit. At the hot-dog concession, Johnnie Faye levelled a finger at his chest. 'Good buddy, I've got a beef. Since the seventh innings you haven't heard a word I said! I don't know if I want a lawyer who can't bother to listen. You owe me an explanation.'

Warren took a shaky breath and said, 'My wife just told me she's having an affair. She might leave me. That's what was on my mind. Not the game.'

Johnnie Faye's face bloomed like a pink rose. 'You should have told me that before, Warren,' she said. She slipped her arm through his. 'You give her half a chance, there's a kind of woman will tear your heart out and stomp the sucker flat. Is your wife like that?'

'No,' Warren said, 'she's not.'

Charm was asleep when he got back home. In the darkness he slid silently into the bed, keeping to his side, listening for a while to her steady quiet breathing. She seemed at peace. Pain pressed against his eyelids. None of this is true. I'll wake up in the morning and it will all be gone.

4

Warren arrived at the house of the late Dan Ho Trunh at nine o'clock in the morning. The Trunhs lived south of the Loop in Blueridge, on a street with small neat brick houses. A small Chevrolet was parked in the driveway and Warren peered inside. It was immaculate. The house was immaculate too. Dan Ho Trunh's tiny young widow and mother were dressed in black blouses and black jeans, and some kids played quietly in another room. Warren offered his business card and explained that he was the lawyer appointed by the State of Texas to defend the man accused of killing their husband and son.

The younger Mrs Trunh, the widow, who looked about twenty-five, invited Warren to have a Diet Coke. Her dark eyes were grave but she kept smiling at him. How could they help?

'By telling me everything that happened the night before Dan Ho left the house. And that morning too.'

They told him nothing he didn't know already. He focused on the widow. 'You stated to the police that your husband was carrying his wallet that day. Did you see him pick up his wallet when he left home, Mrs Trunh?'

'No, but he always carried it.'

'How do you know that he had more than fifty dollars in the wallet that morning?'

'He always did,' the widow said.

'Did your husband have any enemies, Mrs Trunh?'

The widow said no.

Warren scratched his head. This was going nowhere but downhill. He asked if the police still had the car her husband drove that night. No, the widow said, it had been returned.

'May I see it?'

The women led him through the kitchen into the garage, where tools and paints were stacked neatly on plywood shelves. The old Fairlane station wagon, a particularly garish shade of blue, gleamed in the shadows. The inside had been vacuumed. If there had been bloodstains, there were none now.

When he stepped behind the car to write down the licence-plate number on his legal pad, Warren saw that the right rear bumper had been torn away a few inches, and there was a cream-coloured rip along the shiny blue metal in front of it. While he was looking at that, the mother-in-law chattered loudly.

The widow said, 'She is angry at the police for damaging the car. The bumper and that big scratch—they were not there when my husband left that morning. The police did that when they returned the car to us.'

'Oh,' Warren said. The mother was still talking in Vietnamese, using her hands now to emphasise her point.

The widow said, "Naturally they say, 'No, we didn't do that. It was there already." These things are very expensive.'

'Yes, they're ridiculously expensive,' Warren said, while out of habit he made a note about the damage on his legal pad.

He drove from the Trunhs' to Hermann Park and the stables. Behind the shed where Hector Quintana had once lived, Warren found a blackened pot where someone had fried pork cracklings. A rolled-up rag of a plaid blanket lay on the earth. The heat rolled over the ground in waves. There was no one around.

Inside the stables a man shovelled manure into a bucket.

'Armando?'

The man turned, wiping sweat from his forehead. 'Armando is not here,' the man said. He was thin and dark and wore baggy trousers.

'Then you must be Pedro.'

The man nodded.

'Well, you sure look worn out. You finish up, I'll buy you a bunch of chicken *tacos* and a beer. I'm a friend of Hector's.'

At the taco stand Warren brought the plastic plates back to his car, where he had left the motor running and the air conditioning on. To his amazement—although as soon as he thought about it, it made sense—Pedro hadn't known that Hector was in jail.

'Nobody from the DA's office came to talk to you?'

No one, Pedro said, layering fiery hot sauce deep into the taco.

'Hector suppose' to have kill a man?' Pedro didn't stop chewing, but he shook his head strongly. 'I doan believe that.'

'Neither do I, Pedro, but they say he did. With that *pistola* he carried around in his shopping cart.'

'He din' have no pistol,' Pedro said, apparently surprised.

'You never saw it?'

'Never saw no pistol, I swear to you. Who he can borrow it from? We doan know anyone has a pistol.'

'Maybe he bought the pistol,' Warren said.

'He din' have no money for buy a pistol.'

'How can you be so sure?'

'He borrow three dollars from me that day. I trust him. I borrow from him too when I doan got nothing.'

'Would you get up in court and testify to all that?'

Pedro looked unhappy.

'I can't pay you to testify,' Warren said, 'that's against the law. But I can give you some money to eat for a few days.' He slipped two twenty-dollar bills into Pedro's dirty shirt pocket. 'You can't get hurt if you tell the truth. Do you understand? Hector's your *amigo*. If they find him guilty, they could kill him.'

Pedro still said nothing.

'Look, you get up there in court, you talk, you leave. They won't kick you out of the country for having no papers, I promise you. If I can arrange that, will you do it?'

'OK,' Pedro said. But it was not heartfelt.

Warren drove the Mexican back to the stables, gave him one of his business cards and let him out of the car.

'Don't leave the city. Don't even leave Hermann Park without calling and letting me know where you are. Don't let me down, Pedro. Don't let Hector down! *Viva Mexico!*'

Later, Warren went to see Siva Singh at the dry-cleaning establishment. The Indian lady informed him that the district attorney had told her not to speak to anyone about the case.

'Nancy Goodpaster told you that? The woman prosecutor?'

'Goodness me, sir, please don't be angry. I have her card right here.' Taking off her glasses, she dipped into her pocketbook.

'She has no right to tell you that,' Warren explained. 'You do have the right to talk to me. If you want to be fair, you should.'

Singh still refused to talk to him. He put in a call to Goodpaster but couldn't reach her.

HE SPENT THE NEXT MORNING, a Wednesday, at Ravendale, knocking on doors of the apartment buildings near the west parking lot. The few people who were home stared at him in astonishment. 'Do I remember throwing out a half-empty bottle of Old Crow or a pair of tennis socks? Are you kidding me?'

Warren was wearing a suit and tie, so no one thought he was entirely a madman. But no one could remember seeing a man rummaging in the garbage or sitting in the parking lot.

AT HPD HEADQUARTERS in Reisner Street, Warren took the elevator up to Homicide on the third floor. Sergeants Hollis Thiel and Mitch Douglas were the arresting officers in the case. Douglas was tall, in his thirties, and looked like a cadaver. Thiel looked like an older Porky Pig. Warren's private opinion was that both hated defence attorneys with equal vigour.

'Goodpaster call you?' Warren asked.

Thiel nodded. 'She said we could tell you a few things.'

'Just tell me about Quintana in your own choice words.'

Thiel repeated the story of the arrest, which was much as Hector had told it. The clerk in the Circle K had pushed a button with his foot. An alarm had flashed in the nearest police station. The next day Ballistics had called Homicide to tell them that the calibre and rifling in the barrel of Hector's gun matched the bullet that had been found in Dan Ho Trunh's brain. Since Thiel and Douglas were the detectives who had made the crime scene at the Trunh murder, Hector had been brought over to their office in Homicide and read his rights a second time.

'Did he ask for a lawyer?'

'Too dumb to do that,' Douglas said. 'Just sat there and babbled, I doan know what you talkin' about. '

'Did he say he found the gun in a trash can?'

Thiel stroked his jowls. 'That was it.'

'Any other prints on the gun?'

'Smudges.'

'Y'all examine the car where the victim's body was found?' Warren asked.

'Nothing in it. Nancy said to give you a set of photographs.' Thiel slid open a file drawer and plucked out a manila folder. He slid it across the desk. 'The victim was shot in his car through an open window on the driver's side. Ballistics says maybe five, six feet. Your guy must've took the wallet after he wasted him.'

Warren glanced down at his notes. 'By the way, who drove the car away from the crime scene?'

'I did,' Douglas muttered.

'You sideswipe any lampposts going back to HPD?'

'Hey, I already had this out with the old lady.' Douglas unclipped the manila folder and spilt the colour eight-by-tens out on the desktop. 'This one,' Douglas said, tapping a photograph he slid from the pile. 'See it? That bumper was ripped up when we got there.' He laughed hoarsely. 'I told her that.'

Warren stood up, shaking out creases in his seersucker jacket. 'Thanks, guys.' He put the photograph file into his briefcase. 'Tommy Ruiz in the shop?'

Tommy Ruiz was the Homicide sergeant who had arrested Johnnie Faye Boudreau on the night of Clyde Ott's murder.

'I think so,' Thiel said. 'Let me buzz.'

TAR ON THE PAVEMENT was beginning to melt in the midday Gulf Coast heat as Warren eased his car into the low-priced parking lot behind the jail. Ten minutes later he again sat opposite Hector Quintana in one of the visitors' cubicles at the jail.

'Hector, we have to make a decision. And certain things have to be said.'

'What more can I tell *you*?' Quintana asked, glowering.

'It's what *I* can tell you. The DA wants to put you in jail for life or get the State of Texas to inject you with cyanide. She thinks she's got a good case. Problem is, I agree with her.'

Quintana took some harsh breaths. Warren raised his hand to forestall what he thought was coming.

'I'm trying to be objective,' Warren continued. 'That's part of my job. But it's not quite so bad as I'm painting it. Relax.'

Quintana's breathing eased a little but not much.

'The courts are crowded. So the DA is willing to compromise. She'll reduce the charge from capital murder to plain murder. She's offered you forty years.'

Softly, Quintana repeated the number.

'I know forty years sounds like a lot,' Warren said, seeing horror in the man's brown eyes, 'and it is a lot, although with good behaviour you'll do only half of what they give you. But I want to point something out to you. You can't do half of death.'

Quintana groaned and clenched his fist.

'Let me ask you something,' Warren said. 'You've been here a couple of weeks now. You like the life?'

Warren knew that prison could become a normal existence. Jailing, the cons called it. Three meals a day, a bed to sleep in, a TV to watch. No rent to pay. Some thrived on it.

'No,' Quintana said. 'I doan like it here. I want to go back to El Palmito.'

'That may not happen, Hector.'

Quintana quietly began to cry. 'Forty years . . .' he murmured. 'Twenty, if I behave. What should I do, Mr Blackburn?'

'Don't dump that on me, Hector. You've got to tell me.'

'Mr Blackburn, listen to me. In El Palmito I have trouble killing even a pig. People laugh at me, think I'm foolish. Do you think I did such a thing as kill a human being who never harm me, never speak a word to me?'

Warren looked into Quintana's liquid eyes. There was no fright there, no desperation, only yearning and a simple plea. A feeling welled up from somewhere in the most profound part of him. He couldn't explain it. It was a feeling akin to love. If you loved someone, you believed them. You trusted them. In that moment the feeling seemed indisputable.

Pedro had said that Hector didn't own a pistol and had no money to buy one. Words with the ring of truth. Hector's story was a simple one. He never deviated, never contradicted, never blushed. This was not a man who would kill.

Warren linked his fingers together behind his head. This was crazy. He had an understanding with Lou Parker. He had the Boudreau trial looming, the most important trial of his life. If he could win with Scoot, he would be more than back on track. But he couldn't back away from Hector Quintana.

'No, Hector, I don't believe you did it.'

There were fresh tears in Hector's eyes. 'You doan?'

'No, I really don't. I would never lie to you.'

'Then why should I go to prison for twenty years?'

'I can't think of a single reason,' Warren said. His cheeks flushed. 'Now listen to me. I'm going to break the rules. I'm going to tell you what I would do if I were in your shoes. If I were *really* innocent—I'd pray a lot, and I'd go to trial. But it's your life, not mine. The odds against you are big. Stupendous.'

'All right.' Quintana spoke softly. 'I go to trial.'

'You understand what happens if you lose?'

'Yes. They will kill me, put me to sleep. Maybe that's not so bad as twenty years in prison. I don't care. I am innocent.'

There was no way to shake hands through the mesh, so Warren pressed his palm against the cool metal. Quintana pressed back.

Warren gathered up his papers. 'I'll do what I can,' he promised. 'We'll give these guys a run for their money. But for God's sake, if you change your mind, let me know.'

JUDGE PARKER ORDERED WARREN into her chambers after he had spoken to Nancy Goodpaster. Goodpaster looked unhappy. She said to Warren, 'I think you're making a mistake.'

He sat facing the judge's desk. Lou Parker pinched her cigarette between her thumb and index finger as if it were a dart and pointed it at him right between his eyes.

'Let me get this straight, Mr Blackburn. Less than a week ago you asked Nancy here if she'd cut a deal with you.'

'That's correct, your honour.'

'She agreed to forty years. That was a pretty good deal.'

'My client won't go for it, your honour. He says he's innocent. And I happen to believe him.'

Parker rasped, 'Then you're a fool. My memory is that you and I sat right here one day not so long ago and got our signals straight. I told you this was a whale in the barrel for the prosecution. I told you to plead this guy out and not waste my court time. You do this to me, and I promise you'll never get an appointment in my court again.'

'What difference does it make if my client insists on going to trial?' Warren said, ignoring the threat.

Parker raised her voice: 'I'll tell you what difference it makes! You're supposed to represent this man's best interests. Have you talked straight with this man Quintana?'

'I did my best,' Warren said, wondering if that was true.

'How come I don't quite believe you? How come I think you're aiming to use up two valuable weeks of my courtroom time playing to the crowd? And picking up a big fat fee for every day you're in court?'

'I don't know, your honour,' Warren said, letting his annoyance show. 'But I don't think you should question my doing what I think is best for my client, who, I remind you, claims he's innocent.'

'And don't they all,' said Parker, 'until you give them the facts of life. We're not talking about probation here. We're talking about a needle in the arm.'

'He knows all that.'

In the face of his firmness, her exasperation ripened. 'Just how do you plan to benefit, counsellor? This case isn't going to make any headlines—this is a dumb Mexican supposed to have blown away a Vietnamese handyman. So how do you justify this farce?'

When she realised he had no intention of answering her, Judge Parker clenched her teeth and snatched her court calendar. She leafed through it rapidly, then turned to Goodpaster. 'Madam Prosecutor, is the state ready for arraignment?'

'Yes, your honour.'

'The court will take a plea this coming Monday morning, June twelfth, at nine o'clock. Defence motions next Friday, June sixteenth. State has a week to respond. How about a trial date? State ready?'

'The state can be ready in seven days,' Goodpaster said.

'Too soon. But I have an open date on the agenda for Wednesday, July fifth, right after the holiday weekend. On July twenty-first, that's a Friday, I go on vacation to Hawaii. That's the deal.'

Warren jumped to his feet. 'Judge Parker,' he pleaded, 'that's a gun to my head! Including jury selection, you're allowing less than three weeks for the whole case! And only three weeks to prepare! In a capital murder case, that's nothing!'

'You're talking Chinese to a pack mule, counsellor. My agenda's full right through Thanksgiving. You want a trial. Jury selection begins on July fifth. That's *it*.'

Warren tried another tack. 'Scoot Shepard and I are trying *Boudreau* on July twenty-fourth. With all due deference, can't we do *Quintana* when you come back from your vacation?'

The judge stubbed out her cigarette and leaned back in her armchair. 'Never mind that due deference garbage. You're a damned fool. I feel sorry for you.' She flicked her hand towards the door.

IN GOODPASTER'S OFFICE—after she had settled behind her desk—Warren said, 'I want you to remember everything that happened in there today. Make some notes if you have to.'

'Why?'

'Just for the heck of it, Nancy,' he said. 'Just in case I forget. Did you tell Mrs Singh she shouldn't talk to me?'

'I just told her she didn't have to if she didn't want to.'

'Can I see the offence report now?'

'No.'

'What are you scared of?'

'I'm just keeping to the rules. I could have showed you the file if you were going to plead out. But you're not. It's not a game now. It's war.'

THAT EVENING Scoot Shepard left his office in the Republic Bank Building and headed towards the Houstonian Club for an early session of draw poker. All day he'd been chewing tablets to ease his indigestion, but it refused to go away. So did the headache at the base of his skull.

He had passed Buffalo Bayou and was on Memorial Drive heading west. Without warning—if you discounted the last two years of headaches and dizzy spells, and the admonitions of his wife and his doctor—his eyesight blurred. The road went severely out of focus. Scoot felt a jarring pain in his left temple, as if someone had jabbed him with a knuckle. He had suffered a slight stroke. At that moment the road changed from a right curve to a left curve. Scoot failed to see that. His Cadillac hopped the kerb. The car veered, but there was still a leafy old oak tree in its path. Scoot's bumper struck with a thunderclap, the grillework wrapped round the tree and the steering column began to fracture his chest.

DRIVING HOME, DISCONSOLATE over what had happened in Judge Parker's office and what it foretold for his client's trial, Warren felt a new refrain pounding in his head. *I want my wife back*. I need to talk to her. I'm a country boy. We mate for life.

Alone at home, he mixed a vodka and tonic and switched on the TV. There was Charm, ripening in colour, blue eyes levelled at him, lips moving soundlessly. He punched up the volume.

'. . . when we come back, we'll have the weather, and sports. Please stay with us, friends.'

Nice touches. She always seemed to mean what she said. He turned the volume back down then untied his slim file on the Quintana case. Jury selection in three weeks. He studied his notes from the visit to the Trunhs. Maybe Hector had done it. Drunk, unable to remember, blocking out the horror now because he couldn't believe it was possible. The thought was like a block of ice pressed unremittingly against Warren's spine.

On the TV screen he saw Scoot Shepard, doused in brilliant light, talking to reporters outside some courtroom. Surprised, Warren leaned forward from the couch and hit the volume button.

In her gravest tones, Charm said: '. . . so at the age of sixty-four, a great Texas lawyer is dead. A preliminary medical report indicates that Mr Shepard suffered a minor cerebral stroke just prior to the fatal accident. We'll have an update on Channel Twenty-six Eleven-o-clock News. Don?'

Hard to believe, even harder to accept. Warren punched over to the networks, but they were doing weather and sports. He turned off the TV. The silence of the house fell like thunder about his ears. Scoot, you poor cuss. He moaned aloud, surprising himself. And now the Ott case . . . the best shot of my life, gone. Gone like Scoot. Gone *with* Scoot.

He waited up for Charm. In all his life, he couldn't remember feeling this abandoned. He didn't eat, just drank more vodka. At midnight, a little dazed, he went to bed. He was almost asleep when the telephone rang. He snatched the receiver from the cradle and said, 'Charm? Are you OK?'

But it was Johnnie Faye Boudreau. She sounded frightened. Warren had trouble understanding her words. Finally he realised that she was at the club, and someone had just told her of the tragedy. Johnnie Faye's voice rose. 'What am I going to do?'

'You're going to calm down,' Warren said firmly, 'and in the next few days you're going to find a new lawyer to take the case. You have a good case. Any decent lawyer can win it.'

'I want Mr Shepard!' she cried.

'That will be a little difficult,' Warren said.

'Can I see you? Can I talk to you? I need your advice.'

'Yes, of course. I'll be at the club in twenty minutes.'

5

In a garden restaurant near the courthouse the next day, Warren lunched with Judge Dwight Bingham. The judge lifted a forkful of charcoal-grilled catfish to his mouth. He had been born on a plantation near Texarkana and had put himself through law school. A long journey, and he had seen a great deal happen.

'It's you I'm worried about, young Warren. Bob Altschuler's an awfully good prosecutor. He'll run for judge in November. This is a big case. He'll fight hard to win it.'

'So will I,' Warren said flatly. 'Look, Judge, the Boudreau woman thinks she wants me. That's what matters.'

He hadn't asked her. He hadn't pressured. Last night at Ecstasy she had asked, 'You have faith in me?'

'If you told the truth to Scoot,' Warren answered carefully, 'and you keep on telling the truth to whomever you pick as your new lawyer, I have faith in your defence.'

'Could you win my case?'

'Yes, I could,' he said.

'*Would* you win it?'

'Yes,' Warren said.

'Let me think it over. I'm tired now.'

'You'll do the right thing,' Warren told her.

In the garden restaurant, Judge Bingham frowned and touched a glass of iced tea to his sagging cheeks. 'When will Ms Boudreau let you have an answer?'

'I'm meeting her again tonight at Ecstasy.'

'I want to tell you something, Warren. Off the record.' The old judge let out a soft sigh. 'You were there that day in court, the hearing for reduction of Ms Boudreau's bail. All that business about the Louisiana corporation owning that club, her having no money, that was a lot of baloney. I knew it, couldn't prove it, didn't want to be bothered. That's a clever woman. Gets what she wants, twists people around. You watch yourself, son.'

Warren paid the bill over the judge's protests and left the restaurant. To defend Johnnie Faye Boudreau was the chance of a lifetime. But if Johnnie Faye said yes, Warren realised, he would be trying two murder cases back to back. He would be spreading himself so thin that he might tear. He could win it all . . . or break even . . . or lose it all.

WARREN CALLED Rick Levine's office and found out that he was conducting a pre-trial examination of a cop who had made the arrest in a drug case. In the county courtroom, when the judge declared a recess, Warren grabbed Rick by the sleeve of his jacket.

'Got a minute?'

They walked outside to the stairwell.

'Poor Scoot,' Rick said. 'Where does that leave you with *Boudreau*?'

Warren related his discussions with Johnnie Faye and Dwight Bingham. 'If she says yes, what I need is a good lawyer to assist me, to sit second chair. A *very* good lawyer. Will you do it?'

Rick stroked his moustache thoughtfully. 'I'm doing enough charity work now. Is there any money in it?'

'Whatever I get I'll split with you.'

'What's the plea?'

'Self-defence. Clyde Ott threatened to kill her—there are people who heard him say it. And before she blew him away, he picked up a poker from the fireplace.'

'Did she provoke him?'

'She claims she didn't,' Warren said. 'There are no other witnesses to contradict her.'

'I have a lot on my plate in July.' Rick frowned. 'I'd have to get Edith to fill in on this drug case.'

Warren waited, said nothing.

'OK, I'll do it,' Rick said, banging him on the shoulder. 'It's a good case. Plenty of TV coverage.'

'You're going to love our client,' Warren said. 'If she becomes our client.'

WARREN AND JOHNNIE FAYE BOUDREAU sat at a small round table near the horseshoe bar in Ecstasy. Frank Sawyer leaned against the bar, drinking a 7-Up, scanning the Friday-night crowd. Young waitresses were moving among the customers. They wore high heels and G-strings and yellow ribbons in their hair. The music was relentless and cigarette smoke swirled in the beams of the overhead spotlights. Warren's eyes itched.

Johnnie Faye seemed to have recovered from last night's trauma; her laugh was merry. Warren said, 'Well, are we in business? If we are, I'll Xerox a copy of the file for Rick Levine.'

'I asked around about you since yesterday. You've got a lot of people who think an awful lot of you. That's all well and good, but what I need from a lawyer is to hear that I can't lose.'

Warren said, 'Any lawyer who tells you that is a fool.'

'Mr Shepard said it.'

'I don't believe that. You may have misunderstood him. It's a very good case. Not a whale in a barrel, but close.'

'Do better than that, counsellor.' Both Johnnie Faye's blue-grey eye and her hazel eye had clouded.

'Trials aren't simple,' he said. 'Lawyers can make mistakes. So can judges. Witnesses lie, or forget, or become confused. The jury's always right, whether it is or not. Bearing that in mind, we'll represent you as well or better than anyone else in town.'

'You see,' she said, 'you're a good talker when you get wound up! That's what I wanted to hear. I like you, counsellor. Go for it. You and Mr Levine. He's a Jew, right?'

Warren nodded, wondering what would come next.

'Can't lose with a Jew and a good ole boy on my side.'

Warren smiled softly.

WHEN HE REACHED HOME that evening, Charm's car was parked in the driveway. He had hardly seen his wife since Monday, the day he had found her outside the house with her lover. Since that day, everything in Warren's life had changed. He walked through to the bedroom with Oobie clawing at his trouser leg. Charm was in the shower, washing her hair. She came out with a thick brown towel wrapped round her head, another one draped round her body like a sarong.

'You going to the ball game tonight?' she asked, as she began to dress.

'That was with a client in a murder case.'

'Aren't you out of it now that Scoot's gone?'

'I'm trying the case. Rick is sitting second chair.'

'That's good for you, Warren. That's positive. Will you win?'

'You never know, do you? Charm, can we talk?'

'I think that's a good idea.'

But the talk didn't resemble anything he'd imagined. Yes, of course she wanted time . . . not for him to win her back, but to figure out what to do with the rest of her life. She had hired an agent in Chicago. He was going to try to get her an anchor job in a top market: Chicago, Los Angeles, Boston, New York.

'But our life's here.'

'Your life is here, Warren. Not mine.'

'And what about us?'

The pain of the other night bloomed again in Charm's eyes. He wanted to hold her. She raised a hand to keep him back. 'Warren, this is hard for me to say. I want a divorce.'

It was like his worst nightmare. He took a rapid turn round the room to get control of himself.

'So you can marry this other lawyer and move to New York?'

'I'll decide that when I'm ready to decide it,' Charm said. 'I thought of moving out. But you know how I hate apartments. I thought we could share the house for a while. I just don't think we should share the bed. It's a little painful for us both.'

'So who vacates?' He waved a hand at the room.

'That's up to you, Warren. I don't have the right to kick you out. But the guest-room closets are so small. Would you mind?'

After a minute he said, 'I would mind a lot.'

He walked out of the room before tears misted his eyes. In the kitchen he patted Oobie, who hadn't been fed. He poured out dogfood and mixed it in the bowl.

He watched Oobie eat. Yes, I mind a lot.

He sat down in the living room and put his head in his hands. He couldn't stay in the same house with her.

Charm left ten minutes later, calling a muffled goodbye. He heard her high heels hurrying on the walkway.

He went out for dinner at a nearby fast-food chicken restaurant, then came back and worked on the Quintana file for an hour. After that he turned his attention to the Boudreau file, but his eyes began to tire. The two cases blurred, became one. I'm not seeing things clearly, he realised.

In the guest room, he turned down the covers on one of the twin beds, then switched off the bedside lamp at 2am.

He woke at daybreak on Sunday morning. On his way to the kitchen he noticed that the door to the master bedroom was ajar. The bed had not been slept in. Charm had not come home.

'Damn her,' he said softly. And thought, I'll get on with my life. Using the kitchen telephone, he called Ravendale and made arrangements to rent an apartment. By ten o'clock he had moved himself in, with his dog for company.

Late the next afternoon in Judge Bingham's court, Warren M. Blackburn and Richard C. Levine were registered as co-attorneys of record in *Texas v. Johnnie Faye Boudreau.*

TOWARDS THE END OF JUNE, on a rainy afternoon, Judge Lou Parker called Warren and Nancy Goodpaster into her chambers. She directed her flinty gaze at the man who stood between Hector Quintana and death.

'How about clothes for your dude? I don't want this Mexican sitting there in a Harris County jumpsuit making us all look bad. Find out his size and hike your butt down to Kuppenheimer. They've got a sale on. The county will reimburse.'

Without waiting for a thankyou, the judge said, 'Jury selection starts a week from Wednesday. I limit *voir dire* to thirty minutes a side for each juror. I keep a chess clock on my desk. When it goes *ping,* you've had it. No exceptions.'

She stared at Warren sombrely. 'You better think hard about all this. You want to plead your guy out at the eleventh hour, I won't be overjoyed. But I sure won't stop you. That clear?'

'Clear,' Warren said.

Her scowl deepened. 'I'll see you both for jury selection, a week from Wednesday at nine sharp.'

IN THE EVENINGS, in his apartment at Ravendale, Warren watched movies on a rented video cassette recorder. He had rented a package of pots, pans and other kitchen paraphernalia, and had stocked his refrigerator with cold cuts, frozen dinners, and a quart of Polish vodka for the freezer.

The furniture in the apartment was ordinary beige motel-style, but he could leave a mug of hot coffee on the coffee table without anyone telling him to put a coaster under it. The rings on the table grew and overlapped.

He and Rick met several times with Johnnie Faye to hear her story and prepare a trial notebook.

Warren gave her a definition: 'Self-defence is where you use deadly force to thwart the immediate anticipation that you're about to be killed or suffer serious bodily injury, and you have no opportunity to retreat.' Johnnie Faye's testimony was the key. 'This goes in three stages,' Warren explained. 'First you tell us exactly what happened. Then we interview other possible witnesses. Then we woodshed you—prepare you for direct examination and cross-examination under oath. For now, don't leave anything out, no matter how trivial you think it is. Tell us the truth. We're your lawyers. We're here to help you, not to judge you.'

But her tale of the events never varied. The lawyers took notes. Rick then brought the notes back to his office for his secretary, Bernadette Loo, to transcribe them into computer memory. Pure Chinese in appearance, Bernadette Loo was pure Texan in speech and attitude.

The district attorney's office in the person of Bob Altschuler had given them parts of the police report. The prints division had picked up enough ridges and valleys on the fireplace poker to match the fingers of both Clyde Ott's right and left hand. The poker had been found lying on the living-room carpet, directly in front of the sofa. Johnnie Faye's prints were on it too, but that matched her story. Altschuler had also provided Warren with a set of photographs of the living room, a floor plan of the mansion on River Oaks Drive, a transcript of what Johnnie Faye had said to the emergency dispatcher, and a copy of Sergeant Ruiz's notes after he had reached the Ott place and heard her confession.

Warren went to the library of the *Chronicle* and Xeroxed the cuttings on the murders of Sharon Underhill Ott and David Inkman. Any reference to them was barred from coming up in trial, but the defence team needed to know the background.

Late the same afternoon he drove out to the Hacienda Restaurant. Both the waiter and the *maître d'* remembered Dr Ott and Johnnie Faye dining there, and the management provided a copy of the bill that showed they had consumed ten margarita cocktails. The waiter remembered an argument at the dinner table.

On a different evening Warren visited the couple who Johnnie Faye had said heard Clyde threaten to kill her, Dr and Mrs Gordon Butterfield, a cosmetic surgeon and his wife. They had been friends of Clyde's, they emphasised, and described Johnnie Faye as flashy and amoral. But they recalled that particular evening a year or so ago—a charity dinner for the homeless, held at the Houston Racquet Club.

Dr Gordon Butterfield said, 'They were arguing about the money Clyde spent on his stepchildren. In the midst of this argument, the Boudreau woman threw a drink in his face. And Clyde said, "You slut, I could happily kill you for that." '

Warren thanked the Butterfields and left. Later, at Hermann Hospital, he secured a copy of the emergency-room report on the night of December 22, 1988, when Clyde had reputedly punched Johnnie Faye.

PATIENT'S INITIAL COMPLAINT: suspected fracture, nasal bone. (Some swelling observed in dorsum.)
DIAGNOSIS: hairline fracture of left zygomaticofacial foramen.
TREATMENT: none.
PRESCRIPTIONS: Tylenol III.

The young doctor who had treated Johnnie Faye agreed to testify.

Meanwhile, Rick dropped by the bar at the Grand Hotel, but Cathy Lewis—the cocktail waitress to whom Clyde had supposedly paid the $25,000 for knocking out three of her front teeth—hadn't worked there for eighteen months. No one knew where she had gone. 'Call all the hotel bars,' Warren told his partner, 'and try your people at Social Security and the Department of Motor Vehicles. We need her.'

EVERY MORNING WARREN ran along Braes Bayou with Oobie. On Saturdays he had a maid come in to clean. He went to court when it was required, and met with Hector in the jail visiting-room, and with Johnnie Faye in Rick's office or his own. He drew up witness plans and a theory of defence for both cases. Veering back and forth as he did between the two cases put him on edge, gave him dreams that were nightmarish in their confusion. When he awoke, his pillow would be damp with sweat.

If he was back in his apartment by six o'clock he avoided Channel 26—Charm's news channel—and watched the local news on one of the networks. He had left a message on Charm's answering machine to tell her where he was. Twice in the last two weeks she had called and enquired if he was all right, and each time he had said, 'I'm fine, Charm. How about you?' The first time she had replied, 'I'm doing well,' and the second time, 'I'm doing OK.'

He kept the conversations short. He was heartsore, but that was none of her business now. Focus on the Boudreau woman's testimony and suffering Hector Quintana. Take good care of Oobie, because she loves you and depends on you. A dumb and hungry dog was all he had.

But women seemed to smell his availability, if that's what it was. Courthouse gossip got around. One morning in Judge Bingham's court Maria Hahn, the court reporter, nudged his elbow.

Maria was in her late thirties, with an eight-year-old son, a fact that discouraged most of the bachelor lawyers. Tall and leggy, she had short brown hair in a frizzy permanent wave, bright blue eyes, a neck like a Modigliani portrait.

She was always telling jokes and was a favourite of Dwight Bingham's, who called a break in court proceedings whenever he thought she was tired. 'Break for the beautiful Maria,' he would say, and more often than not, Maria, smiling, transcribed it into the record.

She asked Warren how he was doing, and he said fine. Then: 'Warren, I belong to this club, called, would you believe it, The Towering Texans of Houston. There's a big Fourth of July party Sunday night. I don't want to go alone. Want to come with me?'

'Sounds good,' Warren said, after a moment. He liked Maria; she was a cheerful woman. 'Exactly how tall are you?'

'Five-foot-eleven. You?'

'Six-one. Maybe shy a quarter inch.'

'Well, you can't join the team. Men members have to be six-two. But I'm allowed to bring along a short guy.' She squeezed his arm, and chortled. 'Want to hear a real disgusting joke?'

'Do I have any choice?'

'It's a riddle. Why do politicians have one more brain cell than horses do?'

'I can't imagine.'

'So they won't mess up the street during parades.'

Maria howled with laughter like a benevolent witch. 'Give me your new number,' she said. 'I'll call to tell you when and where.'

WEARING SHORTS AND A SAFARI SHIRT, Rick Levine arrived at Warren's converted cottage office. It was the Saturday afternoon of the long Fourth of July weekend. Rick brought Bernadette Loo; she had been sick with the flu and had fallen behind in the transcription of their notes. Johnnie Faye was due to arrive at four o'clock and they would continue to woodshed her for cross-examination. Bernadette set herself up at a desk in the corner alcove where Warren kept his computer and printer.

'Got a question before we begin,' Rick said.

'Fire away.'

Rick unrolled a simplified drawing of the downstairs of Clyde Ott's house on River Oaks Drive. The dimensions of the house were on a grand scale. You entered into a large Italian marble vestibule and directly ahead, in southern style, was a broad marble staircase leading to the two upper floors. To the right was the family room, complete with pool table and oversized television; to the left, through an archway, a vast living room. Opposite the fireplace in the living room, quite a distance away, an alcove on one wall contained a built-in bookcase in front of which stood the leather sofa on which Clyde Ott had died.

Rick's finger pointed at the outline of the sofa. 'Suppose, like our client keeps telling us, Clyde was waving the poker over his head in a threatening manner, and she shot him just as he took a swing at her. Then how come, when he fell, the momentum of his arm didn't sling the poker over the sofa against the bookcase? Or at least onto the sofa? How come the poker wound up two feet this side of it on the carpet?'

Behind them Bernadette Loo tapped away at the computer keyboard, occasionally sipping a cold drink.

'It's possible,' Warren said, 'that Clyde swung the poker in such a way—like, right around his body, strike three—that it wound up behind his body on the carpet.'

Rick nodded. 'It's also possible that she moved the poker after she killed him so the cops wouldn't miss it.'

Right, Warren thought. 'Of course, there's one more possibility. An entirely different set of facts.'

'Yeah, the poker story's a fairy tale. Clyde never picked up the poker and swung at her with it. She shot him, then put the poker in his hand to fix the prints. And then she laid it down in what she figured was the most visible spot and made up that cock-and-bull story.'

'You've got it,' Warren said.

'If we figured it out, Bob Altschuler'll figure it out. You sure you want to put this black widow up on the witness stand?'

'What have we got without her? If the jury believe her, she walks away. And why shouldn't they believe her? Who has the state got to contradict her?' Warren thought a bit. 'But I'll have to woodshed her on the duty to retreat.'

'You told me Scoot said not to worry about that.'

'He ain't trying this case,' Warren said.

JOHNNIE FAYE BOUDREAU arrived at Warren's office at five o'clock in the afternoon. She left her Mercedes in the concrete parking area out in front. When she swept in, wearing a Guatemalan silk blouse and tight white Dior slacks, she cried, 'How're y'all? How's my team?'

Warren introduced her to Bernadette, who was typing a fresh set of Rick's notes. After about ten minutes, when Warren began to review her story about the tussle with Clyde and the poker, Johnnie Faye's smiles faded. She wriggled in her chair. She kept crossing and uncrossing her legs. Her eyes grew flat and cold. Then she glanced up from under dark pencilled brows with a definitely theatrical frown.

'Could I talk to you gentlemen alone for a minute?'

'Bernie,' Rick said, 'go see if you can find us some Cokes and chips.'

A ten-dollar note appeared in his hand and Bernadette left.

Johnnie Faye let out a soprano-sized sigh. 'OK, guys, what's she doing here?'

'She's Rick's secretary,' Warren said.

'Listen,' Johnnie Faye said. 'I don't trust them.'

'Legal secretaries?'

'No, stupid. Don't you know what I'm talking about?'

Rick coughed gently. 'Ms Loo has been with me for three years. Graduated University of Houston. She drinks Coke and Miller Lite. She may look Chinese but she is a trustworthy one hundred per cent American.'

Johnnie Faye rocketed into a tirade.

Slant-eyes were no damned good. The Japs were taking over our banking industry, buying up all the stocks in the Fortune 500 and half of the high-priced real estate. The Chinks were all commies, and the Vietnamese were the worst. 'Send 'em all back where they came from. If I had my way—'

Her face was scarlet. Warren and Rick looked at each other.

'Anyway,' Johnnie Faye finished, 'in case you didn't get my drift, what I'm trying to say is, I don't trust them.'

'We got your drift,' Rick said.

'So when your little friend comes back, I'd appreciate it if you told her we don't need her. Nothing personal, of course.'

A few minutes later, when Bernadette popped open the door and set some cold Cokes down on the desk, Rick said, 'We're finished, my dear. You can go home. Or,' he added, 'go over to the Bamboo Garden and get a good meal. My treat.'

'Good Lord, you know I can't abide that stuff,' Bernadette said. She gathered up her things and left.

'I forgot,' Rick said.

The lawyers then went to work on Johnnie Faye: the layout of Clyde's living room, the poker, her knowledge of how the ·22 worked. In an hour the telephone rang.

It was Charm. She was sorry to bother Warren, but she was in the neighbourhood. Could they talk for just a few minutes?

Her voice startled him, and for a moment he didn't answer.

'Is this a bad time for you, Warren?'

'Hang on a minute—' He put a palm over the mouthpiece and spoke to Rick, who said, 'OK with me—we've wrapped it up for today.'

'I'd like to meet your wife,' Johnnie Faye said sweetly. 'Mind if I stay? Just to say hello and how's tricks.'

In some way Warren was glad that Johnnie Faye would be there when Charm arrived. He didn't want to guess at what she wanted, and yet the possibilities ballooned in his mind. A divorce . . . or getting back together. No doubt it was neither of those. Probably something utterly trivial.

Rick banged out of the door, and Johnnie Faye excused herself to the bathroom to fix her make-up and brush her hair. She came back looking clear-eyed. Warren said, 'We have a few minutes. Let's go through this business with the gun once more.'

One of the troubling questions was: did she reflexively shoot Clyde, or did she shoot him because she meant to kill him? And the lead-in to that was: did she cock the action on the pistol, or, did she just pull the trigger and discharge the weapon? So far she had given several answers. She had cocked the action, she had not cocked the action; she had meant to shoot at him but not kill him. Often she said, 'It went so fast. I don't really remember it too well.'

Now she asked him, 'What happens if I fib a little?'

'Beg your pardon?'

'Look, you're my lawyer. It's all in confidence, right? So I'm asking you—what happens if I really don't remember something or tell it in a way that's *good* for me?'

He considered for a moment. Not that he was in doubt about the basic answer. Only how to express it to her so that she got it and would not forget it.

'What could happen if you lie, Johnnie Faye, are two things. You could get away with it. Or if the prosecutor wears you down and gets you confused, or if there's a witness to contradict you or hard evidence that says otherwise, you could get hurt. Mangled, probably.' He paused, with as much significance as he could muster. 'And there's one thing more. If I put you on the witness stand I'm vouching for the probability of what you say. If I know you're going to lie, I can't put you up there. Those are the rules.'

'Funny game, counsellor.'

Just then he heard the familiar sound of Charm's car rolling into the little concrete parking area. A car door slammed.

'That's my wife,' Warren said. 'We'll finish up after she goes. Think about what I told you.'

After a minute, Charm's quick footsteps approached the door. Dressed in faded jeans and a T-shirt, Charm wore a quizzical expression, and her eyes shot darts at the woman seated by the desk. Warren introduced them.

'I'm real proud to meet you,' Johnnie Faye said. 'Can't say I watch the news a lot, but when I do, you're right up there with that fella whose name I can never remember.'

Charm offered a tepid smile, turned back to Warren and said, 'I thought—'

'You told me just a few minutes. I start trial this week. If you want privacy, we can go outside.'

It had turned a little cooler, down to eighty-five degrees, moving on towards evening. In the parking lot with Charm facing him, he leaned against the bonnet of Johnnie Faye's cream-coloured Mercedes. 'So what can I do for you?'

'I think we should start taking steps towards a divorce. I've talked to a lawyer. Here in town,' she added quickly. 'His name's Arthur Franklin. He'll be in touch with you.'

Warren nodded grimly. 'Don't know him,' he muttered.

'It'll be simple,' Charm said. 'No alimony. We sell the house and split the money down the middle.'

What was happening with Charm seemed like a dream sequence in a movie. 'Are you going to remarry?'

She tossed her head, her blonde hair flaring into a temporary mane. 'I don't want to discuss that, Warren. Give me a break.'

'Anything else you want to tell me?' he asked.

'I don't think so. I take it that's your client in the Ott case.' Charm nodded towards the cottage. 'Formidable-looking lady.'

Warren hoisted himself up to a sitting position on the bonnet of the car. The metal gave a bit under his weight.

'You always sit on your clients' Mercedes?' Charm asked, curling her lip. She was implying a certain intimacy.

He said nothing, just shrugged with nonchalance.

'Well, I'm sure she won't mind,' Charm said. 'I can see she's a careless driver.'

'What makes you say that?'

'The bumper. And the wing.' Charm's reporter's eye flicked towards the front of the car.

He jumped down lightly from the bonnet and turned in the direction of her glance, where he saw that the bumper had separated from the grillework. There was a small dent, with a nickel-sized spot of bright blue paint ground into the cream-coloured paint of the wing.

He kept staring at it, at first not knowing why. And then, slowly, he remembered where he had originally seen that combination of blue and cream. Strange coincidence. How many cars in Houston were painted that peculiarly bright shade of blue? And how many collisions could those blue cars have had with other cream-coloured cars? The breath almost left Warren's body.

AFTER CHARM HAD GONE he walked back inside to where Johnnie Faye waited.

I can't deal with this now, he thought. Be careful, and assume nothing.

'You look upset,' Johnnie Faye said.

'I am,' he admitted. 'But I don't want to talk about it.' A canny idea picked at his mind. 'Are you tired?'

No, she said, she wasn't tired.

'Let's do some more cross-examination,' Warren said. 'You're on the witness stand, under oath. I'm Bob Altschuler. I'll start off with the murder weapon.'

Johnnie Faye nodded.

'Ms Boudreau, you shot Dr Ott with a ·22-calibre pistol, is that correct?'

'Yes.'

'Did you always carry that ·22 in your handbag?'

'Yes, I needed it for protection.'

'No,' Warren said, 'don't justify. Just answer his question. If you add an explanation it makes you sound defensive.'

She nodded.

'Ms Boudreau, is that ·22 the only pistol you own?'

'No.'

He digested that, and said, 'Describe the other pistol, please.'

'It's a ·45. I keep it in my desk drawer at the club, under lock and key.'

'Was the ·22 that you carried in your handbag always loaded?'

'Yes.'

'Did you know it was in your handbag that evening you went with Dr Ott to the Hacienda Restaurant?'

'Well, I knew, but I wasn't thinking about it.'

'Just yes or no,' Warren cautioned.

She frowned. 'Yes.'

'Was Dr Ott aware that you were carrying a gun?'

'I don't know.'

'Good,' Warren said. 'That's the right answer. OK—did you tell Dr Ott you were carrying the gun that evening?'

'No.'

'In the restaurant, you and Dr Ott argued, didn't you?'

'He argued.'

'Was he abusive to you?'

'Yes.'

'And were you abusive to him?'

'No, I just shut up and listened.'

'Was Dr Ott drunk when you both reached his house that night, after dinner?'

'Yes.'

'Were you drunk?'

'Yes, but not as drunk as he was.'

'You had your Mercedes parked at his house, didn't you?'

'Yes.'

He considered what he could ask about the Mercedes. *Is that your only car? Does anyone else drive it? Had any accidents with it lately?* No, don't be a fool. He could hear her mind ticking.

'So when you got back from the Hacienda to his house, you could have gone home then, right away, in your car?'

'Well . . . yes, I suppose so.'

'But you didn't, did you?'

'No. Wait,' she said to Warren. 'Can't I explain *why*?'

'Not unless he asks you, and he won't. He won't ask any questions that begin with "why". But I'll ask you plenty of that on direct examination, and you can talk as much as you like—so you'll already have explained why you didn't go home right away. OK, let's keep going. We'll skip forward a bit. Later, after you came downstairs with Dr Ott, where did you go?'

'Into the hallway, what he called the vestibule.'

'Dr Ott was drunk and abusive and threatening?'

'Yes. All three.'

'You could have gone directly out the door, couldn't you?'

'No.'

'He blocked your path?'

'Yes.'

'You came down the stairs first, and he followed you, but still he managed to block your path out the door?'

'Yes, he caught up with me in the vestibule.'

'Now, Ms Boudreau,' Warren said. 'How did you get from the vestibule into the living room?'

'He shoved me in there.'

Warren stopped to make some notes.

'All right,' he said, 'then you picked up the poker to defend yourself and he took it away from you. He cursed at you, threatened to kill you. Where were you standing?'

'Behind the sofa.'

'And you already had your gun levelled at him?'

'No.'

'When did you take the gun out of your handbag?'

'When he raised the poker like he was going to hit me.'

'And he came running at you with the poker over his head?'

'Yes.'

'He was running at you when you shot him?'

'Yes.'

'He never hesitated? Never stopped?'

'No.'

'You aimed at his head and pulled the trigger?'

'No, I didn't aim at all. I was petrified.'

'You pulled the trigger three times, didn't you?'

'No, just once.'

'But three bullets were fired, isn't that a fact?'

'Yes.'

'You cocked the action when you took the gun out of your handbag, didn't you?'

'I don't remember.'

'Did you know the sear had been filed down on this gun?'

'I'm still not even sure what a sear is.'

'You've practised with that pistol, haven't you?'

'Once, five years ago, when I bought it. I don't even think I hit the target more than two or three times.'

'All right,' Warren said, after he had made some more notes. 'That's enough for today. How do you feel?'

'Fine,' Johnnie Faye said, her eyes sparkling.

'We'll go through it again next week. I'm starting my other trial on Monday, picking a jury. I'll call you.'

THROUGH THE PARTED BLINDS, Warren watched the Mercedes turn and vanish in the long shadows of early evening. He dropped into his swivel chair, tilted it back and swung his boots up on the desk. Coincidence. It had to be coincidence.

From his desk he took out the Quintana file and stared at the colour photograph of Dan Ho Trunh's blue station wagon, at the cream-coloured rip in the metal just ahead of the rear bumper. That rip, Mrs Trunh swore, hadn't been there when her husband had left the house on the morning of his death.

All right. It could have happened any time that day. Trunh could have sideswiped any number of cream-coloured cars.

But there was one cream-coloured car with that shade of blue paint ground into its front left wing. The blue paint was garish, distinctive—probably hand-painted. And the nature of the owner of the cream-coloured Mercedes was equally distinctive. *'Slant-eyes are no good. . . If I had my way . . .'*

He remembered Bob Altschuler casually telling him that unproved tale: *'We think she offed some Korean kid who worked in her club and gave her some back talk when she wouldn't give him a raise.'*

It can't be, Warren thought. It made no sense. There was no connection. No connection, other than the rage she had shown in the office, and her nature, and Altschuler's accusation. And her brothers. But that was too far-fetched.

Can I ask her? Cutely probe? Find out where she was that day, that evening? I have no reason to ask. But if she's innocent she won't know what I'm getting at and she'll tell me where she was—so I risk nothing. If she did it, she'll be evasive, maybe furious. I'll see it, I'll know the truth. And she'll see that I know. I'll be finished as her lawyer and I won't have a nickel's worth of proof.

Warren spent nearly all day Sunday in his office, preparing an opening statement for *Quintana.* In the late afternoon he visited Hector to tell him how to conduct himself in the courtroom. Hector was grave and courteous. Warren left there feeling depressed. This man could not have done it. He's innocent. And I have no way of proving it.

He looked at his watch: it was nearly eight o'clock. He gathered up his things from his office and drove back to Ravendale to change for the party with Maria Hahn.

6

A bearded man at least six and a half foot tall clapped Warren on the shoulder, yelling above the din, 'So, little buddy, how come you're improperly dressed for this patriotic occasion?'

'Didn't know it was a costume party,' Warren admitted.

'What?'

Warren yelled up, 'I said, my sarong shrank in the dryer!'

The bearded giant guffawed, then headed for the swimming pool on the lawn behind the house. Warren followed, *en route* snatching a piña colada off the bar.

It was his second since he and Maria Hahn had arrived at the Towering Texans Fourth of July party. The fifty large guests had all drifted to the back lawn where they could stretch their limbs to the disco beat.

'Nuts,' Maria exclaimed, when she saw that everyone was wearing bikinis and muumuu dresses. 'How come I forgot?'

'Denial,' Warren said. 'I know a lot about that.'

His mind lay unguarded for a moment, and an idea invaded him. There was something he had to do, and he *had* to do it tonight. Tomorrow might be too late. How had he missed it? He set the frosted rum drink down on a patio table and turned back to the house. His watch said 11.25pm.

There was a pink wall phone in the bathroom. Sitting on the closed toilet seat, Warren punched out the number of Ecstasy. It rang five times before the club's name was announced.

'MCI operator. Person-to-person from Corpus Christi for Johnnie Faye Boudreau, ma'am,' he said.

The five-second wait was shorter than he had predicted. 'Yes? Mama, is it you? What's wrong?'

Warren broke the connection.

MARIA'S WIGGLING FEET and shapely calves dangled in the water of the pool; she was talking with two women in muumuus. Warren caught her eye, and she excused herself to come flowing over to him. He had never really noticed how graceful she was.

'I'm having a fine time,' he said, 'but I have to go somewhere else. Take care of something. And I might need some help.'

'Boy, you *are* mysterious,' she exclaimed.

'I need a lookout. And a witness. No questions asked.'

'Just one, my weirdo friend. You going to rob a bank?'

'Photograph a car.'

Maria asked no more questions, seeming to prefer the poetry of the unknown to prosaic reality.

Down the darkened street from the party house he unlocked his car. 'You have your camera with you?' she asked.

'No, I'll have to . . . oh, no,' he howled. 'Charm has it!'

Maria quickly touched his forearm with cool fingers. 'Take it easy. I have a camera. And film. Just stop at my place and I'll get it.'

Half an hour later, Maria had snapped open the back of her Pentax and slipped in a roll of colour film. It was twenty minutes past midnight. Warren headed west for the Richmond strip.

A short time later he spotted the lights of Ecstasy. Warren parked in a slot on the outer concrete edge. In the illuminated doorway of the club under flickering neon script, silhouettes appeared. A hum of laughter followed by a salvo of music broke from the door into the night.

'This car you want to photograph—'

'I see it.' The car was about six spaces from the front door.

'You want to tell me now what it's all about?' Maria asked.

'I really don't. Show me how this flash works, sit tight, and keep the motor running.'

'Jeez, this is like an old movie.'

Warren smiled, but his heart picked up cadence. In the getaway scene of those old movies, something always went wrong.

'I like you, Mr Blackburn,' Maria said.

'How come?'

'I'm trying to figure that out.' Taking the camera from his hands, she said, 'You set it for distance here. When you push this button and the red light shows, all systems are go.'

'I've got it,' he said. 'Maria, I may need you to verify what I'm going to do. Watch me.'

He walked through the warm night air towards Ecstasy. Nothing furtive, he decided. Do this fast.

Maria saw it all. Saw Warren crouch and raise the Pentax as he reached the front of the light-coloured Mercedes on the driver's side. Saw the thin little black man at the door of the club whose head swivelled towards Warren. Saw the man stare, then vanish.

Warren's back was to the club. He flicked the switch on the flash attachment and the red light popped on. Peering through the camera's viewfinder, he focused the bull's-eye on the small blue scratch adorning the Mercedes's wing. He was sweating.

He clicked off one shot, then moved left a pace and did it again. Then one more of the front licence plate and the wing.

Maria heard the lunatic thump of music as the front door of the club opened and the thin black man and a taller white companion stepped out. Maria reached across to the driver's door and shoved it open. Twice, and loudly, she yelled Warren's name.

At fifteen feet Warren had nearly the whole car in frame, including the wing and the front plate. The car went suddenly dark: obscured. Something tugged at the camera.

Frank Sawyer, in black T-shirt and chinos, had one hand clamped round the Pentax lens. The dragon tattoo was flexing.

'What are you up to, counsellor?'

Sawyer's cold blue eyes were accusing.

'Just doing my job, soldier,' Warren said.

Dropping into a crouch, Sawyer hit Warren hard with a boxer's left hand, between the cheekbone and ear. The world was darkening; Warren sank to lightless depths. Sawyer tore the camera off his neck and smashed it onto the ground until it was reduced to junk.

Warren heard distant crunches and spectral voices. His next awareness was of someone dragging him by the elbows. He was being lifted. There was an aroma of fruity perfume. He was in his car. Maria's voice came from a hundred yards away in a mist.

'. . . it's OK, it's OK. For God's sake, take it easy . . .'

His mind and his eyesight began to clear. Cool air washed over his cheeks. Maria Hahn was driving. They were on a boulevard, not a freeway. His head throbbed as if a drummer were using it for a martial beat.

'I yelled,' Maria said. 'You didn't hear me.' The camera was gone, she told him. Sawyer had demolished it.

'I owe you a camera.' Warren raised his head a little, saw streetlights whip by, and felt raw pain.

WARREN OPENED ONE GLUED EYE. A small boy stood over him, watching. The living room was shadowed, the blinds drawn, but clearly it was morning. The boy had freckles and curly brown hair and an interested expression.

He heard Maria Hahn's voice: 'Randy, don't bother him. Let him sleep.'

The boy's face disappeared. Warren's eye closed.

He awoke again at ten in the morning. In Maria's bathroom mirror he observed that the right side of his face was swollen. The bruise on his cheek was a shiny green edged with purple, the colouring of certain large, vicious Texas bottle flies. He walked slowly out of the bathroom. Maria's neck tilted gracefully from a navy-blue terry-cloth bathrobe.

'How you feeling?'

'I've felt better.'

'Looked it too. You hungry?'

'Yes, please.'

At the breakfast table she stirred eggs and fried some bacon. He asked, 'Where's your son?'

'Gone over to a friend's house. Now will you tell me what this was all about? I think I need to know.'

'I can't do that,' he said.

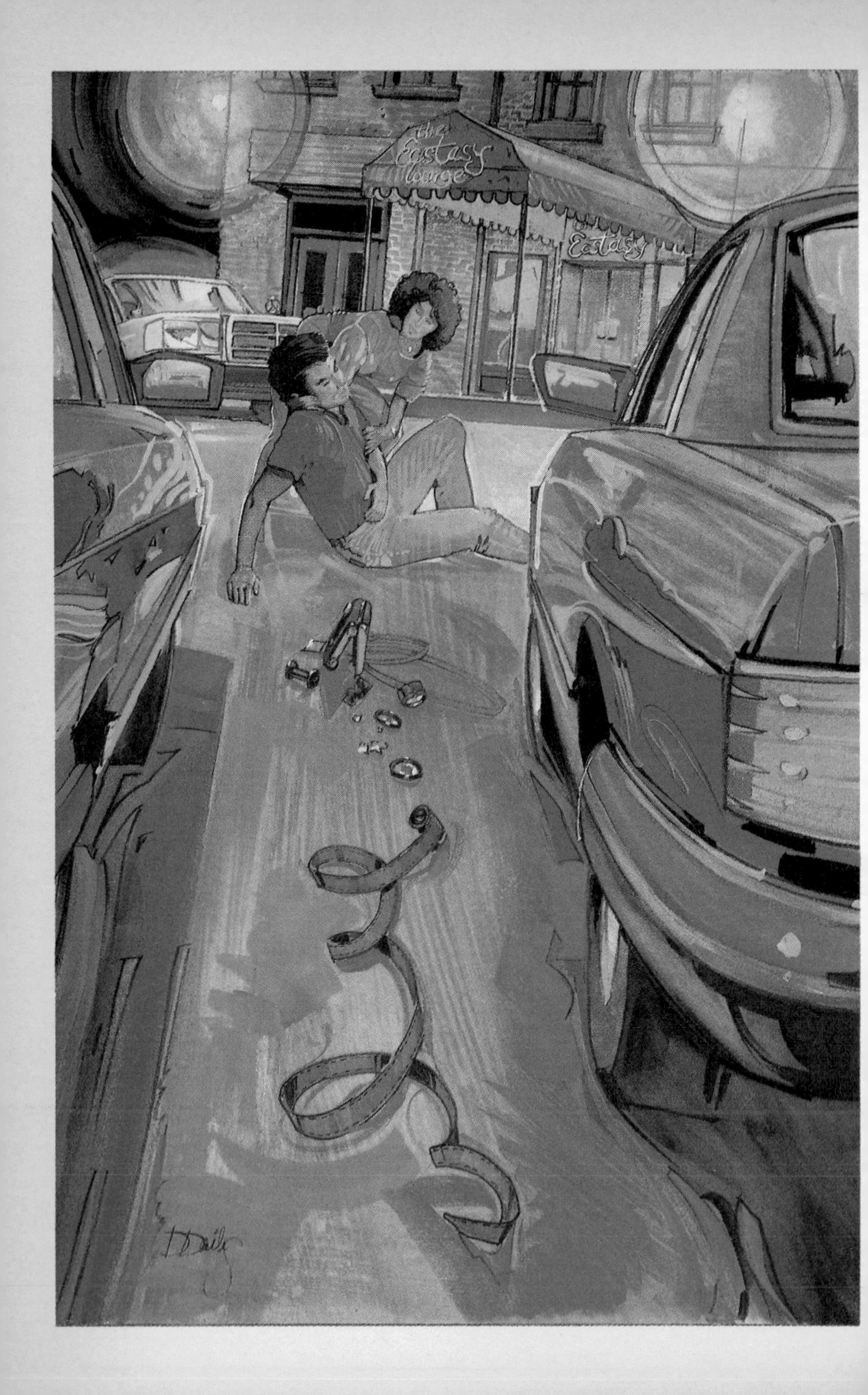
the
Ecstasy
lounge
Ecstasy

'Can't, or won't?'

'Can't. Believe me. Sorry. Just can't.'

Maria took a turn round the kitchen, leaving the bacon to sputter, while she worked at accepting that answer.

'OK,' she said, 'for now. What's your plan?'

He felt cobwebbed, heavy-legged. He had no plan. Doggedly, with suffering brain cells, Warren recalled that he had one task for today. Go to Hermann Park and twist old Pedro's arm to ensure his testimony on Hector Quintana's behalf. As for photographing the Mercedes, that was no longer on the agenda. By now Frank Sawyer was probably under orders to grab a wad of sandpaper and bucket of paint and do a job on the car.

Sorry, Hector, I tried.

Johnnie Faye would surely dump him as her lawyer. She would go before Judge Bingham tomorrow and tell him she hadn't realised that her lawyer was so young and inexperienced. The story would spread. Warren's grand comeback would be a downfall.

'My plan,' he said to Maria Hahn, 'is to dig a cool hole and crawl into it.'

'You can do better than that,' Maria said.

He probably could. And should. He was grateful to Maria. Why was she being so kind to him? He wasn't used to that lately.

'Just as soon as I finish these eggs. They're delicious. They're wonderful. They're the best eggs I've ever eaten.'

Maria laughed and looked at him with friendly blue eyes.

AT NOON, with the July heat building, he drove to the stables at Hermann Park. The pot with fried crackling grease was gone. A black man was cleaning a stall in the stables.

'There were two men here,' Warren said. 'Two Mexicans.'

'They gone.'

'Good Lord, where did they go? Does anyone know?'

The man shrugged.

Gone. Vanished, just like Hector's defence would vanish if he couldn't find Pedro.

He drove back to his office on Montrose for the solace of a cold drink, a darkened room and penitent silence. The red light on his message machine was blinking. The first calm voice was that of Arthur Franklin, Charm's divorce lawyer, who asked Warren to return the call at his earliest convenience. The second voice was Johnnie Faye's. Call me back today, she commanded. We have a lot to talk about, lawyer buddy.

Her apartment was on the eighteenth floor of a new building with a sweeping view of downtown Houston. Warren had expected modern decor, but Johnnie Faye's living room was an old lady's, crowded with memorabilia and fussy furniture. Gold-framed photographs stared gloomily from every wall.

Johnnie Faye wore gold tasselled slippers and a glittering gold pantsuit.

Settling into an ornate Queen Anne chair, she put her feet up on a hassock. A pitcher of iced tea, two glasses and a bowl of lemons stood on the little coffee table.

'Minute I got that phone call supposed to be from Corpus, I knew something was out of line. Somebody wanted to make sure I was there at the club, and deviltry was afoot. But why?' She raised a glass of iced tea in what amounted to a toast to her acuity. 'I told Frankie to keep an eye peeled at the club in case anything odd went down. And it sure did. I think I've got a right to know just what makes you want my car in your scrapbook. But,' she said slyly, 'I'm not about to ask you, because you'd lie. So keep quiet, and listen to me.'

It was all so civilised and polite. He was sitting with a woman who had probably murdered three people—three that he knew of. She was serving him afternoon tea. But where did it end?

'You're still my lawyer, and I need your advice. If I committed another crime, could they bring that up when I go to trial for what happened to Clyde?'

Warren grew wary, but he was obliged to answer honestly.

'They can ask you in cross-examination, if they have reasonable grounds. But they're bound by your answer. They can't then bring in proof that you committed the other crime.'

'Even if the other crime is the murder of that Vietnamese guy you think I killed?'

Warren felt himself growing pale. So it was true. 'Yes,' he said.

'Well, I did it. In self-defence. I had to.'

Warren's heart began to beat out of rhythm. But he said carefully, 'You shot him in the Wesleyan Terrace parking lot outside the dry-cleaners. You used a ·32, and then you shoved it in a trash can in some apartment complex.'

Johnnie Faye said nothing.

'Why?' Warren asked, dumbfounded.

HEADING BACK HOME that day with her booty, Johnnie Faye chose the freeway. A Ford Fairlane station wagon trying to get off it clipped her bumper and headed for the exit ramp to Wesleyan.

She hit the accelerator and drilled after him to give him what for. He popped the wagon into a parking lot in front of the dry-cleaners. She saw him clearly for the first time and realised he was Asian.

She began yelling. Dan Ho Trunh cursed back at her, she told Warren. He hissed through his protruding white teeth and reached back towards his trouser pocket to take something out of it. Johnnie Faye felt a surge of terror. This was the way your life could end, in a parking lot you didn't know, at the hands of an alien stranger. She twisted the knob of the glove compartment and snatched the ·32-calibre Diamondback Colt. In one practised motion she snapped the safety to the off position.

The Vietnamese straightened up, and there was something dark in his right hand and it was pointed at her.

'I guess I screamed,' she said to Warren. 'But I did it to him before he could do it to me.'

Warren believed that she believed what she was telling him. He asked, 'Did you ever hear of a man named Hector Quintana?'

She had found that out a couple of weeks ago. Had a good laugh. Ironic, wasn't it? Made no difference, she had concluded.

Warren stared at her. 'But he didn't do it!'

'Then you'll get him off,' she said.

Simple as that. She was a woman of great faith. Warren felt the blood throb in his temples.

'And let's get something real clear between us,' Johnnie Faye said strongly, fixing him with her thoughtful bicoloured eyes. 'You're still my lawyer. I'm keeping you on.'

'What makes you think,' Warren asked, 'that I still *want* to be your lawyer?'

She seemed amused by the question. 'I thought this was a big deal for you.'

'If they still had hanging in this state,' Warren said hoarsely, 'I'd knot the noose, and not too tight. I'd put the damn needle in your arm myself.'

'Sure,' Johnnie Faye said, 'in your fantasies. But not in reality. You're my lawyer now. Everything I told you is secret between us, even if you quit me. Confidential is the word, right? You can counsel me, you can help me win. *But you can't tell anyone what I told you.* I checked the law. Isn't that so, counsellor?'

His fists clenched at his sides. His breaths were shallow.

'Why do you believe,' he asked, 'that if I defended you in court on the Ott murder, I wouldn't throw you to the dogs? I could mess it up so badly the jury wouldn't even have to leave the courtroom to hand down a guilty verdict.'

'I thought of that,' Johnny Faye said. 'You mess up, they'll see it. You'll be out on your ass again. I'll get a new trial, and someone else to defend me.' She patted his sleeve. 'I know you. You'll do your best. That's the way you are, counsellor. That's why I like you. And I like the idea of having you around me, so I can keep an eye on you.' She yawned, reached for a cigarette.

'What if Hector Quintana's convicted?' Warren asked, his mind ripped with rage and helplessness. 'What if I can't save him? What if he gets death, or life in prison?'

'A sad song don't care whose heart it breaks,' Johnnie Faye Boudreau said. 'You of all people should know that.'

'ALL RISE!' THE BAILIFF CRIED, as Judge Lou Parker swept into the courtroom for the capital murder trial of Hector Quintana.

Her gaze flicked like a bullwhip from counsel tables to jury box to the dozen or so Vietnamese spectators. On this day, courtesy of the State of Texas, Hector Quintana wore a blue suit, white shirt and dark blue tie. Standing next to his client at the defence table, Warren quickly squeezed Hector's arm. For courage.

Goodpaster was seasoned and swift. In her opening statement to the jury she said, 'The evidence will show . . . that the defendant'—she faced him squarely and jabbed a finger at Hector—'set out deliberately not merely to rob Dan Ho Trunh but to murder him for less than a hundred and fifty dollars! The evidence will show cold-blooded, premeditated murder of an unarmed human being.'

Seated now, Hector Quintana threw his shaking hands up in the air. He groaned loudly—the wail of a tortured soul.

The piteous cry echoed through the courtroom. Nancy Goodpaster's mouth fell open. For three full seconds the room was preternaturally silent. Could a guilty man emit such a ravaged sound? Would the jury not grasp the truth?

Judge Parker cracked the silence: 'Counsellor, don't let that happen again! No more outbursts!'

Warren spoke in Hector's ear. 'Don't do that again.' He added, more softly, 'Not today.'

When Goodpaster sat down, the judge waved a pale, many-ringed hand at the defence attorney. Warren cleared his throat and stood to face the jury. 'Hector Quintana is innocent,' he said. 'He's innocent of everything he's been charged with. Not just "not guilty" under the law, but truly innocent. The defence will show that he didn't kill Dan Ho Trunh, and that this entire case is a frightening miscarriage of justice. And we will prove it to you beyond a reasonable doubt.' That was as far as he dared go.

THE NIGHT AFTER HIS MEETING with Johnnie Faye Boudreau he had paced the carpet in his apartment, staring sightlessly at the TV, thumbing through books and tomes on legal ethics. A great deal had been written about attorney–client privilege and the duty to keep or disclose client confidences. One thing was clear. The Code of Professional Responsibility and its fourth canon said: no matter how heinous the secret, to reveal it is forbidden. The lawyer was duty-bound *not* to tell.

Surely in this instance, Warren thought, there are overriding concerns. What about his obligation to Hector Quintana?

The canons allowed him to share his knowledge with co-counsel. Late the next afternoon he went to Rick Levine's office.

'There must be exceptions to the privilege rule,' Rick said gloomily.

'Yeah, there are four exceptions. If your client gives you permission, if a client tells you about a crime planned for the future, if it's the only way you can collect your fee, or to defend yourself against a false accusation of wrongful conduct.'

'You don't think it would be wrongful conduct to let this guy Quintana go to jail for a murder that the dragon lady committed?'

'I do, but there's no accusation against me. That could only be if Quintana is convicted. And I still have no proof!'

Rick shrugged. 'Go to the DA now and tell him you saw the scratches on the two cars. You figured it out on your own. You never talked to her, she never confessed, and you're not violating confidentiality. Then let him run with it.'

Warren laughed bitterly. 'So then she brings charges against me before the judicial committee. The DA insists I take a polygraph, which I won't pass. Then I'm disbarred.'

Rick lit a cigar. 'Go to Nancy Goodpaster or Judge Parker. You have a duty to try and save Hector's hide.'

Warren slammed a fist down. 'Don't you think I know that? Nancy will say, "Where's your proof? What am I supposed to do, Mr Blackburn, drop a case because you say someone other than your client is guilty? The facts indicate otherwise. There's possession of the gun. There's positive ID by an eyewitness." ' Warren sniffed. 'I'm going to withdraw from *Quintana,*' he said.

'And you think Hector's going to understand why you're bowing out right in the middle of jury selection?'

'No, he won't,' Warren said.

'Parker will appoint someone like Myron Moore. Myron will plead your guy out for forty years. Can you live with that?'

'I can't live with *any* of it,' Warren groaned.

That evening, in his apartment, he thought, My obligation is not only to Hector Quintana, and to Johnnie Faye Boudreau, and to the rule of law—above all, it's to my conscience.

I can violate confidentiality, he decided. I can disclose what I know, go to Charm, or to the rest of the media . . .

But how would that help Hector? The jury had taken an oath to decide Hector's guilt or innocence based on the evidence alone. That oath would not change. The law, Warren thought bitterly, protects us from barbarism, and in its place gives us the barbarism of the law. I can't desert Hector now. There's no answer to this, no decent solution. Day to day. Stick with it. Stick with both cases. Wait, like a lion in the brush, for the prey to show itself and make a mistake. Stick close to *her*, for the same reason she wants to stick close to *me*, and see what happens.

LESS THAN TWENTY-FOUR HOURS after he knew who had murdered Dan Ho Trunh, Warren and Nancy Goodpaster began to pick the jury that would decide the life or death of Hector Quintana. Defence and prosecution were each allotted a set number of peremptory strikes—disqualification of jurors with no reason given. Goodpaster used most of her strikes to eliminate Hispanics. Warren had made up his mind not to let any Asians on the jury.

He wanted young jurors. He theorised that the young ones would have more sympathy for an illegal alien, a member of the new legion of homeless.

In the midst of the *voir-dire* session he took Maria Hahn to an Italian restaurant for dinner. 'I haven't done anything about replacing the camera, but I will. I promise. I'm not quite with it these days.'

Maria waved her hand in dismissal, rosy fingernails glittering in candlelight. Later, outside the restaurant, Warren kissed her on the cheek fraternally and said good night.

Two days later, at noon, he bumped into her in a crowded courthouse elevator. She clasped his arm. 'You look awful,' she whispered. 'I'll buy you lunch. Cheer you up.'

Nothing dark or desperate or depressing about lovely Maria Hahn. But what did she want from him? Friendship? Company? What he wanted too. A perfect match.

At lunch, he reached for the bill. 'I invited you,' Maria reminded him.

'Too late.'

'I want my Pentax.'

'Give me until Friday night.'

'It's a date—I'll take you to dinner. And leave your money at home.'

The Quintana jury was picked and sworn by Thursday. It comprised seven men and five women: seven were white, five were black, half were under thirty. Judge Parker instructed the jurors not to discuss the case among themselves or even with family, and to be in court by 8.30am on Monday.

The next day Warren stopped at a discount camera store and bought the Pentax, then went on to Arthur Franklin's law firm in the Republic Bank Building. Charm's lawyer was in his sixties, a Texan who had gone to Harvard. His office smelt of wood polish, Havana cigars and tax-free bonds. 'You're an attorney, Mr Blackburn,' Arthur Franklin began. 'You know these matters are never pleasant, but they needn't be acrimonious.' In the end Warren agreed to all of Charm's terms. There was nothing to argue about. But he felt rotten all over again.

He went home to shower and to feed Oobie, and at eight o'clock he met Maria Hahn at a French restaurant in River Oaks. Warren looked at the menu and said, 'Do you mind if I ask you something gauche? Can you afford this?'

'Sure,' Maria said. 'Not all the time, but life is short.'

She was paid a salary for her normal day in Judge Bingham's court, she explained, but by the page for extra transcripts. She had a second stenograph machine at home in her spare bedroom. Sometimes she worked until midnight. 'The kid has to go to college one day, and you know what that costs. Randy's a smart boy. I was thinking of the Ivy League. Penn or Cornell.'

'A little early for that, isn't it?'

'You have to plan.'

'My wife went to Penn,' Warren said.

Maria smiled easily. 'Good for her.'

After espresso, Maria paid the bill with a credit card and asked him back to her apartment. She lived nearby in a condominium.

Maria's son was spending a month with his grandparents over in Austin. Maria put some Spanish guitar music on the tape deck, kicked off her shoes, then dropped down next to Warren on the living-room sofa. An after-dinner drink warmed him, the sofa was soft; like any stray, his response to these comforts was instantaneous. Extracting the half-finished glass of cognac from his hands, Maria set it on the coffee table then leaned towards him and kissed him. The kiss continued and Warren enjoyed it beyond expectation. She was a beautiful woman. He began to kiss her neck.

'Maria—'

'Oh shut up,' she said quietly.

7

Wearing the austere jet-black robes of absolute authority, Judge Parker peered down from the height of the judicial bench, and nodded in the direction of Nancy Goodpaster. 'You may call your first witness, Madam Prosecutor.'

'The state calls Khuong Nguyen.'

A slightly built man in his fifties seated himself in the witness chair. He was dressed in a pale grey silk sports jacket and perfectly creased dark grey trousers. He identified himself as the owner of the 7-Eleven near the corner of Westheimer and Kirby in River Oaks. When he took over the 7-Eleven, the defendant, Hector Quintana, had been employed for about three months by the previous owner as handyman.

Goodpaster asked, 'Did the previous owner make any recommendation to you regarding Mr Quintana, sir?'

'Objection,' Warren said. 'Calls for hearsay.'

'Sustained. Rephrase the question, Madam Prosecutor.'

'Thank you, your honour. Mr Nguyen, what was your feeling about the defendant after you'd spoken to the previous owner?'

'I still object,' Warren said. 'The answer will depend on hearsay, on a statement made out of court.'

'Don't explain hearsay to me, Mr Blackburn!' Judge Parker glared down, then turned to the jury. 'You're not to believe or disbelieve any remarks attributed to the previous owner. Just pay attention to the reaction of the witness at the time.'

In a cultured voice with a slightly French accent, Mr Nguyen said, 'I was told that Hector Quintana was a good worker but that on several occasions he had been intoxicated.'

Goodpaster asked, 'And as a result of being told that, Mr Nguyen, what did you do?'

'I was forced to let him go.'

Warren jumped to his feet. 'Your honour, I object to this entire line of questioning. It's leading to an attempt to prejudice the jury. I ask that it be stricken and the jury instructed to disregard.'

'Overruled,' Judge Parker said, 'and sit down, Mr Blackburn.'

So that's how it was going to be. Warren had assumed the worst. The worst was happening.

Goodpaster resumed: 'And did you have words with Mr Quintana?'

'I said to him, "I'm so sorry, but I must let you go," and I gave him a week's wages. And he said, "That's not fair." '

'And then what did Mr Quintana do?'

'He became angry and just before he left he cursed at me.'

'You understood he was cursing at you?'

'It was very clear.'

'Thank you, Mr Nguyen. Pass the witness.'

Warren conferred in whispers for a minute with Hector before he rose. 'Mr Nguyen, you mentioned that the previous owner told you Hector was a good worker, but he drank now and then on the job. Nevertheless, the previous owner thought enough of him as an employee not to fire him, isn't that so?'

'It would seem so,' Mr Nguyen said carefully.

'Sir, before you moved here, where did you live?'

'In Singapore. And before that, Saigon.'

'How many languages do you speak?'

'Five. Vietnamese, of course—English, French and Thai. And some Chinese, the Mandarin dialect.'

'But you don't speak Spanish, isn't that so?'

'I have not had the opportunity to learn.'

'And when Mr Quintana supposedly cursed at you, it was in Spanish, isn't that so?'

Mr Nguyen frowned. 'As I said, it was clear.'

'Sir, excuse me, but I didn't ask you if it was clear or not. I asked you if Mr Quintana cursed at you in Spanish.'

'I seem to recall that was so.'

Warren's voice rose angrily. 'Did you understand *one* word Mr Quintana said?'

'Some few words,' Nguyen said.

'Oh?' Warren gambled. 'Repeat them to the jury, please.'

'I do not remember them,' Nguyen said.

'No further questions, your honour.'

The next witness, Rona M. Morrison—a pale, nervous woman in her late forties—was sworn in. Prompted by Nancy Goodpaster, she related that on the night of May 26 she had delivered some skirts and cotton sweaters to the dry-cleaning establishment on Wesleyan, and on the way back to her car had 'just kind of peeked into this station wagon that was settin' there'. And there was a man on the seat who 'looked real dead'.

Goodpaster had some crime-scene photographs stamped by the clerk and formally introduced into evidence, and then handed them to the witness.

'Is this what you saw, Ms Morrison?'

Rona Morrison said yes, then began to shed tears.

Warren scowled. Oh Lord, a weeper. A bonanza for the prosecution. He took over for cross-examination. 'Ms Morrison, did you see anyone else in that parking lot that evening?'

No one that she could recall.

'You didn't see *this* man, did you?' He put his hand on Hector's shoulder and squeezed it.

'No, I didn't see him.'

'Thank you, Ms Morrison. No more questions.'

Goodpaster called the Harris County assistant medical examiner who took the stand to tell the jury that the cause of death was a .32-calibre bullet lodged in the brain.

Warren waived cross-examination of the witness.

'The state calls Sergeant Hollis Thiel.'

Pink-faced, with eyes like hard little brown buttons, Thiel settled into the witness chair. He was at ease.

Goodpaster asked him what he had found in the vehicle.

'Registration papers, which led us to a positive identification of the complainant as Dan Ho Trunh. A box with various electrician's tools. Some dirty shirts and a balled-up jacket.'

No weapon of any kind, Thiel replied, when asked. No wallet, no money.

'Did you detect any signs of a struggle that preceded Mr Trunh's being shot and killed?'

'No, ma'am.'

'Pass the witness.'

Warren stepped in front of the defence table.

'Sergeant Thiel, when you reached the crime scene, the window on the driver's side of the victim's car was open?'

'Yes.'

'You found no wallet on the victim or in the car?'

'None.'

'If Mr Trunh had a wallet, someone took it before your arrival?'

'That's correct.'

'And there's no telling, is there, who took that wallet? It didn't have to be the person who shot him, did it?'

'Objection!' Goodpaster barked. 'Calls for speculation.'

'Sustained.'

'But, your honour—'

'Sustained. Get on with it, Mr Blackburn.'

Warren seethed a moment, then calmed down.

'Let me put it this way, Sergeant. All anybody had to do—anybody who came along—was to open the door and see a dead man and take his wallet. Isn't that true?'

'Objection!'

'Don't answer, Sergeant!' the judge cried. 'Mr Blackburn, that's enough! I'll see both counsel in chambers!'

Two rebukes from the bench on the first morning. Juries invariably followed the judge's leaning, if the judge leaned. And Lou Parker leaned hard. I'm getting killed, Warren thought.

In chambers, seated at her desk, the judge pointed that familiar finger at Warren's chest. 'Now listen here! When I rule, that's *it*. You want to appeal to a higher court and claim error, be my guest. But this is *my* courtroom. You follow?'

Warren considered his options. He was tired of being stepped on by this woman. He said, 'No, Judge, this is not your courtroom. Your only function is to help the two of us'—he waved to include Nancy Goodpaster—'present a true case to the jury. You can rule, but you've got to rule without prejudicing the jury against me and my client. Because until that jury comes in with a verdict, it's Quintana's courtroom. He faces death. I'm not going to hurry this case along so you can get a better suntan.'

Seated next to him, Nancy Goodpaster bowed her head.

Lou Parker was looking at him, open-mouthed. 'Don't say another word,' she stammered. 'I'm not prejudicing anybody, you hear? You'll follow my rulings! Right or wrong, I'm the judge! Now get out!'

She had backed off.

GOODPASTER CALLED PAUL STIMAC, a thin, sandy-haired man.

'Where do you work, Mr Stimac?'

'In the Circle K, corner of Bissonet and Harding. I'm the night cashier.'

On the evening of May 26, Stimac related in a high-pitched voice, a man had come into the store and pointed a gun at him. Yes, the man was in the courtroom. He identified Hector.

'Were you frightened for your life, Mr Stimac?'

Warren calmly objected. 'Irrelevant, and calculated to inflame the jury against my client.'

'I don't think so.' The judge shook her head. 'I think it's relevant how he felt. Objection overruled.'

'Well, I'd been stuck up twice before,' Stimac answered. 'I wasn't too scared. I knew what to do.' He had pressed a button on the floor that would summon the police, then stalled. He handed over the money. The police came.

Warren took over on cross-examination. 'Mr Quintana never threatened you, did he?'

Goodpaster objected. 'Calls for a conclusion.'

'Sustained,' Parker said.

Warren shrugged lightly. 'I'll rephrase. Did he ever say anything to you like, "If you don't hand over the money, I'm gonna blow your brains out."? Anything at all like that?'

'No,' Stimac said, 'he just asked for the money. He looked more scared than I was.'

'Would it surprise you, sir, to learn that the pistol Mr Quintana pointed at you had no bullets in it?'

'Objection,' Goodpaster cut in, 'there's no predicate.'

She meant that you couldn't ask a question implying a fact that had not yet been established as a fact. The gun wasn't loaded, but no witness had as yet testified that it wasn't.

'Sustained,' Judge Parker rumbled. She seemed to be saying: Do your worst, counsellor, but I'm still going to win. I'm the judge and it's my court.

AFTER LUNCH, Officer L. E. Manley took the stand. A young, athletic-looking black man, he testified that he and his partner had apprehended the defendant as he trotted out of the Circle K, pistol in hand. Naturally they took the pistol away from him.

'Yes, this is the same weapon,' he said, after Goodpaster placed it in his hands. 'A .32-calibre Diamondback Colt with a distinctive ivory-inlaid butt. It's had some work done on the hammer and recoil spring. Real easy to fire.'

Warren scribbled some notes. New information. Thank you, Officer Manley.

Goodpaster asked Manley, 'And were there any bullets in the pistol when you took it away from Mr Quintana?'

'No, ma'am.'

'Pass the witness.'

With Manley's help Warren established that Hector had carried no other bullets on his person, and none had been found inside or outside the Circle K. Now Warren asked, 'Tell us this, Officer Manley. This particular gun—you said it had an ivory handle, and an easy trigger pull. In your experience, it's not the sort of gun a man would carry, is it?'

'No, it's not,' Manley said.

'You would say, wouldn't you, that it's a woman's gun?'

'Objection!'

'Sustained,' the judge declared.

'No further questions.'

On redirect questioning, Goodpaster asked, 'Is there anything about this gun that prevents a man from using it?'

'No, ma'am.'

'And the defendant was carrying it that night, wasn't he?'

'Yes, he was.'

On recross-examination, Warren hammered away. 'Can you think of any reason, Officer Manley, why a dirt-poor illegal Mexican alien would be carrying an unloaded gun—a gun of a sort that men don't carry?'

'Objection! Calls for speculation.'

'You can answer, Manley,' Judge Parker said, surprising Warren. Then she added, to the prosecutor, 'Or else he'll just rephrase and worm it out of him some other way.'

Manley shrugged. 'It might have been the only weapon he could get hold of. He might have borrowed it. He might have found it somewhere. Anything's possible.'

Manley was told to step down.

The expert from HPD Ballistics then identified the Diamondback Colt as the tagged weapon that had been handed to him on the night of May 26 by Officer Manley. It wasn't until late the next afternoon that the bullet retrieved from Dan Ho Trunh's brain was brought into the lab. There was an immediate match.

It was now after three o'clock. Judge Parker rapped her black oak gavel, then dismissed the jury until the next morning.

When they had gone, the bailiff put handcuffs back on Hector's wrists. Hector looked worn out and pale. Warren said, 'Listen, it went well. And tomorrow will be even better.'

Hector nodded with terrifying politeness. He knows, Warren realised, knows I'm pecking away at a steel wall.

'Your turn will come,' Warren said, a little desperately.

Hector shook his head. 'They will not believe me. I will die.' His voice was like an axe falling.

'No. Listen! You have to believe in me.'

But Hector turned his back and nodded to the bailiff, who led him away.

JOHNNIE FAYE BOUDREAU entered the courtroom a few minutes after 9am on the second day of the Quintana trial. Warren's eye fell on her immediately.

That was not difficult. She wore a cherry-red double-breasted linen suit over a white camisole, red high heels to match the suit, and her tight skirt was well above the knees.

Johnnie Faye took a seat in a back row and smiled across the room at Warren. He had a powerful urge to clasp Hector Quintana by the arm, turn him in his chair and say, 'That woman in red is the one who murdered the man you're accused of murdering. Go to her, Hector. Ask her how she can live with it.'

Judge Parker entered, the bailiff demanded order, and the state called Mai Thi Trunh as its first witness. Mrs Trunh was on the stand for two purposes: to elicit sympathy and to help prove that her late husband was in possession of his wallet on the morning of his death.

Dan Ho Trunh's young widow wore black. She was a composed witness who spoke slowly and simply, her grief not flaunted but clearly there. Warren was moved by her. Under Nancy Goodpaster's patient questioning, the jury learned a great deal about the Trunh family, all of it irrelevant, but Warren did not object. When a bereaved witness testified, a defence counsel had to shut up and take it. Goodpaster's merciful 'Pass the witness' occurred only a few minutes before noon. The jury was led away by the bailiff.

Warren walked slowly to the rear of the courtroom where Johnnie Faye waited for him in her cherry-red suit. 'That was boring,' she said.

'I suppose so. What are you doing here?'

'You're my lawyer. I came to watch you at work. When do you get to strut your stuff?'

'After lunch. You'll be disappointed.'

'That remains to be seen. Let's go.'

'Where?'

'Lunch.'

'No thanks.'

'That's dumb,' Johnnie Faye said. 'I know you're not exactly crazy about me, but we're going to see a lot of each other. It won't hurt you to be civil. Besides, I want to talk about the case. *My* case.'

'I'm on this case now. When I want to talk to you about yours, I'll call you and we'll meet in my office.'

He saw a quick and exacting look in her eye, the look that Clyde Ott and Dink might have seen more than once. She could easily kill me, he realised. She's capable of it. Like them, I know too much. Then the expression vanished and her eye was as flat as stone. Her blue-grey eye.

SHE WAS BACK IN HER SEAT at the rear of the courtroom when Warren stood and faced Mai Thi Trunh for cross-examination. The theft of Dan Ho's wallet was what turned simple murder into capital murder. The key to the widow's testimony was her statement that her husband always took his wallet with him. Circumstantial evidence. Perhaps during the course of the day he had been pickpocketed, or inadvertently dropped it in the street. Who could prove otherwise?

But Dan Ho Trunh did take the wallet, Warren believed.

'The defence has no questions,' he said.

'You may step down,' Judge Parker said to Mrs Trunh.

Nancy Goodpaster rose eagerly. 'The state calls its last witness—Mrs Siva Singh.'

Behind her glasses the Indian woman looked nervous. She had been born in Jaipur; she and her husband had emigrated to the United States twelve years ago. They owned the dry-cleaners on Wesleyan. Her husband worked in the back.

Goodpaster got down to business. 'Mrs Singh, please tell us where you were on the evening of May twenty-sixth.'

In the Wesleyan Laundry & Dry-Cleaners.

'On that evening, did a Mrs Morrison enter your store?'

Siva Singh described how Rona Morrison had come in to drop off her dry-cleaning, exited, then a minute later, in the parking lot, screamed. Singh had hurried outside to find Mrs Morrison on her knees by the side of a parked station wagon. After she had seen the bleeding body of a man inside the car, she had brought Mrs Morrison inside and called the police.

Goodpaster said, 'Did anything unusual happen *prior* to Mrs Morrison's scream and your discovery of the body?'

'Yes indeed. I was working in the back when there was a noise, which I later understood had been a gunshot. I returned to the front of the store.'

'From behind the counter you had a clear view of the parking lot?' Goodpaster asked.

'Quite clear.'

'Please tell the jury what you saw.'

'A man stood by the station wagon—'

'The station wagon in which you later found the body?'

'The same. The man was perhaps thirty or forty feet away from my point of observation. He seemed to be leaning in the window. Then he turned and ran away.'

Goodpaster looked at her soberly, then asked: 'When the man turned, did he turn towards you, or away?'

'Most definitely towards me, so that I saw his face.'

'You saw it clearly?'

'Quite clearly.'

'Can you describe him to us, Mrs Singh?'

'He was about five foot nine or five foot ten inches tall, with long dark hair, and wore just a pair of trousers with a shirt. He wore no jacket. He looked to be poor and homeless. He seemed most certainly to be Hispanic.'

Warren wrote a note on his pad: who was the man in the parking lot? Siva Singh had seen someone, he didn't doubt it, but not Hector Quintana. Johnnie Faye had been in her car, and even if she had stepped out of it for a moment, there was no way she could be mistaken for a man. Some passer-by, he decided, who had seen the body, become frightened, then bolted. Still, that didn't account for the missing wallet.

'Please tell us what happened the following day, Mrs Singh,' Goodpaster continued, 'at the Harris County Jail.'

Siva Singh described the police line-up. Six men were paraded before her. She identified one of them as the man whom she had seen running away the night before.

'You were certain it was the same man?'

'Quite certain.'

'Do you see that man in this courtroom today?'

'I do indeed.'

'Point to him and describe him, please.'

She pointed towards the defence table. 'He is wearing a white shirt and blue single-breasted suit.'

Goodpaster smiled in embarrassment, and said firmly, 'Mrs Singh, there are *two* men at the defence table wearing white shirts and single-breasted blue suits. Can you be more specific?'

The jury began to titter.

Mrs Singh threw a hand to her open mouth and rose slightly in the witness chair. Then she tore her hand away and stabbed it towards Hector. 'I am mortified! It is he! The man in the blue tie!'

The jurors' laughter surged for a moment, then ebbed away. The judge tapped her gavel.

'Let the record reflect,' Goodpaster said gravely, 'that the witness has identified the defendant, Hector Quintana.'

'Let the record so reflect,' said Judge Parker.

Warren rose to face Siva Singh. 'This isn't the first time we've met, is it?' Warren asked.

'No.'

'I came to talk to you some weeks ago, isn't that so?'

'Yes, that is true,' Singh said unhappily.

'You wouldn't discuss this case with me, because you were under the mistaken impression that Ms Goodpaster, the prosecutor, had forbidden you from doing so. Isn't that so?'

'That is so. I apologise, sir.'

'No, Mrs Singh, it's I who should apologise. I should have got Ms Goodpaster to call you and explain. Please forgive me.'

Singh's dark brown eyes glittered.

'Your glasses are for distance, aren't they?' Warren asked, remembering how she had taken them off to reach into her pocketbook for Goodpaster's business card.

'Oh yes. And with them I can see perfectly.'

'Can you see at a distance without them?'

'Quite well.'

Warren frowned. 'Were you wearing them on the night of May twenty-sixth when you saw the man leaning into the station wagon?'

'Indeed, yes, I was wearing them,' Singh said gravely, 'or I would not have seen him as clearly as I did.'

Warren thought for a moment, then moved a few feet closer to her. 'Ma'am, what is your native language?'

'Hindi,' Singh said, a little surprised and suddenly wary. 'But of course as a child in Jaipur I learned English.'

'And you speak it perfectly. English English, not American English, correct?'

The wariness vanished. 'Indeed, yes,' Singh said, smiling.

'If you'd indulge me, ma'am, I'd like you to shut your eyes for a moment and then answer a question.'

Obediently, Siva Singh shut her eyes.

Warren said, 'As best you recall, how tall am I?'

'Objection!' Goodpaster cried.

Before the judge could rule, Siva Singh's eyes flew open.

'Withdraw the question,' Warren said.

He began to move about the room, pacing. 'Mrs Singh, before the police arrived to talk to you on the evening of May twenty-sixth, did you tell your husband that you'd seen a man running away from that station wagon in the darkness?'

'Indeed, I told my husband.'

'Do you recall what words you used when you described him to your husband? Just answer yes or no, ma'am.'

'Yes.'

'Please tell the jury what you said to your husband.'

She thought a moment, then said, 'I told my husband that the man was perhaps five foot nine inches tall. That he had long dark hair. That he wore just a pair of trousers with a shirt. That he did not wear a jacket. That he appeared to be a poor and homeless fellow. That he was most certainly Hispanic, and that I had never seen him before in my life.'

Warren waited as long as he dared for it to register. Then he said, 'Mrs Singh, aren't those just about the exact words that you used to describe this man to the police?'

'Most probably,' Singh managed.

'And in this courtroom today, when the prosecutor asked you to describe the man you saw running away from the car in the darkness, didn't you use the exact same words?'

'Most probably,' Singh said again.

'Do you have a copy of your sworn statement to the police?'

'Yes.'

'Have you memorised it? Word for word? Phrase for phrase, in the right order, so that there would be no discrepancies?'

'I did not memorise it, sir. But I studied it.'

Warren moved to the other side of the courtroom, next to Hector Quintana. The jurors' eyes followed him. 'Mrs Singh, when you talked to the police and described the man whom you saw running away, you said: "I thought he *might* have been Hispanic"—isn't that so? Just yes or no, please.'

'Yes.'

'And then to my colleague, Ms Goodpaster, earlier today, didn't you say, "He seemed most certainly to be Hispanic"?'

'Yes.'

'And a few moments ago, when you were relating to the jury what you told your husband, you said: "He *was* most certainly Hispanic." Didn't you, Mrs Singh?'

'I may have done so.'

'Isn't it a fact that with each description, as time moves on, you grow more positive?'

'Objection,' Goodpaster called out sharply, a little desperately. 'Badgering the witness!'

'Overruled,' Judge Parker said, to Warren's surprise. 'You may answer, Mrs Singh.'

'I do not know the correct answer,' Singh said.

'What is a Hispanic, Mrs Singh?' Warren said quietly.

'A person from Latin America, sir.'

'How would you describe such a person physically?'

'They are usually dark. Not very tall.'

'You are dark too, Mrs Singh, and not very tall,' Warren said, in his quietest audible voice. 'Are you Hispanic?'

'Most definitely not,' she replied.

'Do you have anything against Hispanics?'

'Not in any particular way.'

Warren pounced: 'You have something against them in a *general* way, is that what you're telling us?'

'It is just that I have noticed that many of the unemployed and homeless men in our city are of Latin origin.'

'Just one thing more, Mrs Singh.' He saw her relax. 'At eight pm the parking lot outside your dry-cleaners is relatively dark, isn't it?'

'There are lights.'

'Was the station wagon parked directly under one of them?'

'No. But it was not too far away.'

'Isn't it true, Mrs Singh, that the station wagon was parked at least twenty feet from the base of the nearest lamp?'

'That may be.'

'You came from the back of the laundry a minute or two after you heard the gunshot?'

'Yes.'

'The man who was running away, you saw him clearly?'

'Quite clearly.'

'Mrs Singh, in the Queen's English, which you learned in Jaipur, and still speak, does the word "quite" mean *very*, or does it mean *sort of*?'

'I beg your pardon?'

'When I asked you if you could see well at a distance without your glasses, you answered, "Quite well." And yet your glasses are to help you see things at a distance, aren't they?'

'Yes, exactly.'

'So what you meant when you said, "Quite well," was really, "Fairly well"—isn't that so, ma'am?'

'That is possible.'

'When Ms Goodpaster asked if you saw the man's face when he turned towards you, and you replied, "Quite clearly"—you actually meant "fairly clearly". Isn't that true, ma'am?'

'I could see him,' Singh said. 'He was dark and scruffy.'

'A Hispanic.'

'Well, I am not sure of that now.'

Warren took a shaky breath and paused to let that register with the jurors.

'And then later, when Ms Goodpaster asked if you were certain that the man you picked out of the police line-up was the same man whom you saw "quite clearly" in the parking lot, you replied that you were "quite certain". You meant *fairly* certain, didn't you, Mrs Singh?'

'He was quite similar,' Siva Singh replied softly. 'And if he is not the same man then I will not forgive myself.'

'Do you think *he* will forgive you?' Warren asked.

Mrs Singh did not answer.

He was torn between ending right there and going on. He glanced at the jury. They were with him. They would not forget.

He wanted to show the jury that Dan Ho Trunh could easily have been followed to the dry-cleaning establishment by someone who knew his habits. A red herring, but he needed it.

'Mrs Singh, was Dan Ho Trunh a regular customer?'

'Yes, he came once a week.'

'Mr Trunh came always on the same day?' Warren asked.

'That is correct. On Friday evening between five and eight pm.'

Thiel had testified that some dirty shirts had been found in the back of the station wagon.

'Which laundry or dry-cleaning of his was in your store, that he was going to pick up? If you remember.'

'Ah, I do indeed remember,' she said happily. 'Five white button-down shirts, a grey suit, and a gentleman's green cotton sweater. They were picked up and paid for on Monday.'

Warren said, 'I'm confused. Do you mean the Monday before the murder?'

'No, sir. The Monday following.'

Warren frowned, still a little puzzled. 'You mean they were picked up by Mrs Trunh, or one of her family?'

'It was most definitely not Mrs Trunh or one of her family,' Singh said. 'But he had the proper ticket.'

Warren stopped.

'Wait a minute. *Who* had the proper ticket, Mrs Singh? Who picked up the shirts and a suit and sweater?'

'I had never seen him before,' Singh said.

'Describe him!' Warren demanded.

Siva Singh looked distinctly uncomfortable. 'He was of medium height. Poorly dressed. He smelt dreadfully of alcohol.'

'Was he Hispanic?'

She hesitated. 'I cannot say with certainty.'

'Was he Asian?'

'Most definitely not.'

'Was he black?'

'No.' She looked down into Warren's hot eyes. 'He had the proper ticket,' she bravely explained. 'He paid.'

Warren wanted to hug her and kiss her. He wanted to dance round the courtroom and click his heels in the air. But he calmed himself.

He said, 'Thank you, Mrs Singh. I have no further questions right now—' He turned swiftly to look up at Judge Parker. 'But I ask that this witness remain on call today in the courthouse. And I would like a conference, your honour, in chambers.'

8

Light-headed, his mind spinning through the possibilities, Warren paced the floor of Judge Parker's chambers. Then he halted and said emphatically, 'I want to question Dan Ho Trunh's widow out of the hearing of the jury. I intend to ask her just one thing. Did she or any member of her family ever have the dry-cleaning ticket in their possession? If the answer is no, and I believe it will be no, then this is not a capital murder case. Some unknown white man stole Dan Ho Trunh's wallet, probably from his dead body, and three days later picked up the clothing. And he probably saw the murder take place.'

'What makes you think *that*?' Goodpaster asked.

'Because Siva Singh heard the gunshot. A minute or two later she went to the front of the store, and there was the man leaning into or out of the car window. The woman's a lousy eyewitness, but she ain't completely blind. So whatever this guy was or wasn't doing, he was *there* when Trunh was shot.'

Guardedly, the prosecutor said, 'Why couldn't Quintana have shot Trunh and thrown the wallet away after he took the money out of it? Somebody else could have taken the ticket.'

'There are a lot of possibilities,' Warren said. He turned to the judge, who sat behind her desk, chain-smoking. 'However it turns out, I've got to find this man. I'll need a continuance. At least a week.' He flexed the muscles in his back. 'I start trial this Monday in the Ott case. I'll need whatever time it takes to finish up in the 342nd.'

The judge tapped her calendar book. 'You expect me to tell this jury to go home and spin their wheels for two weeks?'

'If that's what it takes,' Warren said, 'yes, I do.'

'You've got a heck of a nerve. I'm going to think on this,' the judge said calmly. 'Meanwhile, ask the Trunh woman your question. Maybe the answer will put an end to this ruckus.'

Back in the courtroom, Mai Thi Trunh settled once more in the witness chair. Warren reminded her that she was still under oath even though the jury was not present.

No, she said quietly, she had never seen the dry-cleaning ticket. Normally her husband carried such things in his wallet.

'Permission to approach the bench!' Warren headed there with Nancy Goodpaster close behind.

'Let's keep this off the record,' Judge Parker said, waving away the court reporter who normally hovered near the bench.

Warren declared, 'Your honour, based on the existence of a vital witness I request a continuance until I finish *Boudreau*.'

'No, I can't allow that,' Judge Parker said. 'If you want to halt this trial to produce a new witness, you've first got to show me that his testimony is relevant and necessary. You don't know what this man will say, or if he even exists. You don't know his name or where he lives. He could have left town.'

With cold fury Warren said, 'I know he's white and resembles Quintana. He's probably a bum, so he won't leave town. I know he's got the victim's clothes and might be wearing them. I know a man's life depends on finding him. And I *will* find him.'

'Maybe you will, maybe you won't. I have to balance your chances against the problem of letting this jury stew for ten days and forgetting every word they've heard. I might have to pick a whole new jury. Aside from that, my agenda is full.'

Trying to bridle his rage, Warren gripped the edge of the bench. 'The jury won't forget. As for your agenda, your honour, that's your problem. You'll have to rearrange things.'

'No chance of that,' Parker said. 'I've ruled, and that's final. Let's get on with this trial.'

Warren said sharply, 'I want the rest of this on the record.' He beckoned to the court reporter, who obediently moved forward. 'Your honour, I'm formally asking you to step down. I want a new trial with a new judge.'

The judge bared her teeth. 'On what grounds?'

'On the grounds of prejudice from the bench.'

'Because I overruled most of your fool objections? Because I won't let you hunt for a phantom witness? You're out of line!'

They were no longer whispering. The entire courtroom could hear.

'Because of all that,' Warren lashed back, 'and a lot more. Because the first time we met to talk about my taking this case, you told me not to waste your court time. Hurry it up and plead it out, it's a whale in a barrel for the state—your exact words. And you repeated that in front of me and the prosecutor three weeks later. You thought we had our signals straight. Forty years' pen time was a good deal for a man who claimed he was innocent! You threatened that if I went to trial with *Quintana*, I'd never get an appointment in your court again. *You* were out of line then! That's a clear violation of judicial canons. That's what you get away with day in and day out but not with me. I refuse to go on in this courtroom. I'm walking out.'

Quietly and coldly, Judge Parker said, 'I can hold you in contempt now. Your reputation stinks.'

'Try it. I have a witness right here.' He flicked a finger at Nancy Goodpaster. 'She remembers.'

Confidently, Judge Parker turned to her chief prosecutor. 'You don't remember any of that, do you, Nancy?'

Goodpaster took an unsteady breath and said, 'Yes, I do.'

The judge's face turned a mottled pink. 'I said what he says I did? You claim you heard that?'

'Yes,' Goodpaster said, 'you said it all, your honour.'

The judge spun on the court reporter. 'Get out of here! This is off the record. *All* of it was off the record.'

The court reporter retreated in haste.

Warren said quietly, 'If you won't disqualify yourself, I'll file a motion in another court seeking your disqualification. Right now, this afternoon. I've never been disrespectful to a judge, but there's a first time for everything. I'll nail you to the wall.'

Judge Parker's eyes were the colour of burning charcoal. She drummed her fingers on the court calendar. A minute passed.

Judge Parker said, 'Look for your witness. The law requires you to exercise due diligence. If you can't find him before your other trial's finished, that's it. We resume. Same jury.'

'Thank you, your honour,' Warren said cordially.

THAT EVENING, after he had changed into jeans, he saw in the bathroom mirror the bleary, red-eyed look of a lawyer on trial. I need time out, he decided. There were five full days before jury selection began in the Boudreau case. He punched out Maria Hahn's number. Ten minutes later, with Oobie curled in the back seat gnawing on a tennis ball, he drove out to Maria's condo near River Oaks.

Maria cooked lasagne. She wore old jeans and a blue cotton cowboy shirt. 'How did it go today?' she asked while they ate.

'Good.' He gave her a synopsis.

'So now you have to find this guy. You have a plan?'

She loved plans. 'I'll come up with one,' he promised.

'You need help? Like a wheel man?'

'The last time you were my wheel man it didn't work out so well. Next time I might get killed.'

'Well, now we're experienced. We learn from mistakes. That's what it's all about, isn't it? Randy's away and it's a dead week for me.'

Warren looked at her and she smiled. I could get used to this, he thought.

ON MONDAY, JULY 24, five days after Judge Parker had granted a continuance of trial in the Quintana case, the two lawyers defending Johnnie Faye Boudreau met for breakfast in Rick Levine's suite of offices in the Old Cotton Exchange Building. An hour later, through the blue-grey shade of oak trees, they walked to the criminal courthouse only a few blocks away.

'Now that I see you in daylight,' Rick said, turning, 'I have to tell you that you look like a nag that just finished last in a six-furlong race. What the heck have you been doing?'

He had been hunting for a man who wasn't there.

For five days and nights, with and without Maria, he had prowled the streets of downtown Houston, talking to every bum and homeless man he met. He had gone to all the missions and soup kitchens, the parks, the crummy bars in Montrose and the Heights, the Greyhound and Amtrak stations. He had cruised past the Wesleyan Terrace Shopping Center three times a day. He had tried the city's hospitals and the jail. Without luck.

'OK,' Rick said, 'I understand. And now, concentrate on our worried client.'

'Why is she worried? We've got a great case.'

'Because you've been neglecting her. I told her you were thinking about her night and day.'

'I am,' Warren said.

IN THE CROWDED HALLWAY outside Judge Bingham's baronial wood-panelled courtroom, reporters thrust microphones at the arriving counsel. Johnnie Faye Boudreau, outfitted in the grey shantung suit that she had bought at Neiman-Marcus on the day she had murdered Dan Ho Trunh, assumed a modest position between and just behind her lawyers. 'Mr Levine and I expect a verdict of not guilty for the murder of Dr Ott,' Warren said into the microphones.

'Will Ms Boudreau testify on her own behalf?'

'When the time comes, Mr Levine and I will confer with our client and make the proper decision. Now, if you'll excuse us.'

On the way into the courtroom, Johnnie Faye tugged at Warren's arm. 'Am I going to testify or not?'

'If it's necessary.'

'So why have you been working my butt off and telling me what to say when I get up there?'

'Wait.' Warren stopped to face her, and made sure Rick heard his words. 'I never told you what to say, only how to say it. I told you, if you testify, to tell the truth. Remember that.'

Jury selection began. Johnnie Faye helped the defence team make their choice. Rick in each instance argued with her. Warren said, 'Let her have her way. She has good instincts.'

Maria Hahn recorded the proceedings. Whenever she caught Warren's eye, she smiled decorously.

The jury was chosen by two o'clock the next afternoon, and Judge Bingham then called chief counsel to the bench. 'We can begin now if you like,' the judge said. 'Get through the opening statements. Or do it tomorrow. You two gentlemen decide.'

Altschuler shrugged. 'The state is ready.'

'The defence is ready,' Warren said.

THAT EVENING WARREN and Maria drove in her car to Tranquility Park. Some homeless men were camped there, sleeping or cooking meagre meals under the magnolia trees. None of them wore any of Dan Ho Trunh's clothing. Warren talked to each man: none had been in the Wesleyan Terrace parking lot in late May when a shot was fired. Warren watched their eyes carefully and held a folded ten-dollar note between two fingers.

'Let's try Hermann Park,' he suggested.

In the car, Maria said, 'You made a good opening speech today. Short and sweet.'

'Our case will speak for itself.' Warren thought for a while. 'Whatever happened between you and Randy's father?'

Randy's father was a Dallas Homicide detective who had come to Houston to testify in some case. 'He was a hunk,' she said, 'and I ended up pregnant. I didn't want this guy as a husband—I didn't really love him. I believe in that stuff. But I decided to have the baby. I was thirty-one years old, the timing was right. So I had Randy. No regrets. I love that kid. Now you tell me what happened with you and your wife.'

As best he could, Warren told her.

Maria said, 'I don't get it. You're a wonderful man.'

'Thank you. Most of the time I don't get it either. Maybe I wasn't always so wonderful.'

He pulled the car into a parking space near the stables in Hermann Park, where he had found and lost Pedro.

'You see anyone?' Maria asked.

'No, but we'll poke around.'

The shed behind the stables was empty, but Warren, using his flashlight, noticed some empty beer bottles and a rolled-up bundle of dirty clothing. The door to the stables was locked. Following the beam of the light, he walked across the grass.

Maria touched his arm. 'Someone's there.'

Warren raised the beam until it outlined two men leaning in repose against the wooden fence surrounding the ring. They were smoking and talking softly. A voice said, *'Que pasó?'*

He shone the beam into one of the faces.

'Pedro?'

'Quien es?'

'Me. Hector's lawyer! I gave you forty bucks, remember?'

'Oh, yeah.'

'This is your friend Armando?' Warren asked.

'This is Armando. He don't speak English.'

'So what happened to you, Pedro? I came back to look for you and you were gone.'

'Lost my job, man. Had to go to the mission.'

'Let's get out of here,' Warren said. 'I'll buy you a beer.'

He drove them all to a nearby bar and bought a pitcher of beer on tap. 'Listen, Pedro, and you too, Armando. Hector needs you. His trial's still on. Next week, I get a chance to try and save his life. I need you to get up there and swear that Hector didn't own a pistol. Will you do it? Yes or no.'

'We get in trouble,' Pedro said.

'You mean because you have no papers? I told you before, I'll protect you. You swear that Hector had no pistol, then you go.' For a while the two men talked rapidly in Spanish, arguing.

'OK,' Pedro said. He nodded at Armando: 'But he doan speak English so good as me.'

'If he testifies, the court will provide an interpreter. Where are you guys sleeping these days?'

Pedro shrugged. 'Where we can.'

'You can stay at my place. A nice apartment. Food, beer, all on me. All you have to do is take care of my dog. Free.'

'You got a TV?'

'With cable. Two Spanish-speaking channels.'

'And we doan get arrested? Doan get kick out?'

'You have my word. *Mi palabra de honor.*'

Armando spoke again. Pedro said, 'He wants to know if your dog bites.'

'Not unless I tell her to,' Warren said.

Back at his apartment in Ravendale, Warren said, 'Don't use the telephone to call Mexico, I can't afford that.' He figured they might do it anyway, but this way they would keep the calls to under ten minutes.

Maria said, 'Why don't you ask them if they've seen the guy you're looking for?'

Warren gave a description of the man.

'Lotta guys look like that,' Pedro said.

Warren described the clothes that had been taken from the dry-cleaners. Pedro turned to Armando and chattered in his musical Spanish. Armando chattered back. Pedro said, 'We know him. We seen him at the mission. Green sweater, grey suit. He's a wino. Name is Jim something. Everyone laugh when he tell his whole name, but I doan get it. Few nights ago he get drunk and somebody steal all his new clothes.'

Warren said excitedly, 'Is he at the mission now?'

'No, he come and go. I see him maybe two nights ago.'

'Listen,' Warren said, 'I've got a job for you guys. You find this Jim by the weekend I'll give you a hundred bucks each. Find him in the next few days, I'll give you more.'

Pedro spoke to Armando. 'OK,' he said. 'Cash?'

They shook hands.

In the car on the way back to her house, Maria hugged his arm. 'See? Sometimes good things happen.'

He laughed happily. The next day he started the second trial.

THE PROSECUTION BEGAN its case in the usual manner, with the Harris County chief medical examiner establishing the cause of death: one .22-calibre bullet entering and exiting the brain; a second bullet lodging in the right lung. Death was instantaneous. The shots appeared to have been fired from a position directly in front of the victim.

Altschuler then asked whether Dr Ott had been moving or standing when the bullets had struck him.

'In my considered opinion, when he was killed, Dr Ott was standing still.'

'Pass the witness.'

Warren remembered all too well: *'He was running at you when you shot him?' 'Yes.' 'He never hesitated? Never stopped?' 'No.'* That was Johnnie Faye's story. If Clyde was standing still, it meant there was considerably less reason to shoot him. And it also meant she had lied to her lawyers.

Warren took the medical examiner on cross, but the doctor, who was also an attorney, refused to budge.

'Sir, your opinion that Dr Ott was standing still when the bullets struck him—that's not necessarily a fact, is it?'

'In this instance, yes, it is. There's no doubt in my mind.'

The more Warren nagged at him, the firmer the medical examiner became. 'No more questions,' he finally said, sitting down. Johnnie Faye threw him a dark, questioning look.

Photographs of the body were introduced into evidence, and then Tommy Ruiz, the Homicide sergeant, told of his arrival at River Oaks. He had found the defendant waiting at the front door. She had flipped a cigarette onto the lawn before stepping out to meet him. Ruiz quoted Johnnie Faye as saying: 'When we got downstairs I tried to get out of the house, but Clyde blocked the way. . . I picked up a poker to defend myself and he grabbed it away from me. . . I didn't mean to kill him, but he was coming at me like an old grizzly bear, waving that poker over his head.' A poker had indeed been discovered about eighteen inches in front of a white leather sofa in the living room, Ruiz testified. Dr Ott's body was half on the sofa, half on the floor.

Using a large three-coloured architectural chart, Ruiz described the Ott house in detail. Altschuler made him dwell on the huge dimensions of the living room and of the archway leading from the living room to the vestibule and the front door.

Altschuler said, 'Would it be difficult, Sergeant Ruiz, if a person was standing in either the archway or the vestibule, for another person to run past him—that is, to run *around* him?'

Rick Levine objected. 'Calls for speculation.'

'Sustained,' Judge Bingham said. 'Rephrase, Mr Altschuler.'

Altschuler asked, 'Approximately how many people, standing side by side, could fit across that archway, Sergeant Ruiz?'

'Ten or twelve,' Ruiz replied. 'The vestibule was over three hundred square feet. Basically, it was a large, empty space.'

'The white leather sofa in the living room—about how far was that from the bottom of the marble staircase?'

Ruiz looked carefully at the chart. 'About sixty-five feet.'

Altschuler continued. 'Sergeant Ruiz, you stated that soon after Ms Boudreau met you at the front door of Dr Ott's house, tears appeared in her eyes and she seemed very upset. Did she slur her words or make any movements that would lead you to believe she was at all drunk?'

'No,' Ruiz said, 'she seemed sober and in control.'

IN THE STREET, with Johnnie Faye a few steps ahead of them, Rick looked thoughtfully into Warren's calm eyes. 'This is going to be a little tougher than we thought it would be.'

'Altschuler prepares,' Warren observed.

At lunch, Johnnie Faye's eyes were cloudy. 'I don't get it. What was that last part all about? What's the big deal about drunk or sober?'

Bob Altschuler, Warren explained, was mounting a double-barrelled attack both on her credibility and her duty to retreat. In a few days, Johnnie Faye would take the witness stand. 'And on cross-examination, Altschuler will try to prove that you could have got out of the house, meaning there was no reason for you to shoot him. If you were still a little drunk, as you claim you were, you might not have been able to get out so easily, and it helps to explain why you couldn't control the trigger. But Ruiz says you weren't drunk.'

'So what should I say about it?' Johnnie Faye looked worried. 'Was I drunk or not? And what about that coroner? What about that standing-still garbage?'

The lawyers were silent. Rick coughed. The medical examiner's testimony had devastated her current version of self-defence.

'I told you we had a good case if you were telling the truth,' Warren said coolly. 'So that's what you'd better do.'

After lunch the state called Sergeant Jay Kulik, the HPD fingerprint expert. After he had lectured at some length on fingerprint analysis, it was established that both Clyde Ott's and Johnnie Faye Boudreau's prints were found on the thirty-two-inch-long, three-pound poker. Altschuler asked Kulik to describe in lay terms the exact placement of those prints.

'Her prints were all over it,' Kulik said. 'At the bottom, at the top, and in the middle. Both palm and fingertips.'

'And Dr Ott's prints?'

'One set only, at the bottom—the handle part. No palm prints. Just fingertips of both hands.'

Altschuler produced the poker with its police ID tags, and had it entered into evidence.

'Please stand up, Sergeant. Pick up this poker so your palms don't touch it. In other words, just with your fingers.'

Kulik did so. Obviously, an awkward grip.

Altschuler took a step backwards. 'Sergeant, see if you can raise the poker over your head, holding it only with your fingertips. Can you do that?'

'I can, but I wouldn't. It's not natural.'

Altschuler turned to him again. 'Now, Sergeant, grip the poker in a natural way and raise it over your head. You can swing it a little if you like.'

Kulik drew it back and took a short swing.

'If that poker were taken from you now, Sergeant, and your office examined it, what would you find?'

'My fingerprints and palm prints.'

'And there were none of Dr Ott's palm prints on that poker, were there, when you examined it in your lab?'

'No, sir. None. Just prints of his fingertips.'

'Does that lead you to believe, Sergeant Kulik, that Dr Ott *ever* held that poker up above the level of his shoulders?'

'No, sir, it doesn't.'

Altschuler looked at the jurors to assess whether or not they had understood. Satisfied, he said, 'Pass the witness.'

Warren asked for a ten-minute recess. Ignoring Johnnie Faye, he drew Rick into the hallway. He was pale. 'The poker story is a fairy tale. She put Clyde's prints on it after she shot him.'

'You think the jury figured that out?' Rick asked.

'Altschuler will make it clear enough in final argument.' Warren shook his head gloomily. 'What else are we going to find out that we don't know?'

The next witness was Lorna Gerard, Sharon Underhill's much-divorced daughter. She had been asleep in the house on the night of the murder. Had seen nothing, heard nothing. She had taken some sleeping pills, and the house was so huge.

Altschuler asked the witness if she had known the defendant, Johnnie Faye Boudreau.

'Yes, in connection with my stepfather. She was his mistress. I was with them on several occasions, sorry to say.'

'Tell us about those occasions, if you will, Mrs Gerard.'

Lorna Gerard said that a month after Sharon's death, Clyde had brought Ms Boudreau to Dallas, where they'd all had dinner at a French restaurant in the Anatole Hotel. The woman had said, 'Clyde and I are going to get married.' Clyde had said, 'Maybe.' The woman walked out in a rage. Clyde then said to his stepdaughter, 'I'm getting rid of her, I promise you.'

On another occasion, without Ms Boudreau present, he said, 'I'm frightened of her.' Lorna Gerard had asked why, but Clyde had declined to explain.

Judge Bingham overruled Warren's objection.

A week before Clyde's death, Lorna Gerard continued, she came down to visit old friends in Houston and stayed at the house in River Oaks. 'One afternoon while I was trying to watch TV, Johnnie Faye said to me, "I love your stepdaddy to death, but he can be crazy. When he gets mean and drunk and passes out, I could cut his throat in his sleep." Those very words. There may have been more, but I put my hands over my ears.'

Despite himself, Warren glanced quickly at Rick, who was blinking. Johnnie Faye had never told them of this incident or of the argument in the Dallas restaurant.

Altschuler asked, 'Did you ever see your late stepfather strike Ms Boudreau, or hear him threaten her in any way?'

'No, he just wanted to get rid of her. But she had a hold on him of some kind.'

'Your mother died in nineteen eighty-seven, didn't she, Mrs Gerard?'

'Yes. She was murdered.'

'Did Dr Ott ever tell you who he thought had done it?'

'Objection,' Warren snapped.

'Sustained. Don't answer, madam.'

'Pass the witness,' Altschuler said.

Warren took her on cross-examination. 'Did you know Ms Boudreau as well as your stepfather?' he asked.

'Of course not.'

'You knew her hardly at all—isn't that what you're saying?'

'I suppose so.'

'And it's a fact, isn't it, that you didn't know her well enough to know when she was exaggerating?'

'Well, if you're referring to what she said about Clyde that night in front of the TV—'

Warren said, 'Mrs Gerard, you must have heard people say things like that many times. Do you always take them seriously?'

'I took *her* seriously. You should have seen the look in her eyes.'

'When Ms Boudreau made the remark about cutting Dr Ott's throat in his sleep, where was she standing?'

'Behind me. Near me. I don't remember exactly.'

'You were seated and she was standing, isn't that correct?'

'Yes, that's how it was.'

'Isn't it a fact that if you were watching a movie and Ms Boudreau was standing behind you, you couldn't possibly see what you describe as "the look in her eyes"?'

'Well, I *saw* it. Don't ask me how. I *did*.'

'And then, after the alleged remark, you say you covered up your ears so that you wouldn't hear any more?'

'Yes, I did.'

'So that if Ms Boudreau said anything else, such as "I was just joking" or "didn't mean it", you wouldn't have heard her.'

'She didn't say anything like that.'

Warren smiled. 'No further questions.'

'Nice work,' Rick said when Warren returned to the defence table, just as the judge called a break.

Johnnie Faye pulled her lawyers to a secluded spot down the corridor. Crimson spots burned on her cheeks. 'I don't like the way this is going.'

'You should have told us about that stuff,' Warren said.

'Well, it's all a lie!'

'You didn't have that discussion in Dallas?'

'No way. Listen, that Lorna is a paranoid schizophrenic. She hates my guts! She's making the whole thing up!'

Neither Warren nor Rick said anything. Johnnie Faye fled to the bathroom down the hall.

'Our client's in deep trouble,' Rick said. 'What made us think this was an easy case?'

'Truth,' said Warren, 'is not her strong suit.'

After the coffee break, Kenneth Underhill testified. He was Sharon's dissolute son, a man in his late thirties. He had a drug habit and was undergoing treatment. He stated that twice he had witnessed angry arguments between Clyde Ott and Ms Boudreau. One had been at dinner in The Anatole and he recounted it much as Lorna Gerard had done. The other had been at River Oaks and Ms Boudreau had definitely been abusive.

When Altschuler passed the witness, Warren said, 'No questions.'

Johnnie Faye kicked him under the table, and Warren gasped in pain. She hissed, 'He's lying! What's *with* you?'

Clenching his teeth, bending to rub his sore ankle with one hand, Warren smiled for the jury to see. 'Shut the heck up. And if you kick me again, I'm walking out of the courtroom.'

With the afternoon waning, Dr Gordon Butterfield took the stand for the prosecution. Altschuler's aim was to defuse the issue of Clyde's threat made at the Houston Racquet Club.

'. . . so, after the drink had been thrown by Ms Boudreau, when Dr Ott said, "You slut, I could happily kill you for that," your impression was that he didn't mean it literally?'

'Absolutely not. Clyde calmed down right away.'

'Dr Butterfield, how would you characterise Dr Ott?'

'A hard-working, hard-living, gregarious man. Quick-tempered, but also very forgiving.'

Altschuler passed the witness.

'Dr Butterfield,' Warren said casually. 'Hard-living, among other things, means hard-drinking?'

'Yes, to an extent.'

'Sexually promiscuous?'

'It might mean that.'

'Quick-tempered means he lost his temper easily?'

'Yes, but—'

Warren cut him off: 'You've answered. And losing one's temper means unreasonable anger and shouting, doesn't it?'

'I suppose so.'

'Did Dr Ott habitually use cocaine, to your knowledge?'

Butterfield glared and his cheeks flushed a rosy red. 'He was a *doctor*.'

'Oh? You're telling us, Dr Butterfield, that it's impossible for a doctor to ever use cocaine?'

'It's *very* rare.'

'No more questions.'

Judge Bingham rapped his gavel and announced that the court would adjourn until nine o'clock the following morning. As they all rose and the jury left the courtroom, Johnnie Faye turned a glare of rage on her lawyers.

'What a bunch of garbage! You know that Clyde sniffed cocaine and you're just not smart enough to get that uptight doctor pal of his to admit it! You let Ken—a druggie!—say whatever he wanted to.' She sneered. ' "Pass the witness." I could have any lawyer in town in a big case like this and I wind up with a pair of cupcakes!'

'Try to calm down,' Rick said.

'Calm down? I'm calm! I'm just scared!'

'You don't have to be,' Warren said. 'We haven't told our side yet. We have you to testify. How can we lose?'

After Johnnie Faye and Rick had gone, Warren trudged through the tunnel to the jail to visit Hector Quintana. 'I don't want you to think I've forgotten you,' he said.

Hector, behind the steel mesh, looked listless and weary.

'Have you heard from your wife?' Warren asked.

Not lately. He hadn't written to tell Francisca that he was in trouble. He didn't want her to worry.

'I found your *amigos*, Pedro and Armando. They're going to testify for you. Say that you had no pistol.'

'I been thinking,' Hector said. 'Guys here say it's bad to have a trial. The jury kill you. They say Texas jails so crowded that in a few years they going to cut everyone's time down to *una tercera*.' A third. 'So maybe I should do what you say before. Go for forty years, to jail. Get out in *una tercera*.'

Warren knew that Hector had understood little of what had gone down in the courtroom with Siva Singh. He had been watching the jury. And listening to jailhouse lawyers.

'Hector, the choice is always yours. It's never too late until the jury leaves the courtroom to make up its mind.'

'I am frightened,' Hector said.

As well he should be, Warren thought. His heart felt weak. He summoned up courage and said, 'Don't worry. Have faith in me.'

He left the jail in a chastened mood. For Hector, he realised, I would do anything. But not for Johnnie Faye. She *was* guilty, Warren now believed. She should pay the price.

That night, in his apartment at Ravendale, Warren watched the news on Channel 26, catching the end of the trial report. The expression on his face, as he brushed past the reporters' microphones, was one of stolid acceptance. We look like we took it on the chin, he thought. And we did.

Voice-over, Charm said coolly: 'The prosecution, led by Assistant D. A. Robert Altschuler, will continue presenting its case tomorrow. Boudreau's chief counsel, Warren Blackburn, has refused to comment on whether or not his client will testify.'

At eleven o'clock Pedro and Armando thrust open the door. They had hung around the mission since late afternoon, Pedro reported. The man they knew as Jim hadn't showed up.

Warren said, 'Tomorrow, do me a favour and go to the mission in the morning. Stay there until midnight. *Find* this guy. Call me in the late afternoon and leave a message on my machine—I want to know if anything's happening.'

He left for Maria Hahn's condo.

9

'The State of Texas calls José Hurtado.'

Warren consulted his copy of the witness list where three Hispanic names appeared next to the mailing address of the Hacienda Restaurant. Hurtado was the *maître d'*.

Hurtado set the scene for the jury: a candlelight dinner, *mariachi* music, an arguing couple, and many margaritas. Four margaritas before dinner, at the bar. Six more during dinner. He produced the bill and Altschuler had it entered into evidence.

'Strong drinks, would you say?' the prosecutor asked.

'A margarita is strong. It is not meant for a child.'

'Pass the witness.'

'No questions,' Warren said.

Luis Sanchez took the oath and settled into the wooden chair. He was a thin, grave, pockmarked man of forty.

Sanchez was the barman. He remembered Dr Ott, who seemed already drunk when he walked into the restaurant and consumed three of the four margaritas the barman had served. The doctor and the lady with him had argued. She had cursed at him. 'She kept saying, "You lied to me." She was very angry.'

'Lied about what? Did she say?'

'I didn't hear.'

'And were you abusive to him?' Warren had asked Johnnie Faye. *'No,'* she had said, *'I just shut up and listened.'*

His turn came. 'Mr Sanchez,' Warren asked. 'How many people were at the bar that evening?'

'Ten, twelve. I cannot remember exactly.'

'You mixed and served drinks for all those people?'

'Of course.'

'So you weren't watching Dr Ott and Ms Boudreau all the time, were you?'

'No.'

'And you didn't hear every single word of the argument between Dr Ott and Ms Boudreau, did you?'

'I cannot say. The bar is noisy.'

'If Dr Ott had cursed at Ms Boudreau, or insulted her before she cursed at him, you might not have heard it—isn't that a fact?'

'That is possible,' Sanchez said.

'How many people does it take to argue?'

'Two,' Sanchez said.

'No further questions.'

Daniel Villareal, the table waiter, took the stand. He had served six margaritas at the table, he told Altschuler: three to the gentleman and three to the lady. The lady only drank one of them. She pushed the others across the table to the gentleman.

'What else did the lady drink during all that time?'

'A lot of water. I had to fill her glass twice.'

Warren looked at the jury. The women jurors all had a certain prim look. They would assume that seven or eight margaritas would put a man under the table. Certainly render him incapable of halting the exit through an eighteen-foot-wide vestibule of a woman ten years younger, and in control of her faculties.

Johnnie Faye's face was as wooden as the defence table. Rick whispered in Warren's ear, 'We're getting killed. Don't cross-examine on this guy either. It'll only get worse.'

Altschuler called the last witness for the state: Harry T. Morse. A middle-aged man with thinning hair and a beaked nose, Morse was the assistant manager of Western America, a pistol and rifle practice range seven miles north of the city.

'Do you see anyone in this courtroom who ever came to Western America, Mr Morse?'

'Yes, over there.' He pointed to Johnnie Faye Boudreau.

'Why are you so sure it's she whom you saw at Western America?' Altschuler said, smiling.

'Object as to relevance,' Warren said desperately. He remembered asking Johnnie Faye if she had ever practised with the pistol. *'Once, years ago, when I bought it. I don't even think I hit the target more than two or three times.'*

'Overruled. You can answer, sir.'

'Good-looking lady,' Morse said. 'Kind of memorable.'

Morse said that he had seen her practise at least twice.

'Did you observe what kind of pistol she used?'

'She had three. A ·32-calibre Diamondback Colt, an ivory-handled Colt ·45, and what looked like a ·22-calibre semiautomatic.'

Warren's heart beat a little faster in his breast. He leaned forward intently, resisting the urge to look at Johnnie Faye.

'Three?' Altschuler's mouth gaped in feigned surprise.

'Yes, sir.'

'How are you able to identify those three guns so positively, Mr Morse?'

'She laid them down on the counter when she registered to shoot. I noticed them. We don't get that many ladies, and I never saw one bring three pistols before.'

'When did all this take place?'

'The first time, maybe a year or so ago. The last time, not so long ago. Late April. Maybe early May.'

Johnnie Faye pushed a note at Warren. *Do something!!*

Without taking his eyes from the jury, he wrote under her words: *Nothing to do—yet.*

Altschuler said, 'Mr Morse, do you have your registration sheets for the last eighteen months with you today in court? I'm referring to the names and addresses the people give to you when they come to practise at Western America.'

Morse offered a thick bundle of papers wrapped in rubber bands, and they were entered into evidence for the state.

'Does the name Johnnie Faye Boudreau appear on those sheets?'

'No, sir. And we looked hard for it.'

'Can you account for that, Mr Morse?'

'Well, I saw her sign in. So she must have used a fake name.'

Warren objected as to relevance; he was overruled.

'Just a few more questions, Mr Morse. Did you ever watch the lady sitting over there shoot with her three pistols?'

'Both times. All three weapons.'

'And what did you observe?'

'She hit that bull's-eye a lot.'

'You saw her fire the semiautomatic ·22?'

'Yeah, but it wasn't semiautomatic. Probably had the sear filed down. You pull the trigger and let it go, it goes right on shooting.'

'Was she comfortable with that ·22? Did it look like she was aware of its automatic capability?'

'She was aware. She looked comfortable, like she knew what she was doing. Bang, bang, bang. Like it was fun.'

'Pass the witness,' Altschuler said, glaring at Johnnie Faye.

Hopeless, Warren thought. He had a client who never told him the truth. But he strode forward with confidence, halting a fair distance before Harry T. Morse.

'Sir. You just said that Ms Boudreau fired the pistol like it was fun. You did say that, didn't you?'

'I said it,' Morse replied, glowering a little.

'Do you equate fun with serious intent?'

'Not usually.'

'You do have people who come to Western America just for fun, don't you?'

'Sure.'

'You wouldn't characterise your customers as potential murderers, would you, Mr Morse?'

'Of course not,' Morse said.

'Thank you. No more questions.'

Altschuler stood and said gravely, yet with an air of triumph: 'The state rests its case.'

AT FIVE O'CLOCK Warren and Rick ducked into a small Greek restaurant near the courthouse, where Warren ordered a Greek salad and an espresso. Rick drank a double Scotch on the rocks.

'Look, here's the problem,' Rick said. 'Our case hinges on whether or not the jury will believe the dragon lady when she gets up there to testify. She says Clyde threatened her life, and now it turns out she threatened *his* life. She says she was drunk and had no way to get out of the house—the restaurant people say she was sober, and Tommy Ruiz swears you could have driven a giant truck through that hallway. She says Clyde was coming at her with the poker—the medical examiner claims he was shot standing still. Worse, Kulik says there should be palm prints. And we still haven't got to that funny little business of the poker winding up on the wrong side of the sofa. What I'm saying is, if we want to win this case, you have to talk to her. Maybe say: "I'm instructing you to tell the truth. But you testify however you think you should." '

Warren nodded, trying in his mind to separate the concepts of what was ethical, what was practical, and what a man needed to do in order to preserve sanity and self-respect. He put down his espresso and said nothing.

'Good Lord!' Rick, in alarm, watched Warren's face reflect his thoughts. 'You're not going to sell her down the river, are you?'

'No. I want to win.'

'You want me to handle it?'

Warren shook his head emphatically. 'I'll talk to her.'

LATER, FROM MARIA'S BEDROOM, he called his apartment for messages. Pedro picked up the telephone.

'What are you doing there?' Warren said angrily. 'It's not even ten o'clock!'

'Take it easy, *patrón*.'

The mission had been closed since early morning, Pedro explained. Full of *policía*. Late last night some bum was shot to death in the toilet. Blown away, man. Two other men sitting on the open stalls saw it happen, had even seen the man who killed him. But they didn't know him, had never seen him before.

Warren drew in a deep breath. He asked, 'The man who was shot and killed—it wasn't Jim, was it?'

'No,' Pedro said. No one had seen Jim for days. Might have left town. He did that sometimes, one guy said. Went south, had a common-law wife down there. No one knew which town.

'Did this guy know Jim's last name?' Warren asked.

'Jus' his nickname. They all call him Jim Dandy.'

They promised to go back tomorrow, if the cops were gone. 'And your wife call you here,' Pedro said. 'Say for you to call her.'

Warren hung up. Another murder. He walked into the living room, where Maria was watching television. He wondered what Charm had wanted, then realised he didn't care.

ON THURSDAY MORNING the city sweltered under ninety-degree wet air that pressed like a clammy hand against Warren's forehead. Rick waited for him outside the 342nd.

'Did you talk to her?'

'Not yet,' Warren said impatiently. 'But I will.'

The first witness Warren called for the defence was Dr George Swayze, who had treated Johnnie Faye last December at Hermann Hospital. In a clear voice Swayze read a copy of his diagnosis and treatment for the broken cheekbone, and then, under questioning, said, 'She told me that her boyfriend had done it to her.'

'Did she describe the boyfriend?' Warren asked.

'She said he was a big man. And he'd been drinking.'

On cross-examination, Altschuler asked the doctor, 'Did she say *which* of her several boyfriends had hit her?'

Warren objected to *several boyfriends*.

'Please rephrase, Mr Altschuler,' the judge said.

When Altschuler did, the doctor answered, 'No, she never named the man.'

The next witness was Cathy Lewis, former waitress at the Grand Hotel. Rick had finally tracked her down through the Department of Motor Vehicles. Cathy Lewis told the tale of her affair with Clyde, and his swatting her in the mouth 'with his big hairy paw', so loosening three front teeth that she had to have them replaced.

Cathy Lewis said that Clyde had paid the dentist's bill, and had also given her $25,000 in cash.

'For what?' Rick asked.

'Kiss-off money, and so I'd shut up.'

Bob Altschuler asked, 'Do you have a receipt for that twenty-five thousand dollars in cash that Dr Ott supposedly gave you, Ms Lewis?'

'No, sir.'

'So we have to take your word for it, right?'

'Yes, sir.'

'You've been a cocktail waitress for most of your adult life, isn't that right?'

'Yes, sir.'

'Ever do it topless?'

'For a while.'

'Ever go to bed with men for money?'

'Not really,' she said, before Rick had a chance to spring up and shout an objection.

Altschuler passed the witness.

The last two witnesses of the day were former patients of Dr Clyde Ott. Patricia Gurian—a shapely blonde woman of forty, married—took the stand. Normally, she said, she would see a gynaecologist twice a year for checkups. On her second visit to Dr Ott, the nurse left the room to take a telephone call. Dr Ott began to fondle her.

'Objection!' Altschuler yelled. 'It's not only irrelevant, it's prurient!'

Warren said, 'Your honour, it's a line of questioning leading to show the character of Dr Ott relative to the defendant.'

The judge sighed. 'All right, but get to it quickly.'

Warren stood next to one of the prim woman jurors in the first row. 'What did you do when that happened, Mrs Gurian?'

'I decided to leave.'

'Did Dr Ott try to stop you?'

'Yes, he did. He blocked my path.'

'Were you frightened?'

'Not really, I knew I could call for the nurse.'

'Did he threaten you physically?'

'No.'

'Pass the witness,' Warren said.

'Sidebar!' Altschuler cried, and drew Warren with him to the bench for a private conference. 'That was crazy,' he gasped. 'The woman didn't claim violence! So where's the relevance? Judge, you can't let him put the second patient on the stand!'

Judge Bingham turned to Warren. 'Will this be relevant?'

'I'm not clairvoyant, but I can promise relevance.'

The judge said, 'All right, put her on.'

Judith Tarr—red-headed and in her mid-thirties, took the oath. She had been a patient of Dr Ott's. They had had an affair.

'I was lonely at the time,' Ms Tarr said and shrugged.

Altschuler objected again and was overruled.

Warren glanced at the jury.

'Was Dr Ott married at the time?' he asked.

'Yes, it was about half a year before his wife was killed.'

'Was he ever violent with you?'

'He was a rough man. He drank a lot and took cocaine in my presence. But no, he never hit me.'

'Pass the witness,' Warren said.

He went back to the defence table. Johnnie Faye squeezed his hand. 'Counsellor,' she said, 'I've got faith again.'

Finished for the day, he sat with Johnnie Faye in her rented Chevrolet. Where the Mercedes was, Warren had no idea. Repainted and sold, he guessed. He made no comment.

'Tomorrow morning I put you on the witness stand,' he said. 'Dress conservatively, and go easy on the eye make-up. If I ask you what someone said, give it word for word, as best you can. And give details. If you mention a TV set, don't just say, "A TV set." Say, "A forty-inch Mitsubishi TV," or whatever it is. That way the jury will learn to trust your memory. You understand?'

'I'm with you, counsellor.'

'When it comes time for cross-examination, don't get trapped into arguing with Altschuler. Be calm. Look him in the eye, and if it's an important answer, speak directly to the jury. If you don't know the answer to a question, say so. Most of Altschuler's questions will force you to say yes or no and you've got to do it. But if he asks something like "Do you still beat your dog?"—you've got a right to say, "I never beat my dog." If you're not sure whether the answer is yes or no, say something like, "I don't think I can give an honest yes or no answer to that, sir." If you think I should object and I don't, there's a good reason. Trust me. Is all that clear?'

'Like crystal.'

'Do you have any questions?'

'I got about a hundred,' Johnnie Faye said. 'What about this missing palm print—how do I account for that? What about those lies Lorna told about how I threatened Clyde? What do I say about whether or not Clyde was coming at me across that living room? What about after I came downstairs, my trying to get past him and out of the house, when I couldn't? And all that stuff about my being such a hotshot with that teeny ·22? What do I *say*?'

'I keep telling you,' Warren said. 'You just tell the truth . . .'

He omitted the second part of Rick's dictum to witnesses: 'but you testify however you think you should.' Warren made distinctions. He had to live with himself when this case was over and he returned to save Hector Quintana's life, if he could.

HE WENT BACK TO RAVENDALE at seven o'clock. Except for his dog lying on the sofa, the apartment was empty. The message light on his answering machine was blinking.

The first voice on the machine was Pedro's.

'Callin' in, like you say to do. We talk to a guy knows this Jim. He says he's gone home. Some place called Beaver. Call you later. *Viva Mexico, patrón.*'

The second message was from Charm. She said in a calm tone, 'Please call me at home or at the station, Warren. I need to talk to you.'

Warren dug his old road atlas out of a box and paged through to the list of Texas cities and towns. There was no place called Beaver. There were Beeville and Bellville. Bellville was far to the north near the Louisiana border. Beeville he knew: about two hundred miles southwest from Houston on Route 59.

He called Maria to tell her he would be at her apartment between eight and eight thirty. He would shop on the way. They would broil some swordfish steaks. He set the phone down, drumming his fingers lightly on the table top. The last time he had spoken to Charm had been weeks ago. Now she had called him twice.

Whatever it is, I don't need it. Let Franklin tell it to me.

10

'How old are you, Ms Boudreau?' Warren asked pleasantly.

'Forty. I'll be forty-one on the fourteenth of August.' She looked directly at a woman of approximately her own age sitting in the jury box, and smiled.

'And where were you born and brought up?'

'Odem, Texas, down near Corpus Christi. Just a little town. Cotton, peanuts, scrub-oak country. My daddy had a gas station. My mama helped him run it. Daddy was a part-time preacher too—taught me Scripture. Passed away about five years back.'

'You have brothers and sisters?'

'Two brothers, but they got killed in Vietnam. I guess they were what you'd call unsung heroes. One sister, and she still lives back in Odem near my mama. I visit every chance I get.'

'Tell us what happened to you after you left Odem.'

Johnnie Faye, wearing a simple dark blue dress, told the story of her life to the jury and the packed courtroom. An early mistake in marriage. Struggles to educate herself. She talked about coming to Houston, a frightened country girl. She had to support herself so she danced for a living. Sent money back to her mama who had a heart condition. Made another mistake in marriage. She shifted her gaze to the jury. 'My fault. Chose wrong. I haven't been lucky with men.'

No children. That was an ache inside her. Finally, a good break: a chance to run a nightclub. Which she still did.

'How did you meet Dr Clyde Ott?'

He had come to her club about four years ago. He had a girlfriend who danced there.

'At first you were just friends?'

'Oh, yes. I didn't want to rush into things.'

'But then you became intimate?'

'After a while. Yes, very intimate.'

'How did you feel about the fact that Dr Ott was married?'

'I felt bad, but he told me he was very unhappy with his wife. I fell in love with him. I couldn't help myself.'

'Love is a powerful emotion,' Warren said. 'Tell us, if you will, what your relationship with Dr Ott was like.'

Sharon had died so tragically. Johnnie Faye helped Clyde get through that. But he drank a lot, and sniffed cocaine, which she hated because drugs had killed one of her brothers.

Clyde wanted to marry her. But he had a violent side to him. Once, in front of mutual friends, he threatened to kill her. Several times when he was drunk, he hit her. And then last December he broke her cheekbone. That's when she realised the love affair was doomed.

'But you kept seeing him?'

'From time to time, if he promised to stay sober.'

'Did you still sleep with him?'

'Now and then. I was weak, and he was very dominating.'

'What were his relations like with his stepchildren?'

'He dominated them too. He said, "Lorna's a lush, and Ken's a middle-aged junkie." At a restaurant in Dallas we had this big argument. Clyde told them he wanted to marry me, and that got Lorna all worked up. So he backed off and said, "Well, maybe we won't get married." I got angry, and I cursed at him and walked out of the restaurant. That was dumb. I regretted it right away.'

So she had come to terms with that, Warren thought, and decided to admit it—with a twist. He hadn't had to tell her what to do. Delicately, Warren smiled. Time to test her.

'In Lorna Gerard's presence, Ms Boudreau, did you ever say anything like, "When Clyde gets mean and drunk and passes out, I'd like to cut his throat in his sleep"?'

Johnnie Faye blushed. 'I did say that,' she said calmly, 'One afternoon Lorna was watching TV downstairs in Clyde's house, sitting in front of that big forty-inch Mitsubishi TV set, drinking about her sixth Scotch on the rocks. I needed someone to talk to, because Clyde had walloped me again the night before, just before he passed out. Lorna was real involved in her TV programme and wouldn't listen to me. So I had to grab her attention somehow, and that's all I could think of saying. I tried right away to tell her I didn't mean it, but she put her hands over her ears. I was so ashamed afterwards I cried. I told Clyde about it that day when he was sober and he said, "Lorna hates you 'cause she's got this idea you're trying to convince me not to keep giving her money. Now you've given her another reason to hate you." '

Neat, Warren thought. Again a nice twist. She must have been up half the night working all this out.

Warren moved to May 14, to dinner at the Hacienda Restaurant. He asked if the dinner had any particular purpose.

Johnnie Faye said, 'From my point of view it was a goodbye dinner. I just couldn't take it any more.'

Warren remembered the transcript of Johnnie Faye's tapes with Scoot: *I wanted to marry him, but he kept stalling, and it upset me. . .*

Well, she lied then—or was lying now. Or lying both times. No matter what he believed, there was no basis in fact for him to conclude she was perjuring herself now.

'In the Hacienda, were you drunk?'

'A little bit.'

'Did you argue at the bar before you sat down to eat?'

'Yes, I was upset because Clyde told me he'd been snorting cocaine again. So I yelled, "You lied to me!" I cursed at him too.'

'Did you try to get Clyde drunk at the Hacienda?'

'He kept telling me to order new rounds of drinks. I said, "I don't want to drink any more." He said, "Just do what I say, woman." So I did—I didn't want to get him any angrier than he was. When the drinks came he'd finish his real quick, then he'd say, "If you're not drinking that, hand it over." '

'What happened after you left the restaurant?'

'I'd meant to take a taxi to his place, to pick up my car. But I figured if he drove he'd kill himself. So I drove him in his Porsche. And when we got to his house he said, Come on in, let's talk. '

'Did you talk?'

'Well, we went upstairs for a while. Then he disappeared into the bathroom. When he came out I could see he was crazy. What he did in there, I don't know, but his eyes were red and he was sweating. And he was yelling again. He slapped me in the face. I ran downstairs and he followed me to the living room.'

'What did he do in the living room?'

She described how Clyde had screamed and cursed at her, how she had picked up the poker to keep him at bay, how he had twisted it away from her and raised it above his head.

'Please wait a moment, Ms Boudreau,' Warren said, holding up his hand. 'Sergeant Ruiz has told this jury that when he arrived at River Oaks, you stated to him that you tried to get out of the house but Dr Ott blocked your path. Did that happen?'

'Oh, yes,' Johnnie Faye said, 'that happened *before*. I mean, when we first arrived. I wanted to leave then, and Clyde blocked the way. Of course I could have got round him—*then*. Sergeant Ruiz is absolutely right, it's a huge hallway. But Clyde wasn't going crazy *then*. He was begging me to stay. I felt sorry for him, so I gave in. That's when we went upstairs.'

Warren looked at her steadily. 'You're saying that Dr Ott didn't block your path *after* you both came downstairs, when you picked up the poker and he took it out of your hand?'

'That's right. Long before. I think I may have confused Sergeant Ruiz when I spoke to him later that night.'

'Then why, when you came downstairs *later,* knowing Dr Ott was already aggressive and, as you put it, "crazy"—why didn't you go straight out the door to the safety of your car?'

A spark of fury showed in Johnnie Faye's eyes. But it was gone instantly. Warren didn't think the jury had seen it.

'Because I'd left my handbag on the sofa in the living room,' she explained. 'My car was in the front driveway and the keys to my car—my Mercedes—were in my handbag. My brown handbag which I left on the white leather sofa before I went upstairs.'

Details, Warren had told her. The Mitsubishi. She was remembering, even if the details were part of a new fiction.

'I see.' He took a moment to readjust. 'Ms Boudreau,' he said, having no idea what she would answer, 'please tell us what happened after you came downstairs.'

Johnnie Faye obliged. She had come down the stairs and picked up her handbag from the sofa. Clyde yelled that he was going to beat the hell out of her. She picked up the poker to defend herself. He grabbed the poker from her and gave her a shove that sent her across the room, tumbling backwards onto the sofa. Then he said, 'Now I'll kill you. You've been asking for it.'

Warren asked, 'And then what did Dr Ott do?'

'He rushed across the room towards me, and I reached into my handbag and took out my little pistol. I never intended to use it. My heart was beating *so* fast. Then he stopped, kind of skidded to a halt on the carpet, and stood still. He was maybe six feet away from me. I said, "Don't come any closer, Clyde, or I'll shoot." But I was just bluffing then.'

'You were still sitting on the sofa?'

'Yes.'

'And he was standing still, not charging at you?'

'That's correct. But then I managed to stand up. And he lifted the poker to swing it at my head. So I pulled the trigger of my pistol. I didn't mean to kill him, just maybe scare him or put him out of action so I could get away safely. But the pistol kept firing. I didn't mean for that to happen. I couldn't control my finger. I guess I was panicked or something.'

Clyde fell forward onto the sofa. She ducked out of the way. The poker fell to the carpet.

'And how did you feel at that moment, Ms Boudreau?'

'Terrified. Horrified at what I'd done. Awful.' Johnnie Faye reached into her handbag for a tissue. She blew her nose.

After a pause, Warren continued. 'Ms Boudreau—' He leaned forward. 'After the shooting, did you call a doctor or an ambulance?'

'No, sir. There was so much blood that I suspected the worst. I felt Clyde's pulse. None at all. I realised he was dead. Then I did a stupid thing.' She hesitated, lowering her head.

Now Warren had no idea at all what was coming. But he asked, 'What did you do, Ms Boudreau?'

'I picked up the poker from the carpet where Clyde had dropped it. I don't know why I did that. I guess I was a little hysterical. I kept working the handle of the poker around in my hands. I almost put it back against the fireplace, but then I thought, no, that's even more stupid. So then I dropped the poker back on the carpet just about where Clyde had dropped it.'

Warren almost smiled in appreciation of her arrogance. All the bases were covered, including the missing palm prints. Johnnie Faye's head was raised now. Her glance was unwavering.

'Please tell the jury: before Dr Ott raised the poker over his head, did you threaten or provoke him in any way?'

'No, sir.'

'When Dr Ott raised the poker over his head, did you fear for your life?'

'Yes. I was frightened out of my wits.'

'Where were you at that moment?'

'I was sitting on the sofa. Then I stood up.'

'Did you have anywhere to retreat?'

'No, sir. The sofa was jammed right up against a bookcase.'

'Did you mean to kill Dr Ott?'

'That was the last thing on my mind.'

'You were sober or drunk when you pulled the trigger?'

'Sober by then. On the drive home I sobered up.'

'Ms Boudreau. Mr Harry Morse testified that you visited his pistol range and used a name other than your own. Why?'

'I value my privacy,' she said. 'And I didn't think there was any law against using a different name if you weren't out to cheat somebody. I didn't cheat Mr Morse.'

'Did you own as many as three pistols at that time?'

'I did then. One got stolen afterwards, and the other, the ·45, I keep in my office, in a desk drawer. I'm the only one has a key.'

'Did you have legal registration for all three pistols?'

'For the ·45 and the ·22, yes. Not the other one. Someone gave it to me as a gift. I forgot to register it.'

'What did you need those pistols for?'

'Protection. We were held up five years ago. And someone followed me home once and tried to rape me. After that I carried a pistol in my car. That's the one that got stolen.'

Not stolen. Thrown into a trash can, after you'd killed a man with it.

'One more thing, Ms Boudreau. Mr Morse also testified that when you were practising at his pistol range, he observed you shooting. He said you were a good shot. Is that true?'

'Yes,' she said, 'I'm a very good shot.'

'Then how do you account for the fact that you meant only to wound Dr Ott, yet two of the three bullets you fired hit him in vital places and killed him?'

She was in control of herself, prepared.

'I think he may have moved, just slightly. And I was in a panic. My hands were shaking. I was in fear of my life.'

Warren had had enough. He said, 'Pass the witness.'

'We'll stop here,' Judge Bingham said. 'After lunch, Mr Altschuler, you can take the defendant on cross-examination.'

Back at the defence table, Rick said to him, 'Good work.'

'What are you talking about?' Warren shook his head angrily. 'You think *I* told her to say all that?'

He began to gather up his papers and stuff them into his briefcase when someone tapped him lightly on the arm from behind. He turned. It was Charm. She was thinner. The bones of her face were more clearly outlined. It made her seem older, but it was becoming.

'I called twice and left messages. I need to talk to you.'

'This is a bad time, Charm.'

'I know that,' she said softly. 'I'm sorry, but I thought we might grab a quick lunch.'

Warren hesitated. In the afternoon Johnnie Faye would undergo cross-examination; he wanted time to ponder her story. It was definitely the wrong time for a visit, an unnerving chat.

On the other side of the defence table, Rick cleared his throat. 'I'll go with our client. No problem.'

Johnnie Faye smiled. 'I'm fine. Take your wife to lunch.'

WARREN FELT WEAK. He should have said no. He took Charm to the little Greek place. It had plastic tablecloths and thin, bent forks. He ordered a Coke and a salad, and Charm ordered something he couldn't pronounce. Warren leaned back in his chair.

'So? What's up?'

Charm said, 'I've split up with Jack. That's the name of the man I was seeing. Jack Gordon. About two weeks ago.'

Good, Warren thought. But a part of him thought, Not good at all. Not good for her, and probably not good for me.

He looked up and saw that Charm was disconsolate. She lowered her head and raised one hand to press against her temples. 'I feel so awful,' she murmured.

'Because Jack's gone?'

'Partly. Mostly because I walked out on you the way I did. I made a mistake. Now I'm paying for it.'

When finally she lowered her hand, he saw that her eyes were filmed with tears.

'I shouldn't come to you like this and snivel like a schoolgirl. But I had to tell you.'

'I don't know what to say, Charm.' And that was true.

'Do you hate me, Warren?'

'Hate is the wrong word. I was angry. I was hurt!'

'Did you find another woman?'

'Yes, there is someone else.'

Charm reached into her handbag and blew her nose sharply in a tissue. 'Is it serious?'

Warren said, 'It's still in the fun stage.'

Charm began stuffing things back into her handbag. She spoke nervously, softly. 'I came here to ask if . . . ' She choked a little. '. . . if you'd come home. Not today, but when you were ready. Don't answer now. I know what you'd answer. I can see it in your eyes. And don't pity me. I'll be OK.' She fled from the restaurant.

Warren's mind was jammed, the circuitry overloaded with contradictory thoughts and emotions. But he had no chance to voice any of them. He felt his lungs were filled with sorrow, not air.

He watched her vanish into the hot street. What a good-looking woman, he thought. And I don't want her back.

There it was, not to be denied. He looked at his watch. He had just ten minutes to pay the bill and get to the courthouse for the cross-examination of his client.

GLANCING AT HIS NOTES, Bob Altschuler leaned back lazily in his chair at the prosecutor's table. He said, 'Ms Boudreau, I remind you that you're still under oath to tell the truth.'

Johnnie Faye met Altschuler's gaze without wavering.

Altschuler raised an eyebrow, then studied the yellow legal pad. 'All right . . . I recall that you said drugs had killed one of your brothers. Did you say that?'

'Yes, I did.'

'But you also said, earlier in your testimony, that both of your brothers had been killed in Vietnam. Which is it, Ms Boudreau?'

A mistake, Warren thought. She'll only get more sympathy from the jury. But he knew where Altschuler was headed.

Patiently, and in detail, Johnnie Faye explained what had happened to Clinton and then Garrett. She spoke directly to the jurors. 'So what I meant was that Garrett was killed *by* Vietnam, even though he wasn't actually killed *in* Vietnam.'

'In other words, when you were testifying you said one thing and meant another—is that a fair way to put it?'

'In a way. But about my brother Garrett, I didn't think that was important.'

'It's only important in so far as this jury can see how your mind works when you're asked to state the truth under oath.'

Before Warren could object, she said, 'I *was* telling the truth. I said later that my brother died of an overdose.'

Two minutes into cross-examination, Warren thought, and she's already arguing with Altschuler. She'll get ripped apart. Warren stood, shaking his head sadly. 'Objection. Your honour, the prosecutor is meant to ask questions of the witness, not badger her.'

'Sustained. Don't do that any more, Mr Altschuler.'

Warren glanced sharply at Johnnie Faye, hoping the message had got through, then sat down.

'Ms Boudreau, your nightclub, is that a topless nightclub?'
'Yes, sir, it is.'
'Young women dance naked from the waist up?'
'Yes, sir.'
'And do they ever perform any sexual services?'
'Not that I know of,' Johnnie Faye said.
She was in control again. She had figured it out.
'You said, speaking of Dr Ott's wife, "Sharon had died so tragically." Tell the jury—how did Mrs Ott die?'
'I believe she was shot down outside an aerobics centre.'
'Did you have any personal knowledge of this event?'
'Just what I read in the papers and what Clyde told me.'
'Weren't you extremely friendly with a man named David Inkman, whom the police suspected of murdering Mrs Ott?'
'Objection!' Warren cried. 'No predicate, and it's irrelevant, and there's an outrageous implication!'
'Sustained,' Judge Bingham said. 'The jury will disregard the question and any implication.'
'Ms Boudreau, you owned three guns at one time, and one of them, a ·32-calibre Colt, was unregistered?'
'Yes.'
'Are you aware that's illegal?'
'Yes.'
'That gun was given to you as a gift?'
'Yes.'
'By whom?'
'David Inkman.'
Altschuler veered again, trying to confuse her. 'Tell us,' he said, 'after the first time Dr Ott allegedly struck you, were you concerned for your personal safety?'
'Yes,' Johnnie Faye said.
'And didn't you begin carrying a ·22-calibre pistol in your handbag so that if Dr Ott threatened to strike you, you could protect yourself?'
'No, it had nothing to do with Clyde. I always carried that pistol. I think I mentioned that someone once tried to rape me.'
'Did you report that attempted rape to the police?'
'No.'
Warren paid close attention. She was in trouble, but she was bearing up. Her hands were steady on her handbag.
'How many drinks did you have at the Hacienda on the night of May fourteenth, Ms Boudreau?'
'Two or three.'
'And so Dr Ott had seven drinks, and possibly eight?'
'Yes.'
'Didn't you plan to drink just enough so that you'd stay sober, and didn't

you encourage Dr Ott to drink heavily, Ms Boudreau?'

'No, I didn't do that at all.'

Altschuler's eyes were inky and threatening like those of a deep-water fish. 'What time was it when you came back to Dr Ott's house from the Hacienda on the night of May fourteenth?'

'Let's see . . . Close to eleven thirty.'

'You went upstairs with Dr Ott?'

'Yes.'

'You had sex with him then, didn't you?'

'Yes. He insisted.'

'You mean you didn't want to have sex with him?'

'No. I mean that's right—I didn't want it.'

'He was drunk and under the influence of cocaine, and you were sober. Are you telling us, in those circumstances, he was able to force you?'

'Yes, that's right.'

'Did he threaten you with bodily harm if you wouldn't?'

'No. He just shoved me down on the bed.'

'But you knew, didn't you, when you went upstairs with him, that he wanted to have sex with you?'

'No, I didn't. I thought he wanted to talk.'

Suddenly, amazingly, tears flooded Johnnie Faye's eyes. 'Sir, I shouldn't have gone up and gone to bed with him.' Her voice had choked. 'I'm ashamed that I did that, but I was feeling sorry for him. I'm not perfect. People don't always do the right thing every hour of the day and night.'

Altschuler hesitated. With a witness like Johnnie Faye Boudreau he would normally slash at her character. But now there were tears.

'So that night,' Altschuler asked, 'you had sex with him completely against your will? He *raped* you?'

'No, he couldn't do it. That's what got him so angry.'

'He slapped you in the face?'

'Yes.'

'Were you frightened when he got angry and slapped you?'

'A little.'

'And so you rushed downstairs to get your pistol out of your handbag?'

'No, sir. I needed my handbag because my car keys were in it. I wanted to leave.'

'You had left your handbag on the living-room sofa?'

'Yes.'

'You knew your pistol was also in your handbag, didn't you?'

'I didn't think of that at the time.'

'Are you telling us that on the night of May fourteenth you didn't know your pistol was in your handbag?'

God, Warren thought, he's good.

'I'm not saying that—'

'Stop. Is the answer yes or no, Ms Boudreau?'

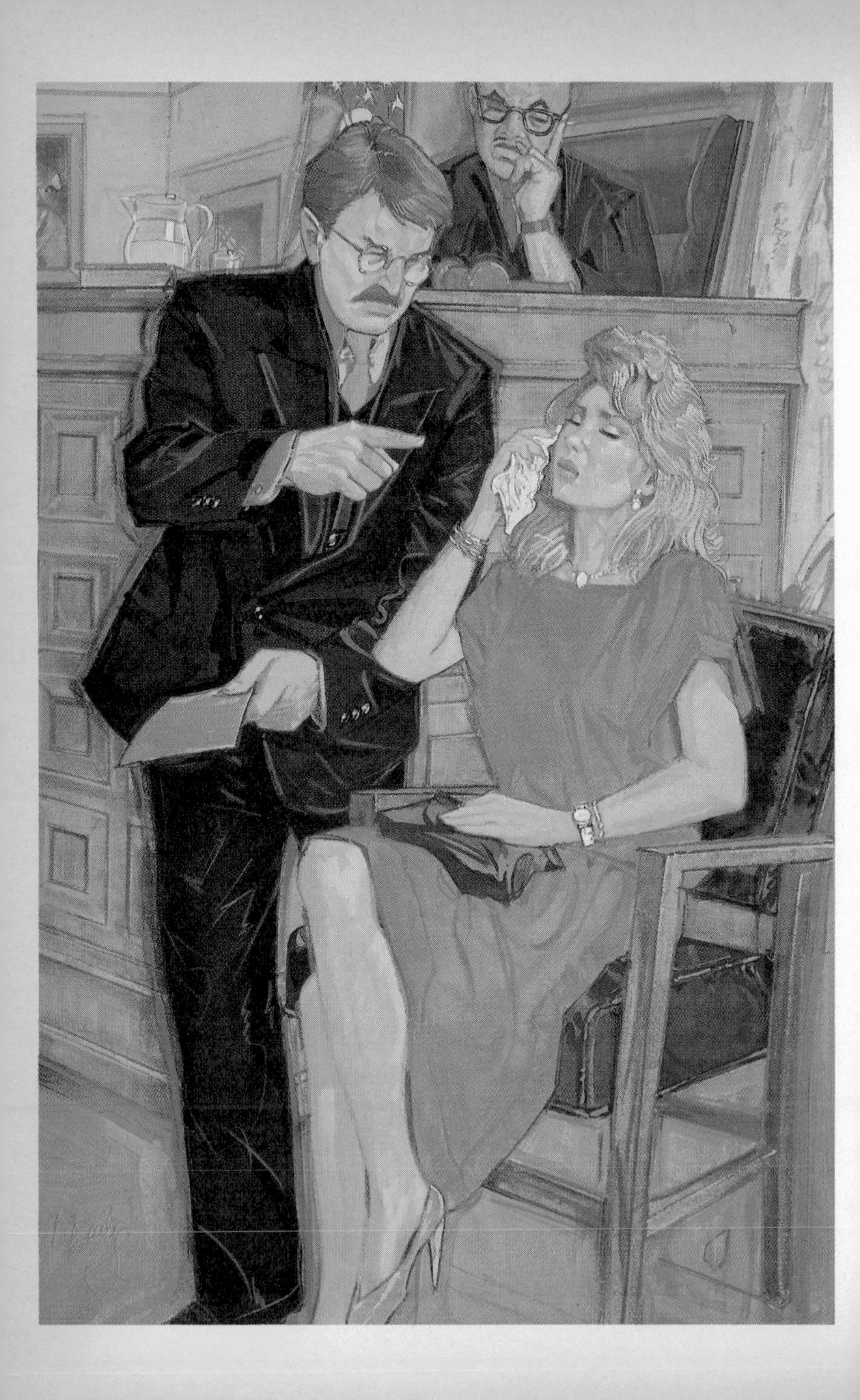

Johnnie Faye wiped her eyes and turned to Judge Bingham. 'Your honour, that's like asking me, "Do you still beat your dog?" I can't give a simple yes or no honest answer. I want to answer truthfully, but he won't let me.'

'Answer as best you can,' the judge said.

'My answer is: I knew it was in my handbag, but I wasn't *thinking* about it being there.'

And she's good too, Warren thought. It was a contest worth watching. But he was not sure who he was rooting for.

'When you went downstairs and picked up your handbag with the pistol in it, Ms Boudreau, you could have left the house then, couldn't you?'

'He came downstairs before I'd got the handbag.'

'You're telling us that you were sober, and you couldn't have picked up your bag and run out of the front door before a drunken man clambered out of bed and down a long flight of stairs?'

'He was right behind me. I heard him shouting.'

'And he blocked the front door so you couldn't leave?'

'No, he didn't do that then. That was long before.'

'Ms Boudreau, less than forty minutes after the murder, didn't you tell Sergeant Ruiz that Dr Ott had blocked the front door *after* you and Dr Ott had come downstairs?'

'Yes.'

For half an hour Altschuler played the theme of her prior inconsistent statement to Ruiz. Johnnie Faye admitted that she might have said certain words to Ruiz, but the facts were incorrect. She had been confused. She was actually in shock.

'So,' Altschuler said, 'you picked up the poker from the fireplace to strike him?'

'No, sir. I picked it up because he threatened me.'

'You meant to kill him with that heavy iron poker, didn't you, or inflict serious bodily harm?'

'No, sir. I meant to keep him away from me with it.'

'And then he took the poker away from you?'

'Yes.'

'He was drunk and stoned, and you were sober, yet he was able to take the poker from your grasp? You couldn't elude him?'

'Yes, he was able, and no, I couldn't elude him.'

'And he blocked your path to the front door?'

'No, sir, not then. He threw me onto the sofa.'

'And then you took the pistol from your handbag?'

'No, sir. Not until he raised the poker and said he was going to kill me with it.'

'That's when he charged across the room at you, isn't it?'

'Yes, sir.'

'And you shot him as he was charging at you, isn't that so?'

'No, sir. I said, "Don't take another step, Clyde, or I'll shoot you," and he stopped short, and he stood still.'

'You had already cocked the action on the ·22?'

'No, sir. I didn't cock it.'

'But when you took the pistol out of your handbag, you released the safety catch so that it would fire, didn't you?'

'I must have done that without thinking.'

'You said you were a very good shot, didn't you?'

'Yes, on a target range.'

'What part of Dr Ott's body did you aim for?'

'His left shoulder, I think.'

'Show us how you held the gun. Just use your finger and point it at me. You can stand up if you like.'

Johnnie Faye stood and raised her hand, fist clenched, index finger protruding. Her elbow was bent.

'Your arm wasn't level?'

'No, sir.'

'Can't you shoot more accurately if your firing arm is level?'

'Yes, you can.'

'So with your arm bent, weren't you taking a grave risk that your shot, which you say was aimed at his left shoulder, might be off a few inches and hit him in the heart instead?'

'I didn't think about the risk. I was frightened.'

'You knew that the gun had its sear filed off illegally, making it fully automatic—you knew that, didn't you?'

'I knew about the sear. I didn't know that was illegal.'

'You pulled it three times, didn't you?'

'No, just once. But it kept on firing.'

'You missed with the first shot?'

'I don't know.'

'You mean you may have missed with the last shot?'

'No, sir. I mean that I didn't know then and don't know now which two of the three shots hit him.'

'Ms Boudreau, isn't it a fact that you could have run around him to the front door and the safety of your car?'

'No, sir, I was on the sofa.'

'Isn't it a fact that you could have used your pistol to keep him at bay while you ran or walked past him?'

'No, sir. Even if I could have done that, he could have used that poker to brain me when I ran by.'

'Isn't it a fact that he never picked up the poker?'

'No, sir, he did pick it up.'

'Isn't it a fact that the reason his palm prints weren't on the poker was because after you shot him you picked up the poker yourself and then pressed a dead man's fingerprints onto it?'

'No, sir, that's absolutely not a fact.'

'Come on, Ms Boudreau—didn't you decide to kill Dr Ott because you were in a rage that he wouldn't marry you?'

'No, that's not true either.'

'What *is* true, Ms Boudreau?'

'That I shot him in self-defence. That if I hadn't done it, he might have killed me. *Would* have killed me.'

'Ah, but which is it? Might have or would have?'

'I was certain then,' Johnnie Faye said, 'that he *would* have.'

'But a moment ago you used the words *might have*.'

'Yes, I did.'

'So there *is* a doubt in your mind!'

Johnnie Faye took a deep breath. 'Sir, ever since this happened on the night of May fourteenth I've been in agony over it. I've hardly slept. I didn't hate Clyde. Taking a person's life is the worst thing a human being can do and if you take the life of someone you once loved, even if you didn't mean to do it, you live in hell for ever. So, yes, there have been doubts in my mind—lots of them. Terrible moments. I cry all night long sometimes. But I believe with all my heart—unless I wanted to take the chance that he would kill me—that I had no choice.'

From the blotch of dark pink colour that spread across Bob Altschuler's face, Warren gathered that the prosecutor knew the jury had been sold some snake oil. But there was little he could do any more, not until final argument. Glaring stonily at the defence lawyer, he passed the witness.

For the better part of two hours the state and the defence tossed Johnnie Faye back and forth between them. Then—with Altschuler's final derisive 'Pass the witness' and Warren's confident cry of 'The defence rests!'—it was over.

Just after five thirty in the afternoon, a weary Judge Bingham tapped his gavel on the walnut bench. 'On Monday morning,' he said, 'I will charge the jury. Then we will have final argument by both attorneys.' He turned to the twelve jurors and the two alternates. 'Don't read the newspapers over the weekend. Please try not to watch the news on television. And don't discuss the case with your family or friends. You'll begin deliberating on Monday afternoon. I suggest you bring your overnight kit in case you have to spend the night here. Now y'all have a nice weekend.'

11

Heat waves rippled above the highway. The land spread flat and brown in every direction. Maria Hahn sat at Warren's side as he drove, fiddling with the tape deck. He tried to banish Charm to the back of his mind.

He was a forgiving man. To forget was more difficult. But that could be done too, he thought. The final question was: what do I want? He was fond of Maria, enjoyed her. He did not love her yet, but could. And with time, if he chose to invest it, would. He saw that clearly.

'Do me a favour,' he said to Maria now. 'Look in the glove compartment. I think there's some Vivaldi there.'

The music soothed him for a while. He had been to see Hector early that morning. Abiding misery had made the Mexican's face a little greyer than on the previous visit. Warren wanted to say, 'I'm working for you. Don't give up'—but the words seemed powdery and without substance. 'How are you?' he asked.

'I can't sleep good,' Hector said.

'Not much longer,' Warren promised. 'Maybe next week.'

'I want to tell you something,' Hector said. 'I lie to you.'

'What about?' Warren asked, his heartbeat quickening.

'The shopping cart. You ask me a long time ago if I steal it. I say I found it.' Hector shook his head. 'That's the only lie I ever tole you.'

Warren thought, My heart will break if this man goes to prison. He promised to come by on Sunday with a newspaper.

A sign flashed by. GOLIAD: 8. BEEVILLE: 38.

'Want a sip of Gatorade, honey?' Maria asked.

'No, thanks.' He smiled.

Honey, she had called him. She was affectionate, needed affection but asked little else so far. I could be happy with Maria, he thought. Content. I could do my work, raise her son, have a kid of my own with her. Grow old with ease. The river would flow. There would be rocks and eddies but it would be navigable.

'You worried about the case?' Maria asked.

Yes, I'm worried that my client will be found not guilty. Not just worried. Crazed. 'It's complicated,' he said.

Outside the courtroom, late yesterday afternoon, Johnnie Faye had caught him by the arm. Her eyes had narrowed. 'You better make a good speech for me.'

He'd nodded. That was his obligation, one way or the other.

Now on Saturday morning he was driving to Beeville to hunt for a man with a nickname. Without him, Warren believed, the Quintana jury would come in with a guilty verdict.

They reached there at eleven o'clock in the morning. It was an old cattle town north of the King Ranch. Warren slid the car off the bypass road and drove down the main street. They passed a motel, a supermarket, a bowling alley. Warren spotted a Mobil filling station. He said to Maria, 'I'll try there first.'

Outside the car, the heat struck a mean blow. A man of about fifty sat at the cash register working on credit-card receipts.

Warren, in boots and worn jeans, stuck a toothpick between his teeth and said, 'Mornin'. Hot day.'

'Sure is.'

'Man in this town, some folks up in Houston call him Jim Dandy. He around?'

The man grinned, showing yellow teeth. 'You the law?'

'Shoot, no,' he said. 'I'm a lawyer. Tryin' to help Jim out.'

'Well, Jim Dandy's around. Was, anyway. Up at Kitty Marie's. You know Kitty Marie too?'

'No, sir,' Warren said.

'Little house on DeKalb Street. Go back up a few blocks past Walgreen's and turn right. Next-to-last house on the block, got a beat-up black Chevy pick-up in front of it.'

'Anything I need to know?'

'Well, Jim Dandy's so poor he'd have to borrow money to buy water to cry with. And Kitty Marie's so ugly she'd run a dog off a meat wagon. So if you were a religious man you might say that God did them both a favour by uniting them. Anything else?'

'Nothing,' Warren said. 'Thank you.'

Two minutes later Warren knocked on the door of the next-to-last house on DeKalb Street. The place looked as if it would fall down if you kicked hard at any one of its rotting grey boards. A woman in her late thirties, with pink rubber haircurlers and buck teeth, opened a screen door. It groaned on its hinges. Warren handed her his business card and asked for Jim Dandy. That old drunken dog was still in bed, she said, but it seemed she couldn't move fast enough to get him out of it.

JIM DANDY SAT at the kitchen table drinking a cold beer, the second of a six-pack that Maria had provided after a dash to the nearest supermarket. Now Maria was outside with Kitty Marie. Warren sat opposite Jim Dandy at the rickety table.

Jim Dandy matched Siva Singh's description, as many men would: closing in on forty, dissolute, long-haired, and pot-bellied. He hadn't shaved in several days. He smelt of yesterday's beer.

'I'll tell you again, pardner,' Warren said, 'while you're still sober enough to hang on to it. You're not going to get in trouble. No one cares you took the wallet. But you have to admit you did it and say what you saw. All of it.'

'Don't sit well,' Jim Dandy said.

'What's your problem? You can tell me.'

'I spent the money.'

'Course you did. No one cares about that. Unless, of course, you don't come back to Houston.'

Jim Dandy kept rubbing his hands as if to warm them. He glanced out at the women in the yard. 'I can't do it,' he said.

'Then you're in the deep weeds, pardner. Then the law might want to know what you did with the money.'

'How's the law gonna find out I ever had it?'

'I'd tell them,' Warren said.

'You'd do a rotten thing like that, hoss?'

'I might. I've got a man facing the death penalty.'

'How'm I gonna get up to Houston?' Jim Dandy asked.

Warren laughed. 'With me, today. And I run a kind of a little hotel up there. Got a couple of *amigos* bunked down there already. You're invited, free of charge. Free beer until the day you testify, free eats as long as you stay.'

Jim Dandy looked Warren up and down, frowning. 'I won't eat nothin' that jumps, crawls, or climbs trees.'

'Supermarket's right around the corner. You shop. I pay.'

'Well . . . you seem like a fair man. OK.'

Warren rose immediately from his chair. 'Tuck the rest of that beer under your arm, and let's go party.'

On the drive north to Houston, with Jim Dandy in the back seat and the windows open, Warren asked him, 'Why'd you go back to the dry-cleaners and pick up those clothes?'

'Seemed like a good idea at the time,' Jim Dandy said.

'Got stolen from you, I heard.'

'Nope. I sold 'em for ten bucks,' Jim Dandy said. 'And I allow they was bad-luck clothes. Fella that bought 'em from me got shot full of holes. Killed real dead right there in the mission.'

AT NINE O'CLOCK SHARP Warren appeared in the 342nd District Court. Everyone rose as the jury filed in to take their seats.

Judge Bingham read the charge. Johnnie Faye Boudreau stood indicted with the offence of murder. 'Our law provides that a person commits the offence of murder if he, or she, intentionally or knowingly causes the death of an individual. Ms Boudreau has admitted to causing the death of Dr Clyde Ott and has pleaded not guilty by reason of self-defence. An accused cannot be found guilty for any offence if she engaged in the proscribed conduct because she was compelled to do so by the threat of imminent death and serious bodily injury, provided that she did not provoke the victim into so threatening or attacking. Our law, in addition, requires that anyone who feels she is facing such a threat has a duty to retreat, if retreat is possible, before taking action against the threatening person. If you find beyond a reasonable doubt that Ms Boudreau provoked the attack, or then had the possibility to retreat and did not do so, and wilfully caused the death of Dr Clyde Ott, you will return a verdict of guilty. If you find that she exercised her duty to retreat, or had no possibility to do so, and did not wilfully cause the death of Dr Ott, you will return a verdict of not guilty.

'Mr Blackburn, you may open for the defence.'

Stepping forward, Warren thanked the jurors for their patience and briefly summarised the facts from the defendant's point of view: a stormy relationship between lovers, a history of abuse by the victim—'a man whose death some may indeed mourn but whose way of life certainly doesn't seem worthy of praise. Johnnie Faye Boudreau has told you of beatings and hospital treatment. Dr Ott was not a kind man. He was a brute.

'As for the defendant, she is a worldly woman—make no mistake about that. She runs a topless nightclub. But she is not on trial for that. She owned three handguns and practised with them at a pistol range. That is not a crime.

'Mrs Lorna Gerard, a subsidised stepdaughter of Dr Ott, quoted Ms Boudreau as having said, "When he gets mean and drunk, I could cut his throat in his sleep." ' Warren smiled with a certain delicate intimacy, and pointed an idle forefinger back and forth among the jurors. 'How many of us have used the words, "I could kill him for that"? Did we really mean them? Do we take such angry statements at face value, or do we accept them as part of human frailty? I think you know the answer.'

He stopped in midflow, and moved from the well of the courtroom back to the defence table, close to Johnnie Faye.

'Beyond that, you have listened to the defendant under oath. You have listened to a brave and independent woman, and a sad woman. She loved Clyde Ott. Not wisely, perhaps, but for a long time. Clyde Ott was rich, but Johnnie Faye Boudreau had a job and she paid her own rent. She never took advantage of Dr Ott's considerable wealth. Whether or not she wanted to marry him and *he* was reluctant, or he wanted to marry her and *she* was reluctant . . . who cares?

'And so we come to the tragic events of the night of May fourteenth. And they are tragic—Ms Boudreau is sorrowing. You could see it. She did not mean to kill Clyde Ott. She meant to keep him from killing her or inflicting grave bodily harm. The state has provided not a single witness to say otherwise. A fingerprint expert testified that there were no palm prints on the poker with which Clyde Ott threatened the defendant. But the defendant herself has admitted that in a semihysterical state, she inadvertently destroyed some of the prints on that poker. Destroyed evidence that would have completely exonerated her! Can she be blamed for that?'

He moved back to the jury box.

'You have heard from Judge Bingham about what our law calls "the duty to retreat". I will ask the men among you: if a raging, two-hundred-and-twenty-pound drunken man came at you with a heavy iron poker, and said he was going to kill you with it—what would *you* do? You might try to run away. Would any of you do that? I doubt it. You might try to reason with him, although we all know what it's like to reason with an angry drunk. Some of you might have been brave enough to grapple with him, some might not. Or, if you had a pistol in your possession, you might do what Johnnie Faye Boudreau did.'

Warren paused before the jury, studying the intent faces.

'And now I will ask the women among you: would *you* have tried to run away? Ms Boudreau couldn't. The archway and the vestibule were wide. But ladies, she was on the sofa, backed against a wall! So, under those circumstances, I ask you: would you fight back with your woman's body? Would you try to reason with him and pray to God that the man with the poker wouldn't splatter your brains on the carpet?' Warren's voice rose in volume. 'Because that's the only kind of retreat that was possible! Take the beating or fight back! Johnnie Faye Boudreau fought back. She shot him, and the shots killed him. She didn't mean to, but that's what happened. And so I ask this jury if we, as Texas men and women, are meant to grovel and beg or accept death or probable disfigurement when we are flatly threatened. And as a result of that question, I ask you to find Ms Boudreau not guilty by reason of self-defence.'

Warren sat down.

That was my best, he thought. I did it. I had to do it.

BOB ALTSCHULER SNAPPED and scolded from the moment he got to his feet and faced the jury. 'Today,' he bawled, 'there's one important man who isn't in this courtroom! One man we need to hear from, and we can't because he's dead! Shot twice—once between the eyes, and once right here!' Altschuler placed his right hand in the region of his heart. 'Clyde Ott—Dr Clyde Ott, a medical man and healer. Folks'—he pointed a rigid finger at Johnnie Faye Boudreau—'this woman who runs a topless nightclub shot him down in cold blood! Don't you *know* that? Don't you feel it in your heart of hearts?' Altschuler shook his head, as if deeply perplexed. 'Let's go through the evidence.'

He focused instantly on Johnnie Faye's statement to Sergeant Ruiz less than an hour after the murder. 'So the defendant, under oath, changed her story! Told us that Dr Ott had blocked the doorway *before* the two of them went upstairs, *before* he supposedly threatened her and picked up a poker. Why should she tell one story then and a different story now? Don't you know why? Because she'd realised that if she didn't change the details of her story, she'd be in violation of her duty to retreat!'

Sighing, he shook his head again. 'On the night of May fourteenth she told Sergeant Ruiz that Dr Ott was coming at her "like an old grizzly bear, waving that poker over his head". Her own words. *Coming at her*. But then a few days ago the county medical examiner testified that Dr Ott was shot *while he was standing still!* So what did Johnnie Faye Boudreau do after she heard that? Changed her story! Now she says Dr Ott ran at her with the poker and then stopped, and that's when she shot him. Didn't you realise, folks, what she was doing? Didn't you realise what she was doing after Sergeant Kulik testified that Dr Ott's palm prints should have been on the poker—and *weren't*? Until her testimony here Johnnie Faye Boudreau never said a word to any authority about having picked up the poker after she'd killed Dr Ott, and in the process possibly damaging his set of palm prints. She made that up! This woman will say *anything*!'

Warren had to tense the muscles in his neck; he had been on the verge of nodding in agreement.

'Now,' the prosecutor continued, 'let's consider all these various threats that the witnesses have told us about. At the Houston Racquet Club, after Johnnie Faye Boudreau had thrown a drink at him, Dr Ott said to her, "I could kill you for that." But he didn't kill her, did he? On the other hand, Johnnie Faye Boudreau, in front of Mrs Gerard, said of Dr Ott, "I could kill him." *And she did.* There's a big difference, don't you agree? Please remember that Dr Ott also said to his stepdaughter, speaking of the defendant, "I'm frightened of her." Think about that. Why was Dr Ott frightened?

'The defence also makes light of the fact that no more than a few weeks prior to the actual murder, Johnnie Faye Boudreau practised at a pistol range with the murder weapon. All sorts of fun-loving people do that. Surely you see past that double talk! Other people may practise with their pistols, but other people do not murder someone immediately afterwards! Johnnie Faye Boudreau used a false name, just in case any enquiry was made, but unfortunately for Johnnie Faye Boudreau, Mr Morse remembered her.' He raised a finger and said, with solemn import, 'And she is a very good shot.'

Altschuler began to shake his head again. Warren was fascinated. Go for it, Bob. Do her in.

'Ladies and gentlemen of the jury, do you believe that she put a bullet into Dr Ott just a few inches from his heart, *and didn't mean to kill him*? Do you believe Dr Ott "moved slightly", as Johnnie Faye Boudreau claims, and that's why the other bullet hit him *between the eyes*?'

Altschuler gripped his head with both hands as if it might explode, as if all he had said was so beyond comprehension that belief in it might render him insane.

Then he became terribly calm. 'And now let's talk about the duty to retreat.' He paused, giving the jurors time to anticipate. 'Johnnie Faye Boudreau claims that when Dr Ott was drunk he was capable of violence. Yet when she got to the house that night, she went inside. She didn't have to go upstairs with him, but she did. He was drunk. Wasn't she frightened?' Altschuler threw his hands into the air. 'No, of course she wasn't frightened! *She had a gun in her handbag!*'

He smiled and raised one finger.

'But wait. You're probably recalling, as I am, that Johnnie Faye Boudreau said she left her handbag on the sofa downstairs. Folks, you've seen the diagram of the Ott residence. You know where the living-room sofa was. It was *sixty-five feet out of the way*. Now I ask you—particularly the ladies—does a woman walk into a house that's not her own, and go upstairs with a man to his bedroom, and first march sixty-five feet out of her way to leave her handbag on the sofa in the downstairs living room? Think about what's in that handbag! Never mind her pistol—I'm talking about her make-up, her keys, her private and precious little things! *She takes the handbag with her!*'

He waited a full five seconds.

'And if she does that, ladies and gentlemen, when she goes downstairs again, trying to flee a man who's threatening her, *why doesn't she just go out of the front door and drive home?*'

Altschuler went up to full throttle. 'She didn't retreat!' With a harsh thrust of his hand, the prosecutor indicated Johnnie Faye, who sat immobile and without expression. 'There sits a true monster! Deceitful! Cunning! Wicked! Manipulative! She's a cold-blooded killer, and I ask you, on behalf of the State of Texas and in the name of justice, to find her guilty of murder. Not murder by reason of self-defence—*wilful* murder.'

Warren wanted to applaud. Amen, he thought. Don't say any more, Bob. You've got her every way. Just sit down. And Bob Altschuler did.

Judge Bingham nodded at the bailiff, and the bailiff nodded at the jury. Obediently the jurors rose and followed the bailiff through the back door of the courtroom to the jury room.

Rick looked at Warren with bleak eyes. Warren turned towards Johnnie Faye, whose face was icy. She was staring at Bob Altschuler, who was sipping a glass of water at the prosecution's table.

'That son of a bitch,' she murmured. 'I'd like to put one between *his* eyes.' She focused finally on Warren. 'Well, buddy, what do we do now?'

'We wait,' he said coolly. 'We sweat it out.'

AT 1.30PM THE BAILIFF LEFT the courtroom to buy sandwiches and soft drinks and coffee for the jurors.

'What about lunch for us?' Johnnie Faye asked Warren.

'I'm not hungry. You can go to the cafeteria in the basement if you like. Don't leave the courthouse.'

'What if they find me guilty? Do they let me go home and get my things in order?'

'You should have done that already,' Warren said. 'They'll cuff you and take you away.'

Her lip trembled. 'And what about an appeal?'

'You can hire a lawyer to do that for you.'

'Will you do it? You know the facts.'

Bizarre. She knows how I loathe her, but she depends on me.

'Yes, I know the facts. And that's why I won't do it.'

He got up and walked through the back door of the courtroom to a telephone reserved for lawyers and reporters. He called his office to pick up the messages from his answering machine. Charm spoke briefly, asking him to call back. Two lawyers had checked in with referrals, and one man had called directly from jail, begging to see him about a drug bust. So he would be working again. I should feel better about it than I do, Warren thought.

He went outside into the corridor to use the public telephone, which was more private, and called Charm at Channel 26.

'Warren!' she said, almost breathlessly, as if he had surprised her by returning the call. 'How did it go?'

He told her the jury was out and it had gone as well as could be expected.

'I have to talk fast,' she said. 'I didn't say everything I had to say the other day. Can we meet to talk again?'

He tried to think that through.

'Don't cut me out of your life, Warren. *Please*.'

He saw some TV cameramen moving rapidly to the courtroom. 'I have to go. The jury may be coming in. All right. Lunch tomorrow, if that suits you.'

She would be outside Bingham's courtroom at noon. Warren hurried back to the courtroom and pushed open the swinging door. The TV cameramen were taping Bob Altschuler.

When they were finished, Altschuler grasped Warren's elbow and moved him firmly to an empty back bench.

'Your client is guilty as sin,' Altschuler said. 'She got Clyde Ott drunk and shot him in cold blood. You know that, don't you?'

Warren thought for a moment or two. 'Off the record?'

'Whatever you say. Whatever you like.'

'You're right.'

'Well, you didn't have any choice,' Altschuler said, sighing. 'I just wish you hadn't done such a good job of defending her.'

'You were pretty good too. I think you've nailed her.'

Altschuler extended his big hand. And Warren shook it.

AT HALF PAST FOUR Warren conferred in whispers with Rick, then took the elevator up to the seventh floor and the 299th. Judge Parker's courtroom was empty except for the judge and Nancy Goodpaster, huddled at the bench working on the court calendar. Goodpaster smiled and mouthed a hello. The judge was suntanned and looked as if she had gained a few pounds.

'Well, if it ain't my friend Mr Blackburn.'

'How are you, Judge?'

'Just fine. Jury still out in *Boudreau*?'

He nodded. 'But the smart money says they'll reach a decision this evening. When can we do *Quintana*?'

'Tomorrow and the next day are pretty free. From Thursday on, my agenda's full. So you get going by tomorrow after lunch or I dismiss the jury and we pick a new one in September. That's it.'

Just then the telephone rang on the bailiff's desk.

Nancy Goodpaster picked it up and listened for a moment. 'Yes,' she said, 'I'll tell him.' She hung up and turned to Warren. 'Your partner wants you. The jury's coming in.'

'ALL RISE!' THE BAILIFF CALLED, and the jury filed in and took their seats. Johnnie Faye Boudreau stood between Rick and Warren at the defence table. Bob Altschuler stood at the prosecutors' table, fingers tapping a light tattoo on the walnut. Judge Bingham asked the jurors if they had reached a verdict, and the foreman said yes, they had. He handed a slip of paper to the deputy clerk.

'You may read the verdict,' Judge Bingham said.

The deputy clerk read aloud: 'We the jury find the defendant, Johnnie Faye Boudreau, not guilty by reason of self-defence.'

The blood fled from Warren's face. Johnnie Faye let out a whoop. She threw her arms round Rick, then wheeled with outstretched arms to hug Warren. But Warren was not there.

He strode, almost ran, out of the courtroom. Reporters trotted after him, shouting questions. The microphones were nearly in his teeth. A tumult of galvanic anger rocketed through him from head to toe. 'The jury has spoken,' he replied, 'for better or for worse. Ms Boudreau is free. I have nothing more to say.'

But he couldn't get away. They were blocking him, clutching at his sleeve. 'Mr Blackburn, what do you mean *"for better or for worse"*? Are you casting doubt on the justice of the verdict?'

'The jury is always right,' Warren said, quoting himself to his former client, 'whether they're right or not.'

Amid the clamour and shrieks of disbelief, he brushed past the reporters and cameramen and headed for the stairwell. The door slammed behind him. Warren's hands felt clammy, his stomach heaved and twisted. If I had real guts I would have grabbed those microphones and said: 'She's free—free to lie, free to murder again.' He wanted to howl with frustration.

But what could I have done? Nothing. And what can I do now? Nothing yet. But so help me God, I'll find a way.

12

Even as he reached his office at nine o'clock on the morning after the verdict, Warren's telephone had been ringing. The message light was blinking; the tape was full. He unplugged it. At eleven o'clock he drove downtown to the courthouse.

As they had agreed, Charm was waiting for him at noon outside Judge Bingham's courtroom. Just after Warren said hello and Charm kissed him on the cheek to congratulate him on the verdict, the courtroom door popped open and Maria Hahn stepped out with Judge Bingham. They were laughing. The judge, halting, thrust out his hand. 'Warren!' he said. 'I see by the papers you've been a bad boy.' He inclined his bald head towards Charm. 'Can't you control your husband, Mrs Blackburn? Get him to keep his big mouth shut?'

But he was smiling. He had enjoyed the case.

Maria Hahn wasn't smiling.

Warren exchanged a few more words with the judge and then said, 'Goodbye, your honour. Goodbye, Maria. See you later.'

He took Charm to the Greek restaurant again. Charm looked pale and even thinner than before. On the way, she said, 'That's the woman you've been seeing, isn't it?'

'Who?'

'Come off it, Warren. The tall one with the great legs. The one who was giggling with the judge.'

Warren was mildly amazed. 'How could you tell?'

'The way she looked at you. And you at her.' Charm clamped her lips shut.

In the restaurant, her eyes moist, her hands trembling, she said, 'Give me a chance, Warren. Don't throw away our marriage for someone you hardly know. I know you. I love you. We have a history. We were partners, and we can be partners again.'

Those had been his thoughts, the thoughts that he had been unable to speak. He had mourned her going, he had been bitter. But that was ending.

'I want children with you, Warren. I'm ready.'

'That's a new tune,' he said.

'I know,' she said, flushing. 'Please forgive me for that.'

'I forgive you,' Warren said. 'But I can't promise you a darn thing.'

'I'll give you time, you know I will. But I can't hang around for ever. I think I have a job in Boston with PBS.'

He saw how the thought energised her. 'Do you want it?'

'If we're not back together, yes. If we can be together, probably not. Your life is here.'

'I have to go now,' Warren said, after he had looked at his watch. 'I'm in trial in the 299th. I can't be late.'

Her eyes glistened. 'Call me,' Charm said.

WITH THE JURY IN PLACE and Hector Quintana by his side at the defence table, Warren stood. He had never been so nervous in a courtroom in his life. 'The defence is ready, your honour, and calls James Thurgood Dandy.'

Jim Dandy, sober and dressed in a new shirt and trousers, slouched in the witness chair. He was almost as nervous as Warren.

'Your honour,' Warren said, 'before testimony, the defence will make a motion *in limine*.'

He was already on his way to the bench, with Nancy Goodpaster following close behind. *In limine* meant 'on the threshold'. Warren said quietly, 'Judge, this witness will testify to having approached the car of the victim, Dan Ho Trunh, and to taking a wallet and its contents from the dead man's hand. But this witness won't testify if his sworn statements prejudice his liberty. I request immunity for the witness on all felony charges of theft, on the grounds of an overriding need to have the facts clarified in a case of capital murder, which takes precedence.'

Judge Parker looked to Nancy Goodpaster. The prosecutor considered. 'State has no objection,' she said.

Jim Dandy was sworn in by the deputy clerk.

Warren went through the customary business of asking name, address, age and profession.

'Jim Dandy is what they call me.'—'De Kalb Street, Beeville. Down south a ways.'—'About thirty-eight.'—'Don't have no profession.'

Warren plunged in like a swimmer from a high board. 'Do you recall where you were on May fourteenth, at about eight pm?'

'Well, I don't know that it was exactly May fourteenth, but about then, and I know what you're talkin' about. I was sittin' against a wall, drunk.'

'Where, sir?'

'Here in town. Some shoppin' centre, guess you'd call it. I bought a pint of Thunderbird there. Set me down to enjoy it.'

'Did anything unusual happen while you were sitting against the wall in that shopping centre?'

'Well, I remember I stood up to stretch myself, and while I was doin' that, I heard a yell and then a shot.'

'And what did you do?'

'I ducked then turned my head around—I was scared someone might be aimin' to shoot me—and there was these two cars there. A station wagon, and the other was a nice big car. Engine was runnin'. They was parked side by side, sorta facin' me.'

'How far away from you?'

'Can't say. Not far, not close. Close enough to see.'

'And what did you see, sir?'

'Didn't see anyone in the wagon. Saw a woman in the car.'

Warren didn't bother looking at the jury: they were not the object of this exercise. He glanced at Nancy Goodpaster. She was hunched at the counsel table, listening intently.

'Mr Dandy, you saw a woman in the car that was parked next to the station wagon? *A woman?* You're positive?'

'That's right. Besides, I told you I heard a yell before I heard the shot. That was a woman's yell, what you might call a scream.'

'The woman in the car was alone?'

'Didn't see no one else with her.'

'Can you describe the woman in the car?'

'Sure can't. I saw long woman's hair and some red lipstick, and that's about all. Then she was gone.'

'Can you describe the car? The make? The model?'

'Not really, 'cept it was big and looked new.'

'Mr Dandy, did the woman have anything in her hand?'

'Looked to me like a gun.'

'Big or small?'

'It wasn't nothin' gigantic.'

A great witness, Warren thought. He never speculated, never embroidered, and he told the truth.

'What did you do then, Mr Dandy?'

'Walked over to the wagon and looked inside. Man was dead in there.' Jim Dandy sighed. 'I took his wallet. He wasn't gonna need it no more.'

'And was there anything else besides money in the wallet?'

'A laundry ticket.'

'What did you do with the wallet?'

'Threw it in a sewer.'

'What did you do with the laundry ticket?'

'Well, a few days later, I figured, heck, dead fella don't need clothes. So I went back there to the laundry and got 'em.'

'Do you remember who waited on you in the laundry?'

'Indian lady.'

'Can you describe the clothes you got from her?'

'Nice grey suit. White shirts. Nice green sweater. Didn't fit too good—so I sold 'em down at the mission.'

Warren, his voice rising, said, 'Mr Dandy, have you ever in your life seen the man sitting beside me?' He put a hand—a hand that almost trembled—on Hector Quintana's shoulder.

Jim Dandy peered across the courtroom at Hector. 'Not that I can recollect. Looks like a Messkin.'

'You didn't see this man in the parking lot that night, or anywhere around the vicinity of the shopping mall?'

'Nope.'

'Thank you, sir,' Warren said. 'Pass the witness.'

Nancy Goodpaster took Jim Dandy on cross-examination for only fifteen minutes. She focused mostly on his certainty that it was a woman in the car. Jim Dandy was certain. 'I was drunk,' he said, 'but, ma'am, I ain't never *that* drunk I can't tell a man from a woman.'

Goodpaster hesitated, then said, 'No further questions.'

To hammer in the final nail of innocence, Warren called Siva Singh for the defence. She quickly identified Jim Dandy as the man who had picked up Dan Ho Trunh's dry-cleaning.

'And could Mr Dandy be the same man you saw running away from the car and out of the parking lot?'

'That is possible,' Singh said quietly.

After Goodpaster declined cross-examination, Warren called for a ten-minute break for counsel to confer.

Goodpaster led Warren back to her office. She sat down behind her desk and faced him. 'I have one problem. How do we know that it wasn't your witness, this guy Dandy, who murdered Trunh? He had motive—the money. He had opportunity.'

'Then why would he be dumb enough to show up in court,' Warren asked, 'and take the risk you'd nail him to the wall?'

'I have no idea,' she admitted.

'He didn't do it, Nancy. I'm not guessing.'

Goodpaster frowned. 'You know something about this case that I don't. Now let's stop fooling around. What is it?'

'I know that the woman in the car murdered Trunh. She threw the gun away in a trash can. Quintana was foraging there and he found it.'

'And there's more than that. I can tell.'

After a few moments, Warren said, 'I know who the woman is. She's admitted it to me. '

'My God! Then stop playing games! Who is it?'

'I can't tell you—it falls under privilege.' He smiled briefly, exhausted. 'And now let's wrap up *Quintana*. You're chief prosecutor in this court. Will the state drop charges?'

Goodpaster sighed. 'I guess we have no choice.' With her sleeve she wiped a light sheen of sweat from her forehead. 'This could have been my worst nightmare come true. That jury could have given your client the needle. I was sure he was guilty.'

'Don't feel too badly. For a long time, so was I.'

Goodpaster laid a slim hand on his shoulder. 'I want to tell you something, Warren. You are a heck of a lawyer. I never saw anyone fight so hard for a client. And I never saw anyone stand up to Her Worship the way you did. You made my week. My year. You must feel awfully good.'

'I do,' Warren admitted, 'but I'm damn tired.' He suddenly felt he might cry. He had to turn away.

BACK IN JUDGE PARKER'S COURTROOM, Goodpaster requested a continuance pending a formal quashing of the indictment by the DA's office. 'The state,' she said, 'is also willing to accept defence counsel's motion for bail on defendant's personal recognisance bond, if the defence so moves.'

'Defence so moves,' Warren said.

'Granted,' said the judge, shaking her head in near disbelief. She rapped her gavel. 'And will y'all go now, so I can dismiss this jury and get on with my agenda?'

Warren walked over to Hector Quintana. 'You can go.'

'Go where?' Hector said.

'Anywhere you like. It's all over! You're free.'

Hector murmured some phrases in Spanish, and then tears glittered in his eyes. He hugged his lawyer fiercely. 'Thank you,' he said. *'Dios te pagará.'*

God will reward you.

Warren couldn't remember ever having been so glad. He laughed and hugged and pummelled his client at the same time.

'I have no money,' Hector said when they had recovered enough to deal with practical matters. 'Where should I go?'

'Don't worry about money,' Warren said. 'Tomorrow I'll give you the money to get back to Mexico or to stay here, whatever you like. But do me a favour and come along with me now. I have something to do. Something that can't wait.'

'I OWE YOU ONE,' Warren said, 'and I'm here to pay. But first you have to indulge me and answer a few questions.'

Bob Altschuler reclined in a swivel chair in his spacious sixth-floor office in the district attorney's building. Hector Quintana was waiting outside in an anteroom.

Altschuler nodded coolly. 'Go ahead.'

'There was a murder in the mission about four or five nights ago,' Warren said. 'A bum, shot to death in the toilet. As far as I know, no one's been indicted. I don't represent anyone involved, and you have my word that I won't in the future. But I think I know who did it. Before I tell you, I need a look at the offence report. Or else I need to talk to whoever's handling it at Homicide.'

For a moment or two Altschuler fixed him with an astute dark look. Then he reached for his telephone. Ten minutes later Sergeant Hollis Thiel was sitting in the French provincial chair next to Warren, hands resting on the paunch under his brown suit.

'Tell me what happened,' Warren said.

Thiel glanced over at Altschuler.

'Tell him,' Altschuler said.

'It's a real zoo over at the mission,' Thiel said. 'Guys come in and out all night. Around four o'clock this guy goes into the toilet. His name is Jerry Mahoney, guy about thirty-five. He's at the urinal when another guy walks in, looks him up and down. Other guy whips out a piece, puts two bullets in the unsuspecting slob, then beats it. Mahoney's dead by the time the ambulance arrives.'

'What was he wearing when he was killed?' Warren asked.

Thiel checked his notes. 'Green cotton sweater, white button-down shirt, no tie, grey pants, brown shoes with holes in both soles. A classy bum.'

'And there were witnesses?' Warren said.

'Yeah. Two bums.' Thiel looked at his notes again. 'One dude named Fred Polson, one named Raul Fernandez.'

'They give you a description of the killer?'

'Yeah, but they don't know him. Never saw him before.'

'Let me guess,' Warren said. 'About thirty years old. Fair hair. Muscles. Wore a black T-shirt. Tattoos on both arms. One's a dragon, the other says "Rosie".'

The new boyfriend did the dirty work now. Johnnie Faye had been in court the day that Siva Singh testified to a man having probably witnessed the murder. A bum with a laundry ticket for a green sweater and a grey suit. The dirty work needed to be done.

Thiel's eyes narrowed to slits. Rustling his papers, he glanced up at Altschuler, who nodded his approval. Thiel looked back at Warren.

'Close, counsellor. One tattoo on one arm is what they saw. Polson says the guy was about thirty-two. He wore a hat so they couldn't see his hair. Black T-shirt is correct.'

'And you found cartridges,' Warren said, 'behind and to the right. A ·45 ejects behind and to the right.'

'I didn't say it was a ·45,' Thiel said. 'But it was.'

'Polson and Fernandez still around?'

'They're around.'

'Why don't you take them to visit a few nightclubs this evening?' Warren said. He handed Thiel a slip of yellow paper torn from a legal pad. 'Here's a list of clubs. Tear it up before I leave this office. Look very carefully in the third one on the list. If you find the guy you're looking for, you have cause to search the premises. Bob will review the transcript of *Boudreau*—my direct examination of the defendant—and tell you where to look. The ·45 may be there, or it may not. But the guy you find will know where it is, and he'll know who gave it to him and told him to ice a man in a green sweater and white button-down shirt. He's tough, but if you offer him the right deal for the right name, you're home free.'

Warren turned to Bob Altschuler. 'I just tried a case in the 299th. Interesting case. You'd like it. Pay the court reporter to transcribe the trial. Pay attention to two prosecution witnesses—Mai Thi Trunh and Siva Singh—and one defence witness—James Thurgood Dandy. You read carefully, they'll tell you why Mahoney was wearing a green sweater and grey pants.'

'Since you know so much,' Altschuler asked, 'why don't you just lay it all out instead of making me jump through hoops?'

'Because this way,' Warren said, 'you can leave me out of it. I'm not a witness. I'm not a source. Can you live with that?'

'Ah well.' Altschuler smiled gently. 'If things work out—why not?'

THAT EVENING WARREN dipped into his wallet and said goodbye to Pedro and Armando and Jim Dandy. He settled Hector Quintana, his new guest, onto the living-room couch at Ravendale. After he'd showered, run with Oobie, and made sure Hector had everything he needed, he drove to Maria Hahn's house. He had called her earlier to set the hour.

Maria's son, Randy, was home from Austin. When Randy had eaten and rinsed his dishes, Maria sent him into his room to watch the ball game on television. She then curled into an easy chair, tucking her long legs beneath her skirt. Her usually cheerful blue eyes were melancholy.

'How are you?' Maria asked tonelessly.

'I won two cases in two days. I feel great. But I didn't like bumping into you that way, outside the courtroom.'

'So what happened with your wife?'

Warren told her everything. It took a while.

'And what will you do?'

'I don't know,' he said.

Maria bit her lip. 'I'm not happy about it, but I guess I understand. We never made any promises to each other. No declarations of love.'

'Listen, I didn't come here to say goodbye. I came here to tell you I have a problem. I want to keep things clear. I don't want to hide anything.'

'Are you moving back in with her?'

'That is exactly what I am not doing. And I promise you, for whatever it's worth, I won't play games. If I come back here, I'll be a free man.' He paused at the door, turning. 'You know something? You saved my sanity. You're a loyal friend.'

'I'm good at that,' she said curtly. 'See you around.'

He went out of the front door to his car, got in, and shut his eyes for a long minute. Then drove back to Ravendale.

ON MONDAY, Warren put Hector on a bus for McAllen, on the border, with the fare to El Palmito, and something more to tide him over until he found work. Hector thanked him quietly. 'You will come visit me one day?'

'Maybe,' Warren said, Mexican style. 'Who knows?'

Hector smiled at that.

'Don't come back,' he said to Hector at the bus station. 'Poor is not good, but I don't think this is better.'

DURING THE EARLY PART OF THE WEEK Warren signed on three new clients. On Friday morning he called Charm at the station and said, 'Would you like to meet?'

She invited him to the house on Sunday. He mowed the lawn while Oobie ran on the grass, fetching a tennis ball that Charm threw. Charm cooked pancakes. After brunch, she said, 'There's something I haven't told you.'

'And what might that be?'

'That agent I hired? He got me the job in Boston. I said yes.'

'Well, that's good, Charm,' Warren said easily, although he knew he had cause to be irked. 'That's what you want. When do you start?'

'Right after Labor Day. Only—I don't know how you feel about it.'

'I feel,' he said, 'that it's dead right for you. If you mean do I feel like starting a law practice in Boston, or commuting to Boston for the occasional weekend in order to sustain a marriage, the answer is no.'

'Are you angry?'

'No. Things will work out. You'll see.' He was relieved. He was surprised by the feeling and kept it to himself.

ON MONDAY MORNING, when he stopped by Bob Altschuler's office to discuss a case, Altschuler shut the door, grinned and said, 'I have news for you. Off the record?'

'Naturally.'

'I read *Quintana*. You did a great job. We picked up a guy named Frank Sawyer last week at Ecstasy—positive ID by the two witnesses that he was the one burned this bum Jerry Mahoney. Couldn't find any weapon, but Thiel and Douglas sweated him. Finally Sawyer's lawyer says, What kind of a deal can we cut?" To make a long story short, we cut the deal and Sawyer says: "This woman made me do it, see? She's my drug connection, and she knew some things about me that she threatened to tell to the law if I didn't play ball. She sends me down to the mission to find some guy in a green sweater and grey suit, some guy that might have ID'd her when she offed a Vietnamese guy. So I did it. I didn't want to, but I had to. I threw the gun away in Buffalo Bayou, but I can show y'all where. And it's her gun." '

Altschuler rubbed his big hands together vigorously. 'So we got the underwater boys and they found the gun. An ivory-handled Colt ·45. And it's hers, registered and all. Like she said under oath: "It's in my desk, and I'm the only one who has a key." We arrested her on Saturday night. She cursed me like I was Satan come up from the pit. You would have loved it.'

'I love it now, Bob. What kind of a deal did you make with Sawyer?'

'Thirty-five years. He's out in twelve. I'm meeting her new lawyer in half an hour. He wants to cut a deal too, but he can kiss my rosy-red bunions. If I can tie this one into Trunh, that's multiple murder—it becomes a capital. Whichever way, I'll take this case to a jury, and if she doesn't get the needle, she'll do life without parole.'

Altschuler extended his hand. Warren shook it.

WHEN HE HAD FINISHED his business with Altschuler, Warren hurried through the heat to the 342nd District Court, arriving a few minutes after noon. In the cool well of the empty courtroom Maria Hahn sat at the court reporter's table, back turned to the door. She was alone in the room, gathering up papers, and Warren sensed she was about to rise and leave. Moving catlike with some speed, he bent behind her chair, put his cheek next to hers above the pulse of her white neck, took a quick breath to try to smother the aberrant beat of his heart, and said, 'I have a riddle for you.'

She didn't turn her head. Quietly she reminded him, 'You said no games. And you made me a promise.'

'I'm well aware of that,' Warren said. 'Here's the riddle. What is a criminal lawyer?'

'I know that one. *Redundant*. I've got a better one: why are they starting to use lawyers instead of white rats in laboratory experiments?'

'Tell me the answer this evening at dinner . . . if you're free. And I'll tell you everything that's happened to me.'

Maria raised an eyebrow. 'Everything?'

'Yes.'

Late that night, after he had unburdened, he said, 'So what's the answer?'

Maria softly sighed. Leading him to her bedroom, bending close as if offering a rare confidence, she said, 'Because there are more lawyers than white rats. If you have any sense, you don't get personally attached to lawyers. But mostly,' she added, with a smile he would treasure, 'because there are some things that white rats just won't do.'

CLIFFORD IRVING

When Clifford Irving was growing up on New York City's Upper West Side, Texas seemed like the outer limits of the universe—a dangerous, rough-and-ready frontier. Even when he was old enough to hitchhike out West, his cautious, urban mother told him, 'Don't go to Texas!' And, over the years, except for crossing the border a few times, he never did.

That is, until the mid-1980s when the author began writing his best-selling book *Daddy's Girl*, about a notorious Houston murder case. 'With some trepidation,' he says, he set out to research and write his nonfiction work there. But, to his delight, he discovered that Texas was neither frightening nor, as he had presumed, 'provincial'. He was so smitten, in fact, that he couldn't resist setting his next book in Houston as well. So *Trial* was born, with the flavour of Texas permeating every page. 'I love it in Texas. I like its frontier spirit,' Clifford Irving says. 'There's an openness that you don't find in most other parts of the country. And Texans are friendly—extremely friendly.'

Home base for Irving, now, is San Miguel de Allende, a town high in Mexico's central mountains. He settled there to resume his writing career after creating a literary sensation, and scandal, during the 1970s. It was then that Irving wrote a book purporting to be the autobiography of Howard Hughes, based on interviews with the famous millionaire recluse. But Hughes disavowed the book and it was never published. Clifford Irving eventually admitted the whole affair was indeed a hoax—and wrote a book about that too!

Always intrigued with the law, Irving is now writing a novel that features yet another twist in the judicial system, this time in Florida. He and his wife, writer Maureen Earl, enjoy the travel that his research requires, but they also like taking trips 'just to enjoy the planet'.

THE FLIGHT

OF FLAMINGO

by Elizabeth Darrell

ILLUSTRATED BY GRAHAM COTON

When Kit Anson agrees to pilot *Flamingo*, a spectacular new flying boat, on her proving flight from England to Mombasa, he is brought face to face with a past that he would rather forget.

Flamingo is the latest design from the workshops of Kirkland Marine Aviation, the company founded by the powerful Sir Hector Kirkland, who adopted Kit when he was only a youth, and offered him a glittering future.

Unfortunately it was a promise which turned sour when Kit was bold enough to expose deceit and treachery behind the respectable façade of the Kirklands' proud name . . .

A riveting story of courage, love and ambition, spanning the great years of aviation history.

1

The Kirkland launch glided through the stillness of a dreamy English summer afternoon towards Sheenmouth Abbey, her gleaming white bows breaking reflections of willow-lined banks and pale, heat-hazed sky into shimmering images which spread in ever-widening circles. Donald Kirkland and his friends were now as dreamy as the atmosphere. They had been upriver to an island owned by their host's father, where they had picnicked, splashed in the shallows, and danced to music from an ancient gramophone while sipping cocktails. It was 1929 and life was there to be lived to the hilt.

Leone Kirkland was not finding it easy to emulate them, as she lay back against the cushions gazing at Guy Kingsford who was, in turn, gazing at Mitzi Fennemore. The ache of loneliness tightened her throat. Today had been a failure. Although several of Donald's friends had made faint attempts to acknowledge the presence of a thirteen-year-old girl, the blond, brooding embryo poet had totally ignored her. Being ignored during school holidays was no new sensation to Leone, it was simply more painful, in this instance. Guy was neither a business giant nor an aviation genius such as her father invited to the ancient abbey he had converted into the Kirkland residence, and he was different from the male friends Donald frequently brought here during university vacations. She had had great hopes of finding a soul mate in this silent young man.

Twisting away to hang over the side of the boat, and sighing heavily,

Leone realised her attempt to drown her misery in the potent cocktails had failed as signally as her efforts to find a companion of her own. Being the only girl in a stronghold of self-absorbed males was unbearably lonely; being ignored by every one of them made her long for Switzerland and the new term.

When the launch slid alongside the private jetty, old Walter, who had been their boatman for years, came forward to hold the vessel steady while they all scrambled ashore. Leone was the last to leave. In a state Donald would term 'half-cut', she somehow managed to walk the jetty without falling into the water, then began to plod behind the laughing group towards the great monastery high on the bank of the River Sheen near the eastern border of Devon.

Entering the great hall patterned with colour from stained-glass windows, where a branched staircase gave access to the upper galleries, she found the entire group halted just inside the entrance, and heard her father's voice.

'Donald, I'm afraid there's been a tragic accident. I must ask you to leave your friends to amuse themselves for a while. Please excuse us, ladies and gentlemen. My staff will be happy to bring anything you may require, and my son will join you shortly before dinner. Drinks will be served in the baptistry at seven thirty.'

Leone pushed her way through the cluster of guests in time to see her father and Donald heading towards the library at the far end of the hall. What kind of tragic accident had occurred? How did it affect Donald? Although her brother was destined to inherit Kirkland Marine Aviation after working his way through Cambridge and the company's design office, he was not yet allowed a hand in controlling the family organisation which built seaplanes. However, if the tragic accident did not concern the business, why should it affect Donald and not herself? She was as much a Kirkland by birth as he. She set off towards the library. Sir Hector had left the door slightly ajar, and as she peered through the gap, Leone caught a glimpse of someone waiting there: a youth, his face ashen, his clothes cheap and ill-fitting.

Leone gazed at the stranger, fascinated, as Sir Hector explained his presence to Donald. 'Geoffrey Anson met with an accident in the workshops this morning. It seems he had been drinking more heavily than usual, lost his footing and fell into one of the machines. He had no chance, of course. The men are all very shaken by the affair, as you can imagine. I've closed the workshop for today.' Shaking his head, he said heavily, 'What a senseless tragedy! He had been warned several times about drunkenness during working hours, so he knew the risks he was running. As everyone knows, the poor man went downhill fast after his wife left him. I was loath to fire one of the most gifted designers in the country, however, even though his work was suffering.'

'Good God, sir,' exclaimed Donald. 'Surely we are safeguarded against industrial accidents.'

'For those who are sober, yes,' came the sharp reply. 'Anson was not in command of himself, so there'll be no obligation for company compensation. Even so, the man had been with us a long time, which leaves me with some sense of obligation, despite the circumstances.' He indicated the white-faced boy. 'This is Kit Anson, Donald. His father's sudden death has saddled him with debts he can never repay. It has also left him alone in the world. A few minutes ago, I offered him a home here, and the opportunity to continue his engineering studies at the company's expense.'

Shaken, Donald stammered, 'Are you saying you've . . . *adopted* him?'

'Not officially, but I trust he'll find it possible to feel like one of the family before long. We'll soon get him polished up to meet Kirkland standards.'

Leone slid back to lean against the stone wall, heart thudding, as the three came from the library, and headed for the stairs. Her father had a reassuring hand on Donald's shoulder. Kit Anson walked behind them.

'I've instructed Maitland to install Kit in the bell-tower suite,' Sir Hector was saying. 'He brought a few things with him, but Maitland has the rest in hand. You'll have to find him a dinner jacket and stiff shirts until he's properly kitted out.' Reaching the foot of the stairs, they all halted. 'There'll have to be an inquest, of course. It'll be no more than a formality and, for young Anson's sake, we'll ensure the affair is kept private. No point in raking up Anson's past history.' He turned away. 'Well, take him up and settle him in, my boy. I'll be studying Willard's latest report, so won't be dining with you. Introduce young Anson to your friends.'

Donald asked stonily, 'What do I introduce him as?'

'Tell them . . .' Sir Hector let out a rich laugh. 'Tell them to take a good look at him as he is now because they won't recognise him in three years' time. He might well be our leading designer one day, if he's inherited his father's brilliance . . . and if he takes full advantage of his new status.'

Leone waited until they had all vanished from sight, then made her way to her rooms. She sprawled on the window seat to gaze at the bell tower rising at the far end of the front façade. Sir Hector Kirkland was known as a ruthless, unforgiving man, who would tolerate neither weaklings nor tricksters. Why, then, had he taken in the penniless son of an employee who had often been warned about his drinking and whose work had suffered because of it?

She decided on action. Still in her crumpled shorts and sun top, she ran on bare feet along the upper gallery to the bell tower. It did not occur to her to knock on the door. Pushing it open, she climbed the six spiral steps to the set of guest rooms. The suite was on three levels, with a marble bath in the smallest of the circular chambers, just beneath the arch containing the original monastery bell. The ingenuity of the modernisation seemed to have overwhelmed the sturdy figure standing by a sconced window set in the curving stone wall. He was staring from it like a resigned prisoner, looking totally out of place.

'Don't you like it here?' Leone asked.

He spun round, startled, and she saw that his square face was still ashen.

'This is the original tower, you know,' she continued. 'The huge cast-iron bell is up there directly above where we're standing. The monks used to summon everyone to vespers, or whatever it was they had. It was also rung as a warning of fire or flood or any kind of disaster.'

After several moments he said, 'You must be Miss Kirkland. My father said there was a daughter as well as a son.'

His voice, surprisingly deep, contained a strong Devonshire accent.

'I'm sorry about your father,' she offered. 'It must be terrible for you.'

When he merely nodded, she flopped onto one of the chairs covered in ruby velvet and drew up her knees to study him over the top of them. 'My mother also died in a tragic accident, you know. I was a baby when it happened, but it means we have something in common, doesn't it? She was drowned when her lover's yacht sank in a storm off the coast of Naples. It caused a frightful scandal.' Hugging her knees tighter, she asked, 'Are you really all alone in the world?'

'My mother's around somewhere, I suppose,' he admitted.

'Doesn't she ever get in touch?' she asked.

He shook his head. 'She married again. Started a new life.'

Fixing him with a stern look, Leone said, '*You're* starting a new life now. Sheenmouth Abbey dates back to fifteen eighty-four and smugglers used to bring contraband goods up the Sheen at night and store them in the grounds. There's a network of tunnels still in existence beneath the building, although Father sealed the entrance when he moved in.'

He appeared unimpressed. 'I've lived in Sheenmouth all my life, so I've heard the yarns. Most of them are nonsense invented by local fishermen to impress summer visitors.'

'No they're not,' she cried furiously. 'The bell in this very tower used to toll the go-ahead for the smugglers waiting further downriver with their cargoes. One of the monks was so filled with remorse after ringing the bell one night, he hanged himself with the rope. Since then, the bell has been known to ring at midnight. It's his ghost.' Undulating her arms very slowly, she uttered an eerie wail. 'Wooooo!'

Too many cocktails were making her behave foolishly. They were also threatening a feeling of nausea. She sat up straight and changed the subject abruptly.

'Are you studying engineering at Cambridge, or at Oxford?'

'Neither.'

'Where do you study, then?'

'At home . . . by correspondence course.'

She gazed at him incredulously. 'You mean you actually send questions and answers back and forth by *post*?'

He stiffened. 'How you give the answers to their questions is immaterial. So long as you get them right, you eventually qualify.'

'You'll have to do something more impressive than that if you're going to be one of us. Father will insist. You do realise that everything about you will have to change from now on?' She studied him closely. Tall and chunky, in greasy, unpressed grey flannels and a faded blue shirt with ragged cuffs, he was as different from Donald as a stray mongrel from a pedigree hound.

'Just why have you been taken in by the grand Sir Hector Kirkland?' she asked curiously.

'For my father's sake, I suppose.'

'Rot,' she declared, getting to her feet so suddenly the room began to spin. 'He has never done anything for someone else's sake in his life. There's a deep mystery behind all this, and I'm going to get to the bottom of it. *I am,*' she emphasised, as she realised that her stomach was about to reject the cocktails, and headed for the door. 'I fully intend to befriend you, Kit Anson, because no one else in this house will. After all,' she reasoned, over her shoulder, 'we're going to be like brother and sister, aren't we?'

'I shouldn't think so,' came his low comment, as she fled for her room.

BY DINNER TIME Leone was feeling fine again. After lying on her bed for an hour making elaborate plans, she dressed in a deep cream layered chiffon dress with a frilled bodice, and sallied downstairs eager for action. As the only guests were Donald's, she was at liberty to dine with them in the refectory, now thickly carpeted and hung with silk-embroidered tapestries. Above the long oaken table hung five circular flambeaux, with wall sconces to match.

The houseguests had gathered in the adjacent octagonal room, to stand around drinking sherry or to sit on scattered church pews lavishly padded and covered in dull green and gold brocade. None made any secret of their curiosity towards the dark young man standing self-consciously beside Donald, the sleeves of his borrowed dinner jacket well down over his square, workmanlike hands.

Leone paused on the threshold, comparing her new brother with the existing one. Donald was the taller by some inches, and as fair as the other was swarthy. She did not know her brother well. A six-year age gap separated them. Donald was easy-going, fond of girls, gins and 'gee-gees', like most of his contemporaries, and confident of his future. Beyond that, Leone knew little of him.

She walked straight up to the unhappy Kit Anson, determined to befriend him. He certainly looked in need of a friend right now.

'Hello, Kit,' she greeted warmly. 'Have you been introduced all round?'

'Yes, but I can't remember anyone's name,' he murmured, frowning.

'Heavens, who can? They call each other "old thing" or "sweetie" or "honeybun". Don't they, Donald?' she asked her brother.

'Mmm,' he agreed absently, his gaze following the advance of Maitland Jarvis, their father's personal assistant. 'Wonder what old Maiters wants.'

The sandy-haired man came up to address Kit in clipped tones. 'Sir Hector would like to see you in his study. Dr Gibbs has the death certificate, and would like to discuss it. It won't take more than a few minutes, Mr Anson.'

Fully confident that his polite request would be seen as a command, the man turned away. Kit hesitated as he looked for somewhere to put his full glass. Leone took it from him, with a sympathetic smile.

When Kit had gone, Leone turned to Donald. 'Isn't it a bit much to expect him to socialise tonight? His father was killed only twelve hours ago.'

Her brother's pale blue eyes regarded her shrewdly. 'Fat lot he'd care. I thought everyone knew there was no love lost between them.'

'Everyone save me. I've never even *heard* of the Ansons.'

'Why should you have? They didn't concern you in any way.'

'They do now. He's suddenly become my brother.'

A strained smile crossed Donald's attractive features. 'Oh, grow up, Leone! You don't have to treat him as one of the family, you idiot.' He dragged her out of earshot of the others. Halting in an alcove, he said, 'This doesn't really concern you. It's a pretty sordid history.'

'Tell, just the same,' she urged.

'I knew old man Anson, of course, but I'd never met the son. Geoffrey Anson was loaned to the company just before the end of the war, when we won the contract to build our first seaplanes for the RAF. He stayed with us when peace came, and became our senior designer. But success went to his head and he began gambling, then drinking when luck wasn't running his way. No one was surprised when Daisy Anson went off with an artist who was working in Sheenmouth one summer. She eventually divorced Anson and the old boy went downhill fast.'

A loud whoop of laughter from a nearby group of his friends took Donald's attention, and he showed every sign of moving off to join them.

Leone grabbed his arm quickly. 'Come on, finish the story. You suggested just now that Kit wouldn't care about his father's death, because they hated each other. Why?'

Donald sighed in a long-suffering manner. 'When Daisy Anson left, they were living in a comfortable place up on the cliffs at East Sheenmouth, but Geoffrey soon owed so much he was forced to sell it. Good money went after bad, until the pair were even forced to leave the cheap rooms they then occupied after old Anson engaged in a drunken brawl with the landlady's husband. Eventually he tried to do himself in.'

'Heavens!' cried Leone, aghast. 'How?'

'Walked into the sea one dark night. Unluckily for him, some local fishermen spotted him and hauled him out.'

'Poor Kit!'

'Poor Kit, be damned! When the old salts turned up at the shack the Ansons then called home, there was the deuce of a row between the half-drowned father and his son. The story goes the young blighter had packed his bag and was on the point of leaving. When they turned up with old Anson, he was furious. He had to abandon his hopes of signing on at the

College of Engineering in Exeter, and take a job instead.'

'So where does Father come into the affair?'

Donald's roving gaze returned to focus on her face. 'In view of the long-standing association Kirkland's had had with old Anson, Father offered the pair, rent free, that disused old boathouse down on our north boundary. It has living quarters above it. In my opinion, it was a jolly decent gesture in addition to giving Kit a job in the workshop. In return, old Anson walked the straight and narrow for a while, turning in some first-rate work on a new design. As a result of generous advice from Father on some prudent investments, the Ansons were gradually able to pay off what they owed. Kit wasn't in the least grateful, however. There are stories galore of heated arguments at the old boathouse between the pair. They hated each other all right. Chaps in the design office reckon it was their enmity which drove the old chap back to the bottle.' He gave a cold laugh. 'Can't really pin anything on Kit regarding the affair this morning, because the blighter was late for work and therefore not in the machine shop at the time. If he possesses any finer qualities at all, which I doubt, he ought to be feeling pretty sick about it. He's basically to blame for Anson's death.'

'That's a terrible thing to say,' cried Leone. 'If it's true, why has Father brought him here to live, and why is Maitland ordering clothes and things which will turn him into someone resembling a Kirkland?'

Donald shrugged. 'I suppose Father feels it's the least he can do for a man who had a rough deal from life.'

'Phoo,' she declared. 'No one *forced* Kit's father to start drinking and gambling. He had only himself to blame for driving his wife away and turning his son against him. Life didn't hand him a rough deal: he dealt the cards himself. Anyway, if Kit has been working at Kirkland's, how is it you've never come across him before?'

'He's only a greaser in the workshop. I have no reason to deal with people like that.'

She frowned. 'You'll have to now, won't you? There's more behind this than Father deciding to be kind. If I were in your place, I'd be very keen to find out what it is. Kit may not be offered the Kirkland name but, for some strange reason, it looks certain he's going to be offered everything that goes with it. Where will that leave you, Donald?'

KIT DID NOT RETURN. After the meal Leone slipped away unnoticed and made straight for the bell tower. Her quarry was not in his sitting room, so she climbed the spiral steps to the bedroom. He was not there, either. In the open wardrobe hung the borrowed dinner suit. Kit's own clothes were nowhere to be seen. Leone might have believed he had run away if it had not been for two cheap suitcases beside the chest of drawers, and a worn leather case containing a draughtsman's instruments.

Up in the circular bathroom she found a cheap shaving brush and razor standing defiantly beside the boxed set from Harrods provided for the use of guests. Hanging alongside the maroon bathrobe was a navy-blue plaid dressing gown with a frayed cord trailing from one of its loops. Leone stared at it. He must have had it for years! Maitland would soon instruct Coombes, the visitors' valet, to dispose of *that*.

Returning to the bedroom, Leone sat on the floor to investigate the two suitcases. The first was filled with textbooks, notes and technical drawings, and an old photograph album. The second suitcase contained clothes. They were all fairly dreadful. Holding up a pair of quite astonishing underpants, Leone sighed. Coombes would faint with shock at the sight of them.

Beneath the folded clothes she came upon a framed photograph of a seaplane, and she recognised the background of hangars and slipways owned by Kirkland's. It was a graceful little machine with high wings, and floats almost as long as the aircraft. Even she had heard of *Diadem*, the company's most famous design. A competitor in the Schneider Trophy Race had blamed his failure to win on the fact that his team had not been flying the sleek little seaplane produced by Kirkland Marine Aviation. To prove his point, the pilot had flown *Diadem* over the designated course on the following day, exceeding the speeds claimed by the trophy winner. The stunt had caused worldwide publicity for Kirkland's. But it was not thoughts of that which occupied Leone as she stared at the framed picture. Inserted into the corner of the frame was a slip of paper. Written on it in a youthful hand was: *Dad's finest design*. So Geoffrey Anson had created *Diadem*! That slip of paper proudly stating the fact did not fit in with the description of a boy who hated his father enough to be glad he was dead. What was the truth about Kit Anson?

LEONE RUSHED DOWNSTAIRS for breakfast next morning, in the hope that Kit would be there for her to question. She was delighted to see his solitary figure at the octagonal table. He got to his feet as she entered, and all she could think of was his terrible underpants. His top clothes were little better: a crumpled grey shirt, grey flannels and a striped pullover with ribbing that had been stretched into flutes. He was still very pale.

Noticing his empty plate, she asked kindly, 'Don't you want any breakfast? I'm *starving*.'

'They brought me some tea, but haven't asked if I want anything else,' he said. 'I wouldn't mind something to eat.'

'Well, have something, silly,' she cried, crossing to the sideboard. Lifting lids she recited, 'Scrambled eggs, mushrooms, tomatoes with bacon, kedgeree, poached haddock . . . oh, and there's porridge to start with.'

He flushed. 'I didn't realise.'

'Don't expect to be waited on for breakfast,' she informed him. 'We all come down when and if we feel like it. Come on! Take what you want.'

He selected porridge, then eggs, bacon and tomatoes.

Watching him attack it hungrily, Leone sighed. For someone who was extremely clever at engineering, he was awfully slow in other areas.

'Where did you go last night?' she asked.

'I went home. Dr Gibbs needed certain documents . . . for the inquest.'

'Heavens, I'd forgotten that. How awful for you!'

'Sir Hector says I won't have to attend. It'll be no more than a formality, apparently, and his legal people will handle it.'

'They always do,' she informed him. 'What are your plans for today?'

'I don't know. I intended to go to work, as usual, but your father told me I'm not to do that any longer. Mr Jarvis is going to arrange for me to attend the engineering college when the new term begins.'

'You must stop calling him Mr Jarvis. Only the servants do that. There's a choice between "Maitland" or "Old Maiters", as Donald calls him. If you're going to be one of us, you'll have to forget you were ever a greaser.'

When he made no comment, she tried another tack. 'Would you like to come riding with me when we've finished eating?'

Dark eyes regarded her warily. 'I haven't had much experience.'

'What does that mean?'

'I've only ridden the Sheenmouth donkeys.'

Her burst of laughter coincided with a forkful of scrambled eggs as she spluttered, 'You really are funny.'

'It wasn't meant to be a joke,' he said stiffly. 'I've fed and exercised them every evening for three winters. It paid for my textbooks.'

'You buy your own textbooks?' she exclaimed, sobering slightly. 'Heavens, how quaint! I don't. Heiterman's provides everything.'

'There's a great difference between your fancy high-class Swiss school and a correspondence course, you know.'

Resenting his preaching tone, she fired up swiftly. 'Congratulations on realising *that*, at least. It's a pity you're not so sharp about everything else, Kit Anson. If I hadn't come down to breakfast, you'd still be sitting there like a bumpkin waiting to be served.'

His mouth tightened in anger. 'Now, look here, you little . . .'

His outburst was halted by the entry of Maitland Jarvis. He nodded a brisk greeting to Leone, then addressed Kit. 'The fitter from Sir Hector's tailor has arrived with samples of cloth. He wishes to measure you, Mr Anson. A manicurist is also waiting to attend to your hands.'

'My hands,' he echoed hoarsely. 'What's wrong with them?'

Maitland gave his irrefutable reply to all such awkward questions. 'Sir Hector has requested it.'

He turned away and Kit got to his feet immediately, leaving his breakfast on the table. Next minute, Leone was alone in the room. She sighed heavily. He had trotted off obediently, like a dog at Maitland's heels.

'Oh, *blast*,' she cried softly. 'He's going to be like everyone else. *Sir Hector has requested it*. So they go off with Maitland and don't reappear for the rest of the day. I thought he was going to be interesting . . . and *company*.'

Within hours he had been absorbed into the brotherhood manipulated by Sir Hector, whose daughter remained as invisible to his eyes as ever.

2

As Meader turned the car at the junction to Magnum Pomeroy, Leone reflected that nothing appeared to have changed much during the three years since she had last been in Devon. The seven-mile drive from Axminster took her past familiar landmarks: villages, churches, open downland white with grazing sheep, to climb eventually to the red cliffs above Sheenmouth sands bordering the waters of Lyme Bay.

At sixteen, Leone was now one of the senior girls at Heiterman's and life had grown very enjoyable among her multinational friends. She had spent school holidays in Athens, Corsica, Florence, Paris, Monte Carlo, and even one exciting Christmas in Tunis. Maitland had always cabled her father's permission to stay with this succession of wealthy families, and she had never failed to express her thanks in her monthly letter home. Whether or not Sir Hector Kirkland bothered to read her letters, she had no idea. Replies were rare, and then couched in unmistakably 'Jarvisonian' terms. Cards and presents arrived on the appropriate occasions, almost always from an exclusive Swiss store. Her father fulfilled his paternal role, albeit through a third party. Between herself and Donald there had been no communication since that summer of 1929, when the curious 'adoption' of Kit Anson had taken place.

Whatever the reason behind her father's surprising move, he was now reaping rich rewards. Some of her schoolfellows had begun sighing over photographs in society magazines of a dashing young British aviator, fast making a name for himself in speed flying. Doubting that the 'Keet Ansong' the girls adored could possibly be the one she knew, Leone had studied the pictures closely, trying to identify the laughing young man in a leather flying helmet with the white-faced boy she could now hardly recall. Yet the text had claimed him to be the test pilot for Kirkland Marine Aviation, who would soon make his all-out attempt at the world speed record. He would fly the exciting new seaplane *Aphrodite* designed by Donald Kirkland, son of the man who owned the company pushing to rival the top manufacturers.

Curiosity had driven her home. The late May sunshine was striking the south side of the building with its bell tower in the eastern corner when Meader drove up to the massive studded door. Leone studied her home with surprise. Had it always looked this impressive and beautiful? As the soft breeze ruffled her hair and shifted the calf-length fluted skirt against her legs, she caught herself sighing with unexpected pleasure.

Clunes and Meredith came from the house to greet her, then take from Meader the vast number of leather trunks and bandboxes stacked atop and behind the car. On being informed that Sir Hector, Mr Kirkland and Mr Anson were all at the works, which disappointed but did not surprise her, Leone told Clunes that she would have a tray of tea in her sitting room, and set off up the stairs.

After taking a shower and dressing in a blue linen dress, she drank her tea. The four tiny sandwiches and the dainty fingers of honey cake remained on the plate as she finally admitted to herself her true reason for coming home. Unable to resist the impulse, she made her way to the bell tower. Presumably, he still occupied the tiered circular rooms. As she climbed the six spiral steps to the sitting room, a wave of apprehension swept through her. Kit Anson had been no more than a gauche white-faced youth of nineteen. Who was this man who had apparently become, within three short years, more a member of her family than she?

He was certainly not a tidy person. Open textbooks, charts, diagrams, newspaper clippings, gilt-edged invitations, a great many photographs of aircraft, and several grease-smeared logbooks all jumbled together to give the impression that the occupant was totally unorganised.

Then she spotted the framed photograph and moved to pick it up. Recollection of him flooded back at the sight of *Diadem* and the slip of paper in the corner of the frame. *Dad's finest design.*

'Well, you've got more nerve than the rest, I'll say that for you,' pronounced a voice containing a faint Devonshire accent, making her swing round swiftly. 'I don't know how the hell you slipped in past the servants without being seen, but I promise you they'll certainly see you on your way out, young lady,' he continued forcefully, advancing to pluck the photograph of *Diadem* from her hand. 'Come on, out you go!'

Next minute, he seized her by the collar of her dress and the seat of her pants to frog-march her across the room then down the steps to the door. Leone found herself halfway along the upper gallery before it occurred to her to struggle. It did no good. He had too firm a hold of her in strategic places. Whether or not he would actually toss her bodily from the premises she had no chance to discover, for Meredith appeared.

'Black marks all round,' her captor told him sternly. 'How is it none of you spotted this little miss sneaking in?'

'But . . . that's Miss Kirkland, sir,' announced Meredith faintly.

'Never mind who she is,' came the firm directive. He halted momentarily. 'Who did you say she is?'

'Sir Hector's daughter, Mr Anson. I understood you to be acquainted with the news of her expected arrival today,' Meredith added.

Loosing his hold on the back of her skirt, Kit tugged at Leone's collar until she was facing him, saying to the servant as he scrutinised Leone closely, 'Are you playing straight with me, Meredith? She hasn't bribed you to say she's Leone Kirkland?'

'Certainly not, sir.'

'If you value your toes enough to prevent their being stamped on, you'll quickly let me go,' said Leone, coming to terms with the situation at last.

As the servant moved off, Kit began to chuckle. 'Be fair. You've changed rather a lot.'

'So have you. You were a stray mongrel.' Laughter was starting to bubble in her own voice, as she said, 'I think I'm entitled to know why I was about to be thrown out of my own house.'

He nodded, dark eyes lively with mirth. 'You are, indeed.' He led her back along the gallery. 'Aviation is a hazardous profession, Miss Kirkland. Although I'm not afraid of a challenge, a chap can be hugged almost to death by squealing girls and kissed practically unconscious by those determined to have their pictures in the newspapers. You wouldn't believe the tricks they employ. One even tried to post herself to me in a giant parcel. So when I walked into my rooms just now and found a neat little blonde making herself at home, what was I to think?' Reaching the bell tower, he ushered her through the door. 'Have I succeeded in making you understand my reaction?'

'You've succeeded in making me think you're disgustingly conceited.'

He grinned. 'So girls are constantly telling me.'

Inviting her to sit down he shrugged off his Harris tweed jacket, then dropped onto a chair as he tugged his green silk cravat loose and tossed it onto a pile of books. Watching him, Leone was filled with fascination. His tanned face was vivid with eagerness for life. Taller and even more muscular than before, Kit had somehow retained an intriguing hint of his origins, yet there was an aggressiveness about him which suggested that anger could rise as swiftly as laughter.

'I can't believe that you and the boy I recall are the same person,' she murmured. 'Tell me what happened.'

Leaning back with one leg resting across the other knee, he said, 'When those summer holidays ended, that boy was sent to an engineering college for the final year of studies. By the time he had gained his qualifications, he had discovered the true love of his life. His benefactor had provided him with funds to afford flying lessons, and when he joined Kirkland's there was just one job he wanted. Taking matters into his own hands, he defied orders and took up the company seaplane to demonstrate what he could do with it. Despite the fact that he damned near broke his neck for several very risky manoeuvres, the stunt so impressed the great Sir Hector that Kit Anson became his test pilot.' Leaning forward, he spoke with sudden feeling. 'I count myself one of the most fortunate men in the world, and I have finally given up pinching myself to prove I'm not dreaming it all.'

'The European magazines suggest you might soon challenge the world air-speed record,' she said. 'Is there any truth in that?'

His face was alive with pride. 'It's not usual for company pilots to compete in that area but I'm going to have a crack at it, yes.'

'In *Aphrodite*?' she asked.

'Of course! She's a siren of a machine; a temptress who offers paradise to the man who dares give her her head and manages to hold on to his own.'

'My brother designed the seaplane,' she said. 'Does he share your love affair with this combination of wood and metal?'

'Ah, designers are a different breed altogether,' he informed her, lying back in the chair and crossing his legs in the perfectly tailored flannels. 'They are bewitched by line and elevation, by thrust and power ratio; they worship at the shrine of positive and negative Gs, wing curvature and structural equilibrium. But when I break the speed record, it will be as much a triumph for him as for me.'

'What *is* the point in trying, Kit?' she asked. 'There must be a reason other than doing it for the fun of it.'

'Certainly. Attention will be focused on Kirkland Marine Aviation as a contender for inclusion among the real giants such as Hawker's and Supermarine. Sir Hector has been highly successful with his foreign investments during this recession, but the company has been suffering like all other British industrial firms. Kirkland's is his favourite baby, and he wanted a means of pulling it out of the red. This could be it. By making the affair as sensational as possible, Sir Hector will save his company. Orders for the standard *Aphrodite* model should come in from all over the world, Donald will be recognised as one of our most talented designers, and I will hold a world record many men covet. Not bad reasons, are they?'

'No . . . but they're all dependent on you. Suppose you fail?'

'I won't. *Aphrodite* is the fastest thing in the air ever produced. I'll take the record, and your father will feel more than satisfied with the stray mongrel.'

'I'm sorry, I shouldn't have called you that,' she said swiftly.

'It's an apt description. Wait until you've more knowledge of me before you change your opinion,' he warned. 'I can tell you with confidence that Kirkland's has an exciting future ahead. With Donald designing, and me testing, there's no limit to the kind of machine we'll be producing a few years hence. By that time, my dear girl, you'll be one of the most courted women in Europe.'

'I'm already doing quite well in that direction,' she told him smartly, and got to her feet. 'You might have reached perfect understanding with a seaplane, Mr Anson, but I suspect your understanding of women is limited to brute-force tactics.'

She descended the steps with as much dignity as the memory of his hand clutching her panties would allow.

BROTHER AND SISTER MET AGAIN after three years, in the octagonal room adjoining the refectory. They eyed each other in surprise. How alike they were now she had matured: tall, slender, blond, and graceful of limb, blue-eyed with golden skins. There was no doubt of their kinship.

'My word, you look very grown-up, Leone,' said Donald, after studying her mauve chiffon dress.

'So I should. I was sixteen in February.' She smiled. 'I like the new moustache. It suits you, despite making you look older.'

'How's school?' he asked. 'What's brought you home after all this time?'

'Actually, I was driven by curiosity. They're probably rather late, but I wanted to give my hearty congratulations.'

He looked startled. 'Good Lord, who told you?'

'Not you, which was a bit mean, I thought. No, it was in all the magazines, so I guess it's pretty common knowledge everywhere.'

'I don't understand,' he said in plain confusion.

'*Aphrodite*, you chump!' she said laughingly. 'The glossy magazines were full of glamorous pictures of Kit. The whole world must be aware that you've designed this terrific seaplane.'

Confusion was replaced by unease on his fair, handsome face, and he tossed back his sherry in one gulp. 'I thought you were referring to Steph.'

Taken aback, she asked, 'Who's Steph—someone in the design office?'

He made a surprising announcement. 'I shall celebrate my engagement to Stephanie Main at the reception to be held here to celebrate the breaking of the speed record earlier that same day. Maitland has all the arrangements in hand. All we need is the go-ahead from our pilot, who's as temperamental as a bally prima donna when it comes to pinning him down to a date.'

Thrown off-balance by news of another milestone in Donald's life which neither he, nor any other member of this household, had bothered to write and tell her about, Leone began to realise that things had not changed much in her home. She was still very much an outsider, it seemed.

'I'm somewhat out of touch, Donald,' she told him, trying to curb her anger. 'Who is my future sister-in-law?'

'Old man Main is the head of Allied Nordic Banking Corporation. Steph's his granddaughter. Her people run an estate in Northumbria: father's a stockbroker, mother's one of the Stanwell-Turners.'

Leone's eyes widened. 'No wonder Father approves.'

'It cuts both ways,' he said tightly.

'Mmm. Brilliant young designer due to inherit a growing aircraft company, and a converted monastery along with huge foreign investments,' she mused, recalling all Kit had told her this afternoon. 'Yes, I suppose she's doing rather well for herself, too.'

Further words were prevented by the entry of Maitland Jarvis in dinner jacket, bow perfectly tied. It was typical of a man who rarely erred, a man Leone had always distrusted without knowing why.

'Good evening, Miss Kirkland,' he greeted with the usual urbane smile. 'Welcome home.' Turning to Donald, he went on, 'Sir Hector has just received secret confirmation that the Italians plan to put their man Benzini forward in a bid for the record sooner than we expected. *Aphrodite* must be ready in time to beat them to it. He'll want a good reason why we can't go for it before the middle of the month.'

'Kit wants another slight modification to the rudder,' Donald told him.

'In that case, do it, boy. Do it!' said a voice. 'Why are you standing here drinking sherry when you should be working on it?'

Sir Hector Kirkland had a neat but powerful frame which looked impressive in suits cut by a master tailor. His thinning fair hair had turned grey since Leone last saw him, but his strong features wore a look which told those who knew him that he was spoiling for action. 'Maitland, ring the bell. We'll have dinner right away, then you can get Johnson back to the works, Donald, and drive him all night, if necessary.'

'There'll be no need for that, sir,' Kit assured him, arriving at that moment. 'It's only a small mod. An hour or so should be adequate.'

Casting him an assessing glance, as if checking that he was properly dressed with everything respectably buttoned up, Sir Hector told him, 'That's all to the good, because I've set the date as June the tenth.'

Kit frowned. 'That allows us only twelve days.'

'Precisely. You've been shilly-shallying long enough over this. I'm not going to permit Benzini to steal our thunder when we're so close to success. Grab this thing by the throat and go for it. Stop being so pernickety.'

'Being pernickety, if that's how you like to regard it, is behind the success of any pilot,' Kit countered. 'It's not only your prestige and the boost to Kirkland's sluggish trade which will be at stake when I take *Aphrodite* up. My life might seem a trifling consideration against all that, but I'd prefer to hang on to it for a few years more.'

For several moments the two men confronted each other, then the older one smiled. 'Now then, boy, simmer down. We're all getting stage fright. I have utter confidence in you, the whole team has. Let's have dinner, then you can take yourself off to bed while Donald puts in hand this modification. Test it tomorrow when you're less jumpy.'

Turning away, her father caught sight of Leone. A minor shock passed fleetingly over his face, then he said in unusually quiet tones, 'By George, how much you've grown to resemble your mother!'

'How are you, Father?' she replied.

'Very tied up with an event of acute importance, as you've probably deduced from all this argument. Dining with us, are you? Come along then.'

To her astonishment, Leone found her elbow being taken by her father, who walked her into the dining hall. As they progressed, he asked how she was and how she liked school. She answered in dutiful tones, reflecting that they could have been strangers recently introduced.

Then he smiled with a semblance of affection. 'Now you're here, have you everything you need?'

'Not really, Father,' she told him impetuously. 'I've always been provided with a personal maid at the homes of my friends.'

'Then you shall have one here. See to it, Maitland,' he commanded, as they all sat at the table. 'No moon-faced local girl, of course. Contact a London agency for one. French, if possible.'

'Certainly, Sir Hector,' said his assistant, shaking out his napkin with such a precise flick of his wrist the starched linen cracked like a whip.

'The jewellers will be sending a man down with the ring on Thursday, Donald,' said Sir Hector, apparently considering his daughter's needs now taken care of. 'You'll place it on the girl's finger as I make the announcement, so the newsmen can take a few pictures.'

Leone asked, 'What's Stephanie Main like?'
'Rich brown hair—masses of it,' Kit offered, 'eyes the colour of vintage sherry. Slender, intelligent. Lovely arms, skin like cream satin . . .'
'That'll be enough to be going on with,' Leone told him tartly. 'I thought you only waxed lyrical over flying machines.'
'Ah, if you want real lyricism, I'll describe *Aphrodite*,' he offered with his wicked grin.
After a meal of soup, asparagus soufflé, local fish with summer vegetables, and various cheeses, during which talk was concentrated on the coming speed attempt, the gathering broke up. Donald was posted to the workshops downriver; Maitland disappeared with his employer. Left alone with Kit, Leone found him looking apologetically at her.
'Not much of a first-night reunion, is it? I'm afraid I'm going to have to leave you, as well. I must go down there with Donald to keep an eye on what they're doing to *Aphrodite*. I have to fly her in twelve days' time.'
'Is flying really as dangerous as you suggested?'
'No, dear girl, flying isn't in the least dangerous. Crashing is. That's what I hope to avoid when I push her to limits no other aircraft has reached.' Touching the top of her head lightly with his hand, he added, 'Good night, sleep tight. Hope the bugs don't bite.'
'What?' she asked softly.
'A little rhyme I used to chant as a boy. I'd forgotten it until now.'
He walked away, leaving her with the thought that while Donald's future bride and aerial goddess could inspire poetic odes to their charms, all she could coax from Kit was the memory of a rather vulgar rhyme from his dubious past. With a sigh, she made her way upstairs.

WHEN KIT WENT for his morning swim he was lost in thoughts of the coming twelve days. The modification had been done the night before, and he intended to take *Aphrodite* up as soon as today's tidal flow provided the right conditions. He knew he was capable of exceeding the present record of just over 407mph, but his love affair with *Aphrodite* instilled in him the strong desire to display her full glory. He wanted the whole world to hold its breath with wonder.
The morning ritual in the Roman-style pool was not due to a passion for swimming; it was to keep fit. To fly an aircraft might suggest no more than the ability to sit in a small leather seat and move one's arms, but a pilot needed to be mentally alert, strong enough to hold his machine steady in an emergency, and physically sound. Kit ate well, and exercised daily. His eight hours of sleep might often be taken alongside a soft female form, but he counted that as additional exercise and a very definite contribution to his general sense of well-being.
Between now and the tenth of June, however, there would be no such exercising, he was just reminding himself, when a girl's voice called out a good morning to him. Turning, he was in time to see Leone Kirkland, in a

stylish scarlet bathing suit, make a perfect swallow dive into the chilly water.

'Hello,' she said, arriving beside him as he floated on his back. 'It's nice to have company.'

They moved slowly side by side until they reached the rail along the shorter side of the pool. Gripping it, she turned to him eagerly. In a scarlet rubber bathing helmet with a tiny peak, and with lashes and lips wet, she looked disturbingly pretty.

'Did they do the modification?' she asked, her legs scissoring in the clear water.

He nodded. 'I shall be testing her later this morning, if the weather holds.'

'I'll come and watch you.'

'I haven't yet heard you ask for my permission.'

She smiled disarmingly at him, all glow and water-drops. '*Please* may I come and watch you?'

'Does your father allow you to visit the workshops?'

'I've never wanted to before. Surely you haven't forgotten that I'm a Kirkland, Mr Anson?'

'I suppose I have,' he admitted, heaving his dripping body up to sit on the side. 'You're a little different from the others.'

'In what way?' she demanded.

'You have curves where the others haven't.'

It did not bring the giggle he had expected. Her voice had lost its earlier vitality when she said, 'The practised philanderer. I had forgotten that.'

'Never forget it,' he advised quickly, touched by the suspicion that her loneliness might lead her to imagine his friendship was deeper than it could be. Sixteen was a vulnerable age. 'Flattery rolls off my tongue like drops of water from your bathing helmet. Ask any girl within fifty miles of Sheenmouth.' Getting to his feet, he looked down at her pale shape in its scarlet costume. 'Come and see *Aphrodite*, if you want to, but don't expect a VIP welcome. When I'm with her, I don't see anyone else.'

Pulling on a robe, he slung a towel round his neck and headed for his rooms, where breakfast was served to him at seven every morning.

While he ate, he read the morning papers. Each of them contained a short paragraph speculating on the Italian attempt at the speed record presently held by an RAF pilot named Stainforth.

With that on his mind, he dressed in casual clothes before making his accustomed sprint down the path to the boathouse. As he approached, he spotted a girl in cream flared trousers and a blue and beige striped top sitting on one of the jetty piles.

Leone smiled as he arrived on the weathered planking. 'Very athletic! Are you planning to *swim* down to the workshops?'

'You know the answer to that, or you wouldn't be here fully dressed,' he replied and looked for the boat, which Walter normally tied alongside in readiness for him.

'I told Walter we'd take *Columbus* this morning.'

'I'm not permitted to use the family boat,' he told her swiftly.

'I'm going to take you, silly,' she announced, jumping from her perch to stand beside him. 'Walter's afraid I can't handle it but, heavens, in Monte Carlo last summer Raoul let me take control of his latest acquisition without a qualm. It was a giant of a thing!'

'Raoul is to be congratulated on his iron nerve,' Kit replied drily, as the throaty roar of a powerful speedboat engine heralded the emergence of *Columbus*, probably the fastest craft on that stretch of the Sheen. As Walter taxied it alongside the jetty, he looked up at Kit unhappily.

'I don't rightly know my duty, Mr Anson, I tell you straight. Miss Kirkland is wanting to take you along, and I don't see there's any way of stopping her, sir.'

Jumping into the smart scarlet and white craft, the girl cried, 'What a fuss you men always make! Come on, Kit. Get in, or I'll go without you.'

'Is that a genuine offer?' Kit asked with feigned optimism. 'I'm no Raoul, I must warn you.'

Revving up with a roar, she put out her tongue at him. Kit stepped in beside her, and took the rope Walter uncoiled expertly from the mooring post.

They shot away with such force Kit was thrown backwards into the scarlet leather seat.

'Whoops! Sorry,' Leone called over her shoulder. 'It takes a while to grow used to the feel of any boat.'

'Let me know when you do, just in case I don't notice the difference,' he said, back on his feet and moving up beside her as she swung round and headed downstream.

This morning the river was empty. The sky was clear, promising a sweet golden day. Dressing-gowned residents of riverside retreats, drawn onto their sun-washed terraces by the roar of the Kirkland boat, waved in friendly fashion as they passed. Leone waved back in high spirits.

Watching her thoughtfully as the breeze ruffled the waves of her short blonde hair, Kit told himself Raoul must have been either a fool or a man of unusually strong principle if all he had taught her was how to steer a boat.

Her head turned, surprising him in his study of her lithe body. Flushing faintly, she asked, 'Do you approve?'

'Of your seamanship, yes. I award full marks, Miss Kirkland.'

'May I watch you fly this morning?'

He smiled. 'If you can bear to hang around for hours while I check that all the conditions are right. Look, there she is,' he added, nodding towards the bright yellow aircraft lying on the water alongside the hangars, workshops and offices of Kirkland Marine Aviation. 'Isn't she the most exquisite creature you've ever been privileged to see?'

He fell silent, studying the present love of his life as Leone swung the speedboat in a starboard turn to head for the Kirkland jetty. Then, as they curved towards the slipways running down from the hangars, a small, powered vessel shot out from behind an ancient barquentine which was moored mid-river. At the wheel was a typical two-weeks-every-summer sailor. He saw the red and white rocket hurtling towards him, and forgot all the rules of navigation. Zigzagging frantically on the same course, he gave Leone only one chance of avoiding him. Swinging the wheel hard over, she straightened from the turn to roar past the terrified novice, trying to throttle back as they closed on the workshops at full speed. Kit knew they would never stop in time. Heaving the wheel round in the opposite direction, she re-entered the starboard turn she had broken but, by now, she was too near the bank. *Columbus* scraped one of the concrete slipways, leaped into the air, then smacked back into the water to career headlong at the yellow seaplane moored just ahead.

'Turn! Turn!' yelled Kit. *'For God's sake, turn!'* He seized the wheel and their combined efforts succeeded in making the powerful craft almost stand on its side with the violence of the turn, but still it clipped one of *Aphrodite*'s floats as it sped past.

There was a bang, followed by the sound of rending metal. Kit twisted frantically to look behind him. His beautiful mistress, his hope of triumph, was starting to tilt. He watched her go over, as people came running from the workshops to stare aghast at the disaster. Kit found himself blinking back tears. Months of work destroyed in a moment. The Italians would have a free field, and his own dreams would remain no more than just that.

3

The team which had created *Aphrodite* tenderly made her whole again. It took time. As the tenth of June drew nearer, the press, who had sensationalised Leone Kirkland's 'madcap spree in the family speedboat', built up tension by setting the British public agog to know whether the attempt on the record would still be made on schedule. Anyone who knew Sir Hector already had the answer to that.

At Sheenmouth Abbey an army of professionals was slowly transforming the rooms into a sumptuous setting for an evening reception worthy of the occasion. A raised platform for the dance band was erected in the great vaulted hall, whose stone floor was to be covered with polished wood panels. And Sir Hector had chosen plaster figures from Greek mythology set in a series of tableaux, each with the goddess Aphrodite as the central subject. Greenery was to be twined round the sturdy pillars of the hall, and white water lilies placed in the several mock-marble pools where small fountains played. The refectory, where a lavish buffet would be offered, received the same thematic treatment: ornate mock-marble benches set beneath arbours of greenery where gods and goddesses posed in near-naked splendour. As a final dramatic touch Sir Hector had decreed that his guests should arrive upriver from Sheenmouth on decorated barges, and be transported from his private jetty to the foot of the monastery steps in small Grecian chariots.

These arrangements, together with the preparation of a covered stand on the promenade beside Sheenmouth sands, where Sir Hector and senior staff of Kirkland's would watch the event in company with high-ranking officers of the RAF, representatives of the Air Ministry, leading aircraft manufacturers, engine designers, investors and socialites, all went ahead without a hitch under the ultra-efficiency of Maitland Jarvis.

Leone was the only person unoccupied during those frantic days leading to the tenth of June. How could she have made such a disastrous start to the visit designed to establish family unity? Donald was ignoring her. Her father's brief warmth during her homecoming dinner was never likely to be repeated. Kit was either down at the workshops, or shut in the bell tower taking the rest essential for the feat he would attempt.

JUNE THE TENTH DAWNED cloaked in mist from the sea. Even Sir Hector Kirkland could do nothing about the weather and, while all the preparations had gone ahead on well-oiled wheels, no one had dared to mention the one factor which could delay everything. The British were accustomed to braving the elements for outdoor events, so the grey damp shroud was no deterrent to those who flocked by train, car, bicycle and small boat to Sheenmouth, bent on having a wonderful day. Along the promenades on both sides of the mouth of the river, seafront cafés almost obscured by the mist were full. By ten o'clock, spectators were crowding whatever open space could be found along that stretch of coast, settling happily to their national pastime of waiting for the weather to clear.

The atmosphere was vastly different in the VIP stand when dignitaries and their wives began arriving just before noon. The mist had lightened from grey to white, and the Met men promised a clear afternoon once it had dispersed, but a cold buffet and chilled wine did little to warm anyone. Leone, in a dress of pale blue silk-embroidered Swiss lace, was so nervous she shivered as she wandered among the guests with the same canapé in her hand for more than half an hour. It was some comfort to know that her father, Maitland, and the staff of Kirkland Marine Aviation, were also inwardly tense as they all waited for a message from Donald, who was at the workshops with Kit and his team. He would telephone to a mechanic waiting in the pier ticket office with the go-ahead.

Before going to bed the night before, Leone had given Kit's valet a sealed good-luck note to put on Kit's breakfast tray. All week, flowers and parcels had been arriving from female well-wishers until the gallery had been filled to overflowing. She hoped Kit had bothered to read her message, and that it had cheered him more than the extravagant tributes from adoring females, many of whom had managed to sneak into the grounds and mob him as he set off for the workshops at the crack of dawn. She had watched the mass worship from her window, and now fully understood his reaction on finding her in his room on the day of her arrival. She was less understanding of the pain such worship had induced in her. The pain was still there as she studied the shrouded promenade. If only it were over; if only he had broken the wretched record and landed safely.

The sun eventually broke through at two thirty. A ragged cheer rose from the main promenade. Small boats put to sea to take up positions near the marker buoys. In them were the officials who would time the seaplane's three runs in each direction, a doctor to administer emergency resuscitation, if needed, Kirkland's mechanics to deal with technical faults, and men from the broadcasting service. The Sheenmouth lifeboat was also run out by its enthusiastic crew.

After that flurry of activity the waiting resumed. Heads were constantly turned towards the river mouth for a first sight of the seaplane and its dashing young pilot. Then, in the mysterious way such things happen, the word was passed round. *They're setting off now!* The information ran through the crowds like lightning, and the vast band of people compressed into a thin line as those at the rear pressed forward, craning their necks for a better view. The whole of Lyme Bay seemed to ring with cheers as the little waterborne procession emerged from the estuary and turned into the open sea lapping Sheenmouth sands.

Heading the flotilla was a boat containing Donald Kirkland, designer of *Aphrodite*, and an expert from Rolls-Royce who had made the engine for the seaplane. Behind them came a boat towing the pontoon on which the delicate, streamlined and immensely powerful machine was secured, watched over by overalled mechanics. Following closely was the Kirkland launch, filled to overflowing with so many people it was not clear whether Kit Anson himself was among them, or with the mechanics on the pontoon.

Leone's heart was pounding and her throat was dry. Remembering that ashen-faced boy in a cheap jacket and grubby shirt, who had stood in the library while her father had discussed him with Donald, tears began to blur her vision. It was now clear what this day was really all about. There was a world record to break; a company to promote. What Kit was about to prove, however, was that he was as good as any Kirkland. The stray mongrel was now running with the pedigree hounds before the eyes of the whole world.

A cry went up as *Aphrodite*'s engine roared into life. Next minute, a thickset figure wearing dark trousers, a flying jacket and leather helmet clambered onto the pontoon, where a short ladder enabled him to reach the small cockpit. Once he had settled inside, little could be seen of him, and the growing roar of the engine was almost drowned by the crescendo of cheers. Everything now lay in the hands of the daring young aviator.

Suddenly, the pontoon tilted, the ropes were snatched away, and then *Aphrodite* slid into the sea. She began surging forward in a great fountain of spray and then sped over the sea until she lifted and became no more than a yellow moth against the pale blue of the sky. Leone's tears multiplied as she watched that flying capsule climb and turn into the sun. It dawned on her, with shocked wonder, that the man crammed inside *Aphrodite* was the first person for whom she had cared deeply in all her sixteen years.

ON THE CLIFFS above Sheenmouth sands, Warren Grant was being practically strangled by his girlfriend, Mona. She clasped him tightly round his neck as she hid her face in his best pullover.

'I can't bear to watch,' she gasped into the rust-coloured wool.

More intent on following *Aphrodite*'s progress, as she circled in preparation for the straight stretch between the buoys marking the speed course, Warren pushed down the brim of his sweetheart's hat, which was obstructing his view through the binoculars.

'Don't be silly,' he murmured abstractedly.

'What if he crashes?'

'Whether you're watching or not won't change the fact. Phew, just look at that fuel ejecting from the exhausts as he turns! That special mixture in the tanks might produce exceptionally high speeds, but he'll have to watch his temperature at full throttle. Just look at that beauty!' he marvelled, studying every line of the sleek machine with floats so long they looked like two additional hulls.

For months Warren had spent every spare moment sitting on the banks of the Sheen near the Kirkland Marine Aviation hangars, studying *Aphrodite* in all stages of development. This morning he had raced to this vantage point on his motorbike. Mona had suffered it all for the sake of spending the day with him, but she had no real interest in something she regarded as her rival in his affections.

Warren's fascination with the quest for the ultimate in aircraft design had been instilled in him as a boy by his stepfather. Lieutenant Beamish Doyle, a Canadian in the Royal Flying Corps, had occupied no more than three years of Warren's life before being killed in Mesopotamia, but in that short time had given the dreamy lad visions of machines which would weave magic in the skies. *Aphrodite* looked set to do just that.

The seaplane had made one run in each direction when Warren's experienced eye detected a forward spurt which told him Anson was now fully under way.

'Here he goes,' he breathed, grabbing Mona's hat from her head to prevent his missing what was plainly to be the first of the really fast runs.

As the streaking seaplane passed the first of the buoys, Warren set his stopwatch. If Anson did break the record, it would be broken yet again before long. Men were sending machines faster and faster through the air. This yellow beauty would have her day, then a new goddess would take her place. What he would give to have a hand in creating her!

'Is he all right?' asked Mona, from the region of his chest.

'Stop being silly and see for yourself,' he told her, twisting to the right to study Anson's turn in preparation for his next run. 'He'll do it! By George, he's definitely going to do it! He must be going well over four hundred.'

Scribbling the time of the run in his small notebook, he resumed his scrutiny. 'Here he goes again.'

All around them people developed a frenzy of excitement as *Aphrodite* flew over the designated distance once more. Then she circled and began to lose height, indicating that Kit Anson had made his bid and was coming in to land. Torn between desire to watch the pilot touch down, or make an amateur calculation of his average speed over the three runs, Warren finally decided to keep his binoculars trained on the yellow seaplane until it rested tranquilly on the water. By doing so, he was beaten to it by the judges, who signalled Kit's success. The spectators had no idea by how much the record had been broken, but it was enough to set them kissing each other, dancing a jig, or surging forward in the hope of hearing the precise details.

Warren sat down on the grass feeling a glow of triumph. A boat that could fly; an aircraft that could float! It was a brilliant combination of design and engineering. What if the technique could be further developed until there were passenger liners which could take to the air? Imagine, he thought, long graceful hulls with massive wings, and four, maybe even six, engines to propel them halfway across the world! Travellers could reach India within a matter of hours; be in England one day and Africa the next. Just imagine it!

'Warren, what's up with you?' cried Mona impatiently. 'He's getting out into a rowing boat now. Aren't you going to watch?'

'No,' he murmured. 'Is there any tea left in the Thermos?'

'Oh, you really are the limit! This is the best bit of the day, and all you can think about is tea.'

She returned her attention to the sands where the conquering hero was being brought ashore. Despite the attempts of two local constables to protect him, Kit Anson was immediately mobbed and lifted onto the shoulders of stalwart admirers who bore him ecstatically towards the VIP enclosure where champagne awaited him. A chant was beginning to make itself heard above the cheers. 'FOUR ONE SEVEN . . . FOUR ONE SEVEN.'

While all those responsible for the day's endeavour congratulated each other, Warren sat on the cliffs drinking lukewarm tea and thinking about that figure of 417mph. Anson had just added 10mph to the world record, to make *Aphrodite* the fastest flying machine ever built. Surely Donald Kirkland must be feeling stunned. At a mere twenty-two years of age, what a glittering future lay before him. With family wealth and influence to back his immense flair, he was the man who would one day design those majestic liners with wings to encompass the world. Lucky devil!

Mona dropped onto the grass beside him. 'Can we go down and watch the VIP cavalcade on its way to Sheenmouth Abbey?'

Warren reached for his leather motorcycling jacket. 'Gosh, no. The road'll be blocked all the way from Magnum Pomeroy to Sheenmouth. Come on. Unless we leave right now, we'll never get through.'

'We're not going straight home?' cried Mona.

'Sorry,' he said. 'I've got a lesson at half past seven.'

'Oh, Warren, surely not! Whoever would want to fly on a day like today?'

On the point of crossing to his motorcycle, his dreams of the future had faded enough to allow him to realise how very upset Mona looked. 'I daren't skip the lesson. Mr Mason would fire me.'

Her drooping carrot-red head shook. 'I wish you could get a proper job.'

'This is a proper job,' he reasoned, taking one of her hands. 'I'm paid for every lesson I give . . . and there's the pieces I do for the *Rowmead Quarterly*. They bring in a bit more.'

Looking him sulkily in the eye, she reminded him that the *Rowmead Quarterly* was published only four times a year, and the editor did not always remember to pay him.

'But they always head my piece *From our Air Correspondent*,' he pointed out in defence of the tiny publication, as he led her across to the motorbike, trying not to betray his urgency. 'I'm sorry, Mona, but I daren't risk losing my job. If I turn up late today, I'll be out on my neck.'

Luckily, most of the crowd had decided to stay for a picnic tea so Warren was able to make good progress through the downhill lanes. He eventually pulled up in the small paved area beside the boat-hire office. Warren always left the bike there, and walked the short distance to the tiny office of the *Sheenmouth Clarion*. Mona's father was the owner/editor of the weekly paper, and therefore a man of some substance. He was also a person of strong opinions, especially where his pretty young daughter was concerned. One of these was that she should not be exposed to the dangers of a motorcycle. Although many local people spotted her on the pillion seat behind Warren, none of them passed the information to Jack Cummings who was universally disliked for his rudeness. The residents felt sorry for the girl, and did nothing to spoil her romance.

As Warren helped her from the pillion seat he found his resolution weakened by the sight of her rosy cheeks and bright eyes. Feeling guilty, he said, 'I could come back later on for an hour, if you like.'

'You won't get through the crowds,' she pointed out, wandering off moodily. He followed her in time to catch her next words. 'Sometimes, I wonder if you really are fond of me, or if you say it to get your own way.'

He overtook her, bringing her to a halt. Unhappy over her disappointment, he drew her into his arms and touched her full mouth lightly with his own. 'I'll get what you call "a proper job" soon, I'm sure.'

'When?' she demanded, pressing her body against his in a disturbing manner. Her mouth was almost touching his, so it was impossible not to kiss her again. She responded with such startling fervour he began to lose his head. Into that forbidden passion came a sonorous sound. The church clock was announcing the three-quarter hour. Putting Mona gently away from him, he exclaimed, 'Gosh, you make it hard for a chap to be good.'

'Do I?' she asked, in thrilled tones.

'I'll say. It's just as well I've got to get going, or who knows what might have happened. It's already a quarter to six.'

For some reason, his words caused her to burst into tears. 'You beast, Warren Grant! That's all you ever think about: *flying*.'

Sighing heavily, he asked, 'Will you let me walk you home?'

'I suppose so. Dad'll ask questions if you don't.'

Jack Cummings believed that girls should be called for and escorted home by their young men, so Warren was obliged to take valuable time accompanying a silent, mutinous girl to her front door. If he lost the job at the Aero Club he really would be in a jam. His rent for this week was overdue because he had bought the paint to finish the model seaplane he had designed. What he would be paid for today's lesson would at least enable him to offer Mrs Bardolph an instalment, to keep her sweet.

The door of the little newspaper office stood open. As Warren offered Mona a farewell, he was accosted by her father. 'Just a minute, young man. I'd like a few words with you before you skip off.'

'Could you make it some other time, Mr Cummings?' he asked swiftly. 'I've a lesson booked, and I must allow for the roads being jammed today.'

'No, I can't make it some other time,' came the stern reply. 'Unlike you, I'm a working man whose time isn't his own. Come in and shut the door! All that racket from people who swarm here to gawp at some fancy show laid on by the Kirkland family. I suppose you took my girl to see it.'

'Yes. Anson broke the record by ten miles an hour.'

'I know that,' Cummings roared, in sudden fury. 'Do you think the editor of the local newspaper wouldn't hear that kind of news before anyone else? Nothing but ballyhoo, in my opinion.'

There was no effective reply to that, so Warren got down to more urgent matters. 'What did you want to say to me, sir?'

'What are your intentions towards my daughter?'

'I don't quite understand,' Warren hedged. 'I'm very fond of Mona.'

'I should hope you are. She's been giving you a great deal of her company over the past six months.'

'Dad,' put in Mona, with obvious embarrassment.

'Keep quiet, girl, and you might find out what this young man with his head in the air plans to do about your devotion.'

'I'm very fond of Mona,' Warren repeated with a show of confidence. 'I'd like to continue taking her out, sir.'

'Then I suggest you buy her a ring, so that she and the residents of Sheenmouth know how she stands.'

'Dad!' cried Mona again.

There was no way out of it this time. 'I'm only twenty-four, Mr Cummings.'

'Old enough to get a girl into trouble, aren't you?'

Warren swallowed. 'I wouldn't do that to Mona.'

'Different from other men, are you?'

He felt his colour rise. 'No.'

'Is there something wrong with my daughter? Does she lack what all other girls have?'

'No . . . I mean, I don't know . . . no, of course not.'

'Then you either buy Mona a ring and set the wedding date, or you'll say goodbye to her right now.'

'Dad, *please*,' begged the girl tearfully. 'He'll ask me when he's able to.'

Her father turned on her, his face harsh. 'He'll ask you now, or go. Where's your pride, girl?'

The clock on the wall above Jack Cummings's head showed Warren it was now six o'clock. He grew desperate. 'If those are your conditions, Mr Cummings, I must accept them. At present, I'm in no position to consider marriage. I couldn't possibly support a wife, much less provide a comfortable home for her. It might be years before we could marry, and other chances could pass her by while she was tied to me.' Conscious of Mona's distress, he tried one last shot. 'I'd like to assure you that I've always treated your daughter with the greatest respect, sir, and I'd continue to do so if you'd allow me to go on taking her out. I really am extremely fond of her.'

Cold eyes looked back at him. 'Goodbye, Mr Grant.'

Mona seized his arm. 'Warren, don't go,' she pleaded.

He slowly shook his head. 'Your father's right. You deserve some kind of promise after six months. I'm so sorry I can't give it to you.'

WARREN REACHED the small house on the outskirts of Sheenmouth after fuming and cursing his way through celebrating crowds. It was gone half past six when he parked his motorbike in the little alley leading to the rear entrance of the terrace of Edwardian houses, and went round to the front steps of number twenty-two, where he rented an attic room. Mona had become part of his life. Without her, it was going to be very lonely.

He let himself in as the chiming clock told him it was now a quarter to seven.

'There you are, Mr Grant,' exclaimed his landlady, coming from the parlour. 'I've kept your tea hot for you. A nice little lamb cutlet with some bubble and squeak, then plum tart and custard to follow.'

He halted halfway up the stairs. 'I won't have time, I'm afraid. There's a lesson booked for seven thirty. Could you manage a cup of tea and a sandwich instead?'

'That's not enough for a growing man,' she ruled sternly.

'Please, Mrs Bardolph . . .' Warren interrupted impatiently. 'If I miss that lesson, I could be fired by Jim Mason.'

'Who else would he get?' she called after Warren reassuringly, as he set off up the stairs. 'I'll get you some tea . . . and a nice thick sandwich.' Then she remembered something. 'Oh, Mr Grant! I had a little accident in your room just after dinner. You left that toy aeroplane of yours right on the edge of the cupboard, so it was no wonder my sleeve caught it. I'm ever so sorry, but it was under my feet before I knew. Still, you can soon make another, can't you? It's not as if it was valuable. Well, I'll go and pop the kettle on.'

Sick with apprehension, Warren raced up the remaining two flights to his room in the roof. He was almost afraid to open the door. Breathing hard, he stared at the dresser where the three-foot model of *Seaspray*, the seaplane he had designed and painstakingly built to scale over the past six months, lay in a pile of balsawood. The pride of his life, the great hope for his future, had been smashed to pieces. He gazed miserably at the pieces painted in silver and sea-green only last night.

Sinking onto a chair, he hunched over in misery. He was doomed to mediocrity, it seemed. After Beamish Doyle had been killed in Mesopotamia, Warren's mother had enjoyed the attentions of a number of men on leave in London. Her various lovers had been generous men, so it was through the continuance of her amours that Vera Grant was able to support her son while he studied aerial engineering. During those student days, Warren had worked as a copy boy on the night shift of a large newspaper and the money earned was enough to allow him to take flying lessons.

Vera Grant had died of consumption early in 1930. Six months later Warren had gained not only his pilot's licence but his engineering degree, and had seemed set for launching himself into a career in aviation when an influenza epidemic had made him one of its victims. Weeks in hospital had cost him his job with the newspaper; a second severe winter had laid him low again and the doctor, diagnosing a permanent weakness in his chest, had advised him to move south away from London fogs.

Warren had bought a motorbike, packed up those few things he valued, and set out for Sheenmouth with high hopes for a job at Kirkland Marine Aviation. But the company was already having to shed staff, and would not give him an interview. Deeply disappointed, he had inserted a small piece in the *Clarion* outlining his capabilities. Mona had been there behind the counter. Their friendship had blossomed immediately and she had helped him through the first part of this year. She had arrived at Mrs Bardolph's one afternoon, full of excitement over a notice she had just been given to insert in that week's edition of her father's newspaper.

'Go up there right away,' she cried, 'before someone else reads it in the *Clarion* on Saturday. You can fly; you're just the person he needs.'

He had, and she had been thrilled . . . *then*. Today, the job at the Aero Club had been dismissed as quite inadequate for a prospective husband. It was, of course, yet it was a godsend for a budding aircraft designer waiting for his great chance. That was to have been in several days' time when Warren had intended to take his model of *Seaspray* to Donald Kirkland. It would take weeks to reconstruct.

A tap on the door heralded Mrs Bardolph with a pot of tea and a sandwich. He felt too sick to eat it now. 'Oh, *hell*,' he swore, as the woman departed. 'Double hell and triple damnation! I'll never get there in time.'

Only by struggling over several stiles with his motorbike, and bumping across fields in a series of short cuts, did Warren manage to arrive at the Aero Club no more than fifteen minutes late. His pupil, a fat, monocled landowner from Magnum Pomeroy, made his annoyance obvious. He also allowed it to affect his deplorable skill to the point of endangering both their lives during the half-hour lesson.

After collecting his money and suffering a severe telling-off from Jim Mason, Warren set out in a very black mood back to his lodgings. He had lost Mona, and could not face the wreck of *Seaspray* tonight. The only thing to do was to drive into Magnum Pomeroy and spend the money he had just earned in the Buck and Hounds.

On leaving the airfield, he gave the machine full throttle and fairly raced along the narrow lane which led to the village, and thence past the old monastery where high jinks would celebrate Donald Kirkland's achievement tonight. Thoughts of that occupied his mind to such an extent that only reflexes saved him from hitting a girl standing beside a large Bentley as he rounded a curve flanked by high summer hedgerows. Swerving, he screeched to a halt with his front wheel stuck in the blackthorn. He had not even begun to extricate himself when the girl appeared beside him.

'Thank heavens you came along,' she cried delightedly. 'Do you know how to repair this car?'

Thinking of all the names he would like to call her, he pushed up his goggles angrily. The sight of her robbed him of speech for a moment: short golden hair, huge blue eyes and a blue lace dress. He found his tongue. 'I could have killed myself trying to avoid hitting you.'

The gorgeous eyes filled with impatience. 'Please listen. The car has broken down. We've been stuck on the road from Sheenmouth for *hours*. When we finally turned off it, a kind of banging started under the bonnet.' Gripping his arm as he straddled the bike, she gave him a dazzling smile. 'Be a dear and have a look at it.'

Deciding that he was quite entitled to be angry with her, he plucked her hand from his arm and gave it back to her. 'I'll be as dear as you please, but, if you'll excuse me, I have an important appointment at the Buck and Hounds.' He backed from the depths of the hedge into the road again.

'I'll come with you,' she declared and, before he could stop her, she had climbed onto the pillion seat and settled behind him, clutching him round the waist and displaying a delectable amount of silk-covered legs.

'Just a minute,' he protested.

'Oh, please,' breathed her sweet voice in his ear. 'I just *have* to get to the abbey, which isn't far past the Buck and Hounds. I've been delayed so long, it's now a matter of life or death. Please, *please* say you'll take me.'

The mood he was in now inspired the reverse reaction. This girl was undoubtedly one of the Kirkland set. Playing knight errant to her might be fun. He would get a peek at the Kirkland home and, if it really was a matter of life or death, her father might give him half a crown for his trouble.

'All right,' he agreed impulsively. 'Hold on!'

Partly because she had told him the case was urgent, but mostly to show her a thing or two, he opened the throttle and attacked the road in unusually reckless manner. This girl plainly loved speed. 'You're absolutely *splendid*,' she cried in his ear. 'How fast are we going now?'

'Much too fast,' he yelled over his shoulder. 'If old Sergeant Phipps sees us, I'll be in jail by Saturday.'

'I'll come and bail you out,' she promised. 'Turn off here, down that lane. *Heavens!* You cut that very fine.'

'Yes, didn't I?' he agreed proudly.

He made a reasonably spectacular arrival outside the massive stone building from whence came the sound of a dance band.

The girl scrambled off, her cheeks flushed by speed and excitement. 'Come on,' she said authoritatively. 'You deserve a drink after that.'

'Thanks, but I couldn't go in dressed in this way.'

'Nonsense! No one will look at you, they'll all be swarming over Kit Anson tonight. *Come on*,' she urged, dragging him from the saddle.

Disentangling his legs from the machine, he asked, 'Do you know him?'

'Who . . . Kit? *Heavens*, he's practically one of the family. Do you want to meet him? *Come on*. I'll introduce you to my brother Donald, and he'll give you a drink while I dash upstairs to change.'

'Your brother Donald?' he asked, his heart quickening.

'Donald Kirkland. He designed the seaplane Kit broke the world record in this afternoon. You *must* have been watching. It was thrilling!'

As they walked in, Warren told himself that before Mrs Bardolph had dusted his room this would have been the chance of a lifetime. He had nothing to offer Donald Kirkland now, and he certainly did not want half a crown from *him* for bringing his beautiful, crazy sister home. He wanted a job. *Seaspray* might have got it for him.

4

Dazed by the noise and colour in the great hall, Warren stood just inside the door, a curious spectacle in breeches, blue-checked open-necked shirt, pullover hand-knitted by Mona, and leather boots and jacket.

'Come on,' said the girl. 'I'll hand you over to Donald, then dash off.'

Following her round the edge of the dance floor, he asked, 'What about this matter of life or death?'

Her gorgeous smile hit him again. 'Kit broke the air-speed record, and I haven't congratulated him yet. When they carried him up in triumph to the stand, I passed out with relief.'

The girl Warren now knew to be Leone Kirkland tapped the arm of a tall, fair-haired man. When Donald Kirkland turned, it dawned on Warren that he was face to face with a man he admired and deeply envied.

'The traffic was impossible,' the girl told her brother, shouting to be heard above the band. 'Then we broke down in the most isolated spot on the Pomeroy road, and I was just growing really desperate when . . .' She broke off to turn to Warren. 'What's your name, by the way?'

Bemused, he gave it in full. 'Warren James Bartholomew Grant.'

She turned back to her brother. 'When *he* came along on a motorcycle to effect a gallant rescue. He's been absolutely *splendid*. I've promised him a drink and an introduction to Kit. Look after him for me while I dash up to change into something more suitable.' She smiled at Warren with devastating effect, then vanished.

'How do you do, Mr Kirkland. It's a very great privilege to meet the designer of *Aphrodite*.' As the other man reluctantly shook his hand, Warren added, 'As a designer myself I fully appreciate the brilliance of your work. Congratulations.'

'Thank you,' Donald replied. He seemed less than impressed. 'Forgive me, Mr Grant, but I thought I knew all the leading designers in this country. Are you, perhaps, with a foreign company?'

If only Warren had had *Seaspray* to offer! 'Actually, I'm an independent designer,' he said, talking fast. 'As it happens, I've just finished developing a new seaplane called *Seaspray*.' He launched into an involved technical description of wing elevation and propeller displacement, and it was some time before he realised that his companion was not listening, but was gazing round the room with a trapped expression on his face. His glance finally settled on a sandy-haired man in a spotless dinner jacket who came across immediately.

'Yes, Mr Kirkland?'

'My sister was apparently rescued by Mr Grant, who brought her home on his motorcycle. She would like him to be given a drink and an introduction to Mr Anson before he leaves. Would you see to it?'

The man turned to Warren with the impersonal politeness of a well-trained subordinate. 'Would you come with me, sir? I'll take you to Mr Anson, then send a waiter to you with cocktails.'

Warren had no choice but to walk away from the man who should have changed his life for him.

Kit Anson was eventually found in an octagonal room which appeared to be furnished with church pews—rather a weird idea, Warren thought. The hero of the day was under siege. Pretty girls gathered in open worship around him. Telling Warren to wait, his companion moved expertly through the group to speak in Anson's ear. The pilot glanced across at Warren, then nodded and stepped out through a nearby door standing open to the evening. Warren was then beckoned by the sandy-haired man, to be told that Mr Anson would see him out on the terrace.

Feeling insulted, Warren walked from the curious room with the intention of offering congratulations to the pilot who had plainly been told to give him five minutes, then leaving Sheenmouth Abbey for an important appointment elsewhere, 'elsewhere' being the Buck and Hounds.

The plan was instantly discarded when Kit Anson smiled warmly at his approach, and said, 'My grateful thanks for allowing me to escape. My head was starting to spin with so many voices speaking at once.'

Warren had seen Kit Anson many times through his binoculars. Now the great man was beside him he was very conscious of his considerable strength, both physical and personal. And he was no more than twenty-two—two years younger than Warren.

'I watched your performance this afternoon,' he said admiringly. 'As I'd studied *Aphrodite* throughout her trials, I knew you'd do it. An extra ten is no mean achievement, though. Congratulations.'

The pilot nodded an acknowledgment, but said nothing.

'I thought I spotted fuel coming from the engines on the turns,' Warren continued. 'That mixture you used was probably a little too volatile at full throttle, although you'd probably never have reached four one seven on anything less. Did you get the breeze up at all?'

There was another nod from the pilot. 'I was petrified throughout the entire flight. The cockpit grew so hot, it was like sitting inside a furnace which could blow up at any time. When I landed, the spray actually sizzled as it hit the sides.'

Warren whistled through his teeth. 'Frightening!'

The other man looked back at him dreamily. 'Exhilarating! I believe I lived half my life up there this afternoon.'

'I've designed a machine called *Seaspray* which would enable you to live the other half,' Warren said, on impulse. 'The drawings are at my lodgings. I tried to interest Mr Kirkland just now, but he plainly thought I was just an upstart who happened to have given his sister a ride home. Her car had broken down on the Pomeroy road. That stuffed shirt was told to palm me off onto you, give me a drink, then send me on my way.'

Kit Anson moved along the terrace. 'Let's take the weight off our feet, shall we? That "stuffed shirt" is Maitland Jarvis, Sir Hector's right-hand man,' he added, as he reached a wall and sat down on it. 'He gives the impression of being little more than a robot, but he can be dangerous. His head is a filing cabinet. You have been duly registered, then inserted under the letter U.'

'Why U?' asked Warren, sitting beside Kit.

'U for upstart.' He gave a faint smile. 'That's what you said, if I remember correctly.'

Warren smiled back. 'Very definitely . . . but the way I'm dressed gives credence to that theory, I suppose.'

'Well, it certainly wouldn't help you to capture Donald Kirkland's interest in any project you might have. You've chosen just about the worst time, anyway. He's preparing to announce his engagement this evening.'

'Just my luck,' said Warren resignedly.

Giving him a speculative look, Kit said, 'Care to tell me about this machine of yours? *Seaspray*, I think you called her.'

Thrilled that his companion had noted the name, Warren needed no second bidding. Going into great depth of technical detail which he knew any pilot would understand, he outlined the development of his own seaplane from its conception, and then they discussed the subject of waterborne aircraft with deep mutual interest until the sun went down and lights went on all along the terrace without their noticing the change.

Finally, Kit stood up. 'That wall is growing very hard on the backside. I suggest we find more comfortable seats where drinks are on hand,' he said. Warren got to his feet also. As they walked together over the flagstones, Kit added, 'You know, I'm really keen to see those drawings of *Seaspray*!'

'I had a model of her until about two this afternoon. My landlady dusted my room without due care, and trod on what she calls my "toy aeroplane". It'd take me a while to put her back together, I'm afraid.'

'What filthy luck!' came the sympathetic comment, as the man of the moment made to lead him inside the abbey.

Warren stopped him. 'Look, Mr Anson, I really don't think I should go in there again, dressed as I am.'

'That's no problem. The Kirklands keep a wardrobe for guests who remain overnight unexpectedly. If you'd like to stay—and I hope you will, because I'd like to continue our discussion—I can hand you over to Coombes, who'll fix you up with what you need. What do you say?'

Sensing that the rapport he had established with this speed champion could lead to a productive relationship, and wanting very much to see Leone Kirkland in her 'something suitable', Warren stammered his thanks.

Kit Anson smiled. 'Good. I'll find Coombes. By the way,' he added over his shoulder, 'you'd better start calling me Kit, if we're going to work on that seaplane of yours together.'

LEONE TOOK A LONG TIME over making herself beautiful for Kit. At first, she had despaired over being stranded by the roadside while he was being hugged to death by as many girls as could lay their hands on him. While waiting for the mist to clear today, she had drunk too much and the excitement and relief when it was over had taken their toll. A doctor among her father's guests had recommended that she should lie down for at least an hour, so she had been taken to a room in a seafront hotel where she had been given a sleeping powder. Meader had been instructed to wait until she had recovered enough to be driven home. Everyone else had returned to Sheenmouth Abbey by boat.

When she woke, it was seven o'clock, and she had practically wept with frustration when the Bentley had broken down. The young man on his motorbike had represented a knight in the shiniest armour imaginable.

Now she was home, it occurred to her that the delay might be to her advantage, after all. Everyone else would have mobbed Kit ages ago, so her own congratulations would receive more attention from him. Impulsively she took from her wardrobe a wildly sophisticated ballgown. The black chiffon dress, cut in a severe, figure-hugging line which swept into a small train covered with black satin roses, made her look at least eighteen. It was sleeveless and practically backless, with a stark décolletage softened by a diagonal line of matching satin roses. Leone decided that the fairness of her skin and hair contrasted so well with the black that she needed no jewels to complete the stunning effect.

With her heart beating fast, she hurried down the stairs, searching the sea of faces for the one person she longed to impress. Kit was nowhere to be seen.

All heads were turning to a platform where Leone's father, Donald and Kit were taking centre stage amid thunderous applause. Attempting to push her way through the clustering guests, she was defeated by sheer numbers.

Standing motionless in the spellbound crowd, she realised that her father was the only one of the three who was smiling. Donald looked nervous; Kit appeared dangerously exhausted. Leone's heart went out to him.

Sir Hector held up a hand for silence. 'Ladies and gentlemen, this has been a day the whole world will remember. As the cheering and shouting fade, I offer a more humble personal tribute to these two young men. Donald Kirkland is someone who must hold the future of marine aviation in his youthful hands. I share that universal claim for his ability. But he is also my own son, so my pride in his triumph is primarily that of a father.' The comment was augmented by a paternal grip on Donald's shoulder. 'I count myself greatly blessed.'

While applause rippled through the hall, Sir Hector loosed his grip on Donald and turned to Kit.

'The fastest man in the air the world has ever known!' A cheer rang out. 'Yes, I share your acclaim for his personal courage and daring, but Kit Anson is also the test pilot for Kirkland Marine Aviation, so my pride in his achievement is also on behalf of the company which I have built up into what it will now be—one of the nation's leaders in marine aircraft development.' Putting his hand on Kit's shoulder, he went on, 'Ladies and gentlemen, three years ago I took this boy into my home and gave him every advantage a young man could desire. It was a risk, like any investment, but I think you'll agree that it has yielded rich dividends.'

Fresh applause greeted this, but Leone stood still, gazing at Kit's face. So this was why he had been brought into her home on that unforgettable day. Kit Anson was simply one of Sir Hector Kirkland's investments. He had just been made publicly aware of the fact. Poor Kit!

Then a movement caught everyone's attention. The girl her brother was bringing up the steps to join him lived up to Kit's lyrical description. Her handspan waist, swelling bosom and graceful neck were enhanced by a dress of rich pink beaded satin which highlighted her creamy skin to perfection. Leone was too distant to check Kit's claim of sherry-coloured eyes, but they were certainly wide and lovely.

She heard her father express his pleasure in welcoming the future bride into the Kirkland family. A stranger was being fêted and acknowledged as Sir Hector's future daughter-in-law, while his true daughter was being ignored. Horrified by a rush of tears, she found her pride rising. She had come home fully determined to take her place here, and take it she would. Tonight was the perfect occasion for something dramatic to happen, and she would be the instigator.

The ceremony was over, and the band was striking up a two-step, by the time she had pushed her way through to the platform. Donald was about to take his future bride onto the dance floor, so Leone crossed swiftly to them and summoned a bright smile.

'Congratulations,' she said. 'Sorry I couldn't join you for the presentation of the ring and family groups all embracing, et cetera, but I was cornered by a persistent journalist who wanted the story from my angle. You know: *Daughter of the house tells of the private anguish behind aerial triumph.* Don't worry, Donald, I was terribly discreet.'

Stephanie, whose eyes really were the colour of sherry, studied her with an amused smile, but Donald glared at her with the same expression of animosity he had worn since her crash into *Aphrodite*.

'For God's sake, Leone, this is a celebration not a wake. Wherever did you find that funeral dress?'

His words cut deep. 'It took some finding,' she retaliated swiftly. 'I scoured Zürich for it and realised it was just right for the sad loss of my dear brother. Now I've seen Steph, it seems I haven't lost a brother but gained a sister.' Maintaining the same breezy manner, she said to the other girl, 'You've no idea how glad I am to get some female support, at last. Being the only woman in this place has been frightfully dreary at times.'

The girl in pink satin gave a dazzling smile. 'I can well believe it, having been the only woman here myself on several occasions. The only solution is to forbid all talk of aircraft and turn their minds to more entertaining subjects, I've discovered. They soon thaw.'

They would, Leone thought furiously, wondering what entertaining subjects this seductive creature dreamed up to bring about the miracle. Her next words suggested that she planned to set to work on Leone next.

'I shan't force my friendship on you, my dear, but I'll be very glad to advise you on the painful business of growing up.' The celebrated eyes took in every detail of the sophisticated black dress. 'One can make so many embarrassing mistakes at the age of sixteen.'

All hope of friendship with this girl died instantly, as Donald swept Stephanie into his arms and joined the dancers.

Leone remained where she was, stunned by the encounter.

Someone appeared before her. 'Hello. I was hoping to find you again.'

'Were you?' she murmured abstractedly.

'I wasn't sure it was you, at first. Gosh, no one's going to look at anyone else tonight, now you're around.'

The warm admiration in his voice was so unexpected it captured her attention. She gazed at a young man with slicked-down brown hair, whose face was vaguely familiar. His eyes were a dreamy blue-grey, fringed by dark lashes. Right now they were filled with exactly the kind of wonder she hoped to see in Kit's when she congratulated him.

'Would you care to dance?' he asked hopefully, just as her brother and Stephanie swung past laughing together.

'All right,' she agreed defiantly.

They had moved no more than several yards when the two-step ended. His disappointment was marked. 'I suppose you're not free for the next dance, are you?'

'I have to find Kit,' she told him, gazing round the vast hall.

'I was introduced to him, thanks to you.'

Her attention was drawn back to her companion. Where had she seen him before? 'Thanks to me?'

'Yes, indirectly. I liked him tremendously. He offered to look at my drawings. I'm a designer, you know.'

'I suppose you're brilliant, too,' Leone muttered.

He shook his head. 'Fame's still a long way off, I'm afraid. I was on my way to the Buck and Hounds to drown my sorrows when you stopped me.'

'Heavens, you're him . . . The shining armour on a motorcycle; the person with a long name!' she exclaimed in surprise.

His smile was still shy. 'I don't know why I said it all. Warren will do.'

'You said you were a designer, so I thought you worked for Kirkland's.'

'No such luck! I'm an unemployed designer, when I'm not giving flying lessons at the Aero Club.'

'Flying, flying,' she cried. 'Is that all men ever think of?'

'Not when they're next to a girl who looks as stunning as you do.'

The wonder of his dreamy, attractive eyes was like balm to ease the multiple blows of that endless day. 'I think you're an awfully nice person.'

Flushing slightly, he said, 'So are you, Miss Kirkland.'

'Shining-armour people are allowed to call me Leone,' she offered and beckoned one of the hired waiters bearing cocktails. They both took a glass from his tray, and drank in silence for a few moments, until the mood was broken by the band embarking on its next number. It was a tune Warren knew, and his face came alive.

' "Lady of Spain" is one of my favourites,' he told her. 'Some of the bands used to let me play with them, you know, and I always enjoyed this number.'

'Heavens,' she returned, trying to take in what he had said, 'you actually played a musical instrument at dancehalls?'

He nodded. 'The trumpet. My stepfather used to play in a band before the war. When he was killed in Mesopotamia, one of his friends brought his trumpet home and gave it to me. Dad had shown me the basics, so I taught myself the rest.'

All at once, Leone saw her chance to make her mark this evening. 'Will you play it now?' she asked eagerly. 'Will you go up there with the band?'

'Good Lord, no,' he said swiftly. 'That's Phil Davenport. He's the best. In any case, he'd never let me.'

'He'll have to if I say so,' she said with great authority. 'Come on.'

Only her determination forced the unwilling young man to mount the steps to where they were almost deafened by the volume of the band in full swing. Over the sound, she shouted her request in Phil Davenport's ear. He shook his head while continuing to conduct.

'Sir Hector would never approve,' he told her.

She stood her ground. 'I'm his daughter.'

Visibly unhappy, the man conducted several more bars before signalling his band to stop. Lowering his voice, he began his professional diplomacy. 'It's not that I have personal objections, miss, it's just that . . .' He glanced over her head to Warren in appeal.

'Yes, of course,' Warren agreed. 'It's perfectly all right.'

'It's not perfectly all right,' cried Leone, holding Warren's arm as he made to leave. 'Give my friend a trumpet and let him play.'

The dancers, waiting in the centre of the floor, were gazing at Phil Davenport in curiosity.

The dark-haired man sighed and handed a trumpet to Warren, who had a short discussion with the musicians. Then, wearing a long-suffering expression, the bandleader lifted his baton and Warren raised the trumpet to his lips.

The resulting magic caused everyone in that hall to fall silent, more spellbound by the music than the sound of their own voices. There was a haunting, poignant quality about the arrangement that caught at Leone's throat. Tears were on her lashes by the time the final note died.

Next minute, there was uproar as the guests went wild with enthusiasm. After a brief word with Warren, Phil Davenport struck up 'Alexander's Ragtime Band'. The result was electrifying. The youthful flying instructor in borrowed clothes became another person as he fingered the gleaming instrument. With a final resounding top note, Warren lowered the trumpet to face an ecstatic reception and cries for more. His bow tie was tugged free, his top stud undone as he prepared for another encore. He looked triumphant as he embarked on a sentimental love song. Those gazing up at him started to sway together. In that enchanted moment, no one noticed a young girl in a sophisticated black dress descend the steps at the rear of the platform and slip outside.

Leone could watch and listen no longer. Tonight, she had found a friend; someone who wanted her company alone. Then her ridiculous desire to make her mark as a Kirkland had led her to give him away to the entire assembled company. All she had succeeded in doing was to set yet another male on a triumphant pedestal in Sheenmouth Abbey.

KIT FOUND EVEN the distant sounds of the party disturbing, so he walked on in the starlit darkness until he was blessedly alone in a silence broken only by nocturnal rustling and the whirr of night wings. The stress of the past weeks was all now taking its toll of him.

In those first few minutes after learning that he had added an entire ten miles an hour to the existing record, jubilation had possessed him. He had flown faster than anyone else in the world. It was a fact still too momentous to take in. Even so, as he tilted back his head to gaze at the stars, tears blurred his vision. If his father was up there somewhere, looking down, perhaps he would be proud of him, at last.

As he turned into the ruin of the abbey chapel, his shoulders began to heave. After today, where would he belong? What road could he possibly follow from here? Had he gained the final summit, or was there another pinnacle beyond this which reached into the unknown? The relief of tears somehow eased the ache in his limbs, but not the one within, which needed the answers to those questions.

The sound of stones rattling on the far side of the chapel caused him to turn, appalled at being caught out in this moment of weakness. A girl stood, framed in the arched stone like a cameo.

'I've never seen a man cry,' she ventured. 'Is it because you're sad, or because you're too happy?'

He brushed his wet cheeks with the back of his hand. 'I suppose it's a little of both.'

'How long have you been out here all alone?'

'Too long, that's quite obvious,' he told her with feeling. 'I've just made a fool of myself in front of you. I thought the days of doing that had long passed,' he added, remembering their initial introduction three years ago.

'I don't think you're foolish; just rather wonderfully human.'

Silence fell between them. She looked absurdly desirable: a child-woman in a dress whose ultra-sophistication only served to emphasise the untouched quality of her youth. Those large shining eyes, that soft wilful mouth suggested innocence waiting to be broken. A dangerous combination, when a man was as vulnerable as he was now.

'I wanted to be the first to congratulate you, yet end up being the last.'

'I doubt that,' he said, as lightly as he could. 'Until someone snatches the record from me, people will go on doing it.'

'And girls will want to kiss you?'

'Most probably.'

'I want to kiss you,' she whispered.

The mesmeric quality of that moon-dappled cloister open to the stars was enough, without this girl's naive sensuality to add to his sense of confusion.

'This is dangerous,' he told her swiftly. 'We must go.'

As he stepped forward, she barred his way. Shafts of moonlight highlighted the shimmer of tears on her cheeks, as she put her hands on his arms.

'Don't make me invisible, Kit. Not you, too. I couldn't bear it.'

The yearning in her voice touched him deeply; so deeply he offered instinctive comfort. Her innocence had been deceptive, however. She was more woman than child, he realised, as the light kiss he offered was returned with growing response. Highly aroused by confusing emotions himself, what had begun as a fond embrace now turned into an extremely provocative sharing of passion. Only when the screech of a hunting owl overhead brought him to his senses, did he break away with a feeling of shock. This girl was only sixteen. What was more, her name was Kirkland. Both facts put her out of bounds to him, dangerously out of bounds.

KIT AWOKE TO FIND HIMSELF shrouded in mist. Heavy-headed, he opened the door of his sports car and scrambled painfully to his feet. Reaching for the hip-flask kept in the car door, he relieved the dryness of his throat. The hair of the dog, he thought wryly. His watch showed that it was 9am. Another hot sunny day, when this mist cleared.

Stirrings of guilt assailed him. Whether Leone had followed him to the ruin, or merely come upon him by chance, he could not decide. Either way it had led to disaster. She was a minor; a schoolgirl! In the cold light of day he could not conceive how his comforting embrace had so swiftly flared into passion, yet it had. It meant he would either have to be very cruel or hold her at arm's length until she returned to Switzerland. He had taken the coward's way out last night. After forcibly escorting her back indoors, he had taken his car from the garages, and driven to this isolated spot to spend what remained of the night. His only hope was that her astonishingly mature response to his embrace had been induced by drink, but he somehow felt it was a vain hope.

Stamping about on the grassy hillside to rid himself of lingering cramp, he shivered. This time yesterday he had been totally dedicated to achieving one single aim. It had brought professional triumph for himself, and the much-needed boost for the company. Donald, as heir presumptive, would now be firmly established as the golden boy of aircraft design. Kit did not delude himself, however. His 417mph would soon be exceeded. The feat was thrilling, prestigious and romantic, but had little lasting value.

The advantages of aircraft which could land on water were very clear, but size, not speed, would determine their future. The *Aphrodites* of the aviation world were built for glory, glamour and national pride. If Kirkland's was to survive into the future, attention must be turned to flying boats. Large, graceful, dependable ships with wings. Runways were unnecessary. They could land on any handy stretch of water, and there were oceans, rivers and lakes galore all over the world.

Blowing on his chilled hands he gazed into the greyness. Fortune had smiled on him three years ago. Sir Hector never did anything unless it would bring some kind of reward for himself. If Kit wanted fortune to continue smiling, it was imperative for him to offer some further return on the three-year investment his benefactor had so publicly revealed last night. The gauntlet had been thrown at his feet on that platform. He must take it up, or ignore it at his peril.

The memory of a young man in motorcycling clothes came back through the confusion of last night. Warren—he could not recall his other name—had designed a seaplane he had hoped to show to Donald. From their conversation, it had been plain he had known what he was talking about and some of his theories were worth pursuing. Apart from the fact that he had digs in Sheenmouth, all Kit knew about him was that he gave flying lessons at the Aero Club. Taking another drink from his hip-flask, Kit settled back in the car to wait for the mist to lift. While he did so, he elaborated on a vague plan based on the brief meeting last night.

THE TERRACE OF HOUSES looked neat and clean enough as Kit trod up the steps of number twenty-two and rang the bell.

The woman who answered it was respectable and suspicious.

'What can I do for you, may I ask?'

'I'd like to see Mr Grant,' he told her quietly. 'Jim Mason at the Aero Club gave me this address.'

Her lips pursed. 'Done nothing wrong, has he?' Nodding her crimped head, she added disapprovingly, 'Fast asleep, I shouldn't wonder. Came back in the dead of night, waking the whole neighbourhood with that motorcycle of his. Then he fell over his feet climbing the stairs.' Making no sign of allowing him entry, she asked who he was.

'Kit Anson.' He tried the softening effect of a smile.

This was one woman who was impervious to his charm. 'Oh, are you? I wasn't born yesterday, young man. That was him who flew the aeroplane across here and broke a record.'

'That's right. Were you watching me, Mrs . . .?'

'Bardolph.' She peered closely at his face. 'You're not really him, are you?'

'Of course. I must see Mr Grant on a matter of some importance. Sir Hector Kirkland also wishes to thank him for rescuing his daughter and escorting her safely home.'

Name-dropping succeeded where masculine charm had failed, and she stood aside to let him in. 'Right up the stairs. Top floor,' she called after him. 'If he wants a cup of tea, he'll have to come down and fetch it. Breakfast was over long ago, tell him.'

Warren was in bed, as his landlady had predicted. He sat up in confusion as he recognised his visitor, colour flooding his face and neck.

'Gosh, how did you trace me?' he mumbled with embarrassment.

'Through Jim Mason,' Kit explained, smiling to put the other man at his ease. 'Finding you was easy; gaining admittance was a definite challenge.'

Warren's colour deepened further. 'I made a terrible noise last night, apparently, so I'm not very popular with the terrace.'

'Were you very tight?' Kit asked, with interest. 'You look exactly the way I've often felt, so perhaps it isn't the best time for a get-together.'

'No, it's all right,' said Warren hastily, climbing from the bed with a hand clutching pyjama trousers that were on back-to-front.

Sweeping his goggles and leather jacket from a chair Warren invited Kit to sit down while he slipped along the landing to tidy up. 'It'll only take a minute or two.' Halfway across the room, he paused, still clutching his trousers. 'I could ask Mrs Bardolph to bring us some tea.'

Kit adopted a high voice. 'If he wants tea, he must come down and get it. Breakfast was over long ago.'

It induced a rueful grin. 'You sounded just like her. Won't be a tick.'

There was a vast improvement in Warren's appearance when he returned. The trousers had been reversed and were now securely tied, his crisp hair had been damped into a semblance of order, and he smelt of carbolic and toothpaste. Kit felt filthy, in comparison, and said so.

'I don't usually make morning calls on people, in this state,' he confessed. 'I slept in my car up on Brickham Hill.'

Warren was more at his ease now. 'Tell you what, I'll nip downstairs for two cups of tea while you clean up a bit.' Taking a fresh towel from a drawer, he tossed it over. 'Second door on your right.'

Feeling a new man, Kit returned to the attic room to find his host, in flannels and a blue shirt, sitting with a tray containing tea and rock cakes.

'Good Lord, I must be losing my touch,' he told Warren. 'Your landlady would have none of me, even when I assured her that I was "him who flew the aeroplane yesterday", yet she plies you with tea and buns.'

Warren laughed. 'Have faith. Delayed hero worship overcame her. These buns—her speciality—are specifically for you.'

'Liar!' said Kit comfortably, sitting in the other chair. 'I'm sorry we didn't meet up again last night. It was my fault. What happened to you? Coombes did fix you up, didn't he?'

'Mmm, rather,' Warren told him, with his mouth full. 'I looked so dapper, Leone spoke to me for five or ten minutes without recognising me.' He drank some tea, then said, 'As a matter of fact, I intended to send a note of apology to you, and to her. You see, once I got up there with Phil Davenport, I was sunk. They kept demanding more and more . . .'

Puzzled, Kit coaxed from his host the surprising story of his impromptu concert on the trumpet. This led to the disclosure of his youth spent in London. Soon, he had learned a great deal about Warren, which strengthened his belief in the plan he had hatched on that misty hillside.

'I came in the hope of seeing your drawings,' he said eventually.

Warren crossed to the table and opened a cutlery drawer. Bringing a roll of papers back to Kit, he looked at him apologetically. 'My draughtsmanship isn't one hundred per cent when done on a flat table in poor light, I'm afraid.'

'To hell with draughtsmanship, so long as the detail and specifications are there. Right, let's spread them out and take a look.'

Half an hour later, Kit knew he was on to a winner. He set about putting the next part of his plan into operation. With barely concealed excitement, Warren listened as he outlined the scheme from start to finish.

'Of course,' Kit concluded, 'you realise that I haven't yet approached the Kirklands, so nothing is definite. You'd like the job, wouldn't you?'

'I'd give my eyeteeth for it,' came the fervent reply.

'You'll be expected to give a lot more than that if you work for Kirkland Marine Aviation,' Kit warned. 'Sir Hector will expect you to devote your whole life to his company.'

Warren grinned. 'Suits me.'

Kit then sat back and spoke of something else he had been considering. 'It seems to me that these digs will be a bit inconvenient. To get to the workshops from here would be a hell of a journey each day.'

'I suppose I'll have to try to find somewhere nearer,' Warren agreed.

Kit looked at him. 'I haven't always enjoyed luxury, you know. Before I moved into Sheenmouth Abbey, I lived in a boathouse about half a mile upriver on the Kirkland boundary. When my father was killed in a works accident, Sir Hector said I could keep the place so long as I undertook the maintenance and repairs. I've only been over to it now and then—too many memories—but it might be the very place for you, Warren. There are two large rooms above a spacious store, which my father and I used to tinker about in. You're welcome to use it. We paid no rent to Sir Hector so, now it belongs to me, the same terms apply. I believe a drawing board and several other useful things are still there. The greatest advantage will be that you can come down to Kirkland's on the boat with me each morning. Well, what do you think? The offer isn't dependent on your getting a job with Kirkland's,' he added. 'You could save on rent, and have much more room to work on designs. There'd be no clumsy landlady to step on your models, either.'

'Gosh, it's really jolly nice of you,' said Warren, flushing with pleasure. 'I can't think of adequate words to tell you how grateful I am.'

'That's just as well. I've taken a leaf from Sir Hector's book, and decided never to do anything unless there's some advantage in it for me. You, Warren my lad, are going to help me to achieve my next ambition.' Kit got to his feet. 'I'll go back now and take the first step towards it. I'll be in touch as soon as there's any news.' Turning at the door, he smiled. 'It looks as though we have the makings of a fine team. Thanks for the tea and buns.'

Warren came across to him swiftly, his colour deepening once more. 'Would you give my . . . my best wishes to Leone, and tell her I'll write to explain what happened last night.'

Feeling sorry for him, Kit asked, 'You really like her, don't you?'

'Rather! Don't you?'

Avoiding an answer to that, Kit said quietly, 'Perhaps you aren't aware that she's only sixteen, and still a pupil at a very expensive Swiss school. She'll be going back there in September for the new term.' Seeing the dismay on Warren's face, he added, 'If you're going to forge close ties with the Kirklands, you'd better cool off where she's concerned. I'd hate you to land yourself in a fix over her.'

5

Kit returned to Sheenmouth Abbey, to shave and take a bath. After sleeping for an hour, he went in search of Sir Hector. He found him in his office suite with Donald and Maitland.

Sir Hector looked up to scowl at him. 'Where the hell have you been?'

'Recovering from last night.'

'You weren't here last night, damn you! Who gave you leave to slip off halfway through the evening?'

'I'm sorry, sir,' said Kit. 'I was doing my duty until well past two.'

'I was doing mine until five this morning . . . like everyone else save you.'

'You and everyone else didn't fly *Aphrodite* yesterday,' Kit pointed out calmly. 'And if *I* hadn't done so, there'd have been no reason for the party. While you and your guests were eating and drinking beneath a marquee on the prom, I was flying round in circles within a red-hot cockpit to make Kirkland's world famous. I was still going round in circles while you and your guests were indulging in more eating and drinking last night. I left, rather than embarrass you by passing out in the centre of a Grecian grotto.'

Sir Hector grunted. 'Very smooth, very smooth. You're beginning to sound like a Kirkland. You're not, and don't you forget it.'

'No, sir. You already have one application for membership under way.' He turned to Donald. 'Where is Stephanie? Sleeping off the excitement of becoming engaged to you?'

Donald's scowl was a replica of his father's. 'She apparently has more stamina than you. We've already played two sets of tennis this morning.'

'In the mist? How did you decide which of you won?' Then Kit relented. 'In all yesterday's excitement, I don't think I actually offered my congratulations. Please accept them now.'

'Thanks.' Donald got to his feet. 'I think I'll find Steph and go for a swim.'

'I was hoping to discuss something with you,' put in Kit swiftly. 'Can you spare half an hour or so? It's business.'

'Sit down, Donald,' his father told him. 'Yesterday's success can't be left to stagnate. Yesterday we made the world sit up and take notice of us. We have to keep it sitting up!' Turning to Kit, he showed signs of testiness. 'I hope this means you've been doing something useful all morning.'

Kit nodded. 'I've been following up a contact I made last night.' He glanced across at the immaculate personal assistant. 'You'll probably remember the fellow, Maitland. He rescued Leone when the Bentley broke down, and she invited him to meet Donald. You brought him across to me with the message that he was making himself a nuisance, so would I give him my autograph then chuck him out. Good thing I didn't, because he told me about a new seaplane he's designed. Seemed very disappointed that he'd been unable to interest you in it, Donald.'

Into the heavy silence which followed, Sir Hector said, 'What is that sly piece of screw-twisting leading to, boy?'

Kit got straight to the point. 'I roused him early this morning, and he showed me the drawings of his seaplane. We discussed it in full detail and, in my opinion, I've come across the very man we want. He has flair and originality, based on a good sound design knowledge, *and* he's a qualified pilot. It's the opportunity of a lifetime for Kirkland's.'

Sir Hector shook his head. 'We already have a top designer in Donald.'

'A top designer of seaplanes, yes,' Kit agreed, with emphasis, 'but Donald admits to being confronted with insoluble problems over the flying-boat project we need to get under way. As you just now said, sir, we have to follow yesterday's success with something truly exciting. Look,' he continued, growing enthusiastic, 'you've wanted to expand to the development of flying boats for some time. The future for such machines is very rosy. Warren and I discussed this very thoroughly, and he's full of ideas. I happen to have touched on the great dream he's had for several years. Put him in our design office with Donald, and we'd have the opportunity to lead the world with our "passenger liners with wings". His expression!'

'Passenger liners with wings,' Sir Hector mused. 'A nice turn of phrase that. Get him up here, Kit. I'll talk to him.'

'It wouldn't work, Father,' cried Donald immediately. 'We can't have two designers at Kirkland's.'

Sir Hector's sharp eyes swivelled to study him. 'Why not? Two minds are better than one.'

'Two minds think in different ways,' came the stubborn reply. 'I couldn't possibly work with him. No, Father, I have to do it on my own.'

'Then do it! Don't keep coming to me with the excuse that there are too many problems each time I ask about progress. Solve the bloody problems.'

'They're insuperable,' Donald insisted mulishly. 'Engineering and construction limitations are the same for any designer.'

'Limitations are there to be overcome! Good God, boy, the wheel would never have been made if man had accepted *limitations*.' Sir Hector leaned heavily on the desk. 'I want a passenger liner with wings. It's the best idea I've ever been offered. You'll make me one, but you'll make it a hell of a sight quicker with this man on your staff . . . if he's as good as I've been told . . . This man will work with you. Do I make myself clear?'

'Yes,' Donald snapped, and immediately left the room.

With his gaze on the door through which his son had just vanished, the victor said, 'Maitland, send a message to this man telling him to see me as soon as he can get himself here. Where does he live, boy?'

Kit gave the address, then found himself being fixed with a cold eye as the personal assistant left on the heels of the son of the house.

'You'd better be right about this.'

'I am. Absolutely right.'

'You haven't yet explained what part you expect to play in this scheme.'

Kit sat back in his chair. 'My part will be to undertake a world promotion tour for Kirkland's, by accepting all the invitations I'm going to be sent to fly *Aphrodite* in displays and competitions. While I'm doing that, I shall canvass orders for the flying boat from international passenger lines. By the time I return, the plans for a prototype should be ready. I shall help to build her, then demonstrate her qualities on a proving flight from here to Africa.'

Excitement flared in Sir Hector's eyes. 'It could never be done.'

'They said that about travelling through the air at 417mph but I did it only yesterday. When that prototype is built, I'll fly it from here to Africa.'

'Damn you, I do believe you have the guts to try!'

'I'll try, and I'll succeed,' Kit told him, with matching excitement.

'By God, you're more of a Kirkland than . . .' He broke off and turned away abruptly. 'Don't grow too damned big for your breeches, boy. Never forget who you are.'

Excitement vanished beneath swift anger. 'I never wish to forget,' Kit cried. 'I made the name of Anson respectable again yesterday. It'll be more, much more, than respectable by the time I've finished with it, believe me.'

LEONE DRESSED FOR DINNER with great care. A quiet family meal, served in the Roman pavilion beside the swimming pool, was to be a private celebration of her brother's engagement. Stephanie would be at Sheenmouth Abbey for the next six weeks while the wedding arrangements were decided.

For Leone, a circle of the deepest red would be for ever round the date of June 10, 1932. Yesterday had been the most momentous day of her life. The memory of those moments in the chapel thrilled her. What had happened had been explosive. The passion she had experienced in Kit's arms last night established a deep bond between them which could never be broken.

She had not seen him since he had marched her back to the safety of crowds, plainly disturbed by the way he had betrayed himself to her. When she had slipped along to his room this afternoon, his door had been locked. She guessed that he might now feel embarrassed, because he had let his pose of sophistication slip to expose his naked desire for love and understanding. It was essential that she should convince him that the secret they now shared would remain theirs alone. When he had taken off yesterday morning and headed into the sky alone, she had known she loved him.

Choosing a romantic dress of sea-green georgette, Leone made her way downstairs. Only Donald and Stephanie were there when she reached the floodlit swimming pool. The engaged couple were chatting quietly together as they lounged in the gilded Roman chairs, enjoying a pre-dinner drink.

'Hello,' she greeted. 'Making plans for October?'

Stephanie smiled. 'I'd very much like you to be one of the bridesmaids, but will you be able to come over from school to attend?'

Telling Dayley that she would have a pink gin, Leone sat beside her future sister-in-law. 'I naturally took it for granted that I'd be asked, so I've planned everything. Heiterman's is frightfully prestigious and all that, but there are colleges in England which are every bit as good.' Taking the glass from Dayley, she said, 'I'll transfer to one near here.'

Sipping her drink, Leone asked her brother if the chapel would be fully restored in time for the wedding. 'It still hasn't a roof,' she pointed out.

Donald gazed gloomily at her. 'You should know better. Father has made up his mind we shall be married in it, so it *will* be ready.'

'It seems a pity,' she reflected dreamily. 'A ruin is far more romantic.'

'Not if a lump of masonry falls on the bride,' he retorted. 'Have you spoken to him about not returning to Heiterman's?'

'How could I? He's been obsessed with *Aphrodite* and the speed record, like everyone else. Still, it was frightfully thrilling. What a pity you arrived too late to see it, Stephanie.'

'I did see it, my dear girl. Kit invited me to the hangar to watch preparations, and I was in the boat with him and Donald when *Aphrodite* was towed out for takeoff. I kissed him for luck the moment before he climbed into the cockpit. You're right, it *was* frightfully exciting.'

Leone drank her pink gin rather quickly and asked Dayley for another. As Kit joined the group, he smiled her way. 'I understand your gallant rescuer yesterday turned out to be a musical genius. The lad asked me to apologise and explain to you that he was literally borne off by enthusiastic guests, who plied him with drinks until he was most decidedly confused.' Sitting beside her, he took from Dayley a glass of pale sherry.

Leone was surprised. 'Have you seen Warren today?'

He nodded. 'We had a long fruitful meeting this morning over tea and rock buns. He's a very talented young man. With any luck, he'll soon be working for Kirkland's.'

'There's no luck attached to it,' said Sir Hector, arriving at that moment. 'I took him on this afternoon. He starts tomorrow.'

'Tomorrow!' exclaimed Donald sharply.

'There's no point in delay. He's a good sound man with ideas and ambition. I liked him. Knows what he's talking about.' Turning to Kit, he nodded. 'You were right. Good thing you met up with him.'

'I met up with him first, Father,' Leone said, primed by two pink gins, and by the tingling proximity of the man who had kissed her so possessively last night. 'He came along on a motorbike, so I stopped him and made him bring me home. He'd been so sweet, I brought him in and asked Donald to look after him while I changed.'

Sir Hector studied Leone keenly. 'Are you in the habit of stopping young men on motorbikes, and hopping on the pillion?'

'I've only had the chance to do it once, so far,' she told him, 'but I expect I could easily form the habit. Stopping them is the difficult part. Once they're safely stuck in a hedge, climbing up behind them is very easy. They can't refuse to take you where you want to go, when your arms are round their waist. Warren surrendered in a very short time.'

'Artful young miss,' commented her father thoughtfully. 'Donald, young

Grant will be at the office by nine tomorrow. Be prepared to outline the main problems, so that he can start giving them some thought. I want you there, boy,' he added, waving his glass in Kit's direction, 'so don't take off like you did last night. The women will have to wait. Dare say you'll survive without them for a few days more.'

'Will the women survive without Kit?' queried Stephanie softly.

'By the way, sir,' said the subject of this speculation. 'I've offered Warren the tenancy of the old boathouse. His present digs are extremely inconvenient for the journey to the workshops, and he'll need the extra facilities for a drawing board, and so on. I know you told me the place was mine, but I thought you'd like to be made aware of his presence there. He'll be on hand should he be needed after working hours.'

'Excellent,' said Sir Hector. 'By God, we'll get this flying boat under way at last. I want an all-out effort from everyone.'

'Father, we have given an all-out effort on *Aphrodite* for the past eighteen months,' Donald said, with some force. 'Surely we deserve a short break. The record was broken only yesterday.'

'And I was delighted. That was yesterday, however, and now I'm looking to tomorrow.'

'But, sir, Steph and I have to work on the arrangements for the wedding. She's on an extended visit so that we can.'

Sir Hector smiled. 'Stephanie is an extremely capable woman, who understands the need for priorities. That's why I'm confident that she'll make the perfect wife for you. Weddings are affairs best handled by women, anyway. Ah, here's Maitland! We'll have dinner now.'

He moved towards the three steps leading up to the pavilion, where the marble table was set for six with a Venetian dinner service in red and gold.

Throughout the four courses which ended, as a concession to Stephanie, with a wonderful mousse of fresh apricots and Grand Marnier, conversation ranged over many subjects which had no connection with flying. A rare warmth spread between them all as laughter, rarely heard at the dinner table in that old monastery, rang out in the still June air.

After coffee and liqueurs beside the pool, Sir Hector had relaxed so much he declared his intention of indulging in a rare early night. Getting to his feet, he gripped Donald's shoulder. 'No need to get up. Stay there with that lovely young woman of yours. Enjoy the rest of the evening. You've earned it, my boy, and tomorrow you'll embark on a project which will consolidate the reputation you established for yourself yesterday. Trust my judgment, Donald. It hasn't let you down yet, has it?'

Resentment passed over Donald's features as he murmured, 'No, sir.'

'Good night, my dear,' Sir Hector said to Stephanie. 'I can promise you a very exciting and distinguished future as a Kirkland.'

He smiled at Donald. 'Weddings are affairs more suited to women. Leave them to make the arrangements and concentrate on your first priority.' Turning to Kit, he said, 'The same applies to you, boy, and it is *not* wenching. That's for leisure time, as I've had to remind you on many occasions.'

Kit stood up with a grin on his face. 'It's part of a flier's job to keep the ladies happy.'

'Cheeky young devil!' was the surprisingly good-natured response. 'When you embark on this proposed world tour Maitland is successfully organising, I suppose you'll spend half your time in dalliance.' Jabbing his finger in Kit's direction, he concluded, 'Be there at nine tomorrow—sharp!'

'I wouldn't miss it, sir, after playing the vital role in getting Grant for the company.'

'Wrong, boy,' Sir Hector declared. 'My daughter had the sense to nab him while he was stuck in a hedge. Isn't that correct?' he asked Leone.

'Yes, Father,' she replied, smiling up at him. 'Kidnapping useful young men is another thing women do well, besides arranging weddings.' She knew she must take this opportunity of a hearing while he was in such a mellow mood. 'Stephanie has asked me to be a bridesmaid, but I shall be back in Switzerland before October.'

'I'll arrange a ten-day leave of absence for you. No problem whatever.'

'Father,' she said urgently, 'I don't want to go back to Heiterman's. I've had enough of Europe.'

'I see no sense in changing a perfect arrangement at this stage. Maitland will request your leave of absence for this frilly-frock affair.' Turning to his assistant standing nearby, he said, 'Perhaps we should run through that report before I turn in. There won't be a lot of time in the morning.'

The two men walked away deep in conversation.

Turning back disconsolately to the others Leone found her brother and Stephanie dancing to the soft strains of music from the hidden loudspeakers round the pool. She moved across to Kit. 'Do you think Father would consider that dancing with me came under the heading "wenching"?' she asked pertly.

He gave her a long level look, then rose and held out his arms. 'I think I'm safe enough. No one would classify Leone Kirkland as a wench.'

'Not even you?' she murmured.

'Especially me!'

Loving every moment of his nearness, she tilted her face up to ask, 'What about your world tour? How long will you be away?'

'Six months, at least. More, if I can manage it.'

'So long?' she cried in dismay. 'When will you set off?'

'Not for a few weeks. Even the redoubtable Mr Jarvis needs a short time of preparation for such a complex project.'

It was some consolation, but she was still unhappy. 'What about the wedding?'

He shook his head. 'Business and matrimony don't mix. I'll have to forgo watching the incomparable Miss Main become Mrs Donald Kirkland. I shall be sacrificing the thrill of discovering whether the mother of the bride succeeds in finding a dress not remotely similar to that of any of the guests.'

Leone stopped dancing. 'Kit, why are you adopting this elaborate social pose with me?'

'This is rather an elaborate social occasion, isn't it?'

'Not as elaborate as the one last night. You were vastly different then.'

There was a fleeting shadow in his eyes as he said, 'Don't judge me on last night, Leone. I was three-quarters drunk, maudlin and . . . and I *did* mistake you for one of my wenches.' Putting his hand beneath her elbow, he led her to the far end of the pool where shadows made the night even more enchanting. For a wild moment, she believed he was going to kiss her again. Instead, he turned her to face him and stood holding her arms while he spoke to her very seriously.

'Don't try to grow up too soon. It can be dangerous. What happened last night is the perfect example of that risk. I'm only twenty-two, yet my name is in every newspaper across the world today. For me, that's only the beginning. Your father and Donald have made it possible for me to pursue the love of my life: exploration of the sky. That is my *only* love, Leone. Life is exceptionally good for me right now, and that's the way I want it to continue. "Wenching", as your father called it, is part of it, and a most enjoyable part. I want that to continue, also.'

'Go on,' she prompted, thrilled by every moment of his heart-to-heart confession.

With fresh determination, he said, 'I intend to make flying history. The name of Anson will be there with Lindbergh and Wright—to say nothing of the incomparable Amy.' Fervour highlighted his dark attraction even more, as he added, 'That's the real me, Leone. Kit Anson is searching for fame, fortune and the pathway to the stars. He's ruthless, opinionated and extremely fickle.'

She smiled her love at him. 'He's also a very accomplished liar.'

Releasing his hold on her, he studied her with exasperation. 'Haven't you listened to a word I've said?'

She took one of his hands in her own. 'Please stop trying to bluster your way through excuses for last night. What happened between us was very, very special. Don't worry, I would never tell anyone. And you're not the first man in my life, you know. Father might think of me as a schoolgirl, but Raoul certainly didn't . . .'

'Dear God,' he exclaimed forcefully, 'the careless, irresponsible Raoul needs a hearty kick on his backside, in my opinion.'

They were marvellous words to her ears. 'I hope you won't be as jealous of Warren's interest in me. Father wouldn't like his new discovery to be treated to a kick in the pants.'

'I've already spoken to Warren about you,' he told her sternly. 'I gather he got rather carried away last night. Leave him alone. Your father won't want his blue-eyed boy to have the wrong ideas where you're concerned.'

Movement towards them heralded Stephanie, saying, 'Hey, you two, what about a swim? It's always heavenly by moonlight.'

'A marvellous idea,' agreed Kit with relief. 'It might cool everyone down.'

Although she resented the other girl's intrusion, Leone had to own it was an inspired suggestion. They split up to don bathing suits which were hanging within the separate changing rooms. Leone chose her usual scarlet. The other girl was in a smart beige costume.

'You didn't dance for long,' Stephanie commented from the adjacent cubicle. 'What was the deep, serious discussion about?'

'Our plans,' she called back airily. 'It's the first real chance we've had. Kit's been so busy with *Aphrodite*, and now there's the new project starting tomorrow. Men never have any time, do they? However did you and Donald meet, by the way?'

'At the Chelsea Arts Ball. A mutual friend introduced us because I was dressed as Queen Nefertiti, and Donald had come as an Egyptian slave.'

'Mmm, and the relationship has stayed that way ever since,' Leone commented mischievously. She picked up her bathing cap and went out.

The two men were swimming energetically. Leone climbed to the highest board and dived, swimming effortlessly underwater to surface beside Kit.

'How about a race?' she invited eagerly.

'All right, mermaid, but I'll win.'

That he did so was only due to his superior physique. His compliment on her prowess pleased her, so she challenged him to a diving contest. On hearing of it, the other pair decided to join in, but were no match for the girl who had spent lonely hours with little else to do but amuse herself in this pool. Tonight, it was especially thrilling to show off in Kit's presence. She used the opportunity to the full, ending her display with a spectacular triple somersault she dared them all to emulate. Only Kit was game to try.

'Go ahead and break your neck,' invited Donald, heaving himself out, 'but be there at nine o'clock sharp . . . with your head tucked under your arm, if necessary.'

Kit laughed, and walked away to climb the steps of the diving board. Leone watched, suddenly chilled by her brother's words. 'Kit, don't,' she called. 'Come back.'

She watched him stretch both arms and poise, ready to leap into the night air. When he cut the water cleanly, it was after only two somersaults. He came to the surface shaking water from his dark hair, laughing at his own faintheartedness.

'I now have to suffer the humiliation caused by misdirected bravado,' he called to her. 'Only a fool willingly exposes himself to it . . .'

'Don't be silly,' she called back. 'You attempted it, which is more than Donald did.'

Her brother, towelling himself down, said calmly, 'I never feel the need to display my prowess to ladies.'

'My God, stripped down to the bare essentials he really is a magnificent specimen,' murmured Stephanie at the rail beside her.

Leone had to admit Donald looked attractively well proportioned as he stood holding his towel, gilded by the floodlighting. Yet, when she turned to Stephanie, she saw that the girl's eyes were on Kit as he climbed from the pool. Sharp jealousy gave birth to suspicion. What exactly was the relationship between this man she now loved, and her brother's future wife? Leone confronted her.

'I get the impression that you know Kit well. How is that?'

Stephanie smiled and gained the steps. Leone followed her. 'We've known each other for more than eighteen months. Kit was the mutual friend at the Chelsea Arts, who introduced me to your brother.'

The information came as something of a shock. 'You knew Kit first, yet chose Donald?'

The other girl gave her a shrewd glance. 'My dear Leone, women don't *marry* men like Kit, they simply enjoy them. Kit is immensely exciting, but his future is so precarious.'

Furious, Leone cried, 'That hasn't stopped a great many women from marrying pilots.'

'Dear girl, you misunderstand,' the other said calmly. 'I wasn't referring to the dangers of flying. Charm is Kit's passport to survival. He works hard on it, believe me, and never more than on your father because, if he ever puts a foot wrong where Sir Hector is concerned, everything will tumble down around him leaving him the way he was three years ago. I shouldn't care to be anywhere near him if that happened.'

WARREN TOOK UP RESIDENCE in the old boathouse. Because of that chance encounter with Leone Kirkland he had a job such as he had dreamed of for years, enough money to live well, and a quaint, comfortable, roomy home. He also had the famous Kit Anson for a friend. Small wonder he lived in a daze for a while, travelling up to Kirkland's by boat each morning to discuss and offer his opinions to Donald and Sir Hector, with Kit backing him up. Then he would return exhausted but happy to his new home by the river.

The flying-boat project possessed practically his every waking thought and there were not enough hours in each day. After two weeks on the job, he had decided to clear the ground-floor storeroom the Ansons had used as a workshop-cum-office so that he could work at night. Leaving the heavy workbench and tools where they were, he moved the drawing board up to his sitting room where the light was better. That done, he decided the flat-topped desk should join it. It was a heavy piece of furniture, so he removed each drawer to take up separately. Then he hauled the desk shell to the next floor by means of a pulley installed for slinging boats up while repairs were done. Afterwards he felt very satisfied with his evening's work, and made himself a mug of cocoa.

Sprawled in one of the old armchairs, he sipped his cocoa while his mind grappled with the main problem facing them on this project. Kit had vowed to fly from Sheenmouth to Africa. The distance was nothing—the whole world had been encompassed through the daring exploits of aviation's pioneers in tiny machines—but what Kit was promising Sir Hector was to take a 'passenger liner with wings' over to that dark continent. And, while it was inconceivable to carry the hundreds accommodated in ships, the new Kirkland's flying boat would have to provide passage for many more than the half-dozen daring souls who could presently be taken across the Channel in floatplanes. Lost in speculation, Warren realised they would first have to design a ship, then an aircraft, merging the two by selecting the essential demands of each. Whereas a seaplane was really a straightforward aircraft with floats rather than wheels, what they now had in mind was a ship which had wings rather than sails. It would be vastly different from *Seaspray* or *Aphrodite*.

At the thought of the famous yellow seaplane, Warren frowned. The only slight damper on his new sense of joy was Donald Kirkland's lack of cooperation. He remained obstinate about not wishing to form a team. So far, the machine he appeared to be advocating seemed to be little more than the standard *Supermarine* model already in service, blown up to several times its existing size and with two wing-mounted propellers to augment the one fixed behind the cabin. His ideas were sound enough, yet showed no touch of the brilliance he had demonstrated with *Aphrodite*. Warren had been so eager to work with this gifted designer that he took the man's refusal to give rein to his flair and imagination as a heavy snub to his own ability. As the senior designer, Donald had the power to approve or veto proposals, but he would not even accept that Warren had sufficient skill to make any.

The only answer was to develop them here at home. Then, with Kit behind him, he would present his findings to Donald when Sir Hector was present. It would probably serve to worsen relations between himself and the heir to the company, but it might start a flying boat on the way to being built. Finishing his cocoa, he went straight to work at the desk without bothering to replace the drawers. They remained in a pile on an old sofa.

The work went so well, he refused an invitation from Kit to drive into Torquay on the following Saturday. He rose early on a morning of grey skies and sheeting rain, made himself porridge, eggs and bacon and a pot of tea, then carried it all to the desk where he promptly let it grow cold while he grappled with a very tricky weight ratio. Solving it was such a triumph, he happily cooked a second breakfast, only to realise that it was practically time for lunch. Adding several apples to his meal solved that problem, and he was about to return to his desk when he heard movements below.

Thinking Kit had changed his mind about driving to Torquay in such heavy rain, he called out, 'Come on up! I've got some good news for you.'

He was dumbfounded when a pale round face plastered by wet red hair appeared through the aperture in the floor to stare apprehensively at him.

'Don't be angry, Warren,' she begged. 'Mrs Bardolph told me you were here . . . and all about the job at Kirkland's. I wanted to congratulate you.'

He helped her up the last few steps. How could he have forgotten this girl he so nearly loved? Guilt swept through him as he saw her sodden state. Water was dripping from her hair onto her cheeks.

'Mona, you're wet through! Take off that mackintosh while I fetch a towel for your hair.'

Returning, he saw the rain had penetrated through to her green and white spotted dress. She was shivering.

'How did you manage to get so wet, silly girl?' He held out the towel. 'Here you are. However did you make your way here on foot?'

Taking the towel, she began to rub her hair briskly. 'Mrs Bardolph knew you were in an old boathouse on the Kirkland boundary, and Jake Meakins at the ferry knew near enough where it was. He told me to get off at Forton, then follow the river up to the inlet. He forgot to say that the path is so overgrown it's practically impassable, in places.'

Feeling even more guilty, he went across to take the towel and begin rubbing her hair himself. 'You should have written, you goose! We could have met somewhere.'

She gazed into his eyes through the tangle of red strands. 'Would you have met me, after what Dad said to you?'

'What made you call on Ma Bardolph?' he asked, to change the subject.

'There was a job vacant up at the tractor works. It wasn't flying, but it was to do with engines. I wanted to let you know about it before I put it in this week's edition. Of course, I didn't know you'd gone up in the world, mixing with the Kirklands.'

'I'm not,' he protested. 'At least, only at work.' She was still shivering. 'You'll catch a nasty cold unless you get out of those wet things,' he told her fondly. 'Go into my bedroom and take off that wet dress. There's a dressing gown you can wear while we dry it. I'll make some tea.' He urged her forward. 'Go on, do as I say!'

While he made tea, Warren recalled the many happy times he had spent with Mona. She had done so much for him, how could he have left her lonely and miserable after that scene with her father?

'Do you like living in this queer place?' asked the girl, as she returned to hang her dress over the back of a chair.

'I do.' He grinned. 'Actually, I haven't got round to much cleaning yet, as you can see.'

Her nose wrinkled. 'It smells a bit damp.'

'That's because it's raining. It's nice on dry days.'

'There's extra space,' she conceded, 'but it was more comfortable at Mrs Bardolph's.'

'I had to pay rent there. Kit lets me live here for nothing.'

'Kit?'

'Kit Anson.'

'Oh.'

He reached for her hand. 'Don't go all po-faced. You'd like him.'

Her smile finally broke through. 'No one's called me po-faced for ages.'

He picked up the tea tray and carried it across to a large lumpy settee, where a low table stood beside it. He poured tea, relating to her the story of how Leone had stopped him and demanded to be taken home. 'We're working on this exciting new machine,' he added, 'because Kit apparently made Sir Hector crazy to have what I had called "a passenger liner with wings". I'm determined that he'll have it, despite Donald's refusal to cooperate.'

'He sounds a very stupid person,' Mona commented. 'Sir Hector sounds greedy and as hard as nails. That girl sounds very selfish and a bit crazy.'

'She's not "that girl", Mona, she has a name,' he told her firmly. 'Of course I don't work with her. In fact, I haven't set eyes on her since that first evening . . . and I don't want to,' he finished enigmatically.

That information pleased Mona, and she drank her tea while remarking on the state of the room. 'It's disgracefully untidy.'

'I've been so busy since I moved in, all I do is eat, work and sleep. The Ansons left some stuff here, and I keep meaning to ask Kit if he wants to sort it out and keep any of it.'

'It's a bit lonely, stuck out here in the middle of nowhere.'

'I've been so busy, I haven't had time to feel lonely.'

She put down her cup and saucer, then turned to him. 'Does that mean you've been too busy to think about me?'

It was a tricky question. He hesitated.

'I've thought about you . . . every day and every night,' she confessed.

'Oh, Mona,' he exclaimed remorsefully, 'you know why I've stayed away. Your father was right about the situation. I *was* beginning to make unfair demands on you. He hasn't any idea you've come here?'

She shook her head. 'I don't think he's heard that you're working at Kirkland's. He'd have told me.'

She leaned forward to take a biscuit, and the dressing gown parted a little to reveal the lace edging of her bodice which lay round the curve of her breasts. Warren could not take his eyes from the sight.

Mona surveyed the room again as she nibbled a gingersnap. 'If it was done up, I expect it could be quite nice. Pretty curtains at the window . . . You'd have to get new furniture, of course.' Her gaze rose to the beamed roof. 'You could put planks across to make a proper ceiling, then it could all be painted a nice bright colour. It needs a feminine touch to make it into a real home.' She put her hand over his. 'I could come at weekends and make it cosy and comfortable.'

It sounded marvellous. Faced with an even more revealing glimpse as the dressing gown parted further, thoughts of just how cosy and comfortable she could make him at weekends warmed his mind.

'I couldn't ask you to do that,' he murmured.

'You don't have to. I'm offering,' she told him just as softly. 'The bedroom is in an awful mess. Fancy leaving coils of old rope in the corner!'

Apparently oblivious of the way he was now fondling her hand, Mona studied the jumbled corner which served as a kitchen. 'That's an utter disgrace! It needs a new stove, and some cupboards to pack away the china. Not that any of those things are worth keeping. Now you've got a proper job, Warren, you can afford to buy a nice tea and dinner set.'

All at once, Warren saw which way her mind was working. She was planning a home for *two*. It came as a shock to realise that there was now no real obstacle to buying her a diamond ring and setting a date for the wedding. With what he presently earned at Kirkland's plus the bonus he had been promised by Sir Hector when the prototype flying boat went into production, his financial future was rosy. He was extremely fond of Mona; he found her sexually beckoning.

She turned shining eyes towards him. 'Oh, Warren, it would be the cosiest little house you've ever known. In time, we could make a garden by clearing some of the trees along the bank. It would be the perfect spot for a couple of dogs, and for . . . well, later on, who knows?' she finished shyly.

He knew, well enough. Since his present enthusiasm was for the activity which came before what came later on, he delayed an immediate response, while taking in the glowing attraction of her face surrounded by the fluffy red hair drying like a halo.

'Darling Warren, I do love you so,' she murmured, her arms sliding round his neck. 'The last three weeks have been the worst of my life.'

Her urgent kisses brought an immediate response in him. He slid the dressing gown from her plump freckled shoulders, as his mouth found hers. Tugging the dressing-gown cord free, he pushed it and the bodice off to leave her dressed in no more than a pair of pants. Unbuttoning his own clothes, he pulled them off before getting to his feet to carry her through to the bed.

The climax came almost immediately. Mona cried out with the pleasure-pain of it, while he lay across her damp body, marvelling. Total contentment lulled them both to sleep before they were aware of it.

Warren awoke to find the sun streaming through the uncurtained window. Turning his head on the pillow, he saw a girl beside him. Recollection came swiftly, and with it a strong sense of guilt. Oh God, what if he had made her pregnant? He sat up quickly, filled with panic. Jack Cummings would march him to the altar before he knew what had hit him.

With passion well and truly spent, he began to count the cost. Even if there were no repercussions from what he had done this afternoon, Mona would expect him to produce the diamond ring, together with the date of the imminent wedding. Putting his head in his hands, he told himself she had planned this all along. He had walked straight into the trap like a gullible fool. Anger swamped him.

His swift movement to leave the bed roused Mona. She smiled dreamily as he glanced around for his underpants or trousers. 'We slept too long,' he said. 'It's almost five. Shouldn't you be getting back?'

Mona sensed the change in him immediately. 'What's wrong, darling? You've grown all distant.'

'Nothing's wrong. I'm just worried about getting you home before your father grows suspicious and asks too many questions.'

Her smile was like that of a mother for a foolish child. 'He can ask whatever questions he likes now, silly, and it won't matter.'

The trap seemed to be closing fast. 'Mona, we both got very carried away,' he told her with a tone nearing desperation. 'You'd better not come here again. It's far too risky.'

Stepping from the bed, she slid her arms around him. 'If you find it too risky for me to come here like this, we'd better get married as soon as possible. Then we can do this all the time without worrying.'

'It's not as simple as that,' he told her, disentangling himself. 'I've only just started working for Kirkland's, and Sir Hector demands I devote all my time to the job. I need to concentrate for hours on end when I get back here each day, and I'm more or less at his call at any time of day or night.'

Mona shivered as if he had thrown cold water over her. Then the silence was broken by a light voice calling Warren's name. Almost immediately, Leone appeared, dressed in riding clothes, with a small basket of peaches in her hand. Her blue eyes widened with shock as she gazed first at his naked body, then at Mona's, and finally at the tumbled bed.

'Heavens!' she whispered in hollow tones. 'I had no idea you were . . . oh, how . . . how . . .'

Turning on her heel, she fled with the basket of fruit still in her hand, leaving Warren feeling exposed and humiliated to face the pain of the girl now crouching on the bed beneath the protection of a sheet.

WARREN SAT UP for most of that night. His new golden future had just been tarnished by two girls: his self-esteem had been wrested from him by one act of spontaneous pleasure. He tried in vain to put from his mind that scene with Mona which now left him feeling angry and bewildered. Turning on him like a wildcat when he had swiftly dressed and tried to comfort her, she had betrayed the other side of her personality for the first time. Warren could still hardly believe such words could have come from the girl he thought he knew. Finally, she had stormed from the place, claiming it was a filthy, disgusting centre for his filthy, disgusting behaviour with any girl in sight, including that wealthy tart, Leone Kirkland.

He sighed heavily. After three weeks without making contact, Leone had to choose that precise moment to pay him a visit. What did she now think of him? A girl of sixteen, no matter how sophisticated, must have been shocked to walk in on a man and a girl stark naked beside a rumpled bed in midafternoon. What if Leone returned to the abbey to relate her experience to Sir Hector or Donald? Would they imagine he was bedding a series of girls, using the old boathouse as a den of vice? What if she told Kit of it? Would his friend feel he had abused his generosity in letting him live rent-free here?

At 3am he decided to make himself some cocoa and stretch out on the settee. The bed seemed an undesirable resting place, for the moment.

The cocoa tin was empty, and there was not enough milk left for a cup of tea. This small deprivation ignited his smouldering temper, as he recalled the rude remarks Mona had made about his living conditions. He had no need of her to make it bright and comfortable. He had no need of any girl. With fierce determination he stacked books neatly, shifted furniture, swept floors, dusted, folded away clothing, took the offending coils of rope from the corner of the bedroom to the workshop below, changed the sheets on the bed, then started putting the four drawers back into the shell of the desk.

They contained bottles of ink, old nibs, packets of drawing pins, blotting paper and any number of india rubbers. The latter brought a faint twitch to Warren's mouth. Old Anson must have altered his designs a great deal to require such a supply of erasers. The last drawer did, in fact, contain several rolled drawings marked by dampness and age. Curious to see the work of the man who had designed *Diadem*, Warren unrolled the stiff sheets covered with precise lines, curves and figures. The series of plans was for a seaplane, but it was not the early *Diadem*. Geoffrey Anson had scribbled the name *Solitaire* beneath the full sketch-plan of the graceful little aircraft, but as he studied the details, Warren experienced a growing sense of unease. Was he holding in his hands the explanation of Donald Kirkland's reticence on the flying-boat project? Had he stumbled upon the inconceivable truth about the heir to Kirkland Marine Aviation?

6

On Thursday of the following week, Warren and Kit worked late in the design office. A heated argument with Donald in the middle of the afternoon had sent the man storming out to streak away upriver in *Columbus*. In Kit's view, the younger Kirkland was lovelorn due to his father's refusal to allow him enough time with his fiancée. Warren had a vastly different theory, of which he was now so certain that it had changed his approach towards his employer's son.

After the events of Saturday, Warren had spent Sunday resolving several issues, the main one being what he should do with Geoffrey Anson's drawings of *Solitaire*. After much thought, he had decided to hand them over to Kit in casual manner, saying nothing of his suspicions. If his theory was proven, Kit was the right person to either speak out or let sleeping dogs lie. For his own part, pretending ignorance was the safest course. Nothing had been said since Monday, when he had given Kit the rolled drawings, so he guessed they must have been put aside without inspection.

Nothing had been said on the subject of Leone's visit to the boathouse, either, so Warren breathed a sigh of relief and, as the days passed with no sign of the wrathful father, it seemed certain Mona had also kept her counsel after Saturday's lovemaking.

After working on a knotty engineering problem until they had solved it, Kit dropped Warren off at the boathouse. Overcast skies were bringing darkness early; Warren felt loneliness more strongly than he had ever done.

Since Mona's visit the place seemed to accuse him. He could have all she had offered—someone to love and care for him, a clean, comfortable home, companionship, and her eager limbs to satisfy the hunger she had aroused in him. With a surge of eagerness he decided he had a letter to write. He would ask her to meet him in Sheenmouth on Saturday to choose a ring, and then to plan a most important date.

There was an envelope lying on the workbench, and he instantly imagined it to contain a letter from Mona. Instead, it was a summons to meet Sir Hector on a highly urgent matter. Warren set out right away, on his motorbike.

It was the first time he had been inside Sheenmouth Abbey since causing a stir with his trumpet concert. It looked vastly different tonight. The hall seemed gloomy. His footsteps echoed on stone slabs, as he crossed to the staircase. Sir Hector's business suite lay on the third floor, he had been told.

Warren was apprehensive. He hoped most fervently that he would not come face to face with Leone. He also hoped he was not about to be told off for daring to cross swords with the senior designer. Perhaps Sir Hector was about to challenge him to explain why he had not yet produced specimen sketches for the passenger liner with wings he had boasted of designing.

Sir Hector's business suite contained every modern item found in thriving company offices. Passing through a large room containing three desks with typewriters, telephones and card files, two of which were occupied by male secretaries, Warren entered Sir Hector's office.

The owner of Kirkland Marine Aviation sat behind a desk laden with files, four telephones, cigar box, gold and tourmaline lighter, and a copy of *Who's Who*. He looked a formidable figure in a plum-coloured smoking jacket and heavy horn-rimmed spectacles. Sir Hector attacked immediately—the shot came from an entirely unexpected quarter.

'Read this!' Warren was commanded, being handed a sheet of paper.

He took it with a slight frown, and read the message stamped on it in printer's ink.

> DO YOU KNOW WHAT YOUR DAUGHTER GETS UP TO IN THE OLD BOATHOUSE? SHE IS A TART. ASK YOUR NEW DESIGNER WHAT GOES ON BETWEEN THEM BEHIND YOUR BACK AT WEEKENDS.

Warren read the words again and again in disbelief that Mona could have done this to him. It could not be the work of her father; Jack Cummings would have wreaked a different form of vengeance from this. Swallowing hard, he realised then just how much Mona had loved him, and how very deeply he had hurt her.

'If the sender is a man, I want his name from you because he is plainly a crank who covets my daughter. If some silly venomous bitch is behind it, I want you off my property tonight.'

Warren tried to think.

'I have not insulted my daughter by telling her of this, but you had better have an explanation for this outrage, or you'll pay dearly, I swear. There'll be no scandal attached to any member of my family.' Sir Hector rose in the full flush of anger. 'You'd better say something very soon or I'm liable to choke the words out of you.'

'It's a lie, naturally,' Warren blurted out. 'Miss Kirkland has never visited me in the boathouse. We met on the night of the world record attempt, when I brought her home on my motorcycle. We have not even spoken to each other since then.' (That was true enough.) 'I'm as appalled and furious over this as you are, sir,' he continued, gradually regaining his composure. 'I admit that I did receive a surprise visit last Saturday from the girl who works in the office of the *Sheenmouth Clarion*. We know each other quite well because of my frequent visits to answer ads, for jobs.' Talking fast to avoid interruptions, he went on, 'Miss Cummings had accepted notice of a vacancy at the tractor factory, and went to my former lodgings to tell me of it. The landlady gave her my new whereabouts so she decided to come on to the boathouse.' He forced a half-smile. 'I thought it frightfully good of her. She was unaware, of course, that I was now employed by you.'

His grim-faced employer said, 'That might explain a girl at the boathouse, but what has it to do with this obscene message?'

Warren took a deep breath. 'A great many men in this area are out of work and desperate, as you know, so isn't it possible that the note could be from someone who passed along the river on Saturday, saw me talking to Miss Cummings, and believed he had the means to vent his resentment and envy of my luck in being employed by Kirkland's? I know it's despicable, but a hungry family and loss of pride make men do insane things. If I knew who he was, I'd deal with him myself, sir.' Struggling on, he ended on a note of remorse. 'I'm extremely sorry that you have been subjected to such a letter, Sir Hector, and I can only give you my word that Miss Kirkland always has and always will be treated with my deepest respect.'

There was no more than a moment of silence before his employer made a typically swift decision. 'I believe you, lad. The shock you had on reading that filth was obviously genuine. The matter is now closed, but I'll say one thing to you. My daughter is a minor. She will be returning to school in Switzerland in September. I'm well aware that she is growing very lovely, but her name is Kirkland. That puts her out of your league—now and at any time in the future. Do I make myself clear?'

'Perfectly, sir,' Warren murmured, hardly believing he had come out of the situation so easily.

'One more thing. It is not through *luck* that you are working for Kirkland's. I want a passenger liner with wings, and you have sworn to give me one.' He sat down. 'Now, what was all the fuss about this afternoon?'

Recognising his chance to put forward his findings without Donald's damping influence, Warren launched into an account of his work with Kit, and also of the sketches and calculations he had been doing in the evenings at the boathouse. When he left Sheenmouth Abbey several hours later, it was with Sir Hector's praise ringing in his ears and a very tasty supper inside him. Still, as he drove his motorbike along the dark lanes, his sense of well-being was not strong enough to cover the growing distress over Mona's act of vengeance. She had succeeded no better in her attempt to destroy him than she had in her attempt to win him.

KIT PUT ASIDE the neatly typed itinerary of his imminent tour with a sense of excitement. Whatever else Maitland was, there was no doubt of his thoroughness and efficiency. It was to be a long, hectic tour and getting away on it would be a godsend. Leone was endangering them both by her adolescent infatuation. Donald must surely be aware of it; Stephanie most certainly was, and delighted in taunting him over it. He would be glad to put distance between himself and her, too. They had been lovers on numerous occasions, even after Donald's courtship had begun, but she seemed to think the affair could continue now, with Donald's expensive solitaire on her finger and a wedding being planned. He was finding it difficult to hold her at arm's length.

Sealing the final envelope of the letters he had been writing, Kit was thinking of turning in when he spotted the two rolls of drawings Warren said he had discovered in a drawer of the old desk at the boathouse. Everything about that place held black memories for Kit. Picking up the rolls, he was tempted to stuff them in the hearth and put a match to them. Any reminder of his father was deeply disturbing . . . and yet he could not somehow bring himself to destroy his work. He pulled free the tapes confining the broad sheets, and spread them out on his desk.

The series of plans and detail sketches were for a seaplane named *Solitaire*. Kit frowned. He had heard nothing of the model, so it must be one abandoned on the drawing board. With professional interest, he studied the lines and dimensions on the first sheet, to see if he could figure out why the project had been dropped. One by one, he absorbed every detail of all the drawings and calculations made in his father's shaky hand. Then he reached for the second roll and searched every line on the sheets contained in it. The room turned cold; his body grew icy. His mind tried to shy from the hideous truth, but it confronted him on all sides. Here in his hands, he finally had the reason for Sir Hector Kirkland's generosity in taking him in on that day three years ago! The answer had been in the old boathouse.

So many things now made sense—sickening, humiliating sense. A great cry of protest began to build inside him. Anger began; a brand of anger which drove him from his room to seek and destroy.

Kit found both his victims in the library. Father and son turned in astonishment from what was plainly an unhappy discussion.

'I didn't hear your knock,' snapped Sir Hector.

Kit took a step towards the two figures standing before the bookshelves. 'You bastards! You cheating bastards!' His hands holding the rolled plans were shaking. 'For three years you've made me lick your boots for fear of being sent away as suddenly as I arrived, and all the time you've been hiding your abominable secret from the world. I did the refinements on *Aphrodite*. I suggested the modifications, it was my advice handed to Rolls-Royce when they were asked for a revised stress factor.' Turning to Donald, he cried, 'You couldn't design a toy soldier, much less a seaplane conceived by one of the most talented men this country has ever known.' He seized Donald by the lapels of his smart jacket. 'I'll force you to confess, even if I have to choke the truth from you.'

Struggling from Kit's hold, Donald moved back fast.

In disgust, Kit threw the rolled plans at their feet. 'There are the drawings for a machine my father named *Solitaire*. You stole the design, changed the name to *Aphrodite*, and claimed worldwide credit for it.' Concentrating on Sir Hector, he continued. 'Your son hasn't the guts to do such a thing, so it's obvious the damnable crime was hatched by you. Geoffrey Anson was a brilliant man. He was also a drunkard and a gambler, but you robbed him of his right to redress in the eyes of the world. I'll never forgive you for your pretence of friendship when he was killed, in that same workshop which built his last and most triumphant machine. When I've finished with you both, the whole world will know what you've done.'

Sir Hector smiled. 'Spoken like a true nobody! You burst in here, throw some rolls of paper at my son's feet, and create a histrionic scene crying vengeance. I'll overlook it just this once. Now get out!'

'Father, he knows,' cried Donald. 'Don't you realise, *he knows*?'

'Knows what?' barked his father.

'He's not a fool!'

'He's more than a fool, he's a bloody imbecile.' Swinging back to face Kit, he said, 'You'll pick up that paper you've thrown on the floor and tear each sheet into pieces in front of us. Then, you'll apologise for your insufferable behaviour.'

Kit looked back at him with murder in his heart. 'Go to hell!' He bent to pick up the plans. 'When the news of this breaks, you'll be finished.'

'News? What news? Stick your head under the tap and sober up, for God's sake. Living here for three years has given you delusions of grandeur. In three years you've advanced from being a greaser in my workshops to becoming the holder of the world air-speed record, living in a suite of rooms in this house and preparing for a tour of half the world. What more do you want, you ungrateful brute? I'll give you a choice. You can tear up those drawings and apologise for being insolent, and I'll allow you to retain your quarters here in addition to making the tour, as planned. Alternatively, you can leave these premises within the next sixty minutes or risk being physically ejected by my son and Maitland at the end of that period. You'll

have no money. I shall ensure that no one will be willing to employ you. The newspapers will be told of your parentage and unsavoury background, which will explain your reversion to type. *You'll* be finished, not us.'

'You're not God, although you tend to think you are,' Kit retaliated, gripping the plans his father had drawn; the evidence of a crime no one would believe. 'You'll probably do your damnedest to make things impossible for me in this country, but even Hector Kirkland can't bribe the whole world. My reputation is such that any number of foreign companies will be delighted to persuade me to work for them. While I'm deciding which offer to accept, I'll need finances. I'll sell you the Anson *Solitaire* for ten thousand pounds,' he said, holding out the two rolls of drawings. 'It will let Donald off the hook on that one, at least, until he puts the rope round his own neck over this flying boat Warren will be expected to design for him.'

'Give it to him,' Donald told his father, in shaky tones. 'Pay him off—give him anything he wants to keep quiet. Then toss him out on his ear.'

Sir Hector ignored his son while he looked Kit over with his habitual scrutiny, as if checking that he was clean and presentable. 'I wondered how long it would be before you got to the root of the matter. So it's now blackmail, is it?' His expression hardened. 'All I need do is ring this bell, and I can have Maitland throw you out into the Sheen. If you're not on your way to pack by the time I've counted ten, that's exactly what will happen. *Get out!*'

Kit left the library on the count of five. In the grip of fury he raced up the stairs to his rooms, threw into a bag his books, case of drawing instruments, the family photograph album, the rolls of drawings, the silver-framed picture of *Diadem*, and the keys to his car. Then he made the greatest mistake of his life.

Going up to the offices, he let himself into the deserted suite, switched off the theft device, and opened the safe hidden beneath a stone slab. Taking several thick wads of five-pound notes to stuff into his bag, he closed the safe again, reset the alarm and locked the door behind him. He descended the fire escape and hurried down the path around the north wing of the abbey, to the garages. There he encountered a tawny-haired girl in a ruby velvet evening coat over a long dress of shimmering silver beads, who was climbing from a dark green coupé rather unsteadily.

'Well, well, well,' she mumbled, her eyes very bright in the light. 'Where are you going to at this time of night, lover boy?'

Throwing the bag into his car, Kit flopped into the driving seat, and started the engine with a roar. Stephanie came alongside.

'This damned monastery is too cloistered for my taste,' she confessed. 'I've been to Torquay for some fun, but they're all in bath chairs there. C'mon, Kit, let's set each other alight, like we used to.'

He leaned across to throw open the other door. 'Get in,' he invited. 'I'll set you so well alight, they'll see the glow for miles around.'

The car raced away from Sheenmouth Abbey and onto the Magnum

Pomeroy road, but he turned in the other direction which led to the river and the collection of villages alongside the Sheen. The night breeze buffeted him as the madness possessing his mind found relief in action. He imagined he was out to break the speed record in a machine his father had designed. He was reaching full throttle now. He saw the dark water flying past below him, he knew he had done it. Once more, he felt that incomparable sense of total fulfilment. Diving, he took *Aphrodite* in to land on the shimmery surface of the water. Then there was a terrible sound of screaming in his ears. It was followed by complete silence, and darkness.

LEONE AWOKE THAT MORNING with a sense of foreboding. Since her visit to the old boathouse last Saturday, she had not been sleeping well. The memory of that naked pair facing each other beside that tumbled bed excited and disturbed her. She deeply envied the girl her knowledge of life; she yearned for something her woman's body demanded but her schoolgirl's mind did not yet totally understand.

During those five days and nights, she had grown feverish to the point of desperation, because Kit had either stayed late at the office downriver, or remained in his locked room occupied with plans for his tour. Those few occasions on which she had been in his company had only served to increase her longing for him.

This morning, she made her way down to the pool, where she had so often been certain of encountering Kit taking his morning swim. The blue water lay disturbed by no more than the slight breeze. The gilded loungers and the changing cubicles were deserted. A strangely ominous silence seemed to hang in the air.

With her heart heavier than ever, Leone wandered back indoors. As she crossed the hall her bleak thoughts were interrupted by an imperative call from her father, who stood in the doorway of the octagonal room with Donald. They looked very straight-faced.

'You'll have to know this,' her father began, without preamble, 'so there's no time like the present. I'm afraid we've been very badly let down and deceived by the boy I took in and treated like a son. Last night, he burst in on us during a private conversation. He was aggressive and arrogant enough to demand from me the sum of ten thousand pounds, claiming it was his due for the speed record for Kirkland's. When I reminded him I was already financing a world tour which would enhance his reputation and boost his personal wealth considerably, he turned extremely nasty. He threatened to blacken the name of Kirkland and seek employment with a rival company unless I handed over the money. I was compelled to eject him, with the advice either to apologise, or seek employment elsewhere. He has gone, my dear, and I trust we see and hear no more from someone with such total lack of loyalty or gratitude.'

Leone was torn by conflicting feelings as she gazed first at her stony-faced parent, then at Donald's ashen features. It could not be true, it could not.

Yet why would her father fabricate such a wildly improbable story? 'He's not really like that,' she heard herself say, in a hollow voice. 'He'll come back. There must be an explanation. He *must* be intending to come back and give us the truth.'

Sir Hector's expression darkened further. 'The truth is that we've had our charity flung back in our faces. Like father, like son.'

A flurry of movement in the hall heralded Meredith accompanied by a brace of uniformed policemen.

'What is it, Meredith?' Sir Hector snapped.

'These men insisted that the matter was urgent, Sir Hector.'

'I'll see them in the library.'

'It concerns the whole family, sir,' the police sergeant said. 'I'm afraid there has been a motor accident. Unfortunately, the car wasn't discovered until the first ferry set off up the Sheen this morning, so they'd been trapped in the vehicle for some hours and were suffering from loss of blood as well as exposure. They're both safe in East Sheenmouth Cottage Hospital now. Mr Anson came off worse due to being pinned beneath the vehicle. There's an arm and leg broken, as well as serious concussion and a great many lacerations. He was lucky, nevertheless, to escape with no worse. Miss Main has minor injuries, but is suffering from shock.'

'Miss Main?' thundered Sir Hector.

'My God, he took Steph with him.' Donald seemed beside himself. 'He did it to get at me. It won't stop there, you know it won't. We should have given him what he wanted, done as he said.'

Leone's cry of protest was infinitely anguished. How could she understand this?

The sergeant took the leather bag held by his subordinate. 'We had to go through this for identification, sir, and I thought it best not to leave it at the hospital. Apart from a few personal belongings, there's a large sum of money in it. It's not safe to leave so much lying around unguarded. I had to count it. It's regular procedure, so that someone can sign a docket to put with our records. There's nine thousand, nine hundred and twenty-five pounds altogether,' he told Sir Hector. 'All in fives.'

'Oh God,' exclaimed Donald, turning even paler. 'He meant what he said. He won't stop now until he's . . .'

'Be quiet,' snapped his father, holding out his hand for the bag. 'Where's the receipt you want signed?'

'Just here in my pocketbook, sir . . . oh, and there was something else I thought best not to leave at the hospital.' The constable held up two rolls of papers tied with tapes. 'These seem to be plans and suchlike, Sir Hector. I thought you'd prefer to have them here in case they're important.'

'They're damned important,' cried her father in triumph. 'These are the plans for Kirkland's new seaplane, still in the stage of development. My God, if these had reached the hands of my rivals . . . Sergeant, I want Anson and that woman placed under arrest. Immediately. Not only did he steal these drawings, he most certainly took from my safe the sum he last night demanded from me with threats. Miss Main is his accomplice in crime.'

'No!' cried Donald. 'Steph would never do that.'

The policeman questioned the charge. 'You do understand, sir, that I'm speaking of Mr Kit Anson. The famous pilot who recently broke the speed record in your seaplane. You want him *arrested*, sir, and charged?'

'I do. The man is a thief, a liar and a drunkard. Last night, he assaulted my son. You may add that to the charges against him. I want him under lock and key immediately.'

'Not while he's in a hospital bed, sir,' the confused sergeant ruled. 'He needs medical attention.'

'Then put a man beside his bed until he *is* fit to be locked up! I intend to telephone the editors of several national newspapers. When this story is printed, the cottage hospital will be swarming with reporters intent on digging out every detail of this disgraceful affair.'

Leone heard all this through a daze of misery.

The uniformed men departed, leaving the rolls of drawings but retaining the money to be used as evidence. The minute they were gone, Donald, in a state bordering on frenzy, condemned his father's action and pleaded with him to reconsider before it was too late.

'Pull yourself together, boy! Don't you realise that he's cut his own throat by smashing up that car?'

'But you can't punish poor Steph.'

'She did you a very good turn by going off with him. You have every excuse to end a relationship which was making a fool of you.'

'Father, I love her.'

'Love?' he roared. 'There's only one thing worth loving in this world, and that's success. Where's your bloody pride, man? This sister of yours isn't full of protests. She's accepted the evidence of their treachery. She has Kirkland pride. If *she* were my heir, I might have some hope for the future.'

Leone walked away from their angry exchange. Opening the door of the bell tower she stepped inside. The circular rooms still held the scent of his presence, echoes of his voice and laughter hung in the air. How hard he had worked to charm her! How easily she had succumbed!

Up in the bathroom the smart silk dressing gown hung on the door. The memory of an old plaid woollen one, several sizes too small, returned. Going back to his bedroom, she opened the wardrobe. It was filled with expensive clothes and racks of handmade shoes. On the dresser were silver-backed hairbrushes, and a box containing fancy studs and cuff links. Only one item appeared to have been taken. A picture in a frame. *Dad's finest design.*

Kit Anson had vanished with no more than the meagre possessions he had brought with him. He had left here all those things which had made him the person she had believed him to be. She slowly sank down onto the bed. By revealing herself, she had become a target for the cruellest darts life could produce. She would not return to this place until the wounds had healed.

7

Sir Hector Kirkland died on Christmas Eve 1937—of a heart attack. At the funeral on December the thirtieth, attended by more than three hundred people, Leone made an unexpected appearance. She had left England shortly before Kit Anson's trial, and had not returned since. Now about twenty-two and the owner of a villa overlooking Lake Lugano, she was gaining a reputation for breaking engagements to wealthy eligible men. Although she looked pale and distrait during the service and subsequent gathering in her father's London mews cottage, masculine interest was nevertheless captured by her blonde beauty. It contrasted strikingly with the severity of her black, sable-trimmed suit.

The funeral service for the man Leone had never been permitted to love had been long and solemn. Afterwards the traditional gathering of principal mourners for drinks and cocktail fare had been equally long and solemn. Leone had recognised only three people present: her brother, Maitland Jarvis and Warren Grant. After five years, they seemed like strangers. Warren was now a successful designer of almost thirty, with eyes as dreamy as before and shyness even more pronounced.

She and Donald now sat together in their father's sitting room, in silence, stunned by the terms of a will intended to ensure that Kirkland Marine Aviation would continue as Sir Hector wished. Sir Willard Jameson, the family solicitor, had explained the legal document to them.

Wearing a ruby velvet gown, Leone was warmer than she had been all day as she gazed reflectively into the fire. The will had been made five years ago, after events she had deliberately shut from her mind until now. She had returned to school before Kit's trial, when, on the strength of overwhelming evidence given by Sir Hector, Donald and Maitland Jarvis of the events of that night in July, plus the presence in the wrecked car of the exact sum missing from the Kirkland safe along with secret plans of a new seaplane also missing from Sir Hector's office, Kit Anson had been found guilty of assault, theft and attempted industrial espionage. There had been an additional charge of forcible abduction brought against him by Stephanie Main, who had convinced a jury that her former lover had been insanely jealous since her engagement to Donald Kirkland and had forced her into his car. For that, he had received an additional prison sentence and been ordered to pay compensation for the injuries she had sustained through his reckless driving.

Thinking now of that first vulnerable adolescent love which had been so cruelly crushed, Leone recalled the morning when the truth had been revealed. Her father had applauded her silence and condemned Donald's cries of distress, saying that he wished she were his heir instead. He had done the next best thing. Tonight, she and her brother were joint owners of Kirkland Marine Aviation.

'I think there's only one satisfactory way out of this absurd situation,' said Donald, breaking into her reverie. 'With New Year upon us, nothing can be done for a day or two, but as soon as Sir Willard returns from Scotland, I'll get him to draw up the necessary papers. It's out of the question for me to buy your shares in Kirkland's. I haven't that kind of cash available, for one thing, and the company is going to demand all I can lay my hands on in order to get *Flamingo* successfully launched. After taking almost four and a half years to develop and produce her, it's imperative to win massive orders. Father put everything behind this flying boat, so we have to earn back our investment at least twofold. There's only one way open to us. You retain your shares, thus reaping the dividends, but give me written power of attorney on all company decisions.'

Pouring herself a modest amount of brandy, Leone said, 'How well is Kirkland's doing?'

'Although the *Aphrodite* affair created worldwide interest, we were unable to take full advantage of it. Warren offered to undertake some of Kit's tour engagements in Europe, but he was inexperienced in seaplanes and couldn't show off the machine's full potential.'

'He also had the wrong name, hadn't he?' she suggested in quiet tones.

'We had to do something quickly,' Donald continued. 'Warren produced drawings for a light racing seaplane he'd designed and called *Seaspray*. Father put it into production, and we've since sold models all over the world to wealthy men who fancied the new sport of air racing. You can leave your half of Kirkland's safely in my hands, Leone. Once *Flamingo* is successfully launched, you can rest assured that Father's death will not reduce the flow of cash you need to comb Europe seeking that elusive soul mate.'

Put into words, her future sounded bleak. She faced him frankly. 'What about *your* soul mate? She appears somewhat elusive, too.'

He scowled. 'I don't need one. As soon as *Flamingo* hits the market, I shall announce my engagement to Anita Bergenstein.'

'The American heiress!' she exclaimed. 'You dark horse! Is Anita the love of your life, or a much-needed injection of cash for an ailing company?'

'Kirkland's is not ailing,' he said, firing up immediately. 'Father risked all available capital on his dream of a passenger liner with wings. We gave him one. Now, we're left with the task of making the dream work.'

'We?' she queried.

'Warren Grant played a strong role in designing *Flamingo*, so I suppose he's almost as responsible as I am for her success.'

'So it's an all-male concern.'

'What else could it be?' he demanded irritably. 'That's why it's essential to get the deed of attorney drawn up as swiftly as possible. As the will stands, it means I can't make a move without you. It's absolute madness.'

'I mean to observe Father's wishes, Donald. I've decided not to give you power of attorney.'

'You're mad . . . How can you? It's ludicrous. Leone, you can't do this to me, you can't tie my hands so tightly. Often, company decisions have to be swift or the chance is lost. If I were forced to telegraph every chateau and ski lodge in Europe for your go-ahead on something you knew nothing about, it would mean certain death to the company. Is that what you want?'

'No, Donald, I want to help you to run it.'

He gripped his hair in anguish. 'Dear God, you know nothing about aviation.'

'I'll learn.'

A cold laugh escaped him. 'The only interest you've ever shown in the subject was to make a fool of yourself over the company's test pilot five years ago. There's a hell of a lot more to it than that.'

Calm in the face of his contempt, she said quietly, 'That was another of my serious mistakes. It won't happen again, believe me. You won't have to telegraph every chateau. I've decided not to return to Europe. It's time I did something more fulfilling than putting my trust in men who never live up to my expectations. I intend to go home to Sheenmouth Abbey, which is also half mine now, and start learning the art of making aircraft.'

'Learn the art of . . . you're *mad*!' he cried again, despairingly.

'No, Donald, I think I've just discovered my sanity. For years, I've been the invisible Kirkland but, oh boy, is the world about to see me now!'

WARREN HAD SLEPT BADLY AGAIN. Since Hector Kirkland had died, he had been deeply worried. As he climbed from the motorboat on the first day of 1938, hunched against the cold wind whistling up the estuary, he was preoccupied. *Flamingo* had been created during months of anguish, when all else had been sacrificed to the drive for design perfection. Every single moment had been worth the cost to his health and happiness. He had truly created a passenger liner with wings, as he had dreamed of doing. A hangar had been built to cope with an aircraft of mammoth proportions, and extra hands had been employed. The precise cost of this beautiful water bird was probably known only to Sir Hector's worried accountant and banker, but Warren was unhappily aware that the company could stand or fall on this one aircraft. She was a fine machine, but who, or what, would convince customers that *Flamingo* constituted the finest investment they would find in the world today? Donald had neither the personality nor the drive to sell her. Warren had reluctantly test-flown his own prototype, but he was unhappy in marine aircraft and *Flamingo* was incredibly heavy to handle for a man more used to light monoplanes. He was well aware that he could never dazzle prospective customers with a flying display. That needed a Kit Anson.

Warren entered the vast hangar. Guilt always rose swiftly whenever he thought of Kit. Although he had not been present on that fatal night five years ago, he was reasonably sure that the cause of the quarrel between the Kirklands and their test pilot had been Kit's discovery of their theft of his father's design. The so-called 'secret plans' found in the crashed vehicle must have been those handed over by himself to Kit. No one had suggested he should give evidence at the trial. He had known the accused man for too short a time. So, he had stayed silent, reasoning that if Kirkland influence could succeed in discrediting a man of Kit's standing, going to court with the story of design theft would result in no more than losing his own chance of a lifetime. Kit had not attempted to exonerate himself, possibly also knowing that the facts would never be believed in the face of such incriminating evidence. His reputation and character had been torn to shreds before the awarding of a two-year prison sentence. Guilt had prevented Warren visiting Kit in jail, although he had written to him, declaring his belief that a dreadful mistake had been made.

In company with the three men who had worked most closely with him, Warren spent several hours fussing over the giant aircraft. They eulogised, examined, polished and oiled until they could delay departure no longer. Warren felt even more depressed by the dismal afternoon.

Ownership of the old boathouse had been transferred from Kit to himself by Sir Hector after the trial, and Warren had now made it bright and comfortable.

The overhead apartment was nice and warm to greet him. Mrs Chubb, his housekeeper, had put more coal on the fire before leaving for the day and there was an appetising smell filling the tiny kitchen. Several cups of tea, while he read back numbers of aeronautical journals, finished off his meal, and by nine o'clock he had washed himself in 'Grant's Patent Showerbath' before donning pyjamas and dressing gown to sit before the dying embers in gloomy contemplation of his future. So deep were his thoughts, it was a moment or two before he registered the knocking noise being made on the underside of the trap-door entrance. He crossed to the rope pulley in faint alarm. The only reason anyone would come for him at five to ten on New Year's Day was because an emergency had arisen over *Flamingo*. He tugged the rope which raised the door, then stared in astonishment at the face looking up at him through the square opening.

'May I come in?' asked Leone, not waiting for his reply and climbing up to stand beside him. Casting a glance round the room, her voice took on an enthusiastic tone. 'My goodness, you've made this extremely cosy. It used to be so tumble-down, if I recall.'

So far as he knew, she had only been there once before. His embarrassment doubled. 'I thought you were still in London, Miss Kirkland.'

Her large blue eyes appealed to him. 'You used to call me Leone. We agreed to be friends, didn't we? May I sit down?' Flopping down into the chair he had just vacated, she stretched her elegantly booted feet towards the fire. 'Mmm, you've been keeping this chair nice and warm for me.'

'Look,' he said awkwardly, 'I think I'd better slip next door and get into something more suitable.'

'Suitable for what? Do sit down. I want to arrange something with you, and I can't if you persist in hopping about like that.'

Flushing a little, he sat carefully in the other chair. 'Are you planning to stay at the abbey for a few days before going back?' he asked. 'Donald didn't think you'd bother to travel down to Sheenmouth, especially at this time of year. He said you'd never liked it.'

'I'm planning to do things to the abbey so that I shall,' she replied enigmatically. 'Warren, you'll know this eventually, so I'll tell you now that Father left everything he owned equally between Donald and me. I've decided not to return to Lugano. Instead, I'm going to run Kirkland's in harness with my brother.'

Warren could do no more than gape at her.

'I know what you're thinking. Donald feels the same way about it. It'll take a long time for me to learn something of the technical side of the business, but I can be very helpful on the clerical and social aspects. From the little I've heard from Donald so far, I gather there's an urgent need to stir up interest in *Flamingo*.' Her lovely smile broke through again. 'My decision will create something of a stir in press and business circles so, while Kirkland's is hitting the headlines on that score, we'll do something with the flying boat. Between us, we should come up with an original idea.'

'Yes,' Warren began thickly, then cleared his throat. 'Yes, between us we should.'

She paused to say, 'You're still as nice as you were when you rode into a hedge to avoid hitting me. I think you must have lied when you said you couldn't mend the Bentley, however. An aircraft designer must surely know about cars, too. I'll forgive you, if you'll agree to do something for me.'

'Of course . . . anything,' he murmured.

'Will you give me flying lessons?' she asked. 'Donald has never thought it necessary to learn, but I feel the owner of an aviation company should show confidence in what it manufactures by taking to the air herself, don't you?' She moved across to the trap door giving off a waft of French perfume.

After Leone had gone, Warren put more coal on the fire. He was too worked up to consider going to bed yet. He would ring Jim Mason at the Aero Club in the morning to hire one of his trainers. It would be good to have something to take his mind off *Flamingo* for a while.

8

Leone reflected that she might have bitten off more than she could chew by insisting on helping to run the company. After six weeks at the helm of Kirkland Marine Aviation, she still had no idea how to steer it. She could speak French, German, Italian and Spanish, she could converse knowledgeably on art, music and literature, she could paint attractive watercolours, play a bruising game of tennis, ride with skill, and choose clothes with individuality and flair. She could now pilot a plane. None of these talents were of the least use when learning to understand aircraft manufacture. She had been conducted over *Flamingo* by Warren several times, but still found it impossible to understand his eulogy on statistics and design developments. She readily accepted the word of the two designers that the aircraft was a potential champion of the air. How to prove the fact was the problem facing them all at today's meeting. It was already well into February, and the promotion would need to enter the planning stage now if *Flamingo* was to be launched in the spring.

At present, the best suggestion had been made by Maitland: that a demonstration flight over Sheenmouth, followed by a lavish party at the abbey along the lines of June 10, 1932, when *Aphrodite* had taken the speed record, would be easy to organise. But Warren had flatly refused to fly his creation, saying that he was no Kit Anson. The matter had been left in abeyance, as it seemed to be no more than an unimaginative repeat of a triumphant, world-shaking event. A better idea eluded them until Warren got to his feet and looked directly at Donald. 'Kit Anson vowed he'd fly our passenger liner with wings from here to Africa when she was built. I think we should arrange a proving flight along those lines, fill *Flamingo* with likely customers, and bally well show them what a bloody fine aircraft they're being offered.'

There was a short silence. Leone's mind immediately filled with all manner of exciting ideas. Her brother asked, 'Will you fly this route?'

Warren shook his head. 'I'm not happy in seaplanes, you know that. Besides, I'd have to be on hand to answer queries from the passengers as we progressed. I couldn't fly and sell *Flamingo* at the same time.' He fiddled with a pencil until it snapped. Looking abstractedly at the broken pieces, he said, 'As we'd need an entire flight crew with stewards to wait on passengers, serve drinks, and so on, I suggest we approach one of the smaller airlines to see if we could hire one of their experienced crews for the occasion. Searching for individual people would be time-consuming and chancy. Even if we were fortunate enough to get the top man in each field, they might not work together well as a team.'

There was another short silence before Donald asked, 'What would it cost, Maitland?'

The sandy-haired assistant replied calmly, 'I'll have the answer for you in two days, Mr Kirkland. I take it you're speaking of *total* cost—fuel, catering, docking charges at the stops *en route*, in addition to the hire of a crew. I should need details of the proposed route.'

'That's no problem. Here, Warren, come and take a look.' Donald crossed to the wall at the far end of what had been his father's office, and tugged a cord until the rotation of maps produced one of the area under considera-tion. Leone walked over to join the three men. An idea was fast taking shape in her mind, and it was essential that she should know the route they planned before she placed it before them.

'Naples, Athens, Cairo, Khartoum, Mombasa,' Warren quoted, moving his hand over the map.

'Out of the question,' Donald said immediately. 'It'd be far too expensive.'

'Maitland hasn't done his sums yet,' came the protest. 'Whatever we do is going to cost a lot; *Flamingo* is a long-distance boat. That's what we'll be out to prove. I defy any man to take a trip like that and fail to fall beneath the spell of one of the finest marine aircraft ever built.'

'What of the women who'll be making the trip?' put in Leone. 'You surely weren't proposing to fill *Flamingo* with cigar-smoking top businessmen, who'd eat and drink their way to Africa and back while making private deals among themselves, then thank you for the most enjoyable trip they'd made at our expense? It's essential to include some women. Wives, wealthy widows with money to invest, an actress or two and some eccentric socialites will give this flight the sense of excitement and novelty we want to create.'

Walking to the window overlooking the Roman pool, she said eagerly, 'A flamingo is a graceful water bird with feathers the colour of beautiful pinks. It is found in Africa. See how appropriate it is that our *Flamingo* is flying to Africa! We must decorate the interior in contrasting pinks, and the cuisine must reflect the same theme. New drinks with names to suit the stops *en route* will be served. Special dishes must be presented—*Steak Athenia* . . .' The blank expressions on their faces drove her to demand, 'Do you want to sell this machine, or not? The trip is the ideal solution, but it has to have a quality of opulence which will flatter those who travel in *our* boats. For God's sake, the men you want to persuade to invest in our machine have got to have the trip of their lives. They have to leave *Flamingo* on their return totally seduced.'

'Leone,' cried Donald, 'we're trying to discuss an important question here, and you rant on about creating a pink, aerial, upper-crust restaurant!'

'Why not, Donald?' she cried. 'Why not a flying restaurant, a flying bar, a flying club . . . a flying Orient Express? Why not imply that to fly by *Flamingo* makes passengers into pampered darlings throughout the journey? That *is* what she's supposed to be, isn't it—a passenger aircraft?'

Warren said in thoughtful tones, 'I think Leone's on to something. Your father told me all along he wanted a "passenger liner with wings", so she has to have all the glamour and luxury found on ocean-going ships.' He turned to her. 'Any additional ideas?'

She responded with a smile. 'I haven't spent the past five years as an exile in Europe without making my mark. Naples, Athens and the Mediterranean are more familiar to me than Sheenmouth. I'm known at all the grandest hotels, so a word from me would have the management of each eating from my hand. Our passengers will stay in their best suites, dine at tables decorated suitably while being served with any dish I care to order. Maitland can do the sums, Donald can concentrate on invitations, Warren can worry over the hired crew, but the glamour aspect is very definitely my province. Well, what do you say?'

'There's just one snag. Where do you imagine the company will find the money for these frills and furbelows in flamingo-pink?' asked Donald.

'I'll provide it,' she told him. 'The sale of some jewellery and furs should fetch more than enough. I no longer have use for them. They're part of a life I've put behind me.'

KIT BEGAN HIS DESCENT, flying parallel with the sand-fringed coastline lapped by translucent turquoise sea. Lisbon was no more than fifteen minutes away. He arched his back to ease the stiffness after the long flight. The machine was old and tired and needed a complete overhaul. An obsolete floatplane flown by a pilot no one else would employ hardly constituted a great asset, he thought to himself as *Gina* glided down towards the mouth of the Tagus, where Western Mediterranean Air Services slipways and hangars nestled the shore.

Gina was an ex-RAF floatplane used for transporting cargo. Today, Kit had aboard a full load of wine from Madeira ordered by a Portuguese aristocrat for the forthcoming wedding of his daughter. The precious bottles, stored in straw-lined crates bolted to the floor of the cargo hold, were the only items of value aboard—apart from the life of Morris Snaith, his navigator and radio operator, who had never been in prison and whom anyone would be glad to employ.

Morris was Kit's regular navigator; an Englishman who had married a beautiful Portuguese girl. The two men liked each other, and worked well together on these flights.

The tricky business of docking was completed satisfactorily. It had been an uneventful flight, and they were tired. Leaving the aircraft, they headed across the hangar aprons to the company building, where they took the lift up to Tom Digby's office.

No more than thirty-five, Tom Digby, their boss, was an aerial buccaneer of an admirable kind. A big, rangy, freckle-faced man with bright red hair, he had flown in combat during the Spanish Civil War, lost the sight of one eye during a crash and, having accumulated a fortune from his former mercenary career, he had crossed into Portugal and started an airline of his own. With flair, and the help of influential friends, he was building a formidable company.

Right now, he appeared to have something to celebrate. He greeted them genially, listened to their flight report and then astonished them by offering them a drink. Leaning back in his chair with a generous measure of whisky in his hand, he explained his generosity.

'I have just won a prestigious contract. Not only will it boost income, it'll give the company exactly the kind of publicity it needs. You two lads will earn a tidy little bonus for making the flight of a lifetime.' Raising his glass, he smiled. 'I was asked to tender a quote for the price of a first-class crew to take a prototype passenger boat on her proving flight. Much as I hate to feed your inflated egos, you two are my best pilot and navigator. This proving flight is something really special, so I'm prepared to send my prime men. I'll give you young Joss Hamilton as your copilot, Kit. Morris'll be your navigator, and the rest of Joss's crew will back you up. I'll arrange to get you two and Joss over to England in April for flight trials. The rest can join you a week before the actual trip, which is scheduled for early May.'

Kit's excitement faded. 'For the company's chance of a lifetime you're risking it by sending me, aren't you?'

Tom gave him a level look. 'Whatever else was questioned, it was never your skill as a world-class pilot. That's what I'll be sending over. This is going to be something very special. Naples, Athens, Cairo, Khartoum and all points back to Sheen . . . back home,' he amended, his gaze on Kit's face.

Something inside Kit began to freeze up as he asked, 'Is the manufacturing company of this new boat Kirkland Marine Aviation by any chance?'

'You know damn well it is,' Tom told him quietly.

Kit rose to his feet. 'I won't do it, Tom.'

His friend rose. 'We'll lose the contract. Only a superb crew will ensure total success. I happen to employ a bunch of men who could do the whole thing with their eyes closed, and the boost this company would get from world news coverage comprises the best piece of luck to come my way for years.'

'I won't do it, and that's flat,' Kit told him. 'What do you imagine would happen when *I* cruised up the Sheen and presented myself as their hired pilot? No, Tom, send Joss over to captain the crew of their machine, because nothing in the world would make me do it.'

He left the office, slamming the door on his friend, the Kirkland family, and Warren Grant's *Flamingo*.

KIT DROVE ALONG the rutted coastal road to the isolated two-roomed villa he rented from a local landowner.

The place smelt airless, so he left the door ajar and opened the windows despite the chill of the day. Filled with a sense of pointlessness, he gazed round the room as if seeing it for the first time. This opportunity he could not take suddenly became unbearably beckoning. Five years ago he had vowed to take a flying boat in triumph to Africa and back. Now he could fulfil that vow and make aviation history again. Walking into the bedroom, he took from the wardrobe a bottle of whisky, and began to drink. After his two years in prison, he had returned to the world on a bitter November day in 1934 to find unemployment rife, and Europe in turmoil. He had signed up to join the young Englishmen flocking to help the International Brigades to fight the Fascists in Spain. Such irregular bands welcomed any man willing to risk his life, and he was sent out to join a squadron of buccaneering pilots who flew any machine available to them in bombing and machine-gunning raids. To be in the air again, albeit in slow, outmoded wartime models, was Kit's first sensation of freedom since leaving prison. One of his fellow aviators had been Tom Digby and Kit had confided to his new friend a truth he had spoken of to no one save his solicitor, at the time of the trial.

Kit had been flying alongside Tom when his friend had been shot down, so had been able to pinpoint the site of the crash for the Spanish rebels who went into the mountains and brought the wounded man home. Realising that his flying days were over, Tom had decided to start his own airline in neighbouring Portugal. He had asked Kit to join him as his chief pilot, and they had now been in operation for six months. The possibility of another war in Europe seemed stronger with Hitler's every move. There was little doubt in Kit's mind that his combat experience in Spain would one day stand him in good stead, yet his love for marine aircraft kept him yearning for something beyond his reach. Today, Tom had offered it to him on a plate, and he was forced to refuse it.

He tipped the bottle again, and then stared steadfastly at the photograph of *Aphrodite*. Dad's finest design flown by his own son! Sir Hector was dead, so only he, Donald and Tom Digby knew the truth now. God, but it would be wonderful to vindicate the Ansons and make the surviving Kirklands pay for what they had done.

Gulping more whisky, he began to grin. Imagine terrifying the wits out of young Donald by taking command of his brand-new prototype on its proving flight! The grin turned into a chuckle. Imagine being the pilot hired to take assorted VIPs halfway across the world, in a flying boat upon which all Kirkland hopes were centred! The chuckle then turned into full-blooded laughter. Then he felt himself falling.

He hit the ground with a tremendous thud. Hands seized his arms and legs, then he felt himself being lowered into a remarkably uncomfortable seat and next minute a cold deluge hit him.

'Come on, man, sober up!' commanded a voice in his ear. 'We're not letting you alone until this has been thrashed out.'

As cup after cup of black coffee disappeared down his throat, he reluctantly faced the fact that he was in his villa in Lisbon feeling very sorry for himself.

He studied his three friends morosely. 'You're wasting your time. I won't do it. One sight of the name Anson on the flight list would cause a storm of protest.'

'I don't have to supply your names,' said Tom calmly. 'Just so long as I list your official ranks—Captain, First Officer, Navigator and so on—then supply age, qualifications and experience. I don't think anyone at Kirkland's would care what you're called.'

'They'll bloody well care about my face, when they see it, Tom.'

His friend grinned. 'By then, time will be running too short for them to do anything about it. They'll be stuck with you, old son. Aren't you avid to see whether or not they panic when brought face to face with Kit Anson after all these years?'

Looking round at Morris's lean, hopeful face, Joss's youthful eagerness, and Tom's confident, amused expression, he heard himself say, 'It's no good, I won't do it. *And that's final.*' Somehow, even to his own ears, it did not sound in the least final.

9

The morning was like polished glass; everything stood out clean and sparkling in the welcome sunshine. Leone rode home fast across the downland. It was pure joy to get out into the fresh air after the past two dismal, rainy days. As the departure date drew nearer, tempers were growing shorter, including her own. Warren was fussing and fretting over the proficiency of the hired crew; Donald was predicting disaster from every direction. Only Maitland remained calm, and supremely assured.

Cantering over the moist turf in jodhpurs and scarlet jumper, with the breeze ruffling her hair, she found herself able to think clearly. She had gained her own way over the glamour aspect of the flight. Warren had been a surprising ally, whether through enthusiasm for the idea or for herself she was unsure. That he was growing fond of her was very apparent. She told herself that she should do everything to discourage him. He was a sweet, shy person, who laid himself open to the kind of deep hurt she had so often suffered through misplaced affection. Only when dealing with his beloved creation did Warren grow assertive, stubborn and almost ruthless. He, at least, should be happier after today. The crew hired by Maitland was to present itself at Sheenmouth Abbey this morning.

Donald had invited an impressive selection of guests, all of whom had leaped at the opportunity to make this maiden flight. He had even secured the acceptance of an *émigrée* Russian countess, Countess Renskaya.

The sale of her furs and jewels had brought Leone a large sum, and further funds had been gained by disposing of the London apartment. Leone's approaches to the hotels they would use *en route* had been highly successful. The notion of a party of influential guests arriving by pink flying boat, which would anchor offshore, appealed to their love of the grand style. They rose to the challenge magnificently, and Leone was delighted.

After handing Jemima over to Porter at the stables, Leone entered the abbey and made her way through the ground-floor corridors to the central vaulted hall. Crossing the stone floor, she saw her brother coming from the library. He looked rather pale.

'You look very odd,' she commented. 'Is something wrong?'

Donald shook his head slowly. 'The pilot we hired to fly her has arrived.'

'The man from Portugal?'

'He's . . . it's Kit Anson. He's in the library with Warren now.'

'He's in the library? Kit Anson is in our library at this moment?'

'Yes.'

'Then he can leave immediately,' she said, through a tightening throat.

'No he can't. We've engaged him to fly *Flamingo*.'

'We've engaged a pilot from a Portuguese airline.'

'He *is* a pilot from a Portuguese airline.'

'We'll have to get a different one.'

'Maitland signed a contract. Don't blame him. He had no idea this could happen. The airline based in Lisbon is a reliable company which offered us the best terms for an experienced crew. There were no names given on the contract, just ranks.'

'Then we're under no obligation to accept him. Don't you see that? Tear up that contract and we'll go elsewhere.'

'There isn't *time* to go elsewhere,' he told her wearily. 'I have a prototype flying boat on which the future of Kirkland Marine Aviation and this family depends. So much ballyhoo already surrounds this flight to Africa, we can't possibly postpone it while we find another pilot and crew of equivalent skill and experience. The harm's been done, you must see that. Anson simply has to pilot the machine. He'll be up in the flight cabin all the time, with no chance to leave it and mix with the passengers.'

'Donald, he stole Father's money, some drawings, and the girl you loved. Haven't you any pride at all?'

Goaded from his stunned acceptance, Donald said furiously, 'OK, go ahead and fire him!' Waving a hand at the library door, he repeated, 'Go ahead and fire him. Tell yourself you're Father's daughter, if that's what you want to believe, but he'd take this on the chin and turn it to his own advantage. What's done is done, was his philosophy.'

The sound of his footsteps receded, and soon the distant sound of a slamming door cut him off completely. Leone was left in that great hall with his last words ringing in her ears. Surely her father would want her Kirkland pride to overrule Donald's weakness now.

She pushed the library door open.

Somehow she expected to see an ashen-faced boy dressed in cheap tweed. Instead, standing beside Warren was a tall man in a well-tailored dark green uniform embellished with gold insignia on sleeves and lapels.

As she halted just inside the door, he studied her for a moment or so before moving forward. 'Five years have wrought changes in you, Leone. I would hardly have known you.' He offered his hand. 'How are you?'

Nothing had prepared her for what she felt on confronting him again. The shock of his betrayal might have been inflicted that moment, it hurt her so unbearably, as she stood there still loving him.

Kirkland pride finally came to her rescue. 'You're fired.'

Warren moved up to them. 'Leone, there's no time . . .'

'Keep out of this,' she told him, her gaze still on Kit. 'Your application is rejected, Mr Anson.'

'*Captain* Anson,' he informed her quietly. 'You'll never find another crew by your departure date.'

'You knew that all along! You deliberately omitted the names on that contract so that we'd be forced to let you take this vital flight.'

Warren was shocked. 'You don't know what you're saying.'

Rounding on him, she said tautly, 'I'll deal with this my own way. It doesn't concern you.'

'Oh yes it does,' he returned heatedly. 'I designed *Flamingo*, and I insist she be given every opportunity to display her top-class qualities. Kit's the right man to do that. He was in on her conception and he's one of the finest pilots in the world when handling marine aircraft.' Putting his hand on her arm, he continued forcefully. 'Our only concern now should be the success Kit can make of this proving flight . . . not some silly affair which happened five years ago.'

'Some silly affair!' she cried, shaking his hand off. 'He stole ten thousand pounds, the plans for a new seaplane, and my brother's future wife. He threw Kirkland generosity back in our faces!'

Kit's expression hardened. 'My God, they really hated me, didn't they?'

Trying to retain control, Leone said breathlessly, 'I won't have you on this flight, neither will I have you in this house a moment longer.'

Kit gazed at her for a long while, then he said, 'You've plainly been indoctrinated with the Kirkland ten commandments. I'll leave your house right now, but only to go down to the workshops to look over *Flamingo*. Whether you like it or not, you'll have to accept that I shall be flying her to Africa and back. If you find that impossible, you had best stay here in your ivory tower, while the rest of us make aviation history.'

ALTHOUGH THE WEATHER was extremely chill for May, it discouraged none of those bent on seeing *Flamingo* set out. Newspapers had been full of the details. A flying boat with pink seats and walls, filled with financiers and diamond-decked ladies destined to be served *haute cuisine* meals in midair, was a dazzling enough prospect for anyone. But, with the revelation of Kit Anson's contract to fly the prototype, came speculation on the astonishing liaison between this man and the Kirklands.

For days, the stretch of water between Sheenmouth Abbey and Kirkland Marine Aviation had been patrolled by the press. The abbey itself had been under virtual siege, and on the morning of departure the roads leading down to the coast had been jammed since breakfast. By ten, just an hour before the scheduled departure, spectators crowded the banks of the Sheen near Kirkland's to await the arrival of the passengers.

With attention focused on the Sheen and the abbey, the crew of *Flamingo* hoped to be able to reach the workshops via the narrow road across Giddesworth Downs without trouble. However, coming from their hotel on the promenade, they were immediately mobbed. The appearance of these tanned young men in green and gold uniforms, led by the notorious Kit Anson, put the girls in a frenzy of excitement. Young Joss Hamilton was pushed over in the rush, Morris was dazed and Digger Rathbone, the Australian engineer, kissed as many as he could.

Kit experienced an unpleasant sensation of *déjà vu*, as he fought his way through the press of eager young women into the first of the waiting taxis. *Flamingo* was as superb as Warren had claimed. The friendship between himself and the young designer had instantly revived and, apart from the thrill of flying a world-class boat, was the only aspect which had made his return home bearable.

Joss, Morris and Digger piled into the back seat, Kit sat in front, and the taxi slowly climbed up to Giddesworth Downs and then began its descent to the main gates of Kirkland Marine Aviation.

The car finally pulled up at the entrance to the main hangar.

Kit climbed out and walked purposefully through to the slipway. *Flamingo* had been launched, and was anchored midstream awaiting the crew and passengers. Making for the small boat which would ferry them over, Kit asked himself savagely what he had imagined he would prove by returning to Sheenmouth. His decision had merely caused the press to reprint the lies they had reported five years ago. It had done nothing towards repairing his professional reputation.

WARREN HAD BEEN INSIDE *Flamingo* since early that morning. He had supervised her launch half an hour ago, and now sat watching the approach of the boat carrying the crew. On this, the greatest day of his life, he was feeling suicidal with nervousness.

The crew clambered aboard in silence, and made their way to the upper deck, led by Kit. Warren followed, and watched in silence as his friend took the pilot's seat on the flight deck and embarked on the lengthy preparation for takeoff. When Joss scrambled up to take his place, the youthful first officer became a different person. His wide, innocent-looking eyes missed nothing, and his brow beneath the fine, pale hair was furrowed as he compared instrument readings with the list in his hand.

Their assured voices helped Warren to relax. The sun was shining spasmodically, and a chill breeze was ruffling the surface of the water. Just the conditions *Flamingo* liked best. Spectators were thronging both banks. On the cliffs above Sheenmouth sands, he could see dots moving around. Momentarily, he recalled himself up there with Mona.

'Come on,' said Kit, getting to his feet. 'It's time you left us. The launch is here. Get down those steps and welcome everyone aboard.'

Warren turned; Kit halted him with a hand on his arm. 'How long was it before you realised that Donald was no more than a good draughtsman?'

As Warren stood nonplussed, Kit frowned. 'I'm pretty certain why you've allowed everyone to believe this boat is a dual creation, but I know you must earn total credit. *Flamingo* will be a sensation, I promise you. I hope you'll then feel strong enough to defy Kirkland greed and stand on your own brilliance. I'll do everything I can to help you.' Holding out his hand, he smiled. 'Good luck and happy landings.'

As he shook Kit's hand, Warren's old sense of guilt rose. On the brink of confessing what he had known for almost six years, he was prevented from doing so by Kit gently pushing him back into the cabin. The metal door which shut off the flight deck from the upper cabin closed, excluding him from any control over his splendid creation.

LEONE'S LEGS FELT WEAK as she stepped from the launch into the spacious lower cabin. Any pleasure and excitement she had felt over this flight was buried beneath the distress of Kit's re-entry into her life. The past four weeks had been hell. With all the meticulous planning done, and with invitations accepted, they had had no choice but to agree to the unacceptable.

Wearing a pale green braided silk costume trimmed with silver fox she dutifully donned both smile and poise to welcome the ladies aboard. Their arrival prompted the appearance of two handsome Portuguese stewards who proceeded to assist the removal of coats with a smiling deference which equally impressed the men when they climbed aboard accompanied by Donald and Maitland. The guests stood in small groups gazing about and discussing the merits of all they saw. Some chose to wander round the large hull, opening doors to inspect every aspect of the craft under their scrutiny. Before long, the interior of the aircraft resembled a cocktail party.

The chatter was brought to a sudden halt by a burst of thunderous sound, which set the hull shuddering around them. The passengers could see fine spray flying past the windows. Those on the upper deck called down that there was a better view from where they were. There was a rush for the steps.

Leone went across to Warren. 'This is little short of a nightmare. I never expected them to roam all over the aircraft like curious children. Just look at them! What can we do?'

At that moment, a member of the crew appeared at her side. She recognised him as the copilot, Joss Hamilton.

'The captain is ready for takeoff, Miss Kirkland,' he announced.

'We're not, I'm afraid,' she confessed ruefully. 'When we've managed to get everyone settled in seats, we'll let you know. Then we can start.'

The boy looked unhappy. 'I'm afraid you can't do that. It's the pilot's prerogative to tell you when he intends to leave. He's in total command once everyone's aboard.'

Tired, Leone sank onto the nearest pink seat. 'Tell him to take command, in that case.'

Young Hamilton looked relieved. 'Thank you, Miss Kirkland.'

As he pushed his way back through to the steps leading to the flight deck, Leone reached up to Warren. 'Sit here and hold my hand.' As he sat down, she produced a strained smile. 'As soon as we're safely up, I'm going to have a giant pink gin. The only way to get through the next fourteen days might be to get blotto, then stay that way, don't you think?'

He shook his head as he took her hand in a firm clasp. 'There's too much at stake—for us all. I have to prove to myself that I really have designed a championship-class aircraft. Donald has to sell it in large enough numbers to save the company. You have to vindicate your claim that you can earn your half-share in Kirkland's by making a valuable contribution towards running it. In addition, Kit has to demonstrate that he's still one of the finest pilots of marine aircraft in the world, despite what it chooses to say of him.'

Right on cue, Kit's voice filled the hull over the relay system. 'Ladies and gentlemen, this is Captain Anson. Please take your seats immediately. I am about to taxi to our takeoff position, and it is *essential* that everyone should be sitting during that procedure. There will be ample time for you all to inspect this splendid aircraft during the coming days and ask any questions you wish of myself or any member of my crew. Please occupy the nearest available seat now, as we shall be under way in two minutes. Thank you.'

The passengers sat obediently, as *Flamingo* began to move slowly down the Sheen towards the open sea. Leone gazed from the window as water began to surge up over the broad white hull as their speed increased. They were on their way, and there was no turning back.

LUNCH WAS SERVED by the impeccable Portuguese stewards as they crossed the coast of France.

From the moment of departure, the passengers had been charmed. The takeoff had been highly exciting. *Flamingo* had risen from the water in a remarkably short time for such a large craft. Now, three hours into their journey, and with a splendid meal inside them, the time had come to mix, investigate and ask questions. Most of the male passengers had flown before. Two were ex-RFC pilots. They, and the representatives from aircraft companies around the world, kept Warren under siege with questions on performance and statistics. The bankers and financiers mainly centred around Donald. Maitland, Leone noted with grim glee, was very definitely unhappy in the air. It would not be long before he would be driven to seek a quiet corner in which to ride out his misery.

Her own role was to chaperone the ladies. All but two of the twelve had never before taken to the air, and were finding the experience eye-opening. What spaciousness; what comfort! What *divine* stewards, my dear!

One, however, Mrs Harmesworth, wife of a director of Anglo-Asiatic, had a complaint. 'We have been in the air four hours already,' she said to Leone, 'yet the captain hasn't introduced himself to us and ensured that we're all comfortable.'

Growing wary, Leone said, 'He's the pilot, Mrs Harmesworth, and can't leave the controls.'

'Surely there's a first officer; another pilot aboard.'

'Naturally.'

'Then Captain Anson should have made his rounds by now,' was the firm declaration. 'My husband has observed that the operational crew appeared to be making themselves very scarce on this flight, for some reason.'

'The reason is because I requested them to do so,' Leone said, furious with the woman and trying hard not to show it.

'Good gracious, did you? It's usual for the pilot to speak to his passengers, Miss Kirkland. After all, if we have to place our lives in their hands, they should have the courtesy to let us see in whom we've put our trust. In this instance, it's more than ever essential that we should meet this man. No one denies his skill as a pilot, of course, but he has been in *prison*, hasn't he?'

Sensing the kind of trouble it was her duty to avert, Leone summoned all her self-control. 'When you meet Captain Anson, I'm sure you'll feel every confidence in his ability to fly us safely to Africa and back,' she said.

'*That* has never been in any doubt, Miss Kirkland. It's his other qualities I tend to question.'

Swallowing, Leone beckoned the steward across. 'Tell Captain Anson his presence is required in the cabin . . . *at once*,' she snapped. Then she got to her feet. 'Mr Grant is signalling for my assistance. Excuse me.'

When Kit appeared from the flight deck, his height seemed to fill the narrow walkway as he came towards her. 'Rather a rapid change of management policy, isn't it?' he asked.

'Some passengers have hinted that they'd feel safer if you put in an appearance, that's all.'

'It's usual,' he conceded, 'although it sometimes has the reverse effect. They worry about who's flying the machine while the pilot's socialising.'

Leone said sharply, 'There's no question of your *socialising*. A polite word here and there is all that's required of you. Put a foot wrong, and your employment can be terminated, you know.'

He shook his head. 'Sacking me would cause the kind of publicity you'd do anything to avoid. My place is to captain this entire flight to the best of my ability. That requires me to assume total command on board this flying boat, which means that I can overrule any instructions given by Donald or by you. Stop playing the part of company executive, my dear girl, and face the fact that you haven't the first idea what it entails.'

Before she could speak, he slid past her, saying, 'While I reassure the passengers, you should take the opportunity to powder your shiny nose. On this vitally important flight, even Leone Kirkland can't afford to put a foot wrong and look less than immaculate.'

He left her suffering the first of the wounds she had expected during the coming weeks.

TEA WAS CLEARED AWAY as they passed over the sparkling Mediterranean, and still Kit remained in the cabin. She could see him presently sitting with Donald and the men from the Air Ministry, deep in conversation. He had run the gamut of eager ladies who had been visibly charmed and gratified by his attentions. He was doing his job supremely well; she should be pleased. Why, then, was she furious with their reaction to his easy attraction?

She headed for the washroom reserved for Kirkland use. After touching up her face, she emerged to see Kit climbing the steps to the flight deck again. Donald came hot on his heels, looking angry.

'He said he was carrying out your orders. *Did* you tell him to wander around speaking to anyone he fancied?'

'No, I did not! That Harmesworth woman made a song and dance because he hadn't made his rounds. I had no option but to send for him.'

Donald scowled, then looked through the window. 'We're coming in to

Naples now. I hope to God he knows what he's doing at those controls.'

'Of course he knows,' she murmured, moving forward to stand beside him. The fabled bay with its ancient terraced city stood out brightly against the purple background of Vesuvius. Her brother bent over for a better view through the porthole.

'It looks as though half the town has turned out to watch.'

As *Flamingo* swept round in a turn which would put them on course for landing, Leone was surprised at the enthusiasm of those crowding the tiny jetty which had been placed at their disposal by the port authorities. Soon, they were no more than a few feet above the water. Then, with a gentle thump, *Flamingo* began to skim the waves, sending high-flying white foam over the windows. With a loud roar, the plane decelerated until she slowed to no more than a cruising glide. The foam subsided and Leone then saw that the spectators were holding aloft banners with bold lettering on them: Italian phrases of welcome for Kit Anson, the hero of the skies. Her throat tightened.

'Donald, look!' she directed in faint tones. 'What does it mean? Why are these people making such a fuss, and how did they know about him?'

'They've read the papers, like everyone else,' Donald said. 'I imagine the fuss is because Naples was Benzini's home town.'

Leone frowned. 'Benzini? Wasn't he a rival for the air-speed record?'

'He killed himself in an attempt to take it from us in nineteen thirty-three.' When Donald turned to her she was astonished to see something remarkably like apprehension on his face. 'Whose trip is this, ours or Kit Anson's?'

10

Warren stood on the balcony of his hotel room in the beguiling warmth of that May night, gazing down on the lights of a festive city. It was a moment he knew would live with him for ever. Until now, he had felt it did not matter who laid claim to *Flamingo*'s design so long as the craft was built and allowed to fly. Suddenly, on this unforgettable night, he wanted *Flamingo* to be his alone. Even so, he knew it was too late to claim her, as Kit had discovered it too late to claim *Aphrodite* for his father. His friend had paid a terrible penalty for trying; Warren would not risk a similar fate. Unlike Kit, he had an additional reason for dreading a break with the Kirkland family: he was in love with the female half of it. But on this very special evening, when romance hung in the air, he might have shown her a more heroic image without Donald there to steal half his claim to it.

As if that were not bad enough, there was a third hero tonight. Kit Anson had been greeted with banners, cheering crowds and showers of blossoms. He was presently being fêted by the men of Benzini's team, his widow and family, and the people of a Neapolitan suburb.

In evening dress, Warren trod down the wide marble staircase towards the grand salon lit by massive porcelain and crystal chandeliers.

He spotted Leone at the same time as she saw him. She came across swiftly, and he was reminded again of their first meeting. She was now dressed in sophisticated black. Her dress shimmered with jet beading until it flared into a swirl of ostrich feathers from the knee, and the deep V of her bodice accentuated the gracefulness of her throat fully revealed by hair drawn back into a chignon. Her smile warmed him like a heady red wine.

'I'd forgotten how handsome you can look when you're all togged up,' she said, tucking her hand through his arm. 'From what I've heard, you impressed all the men very greatly during the flight. Now you have to win over the ladies.'

His heart sank. 'You know I'm hopeless at social chitchat.'

'Leave the talking to them,' she advised. 'Smile devastatingly whenever you can, and encourage them to rattle on as long as possible. You'll come into your own after dinner. I've already told everyone how marvellous you are on the dance floor. When you sweep them off in your arms, remember to look as if you think each one is absolutely divine.'

'Leone, I . . .'

'I've also had a word in the ear of the orchestra leader,' she ran on enthusiastically. 'He's quite happy to let you play a solo or two with them.'

'Oh no,' he said determinedly. 'That's right out of the question. I suppose my dancing is up to scratch. I'll partner them all, Leone, but I won't play with the orchestra. I'm here as an aircraft designer, not an entertainer.'

Her lips brushed his cheek, accelerating his downfall. 'You're a darling,' she breathed, 'and you must see how important it is to show them you're *human* beneath all that aeronautical brilliance. When you get up there and play your golden horn, they'll be stunned and thrilled.'

'I can't . . .'

Tilting her lovely face to his, she added softly, 'Yes, you can. It's already arranged, and I'm counting on you to provide the final touch to their delight in this first day.'

They were ushered in to dinner by the *maître d'hôtel*, who treated Leone and several others in their party as old friends. There was a ripple of delighted appreciation as they all took in the sight awaiting them. A local florist had created *Flamingo* in white blossoms, suspended above a horseshoe arrangement of tables. These were set with pink linen garlanded with white flowers and decked with silver cutlery and rose-coloured Venetian glasses.

Warren found himself seated between Countess Renskaya, in silver pleated silk with rubies, and a shy woman in olive green, reputedly a millionairess. He found the meal an ordeal, despite the novelty of the many dishes.

When the long dinner ended they gathered merrily in the ballroom where dancing was already in progress. Warren dutifully offered to partner any lady who wished to dance. His difficulty with small talk was aggravated by

the sight of Leone gliding past in a succession of male embraces. Mutinous after enduring a second dance with Mrs Harmesworth, he crossed to where Leone was being held by a fiery Italian releasing what could only be a torrent of passion in her ear.

Leone seemed pleased at the intervention, made an excuse to her companion, and walked towards the tall open doors leading to the terrace. Warren followed. She walked to a far corner bedecked with geraniums. The scent of lemons wafted on the slight breeze and in the distance there were voices raised in laughter and song. Almost a thousand feet below them, the sea whispered as it met the shore. All round the terrace, couples in shadowy embraces murmured in the language understood by every man and woman in love. There were no words between himself and Leone as she stood lost in some vision which lay beyond that darkened bay, and he stood no more than a few feet behind her, fighting the pain of it all.

Eventually, she asked softly, 'Are you still there?'

'Of course.' He moved closer, wondering if he dared draw her back against him.

She turned, and her eyes were a deep luminous blue as she gazed up at him. She looked lonely, lost and unbearably lovely. To his dismay, Warren realised there would be no one but her for the rest of his life despite her

passion for the man who had been practically destroyed by her family.

Stepping so near they were almost touching, she suddenly asked desperately, 'Would you like to kiss me?'

Anger raced through him. 'No thanks, I don't kiss by invitation.' He took a deep breath. 'And I'm not a substitute for Kit Anson, either.'

The outburst shocked her deeply. For a moment she held her breath, then spun swiftly to face the sea. Warren stood with his heart thudding, knowing he should now walk away. Instead he seized her bare shoulders, tugged her round to him, and kissed her. She froze in his arms, then her body slowly melted against his, as if in relief. Breaking apart eventually, they regarded each other with mutual wariness.

'That was quite a kiss from someone who doesn't do it by invitation,' she breathed. 'Was it inspired by anger?'

'No, something quite different,' he told her roughly. 'Why do you profess to hate him so much?'

'Who?' she asked, still seeming breathless.

'You know who! You put on a very good act most of the time, but I saw your expression when you walked into the library and found him there.' When she remained silent, he went on angrily, 'I can see the truth only because I'm in the same condition over you.'

The words were out and there was no way of retrieving them.

She could have been talking to herself with her next words. 'I don't understand it. It's madness; it's totally inexplicable. He betrayed us . . . the whole family.'

Warren stood in the scented darkness knowing that the moment to tell her the truth about Kit Anson hung there between them. He remained silent.

'All I can do is protect myself with cold words and hostility. Somehow, I have to get through this flight which is so important to us all. Help me, Warren,' she pleaded. 'If you truly do love me, help me to survive this passion for someone who has no idea of loyalty. You're the only person I can trust.'

Warren was spared the need to answer by the arrival of Maitland with a message from Donald. The Frenchams were asking for Leone; would she go immediately. The girl summoned a smile and donned her social guise as swiftly as she had shed it.

'Tell my brother I'm on my way,' she said brightly.

Warren was left on the terrace to watch her disappear into the bright lights and even brighter laughter.

NEXT MORNING the launch was waiting by the sun-washed jetty, and the crew were soon out to where *Flamingo* rode the slight swell. Conditions for takeoff were perfect. Once aboard, Digger went on his inspection round, Morris organised his maps for the route they would be covering, and in the cockpit, Kit broke the news to his youthful assistant. 'I have a head like a blacksmith's forge. You'll have to take her over this leg.'

To his surprise, Joss responded, 'I knew you'd never attempt to fly today.' His boyish smile broke through. 'It was some party, wasn't it?'

'My head tells me it must have been, but I honestly don't recall many details. Thank God our passengers were nowhere near. Much faith they'd have in their captain for the rest of the flight!'

Joss, occupying the pilot's seat, began studying the instruments intently. 'When the fabulous Kirklands, their wealthy influential passengers, and the prototype of a sensational new aircraft can all be ignored in favour of Kit Anson, I'd say no one in the world could fail to have less than total faith in him. Shall we do the checks now?'

Kit took the right-hand seat and concentrated on the ritual of pre-flight instrument checks. That completed, he left the cockpit to stroll through the aircraft for a final word with his crew. Walking onto the boarding bay, Kit looked across at the jetty where the launch was waiting to ferry the passengers out. It was still tied up. He frowned. Departure was scheduled for ten o'clock. It was now a quarter to ten.

By ten thirty he was in a morning-after-the-night-before rage. Radioing the harbourmaster's office to send a boat for him, he returned to shore to telephone the hotel.

It was Maitland who spoke. 'Hello. Who is this?'

'We're half an hour behind schedule, Maitland. What the hell is going on up there?' Kit asked heatedly.

'There appears to be some difficulty in rounding everyone up,' came the unruffled reply. 'Miss Kirkland is doing her best to urge Countess Renskaya and Lady Frencham to dress. Most of the men were here at nine thirty, but several have wandered off again . . .'

Kit could hardly believe his ears. 'This isn't a Sunday-school outing, it's an intercontinental proving flight designed to impress prospective investors! *Flamingo* will be taking off at eleven fifteen—an hour and a quarter late—and anyone not aboard by then will have to find alternative means of returning to England.'

He slammed the receiver down, and stormed back to the flying boat. Silence then reigned on the flight deck as the minutes ticked past. At eleven, movement on the jetty heralded the laden launch on its way out to them.

The recalcitrant passengers were full of high spirits, which hinted at immense tact on the part of the Kirklands. It was not extended to the pilot, apparently, for Donald immediately strode through to the cockpit, to let fly.

'Just who the hell do you think you are?'

It was the wrong tone to use towards a man in the wrong mood. Kit answered with matching animosity. 'I'm the captain of this aircraft. As such, I insist you leave the flight deck immediately. We shall be departing within minutes, and passengers are forbidden here during takeoff.'

'I'm the one who gives the orders,' Donald cried furiously.

'Not aboard this aircraft. A flight captain has total command. You should know that strict aviation ruling without being told.'

'You're no longer captain of this aircraft,' raged Donald. 'I terminate your employment here and now.'

'That suits me,' Kit snapped, 'but you'll find Mr Hamilton will also insist that you leave the cockpit. He knows the rules as well as any pilot.'

Digger rose menacingly to his feet and Donald left. Kit glanced over at his second-in-command. 'Sorry about that. It hasn't unsettled you, has it?'

Joss shook his head. 'I'll make this takeoff a really good one, as it's going to be my last in *Flamingo*. If you're fired, so are we all. Will you make the departure announcement to the passengers, or shall I?'

'I think my fragile condition will just about allow me to do that,' Kit murmured, reaching for the speaking tube. 'Good morning, ladies and gentlemen. We are now ready for departure to Athens. My first officer, Mr Hamilton, will be at the controls today. He is now indicating his readiness for takeoff, so I'll leave you safely in his hands to enjoy the flight.'

The roar of aircraft engines was always as sweet as the song of a bird to Kit, and his anger gradually melted away. After circling above Naples, Joss set course and relaxed.

'Boy, it's warm in here,' he murmured.

'We'll change into tropical kit in Athens,' Kit commented, getting to his feet. 'If any of you should want me, I'll be chatting to Mr Kirkland.'

He found Donald with Maitland and Leone, in the small forward cabin reserved for their use alone. Maitland looked ashen. He was plainly suffering from airsickness once more. Sliding into the empty seat beside Leone, Kit took off his cap to hook it over one knee as he faced Donald.

'I imagine you're all now discussing the best place in Greece to find a replacement crew—one that is highly experienced with flying boats,' he said.

'How dared you speak to me in that manner in front of those men?' choked his adversary, still white with anger.

'Those men are members of my crew that I command. It's essential to hold their respect, so how dare you speak to me that way in their presence?' Kit retaliated. 'We were preparing for takeoff, which is a vulnerable process. Young Joss could have been dangerously unsettled by that scene. If you had something to say to me, you should have waited until now and asked me to leave the flight deck first.'

'Waited and asked!' thundered Donald. 'I own Kirkland's; I own this aircraft. You are simply one of my employees.'

'As the pilot of *Flamingo*, that may be true,' Kit agreed, trying not to lose his temper. 'Right at this moment, however, I'm Kit Anson, who lived and worked with you for over three years and who knows a damned sight too much for your sense of well-being. Now we're here in private, I suggest that you drop your insufferable arrogance and discuss our differences sensibly. If you sack me at Athens, my crew will also leave.'

'How dared you telephone such a message to Maitland?' Donald demanded.

'I'd have telephoned it direct to you, except that you've been in the habit of speaking to me through a third person. Now I'll give you a few facts. Although the sky is endless, we can't fly through it as we please. Pilots have to know who else is moving around, where they're heading, and when they're likely to be passing through certain areas. Where flying boats are concerned, there are additional important factors such as tides which govern the ability to land or take off.' Kit leaned forward to emphasise his next point. 'This flight has been planned down to the last detail, with every port of call told of our intentions and requirements. Kirkland Marine Aviation gave an assurance that *Flamingo* would maintain her schedule, yet this morning we disregarded our own assurances to our host company in Naples. We were almost ninety minutes late in departing, simply because you allowed twenty-four people to run wild this morning.' Getting to his feet, he settled the cap back on his aching head. 'I must insist that you get your passengers aboard on time in future, or you might find not only the crew gone but the flying boat as well.'

Donald rose to face him with terms of his own.

'Then, in future, you'll behave in a decent and responsible manner. I heard details of your disgusting public exhibition last night, and the fact that your reserve pilot is presently at the controls speaks volumes.' He added curtly, 'Now get back to your duty.'

Kit's eyes narrowed. 'Yesterday upset you, didn't it? Afraid of what I might say when I'm too drunk to care? Poor Donald. Two years behind bars might have been harsh, but I've served my sentence and been freed. Yours is likely to go on for as long as you have a conscience.'

As he walked away he heard Leone ask, 'What did he mean by that?'

'Who the hell knows?' came the ragged reply.

THE FLIGHT OF *FLAMINGO* continued without a hitch. Athens . . . Cairo . . . Mombasa, where they remained for three nights' rest.

Half the flight was over, and business prospects looked extremely good. All in all, the sun was in its heaven and shining right down on Kirkland Marine Aviation, so everyone was totally relaxed during the flight to Lake Victoria, the first overland stretch of the trip.

Warren thought Donald had calmed down a lot since Naples, despite the absence of Maitland. Armed with smelling salts and a bottle of sedative liquid provided by an army doctor in Cairo, he had been put on a ship heading for home. Donald seemed quite confident without him.

They had left Mombasa early that morning and were three hours into the flight, when Joss reported receipt of a 'mayday' call. The young pilot looked up at Kit. 'We're being asked to go to the aid of three people from a light aircraft, which crashed in thick jungle near Lake Kiju. Two of them are injured. The crash occurred when the pilot was attempting to reach a nearby mission hospital with a passenger suffering from a deadly virus. He'll die if not treated within twelve hours, they say.'

'Why us?' asked Kit tersely.

Joss frowned. 'It's impossible for anyone to reach them overland, and the river's so difficult it'd take a week to get a doctor up there by canoe. By then, they'd all be dead.'

'No seaplanes available?' Kit asked.

'Two, but with insufficient range. We were known to be in the area, and they want to know whether we could make a landing on the lake.'

Kit reached for the speaking tube and asked for Warren Grant to come to the flight deck, then gave his attention to Morris who was pencilling a circle on his map. Warren joined them. A small expanse of water encircled by thick jungle was a difficult proposition.

Kit looked at Warren. 'You're the man who knows this aircraft better than any of us. Could she do it? Could she land there and, more importantly, take off again, on such a short stretch of water?'

'She'll do it, Kit, if you can make her.'

Kit said to Joss, 'Tell them we're altering course in order to take a look. If it's possible to attempt a rescue, we will. Set the course Morris gives you. I'll take over just as soon as I've told Mr Kirkland our intentions.'

'I'll tell him,' Warren offered. 'You have far more important things to do right now.'

'Thanks,' said Kit briefly. 'If you'd like to come back after speaking to him, I'd be glad of your company. You designed this plane and you're entitled to be up here during her moment of glory.'

Warren left the flight deck possessed by supreme elation. With one of the finest pilots of marine aircraft at her controls, *Flamingo* would save the lives of three people, and hit the headlines. She would remove any last hesitation in the minds of those aboard. His dream had not only come true, it had exceeded his wildest hope.

11

Leone was enjoying a pre-lunch pink gin with her brother when Warren came up to them from the direction of the flight deck. Smiling, Leone said, 'Join us for a drink. There's just time.'

'You'll have to delay lunch,' he interrupted with an air of excitement. 'We've received an SOS asking if we can go to the aid of three people stranded in the jungle. The only means of reaching them is if we can land on a small lake. Kit's agreed to take a look and attempt a rescue, if it's possible. He's altered course. We should be over the lake in about fifty minutes, so I think the meal should be delayed until the emergency is over.'

Donald looked tense. 'He has no authority to do this without my permission.'

'Your permission is superfluous,' said Warren. 'He's captain of the aircraft, and the responsibility for such decisions is his alone. Anyway, can't you see what a splendid piece of luck this is?'

'A piece of luck?' asked Leone. 'What if it isn't possible to land?'

'Kit says he'll then fly as low as he can, while we drop food and anything else we are carrying which might keep them alive a little longer.'

Donald stirred restlessly. 'So much for his highhanded lecture on sticking to a schedule and not flying around the sky willy-nilly.'

'Mombasa knows exactly where we are, Donald, and he's not doing this for fun,' Warren said. 'I'm thrilled . . . *Flamingo* is the one flying boat able to land on that short stretch of water, and Kit is a pilot able to make that manoeuvre. The feat will make world headlines. Not only that, the prospective investors aboard will actually be participating in the event which will demonstrate *Flamingo*'s unique ability. It will ensure the survival of the company, also the survival of three desperate souls. I'm going back to give Kit any assistance he might need. Perhaps you would tell people what we're about to do.' At the door to the flight deck, he turned. 'You might also be generous enough to congratulate your pilot after he's pulled off something a lesser man might shy from attempting.'

'Bloody cheek!' breathed Donald as Warren vanished. 'This trip has caused him to get a bit above himself, if you ask me.'

'Warren's always like that over anything concerned with his precious *Flamingo*. Because you remain aloof over your brainchild, you don't understand how het up he gets in defence of his work,' Leone told him. 'Come on, let's tell everyone what to expect, then pray he pulls it off.'

They moved through the cabins breaking the news, and apologising for the unavoidable delay in serving lunch. Everyone reacted with great enthusiasm, watching for the first glimpse of the lake ahead.

Leone sat by a window, staring at the dense green jungle passing beneath them. Kit had descended at least ten thousand feet, and maintained a steady downward run towards that blue pin-dot on the map.

Then it was visible, lying like a tiny diamond in the rippling emerald vegetation. Suddenly, green gave way to gleaming tawny water as *Flamingo* crossed the lake, throwing a giant shadow over its surface. Dangerously soon, they were again above vegetation at the far end of the waterway. The flying boat began a wide turn which would bring them on a course to cross the lake from the opposite direction. That repeat run produced a cry from some of the passengers, drawing Leone's attention to movement on the banks bordered by mangroves. Someone was waving what looked like a shirt or jacket.

Flamingo was making another turn, climbing as she did so. Next minute, she was heading away from the lake. A chorus of voices filled the cabins.

'He's going away!'

'Surely we're not going to leave them to die!'

Amid these cries came a familiar voice sounding confident and relaxed. 'Ladies and gentlemen, this is Captain Anson. As you'll have seen, there appears to be at least one survivor who has managed to reach the lake from the scene of the crash. We must hope all three are there. I've made two runs to familiarise myself with the stretch of water available, and I'm now preparing to run in for a landing. It's very fortunate that *Flamingo* has the virtue of being able to settle onto a remarkably short stretch of water, no other flying boat could attempt a rescue here. All the same, I must advise you that the next fifteen minutes may be slightly uncomfortable. It is imperative you all remain seated. Thank you for your cooperation.'

The announcement struck everyone silent. Leone was trembling. Despite the calmness of his voice, she knew what Kit must be feeling at this vital moment. They were turning once more and, as the sun flashed through the windows to her right, then through those to her left, Donald slipped into the seat beside her. 'I hope to God he knows what he's doing.'

They were dropping quickly; *Flamingo* began to shudder and weave as she slowed drastically. The engine noise grew deafening, the china in the galley began rattling continuously . . . Next minute, there was cloudy brown water no more than fifty feet below. *Flamingo* dropped like a stone, steadied with a great roar of power, then dropped again to hit the surface with a thud which brought cries of alarm from the passengers. The hull was filled with an earsplitting roar as reverse thrust was applied. With outstretched arms, Leone stopped herself from tumbling headlong into the opposite seat as the aircraft began to shudder violently. As they continued to hurtle forward, the cabin grew dark. Water rose high over the windows to give the impression that they were sinking.

'Dear God, we're going down,' cried Donald. 'He's crashed!'

Leone clung to her brother, then she sensed a less agonising note to the roar of the engines. Kit had done it. Gradually, *Flamingo* eased into a glide, the engines quietened and the brown water subsided enough to let in light through the top half of the windows. Everyone stood to peer through at the view. Thick jungle surrounded tawny water scattered with floating vegetation. The banks were merely stretches of tangled mangrove roots which separated water from solid earth. The whole place bore an air of menace. Somewhere out there, three men had been facing a terrible fate.

'He's done it,' said Donald. 'He's damn well done it!'

From every part of the hull came elated voices as the aircraft came to a stop. Into the buzz of conversation came Kit's voice.

'Sorry about the rough ride, ladies and gentlemen. I trust no one suffered bumps or bruises. As we are likely to be here for some time, while two members of the crew go ashore in the hope of picking up those awaiting us, you may now move about the aircraft as much as you wish. If anyone among you has any knowledge of medicine, I'd be grateful for assistance. Thank you.'

Donald looked at Leone with a slight frown. 'He sounded pretty cool about it all. Come on, we'd better go forward and see what's happening.'

Leone followed her brother along the central gangway to the cargo door. The Australian, together with the young copilot, was climbing into a dinghy which contained water, a first-aid box, and a folding stretcher. Kit's shirt was stuck to his back and his face looked set and worried as he watched his men start to paddle away towards the area where waving had been seen from the air. Smothering heat set them all sweating. Next minute, mosquitoes came swarming in; Kit had no option but to close the hatch swiftly.

He made his way to the flight deck with Leone and Donald in tow. Warren was standing beside Morris when they arrived there. They indicated to Kit a point some twenty yards from where the small boat was heading. A khaki-clad figure had materialised from the dense vegetation, gesticulating energetically. The boat veered towards it and the first officer scrambled across the mangrove roots, while his companion fastened the craft to a low branch. Before following Joss ashore, the Australian waved a small flag from side to side three times. Excitement rippled through the cockpit.

'They're all alive,' breathed Kit. 'Thank God for that!'

Leone felt close to tears, but the arrival of a brisk figure took care of her threatened weakness. Mrs Harmesworth, flushed by heat, pushed past Leone to walk up to Kit.

'Captain Anson, I've come in response to your request for assistance,' she told him, in a voice brimming with authority. 'I was a VAD during the war. I'll do whatever I can to help those poor people you've rescued.'

Kit smiled warmly at a woman who had irritated everyone during the course of the flight. 'I'm very grateful, Mrs Harmesworth. We've been signalled that all three are alive, but we won't have any idea what state they're in. Perhaps you'd prepare impromptu beds for them. The medicines we carry are very basic, but anything you can do will certainly aid their chances of survival.' He glanced at his navigator. 'Morris, show the lady what few comforts we have available, will you? Then you'd better get along to the galley to see what food can be provided.'

'I'll see to that,' volunteered Leone.

Kit's glance met hers briefly and impersonally. 'Thanks.'

IT WAS FRUSTRATING that there was very little on board by way of invalid food. The best Leone could do was to tell the chef to stand by with his supply of eggs, milk and sponge cakes.

As she left the galley, she bumped full tilt into Warren.

'Sorry,' he exclaimed, holding her steady. 'They're coming alongside now. Let's get down to the cargo hatch.'

Kit, his navigator and Donald were there ready to help them all aboard. As Leone and Warren reached the large hold where mosquitoes were again swarming through the open hatch, the dinghy appeared alongside. The figure being assisted from a seat in the stern, wearing khaki shirt and trousers, and a pith helmet, was a woman. Leone could see little of her face, because she was anxiously watching the transfer of the stretcher bearing the unconscious body of a bearded man. The second man, conscious but clearly in great pain, was passed cautiously up to those inside the cargo bay. Leone went forward to the woman in crumpled khaki. 'Perhaps you'd like to come along to one of the cabins and recover a little,' she said.

Silver-green eyes stared from a freckled face streaked with grime, as they took in the sight of Leone's peppermint-green sleeveless dress in fine Swiss lawn and her elegant handmade Italian shoes.

'I must first see that my brother and Paul are comfortable,' the woman said in accented English, turning to the injured pair lying on blankets while their rescuers clambered aboard, then hauled in the dinghy. While Donald and Warren closed the heavy door, Kit addressed the woman in quiet tones.

'There are limited medical supplies and a passenger with nursing experience at your disposal. We shall do all we can for you during the flight to Mombasa, where I'll arrange for an ambulance to be waiting. Are you hurt in any way?'

'No.'

'How sick are the men?' he asked then. 'Can you give us details?'

'They are Paul Christianson and my brother Knut,' she said. 'They have made a study of rare fever since two years in Africa. Now Paul has this fever. I am called to fetch them to the mission hospital. There is a bad storm. We make the crash. I am not hurt at all, but Paul now also has the bleeding inside, I think. Knut has the broken foot and much pain in the back. He will live. Paul maybe will die. I am not certain.'

Kit turned to Mrs Harmesworth. 'Did you catch all that? Will you need assistance?'

She glanced up at him. 'I'd be glad of help from one of the stewards.'

Donald organised the transfer of the men, while Kit questioned the woman further. 'Were you piloting the aircraft when it crashed?'

'Yes.'

'If both men were injured, you must have got them to the lake single-handed.'

'Yes.'

'That's a remarkable achievement.'

'I wanted to live, that is all.'

'We all want to live, Miss . . . ?'

'Sylva Lindstrom.'

'You're surely not the Norwegian girl who did the Arctic flight in nineteen thirty-four! Didn't she also take the record for the polar run from Nicholson last year?'

'Yes, I did . . . and I am she.'

He whistled. 'Great Scott! Tell me I'm not dreaming! Whatever are you doing in Africa?'

'Flying . . . or crashing, to be most truthful.' She turned away from him, saying, 'Now I must drink some tea before we speak together more. Thank you for coming to save us. I think you must be a special pilot yourself to make such a landing.'

He smiled. 'Wait until you've experienced the takeoff before making final judgment on that. It's liable to be pretty rough.'

'So was the landing, my friend.'

Feeling overdressed and inadequate, Leone led the woman to the tiny cabin reserved for the Kirklands.

Of all the people they could have picked up in equatorial jungle, it had to be another record-breaking pilot, and a female one, at that. There was no doubt her presence would increase the sensational aspect of the daring rescue. Donald and Warren would be pleased. Kit even more so.

His voice reached her over the relay system. 'Thank you for your cooperation, ladies and gentlemen. The crew and I are now preparing for our return to Mombasa, but I must warn you that takeoff will be less smooth than usual. As the surface of the lake is too calm, I shall have to create an artificial swell by making *Flamingo* imitate a wounded duck. There's no need to feel alarm. The aircraft will be fully under my control. Please take your seats now. Thank you.'

The great engines burst into life. *Flamingo* taxied slowly forward, turning as she did so in order to face the full length of the lake.

At that moment, Sylva Lindstrom appeared. Leone regarded the Norwegian with a faint sense of shock. Washed, and the pith helmet removed, it was now possible to see that she was no more than twenty-five. Her deeply tanned face with its sprinkling of freckles and the warm brown hair coiled in braids round her head gave the girl an air of Nordic peasantry.

Having completed the turn, *Flamingo* moved forward in a very definite zigzag pattern to create deep furrows. It was as well that Kit had warned his passengers, for the sensation was rather alarming. 'A wounded duck' had been an excellent description, and *Flamingo* dipped and floundered her way to the far end of the lake in this fashion. Another sharp turn, then they were swiftly into maximum acceleration, causing *Flamingo* to bump and bounce over her own artificial swell. The hull began shaking alarmingly, and the interior was suddenly blacked out by great walls of brown water.

Then, as Leone became convinced that instead of going up, they were diving to the depths of Lake Kiju, she felt that unmistakable surge which told her the nose was lifting from the water. With dramatic suddenness, the cabin was flooded with brilliant light as water dropped away from the windows, and soon she could see green vegetation barely a few feet below. They were up and clear! *Flamingo* had just proved her own greatness, and Leone felt like crying.

Sylva Lindstrom looked across at her, her light green eyes blazing with excitement. 'He *is* some special pilot.'

'He should be. He's Kit Anson,' Leone told her, still very emotional.

'Kit Anson who took the speed record, then disgraced himself?' marvelled the girl. 'What can he be doing in Africa?'

'Flying . . . and *not* crashing,' was Leone's response and she turned to gaze out as *Flamingo* climbed gently into the sky.

FLAMINGO RETURNED TO MOMBASA already destined for the annals of aviation history. That a flying boat her size, with such a collection of distinguished people aboard, should effect a dramatic rescue from so small a lake was a sensation in itself. When it then became known that the notorious Kit Anson had been at the controls, and that one of the lives he had saved was that of Sylva Lindstrom, the fearless female pilot, sensational was too mild a word for such a journalistic scoop. On their arrival at Mombasa, the jetty had been packed with pressmen and excited sightseers.

Kit felt very tired after the long flight. When he finally left the aircraft to take a taxi back to the beachside lodging he had occupied before, journalists followed him and the crew. Kit spoke to them for twenty minutes, posed for photographs, then told them he was in dire need of a bath and sleep. To his relief, they went in search of fresh victims.

The bath was soothing, but he lay reliving the drama of the day over and over again. *Flamingo* had risen effortlessly to the challenge, as Warren had vowed she would, but Kit Anson had been obliged to struggle.

Two years in prison, then two more as a virtual down-and-out, had taken their toll. In Spain, he had flown obsolete war aircraft with wheels instead of floats. Only when Tom had set up Western Mediterranean Air Services had his own experience with marine aircraft resumed. He had quickly got back into his stride; however, he was not the man he had once been. What he had done that day had been extremely risky, and he had known it. The aircraft was admirably equipped to perform such manoeuvres, but he had taken a big chance on his own ability to carry them off successfully. The event was being hailed as heroic, but only he knew why he had ignored common sense and professional caution to perform a feat which now had him marvelling at his own madness. It was his professional reputation as much as the three Norwegians that he was determined to bring back from the dead. He had succeeded, but he lay offering a prayer of thanks to the patron saint of aviators for watching over him as he had challenged his own skill.

12

Flamingo made her triumphant way home. Not only was it a long, gruelling flight, there had been the additional stress of the daring rescue to take toll of the crew's stamina. All the same, it had been a long time since Kit had felt relaxed and at peace with himself. As he took off from the blossom-covered island of Madeira on the final leg to Sheenmouth, he smiled.

'Is there some joke I'm missing?' asked Joss beside him.

Kit's smile deepened. 'Yes. Both floats have just dropped off, and you're going to be asked to do the landing at Sheenmouth.'

'Oh, very jokey,' came the light-hearted response. '*Nothing* could fall off this gorgeous machine. She's perfect, and . . . this flight has been a stupendous success, hasn't it?'

'Not half!' Glancing at the youngster, he asked, 'Sorry it's almost over?'

'Things are going to seem pretty dull when we get back to routine.'

'I think we deserve a week off first, so I'll tell Tom he'll have to wait for his super crew.'

Kit then noticed dark clouds on the horizon; a huge bank of them obscuring the sun.

'Hello,' he murmured. 'I don't much like the look of that up ahead.'

Joss studied it through binoculars. 'It's a storm gathering, all right. On our present course, we're liable to hit it fair and square.'

'Mmm. Which direction does it appear to be taking?'

'It's hard to tell,' the youngster replied. 'If anything, I'd say it's cyclonic. Could move anywhere, at any moment.'

'Damn!' Kit said with feeling. 'An entire trip flown in near-perfect weather, then we have to hit something like this just a few miles from home.'

'Home' to Kit meant Sheenmouth; Joss automatically assumed the word to mean Lisbon. 'We ought to get there without much trouble,' said Joss. 'I know it'll mean a detour, but that's surely better than risking a great deal of bumping about on the edge of that monster.'

Kit nodded. 'I agree. Ask Morris to give us a new setting, will you? And tell him to make it snappy, because that swirling column of cloud is coming straight for us.'

Joss left his seat and Kit picked up the binoculars. There was no doubt it was a fearsome clash of elements of the kind every pilot avoided at all costs. It did appear to be approaching alarmingly fast and, if anything, veering east towards Portugal. A wide detour to the west would merely add an hour or two to their flying time to Sheenmouth.

Joss returned to set the new course. Already, the sun was dimmed, and the first sensations of turbulence in the atmosphere caused *Flamingo* to tremble slightly. Almost immediately, the tremble became a shudder. Patches of flying cloud whisked past the windows, and the main section of the cloudbank was now like a huge satanic mountain directly in their path.

Apprehension crept through Kit's veins. Either they had made a severe misjudgment, or the storm was now moving in an entirely different direction. They were heading right into the heart of it.

'God!' he swore. 'Five minutes ago that bastard looked set to hit Portugal. Now it's swung to the west. We should have run for Lisbon, instead.'

Joss looked across at him. 'We are.'

'Are what?'

'Running for home. Morris estimates we'll be there within two hours.'

Kit realised what had gone wrong. Morris had unwittingly been asked to give them a course straight into danger. There was no time for explanations, recriminations, or even the plotting of a new course. Hurtling towards *Flamingo*'s nose was a mass of electricity generated by the violence of the elements. All Kit could do was prepare to fight it while shouting for Digger to send a radio message giving their position and predicament. Even as he did so, lightning sizzled towards them. Digger yelled that the radio was crackling so much he could hear no response from it.

They were in dire straits. Hitting the full force of the cyclone was like flying headlong into the sea. The cockpit grew dark. *Flamingo* rose and plunged as if tossed by forty-foot waves, and rain thundered on her sides with deafening force. The cockpit lights failed to come on, so Kit sat in darkness gripping the column and trying to estimate his altitude.

Light suddenly pierced the gloom. Joss had snatched the rescue lamp from its bracket, and was struggling to cross the cockpit. Another violent plunge threw him off his feet, and the lamp smashed against the bulkhead. The darkness was pierced by vivid bright flashes, which raced along the nose towards them. Kit ducked the lightning instinctively, slackening his hold on the stick just as the aircraft was tossed in the air. Next minute, they were in a steep dive and the nearside starboard engine had flames streaking from it. Hauling on the stick and yelling to Digger to send continuous distress signals, he fought to pull out of the dive. They yawed to port when the flaming engine failed completely, and Kit braced himself to stay in his seat.

A bolt of lightning struck the propeller of the offside starboard engine and the subsequent reduction in power dispelled Kit's last hope of forging through the storm before having to put down on the sea. They were losing height spasmodically and he had his work cut out to avoid stalling or entering a dive which he now had insufficient engine power to counter. He yelled to his copilot, 'Tell all crew members to prepare for an imminent emergency landing. We're going into the drink, Joss.'

He hoped to God they were still over the sea. They had a chance with water beneath them; very little with solid earth. It was the most terrifying of all the hours he had spent in the air. His nerves were so tense they sent a message of instant alert when the dark grey obscurity began heaving in great watery ridges only a few feet below.

'Flaps!' he roared to Joss. 'Here it is.'

Although he fought valiantly, there had been too little warning. *Flamingo* hit the sea with bone-shaking impact, bounced high, then raced forward into a huge rising wall of water.

IT SEEMED AS IF there would never be another sound in the world save the awesome roaring, as seawater surged into the punctured hull. The only indication of life around Leone was a vague blur of life jackets moving in the near blackness. The sea was icy. In the air, she had been petrified. Now that she found herself alive and apparently unhurt, calmness had overtaken her. The first priority seemed to be to escape from *Flamingo* before she sank, taking them all down.

Treading water, she called out, 'Is anyone there? Is anyone else there?'

'Here . . . Yes . . . Oh, thank God,' came voices from various directions.

'Let's all gather over by the bar,' she suggested. 'See where the fire outside is being reflected in the mirror? Make for that.'

Swimming towards the spot, Leone reached the bar. She waited for the others to join her. Before they could, however, the aircraft shifted dramatically, and Leone was thrown against the bulkhead. The blow must have knocked her out. The next thing she knew, she was floating on her back and there was a bright light swaying in the air some distance away.

A man's voice cried out, 'Anyone left in there?'

'I am,' she cried desperately. 'Leone Kirkland.' She made for the light. The man holding the lamp was Digger Rathbone, the Australian engineer.

'There are others with me,' she panted.

'No, you're the last,' he told her. 'We pulled out everyone we could find. They're all in the boat. Come on, it's safer out here. Give me your hand.'

He pulled her up to the edge of the open hatch, and she stood precariously on that small foothold. She shivered as the wind buffeted her. The sea stretched away in a series of huge cold grey-green undulations overhung by cloud. Rain lashed down to bite into her flesh like ice needles. A small lifeboat crammed with people was being dashed against *Flamingo*'s broken hull by the waves.

'Get in, Miss Kirkland, we daren't hang around here much longer.'

'Where is my brother . . . and Mr Grant? I can't see them in the boat.'

'I don't know,' Digger confessed bluntly. 'The crew will find them. You're endangering lives with this delay.'

'Send the boat off,' she cried against the driving rain. 'I'm a very good swimmer. I'll stay and help you look for them.'

The engineer untied the rope. The tiny craft raced away on the crest of a wave, then vanished from sight as if swallowed up by the sea.

'Where's the other boat?' she demanded of the grim-faced man.

'Lost . . . and the dinghy would overturn in this swell. All we can do is use it to cling to, once we're sure there's no one else left alive here.'

Only then did she dare ask, 'Is Kit . . . ?'

He gave a slow shake of his head. 'Can't reach the cockpit. The nose has practically sheared off.'

'I see. Can you swim well, Mr Rathbone?'

'Champion of Millamoola Cove,' he shouted above the roar of waves. 'Digger to my friends. Keep with me, and we'll see what we can do.'

Leone found it difficult to stay with the Australian as he dropped from the hatchway to swim beneath the flaming wing sticking from the water like a fiery finger pointing to heaven. The most fearsome prospect was that of being thrown against the hull, then sucked beneath it by the force of the waves. She used all her strength to move forward. Her companion was heading for the upper cabin near the nose, where Donald and Warren might well have been at the moment of impact. As they neared it, she guessed the chance of anyone being alive in there must be slight; that part of the hull above the water level was blackened and charred. Yet, even as she prepared to swim on, she caught sight of movement. A body was floating nearby, in danger of being pulled beneath the wreck. Without hesitation, she struck out towards it, to discover that the bobbing figure kept afloat by the life jacket was Warren.

She seized hold of the straps across his shoulders and towed him slowly away to where she had last seen the Australian.

'I've found Warren,' she yelled.

The engineer beckoned to her. To her surprise, he was smiling, albeit somewhat grimly. Next moment, she discovered the reason. Three yards from him, her feet touched a solid surface which allowed her to stand when in troughs between the giant waves.

'Sandbank,' he yelled. 'We can't be far from land.'

The next wave swept them up again, but he signalled Leone to be ready for the next trough. When it came, he seized Warren's harness with one hand and pushed Leone up to the roof of *Flamingo* several feet from where the nose had been wrenched almost completely from the body of the craft. Finding a secure perch, she assisted her companion to pull Warren up.

'Is he alive?' she cried.

'Just knocked cold on impact, I guess. He's bloody lucky you saw him when you did. Do what you can for him while I take a look around. My mates are in the cockpit.'

She took a deep breath. 'Yes . . . of course.'

His hand covered hers momentarily. 'I would never have believed you had it in you to do this. Stay where you are. It's safer than a boat, and they'll find you the minute the storm clears.' His drawn face creased into an encouraging smile. 'You are a damned wonderful girl.'

His friends' bodies were in the cockpit; Kit's body was in there. Tears joined the rain on her face as she sat clutching Warren on that white wreck stranded in a grey ocean. Minutes passed until her attention was taken by a moan, and she glanced down to find blue eyes clouded with pain and bewilderment gazing up at her. Bending to put her cheek against his, she sobbed, 'Oh, Warren . . . dear Warren, your lovely *Flamingo* is dead. I'm so sorry. So very sorry.'

THE SENSATIONAL NEWSPAPER REPORTS on the crash of *Flamingo* with the tragic loss of life had now diminished in favour of the German–Czech crisis over Sudetenland. However, the financial columns continued to speculate on the future of Kirkland Marine Aviation, now solely owned by a twenty-two-year-old girl after the death of her brother, along with two Portuguese stewards and two passengers.

The sandbank had saved the lives of the flight crew. The navigator and first officer had suffered less than the pilot, who had remained at the controls until impact. Kit Anson had broken both legs, and received head injuries from which he might not fully recover. Doctors said he would never be fit to fly again. He was now in a Lisbon hospital, too ill to know anything outside his own shocked half-world. Donald Kirkland's body had been flown home for burial at Sheenmouth. His sister had requested a quiet private funeral.

There was to be an inquiry into the cause of the crash, but faith in the prototype had been shaken; investment in its manufacture was now less likely. If the inquiry proved the disaster to be due to pilot error and/or adverse weather conditions, some financiers might still put money in the aircraft or the company. However, if there was the slightest evidence of a major fault in *Flamingo*, the future for Kirkland's would look extremely black.

On a stifling July morning, Leone sat in Sir Willard Jameson's suite of offices facing the family solicitor, in company with Spencer Bligh, senior partner of the accountants Larchforth and Bodmin.

'Miss Kirkland, your brother's death leaves you as Sir Hector's sole heir,' Sir Willard explained, in grave but kindly tones. 'Mr Donald Kirkland had made no will, although I had often pressed him to do so.' He sighed. 'The terms of Sir Hector's will state that everything should pass to his daughter if his son should die intestate. I'm afraid that means you inherit both Sir Hector's and your brother's debts, in addition to their assets.'

She stared at him. Had her father accumulated debts? It seemed inconceivable. Yet, as Sir Willard and Spencer Bligh unfolded the state of her finances, it appeared that both her father and brother had run up huge liabilities in the name of Kirkland Marine Aviation. Sir Hector had prudently invested large sums abroad, but they were in holdings for which interest would only be paid every five years.

'We could, of course, realise on these investments, Miss Kirkland,' the accountant told her in sombre tones, 'but I would strongly advise against such a move. They are your security for the future, my dear lady.'

Leone did not understand. 'Sir Willard has just told me I've inherited debts. Presumably, they have to be settled by selling some of those shares.'

The two men exchanged a glance, as Willard enlightened her.

'The "debts" were all incurred to finance Kirkland Marine Aviation. Sir Hector built up the company from nothing, and was very proud of the achievement. When Mr Kirkland's seaplane gained the speed record in nineteen thirty-two, your father's confidence in his company seemed vindicated. However, the trial and imprisonment of the pilot took its toll of orders for the aircraft. Regrettably, Sir Hector allowed emotion to override perspicacity. Against our advice, he began work on a new flying boat.'

Sir Willard continued. 'Your brother had little choice but to incur additional liabilities in a bid to sell *Flamingo* to investors. Both Mr Bligh and myself advised him to rid himself of the company which was draining his wealth.' He shook his head sadly. 'It's a great pity our advice was not heeded, Miss Kirkland, for we now have an ailing company to dispose of.' He took some sheets from a pile of documents. 'I have drawn up a plan to close the workshops forthwith and terminate the employment of the work-force. Mr Bligh has made a fair assessment of what we can get for the company, dependent on the findings of the inquiry . . .'

'Sir Willard, may I interrupt to ask who you mean when you mention "we"?' put in Leone. 'You spoke just now of my being the sole heir. Surely I am the only person to make any kind of decision concerning the company.'

The solicitor raised thin eyebrows in surprise.

'I want to hold on to Kirkland's, even if it means selling those foreign investments you prize so highly. I have every confidence that the inquiry will absolve from blame both the machine and the man who flew her. When that happens, orders will surely come in for our flying boat. I have every intention of meeting them.'

There was stunned silence from the two men as Leone repeated firmly, 'I want to continue manufacturing flying boats, whatever it costs.'

Sir Willard sighed. 'Very well. But please take a few weeks before making your final decision. It is not one you should make in haste, dear lady.'

Leone gazed back at him frankly. 'As I waited on the wreckage of *Flamingo* for rescue or death by drowning, Sir Willard, it dawned on me that my life is destined to be linked with marine aircraft. The greatest turning points in it, so far, have been created by these machines and the people who are connected with them. I believe the decision has been made for me.'

ARRIVING HOME late in the evening, Leone had a light supper then sat on in the midsummer dusk considering all she had been told.

The future really depended on the vital *Flamingo* inquiry. If technical fault was ruled out, surely the proving flight, with its dramatic lake rescue, would bring investors back. Meanwhile, she must manage to survive without withdrawing those foreign investments. They would be needed to finance expansion when orders for *Flamingo* rolled in. Only when that happened would she decide whether to take on partners, or whether to go public with the company she had now taken to heart.

By morning, she had formed several ideas which would help ease the financial problems. After breakfast she decided to act on one plan without delay. Making her way to the large office which had been Sir Hector's sanctum, then Donald's, she rang the bell, then stood waiting. What she had to say to Maitland would be easier if she faced him eye to eye.

He arrived with a folder beneath his arm. There was little change in his expression as she said, 'Did you know that I tried to persuade my brother the company couldn't afford you, when I joined it? Donald insisted that he couldn't manage without you, yet he did so quite easily when you were so airsick he had to send you home from Cairo by sea.'

'A constitutional weakness I deplored but could do nothing to remedy,' he replied coolly.

'Unlike my brother, I'm prepared to make economies which, in view of the unhappy legacy I'm facing, are essential. I wish I could say I regret having to dismiss you, Maitland, but the prospect of an end to your unctuous self popping up wherever I go is extremely attractive. I shall pay you a month's salary. I'd like you to be gone by tomorrow evening.'

He stood unruffled as he said, 'I don't think you would, Miss Kirkland. I know far too much.'

'I'll agree with that,' she told him calmly. 'In fact, you are almost too perfect for this world. I aim to find someone to replace you, and intend to learn the business myself. In time I shall find out all there is to know.'

'Even the truth concerning your father and Geoffrey Anson?' he asked.

Leone grew still, her sixth sense telling her that the faintly sinister quality she had always suspected in this man was about to be revealed. 'Especially that,' she told him, hiding her apprehension.

'I thought you might.' Maitland folded his arms confidently. 'Anson was a drunkard and wastrel, but he was undisputedly a brilliant designer. Sir Hector needed a new seaplane, but the man was going to the dogs after being thrown from his lodgings. Your father offered him the old boathouse to live in, and gave Anson junior a job as a greaser in the workshops. In addition, he passed on a valuable investment tip to Geoffrey. Sir Hector told him of a new company being floated which was certain to hit the jackpot. The gambling streak in old Anson now saw a new form of sudden chancy wealth, and he put his every penny in shares. Your father invested modestly. The company overstepped itself and crashed. A friend of Sir Hector gave him advance warning to sell, but he neglected to pass on this warning to Anson. The old boy lost everything. When he heard, he drank himself silly, then came here to the abbey to confront the man he held responsible. Your father and I had gone down to the workshops early that day; most of the men were outside taking their breakfast break. Anson no sooner clapped eyes on Sir Hector than he went for him. Sir Hector told the man to pull himself together. That's when Anson let fly, threatening he'd sell his design to a rival. At that, Sir Hector's temper got the better of him. He hit out.'

Allowing a pause to highlight his words, Maitland then continued. 'Your father's blow knocked Anson off-balance and into the racing machinery, where he was instantly cut to pieces. Fortunately, I was the only person who saw what actually happened.' He smiled. 'Sir Hector always appreciated my silence.'

Leone stood for long moments gazing into the past. At last she understood. Guilt had led her father to offer a home to the destitute boy whose father he had accidentally killed. How could he have known that boy would become a man earning more respect from the world than any Kirkland? Was that why he had subsequently destroyed the son, as well? She turned away in anguish. In her own way, she had passively approved the order to place him under arrest. That made her as guilty as her father.

With her back to Maitland, she said, 'I want you gone from here by tomorrow evening.'

After a short silence, he said, 'Do you really want the truth published in every newspaper, and passed from lip to lip in social and business circles?'

Turning to face someone she had always resented for the place he had held in the Kirkland household, she said, 'You've been dealing with the men of this family for the past twenty years. There's a new breed of Kirklands now, Maitland, and I'm the first of them. You may gossip with whom you wish, you are at liberty to drag the name of Kirkland through the mud. It's been there before, and survived . . . but this will be the last time. You'll never know how marvellous it is to feel free of your presence in my home. When you've gone, I shall open all the windows and allow the breeze to blow away the ghosts. The rest of them are going to be *mine*.'

13

After a glorious October, when the banks of the Sheen had been ablaze with autumn colours, the November of 1938 came in grey, damp and with the threat of war; Czechoslovakia had just been sacrificed to placate Hitler in his demand for Sudetenland. No one in Britain wanted a war; what Britain needed was a continuing peace, a run of prosperity. What it got was an outbreak of virulent influenza during that bleak month.

Warren lay in bed feeling desperately ill. He had succumbed to the flu several days ago, and today his condition had worsened. He had been too ill to eat for two days, and the fire had gone out early yesterday evening. Another night lay ahead of him without light or warmth.

He had been dreadfully tired for months. Ever since Leone had dragged him from the sea in May. The disaster haunted him. People had died in *his* aircraft. Donald Kirkland had died. What would the inquiry unearth? What had happened to the dream he had had? A roundabout of facts and images circled in his heated brain—he rolled over to blot them out, and felt himself falling, falling, falling.

He awoke to find himself in an enormous bed in a room of elegant luxury. Old stone walls and mullioned windows, seventeenth-century paintings, brocade curtains, thick carpet dotted with Persian rugs, heavy gilt chandelier, antique furniture. He could only be in Sheenmouth Abbey.

Leone came in with a Dr Gibbs, who had apparently been attending him every day for almost a week.

'Give me a call when you've finished,' she told the medical man. Then, with a smile for Warren, she went out.

'Well, how are you feeling?' asked Dr Gibbs.

'Better than before,' Warren confessed.

'I imagine so,' came the dry comment. 'You've had pleurisy, Mr Grant. It was touch and go until yesterday. Your constitution is none too sturdy. I suppose you've been fretting over the business of the inquiry, and not looking after yourself properly.'

'I've been very worried, yes. The result ought to be announced soon. It's been more than six months.'

The man in tweed nodded. 'Miss Kirkland went to the boathouse to tell you the news. Lucky for you she did. You were in a critical state.'

His heart lurched. 'The news? She's heard the verdict?'

'She has indeed. Now, I'm prescribing a mixture . . .'

Warren heard nothing of Dr Gibbs's mixture. Why had Leone said nothing just now? Was she keeping the blow from him until he was well enough to take it? Surely they had not discovered a design fault.

'As you appear to have listened to nothing I just said, Mr Grant,' said the doctor, 'I have written down the dosage instructions. I'll call again on Thursday.' His smile was friendly and encouraging. 'No reason to get in a stew. You'll find Miss Kirkland's news very pleasant hearing.'

Leone came in several minutes after the man had gone. She crossed to the bed to sit on it and take one of his hands.

'Stop looking so apprehensive. They placed full blame on the freak weather conditions. The crew have been cleared of any possible error or negligence, and *Flamingo* remains as marvellous as you've always claimed.' She smiled, and it was like the sun coming out. 'Preliminary enquiries are already coming in, which suggests that public faith in your beautiful boat remains unshaken. Warren, I'm such a new girl at all this, but I imagine it means we're back in business. If we want to be, that is.'

It was too much for him in his weakened state. He turned his face away, and lay trying to accept that his dream was intact. He rolled his head to look at Leone again. 'How is Kit?'

'I only know what the newspapers report of his condition. Now that he's emerged from the coma, the Portuguese doctors say they'll soon know if their fears are correct. Oh, Warren, what does a man born to fly do with his life when he's no longer able to use that great gift?'

He squeezed the hand holding his. 'Kit's a fighter.'

'This is probably something he can't fight.'

Leone stood up, moved restlessly across the room, then sank into a small chair. 'There's something I want to tell you. For several months I've been expecting to read it in every newspaper in the world, but Maitland is either biding his time, or has given up all thought of what he threatened. All the same, I want you to know this.'

Warren struggled to a sitting position.

'When I told Maitland to go, he gave me the answer to why he was always so favoured by Father and Donald. He . . . he . . . Geoffrey Anson was pushed into the machinery by my father,' she confessed in anguished tones. 'They had a quarrel over investments which Kit's father had been advised to make, but which had crashed. Poor Anson got drunk, then assaulted the man he held responsible for the loss of all he owned. Father apparently thrust him away and . . . and Anson lost his footing to slip down into the racing machinery. Maitland was a witness to it, and blackmailed first Father, then Donald. He expected to use the same pressure on me, but I . . . I truly didn't care if he made the news public. It didn't really seem important to uphold Kirkland integrity which was a myth.'

Warren felt giddy. 'How do you know he was telling the truth?'

She shook her head. 'It's true, it's true. It all makes sense now. Why Maitland was so privileged, why he was so generously paid. It also explains why Kit was taken in by a man with no benevolent tendencies whatever. It was Father's guilty conscience prodding him to do something for the son of a man he had virtually killed with his own hands.'

'No, don't think of it that way,' Warren urged with compassion. 'It was an accident, Leone, purely a terrible accident.'

'Then why didn't Father reveal the facts at the inquest?' she cried. 'There was no mention of pushing anyone, or of causing old Anson to lose his entire investment. No, Warren, Father covered up his actions completely,' she continued, near to tears.

Her distress tore him apart. 'Why didn't you tell me all this before? I'd have sent Maitland packing pretty quick,' he said. 'Why have you tortured yourself all this time? I thought you trusted me enough to confide anything.'

Spreading her hands in a weary gesture, she said, 'I've stopped telephoning Lisbon. I'll keep out of Kit's life from now on. He's free of the Kirklands and their abominable power.'

Loving her as he did, he longed to ease her pain. Putting out his hands, he said coaxingly, 'Come over here. We've had some good news. Try to concentrate on that instead.'

She came to sit on the edge of his bed again. 'Warren, I've wasted the first twenty-two years of my life.' She seized his hand. 'I can't undo what we all did to Kit, but I can ensure that no Kirkland ever does such things to anyone else. I want to make my future worthwhile, and the opportunity is staring me in the face. I want to hold on to Kirkland's. I want that more than anything. I've just sold my villa in Lugano. I intend to make my home here in a place I never dreamed I'd come to love, and the company workshops are just down the river. What could be more convenient?' she demanded, the words rushing out. 'Now the inquiry's over we'll be able to go into production with the flying boats, and I could sell some foreign investments to build a new hangar and workshop to cope with the orders. There's just one gigantic snag.'

'Yes?' he murmured.

'I can't run the company on my own. Since Maitland left, even the day-to-day volume of affairs has turned into a nightmare. I've an excellent secretary, but it's daily more evident how very knowledgeable and efficient that snake was. It'll take a man to handle the industrial aspect of aircraft production.' Letting out her breath in a deep sigh, she went on, 'I need you, Warren.'

What a moment to choose for such a declaration, he thought wildly. A man sitting in bed in winceyette pyjamas, still half stupid with the relief of knowing he was not being held responsible for the deaths of five people . . .

She elaborated with growing enthusiasm. 'I've already worked out where we'd put the new buildings. That spare land to the south of our hangar is large enough—we'll have to take on another foreman for the second workshop, and you'll now be head of the design office instead of Donald. I'll take on the clerical and social side of the business. Most important of all, though, is the addition of a managing director—someone fairly young, who knows the ropes and shares our enthusiasm for *Flamingo*.' She searched his face anxiously. 'Sir Willard insists no one would take me seriously without a man at my side . . . and you're the man I want. What's your answer?'

Feeling the effects of a vastly different kind of fever, he stammered, 'I'm not sure what . . . are you offering me a business partnership . . . or are you proposing to me?'

'Both, silly,' she said, smiling. 'Although I suppose you'll get on your high horse and claim you never get married by invitation, either.'

IN MARCH 1939 the Spanish Civil War ended and throughout the early summer months of that doomed year Hitler continued amassing his weapons, and conscripting men into his three fighting forces.

Also during those early summer months of 1939, Kit was recovering from his serious injuries. The broken legs had mended, in time, but he had had to learn how to use them again. The head injuries he had sustained had severely impaired his powers of coordination, but a Swiss doctor specialising in such cases was working in Lisbon at that time, and had taken over his case with enthusiasm. Without his friends in Lisbon, Kit doubted he would have had the will to continue. Tom Digby, who was paying the sizable fee demanded by Dr Kleist, visited regularly, and so did Morris, Joss and Digger.

Through them, Kit had heard the result of the inquiry a few weeks before Christmas. Because he had only recently emerged from his coma, he said nothing about the misunderstanding over the location of 'home' when setting course. Later, he had reflected that there was no point in raising the issue. They would have hit the storm anyway, if only on its fringes. He had been delighted to hear that orders were being placed for *Flamingo*-class flying boats, and that Warren and Leone were to marry. Warren deserved his success. Leone could not possibly run the company on her own, and Warren certainly understood aircraft manufacture. The news of Donald's death allowed Kit to enjoy a certain grim satisfaction that the parasite of the family had met his end. Warren could now claim full credit for any future designs.

So Kit persevered and soon began to win through, although he did not know how he would ever repay his friend for the sum he was spending on medical treatment. Tom silenced him by saying he was repaying Kit for saving his life in Spain. A more fruitful conversation between them had been on the subject of *Flamingo*, because Tom had contracted a salvage company to take her off the sandbank. The flying boat was presently in one of his own hangars being put together again.

'Kirkland's doesn't want the wreck of their prototype,' Tom had told him with a grin. 'If I get a move on, Western Med could be the first company to put a *Flamingo*-class flying boat into service. What d'you think of that?'

Kit was pleased for Tom, naturally, but now he was out of hospital the spectre his illness had kept at bay rose up to confront him. Would he be able to fly the rebuilt *Flamingo*? Would he ever fly again? What was he going to do with his life? he asked Tom Digby.

'I'd do anything for you, Kit, but nothing on earth would induce me to allow you behind the controls of one of my aircraft,' Tom said emphatically. They were facing each other across the desk in Tom's office.

Kit got to his feet. 'Wait until I go up and fail to return before you pass judgment on my ability. I need this chance to prove myself, Tom. No other man is likely to give it to me.'

The other man shook his head. 'Neither is this man. I'm sorry . . . more sorry than I can say.'

Desperate, Kit asked, 'What about *Gina*? She's so old and shaky, you won't be risking much.'

'You're not old and shaky, Kit. You'd be risking everything.'

Kit caught his arm. 'Let me just taxi her out to sea and back. I'd see how I managed to handle the controls, but I'd not attempt to take her up . . .'

THE FOLLOWING FOUR WEEKS proved to be some of the happiest Kit had ever known. With Tom in the right-hand seat, he did no more than taxi *Gina* from the jetty to open sea and back several times during the first two days. On the third, he declared himself ready to take her up. With Tom's remark that they were two crocks preparing to take another into the air ringing in his ears, Kit taxied *Gina* out to a lively sea on a day of endless visibility. Even with these ideal conditions, however, he was deeply dismayed by the clumsiness of the takeoff. And by the time he taxied her to where Western Med had its base, he was sweating, and ready to admit defeat. Back alongside the jetty by the warehouses, he cut the engines and looked across at Tom.

'All right, I know what you're about to say,' he told his friend heavily. 'And you're absolutely right.'

'I was about to say that you've just proved me wrong. If I could do what you've just done, I'd be back in the pilot's seat like a shot.' Tom smiled. 'It was a bit rough, but at no time did I have the urge to take the controls. The first solo's always daunting. You'll do better tomorrow.'

'You're crazy!' exclaimed Kit, light-headed with success.

With every subsequent flight, Kit found his inborn skill slowly returning. With it came confidence, and a sense of growing elation.

Then, during the third week of August, two things occurred which were to change Kit's life irrevocably. The free world was stunned by the signing of a nonaggression pact between Russia and Germany. Real fears of wide-scale conflict now set Britain and Western Europe building defences. No one any longer doubted that a second attempt by Germany to establish herself as the world's major power was inevitable.

In Lisbon, capital of a neutral country, there was a sudden influx of additional staff at foreign embassies, plus an unusual number of influential civilian visitors taking an unscheduled holiday. No one was fooled for a moment by this evidence of diplomats and spies taking up positions in this tiny country giving easy access to the Mediterranean, and to the Atlantic leading to the English Channel.

Kit was deeply concerned as he drove from his cottage to the Western Med offices three days after the news of the Russo-German pact. As an Englishman, his first duty would be to return home and join the fighting forces. He was worried and distracted as he parked his car and made his way up to Tom's office. Awaiting him was the second development which was to affect him so dramatically in the years to come.

They discussed the situation with matching consternation for several minutes, then Tom changed the subject. 'Perfect flying weather today, old lad, so I've a favour to ask. I'd like you to test-fly *Flamingo* for me.'

After several seconds Kit said, 'Would you mind repeating that?'

'She's ready, I need her, and you know her better than anyone.'

'Give her to Joss. He knows her,' Kit suggested immediately.

'Can't. He's gone to Alex. You happen to be the ideal man for the job.'

As Kit got to his feet, his friend asked, 'Not afraid, are you?'

Kit shook his head. 'Just knocked sideways. I never dreamed . . . I mean, you really have thought seriously about this?'

'The job of test pilot carries a salary. It should put a stop to your annoying habit of touching your friends for a fiver each time you need to fill up that car of yours.'

'You've paid out so much on Kleist's bills already. I can't accept any more from you.'

'Dope! Kleist gave me back my best pilot, so it was a good investment.'

THE REBUILT *FLAMINGO* looked so different painted yellow as she rode at anchor just off the slipway, yet her sleek lines were unmistakable. When Kit climbed onto the flight deck and walked through to the cockpit, that sense of unity with her he had had throughout the flight to Africa returned. She was a work of art, a marvel of engineering, and she was his again.

With Tom and an engineer aboard, he taxied out to open sea and put the machine into her spectacular, powerful takeoff manoeuvre. As *Flamingo* surged forward at his touch, he was back on Lake Kiju heading for those trees at the end of the short waterway. Spray flying, hull bumping and shuddering, and engines growling their power triumphantly, *Flamingo* raced for the wall of jungle, then lifted from the water to climb up and over the top with mere feet to spare. He had done it!

A voice beside him returned him to the present. 'What's the rush?'

He turned to Tom with a ridiculously proud smile. 'She's always like that. She's going places, this beauty.'

14

Britain and France had been at war with Germany for eight months. Early in the April of 1940, German troops swept in to occupy Sweden and Norway. Several weeks later, Holland and Belgium were also lost. By the middle of May, Europe had fallen, and the war had now arrived on the doorstep of those islands which had remained free for centuries. The people of Britain prepared to defend their freedom down to the last man, woman and beast of burden.

When Kit arrived in London at the end of May, he was struck by the change in the city. Most people were in uniform, sandbags were piled round the entrances to a great many buildings, barrage balloons formed a curious herd of grey elephants above the streets. After the colourful Mediterranean, Kit found this evidence of battle preparations disturbing. He found it difficult to accept war in his homeland.

After booking a room in a cheap boarding house, he set out for a nearby recruiting office. Following the sign indicating the RAF department, he went up the stairs, and entered a room to find himself facing a man he knew extremely well from his days of speed flying.

Squadron Leader Max Harvey rose slowly to his feet. 'Good God, the last time I saw you, you were being carried shoulder-high, pursued by screaming girls, after taking the record in *Aphrodite*.'

'Hello, Max,' greeted Kit warmly, shaking hands with him. 'It's good to see you again, but what the hell are you doing behind a desk?'

'Didn't you hear?' the short, fair-haired Cambridge graduate asked him, as he indicated a chair. 'Take a pew. I had a crack at taking the record from you twelve months later. The machine didn't stand up to the strain. I went down in the Solent and spent a year in hospital.'

'Tough luck,' sympathised Kit with total understanding. 'I'd forgotten. So much seems to have been happening since those early but thrilling days.'

'Hasn't it just! I heard you were finished after that *Flamingo* business.'

'I damn near was. It's a great stroke of luck meeting you here, Max. I've been flying again in Portugal since last August—marine aircraft at first, but more recently some wheeled transports for a freight company operating between Lisbon and Seville. I took the proving flight of the Kirkland's boat, as you know. Although I'm best with marine craft, I've put in a decent number of hours with other aircraft. I'm over here to offer my services to the Royal Air Force, if they'll have me.'

'Your qualifications speak for themselves, so all you need do is pass the medical and you're in. Look, you tootle along to the doc, and we'll meet up again at eight for dinner and a good old chinwag. What d'you say?'

Kit stood up, smiling. 'Thanks, I'll look forward to it.'

KIT SPENT THE NIGHT in the lumpy bed of his room overlooking a fishmonger's warehouse. In a sultry early summer temperature, he had to decide whether to open the window and endure the stench, or shut it and stifle. He had enjoyed the convivial hours with Max Harvey, but Max had set him a puzzle to keep him from sleep. In somewhat enigmatic manner, he had confided to Kit that he had spoken to one of his superiors about him during that afternoon.

As a result, he had been charged to ask Kit to report to an address in Whitehall the following morning, where a Wing Commander Dryden would like to talk to him. Mystified, Kit had been unable to discover from Max the reason for the request, and he was still puzzled when he eventually strode through the summertime streets to reach the sandbagged entrance of the address he had been given.

Colin Dryden proved to be a quiet, intelligent man in his late forties.

'I have some rather negative news for you, I'm afraid,' he revealed. 'I've been advised by the medical board that they're obliged to turn down your application to fly for us.'

'I see,' said Kit, leaning back in the dark red leather chair and trying to mask his disappointment. 'Are you telling me the service is declining my services?'

'Not at all, not at all,' was the calm reply. 'My department works hand in glove with the other two services on rather special assignments. Max Harvey spotted your potential usefulness right away, hence this meeting. We pounced on you, Mr Anson, because you're exactly the chap we need.'

'For what?' he asked warily.

'To be our man on the spot in Lisbon.'

Getting to his feet, Colin Dryden came round to sit on the corner of his desk as he explained. 'We have evidence that Mussolini is liable to bring Italy into the war against us very shortly. Hitler is certain to take advantage of that friendly access to the Mediterranean and, with the Balkans mostly in his hands, our strongholds there could be overrun or, at best, cut off, before we could move to save them. We already have men firmly established all along the Med who can give us advance information, but a man flying between neutral Lisbon and neutral Alexandria, under cover of a civilian airline, could be of enormous help. He could see things from the air which our men hiding in forests or mountain caves could not. He could transport vital commodities in a flying boat able to rendezvous with small boats along coasts too isolated to patrol, and he could even pick up packages or the occasional person from places offering no other means of escape.'

Kit was stupefied. 'You're suggesting that I should use Tom Digby's aircraft for spying purposes? You're mad!'

'No, Mr Anson, just very desperate.'

Kit got to his feet. The whole idea was fantastic.

Colin Dryden touched his arm. 'I see this has come as something of a shock to you. You have time to think about it, naturally. Shall we meet again at eleven tomorrow morning?'

Still in something of a daze, Kit walked to the door, only to be halted by words which constituted another shock.

'You should take into account one other aspect of my proposal,' the RAF officer said. 'The only uniform you'd be wearing for this job would be that of your airline, so the Geneva Convention would not apply to you. If you should be caught by our enemies, you'd be shot, of course.'

AT FIRST, KIT DECLINED Dryden's proposal, on the grounds of his refusal to betray a friendship he had already used beyond acceptable limits. But his decision changed when the war situation worsened dramatically. Well over a quarter of a million troops had been brought from Dunkirk as France surrendered. Reading of that courageous action by civilian volunteers, Kit realised the true seriousness of what he had been asked to do. The wing commander had been delighted by his change of mind, and several days of discussions and meetings had followed to familiarise the new recruit with the ways in which he would pass any information and how he would be contacted by agents based in Portugal.

Now, in the rattling lift taking Kit up to Tom's office, the notion of his being some kind of aerial spy seemed utterly preposterous. It did nothing to aid the difficulties of the imminent meeting which *must* result in his being taken back as a company pilot flying the Alexandria run.

The door to Tom's office stood open, so he hesitated on the threshold watching the red-haired man seemingly absorbed in reading a file on his desk. Tom sensed a presence in the doorway and glanced up.

'Hello, Tom. May I come in?'

'The door's open.'

Kit settled in a chair. 'I need a job, Tom. Not just any job. It has to be as a pilot with Western Med on the Alex run.'

'I've been giving that run some thought,' put in Tom. 'It's pretty obvious that passengers are going to be a hell of a lot scarcer in the days ahead. There's nothing for it but to cut the service drastically.'

Dismayed by that news, Kit decided to explain. 'When I've told you . . .'

'Instead, I thought I'd switch to freight,' Tom continued blithely. 'The demand for food and other commodities is going to be huge. I'll make a fortune by ripping out seats and making my boats into freight carriers. It'll make things much easier for you, old lad. Passengers have eyes and ears. They'd report your curious activities to unfriendly authorities here and in Alex. No, my friend, if you really are hell-bent on this glamorous spying caper, you'll do it far easier if *Flamingo* is used for freight.'

As Kit stared at him, lost for words, Tom grinned. 'Colin Dryden's an old friend of mine. We went to the same school. One of his people contacted me yesterday, and I agreed to the scheme right away.'

'You . . . you *knew*?' Kit stammered. 'Then why the devil did . . .'

'I wanted to see how long it would be before you let me in on this vital secret. Colin guessed you'd tell me. He's a good judge of character.' He rose to his feet and held out his hand. 'Welcome back to Western Med, Kit . . . I'm thinking of changing the company name to Spies Anonymous.'

15

Looking at the clock on the wall, Leone was relieved to see the hands pointing to twelve thirty. The benches were all now empty; she could go home. Her work on a refugee interrogation group in London was over for this week. She began collecting her things together.

The head of her particular group, Wing Commander Curtiss, fell in beside her as she walked from the room. 'I'd like to invite you to lunch,' he said. 'A friend of mine is very anxious to meet you, so when he knew you'd be in London today he expressed a hope we could all lunch together. I'd be very pleased if you could manage it. I'd enjoy your company, anyway.'

'Who is your friend?' she asked.

'I'd sooner leave him to tell you himself.'

Leone decided she could afford to take time to enjoy a civilised lunch with this charming man and his mysterious friend. They strolled the short distance to the restaurant, enjoying the July warmth.

A waiter seated them in a corner alcove and Philip Curtiss ordered dry martinis. Then he leaned back comfortably to ask, 'How do you manage to cope with everything? Each Tuesday and Wednesday you work for us on the refugee committee, taking additional translations home to do in your spare time, yet you somehow control a large aviation company in Sheenmouth. You must be astonishingly efficient. I suppose you lost most of your work force when the war began?'

Leone nodded. 'We were visited by men from the ministry and the entire company was requisitioned for war production, whether we liked it or not.'

'So what happened to your flying boats?' Philip asked.

'The two under construction were assigned to your RAF squadron, with instructions to complete them as soon as possible. The men were replaced by local women directed into factory work. It was total chaos for several weeks,' she admitted with a smile, 'but the war has proved a godsend to Kirkland's. The company is making substantial profits from government contracts as well as establishing firm links with major suppliers all over the country.'

'So what happens when the war is won?'

'Kirkland's will make marine aircraft again,' she told him firmly. 'My husband has a dream of a passenger liner with wings. Together with my brother, he made it come true with *Flamingo*. He still has his dreams, and I share them. We'll make them reality when the war's over.'

'Ah, Philip, how very good of you to achieve what I proposed,' said a voice beside them.

Philip Curtiss rose swiftly to shake the newcomer's hand. The elderly man in dark clothes was introduced to Leone as Sir Melville Pyne. He greeted her, then turned to present his wife. Leone experienced a severe shock on recognising the woman.

'How are you, Leone?' asked Stephanie, who still possessed the beauty which had so attracted Donald . . . and Kit.

'Fine,' she replied, trying to recover. 'I had no idea you'd married. I must have missed the announcement in *The Times*.'

'I didn't miss a single detail in the press about yours,' Stephanie replied. 'How is Warren? Such a sweet, *ingenuous* young man, I always thought.'

Leone returned her smile, then turned her attention to choosing between lamb casserole or steak with salad. That done, she reflected that Stephanie had done well for herself. Whatever Sir Melville did, he had brought her a title, enough funds to dress well and to flash an impressive emerald ring.

With their meals before them, Sir Melville revealed the reason for his interest in meeting her. 'Mrs Grant, my wife says your home has an amazing network of tunnels and small chambers beneath its foundations. Is that so?'

'Well, yes. They were reputedly used by smugglers to store contraband goods taken from wrecks. Of course, to my knowledge no one has used them for years. The access from within the abbey has been locked and barred ever since my father bought the place. There is another way in: from the grounds.' She asked lightly, 'You're not proposing to smuggle black-market goods up the Sheen estuary, are you, Sir Melville?'

Dabbing his lips with his napkin, he surprised Leone further by saying,

'You could call it smuggling, of sorts, dear lady.'

Philip entered the conversation at that point. 'Perhaps I should have told you that Sir Melville is an art historian of great international repute.'

'If you're hoping to find something of interest beneath Sheenmouth Abbey, I think you'll be disappointed,' Leone told him. 'My father would certainly have removed any treasures before closing up the tunnels.'

Sir Melville sipped his wine. 'I'm hoping to put treasures *in*, Mrs Grant, not take any out. Let me explain, if I may. This country of ours is presently facing the prospect of occupation by the enemy. It is, therefore, imperative that we act to save the vast number of paintings and artefacts which comprise our heritage. I have been appointed head of a committee charged with finding suitable wartime quarters for works of art. Mrs Grant, if you would permit us to send someone to survey your subterranean storerooms and, if they are suitable, allow us to place objects of great value within them, they would be saved for posterity.'

'Gracious!' she exclaimed in alarm. 'I shouldn't care to be responsible for works of art worth a king's ransom.'

'You would not be asked to do that,' the historian assured her. 'We would provide guards who would work in shifts, and also make regular checks on the condition of anything we might be permitted to store there.'

'Then I agree, Sir Melville,' she said decisively. 'Send your man down, by all means. If he feels the site is suitable, you're welcome to use it.'

The thin face flushed with pleasure. 'Most kind of you. *Most* kind.'

Leone shrugged. 'One grows used to changing rules. In my father's day, Sheenmouth Abbey was as overwhelmingly masculine as the monastery it had once been. Now the war has changed everything. The ground floor of one wing has already been turned into schoolrooms for evacuees; the bell in the tower of the east wing has become the responsibility of our one remaining manservant who, as an air-raid warden for the district, has orders to ring it in the event of fire, danger, or invasion by the enemy from the sea. The people of Sheenmouth use the great hall for meetings and concerts, and the Magnum Pomeroy Home Guard sometimes practises repelling enemies in the lower meadow.'

'I'd never recognise the place now,' mused Stephanie, in light-hearted manner. 'Is there anything you *don't* do for the war effort, Leone?'

'I haven't got round to knitting khaki balaclavas . . . or providing other comforts for our troops, as some women do,' she replied evenly. She had had enough of the woman who had helped to condemn Kit all those years ago. She smiled at Philip. 'The lunch was very nice, but I really do have a train to catch. Forgive me if I leave you now.'

While Philip settled the bill, and the older man headed for the cloakroom, the two women were left together beside the table.

'Stephanie.' Leone was sharp. 'We've been at this table together for well over an hour, yet you've expressed no regret over Donald's death.'

Stephanie rose. 'Donald was firmly put out of my thoughts from the day I went off with Kit.' Those renowned sherry-coloured eyes lit up. 'I fully intended to stay with him for as long as it amused me, you know. How could I have guessed the fool was so drunk he couldn't control that car of his?'

Growing cold, Leone said, 'You charged him with forcible abduction. If you thought anything of him, why did you do that to a man who was already facing ruin?'

'My dear girl, I owed Kit nothing. Didn't I once say to you that men like him were simply for women to enjoy?' Looking closely at Leone, she asked, 'You still don't carry a torch for him, surely? After what he did to your family? You're incredibly foolish, if you do. He's worthless.'

The two men arrived back at the table then, and Leone turned to Sir Melville, shaking. 'I will be glad to do anything to help your committee . . . but please don't ask me to meet your wife again. I'm prepared to do a great deal for the war effort, but being civil to someone my family has cause to despise doesn't come under that heading.' Turning to Philip, she added, 'Thank you for lunch. Goodbye.'

LEONE ARRIVED HOME an hour before dinner. Warren had not yet come up the river from the workshops, so she went to their room to take a shower then change into a georgette evening gown patterned in flame, yellow and beige. It was one of Warren's favourites.

'I thought I might find you here,' said Warren from the door.

She went to him with a smile, and linked her arm with his. 'I met someone today who asked if we'd give permission for works of art and other treasures to be stored in the old smugglers' tunnels here. He's sending a man down to take a look. We might have to put him up overnight—I thought the bell tower would be just right.'

'How did this person know about the tunnels?' Warren asked.

'Oh, Sir Melville Pyne heard the tales,' she replied evasively. 'You know how the locals yarn about this place . . . Dinner will be ready soon. Hurry and change.'

Warren began unbuttoning his shirt. 'How was London?'

'The same as usual. Sandbags everywhere. People all in uniform of one sort or another. Strangely hushed with such limits on traffic.'

With a sigh, she began picking up the clothes scattered on chairs and floor. He was hopelessly untidy. 'I thought you promised to fold your things neatly,' she remonstrated.

'Sorry,' came the unrepentant reply above the sound of running water. 'I was thinking about something else.'

Folding her husband's flannels and grey knitted cardigan, Leone held the woollen garment to her cheek momentarily. Her marriage was a good one. As business partners they worked together very successfully; as husband and wife they were happy and fulfilled. She loved him for loving her, and cherished the loyalty she knew he would never forsake.

Warren returned. 'Am I forgiven over the clothes?' he asked.

'Not in the least . . . but that won't change *you*,' she told him lightly.

'I've no desire to change you. I adore you just the way you are.' Taking underwear from his drawer, he continued. 'I had a call this morning. An RAF squadron has acquired a *Flamingo*-class boat which they want to use for something rather hush-hush. I've been asked to go to Scotland to see what mods could be done on it.'

'How thrilling. When?'

'They'd like to start on Wednesday. I agreed to go up there.'

She smiled fondly. 'It wasn't a request, Warren, it was an order. I'll miss you while you're away,' she added, smoothing the dinner jacket across his shoulders. 'How long will you be gone?'

'It depends on the complexity of the problem. They've given me no clues.' He caught her round the waist as she made to walk away, 'I'll miss you, too.'

'You won't have time. You'll be so engrossed in designing some clever modification, everyone and everything will be forgotten,' she claimed.

'Even when I'm working, I never entirely forget you. The same way you never entirely forget Kit,' he added significantly.

'I . . . what makes you . . .' she floundered.

His right hand touched her hair gently. 'You've made a commendable effort to stay out of his life, as you vowed to do. I didn't think you'd be strong enough to keep it up. But, loving you as I do, I know you haven't managed to keep him out of your thoughts. Something happened while you were in London; something which upset you.'

She should have known he would see through her pretence. With a sigh, she said, 'Sir Melville Pyne's wife was Stephanie Main.'

He whistled. 'Poor darling,' he said, kissing her temple. 'She was the one who knew about the smugglers' tunnels, of course.'

'Of course. Warren, she joked about them and she was extremely offensive about Donald . . . and even more so about Kit. I suppose I was foolish to allow her words to get under my skin, but I'm afraid I was rather rude to Sir Melville and Philip Curtiss.'

'Attagirl!' he said warmly.

Her smile was rueful. 'When you're Sir Warren you won't approve of such conduct from your wife.'

His arms tightened around her. 'Anything you do is all right by me . . .'

THEY ALL STOOD in the hangar beside the huge hull of the *Flamingo*-class flying boat, *Florida*, completed by Kirkland's twelve weeks before.

'A truly spectacular aircraft,' commented a squadron leader named Fletcher. 'When I first saw her fly, I couldn't believe that initial climb. She leaves the water before you know it.'

Warren nodded. 'You should have seen the takeoff from Lake Kiju during her proving flight, after we'd rescued three people from the jungle.'

'We all read of it,' put in Wing Commander Gregg, who was hosting Warren during his visit to the RAF station on the west coast of Scotland. 'It might come as a surprise for you to hear we have on strength young Hamilton, the copilot of that flight. He was sent up to us because he's had experience of these craft. You'll meet him later on. Now let's go up to the office. I'll give you some idea of what we're after.'

They climbed to a large area enclosed by windows, and sat round a table on which lay numerous rolls of drawings.

'Although I can't give you actual details,' the wing commander began, 'I can reveal that your aircraft is to be used for special missions in the months to come. Mr Grant, your flying boat has to be modified so that she can carry up to fifty men, with supplies, guns, et cetera. We require bays suitable for the transport of vehicles, inflatable boats or even small snow-caterpillars.' He gave a grim smile at Warren's expression. 'Yes, I know it's a tall order, but we'd like you to do some sums and drawings which will add up to the nearest answer to our requirements. Here comes the punch line. The brass hats don't want to lose that fast climb on takeoff.'

'You don't want much, do you?' commented Warren heavily.

Brian Gregg sighed. 'This office will be placed at your disposal night and day for as long as you need. Our mechanics and engineers will be on hand round the clock, should you want to consult them. If there's anything else you deem necessary, we'll do our utmost to get it for you.'

'There is one thing,' ventured Warren.

'Yes?'

'If you hear of anyone with a magic wand, race him up here on the double.'

Warren retired early to his room in the officers' quarters that night to study his design plans and make initial weight calculations. He was still working when dawn broke. People came and went during the day with mugs of coffee or tea. He declined lunch but Brian Gregg himself arrived in the upstairs office to drag him away for dinner.

When Warren entered the anteroom Joss Hamilton got to his feet with a smile and an outstretched hand. 'Hello. It's marvellous to meet up again like this.'

'You look extremely smart,' said Warren, shaking his hand warmly. 'When did you come over from Portugal?'

'Right at the start. Well, I had to really, hadn't I? What'll you have to drink?'

Sitting next to Brian, Warren said apologetically, 'I'm afraid I've never really taken to the swanky drinks. I prefer a glass of ale.'

'Ale coming up,' responded Joss. With a grin in the direction of his CO he added, 'The swanky drinks are only indulged in by those who stay on the ground, or who can afford them.'

'Impudent so-and-so!' growled Brian. 'Didn't they teach you manners in that ropy Portuguese airline?'

Joss laughed. 'It was a damned sight warmer and more comfortable flying for Western Med than it is here.' Turning to Warren, he asked, 'Had you heard that *Flamingo* is back in the air again?'

'No,' Warren exclaimed. 'We've had no contact with Tom Digby since he offered to take her off the sandbank and rebuild her.'

Joss wiped the froth from his mouth after drinking. 'Actually, she's been flying for about eleven months. Kit did the test flights last August.'

Warren felt his stomach tighten. '*Kit* flight-tested her? But my wife was told by the doctors in Lisbon that he had such serious injuries, he would never fly again. In fact, they suggested he would be fortunate to walk, much less fly in the future.'

'Gosh, you're dreadfully out of touch. He was treated by a mad Swiss doctor. He made a good recovery. After some hair-raising capers with an old flying boat, Tom gave him *Flamingo*. It was the best medicine he could have had.' Taking another pull at his beer, Joss added, 'I had a letter from the lads this week. She's been adapted for freight, and is regularly flying to Alex with Kit piloting, Morris and Digger forming his crew. It takes some guts to pull back after being declared half dead, I reckon.'

'Yes . . . I'll say,' Warren agreed, somehow shaken by the news. Kit had apparently bounced back again. The old sense of guilt washed over Warren. There had really been nothing to stop him making discreet enquiries about his friend's progress, without Leone being aware of it. It was too late now.

16

By the middle of September the Germans had well and truly launched their campaign for the conquest of Britain. The first stage of their plan was to knock the RAF from the skies so, day after day, aircraft were locked in battle over the east and south coasts of England.

Magnum Pomeroy airfield, where Warren had given lessons to eager pupils including Leone, became an RAF station overnight and was to remain such throughout the war. Leone did not need to be told of the fact; she heard the Hurricanes fly over late the previous evening, and guessed that they had found a haven on the club airfield.

Warren was back in Scotland for a few days, to advise on difficulties encountered when making the modifications to *Florida*. When he was absent, Leone always ate breakfast in their room. Sitting by the open window with a tray, she gazed out over the lower meadow to the grey-veiled river. She had believed Kit to be disastrously disabled. Warren had returned from Scotland with the news that he was miraculously flying *Flamingo* on a regular service to Alexandria. She had been unbearably restless since hearing that, and she was not sure why Warren had told her. He must have known the news would bring her both joy and pain.

The chiming of the clock told her it was time to stop daydreaming. Dressing swiftly in a green cotton skirt and patterned blouse, she headed for the offices on the third floor. The post had already arrived and her efficient, silver-haired secretary, Virginia, had gone through it. After a friendly greeting and brief comment on the arrival of the Hurricanes the previous evening, Virginia pointed out a letter from Sir Melville Pyne notifying them that transports would soon be arriving with 'the merchandise we discussed at our meeting'.

'Not a moment too soon,' commented Leone drily. 'If things carry on as they have been, Britain will be flattened and all our treasures destroyed.'

After an hour with paperwork, restlessness sent her outside. Draping a jacket across her shoulders, she went down to the jetty. Walter was leaning on the rail smoking his favourite pipe. He straightened and smiled.

'Mornin', Miss Kirkland,' he greeted, having never managed to grasp the fact that marriage had taken away the status created by that name. 'You goin' down to the works?' he asked.

She nodded. 'I have a few things to check.'

In no particular hurry to arrive, Leone sat with her hand on the tiller, letting *Miranda* purr along the stretches of the Sheen. The river was quiet these days. The few summer visitors had returned home, and many residents had handed over their boats for more vital purposes.

At that moment, however, the peace was shattered. From up on the hills of East Sheenmouth came the wail of the siren. Almost immediately, the concerted roar of twelve Hurricanes from Magnum Pomeroy drowned out the sirens, as they climbed fast and headed out to sea. They vanished swiftly, but Leone was little more than half a mile from the company buildings when she saw them returning. The aircraft looked bigger and different. They were also approaching in unusual formation, one behind the other . . . Alarm rose within her; a whistling sound was quickly followed by a thunderous explosion. Before her eyes, part of Kirkland's original hangar flew into pieces within a cloud of dust and smoke. Leone turned cold when a second explosion caused the roof of the main workshop to collapse. Inside those hangars and workshops were people she knew: men and women dying as she watched.

Close enough now to feel the blast of air and the warmth of the flames, Leone realised the danger and automatically turned the tiller. There was a fire-fighting and rescue team stationed at the factory, and Sheenmouth defence forces would cope with the casualties. Children were taking lessons at the abbey at this moment. Suppose the German bombers should fly over it and mistake the building for another factory?

Revving the engine to full power, she raced back, her ragged nerves jumping at the swift scream of diving aircraft as half a dozen fighters came streaking down from a blue sky crisscrossed with white vapour trails, then flattened out in pursuit of their quarry. The Hurricanes had returned. At least, half of them had.

Her mind raced with so many wild thoughts. Kirkland's was gone—destroyed in a matter of minutes after years of creation and growth. Her workers, people she knew and liked, had just died in the most savage manner. Through her muddled, feverish thoughts, she heard the thud of further explosions up beyond Sheenmouth Abbey, and the whine of battling aircraft. She was in such a state of nerves, she took the boat too close to the jetty, removing a chunk of wood from one of the piers. Walter hardly noticed; he was more concerned with her safe return.

'Thank the Lord, Miss Kirkland,' he cried in a voice roughened by fear.

Scrambling to the jetty, she said, 'They hit Kirkland's, Walter. There's nothing but rubble and flames.' She started along the jetty on wobbly legs. 'Better get *Miranda* inside the boathouse, and stay there yourself, Walter. It would be foolish to move around in the open until the all clear sounds.'

She was walking over the lower meadow when a dark shape loomed towards her over the western boundary of her land. The bomber was being chased by a Hurricane. Even as she dropped flat, Leone saw two bombs being shed by the doomed German crew. No more than seconds passed before twin explosions rocked the ground beneath her, and her head came up to stare in rage and horror as the north wing of the abbey disappeared. Soon after, a fresh explosion beyond the hilly woodlands to the south indicated that the bomber had crashed.

Leone scrambled to her feet and began to run over the meadow towards the terrace, for the first solemn notes of the great bell were floating in the clear morning air. The tennis courts and Roman swimming pool had become a crater and there came the sound of screams and cries from the west side of the monastery.

'Oh, dear God, the children,' she breathed.

Turning, she ran along the terrace to the main entrance. On she went past the octagonal room, then into the transverse corridor. Here, it was darker still. She pulled up just in time. There was no heavy oaken door leading to the rooms used for lessons. In its place was a wall comprising stone, glass and huge splinters of wood. Above it, about twenty feet up, she could just glimpse some of the furniture in the bedroom where she had proposed to Warren. The ragged edge round this gap in the ceiling was cracked, and one huge section hung dangerously at an angle. Beyond the rubble she could hear the cries of women trying to calm children.

Leone began to climb the wall of rubble. Her hands and arms were scratched as she clambered over the shifting surface, and dust set her coughing. However, she had ceased to be afraid. Foot by foot, she mounted that precarious hill. Something needed to be done. She must do it.

Reaching the top, only two feet from the ceiling, she peered over into the room beyond. The windows had been blown inward by blast from the second bomb. Many of the children had blood on their skin and clothes. In a far corner, alongside one of the teachers, who looked unnaturally still, lay two of the more seriously injured pupils. The three teachers who were still on their feet seemed as bloody as their charges.

Leone's heart sank. The room beyond this one had caved in to form an impenetrable wall. Outside the empty windows of the first room was another crater, making the sheer drop from there a frightening prospect. The teachers might make it, but children never. They were all trapped.

Spread-eagled on that mound of debris, Leone cast an apprehensive glance at the tilting block of stone above her, and moved fast, descending in a slither of stone and dust onto the floor. She scrambled to her feet.

'My word, it's you, Mrs Grant,' exclaimed one woman, in astonishment.

Giving a faint smile as she dusted herself down, Leone said, 'It'll take far too long to bring sufficient rescuers by the outside route, so there's really only one way out for you all.' Glancing round at the children, she asked quietly, 'How badly hurt are they?'

An elderly teacher, holding back tears with a struggle, said, 'Some are quite badly cut. Miss Cadbury is dead. The two unconscious children lying over there with her seem to be in a critical condition.'

Leone told them, 'You've all been marvellous, in view of the state you're in. I have a proposal to put. There is a way out which we could use, if the children could manage it with our help. From this room runs a network of underground passages leading to a concealed door in the grounds.'

'The smugglers' tunnels!' cried one of the teachers.

'Yes, indeed. If we each carried a child who might be unable to walk, could you persuade the others to form a line and follow us through dark passages as far as the exit? It's quite a walk, I must warn you.'

The three women exchanged glances, then the tearful one nodded. 'If we tell them we're taking them through tunnels once used by smugglers, they'll see it as an exciting adventure.' Looking at her colleagues, she said, 'We'll put Terry Symes at the end of the line to keep any stragglers going; Lilian Thwaites can lead them right behind Mrs Grant.'

'There are candles and a supply of matches in this cupboard,' Leone said, going to it and opening the door. 'It's providential that I had cause only a few weeks ago to open up the tunnels from this room after years of disuse. The candles were placed here recently. We'll give one to as many children as possible, so there'll be enough light to banish any fears of the darkness.'

'What about Miss Cadbury and those two poor creatures with her?' asked one teacher.

Leone sighed. 'They'll have to be left until we can return for them.'

'I'll stay with them,' decided the woman.

While the teachers lit candles to distribute, Leone started the 'adventure' off by revealing the secret entrance hidden beneath a layer of glass fragments. Leading the way, she trod down the ten steps to reach the passageway. It was a procession she would never forget, illuminated by flickering light from candles, and accompanied by the echo of young, awe-struck voices. When she eventually reached the exit, she halted and looked back at the ragged, bobbing line of candles slowly advancing.

'I'm now going to open the secret door only I know about. You must tell no one else. You'll be very surprised when you see where you are, but you'll understand why the smugglers used to hide their barrels here.'

The door did not open easily. Soon, however, she was stepping out into the boathouse where Walter had moored *Miranda*. The old man was nowhere to be seen. Walking out to the lower meadow, she discovered why. Flames and smoke were billowing from the woods where the German bomber had crashed. Walter was staring at the sight as if hypnotised.

Shouts drew Leone's attention to the abbey. Men were starting towards them, members of the Home Guard detachment which exercised in the grounds. Never had she been so thankful to see them. In no time, the two teachers were being led away with their pupils towards the south wing for first-aid treatment. Leone then led the three men who remained with her back into the tunnels to bring out those left behind.

Explaining the situation swiftly as she hurried along, Leone began to feel the effects of shock. Mounting the steps, she emerged into that scene of chaos once again, and crossed on rubbery legs to the corner containing the lifeless Miss Cadbury, two unconscious children, and the teacher who had voted to stay with them. Despite her brave resolution, the waiting had proved too much for her. Her face was ashen and beaded with perspiration as Leone and the men approached.

'You can come away now, Ethel,' advised one of them. 'Just you go along with Mrs Grant, m'dear. We'll see to what has to be done here.'

In deep shock, Ethel Green must have seen them as the enemy. Rising from her crouch beside the three bodies, she flew towards the door she normally used. It was no longer there, of course. Encountering instead the wall of rubble, the hysterical woman began to claw at it frantically. Leone ran across to pull her away, but she was too late. The gigantic pile of debris began slithering ominously. Leone heard the avalanche roar down to engulf her just as a wrenching groan of masonry heralded the plunging of the slab from overhead. She was swept off her feet, as part of Sheenmouth Abbey descended to bury her alive in a black, suffocating world.

WHEN WARREN ARRIVED at the East Sheenmouth Cottage Hospital, the doctor conducted him into the same private room in which Kit Anson had slowly recovered from his car accident, way back in 1932. Warren was appalled at Leone's appearance. Her face, arms and hands were black and blue with bruising, and slashed with red cuts. She was in a drugged sleep.

As he stood watching her, the doctor spoke quietly. 'Your wife was buried beneath a considerable pile of debris, Mr Grant. As you can see, she has received extensive contusions and was cut by glass. However, the most serious injuries were internal. The weight of the rubble caused quite severe damage to the womb and pelvis. We operated as soon as she was brought in, but I'm afraid there was little chance of total repair. I don't know how important this news will be to you, but your wife took it with commendable calmness. She will be unable to bear children.'

'I see,' said Warren, still appalled by what had happened so suddenly to the girl he loved so dearly. The idea of having children had never entered his mind. He had been so content with Leone and his work, it had not occurred to him that anything else was necessary to his happiness.

He sat by her bedside for half an hour, but she did not waken. The doctor suggested that he should go home for a meal, then return in an hour or so.

When Warren arrived at the hospital early in the evening, with an armful of yellow and bronze chrysanthemums, he found Leone awake.

'Hello,' he greeted gently, bending to kiss her. 'I hear you were a female Pied Piper yesterday. The whole town's very proud of you, but no one's as proud as I am.'

She studied his face searchingly. 'They told me Ethel Green died during the night. I didn't save her.'

'You tried,' he pointed out, sitting on the edge of the bed and taking one of her bruised hands in his. 'Her weak heart couldn't take the shock.'

'The two children are going to be all right.'

'And so are all those you brought out through the tunnels.' He forced a smile. 'How could we guess they'd ever be put to such use, especially by the only female Kirkland? Poor old Walter was in tears this afternoon when we went down to the workshops.'

'How bad is it, Warren? Tell me the truth.'

He avoided a direct answer. 'Eddie and I worked out several ways of continuing almost full production. The girls are all raring to go again.'

She was one step ahead of him. 'I asked the doctor how many had been killed. *Twelve*, Warren. Did you know?'

'Yes. Eddie told me.'

'I saw it happen; saw the place cave in knowing people were underneath. It's a sight I'll never forget.'

He had no words to follow that, so he simply kissed her hand, thanking God that she had not been one of the dead. 'You've been through quite an ordeal,' he pointed out. 'Take all the rest you can. I can handle the business, with Virginia's help.'

'Have they told you yet? About my injuries.'

'Oh . . . yes, darling, they have.'

Her eyes began to shimmer. 'Perhaps it's just as well. I might easily have been a dismal failure and our poor lonely child would have had a wretched time of it.'

Moved by her tears, he told her fiercely, 'You're all I want, darling.' Almost in tears himself, he said, 'Do you know that each time I look at you, I count myself one of the most fortunate men in the world?'

17

The eastern Mediterranean was slowly being brought under German control. Yugoslavia had been occupied, then Greece. British forces had been taken off in a massive rescue operation at the end of that April of 1941.

Flying through the area, even under neutral colours, became inadvisable if not downright suicidal. Throughout May, however, Kit and his crew continued to fly *Flamingo* to Alexandria. They ran great risks each time, and it became increasingly difficult to smuggle any large package ashore, or British servicemen picked up *en route*.

By the final week of May Crete was invaded and the defending British force was helpless. They faced capture and internment for the rest of the war, which was certainly going in Hitler's favour.

When *Flamingo* took off on what Tom and her crew all agreed would probably be her last flight, Kit experienced a curious sensation of having reached a crossroads. He hated the idea that the flying boat had already known her finest hour . . . or that he had known his. Yet it looked very much that way.

The engines droned on for several hours, and the sun climbed high until it was almost overhead. On the blue surface below there was a great deal of shipping. After refuelling at Tunis, they took off for the second leg to Alexandria. Aldo Diaz, the Portuguese second pilot, took the controls for the first few hours of the long haul, while Kit dozed uneasily in the cabin.

When Digger made tea for them all, Kit took over from Aldo, feeling unrefreshed and belligerent. If this was to be their last flight, he would use it to gain one last piece of information. He determined to take a look at Crete as he passed.

At some distance from the island it became apparent that something was afoot. The sea was alive with an unusual number of small craft, and there appeared to be a complicated aerial battle under way. Heading straight for this activity, Kit took it in with a growing sense of excitement.

'Take a look at this,' he invited, over his shoulder.

Morris and Digger came up behind him to watch the activity below, which left crisscrossing furrows as boats passed back and forth, and the activity ahead, which left the heavens crisscrossed by pale vapour trails. Amid the fighters, small clouds of gunfire came from batteries on the island. As *Flamingo* steadily approached, the sound of distant thuds signalled artillery attacks.

'God, there's a whole war going on out there,' exclaimed Digger. 'We're heading right into it. You really are crazy, mate.'

'Not that crazy,' Kit assured him, keeping his gaze ahead. 'This boat isn't fast enough to join in. I'd like to find out exactly what's going on, just the same. They might like the latest report when we dock at Alex.'

'I don't like the look of it,' said Morris.

'I bet our troops trapped on that island like it, though,' Kit countered. 'Whatever's happening, it must be designed to help them. Get Aldo up here. I'll need him.'

The belligerent aircraft were so intent on their own battle that *Flamingo* approached apparently unnoticed. Aldo tapped Kit's shoulder and pointed to the left.

'Great Scott, flying boats!' said Kit, in surprise. 'They're ours, too.'

He studied the pair of Sunderlands with RAF markings, which were presently flying in opposite directions on a straight course between Crete and Alexandria. They must be ferrying arms and supplies, he decided. Thirty seconds later, he saw the puff of an artillery shell appear by the wing of the southward-bound flying boat, quickly followed by the glow of flames. Fire soon engulfed the starboard engine.

'She's been hit,' he exclaimed. 'There's no way she'll reach Alex now.'

He pulled out of a starboard turn and began to head towards the aircraft from which smoke was now pouring. She was going down very fast.

'Too fast,' Kit said thoughtfully. 'It can't be just the fire. She must have been hit elsewhere. The pilot's making an emergency landing.'

'You're going down after him, aren't you.'

It was a statement rather than a question from the young Portuguese. Kit advised Morris and Digger to get below, ready to open the hatch when *Flamingo* halted beside the doomed flying boat.

'We'll take the crew aboard as soon as they abandon ship,' he added. 'If the fire really takes hold, there could be an explosion. I don't want to be there if there is, so make the business snappy.'

While his friends clattered down to the lower deck, Kit concentrated on the aircraft he was pursuing. It suddenly dropped like a stone, bounced on the choppy surface, then slewed to one side as the port wingtip dipped deep into the water. With a great shuddering smack, *Flamingo* touched down to send a surge of water up almost as far as the cockpit windows as she raced towards the crashed aircraft. What he then saw filled Kit with alarm. From the hatches which still remained above water, men in khaki were leaping into the sea in a continuous procession. He had been wrong to imagine supplies in that flying boat; she was packed with soldiers.

'God, she's a troop carrier,' yelled Digger from below. 'We'll never manage them all with this cargo on board.'

'Ditch the cargo,' instructed Kit, as he took *Flamingo* on a line which would allow them to approach as near as he dared. 'Start pushing overboard now anything you can handle.'

As they dropped speed to no more than a gentle glide, his crewmen opened the cargo hatch. The scene was extremely distressing. Heads were bobbing in the water all round the doomed aircraft, yet men still spilled from the hull. Then Kit saw the flying boat keel over and vanish. Next minute, there was nothing but a swirling eddy to mark where she had been—that, and some fifty men desperately splashing their way towards *Flamingo*.

Leaving Aldo at the controls, Kit took the steps to the lower deck, snatched two life belts, then hauled open the forward hatch to throw them towards the men struggling to stay afloat. Racing through the hull to where Morris and Digger were frantically jettisoning anything they could, Kit did the same with the life belts in the aft section. Next, he inflated the dinghy and pushed it away on the rise and fall of the waves.

The collection of pale faces drew nearer. Kit stood in the forward hatchway, ready to throw ropes as soon as the men swam near enough to seize the ends. The survivors began arriving in small batches as the waves swept them close. Kit threw lifelines and hauled—urgency allowed no time for words. The dinghy came alongside to deliver seven survivors.

A diving fighter suddenly flashed past, raking *Flamingo*'s hull with bullets. A spasm of fury gripped Kit. *Flamingo* was the only hope of survival for those already aboard; the only means of returning to Alexandria. He tried not to look at those terrified faces in the water as he resolutely tugged the forward hatch back into position and punched the button which closed the cargo hatch automatically. Thrusting his way through the crowding troops, he charged up to the flight deck, shouting to Aldo to start up the inboard engines for takeoff. Even as he settled in his seat, another burst of fire hit *Flamingo* on the port wing. Increasing throttle, he prepared to leave, feeling like a mass murderer. Reason told him it was better by far to save half than none at all, yet even that possibility hung in the balance while the attacks continued. If only he had the means of firing back!

Never had he been so glad of *Flamingo*'s superb takeoff. Their German attacker, plainly unprepared for such a rapid climb from a flying boat, now raced past so close that only Kit's swift manoeuvring prevented a midair collision. Although *Flamingo* responded, she did so sluggishly. For a few alarming moments Kit believed she would stall and plunge back into the sea. She held, but there came a cause for even greater concern, as a second dark diving shape flashed past too close for comfort.

'God!' he swore, coaxing the machine into a climb again. 'They're all turning on us.'

'No, they're not,' roared Digger. 'That bloke's an Aussie. His plane's got a 'roo painted on the side!'

Taking *Flamingo* in a wide turn to gain more height, Kit scanned the sky around him. Sure enough, the German aircraft that had been attacking was now the victim of the Spitfire. It was not long before the Aussie pilot had his revenge, and a cheer rose from the soldiers on the lower deck.

Kit's gaze dropped to the sea, where tiny dots were now closing on a lozenge-shaped dinghy. Heading back to the spot where the other flying boat had gone down, he began to prepare for another landing. He shouted instructions to the friends comprising his crew. 'Open both hatches as soon as it's feasible. Each of you take some of the men as helpers, then pull the survivors aboard just as fast as you can. Leave the bodies. I want to be off again before our pal above is obliged to end his protection.'

Kit remained at the controls this time, wondering how he would get *Flamingo* up with such a load aboard. She was about to be a passenger liner with wings again, and this was going to be her finest hour. With a prayer, and a great deal of luck, added an inner voice. The wait seemed interminable as Kit sat in the cabin with little idea of what was happening below.

Finally Aldo appeared. 'They are all aboard. They are not reinforcements, Kit, as we thought. Crete is being evacuated. Two British squadrons are going back and forth, to fly off as many as possible before they fall into German hands. These men are pretty damn grateful.'

Kit prepared for the most doubtful takeoff of his life, knowing how many lives he would be risking in the process. As *Flamingo* began to move forward, it was as if he were driving her through glue. On and on they ploughed, with *Flamingo* noisily announcing her anguish, until the normal time for lift-off had been reached and passed. With his throat tightening, Kit fought to make the machine rise but, for once, she resisted his will. Still she bumped across the waves with engines roaring in complaint.

'Come on! *Come on*, you beautiful creature,' he murmured desperately. 'We can do it, you know we can.'

Of course they could! Well past the usual short run, *Flamingo* finally heaved herself a few feet into the air. Kit hauled on the controls. The climb was laborious. It was enough, however. Kit knew they were past the danger point; she would not let him down now. Whispering words of love to her, he levelled out above the undulating waves. All at once, he felt like the young man who had long ago flown another mistress in triumphant manner across Lyme Bay. In the manner of the water bird after which she was named, *Flamingo* cast a rippling shadow on the blue beneath as she turned and headed for Alexandria.

Aldo gripped Kit's shoulder in congratulation.

'Bloody marvellous!' exclaimed Digger from the rear. 'I never thought you'd do it.'

Morris spoke into the sudden quietness. 'What a time to choose to demonstrate to us all that you're still one of the best marine pilots around.'

THEY REMAINED IN ALEXANDRIA for three weeks. The repairs were eventually completed, and *Flamingo* was scheduled to leave at dawn on a late June morning. The first leg to Tunis was enlivened by no more than a passing squadron of British bombers, whose pilots first eyed them suspiciously then gave friendly waves. When they arrived, Aldo took them safely into the company mooring, and Kit headed for their agent's office. Raymond Leck, a Eurasian, was engrossed in some papers when Kit walked in, hot and thirsty, with his shirt sticking to his back.

Dropping a small package onto the agent's desk, he said, 'There you are,

Ray, me lad. The latest copies of *Picturegoer* straight from the delicate hands of the NAAFI girl in Alex, as usual. Have this lot on me, as a farewell gift. I shall not pass this way again.'

The man frowned at Kit. 'You already know?'

'Know what?'

'About the trouble with Western Med.' He held out a sheet of paper. 'This came in from Tom Digby two hours ago. Read it.'

Kit scanned the terse communication. A diplomatic storm had arisen over *Flamingo*'s rescue of thirty-eight armed soldiers during a military engagement. The Germans in Lisbon had seized their chance to accuse Western Mediterranean Air Services of antineutral activities, using the incident off Crete as proof of their claim. All Western Med machines were temporarily grounded, and *Flamingo* was almost certain to be impounded on her arrival. The local authorities would have no choice but to place her crew under open arrest until the charge could be investigated. The message ended with Tom's recommendation not to return to Lisbon.

Kit reread the message, then looked across at the other man. 'Without us, they have no leg to stand on, Ray. All other crew members are Portuguese. So long as we stay away, Tom will be in the clear.'

'What will you do?'

Kit gazed through the open window at *Flamingo* being refuelled. 'Go on to Gibraltar.'

'Then what?'

'That's up to my crew. I'd better tell them about this now.'

Digger, Morris and Aldo took the news philosophically. They had known all along the risks they were taking.

'What do I do with *Flamingo* and her crew?' Kit glanced at each of their faces in turn. 'Any suggestions?'

Then Digger spoke. 'I don't think we'll come up with a better suggestion than yours.'

'I haven't offered one yet,' said Kit.

'Well, it's obvious what you're asking, mate.'

'If you take *Flamingo* to England, do we want to go with you? That *is* what you want to know, isn't it?'

'I suppose so . . . We could offer her services—and ours—to the RAF.'

'What else can we do with her?' asked Aldo. 'All Tom's aircraft are grounded. I come with you.'

'What about you, Digger?' Kit asked.

'I told you at Alex that I'm in it now. When I saw those poor buggers being shot up in the sea, I knew whose side I was on.'

'Morris?'

'We've been together for some time, and had some hairy experiences,' Morris told him. 'That makes a person very aware of how his companions feel and think. You know damn well I wouldn't go back to Lisbon on my own, don't you?'

Kit smiled. 'I knew you'd come with us.'

'I had to, really,' said Morris casually. 'I couldn't let some other poor soul navigate for a pilot who thinks he can land his machine anywhere, at any time. No man has the right to inflict such a fate on another.'

'Cheeky bastard!' commented Kit, getting to his feet. 'Come on, I think this calls for a drink. We'll need to drink to *Flamingo*'s new role. This time, she'll be flying under her true colours, and she'll be able to fight back.'

THEY FINALLY LEFT at four the following afternoon. Their plan was to fly to Plymouth, where there was a flying-boat base. They were all quiet as the aircraft banked away from their usual course to Lisbon. Making this decision had been one thing; acting it out brought home its finality. The only regret Kit had was being unable to bid Tom a decent farewell.

Kit took the controls from Aldo just before they reached the Brittany coast, the closest they would pass to German-occupied territory. However, there was no challenge to their progress through a clear evening sky.

Morris came forward with the news that the English coast should soon be visible ahead. Kit found himself ridiculously emotional as he strained his eyes for the first sight of it. At that moment, something came at them without warning. With his heart jumping, Kit realised that an aircraft had approached to catch him totally unawares. Hot on that shock came another. A second fighter flashed across the top of the cockpit.

'I see them,' yelled Digger, from his position at a porthole. 'They're Hurricanes. Must be a welcoming committee.'

'I'd have preferred a small crowd waving flags,' Kit said drily.

Even as he spoke, he noticed one of the Hurricanes flying alongside the port wing. At the same time, Aldo remarked that the other was on their starboard flank. Both pilots were making signals which suggested they wanted him to land. He shook his head, pointing in the direction of Plymouth. The response to that was startling. After veering away, the two fighters flew towards *Flamingo*, their guns chattering in unison.

'Stupid bastards,' fumed Kit. 'Signal our neutral status, Morris. Keep on until their thick heads register the fact.'

They could as well have signalled *Merry Christmas* for all the good it did. After several more close bursts of fire, Kit had to bow to their demand that he should land. Fuming and cursing, he embarked on a long shallow descent which would place *Flamingo* as close to the coast as possible. It was not until *Flamingo* touched the surface, then ploughed forward with decreasing speed, that Kit grew aware of red cliffs faintly visible ahead and experienced a sense of unavoidable destiny.

'Where in the name of God are we? It is England, isn't it?' asked Aldo.

'That's right,' Kit told him.

'If this is England, why have we been forced down in such manner?'

'I don't know,' Kit answered. 'Whatever the reason, *Flamingo* has come home. This is a small seaside resort called Sheenmouth.'

18

They had finished dinner and were taking a stroll through the gardens.

'I adore times like this, don't you?' Leone murmured.

Warren squeezed her hand. Halting, her gaze took in the copse through which a path had been cut to the old boathouse. Warren spent a great deal of his time there, on secret Air Ministry work. She smiled fondly at him. 'Clever old thing. You've become what is generally known as a boffin.' Slipping her arm through his, they started back towards the abbey.

Warren laughed. 'Boring Old Fool Full of Idiotic Notions, is how Mona translated it.'

Leone also laughed. 'You'll be *Sir* Warren before long.'

When they were inside their suite, he drew her into his customary close embrace. 'Let's take the phone off the hook. Who knows when we'll spend a night together next?'

She nodded and drew away to unfasten her long dress of blue and white voile. The telephone rang. Reluctantly she picked up the receiver. A man's voice apologised for disturbing her. 'This is Sublieutenant Grimes, ma'am. I captain a patrol vessel stationed at East Sheenmouth.'

'Yes, Mr Grimes. What can I do for you?'

'Well, ma'am, there's been a rather awkward incident. It's those darned Polish pilots up at Magnum Pomeroy. Two of them forced down a neutral unarmed flying boat half an hour ago, despite clear identification markings and signals flashed from the incoming crew. The Poles' excuse is that they didn't understand the signals, and they thought it was an enemy spy machine. I ask you!' he added in tones of disgust. 'We went out to intercept the aircraft, and brought it in to your slipways so that we could board and search. I thought you should be informed of the fact that it's one of yours.'

'One of mine?' she echoed.

'Yes, it's a Kirkland's machine, all right,' the voice on the line continued. 'She's been flying for a Portuguese company, but was apparently shot up in the Med and couldn't return to Lisbon.'

Sinking onto a stool, she asked faintly, 'What's the pilot's name?'

'There are two,' he replied. 'One's a Portuguese called Diaz, the other's a Captain Anson. He's English like his navigator. There's an Australian aboard who claims to know you, Mrs Grant.'

'Digger Rathbone,' she murmured.

'That's right.' His surprise was evident. 'You really are old friends?'

'With the entire crew.' Excitement ran through her as she asked, 'Have they been taken anywhere for the night yet?'

'I'm just about to send them up in a Jeep to Wing Commander Keen. He's offered to give them a meal and a bed.'

'Send them here instead,' she told him swiftly. 'I've plenty of room. Both my husband and I would very much like to meet them again.'

She replaced the receiver with her mind in a whirl. When Warren came from the bathroom, she stared unseeingly at him. 'Warren . . . *Flamingo* is down at our slipways. Her crew . . . I've . . . I've invited them here for the night. They're on their way in a Jeep.' She relayed what she had just been told. When she finally ran out of words, he stood looking at her.

'I can tell from the state you're in that Kit's with them.'

She swallowed. 'Yes, he is . . . Warren, Kit can't destroy what we have. Let's just meet up for old times' sake. You two were good friends.'

He turned away to walk to the wardrobe, his expression desolate. 'Get dressed, darling. They'll be here soon.'

With shaking hands, she slipped back into the dress she had just discarded, then did what she could to her face and hair. Telling Warren that she must organise rooms, she suggested that he should greet the men and dispense drinks before they freshened up ready to eat.

Her mind worked feverishly. When Maitland had told her the terrible facts of Geoffrey Anson's death, she had vowed to keep out of Kit's life from then on. Fate had brought them briefly together again, and she must make her peace with him. Somehow, she must get him alone long enough to . . . to what? To apologise because her own father had pushed Kit's father to his death in pounding machinery? To confess Kirkland guilt for all he had suffered as a boy? Small wonder her nerve failed her when they were about to come face to face.

When that moment could be delayed no longer, Leone found their guests in the small sitting room. Everyone rose at her entry, and her gaze flew straight to the dark, muscular man in the crisp green uniform. He looked tired, and a good deal older than when she had last seen him.

'Hello, Kit,' she greeted, in carefully controlled manner. 'What an incredible twist of fate that Peter Keen's mad Polish boys should have forced you to land right here.'

'Yes, incredible.' He nodded.

It was clear that the friendship between Warren and Kit had survived the years. The two men talked eagerly about the great love of their lives as Leone renewed her acquaintance with Morris Snaith and Digger Rathbone, who introduced their new second pilot, Aldo Diaz. By the time they all sat at the table, a relaxed atmosphere prevailed.

'I'm still not clear why you were advised not to return to Lisbon,' Leone said. 'Surely the Germans couldn't have had you all arrested just for picking up drowning men. It was not as if you'd taken part in the battle.'

'We'd done a few other things over the past year,' Morris told her quietly, 'so they were hoping to use this incident as an excuse to mount a full investigation. Without us, Tom can't be charged with anything.'

'A few other things?' she asked with curiosity.

Kit changed the subject adroitly and soon Warren commented on the fact that it was almost 2am and his guests looked ready to turn in. They seemed to welcome the prospect, and said good night before splitting up to go to their rooms. Leone regretted her impulse to give Kit his old suite, as she and Warren walked with him to the bell tower. Too many painful memories were attached to that set of circular rooms.

They halted outside Kit's door, and he asked, 'What about those passenger liners with wings, Warren; the dreams?'

'Oh . . . I haven't forgotten them,' Warren murmured. 'They simply seem to have vanished beneath the drive to make machines that will kill.' He sighed. 'Sometimes, I'd give anything for the old days at Ma Bardolph's making balsawood miniatures of my designs. We still have a *Seaspray* we made to order for a customer who died before he could collect it. She's a two-seater, with a shortened wingspan and racing lines echoed in body and floats. I was proud of her.'

'I'd like to see her before I leave,' Kit said.

Warren shook his head. 'She's dismantled and stored in the old boathouse for the duration.' With a sigh, he turned away. 'We mustn't keep you awake talking about old times. Good night, Kit. I'm rather glad those crazy Polish boys forced you down so that we'd have this meeting.'

'So am I,' came his surprising reply. 'Good night.'

As he opened the familiar door, Leone caught herself quoting, *'Good night, sleep tight. Hope the bugs don't bite.'*

Kit turned back. 'Fancy you recalling that old rhyme!'

'Like you, there are lots of things I remember,' she said, her throat thickening with pain and regret.

In their own suite of rooms, Warren declared that he was tired and had a tricky development to tackle on the morrow. He made no attempt to embark on the lovemaking which had been interrupted by the telephone call, merely murmured a good-night before turning away. Leone was glad. He would not see the tears gathering on her cheeks.

THEY HAD BREAKFAST in the octagonal room. Rested and fed, their guests were eager to go downriver to their aircraft, and were soon on the terrace ready to depart. Warren walked down to the jetty to rouse Walter, leaving the men to bid Leone a grateful farewell. Feeling desperate, she seized the hand Kit offered in parting.

'Do come and see what they did to the west wing,' she urged. 'Walter will be ages bringing out the boat.' Words rushed from her as she led him round the corner to where the swimming pool and tennis courts had been. Now there was a great stretch of earth filling the bomb crater, where vegetables grew. They turned a second corner to see the damaged area, shored up with stout props for the duration of the war. Kit studied it for several moments.

'You were buried under *that*?'

She nodded.

'And you really did lead a host of children to safety through those old underground passages?'

She nodded again.

'I never believed in their existence, despite those old yarns.' Regarding her with speculative interest, he said, 'As Warren told me last night, I've been out of the country too long. Things aren't the way I remember them, Leone.' He pursed his lips thoughtfully. 'You appear to have made Warren very happy. I never thought you would . . . but you've changed.'

'Have I? In what way?' she asked.

'I can't say exactly. You've grown quieter, perhaps . . . more human. It was there beneath that Kirkland pride when you were a girl. Warren seems to have brought it to the surface. Marriage suits you. So, apparently, does hard work.' He began walking back towards the terrace. 'You've become a woman of purpose, instead of an aimless social butterfly basking in the name your father so revered.'

'Kit,' she blurted out, catching his hand. 'Please wait a moment.' As he turned and disengaged his hand, she almost faltered in her resolution to say what she must. 'I never dreamed I'd ever have the chance to speak to you again. I can't let you go until I've . . . ' The wariness of his expression robbed her of fluency.

Distrust was back in his dark eyes. 'We have a flight to Plymouth ahead,' he reminded her.

'Please,' she begged, 'please listen. After the crash, I telephoned the hospital in Lisbon three times a week for news of you. The reason I stopped was because . . . because I finally learned what you once advised me to ask Donald to explain.' Gazing entreatingly at him, she confessed. 'The guilt for what he told me has haunted me ever since. Please believe that I knew nothing of the terrible affair until that moment. With all my heart, I apologise for what my father did to yours. It's impossible for you to forgive it, I know, but can there be peace between us, at least?'

Kit frowned, plainly disconcerted by her confession. Eventually, he gave a sigh and a shrug, and resumed walking back to the terrace. 'There's no need for you to make apologies. You were only a child when it happened, and were in no way involved apart from blindly believing what Sir Hector and Donald chose to tell you of the affair. When I first saw those drawings Warren found in the old boathouse, and realised that *Aphrodite* was really my father's *Solitaire*, I suppose I went slightly crazy. I threatened to reveal their theft of Dad's design, and expose Donald as the fraud he was. Your father had me over a barrel, of course, and told me to get out within the hour. He laughed in my face when I offered to sell him the design for ten thousand, and when he threatened to dump me in the Sheen unless I went quietly, I foolishly stole the sum I considered to be my due. I played right into his hands, and fate decided to assist him by staging a car crash.'

He paused momentarily, frowning. 'My rage was mainly for the fact that no one would ever know the full record gained on that tremendous day—a man winning laurels in his own father's seaplane. It would have restored the respectability of the Anson family.' He gave a hint of a smile. 'My rage is now directed elsewhere. When I saw helpless men being machine-gunned in the sea, I knew what was really important. War tends to put a great many things into perspective, doesn't it? All the same, I'm glad you finally know the truth. Yes, there can be peace between us, Leone, if that's what you want.' He drew away. 'Goodbye. Take care of Warren . . . and of yourself, of course. You're doing a great job here.' As he walked briskly off to join his crew, Leone felt as if the west wing had collapsed on her once more.

SETTING EYES ON *FLAMINGO* AGAIN gave Warren a great thrill. As the launch approached the jetty, the flying boat seemed a vision from the past.

'Gosh, she's fantastic!' he breathed.

Kit laughed. 'Of course she's fantastic. Surely you hadn't forgotten.'

Warren shook his head. 'Not exactly. I've been modifying one up in Scotland—the third off our production line—but she's camouflaged and armed. Can't think of her as mine as I do this one.' Recollection of *Florida* caused him to turn to the men with him. 'Good Lord, I should have told you last night. I met young Joss Hamilton. He was given command of the boat because he knew the model better than any pilot in his squadron. The last we heard from him, he had just returned from a special flight to Norway. People are being brought out from there regularly. The Germans are using Norway's resources to their advantage, and her unfortunate scientific or engineering experts are being forced to work for them.'

Calpurnian came alongside the jetty and they climbed ashore. As they approached *Flamingo* they were met by a member of the crew of the launch which had escorted them in last evening. He greeted Kit with a smile.

'Hello, sir. Lieutenant Grimes has a message for you from the base at Plymouth. Would you step over to the office for a moment?'

Warren went aboard with Aldo, Morris and Digger, while Kit crossed to the office beyond Kirkland's. For half an hour or so Warren wandered the aircraft, noting with interest how she had been adapted from the original luxury passenger boat.

Kit returned to tell his crew that Plymouth had given them permission to proceed and land there before noon. Knowing they were anxious to be on their way, Warren bade them farewell and the best of luck. Then he remained to watch *Flamingo* get under way and taxi down to the mouth of the river. Only when his flying boat had become no more than a dot in the morning sky did he walk slowly back to the old boathouse with the intention of starting work. He found Leone standing in his drawing office and she looked ashen.

'I guessed you'd come directly here,' she said. 'I need to talk to you, and I can't wait until you finish being unbelievably brilliant and emerge again into the real world the rest of us inhabit.'

'That's rather unfair, isn't it?' he asked. 'I've never locked the door when I'm working. If you've not come down here, I assume it's because there's never been an urgent enough reason for you to disturb me.' He moved towards her. 'Now there is, I take it.'

She passed a hand over her brow distractedly. 'I'm sorry, Warren. I can't think straight. I've had a terrible shock. I can't believe it, yet if it's true . . . I don't know how I'll live with myself. Or with you.' She confronted him, white-faced. 'Did Donald design *Aphrodite*, or did he steal *Solitaire* from Geoffrey Anson?'

It knocked him right off-balance. Kit must have told her . . . but why?

'I joined Kirkland's long after that seaplane was designed and developed,' he caught himself saying.

'The drawings you found here and handed to Kit—were they for a seaplane designed by his father?'

'What has Kit said to you?' he demanded harshly.

'He said . . . Oh, Warren, he completely misunderstood what I was telling him. I took him aside as he was leaving this morning, and apologised for what my father had done to his. He . . . he thought I was referring to something quite different, and explained that his rage over the theft of his father's design had diminished with time.' Coming towards him, she held out both fists in appeal. 'Dear God, it isn't true, is it?'

It rose up to confront him finally: that sense of guilt he had always suffered over an affair which had broken a man at the height of his brilliance.

'I found some drawings here when I was clearing the place out,' he offered carefully. 'I handed them to Kit.'

'Without looking at them? Were they drawings of a seaplane?'

'It was years ago, Leone.'

Her face grew even paler. 'Warren, this is one of the most terrible moments of my life. Tell me the truth.'

He knew it was also one of the most terrible moments of *his* life. 'The drawings were for a seaplane Geoffrey Anson had named *Solitaire*. I wasn't familiar with the finer details of *Aphrodite*'s design. She had been developed and built before I ever joined the company . . . but I did see remarkable similarities between Anson's drawings and Donald's aircraft.' He sighed. 'I'd just been taken on by your father and knew I had to tread very carefully if I wanted to keep my job. As it was really not my concern, I handed the plans over to Kit. For all I knew, old Anson had made some kind of deal with Sir Hector, allowing Donald to take credit for the design.'

'The drawings, found in Kit's car after the crash; were they the ones you handed to him?'

'I don't know. I suppose . . . well, they could have been,' he agreed slowly.

'Those policemen brought them back to the house and handed them over to Father. The only proof of Kit's claim was handed back to those who could charge *him* with theft.'

'I wasn't there in the abbey that evening. I have no idea what was said,' he reminded her.

'You kept quiet when a man was tried and sent to prison for something he hadn't done.'

'Nothing I could have said would have helped him,' he said miserably. 'He didn't even attempt to defend himself.'

'You could have told *me* the truth,' she whispered hoarsely.

He swallowed. 'You were a schoolgirl then.'

'Why didn't you tell me later, when he arrived here to take the proving flight?' she demanded wildly. 'You were my friend. I trusted you.'

'I wasn't your friend, Leone, I was in love with you. There are different rules for each relationship.'

'All right, but when I asked you to marry me, why didn't you tell me then? Donald was dead, and I was vowing to keep out of Kit's life.'

He stood silent, knowing the answer would not appease her. How could he be afraid of losing her to a man who did not want her? Yet he had been. He still was afraid.

'I'll never be able to forgive you, Warren.'

He shook his head, saying quietly, 'It's yourself you'll never be able to forgive. Loving him as you've done all these years, you nevertheless believed him to be guilty.'

19

Over the next few months, *Flamingo* was modified yet again. Machine guns, bomb bays, additional radio equipment and camouflage paint turned her into a warplane, yet she was different from the Sunderlands and Catalinas of the Plymouth squadron. Her guns were recessed and removable; her identification markings could be changed from military to civil, at will. Her crew had two uniforms—RAF blue-grey with badges of rank, as well as the smart navy blue with gold insignia of a civil airline. Kit was given the title of flight lieutenant and the rest of his crew appropriate ranks, but they were chameleons changing appearance to suit the job on hand, for they were earmarked for special duties and received their orders from Colin Dryden's department.

Kit found his new life stimulating. He never knew if he would be flying high-ranking men to secret meetings on neutral soil, or making risky flights over occupied territory to pick up Colin Dryden's agents.

Christmas 1941 brought events which both shocked and cheered. The Japanese entered the war, Hong Kong fell, and America took up arms after the destruction of their Hawaiian naval base. Hope rose again.

One bleak February lunchtime when Kit was in the mess reading of the fall of Singapore, a steward called him to the telephone. A quiet voice said, 'Hello, Kit. I wasn't sure I'd be able to ring you casually like this.'

'Leone?' he questioned experimentally, taken by surprise.

'I'm in Plymouth for a business meeting.'

'Oh.' Still surprised that she should ring him, he asked, 'How's everything at Sheenmouth? Nothing wrong, is there?'

There was further hesitation before she said, 'I'm ringing from a call box. The meeting is likely to continue for most of the afternoon, so I've booked a room for the night. Kit . . . would you have dinner with me?'

'Only if I pay,' he said down the line.

'Can you manage seven? It's awfully early, I know, but the hotel allows its restaurant staff to get home before the raids start.'

'Which hotel?' he asked then.

She named the most exclusive, in the centre of the city.

'OK. I'll come just before seven,' he promised. 'Pity old Warren isn't with you. We could have had a real get-together about old times.'

'That's what I have in mind,' she said quietly. 'Until seven, then.'

WHEN KIT ENTERED THE LOUNGE, he found Leone walking towards him. She looked pale, but very striking in a dark green cocktail dress. Her shining hair was swept into a thick roll like a halo around her head, and scarlet lipstick emphasised the whiteness of her skin. How different from the girls he had been dating recently, he told himself wryly.

'I saw you come in,' she greeted, unsmiling.

'Eagle eyes! I'm dressed like almost every other man here. Would you like a drink before dinner?' He led her to the bar, ordered a dry martini for Leone, and a whisky and soda for himself.

Leaving her drink untouched, she regarded him with eyes deeply troubled. 'Do you recall our conversation just before you left that morning, about Donald's theft of your father's design?'

He knew which morning she meant, and nodded.

'We were unwittingly speaking of two different things. I knew nothing of the theft of *Solitaire* until you mentioned it.'

Kit racked his brains to recall the details of that conversation last July beside the shattered west wing of Sheenmouth Abbey. 'You apologised for what your father had done to mine. I told you it was unnecessary, because you'd been little more than a child when it had all happened.'

'I was referring to something else, Kit.' Her hand, with its heavy gold wedding ring bestowed by Warren, encircled the stem of her glass for a moment. 'You said there could be peace between us. I want that more than anything in the world, but when you hear what I must tell you, you may find it impossible—*ever*. No, don't say anything until I've told you what Maitland revealed to me; what he had used to blackmail both Father and Donald into maintaining him in a very comfortable manner.'

So he sat silently, while a beautiful young woman sitting on a stool in a cocktail bar told him that her father had been the cause of his own losing every penny of an investment; that he had subsequently countered his victim's drunken fury with a physical blow which had sent him staggering into racing machinery.

'When Maitland gave me those appalling facts, I finally understood why you had been taken into my home and given Kirkland largesse,' she continued. 'I persuaded myself that Father had possessed something of a conscience. When you unwittingly spoke of the theft of your father's design that morning, I knew my assumption was wrong. Far from being guilt-ridden over Geoffrey Anson's gruesome death, Father had seen it as the perfect opportunity to endow Donald with the brilliance he lacked. You were absorbed into the masculine machinery of the abbey purely for the purpose of keeping you under Kirkland control. You then heaped further glory on my family by flying their damned stolen aircraft faster than any man of the day,' she added brokenly. 'After such treachery, how can there ever be peace between us?'

Kit was shattered. Swallowing his whisky in a gulp, he slammed the glass back on the counter as he got to his feet. 'You're damned right, there can never be peace between us. You might have changed your name to Grant, but you're still a Kirkland and always will be, so far as I'm concerned.' Throwing some banknotes in the direction of his glass, he headed for the door. Before he reached it he heard familiar shuddering thuds beneath his feet, the thunder of engines overhead, and the wail of sirens. German raiders had arrived.

He was pushed aside as people dashed for the safety of an air-raid shelter. The hotel lights dimmed, then came on again; next minute, an earsplitting roar was followed by a blast of dust-laden air and the scene was plunged into darkness. Women began screaming; male voices rose urgently. Kit moved forward, calling Leone's name. Choking on the flying dust, and pushing through a mill of people all endeavouring to find each other, he groped his way across the room, and then saw her, backed against a wall. He took hold of her arms and spoke gently.

'Leone, everything's all right now. I'll take you out of this.'

Her eyes saw only him. She grew so limp she would have fallen if he had not supported her. Clinging to him, she clutched the dusty uniform jacket with both hands.

'You're safe! Thank God. Oh, thank God.'

Holding her close, he led her through to the dining room. There, staff were bringing candles and oil lamps, and two women wearing Red Cross armbands were dealing with the casualties. Thankful that Leone appeared to be suffering from no more than shock, Kit took her to the table where one of the waiters was dispensing tea. He had to hold the cup to her lips because she was shaking so much. Between her sips, he drank from the cup to moisten his dry throat.

Bombs were still falling, but more distantly now. The enemy aircraft would be turning for home soon.

'What's the number of your room?' he asked. 'I think you'd be better off up there where it's quiet.'

'Key's in . . . in the . . . bag,' she stammered.

Opening the bag on her arm, he took out a key with the number 19 on it. He coaxed her towards the stairs. Progress was slow, but Kit eventually opened the door of what proved to be a suite of rooms. Two lighted candles stood on a low polished table. Several more, in heavy candlesticks beside a box of matches, awaited the guest. Still supporting Leone, he lit all the wicks to provide as much brightness as possible. Only then did he set her down in one of the armchairs, stripped a blanket from the bed and tucked it round her.

'Are you warm enough?' he asked.

'Warmer than before. You must think me very feeble,' she added.

Intent on his task, he said, 'I've seen strong men in shock. This kind of reaction is involuntary and nothing to do with feebleness.'

'You're covered in dust,' she murmured. 'Your hair is full of white plaster.'

He glanced up. 'You're not exactly bandbox fresh yourself, madam.' He was prevented from elaborating because he realised that she was looking down at him with an expression no strong man in shock had ever displayed.

'I ought to get back,' he said, walking to the window. 'The station might have been hit.'

'Not while the raid's still on, wait for the all clear,' she begged. 'Come over here, Kit, you look shaken, too.'

'I'm no hero.' He turned back into the room. 'Of course I'm shaken.'

'I'm sorry,' she said in distress. 'I'm so sorry.'

'Oh, for God's sake don't start apologising on behalf of the Germans, as well,' he snapped, surprising himself by reopening the hostility from which he had been walking away half an hour ago. 'Give up trying to shoulder the blame for everyone's bloody sins. No one expects you to do that, least of all me.' He began to pace the room. 'I don't know why you decided to make a full confession of your father's iniquitous crimes against the Anson family. Both he and my father are dead. Geoffrey Anson can't be brought back to life; *Solitaire* can never be claimed as his. What proof I had of the theft must have been destroyed, and no one would believe my word against that of a Kirkland.'

'Warren studied the drawings. He knew the design had been stolen.'

That halted him. '*Warren* knew . . . right from the start?'

Her pale face grew even sadder in the candleglow. 'He says no one would have believed him, either.'

Deeply affected by the revelation, Kit gazed at her in protest. 'Why didn't he say something to *me*? At the time of the trial, while I was in prison . . . even during the proving flight. We were good friends.'

'He could have told *me*,' she added softly. 'We were also good friends.'

Kit shrugged. 'What does any of it matter now? The three main characters are dead, and you were just a precocious adolescent, who so badly wanted to be a Kirkland she echoed the censure of the males who dominated the scene.'

'No, you're wrong,' she cried. 'You have no idea how wrong.' Getting to her feet, Leone came right up to him.

'Father told me of your supposed ingratitude and treachery, said you had left Sheenmouth never to return. Loving you madly, as I did, I couldn't believe him. Then two policemen walked in carrying some rolled drawings, and a bag containing the exact sum I'd just been told you had demanded as your due for gaining the speed record.' Tears formed in her eyes as she put her guilt into words. 'I stayed true to you even then, Kit . . . but when they revealed that Stephanie had been found in the car with you, I accepted your treachery instantly. Young love is stormy and intolerant. I wanted to make you suffer as I then suffered. Being a Kirkland, my pride overruled my heart and I allowed Father to destroy you. My father and brother are dead, but I'm still paying for what I did. I knew I loved you when you returned to fly *Flamingo*. I love you now.'

She was so close he could feel her breath on his lips. He looked and saw a child bursting into a circular room, declaring that she was determined to befriend him. He saw a girl masquerading as a woman in a moonlit ruin, begging with tears on her cheeks to be kissed. He saw a beautiful social butterfly yearning for fulfilment in a pink-lined aircraft of which she was half-owner and therefore his employer. He saw an intelligent, courageous woman asking for peace between them, yet making it more and more impossible with every word she uttered. He saw another man's wife.

'I should go back to the station,' he murmured.

He must have betrayed himself. Recognition was there in her eyes, and in the way she said without dismay, 'Yes, I know you should.'

It was as if the span of those aggressive years now demanded a lingering surrender. His kiss was little more than a searching, experimental contact at first. Then, as his arms closed around her, their last hope of peace was driven away by a passion more violent than any between the Ansons and the Kirklands, and as potentially destructive.

20

Leone was engaged in translating a long document into French for Philip Curtiss, when her secretary buzzed through to say Flight Lieutenant Anson was on the line. Joy raced through her as she snatched up the receiver. It was May, and they had met only once since that night in Plymouth.

Careless of whether or not she was being overheard, Leone made no secret of her feelings with her first words. 'Kit! What a wonderful surprise. Where are you speaking from? How long do we have?'

'Leone, I have Wing Commander Dryden here in my office,' his voice warned, dousing her excitement drastically. 'Sorry to ring you during office hours. I hope I'm not interrupting anything too vital.'

'A very boring French translation,' she told him, her own voice growing flat with disappointment. 'What can I do for you?'

His reply was quite unexpected. 'When I arrived in Sheenmouth last year, Warren mentioned a *Seaspray* which had been designed to seat two, but was never delivered due to the customer's demise. Does he still have it?'

'Down in the old boathouse. It has been dismantled and stored there.'

'Then I suppose I ought to talk to him about it. Is he at home?'

'Is this . . .' She cleared her throat. 'Is this an official matter?'

'Of course it . . . yes, naturally,' he amended, plainly finding this as difficult as she. 'It's also rather vital. Leone, we believe *Seaspray* could be the answer to a prayer, but we shall have to discuss the matter more fully. We'll fly down to Sheenmouth in *Flamingo*. Should be with you by about three this afternoon. Perhaps you'd warn Warren, and we'd appreciate a boat waiting to bring us up to the abbey. Adieu until then.'

He rang off, leaving her staring at the receiver. In a few hours, he would be here. He would behave as if they were merely old friends, and he would discuss aeronautics in a civilised manner with the man he had betrayed. She would be with them, and they would expect her to handle the impossible situation the way they undoubtedly would. When it came to flying machines, all else was unimportant!

Slamming the receiver onto its cradle, she rose to her feet. Damn Kit! Damn Warren! Damn this wing commander! They had no right to do this to her. How dare Kit ring up and announce that he was arriving this afternoon to discuss some mysterious project with Warren? This incomprehensible relationship between men and the aircraft they flew still took precedence. It was still a masculine world she lived in.

When they all gathered in the blue and yellow room where Leone dispensed tea, there was no attempt to exclude her from the discussion, her position in the aircraft-manufacturing industry being enough to guarantee her reliability.

'Here's the problem in a nutshell,' Colin Dryden said to Warren, leaning forward in his chair to emphasise his urgency. 'You've done mods on *Florida* so that she can operate to and from Norway on special flights, and must know a fair bit about the type of passenger we bring out. This one is rather more tricky. We have just ten days in which to do the job, and only one hope of reaching him. It's a pig of a prospect, but if we can even make an attempt at it we must. That's why we have to commandeer your seaplane, if she's fit to fly.'

Warren nodded.

'When the Jerries first occupied Norway, our passenger happily continued working in his laboratory.' Dryden's mouth twisted cynically. 'Four weeks ago, everything suddenly changed. Our man was told he would be sent to Germany to work with scientists there on further development of his successful breakthrough on bacteria. It then dawned on him that his findings were to be used in the field of germ warfare.'

'So he wants to come over to us?' asked Warren.

'Yes,' Dryden confirmed. 'He is due to be shipped to Germany on the twenty-fourth of this month, which is ten days from now. He has just one chance of being picked up by us. Thirty miles south of his laboratory there's a narrow fiord. The leader of the local partisans says they can get him from his quarters at the end of his working day, and down the steep sides of the fiord under cover of darkness. It's up to us to do the rest, but it's a very tall order, I fear. Halfway along the fiord there's a bottleneck. This rules out a flying boat with a huge wingspan. A small seaplane could be taken through, with a genius at the controls, but the craft has to be a two-seater.' Casting a glance at Kit, he added, 'I have the genius to fly the damned thing, but no machine with the right combination of properties. Your dismantled racing model is our last hope, Mr Grant.'

Warren suggested that they should all take a look at *Seaspray*, and the men rose to their feet, eager to be gone. Leone did not accompany them.

At ten pm she was so tense she buzzed the boathouse. Warren took a long while to answer, then sounded abstracted in answer to her question on what was happening.

'We're assembling the seaplane. It'll probably take us all night, so don't wait up.'

She spent a restless night. In the morning, she had to fight the urge to go immediately to the boathouse. They would not want her there. It was a day of gusting wind and rain which cleared to bring sunshine later in the afternoon.

Walking in the grounds, Leone heard what she thought was one of the boats out on the river. It proved to be *Seaspray* taxiing experimentally. Warren was in the rear seat to explain the aircraft to Kit, who was piloting. The seaplane taxied back and forth for a while, then the engine suddenly roared into full revs as Kit took her in a bouncing run over the choppy surface and up into the air above the abbey. The significance of that flight hit Leone then. Kit really was going to attempt to bring out this scientist within the coming ten days.

WHEN FIVE OF THE PRECIOUS DAYS had passed without any word from Kit, Leone rang Wing Commander Keen at Magnum Pomeroy airfield, where Kit and Colin Dryden had been given accommodation, and asked for a favour. Two hours later, the telephone rang and Kit's angry voice asked if she had gone completely mad.

'No,' she replied, with a touch of bitterness. 'I simply thought it was time to remind everyone of my existence. Don't you think it's time one or other of you had the courtesy to consult me about *Seaspray*, what work is being done in *my* workshops, and whether or not she's to be "commandeered" by Colin Dryden for your stupid death-or-glory antics. After all, I . . .'

Kit interrupted her. 'All right, Leone, calm down. I'm sorry. It's a hellish situation for us all.'

'I must see you.'

After a short silence, he said quietly, 'Drive along the Forton Road. I'll be beside the old watermill in about thirty minutes.'

He was there when she arrived. He looked tired and worried, so she was immediately repentant for putting him in an embarrassing situation.

Kit managed a pale smile as he settled in the seat beside her. He suggested that she should drive onto the downs beyond Forton. As the sun went down they left the car to stroll hand in hand along the smooth turf of the downs, now illuminated by the rising moon. Leone asked, 'Are you going to do it, this flight through a fiord which requires a genius at the controls?'

'Yes.'

'When?'

'I can't tell you that.'

'Oh, for heaven's sake!' she cried. 'I know the rest. Don't start being so ridiculously secretive now.'

Taking her by the shoulders, he gave her a gentle shake. 'Listen! I can't tell you, because I don't know myself. It must be before the twenty-fourth, but the weather has to be considered. As you can see tonight, the moon is in its brightest phase. I'll need as much light as possible, so a cloudy overcast evening is one to avoid. It'll be a last-minute decision.'

Moving into his encircling arms, she murmured against his jacket, 'I hate the whole idea.'

'So do I, but I hate the idea of germ warfare even more.'

They kissed passionately, then he circled her with an arm to lead her back towards the car. 'We're going up to Scotland tomorrow—both of us—in *Seaspray*. Colin's arranging for a ship to take us to a point well within the seaplane's range. I'll fly in, pick up the Norwegian, then get back and land as close to the destroyer as possible. I feel sorry for poor old Warren. He'll have to kick his heels aboard the ship, wondering what's happening. I'll know.'

'Kit, what will . . .' she began swiftly, but he cut her off with a gentle kiss on her mouth.

'You forced this meeting in order to prise the facts from me. Now face them, like a true Kirkland.'

'I'm not a Kirkland, I'm a Grant,' she reminded him hollowly.

'Don't I know it,' he responded. 'If you weren't, I'd have had you in a bed in the Buck and Hounds long ago.'

She heard *Seaspray* depart the following morning; saw the grey seaplane circle twice over the abbey as if in salute, before heading north for Scotland. In the dual cockpit were the two men in her life. For the first time since hostilities began, she knew the fear and prayers of millions of women whose loved ones might have said their last words and bestowed their last kisses.

THEY SLIPPED AWAY from the Scottish coast without ceremony. Warren remained on deck after everyone else had gone below. Lashed securely to the stern was *Seaspray*. Leaning back against the side, he studied the sleek lines of the special aircraft he had modified for sporting purposes. When he had rather shyly shown the famous Kit Anson his first drawings all those years ago, in Mrs Bardolph's attic room, neither of them had guessed how strangely their lives would be linked; parting yet inevitably coming together again in dramatic circumstances. None more dramatic than these.

Moving across to his aircraft with the intention of checking her over just once more, he got no further than a quick inspection of the floats, when a voice made him turn almost guiltily. Kit stood beside him.

'Irresistible, isn't it? I did the same with *Aphrodite*. Although you know she's bloody perfect, you can't stop fussing over her.'

'I'm not sure she likes being tossed around like this,' Warren muttered awkwardly.

'It's a bit undignified for such a delicate creature, I agree.' Kit began checking a few points also, while Warren watched him. A sturdy man in uniform trousers and a thick rollneck pullover, he seemed perfectly calm as all his attention focused on the machine he would fly. What were his thoughts and feelings beneath that outer confidence? Warren wondered. For a while they worked silently together, checking details. Then Kit spoke over the sound of the wind.

'If life had panned out differently, we would have made a good team, wouldn't we?'

Warren ceased inspecting the ailerons. It was suddenly clear that Kit was attempting to make peace between them. Wary, at first, he then realised it was once again as it had been on that first evening at Sheenmouth Abbey, when an instant rapport had sprung between them. Regrets flooded through him. 'I should have burned those drawings instead of handing them over. A small decision which had overwhelming repercussions.'

'Over the years I've found that fate makes the decisions,' Kit said quietly. 'We believe that we're in charge of our own lives, but that's not so. Your decision over the plans for *Solitaire* had very little effect on the ultimate outcome. For years, I burned with a sense of injustice. One day, I realised it scarcely mattered whose name was associated with that seaplane; it was the machine itself that was important. In the centuries to come, my father's design will simply be a single rung in a massive aviation ladder leading to bigger, faster machines.' He gave a rueful smile. 'This Norwegian scientist won't give a damn about the name Warren Grant. All he'll care about is that a flying machine is able to penetrate an inaccessible fiord, in order to save his life tonight. He won't give a damn about the name of the pilot, either. He's right, too. It's what we do, not what we're called, that's important.'

'Except when the name happens to be Kirkland,' Warren said, unable to help himself. 'Leone's burdened with the obsession to right all the family wrongs.'

Kit's dark eyes studied him for a moment across that windswept deck. 'You think that's all it is?'

Warren had imagined this moment many times over, and knew exactly what he would say to the man who threatened to steal his wife. Now he sensed that Kit was somehow saying farewell to him, and the chill of foreboding crept through him.

'She's seeking the echo of a youth that never was,' Kit said. 'You love her; you must be able to see that.'

'You love her?' Warren challenged.

Kit nodded. 'Probably because I'm seeking the same thing. I'm sorry, Warren, deeply sorry.' Getting to his feet, he added, 'Don't be too cruel to her. She's going to need you one day.' Turning away, he said in more normal tones, 'I'm going to get my head down for a while. Look after *Seaspray* for me. I'm going to need *her* tonight.'

Warren remained on deck, gazing unseeingly over the grey sea. *It's what we do, not what we're called, that's important.* Right now, he'd have given anything not to have designed and built this particular aircraft. The scientist meant nothing to him, but the man preparing to rescue him was the only true friend he had ever really known.

THERE WAS A COLD SKY, scattered with brilliant stars. The moon rode high as Kit pulled on his leather helmet and walked to the stern, where an entire team clustered round the aircraft. Men clapped Kit on the back, the ship's captain shook his hand, reminding him of the arrangements for his rendezvous with the destroyer. Then he was helped up the ladder to the forward cockpit and settled in the cramped seat.

From the specially designed ramp, foot by foot, *Seaspray* was lowered until the sea began to wash over the tips of the floats. Soon, Kit felt the familiar rocking which indicated that he was waterborne. Drifting slowly from the destroyer, Kit experienced a momentary sense of desolation.

His hand went to the ignition switch. *Seaspray*'s single engine roared, and she hurtled into the air almost before he was ready. Once up, he found the balance of power growing as she responded obediently to his demands. Putting himself on a course for the fiord, he glanced over the side at the dull silver sea. The destroyer was no more than a distant dark shape. Strangely, the sense of loneliness now took on a different aspect. There was excitement in isolation. He was once again Kit Anson, that youthful seeker of aerial laurels, attempting to do the impossible.

Fanciful thoughts were swiftly banished when he realised the dark smudge ahead must be Norway. In brilliant moonlight, he neared the coast then searched for the gleaming ribbon of the fiord, and eventually spotted it. He changed course, losing height and dropping between steep barren walls where visibility was restricted. With the hood pushed back the cold wind buffeted him, yet he was sweating profusely as he flew on through that shadowed place.

A blank wall of rock was suddenly there ahead, rearing up as high as he could see. His heart raced; he had come upon the dreaded bottleneck. There was no time to 'jump' it, as he had planned. *Seaspray* would never climb fast enough. He told her this in stern tones, as they raced headlong at the wall, searching for the fissure which would offer them passage through it.

When he saw the cutting, he gripped the control column and tensed himself for the sound of tearing metal. Yet the seaplane flew on, her backswept wings, designed for speed, missing the hazards as Kit's nerve held. Hair's-breadth manoeuvring was essential to negotiate the bottleneck's slight irregularities, and the little aircraft responded to his touch with total obedience. The bottleneck lay behind him. He had done the impossible. Leaning forward, he kissed the instrument panel. 'You little beauty, we made it. Together we made it!'

Triumph was brief. He was only five miles from the rendezvous, and what he had just done could not be attempted again, with additional weight to make precise manoeuvres that much slower. Somehow, he must go up and over the hazard. He had precisely fifteen minutes in which to think of a way to achieve the climb needed to do it.

The partisans had been instructed to float flares on the water when they heard the seaplane approach. Kit looked for these pinpricks of flame in the blackness below. There was no sign of light or life. Frowning, he prepared to turn and overfly the spot once more.

There was insufficient airspace for a turn within the chasm, so he climbed towards the bright moonlight flooding the crests. After the gloom of the fiord he found a magical lunar atmosphere above the snow-tipped range. As he made a wide turn, the peace was shattered by rifle fire. He dived for the protection of the fiord, the familiar ring of bullets on metal telling him *Seaspray* had been hit by his unseen attackers. As he pulled out of the crazy dive, faint blobs of light appeared a few miles ahead. They spelt a clear message: the scientist's absence must have been noticed sooner than expected, and the German pursuers were on the lip of the ravine. How long would it take them to climb down to the spot now clearly marked by flares?

Seaspray was now on a steady downward glide towards the dancing lights on the black fiord. The floats cut through the water easily, until the machine slowed to a halt.

Struggling up to perch on the fuselage, Kit saw a small rubber dinghy containing three shadowy figures appear from the darkness. An overcoated man was bundled up the ladder to the rear cockpit.

One of the partisans called softly, 'We have no time to thank you for your courage. Please go quickly. Our enemies are not far behind us. If they have ropes, like us, they will be down here at any moment. Good luck.'

Kit's engineering knowledge then allowed him to see a possible solution. Leaning over the side, he asked urgently, 'You have ropes with you?'

'For climbing.'

'Are there any trees down here?'

'Many trees,' answered the man.

'Good. I can take off all right, but I need to climb very fast. With the aid of your ropes, I think I can do it.'

Briefly he explained his theory. They understood and paddled away swiftly into the darkness.

It seemed an age before faint splashing heralded the return of the boat.

Acting on Kit's low-voiced instructions, the partisans began tying the ends of two ropes round *Seaspray*'s tailplane. As they were engaged in this, however, several of the drifting flares came close alongside. Almost immediately, a volley of shots rang out. One of the Norwegians jumped into the water to swim across and douse the nearest flares. More shots were fired; one hit the dinghy. It collapsed and began to sink. Fortunately, the ropes were now fast round the tail. Knowing he must go now or not at all, Kit increased revs and concentrated on the luminous dials in front of him. This would only succeed if he gauged the precise moment to give the signal, and those men on the bank acted on it immediately.

With his gaze glued to the dial indicating engine power, he reached for the distress pistol kept in the pocket beside his seat. *Seaspray* was now uttering a tremendous roar, and the crucial moment was near. The hand on the dial crept nearer the red danger zone and still he waited, heart in mouth, until *Seaspray* began to groan with structural stress. He dared delay no longer. Up went his hand holding the pistol, to fire a distress flare.

It burst high above him, filling the darkness with blinding white light, and *Seaspray* shot forward at speed, as the ropes attached to trees on the bank were severed by the partisans' knives. The makeshift catapult worked. So suddenly released, *Seaspray* hurtled through the air with such force she was off the water and climbing almost before Kit could recover from the impetus. Up and up they went, he almost lying flat on his back due to the angle of climb. Then the aircraft began to labour, and he risked a glance over the side. In every direction stars appeared to be twinkling. He gently levelled out until he was flying steady on a course for the destroyer. He had done it!

As *Seaspray* purred onward, he grew aware of a dull burning pain high up between his shoulders. A vague recollection of a thump at the back of his neck, during the nerve-racking moments while timing the precise second to sever the ropes, suggested that he had been hit by a bullet fired when he could hear nothing but *Seaspray*'s engine roar. His elation dimmed slightly. However, he did not appear to be losing blood, so the wound must be slight.

It was growing cold in this hour before dawn, so he decided to close the hood until nearing the ship. His right arm felt a leaden weight as he tried to raise it, and he was forced to close the hood with his left. The awkward movement caused the seaplane to wobble, and Kit then realised that he could no longer grip with his right hand. He tried to move his right leg. When that proved impossible, the word 'paralysis' swam through his weary brain. Had fate demanded a higher price for his success tonight, after all?

Knowing nothing could be done until the ship's surgeon could take a look at him, he tried to concentrate on the probable difficulties of landing beside the vessel, so that *Seaspray* could be hauled aboard via the ramp. Warren's seaplane had no radio transmitter fitted, so he had no verbal contact with the destroyer. All he could do was fly round the vessel several times, until it became apparent to those watching that he had a problem. He must hope that they would stand by when he finally reached the sea. At that point, he told himself to stop anticipating trouble. He had solved one insoluble difficulty tonight; he would get round this one when the time came.

Time passed until he saw the dark ship on the dull silver sea ahead, waiting patiently for him. Dawn was breaking to the east, and he was looking forward to a rest. But a glance at *Seaspray*'s fuel gauge showed that the fuel tanks were almost empty. One of the floats must have been hit, leaving petrol to dribble out all through the return flight. He made a swift decision to enter a gentle descent now, even if he touched down some distance from the ship. He could always taxi the last stretch.

In the cramped cockpit Kit moved his leaden right arm to one side as he held the aircraft in the dive with his knees. It was at that point that he realised he was no longer able to swivel his head. Perspiration swamped him as he accepted that he was paralysed down one side of his body. All he could do was continue this shallow descent until he was low enough to glimpse the sea beyond her nose, then do his utmost to bring her to rest on the surface. The navy would have to take over from there.

All at once, there was the sea right below. He dragged heavily on the column to pull *Seaspray* up, but she did not take kindly to such violent commands after all she had done tonight. Lurching upwards in a gigantic loop, she then smacked down on the water with a thud which jerked Kit's useless arm across his body to jam his left hand between the column and his knees, rendering him totally helpless. It was in that state that he saw the shimmery image of hooded lights, a ramp running down to the sea, and a great dark ship towering ahead.

Seaspray raced on impetuously, and he could do nothing to curb her. She hit the ramp with a force which set her screaming as metal rasped on metal. Slewing round, her propeller continued to race as she ploughed crazily in a circle to smash against the grey wall of the warship not far from the ramp. Men rushed to the side of the ship. Klaxons sounded; ropes were lowered. Several dangled inches from him, but Kit could only watch them and hope someone would swiftly realise his plight.

The scientist was rescued from the rear cockpit nearest to the ramp, then two seamen started down the ropes towards Kit. As he watched their precarious approach, a figure rose up from a position on the wing.

'What's wrong?' cried Warren above the general noise. 'Are you hurt?'

'Can't . . . move,' he managed.

A slight hesitation. 'I'll get some others.'

As Warren vanished, Kit had his first indication of the true situation facing him. The glow of fire was suddenly alongside. The leak in the float must have spilled the remaining fuel on the water, which had then ignited to drift and surround the wreck. Kit began to scream for someone to help him. Warren was there, having abandoned his quest for assistance in the face of this direst of dangers. Clambering up to straddle the fuselage behind the cockpit, he bent to grip the collar of Kit's flying jacket. 'Come on,' he yelled, tugging hard but in vain. 'You've got to get out quickly. *Come on! Come on!*'

Kit tried to tell him to shift the useless right arm and so release the hand which he could possibly use to push himself up, but there was too much noise as hoses were played on the flaming sea and the crew shouted warnings to their fellows dangling on the ropes. It was now unbearably hot in the cockpit as flames began to lick around the grey fuselage. The night flared into a lurid hellish glow, as Kit willed his friend to find superhuman strength. When he accepted that there was no hope of it, he sobbed a command for Warren to jump clear while he could. The man refused to go, continuing to drag at Kit's coat like a madman, even when *Seaspray* began to sink beneath that layer of flames on water.

LEONE HAD LIVED A NIGHTMARE of fear and anxiety during the last two days and three nights. Her nerves were stretched to breaking point on this third morning, when the telephone rang. She snatched it up in the hope of hearing Kit's voice. It was Colin Dryden.

'I'm using military priority to make this call, Mrs Grant,' he told her quietly. 'I regret to tell you that there was an accident early this morning, in which your husband received serious burns. He is in a ward of the naval hospital here, being given the best care available. The doctor assured me he is in no danger, but we thought you might care to come and see him.'

Bewildered, Leone could not take in what she was being told. 'My *husband* . . . in an accident? What kind of accident?'

'I'd prefer to explain when you get here, ma'am.'

'Yes . . . of course. I'll come right away,' she murmured, her mind in total confusion. 'Was Flight Lieutenant Anson involved in this accident?'

'I'm afraid so. Your husband very courageously fought to save Kit's life. Doctors are continuing the fight at this moment.'

Leone flew to Scotland in the company Auster, but she found the Kirkland name held no sway with the Almighty. Kit died an hour before she reached him.

Epilogue

On an August afternoon in 1948, Sheenmouth was decked with bunting and the sands were as crowded as the promenade. Visitors had swarmed to Sheenmouth to see the Air Show and, for once, the weather was perfect.

Yet nothing was quite the same as it used to be. Kirkland Marine Aviation had become Grant Kirkland Aviation Limited. The original works by the river continued to produce marine aircraft, but the new factory up on the site of the original Magnum Pomeroy Aero Club concentrated on civil airliners. Warren Grant had gained a knighthood for his work on amphibious aircraft, which had been used extensively in the Far Eastern campaign. He and his wife had also made a fortune from government contracts throughout the war. They had brought prosperity to the area, although there were still people who grumbled about the noise of aeroplanes performing endless manoeuvres.

Old-timers still talked of the days of Kit Anson, Sir Hector's first test pilot, and his war exploits. What was indisputably true was that Kit had piloted Sheenmouth's famous *Flamingo* flying boat to pick up survivors from Crete, for which he had been awarded his first decoration. He had then flown her to England to use on RAF special assignments. What no one knew for certain were the details of his last flight, which had earned him a posthumous DFC. Whatever the truth about that affair with the Kirkland family, no one could deny he had been the stuff of which heroes were made, and had shone as brightly as the stars he had never given up trying to reach.

Today's aerial show began with *Aphrodite*, rescued from the scrapyard and restored by Sir Warren personally. She looked slow by today's standards, but she had had her days of glory. Following her were two noisy giants, side by side, still in their camouflage with RAF markings, *Flamingo* and *Florida*. Next came a formation of Hurricanes which had been based at Magnum Pomeroy, and another of Spitfires for which components had been made at Kirkland's. Several heavy bombers from the existing RAF station beyond Forton thundered past above the sands, tailed by a long line of *Clarions*, the swift, compact passenger planes being turned out in the new factory at Magnum Pomeroy.

Then, at last, came the star of the show, Sheenmouth's latest pride and joy. A new flying boat developed by Warren Grant from an original design by Geoffrey Anson, and named *Solitaire*. Taxiing from the mouth of the river came the majestic craft painted blue and silver, looking like a great passenger liner with wings. When she rose effortlessly from the sea and headed towards the sun, the cheering people slowly grew hushed, silenced by an emotion they could not name.

The cocktail party at Sheenmouth Abbey that evening for VIP guests and personal friends of Sir Warren and Lady Grant indicated the total success of the day. *Solitaire* had been triumphant in advance of her debut, for orders had been placed at the semiconstruction stage. More were certain as a result of today's show, and a decision would then have to be made on whether or not one of the workshops at Magnum Pomeroy would have to switch to making components for the flying boat rather than for the standard *Clarion*. First, however, the directors were taking a holiday.

Leone reminded Philip Curtiss of this when he invited her to a luncheon of the Royal Aeronautical Society. 'We shall be in Africa,' she said firmly. 'Sorry, Philip.'

The group captain laughed. 'You've always been a woman who makes irreversible decisions, Leone.'

'Not where my husband is concerned,' she responded drily. 'The minute I start to pin him down, he escapes to the old boathouse and becomes engrossed in something else.'

'Good thing, too, or he would never have discovered those old plans of Geoffrey Anson's and created *Solitaire*.'

'Yes, of course,' she agreed, so used to the white lie it no longer threw her.

'I bumped into Sir Melville yesterday,' Philip continued. 'Did you know he'd suffered a stroke?'

'Yes, I visited the house soon after Stephanie left him for her American diplomat. I wanted to thank him and the members of his committee for commissioning a stained-glass expert to restore the abbey windows, in gratitude for storing their treasures here during the height of the bombing. I thought it very generous.'

Colin Dryden approached at that point, and Leone soon excused herself to the men. Nearby was Mona Hamilton, who had been widowed in 1944 and now ran the *Sheenmouth Clarion* while rearing two children.

'I saw your Ben wandering around with a dreamy look on his face,' Mona said with a smile. 'I recognise that expression all too well. He'll be flying the minute he's old enough, Leone.'

'I suppose it's inevitable,' she agreed. 'He's surrounded by all the temptations, isn't he? Isn't it curious,' she added, 'that my life has been dominated by aircraft from birth, and I now devote almost every day to the production of them, yet I've never experienced this love affair men seem to have with them.'

'You're a woman, that's why,' declared Mona. 'We've got our feet firmly on the ground, thank God. Let the men have their love affairs with machines. Women have a love affair with life, and that's far more important.'

Mona's words stayed in Leone's mind as she wandered the abbey entertaining her guests. Did she yet have a love affair with life?

Leaving the last few official guests with Warren, Leone mounted the branched staircase to the bell tower. Kit's presence was there immediately, as it always was when she looked round this room with the writing desk and chairs covered in ruby velvet. No one had occupied it since that night when *Flamingo* had been forced to land at Sheenmouth by Polish fighter pilots. So close did she suddenly feel to that young man who had led her along such a stormy path, tears she had not shed for a long while rushed to her eyes.

He and his father had been betrayed by men who had exploited his trust, but today the Kirkland debt had been paid. It had taken seventeen years, but *Solitaire* had flown over Sheenmouth in triumph this afternoon, with Geoffrey Anson's name accredited to her.

She remained swamped by memories until Warren came in to fold his arms round her. 'It's really been *his* day, hasn't it?' he murmured.

She nodded, still unable to speak. Then he said gently, 'Don't you think it's time we used these rooms; time we let him go?'

Her hand went up to feather his face, scarred by burns suffered on that last night with Kit. 'Not many men would have made a gesture as generous as you did this afternoon.'

He caught her hand in his. 'Geoffrey Anson was a great designer who deserved recognition for his skill.'

'But you really did it for Kit, didn't you?'

'No,' he confessed quietly. 'No, Leone, I did it for you . . . in the hope that there'd be peace between the Kirklands and the Ansons, at last.' His steadfast gaze was full of hope. 'Is there?'

Her answer was the farewell she had never been able to make before. 'Yes, darling. I found it here just before you came in.'

He let out his breath in a long sigh of relief, then took her arm to lead her in understanding silence along the upper corridor, past the rooms occupied by Ben, whom they had adopted as an orphaned evacuee four years ago. He was now fourteen, strong and happy, with his gaze already on the skies. Leone's mouth softened into a faint smile. Ben was another stray mongrel who had been taken in and polished up to meet Kirkland standards. This one was here to stay, however. Stay until he fell in love with a goddess of the air, she reminded herself hollowly. Then she recognised that missing element which would make her life complete.

'Warren,' she began quietly, 'isn't it time we thought of adopting another child—a girl?'

He grinned. 'I wondered how long it would be before you felt outnumbered by men, and wanted to even the balance.' He kissed her with that steadfast love she had found so supportive. 'We'll discuss the details when we're in Mombasa next month, darling,' he promised. 'Now, please can I take off this penguin suit and get into something more comfortable?'

ELIZABETH DARRELL

'Even though the Second World War began when I was only eight, it's a very vivid period in my memory. I only have to hear the Glenn Miller Band or the Harry James Orchestra, and I relive it all.' Elizabeth Darrell's ability to capture the atmosphere of a bygone age is a feature of all her books, including the historical romances that she writes under her other pen name of Emma Drummond. 'I try to imagine the details of everyday life: how people would have dressed; how they would have spent their leisure; even what their moral concerns would have been.'

Elizabeth Darrell and her husband Ken became interested in flying boats many years ago, when they saw one moored on the south coast. 'I thought it was the most beautiful machine,' she remembers. Flying boats didn't feature in a book, however, until a visiting American publisher expressed a desire to know more about the 'passenger liners with wings' which were more spacious and more luxurious, Elizabeth points out, than today's Concorde. She began researching the background of *Flamingo* with a visit to the Hall of Aviation in Southampton, where a team of volunteers are restoring a flying boat named *Southern Cross*. Elizabeth is pictured above at the controls of the plane. Through the Flying Boat Association, she also contacted an ex-pilot living in Lymington whose reminiscences were very useful in the writing of her novel. The catapulting of a flying boat out of a confined area such as a fiord, the manoeuvre which Kit performs with *Seaspray* is, for example, based upon a true incident. 'If there was too little room or too few waves, the pilot found it impossible to get sufficient lift for takeoff,' Elizabeth explains.

Elizabeth and Ken, married for over thirty years, have two grown-up daughters, and share a variety of interests including amateur dramatics. Recently, in their home town, Bournemouth, they staged a selection of dramatised extracts from Elizabeth's novels, including *At The Going Down of the Sun*, an earlier Condensed Book selection.

PICTURE CREDITS: Page 223: Padraig O'Flannabhra. Page 351: © 1990 Phillippe Diederich.

161D